Pasticcio opera in Britain

Manchester University Press

Pasticcio opera in Britain

History and context

Peter Morgan Barnes

MANCHESTER UNIVERSITY PRESS

Published by Manchester University Press
Oxford Road, Manchester, M13 9PL

www.manchesteruniversitypress.co.uk

British Library Cataloguing-in-Publication Data
A catalogue record for this book is available from the British Library

ISBN   978 1 5261 6518 3   hardback

First published 2024

Typeset
by New Best-set Typesetters Ltd

For Trystan

Contents

Illustrations

Acknowledgements

This book has had a long gestation and many of those to whom it is indebted will be unaware of their contribution. My thanks begin with Cathie McKimm and Randal Shannon with whom I first created a pasticcio opera in 2004, and extend to Professor Cormac Newark who commissioned another in 2007 and gently explained that I was not the first to have discovered this method of creating opera. Until speaking to Cormac I had never heard of pasticcio and that our definition of the practice has been too closely tied to the word is one of the arguments made in this book. Among later professors to whom I am profoundly grateful for their scholarship, stylistic expertise and, above all, their generosity with their time are David Britton, Derek Connon and Daniel G. Williams at Swansea, Clair Rowden at Cardiff and Sarah Hibberd at Bristol. All have contributed to shaping the work in very different ways.

John Whythe was kind enough to help with proof-reading, Jennifer Wilson kept the biography up to date even when ill, Dawn Marshall resolved the many technical crises faced by every writer in our unwinnable war against system updates; my earliest research was read by Gwyn Williams. All of these people I have been extremely fortunate to know. The ultimate thanks are due to Manchester University Press who have shown monumental patience with my inability to stop revising the material. Matthew Frost commissioned this book and has shown unwavering faith in its significance for music history; his enthusiasm, approachability and support have never wavered throughout and working with him has been a great joy. David Appleyard took over for the final stages, seeing the book into production and his kindness and support have been constant. To my copy-editor, John Firth, I also owe a debt of gratitude for his meticulous revisions and cheerful comments. To Michelle Houston, Paul Clarke and Alun Richards my deepest thanks for their hard work on this project, their kindness and their consummate professionalism.

Introduction

0.1 *The Rehearsal of an Opera* by Marco Ricci, 1709, believed to be the
pasticcio *Pyrrhus and Demetrius*.
Source: Google Art Project (2328395) released under Creative Commons
Licence.

A pasticcio opera is one constructed out of pre-existing music, text or both.
Some pasticcio operas select existing accompaniments to serve an original
libretto and thus tell a new story, others set a pre-existing libretto to new
or pre-existing music; a range of combinations are found. Like many another
literary term, pasticcio derives from Italian cooking, meaning a pie or pasty

enclosing a range of good things, already cooked for use in other dishes.[1]
The word pasticcio is hypocoristic: insiders' slang for a widely used creative
process, not unlike the word opera itself, which was used as short form in
the seventeenth century for dramma per musica, dramma de recitarsi in
musica, dramma giocosa per musica and so on.[2]

In this study I adopt Percy Scholes's distinction between pasticcio and
pastiche; in its current usage, pastiche describes new art self-consciously
imitating pre-existing art, but does not necessarily mean the reuse of pre-
existing materials to create that art.[3] Pasticcio means just that and therefore
this study uses the Italian word. Its plural is pasticci and pasticciere is used
for the creator of a pasticcio, pasticcieri in plural. This is preferable to
describing those who create such operas as composers, compilers or arrangers
because, despite the contemporary use of those terms, pasticcio operas exist
which were created by singers, literati, impresarios, theatre staff including
managers, copyists and orchestral players, scholars and even royal dilettanti
such as Catherine the Great.[4] It is not necessary to be a music specialist to
create a successful pasticcio opera.

Reinhard Strohm, noting that the word pasticcio was used in Johann
Joachim Quantz's autobiography relating to the year 1725, suggests that it
was probably current in Italy a decade or two before.[5] He argues that it
was initially used in a highly defined sense to mean a 'true pasticcio' and
continued to have a reasonably strict usage until the middle of the century.
Thereafter, its usage broadened, being applied to a spectrum of operas the
only common factor among which was that they were not wholly created
by setting original music to an original libretto. It also began to be used
for comparable practices in other artforms including sculpture, painting
and, by the 1870s, diplomatic policies. Despite the word only gaining currency
in the early eighteenth century, the practice itself had been core to opera
creation since at least the 1630s. Similarly, even after the word began to
decline in opera after the 1870s, the practice itself continued long into the
twentieth century and is enjoying a tentative revival in the twenty-first. This
book is a study in the practice as a whole rather than just those operas
which carry the name pasticcio.

I propose that pasticcio is essentially a construction method, not a discrete
genre of opera in the way twentieth-century music history often presented
it. Those writing about opera in the first two thirds of the twentieth century
acknowledged the widespread use of assembly or compilation as techniques
but discussed the practices as if they were a single genre, an approach which
substantially underplayed their ubiquity. There are many ways of creating
an opera from pre-existing parts and I argue in this book that no single
type of creative process enjoyed exclusive use of the word pasticcio during
the centuries in which it was used.

Throughout the eighteenth century, some pasticcio operas designated themselves as such on their playbills, newspaper advertising or on the front pages of published libretti; this was done to let audiences know that they could expect the very finest and most popular arias, especially selected from the very best operas by the finest masters and sung by leading singers. It was not done to distinguish the opera from new compositions, still less to warn audiences that what they were about to see was not staged according to the original texts of the original authors. A large proportion of pasticcio operas, however – probably the majority – did not designate themselves as such in their literature. This was partly because they had other facets which theatres or publishers thought would resonate more with their audiences or readers, such as the opera being a pastoral comedy, a classical tragedy, a masque or burlesque and so on.

Another reason the word was so often omitted was that the majority of London's operas were created from pre-existing parts to greater or lesser extents: a pasticcio designation was not essential information any more than modern opera companies need to advertise their faithfulness to an original score and libretto; compilation was assumed then as fidelity is now. The English translator of Niccolò Piccinni's *La Buona Figliuola* in 1766 claimed it was 'the first attempt of bringing an entire musical composition on the English stage', meaning an unamended complete original. The claim was not true but that such a thing could be claimed indicates how seldom 'entire' scores were experienced.[6] Nor was this omission unique to Britain: French opéras comique such as *La statue merveilleuse* (1718 and revived frequently), *Les trois commères* (1723) and *Les pèlerins de la mecque* (1726, revived 1729) were well known to be assembled works though no descriptor of this was felt necessary in the playbills.[7]

I propose in Chapter 4 that a generation of opera writers in Britain, from the end of the nineteenth century into the early twentieth, misunderstood both the broad application of the term pasticcio in the eighteenth century and the contexts of its use. Writers such as Henry Davison, son and biographer of the critic James William Davison, Frederick Corder, censorious biographer of Henry Bishop and Oscar Sonneck in the United States, held the preconception that original operas had always been considered artistically higher than pasticci and that absolute fidelity to the original texts had always been the aim in staging operas, even if practical circumstances prevented this from being achieved.[8] This perspective led them to confine the term pasticcio exclusively to those operas that designated themselves as such and, as the true pasticcio was the type that did so most frequently, that was the type that came to define the word for this generation. This interpretation created a temporal and generic containment for assembled operas, a containment iterated in music history up to the 1960s. Yet this generation's stance differed considerably from the previous generation of music reformers, the initial propagators of Romantic normativity. This earlier generation saw pasticcio as very much alive and hydra-headed: indeed, without their rigorous critical surveillance, they feared that opera practitioners would resort to pasticcio even more than they already did.

This new, more limited definition of pasticcio generated an impression that assembling operas occurred much less than was actually the case; pasticcio was seen as an occasionally used genre, mostly limited to the eighteenth century, which must have died out at some early point in the nineteenth century. This became received scholarship and is seen in the writings of Stanley Sadie and Winton Dean, as discussed in Chapter 5. Yet it continues to find echoes in scholarship as recent as that of Curtis Price and Jennifer Hall-Witt.[9] A snapshot of this containment process can be seen in a transcript of the questions following a lecture given by E.J. Dent to the Royal Musical Society in 1944. Dent had made the grand claim that pasticcio was peculiar to London; finding his feet held to the fire over this by an intractable questioner, he resorted to defining pasticcio ever more narrowly:

> Mr. HOWES: Could the lecturer elaborate a little the point about the pasticcio and its origin? I always thought it was an Italian practice occurring at a particular stage of development in Italian opera through people like Gluck.
> The LECTURER: There is a bibliography in the catalogue of the Brussels Library. Alfred Wotquenne worked on all those things about forty years ago. All one could do would be to make a bibliography. I think it would be rather a waste of labour except from a librarian's point of view.
> Mr. HOWES: You indicated that the pasticcio was not an Italian practice but that it almost arose in this country.
> The LECTURER: Can you produce any evidence of pasticcio in other countries?
> Mr. HOWES: No, but it was surely in fact common all over the Continent; yet now you produce this revolutionary doctrine that it was done for London.
> The LECTURER: I am not quite clear perhaps on your definition of pasticcio. The London type of pasticcio meant that the foreign singers came over to England and brought their own arias with them. The local poet then took a libretto of an opera, remodelled it to a certain extent to include all the plums, and the favourite arias were put in wherever suitable. But Mr. Howes alludes to Gluck. Gluck had the practice of utilising songs from his own previous operas when writing a new one. That is not the same thing as a pasticcio from a variety of different composers. In Italy, an opera originally composed, say, by Scarlatti, might be revived with half the arias of Scarlatti and several new arias written by a later composer building on an already constructed opera or perhaps utilising old work of his own to some extent

to fill up gaps. The real pasticcio is a complete jumble of songs by any number of composers.

Mr. HOWES: Did that originate in London?[10]

While all of these are recognised as types of pasticcio or pasticcio practices today, Dent does not explain what Gluck's autopasticcio was otherwise called or give a term for the Italian variant of Scarlatti. His selection of the first example as the true or 'real' pasticcio is telling as, I suggest, there are no substantive differences between the methods described. The local poet is remodelling the libretto to accommodate new arias preferred by the singers and the later composer is remodelling Scarlatti's opera to do the same. When the operas were performed or the texts printed, who exactly made the alterations or selections was not apparent unless the playbill or a review stated particular arias as the singer's choice. That Dent's definition of pasticcio was off-the-cuff makes it more revealing of mid-century scholarly thinking, perhaps, than a considered written response. By extrapolating one technique out of many and labelling it the 'real pasticcio' Dent safeguarded the definition of pasticcio as an aberrant operatic genre with a limited floruit; textual fidelity could still be presented as a timeless norm and the more respected method of constructing performances.

This perspective in the first two thirds of the twentieth century was bolstered by the kinds of pasticcio opera produced at that period, as discussed in Chapter 5. On one level, these were standing examples of the practice continuing, but they tended to be set in the eighteenth century, used eighteenth-century music, or were revivals of eighteenth-century pasticci. To avoid embroilment in copyright issues, a deliberately precopyright, antique patina was given even to new pasticci. The academic containment of pasticcio was thus shared even by its practitioners. Mid-century pasticci stood against a background of expanding copyright advocation and a punitive regime of enforcement. Music dissemination companies including publishers, recorders and broadcasters were heavily invested in copyright expansion and performance licensing; they were keen to narrow the possibility that anything other than single-authored works had ever been the norm in operatic repertoires. But, during the last third of the twentieth century, eternal verities of all sorts were on the back foot.

A new generation of music historians including Gordana Lazarevich, Reinhard Strohm, Ellen Rosand, Judith Milhous, Robert D. Hume, Gabriella Diderikson, Curtis Price, John H. Roberts and many others, writing from the 1970s onwards, challenged the timelessness of the normative value systems applied to art by scholars such as F.R. Leavis in literature and the musicologists mentioned in earlier paragraphs. Scholars such as Rosand

and Hume recognised that the practice of assembling operas from pre-existing parts predated the emergence of the word pasticcio by a century or more.[11] In 2016, Christine Siegert noted the problematic nature of pasticcio for a musicology based on prioritising originality and the privileging of music over the story and scholars have recognised the necessity of viewing pasticcio in its contemporary and transnational contexts.[12] Pasticcio was clearly disruptive of normative value systems and contributors to the 2021 multi-disciplinary and international Pasticcio Research Project identify an unwillingness in twentieth-century musicology to leave behind normative ways of looking at music as being causal in the academic marginalisation of pasticcio.[13]

Another innovation of late-twentieth-century scholarship was greater academic legitimacy for performance studies. Modern musicology began to separate the history of musical texts from the history of musical performance; previously, musicology had been conditioned by the culture of a mass-literate society and it was regularly assumed that performance had always been animations of texts, as discussed in Chapter 4. Performance history relied on sources formerly regarded as unreliable or even inadmissible such as reviews or chance references in correspondence, manuscript submissions to the Lord Chamberlain's office, playbills, handbills and other ephemera. The new approach found that when performances in the eighteenth and nineteenth centuries were compared with the printed texts of operas, it becomes inescapable that a proportionally greater number of operas had been changed for performance from their argued original text than had been staged strictly according to that text.

In this book, I have called all operas pasticcio that were either conceived as such, with or without the contributors' knowledge, or that *became* pasticcio works in performance over successive revivals. A list of the types of opera considered in this book to be a form of pasticcio is given below. I have referred to the tools routinely used to create such operas, the interpolations, aria substitutions, transpositions, incorporations of new plot or revised characterisations, as pasticcio practices. Where the alteration from an original opera is demonstrably slight, consisting of no more than one or two substitutions or some transpositions, I have not referred to it as a pasticcio but as an original with a few pasticcio practices. I have taken this approach regardless of whether or not the opera designated itself a pasticcio. I have also used the word anachronistically to describe any opera created in the ways described before the word pasticcio was current. Similarly, I have used pasticcio to describe operas created in this way after the word itself tended only to be used in a contracted sense.

My reasons for taking this approach are twofold: firstly, once the word pasticcio had been contracted to describe only the true pasticcio, scholars such as Edward Dent then struggled to find a contemporary collective term for all operas which had been created using assemblative methods. I argue that pasticcio came closest to being that term in the eighteenth and nineteenth centuries, just as Christina Fuhrmann found that fidelity was the word most frequently used during the nineteenth century to describe the reproduction of authorial intentions.[14] In the nineteenth century the word pasticcio could certainly be used pejoratively by music reformers in the press, but it *was* used widely. Secondly, I believe anachronistic use of the word pasticcio is justified when the method used to construct an opera can be shown to be identical with what will, in the future, be called a pasticcio, or with what was once in the past called a pasticcio. There are precedents: Ellen Rosand argues that many Venetian operas would have qualified as pasticci had the term been in use.[15] Ballad operas have also been retrospectively designated pasticci by Madeleine Smith Atkins, Vanessa L. Rogers and others.[16] To avoid calling a pasticcio a pasticcio because it identified itself as something else in its marketing creates the impression of a material difference where none exists.

Although this approach is a terminological convenience for the reader, such an all-embracing definition of the word has the effect of englobing a vast proportion of opera, indeed nearly all art, as forms of pasticcio. I suggest this potentiality has always been there, and its avoidance in approved scholarship was motivated by a desire to protect artistic metanarratives and Romantic tenets. Thomas Betzwieser, in a discussion of Gluck's *L'innocenza giustificata* (1755), noted that 'we would very likely tend to label the work as a pasticcio … But if we did so, we would certainly open Pandora's box, since we would have to place most of Gluck's operas under this category.'[17] Yet the approach of the Pasticcio Research Project, of which Betzwieser is part, is inclusive rather than exclusionary: Betzwieser emphasises that this approach is necessary in any modern examination of pasticcio:

> When researching the issue of pre-existing text and music, and pasticcio, respectively, a great deal of musical genres come into consideration. It seems that the whole 18th century is dominated by the pasticcio phenomenon. We can verify pasticcios in both opera seria and opera buffa, in French tragédie lyrique and opéra comique, in English ballad opera, in operatic adaptations characterized by insertions and arrangements or lingual transfer (as French parodies); furthermore, it is present in oratorio as well as in other sacred music, and last but not least in instrumental music.[18]

To this I would add the seventeenth, nineteenth and twentieth centuries: letting go of earlier scholarship's containment of pasticcio as a single genre also means opening up its temporal parameters. If we accept that a pro-portionately vast number of operatic performances were created from pre-existing parts, then our understanding of originality and authenticity necessarily changes too. If pasticcio is King Kong crammed into a marmoset's cage, this study is an experiment in what happens if the monster is released. I suggest that most scholarship on pasticcio in the twenty-first century is, consciously or unconsciously, an interrogation of its caging within a neoromantic legacy; this study is no different.

The question of what constitutes a pasticcio opera is inextricable from that of what constitutes an original one. Originality has been conceived differently in different periods, as discussed in Chapters 2 and 4, and composers who created pasticcio operas were usually the creators of original operas as well; many pasticcieri viewed their assembled operas to be just as original as their composed ones. Yet since the Romantic Movement, musicology has not conceived original operas as a single genre within the wider artform.[19] Despite framing discussions of pasticcio against conceptions of originality, it is not my intention to imply an antagonistic binary between the two approaches to operatic construction in any period. Indeed, the overlap between the two is arguably greater than the ground on either side. Both the true pasticcio and the opera that has only ever been performed with absolute fidelity are few in comparison with the host of operas which have been changed in various ways but where the original is still discernible.

Scope of the study

The study as a whole focuses on Britain, but as so much of Britain's opera was Italian, Chapters 2 and 3 are concerned with operatic developments in Italy and Anglo-Italian interaction. This part of the introduction explains the key areas of examination across all four of the centuries studied. Tracing pasticcio from the emergence of opera down to its tentative revival in the twenty-first century is a timeframe longer than usual for this topic; postmodernist theory taught us to be wary of the metanarrative and the long timeframe of this study is not an attempt to create one. Care is taken to avoid inventing or implying transhistoricism where none exists, or technological determinism. Rather, the long timeframe allows a new understanding of pasticcio to emerge by relating it to other cultural developments with similarly long timespans. These include Western society's transition from a proto-literate society with a flourishing oral culture to one of mass literacy with deeply equivocal attitudes to its oral traditions.[20] Other long-timeframe changes include society's evolving technologies for the visualisation of stories and the understanding of music as property. Pasticcio is therefore studied diachronically but also as a feature of other artforms besides opera.

The use of the pasticcio method to create opera has always received validation from its use in other contemporary artforms. Pasticcio was practised in sculpture, the conservation of antiquities, painting, architecture and in the construction of commodities such as wine and furniture. In performance genres it was, and sometimes still is, found in oratorio, mass settings, pantomime, ballet scores, tableaux vivant, puppet shows, musical theatre, spoken theatre and film scores. Pasticcio in sculpture, antiquities and wine are discussed in the study as part of its recontextualisation. The hostile criticism of pasticcio in opera meted out by music reformers during the nineteenth century was echoed by the critics and connoisseurs in these other arts and commodities: even the same quasi-religious language was used to elevate the single-authored and the 'original' above the collaborative and assembled.

One reason why the creation of art and commodities depended so much on compilation from pre-existing parts is that, prior to mass literacy and mass production, this approach had been embedded in Western society for millennia. Roman society had a pasticcio form of poetry and took a pasticcio approach to rhetoric, medieval hagiography was often composed of pre-existing narrative tropes, metalepsis is arguably a pasticcio figure of speech, adapting a pre-existing phrase to create a new meaning. Chapters 1 and 2 argue that pasticcio is an inheritance from oral culture but one which, intriguingly, survived in opera despite society's transition to mass literacy, and despite the intensive pressure it was put under to conform to an increasingly text-based culture.

Storytelling was the most widely practised artform in early modern society and Chapter 2 discusses the orality of early theatre practice and how pasticcio was a feature of this. Rising literacy in the seventeenth century brought change and Chapters 3 and 4 argue that an increasingly literate culture saw an intensification in the visualisation of narratives across all nearly artforms. In opera this meant that scenography and special effects played increasingly important roles in telling the story, but required 'reading' rather than absorbing.

The role of pasticcio in opera has also been governed by evolutions in the understanding of the self. Such evolutions occurred every few generations over opera's four centuries as new ways of performing the self gradually replaced older ones. Chapter 3 traces eighteenth-century reactions against the entrenched sectarian identities inherited from the English civil wars, a reaction expressed partly through performances of civility and national unity. I argue that eighteenth-century people consciously constructed their identities using pasticcio methods. This partly accounts for the explosion of pasticcio in the performed art of this period, identified by Betzwieser.

Yet this performed self was itself subject to a reaction between the 1780s and the 1830s, during which period the Romantic 'inner self' changed public and private behaviour, most noticeably in constructions of gender.

The parameters of acceptable behaviour in early nineteenth-century opera characters, their motivations and the credibility thresholds of their actions were reshaped by this reconceptualising of personal identity, discussed in Chapter 4. Pasticcio practices such as aria substitution and transposed vocal parts were used to reconfigure characters whose behaviours were out of keeping with current expectations. A further evolution occurred with the emergence of what might be called the psychologically aware self in the twentieth century.

Another development with a long timespan which changed attitudes towards pasticcio was the economic shift from hand-produced goods created in small forges, mills, farms and studios to mass production in the factories of the nineteenth and later centuries. Material objects moved from being things of rarity and value to single-use, disposable commodities. So much of elite identity was bound up with owning objects and valuing experiences unaffordable to the majority, that the comparatively sudden accessibility of luxury goods and experiences in the nineteenth century led to panicky attempts by connoisseurs to shore up the prestige of luxury commodities over mass-produced ones. A new cultural value was added to hand-crafted, bespoke construction methods. I suggest that the idea of a single genius behind the creation of an opera was one expression of this, and that the hostility of nineteenth-century critics towards pasticcio sculpture, antiquities, wine and opera reflected a widespread elite reaction against the accessibility of these products and experiences. Pasticcio performances may not have been mass produced but they certainly became prolific in the nineteenth century, as discussed in Chapter 4. As the product of multiple hands, pasticcio was on the wrong side of this economic change as it would be on the wrong side of copyright legislation in the twentieth century.

I propose that the discontinuation by leading opera companies of new pasticcio operas between the 1870s and 1914 was not the result of pasticcio going out of favour; indeed, the rise of operetta and musical comedies indicate its continuing popularity. As Paul Rodmell has shown, a combination of copyright, performance licensing and legal restraints meant that a small number of touring opera companies acquired the rights to a comparatively small number of operas.[21] Although they were toured across Britain in this period, and more people experienced the artform than ever before, the repertoire continued to contract: more and more people were hearing fewer and fewer operas. A contributory factor was the difficulty new works experienced in finding purchase in this ever-narrowing canon. Rodmell shows that Britain's touring companies took great pains to commission and promote new British operas, but failed to sustain them in the repertoire as audiences repeatedly sought older, continental, canonical favourites.[22]

Nevertheless, opera did not dispense with pasticcio as musicology once believed: detailed evidence for its continuation throughout the nineteenth and twentieth centuries is presented in Chapters 4 and 5. Operas which designated themselves as pasticcio were programmed in London theatres in the 1920s and 1930s, with some being broadcast on early television. Chapter 5 shows tutor/pupil lineages connecting pasticcieri such as Francesco Bianchi in the 1780s through Henry Bishop and the Loder family to Herbert and Eleanor Farjeon in the 1930s, all of whom created pasticcio operas. Copyright legislation intensified during the twentieth century and this was a further disincentive for pasticcio, but as the internet developed the conceptualisation of copyright faced challenges in the late-twentieth and twenty-first centuries. It is far from coincidental that pasticcio was rehabilitated academically during the same period in which copyright receded as a legislated force.

By viewing all three of these long-term developments – orality and literacy, identity change and the commodification of music – through a wide lens, it is possible to see where pasticcio sits in Western performance traditions. I have moderated this temporally panoramic view with periodic close-ups in the form of case studies of particular operas or people. These enable us to see how broad artistic trends are reflected in specific moments or in actual performances. Yet this long-lens approach is not without its problems: stadial approaches to history can still exert a gravitational pull when writing about long periods of time, a tendency, as Paula McDowell describes it, to present societies as 'progressing naturally through a series of phases, each with its own characteristic institutions, economy, and social arrangements'.[23] Stadialism risks marginalising the prevalence of practices prior to the time they were held to typify, or underplays their continuation following it: pasticcio opera is a prime example. I have avoided stadialism as much as possible: each chapter is aligned with an historical period but these correspond only loosely to a century because historical changes rarely oblige by correlating with double zeros. Another difficulty is that while the reader may be confidently assumed to have knowledge of operatic history, it would be foolhardy to assume this extends to theories of orality, other artforms or copyright legislation. Consequently, excursi are periodically given to provide the necessary context for the arguments.

Lastly, my decision to use BC/AD rather than BCE/CE is prompted by the recent movement to decolonise academic writing; changing the acronyms does not make the dating neutral or secular if it retains a Western Christian numbering system. Secondly, changing the Latin to English carries a hegemonic assumption of anglophone universality, while opera, of course, is the least monoglot of artforms.

Categories of opera discussed as pasticcio

The desire to categorise pasticcio, to classify the shades of methodological difference between its varied approaches, has characterised its literature from at least the early eighteenth century. The problem with such categorisation is that from the dozens of ways in which a pasticcio can be made, hundreds of sub-categories emerge, variations of variations, as well as overlappings. Many a true pasticcio is also a collaborative pasticcio, but also a self-pasticcio as each contributor is supplying work they have previously used elsewhere. Following its initial run, subsequent revivals change the opera again, making it a pasticcio by substitution. An opera such as *La villanella rapita* (1783) thus inhabits many categories. I propose that categorisation reflects the need of text-based societies to contain and understand the diffusion of music and stories in patterns which derive from oral culture. Not only do pasticcio categories divide and overlap but they inhabit multiple other classifications of structure and genre at the same time: a pasticcio could call itself a 'dramatick opera' or an adaptation but also be a burlesque *and* a pastoral comedy at the same time; a true pasticcio could call itself a masque but also be a tragedy, an opera seria as well as being a political satire.

Confronted with this, writers including Curtis Price and Donald J. Grout tended to limit inclusion under the term to those operas that designated themselves pasticci.[24] The list that follows includes operas considered in the study to be pasticci on grounds of their construction alone, even though they may have designated themselves a masque, burlesque, adaptation or something else. A list can be still of value as an introduction to the variety of methods whereby an opera can be constructed.

Contrafactum and quodlibet

Prior to the emergence of the word pasticcio, each genre of music had its own term for the pasticcio practices it used, as Peter Burkholder noted.[25] Contrafactum, literally 'against the way it was made', was the singing of new words to a musical setting which had previously served a different text; it was used in liturgical settings, madrigals and other genres of Renaissance music. Quodlibet, meaning 'whatever pleases', was the combining of different existing melodies, even sacred and secular ones, to support a new text-setting; it was a free space outside categorisation and genre. Various terms were used at different times and places to describe the pasticcio practices of the medieval cantus firmus and motet.

The 'true' pasticcio

These operas are distinguished by having been conceived as pasticci from the beginning. The process usually started with choosing a story, following which libretti and accompaniments were selected. They could be created collaboratively by a team of theatre staff, friends or impresarios, or by a single pasticciere: *Arione*, performed in Milan in 1694 using a libretto by Oreste d'Arles, was created by a single hand. In a triumph of the arranger's art, arias by twenty-seven different composers were woven into a tight unity. The pasticciere is unknown but hotly debated.[26]

The use of multiple composers is what seized nineteenth- and twentieth-century imaginations but accompaniments were not always drawn from a large number of composers: Handel chose from only two or three. His *Elpidia* (1725) is an example: the libretto was adapted from a 1697 text by Apostolo Zeno and the music taken principally from Leonardo Vinci and Giuseppe Orlandini.[27] Like most pasticciere, Handel wrote some music and text himself to ensure coherence: he possibly wrote the sinfonia, definitely wrote two of the duets and probably the recitatives, but he took great care to ensure stylistic unity by making the music recognisably his own.[28] Examples of true pasticci can be found in Venice at least as early as 1643 with Giulio Strozzi's *La finta savia*, which made a selling point of containing the music of four separate composers. Modern examples include Jeremy Sams's *The Enchanted Island* (2012), performed at the Metropolitan Opera, New York. It was not always a new story that was created; an existing libretto could be taken wholesale and reset with music selected from a number of sources; such were the numerous true pasticci created using libretti by Pietro Metastasio, with some being set well over a hundred times.

Revivals with substitutions

These were operas that evolved into pasticci over time and they were almost certainly more frequent than true pasticci in the eighteenth and nineteenth centuries. They began as original works but aria substitutions, plot and character changes, together with the interpolation of new material, occurring to greater or lesser extents with each successive revival, could make the original all but unrecognisable. Pietro Auletto's *Orazio*, studied by Frank Walker in the 1940s, is an example. Initially an original opera of 1738, it was performed all over Europe but edited differently in each European city. It was then re-edited over successive revivals so that radically different variants developed in each city. New arias appeared and others dropped out, so that Walker noted that by 1760 only a fifth of the original music was still included.[29] Dent's Scarlatti example is this kind of opera, but while he categorises it as something other than a pasticcio, Walker argued that it was. This pasticcio method continued into the twentieth century: Emanuel Chabrier's *L'étoile* experienced the same evolution between 1877 and 1925 before its original was reinstated in the repertoire. It was never, to my knowledge, given the name pasticcio either by critics or those staging it, but its title changed twice and even the rigorous copyright laws of that period did not prevent a very traditional pasticcio practice from occurring.

While the original libretto, scoring and even the dramatisation might alter out of recognition, the story itself was usually the stable component and, in proto-literate societies, an embedded oral culture still privileged the story itself over the forms of telling it. This is discussed in Chapter 2. We might consider operas such as *Orazio* as a performance tradition rather than a text, and definitely rather than a 'work' as, despite being regularly printed, the story was felt to be unowned, while ways of telling it belonged to numerous theatres, embedded in their ever-shifting repertoires.

As well as individual arias, whole sequences, scenes or acts could be substituted in revivals. Ferdinando Bertoni staged his opera *Cimene* at the King's Theatre in January 1783 but lifted the action finale for the end of Act I almost completely from the previous season's *Ifigenia in Aulide*, which had only been performed once.[30] In 1832, Hilary Poriss notes that Maria Malibran and her fellow singers substituted Nicola Vaccai's tomb scene from *Giulietta e Romeo* (1825) for Bellini's in *I Capuleti e i Montecchi* (1830), a substitution which remained performance practice until at least 1897.[31] Bertoni and Malibran's substitutions of large sequences in operas may have derived, ultimately, from France's fragments d'opéras and similar capriccio genres in Italy, where one-act operas, acts or scenes telling different parts of the same story, or exploring the same themes, were gathered into an evening; in these, variety rather than unity was the aesthetic aim.[32] They ran throughout the eighteenth century and in many ways anticipated the nineteenth century's mixed bill.

In many cases, singers were associated with a particular aria, even identified as its owner, and audiences grew to expect that they would sing it in whichever opera they were performing. Such arias tended to disappear from an opera when different singers were cast, so each new revival brought new arias. That said, examples are also plentiful of insertions remaining attached to a particular opera over many revivals, becoming a tradition. Such was Pergolesi's 'Splenda fra noi', inserted into *Orazio* in 1742 and continuing in most European performances up to 1760.[33] Poriss shows that 'Il soave e bel contento' from Giovanni Pacini's *Niobe* (1826) was inserted into many operas including Gioachino Rossini's *La Donna del lago*, *I Mose in Egitto*, *Otello*, *Sigismondo* and *Semiramide*, and Saverio Mercandante's *Elise e Claudio* and *Didone Abandonate*, throughout the nineteenth century, and became a signature aria for Giuditta Pasta.[34] She argues that the points in an opera at which insertion or substitution occurred became traditional: where demonstrations of singing are called for – the lesson scene in Rossini's *Il barbiere di Siviglia* (1816) being the obvious example – but the very first aria of an opera or where a 'national song' was called for to convey the locale, were others.[35]

Self-pasticcio

This very frequent form of pasticcio was satirised in Antonio Salieri and Giovanni Battista Casti's *Prima la musica, poi le parole* (1786). Sometimes termed autopasticcio, it is where a composer receives a libretto (old or new) and sets it using music from their previous works. Antonio Cesti's thirty reworkings of his *Orontea* (1656) serve as one example, but Handel's *Oreste* (1734) is another. If the pasticciere is a librettist or littérateur of some kind, they might do the same, reusing earlier aria texts, narrative tropes or sometimes whole scenes. Sometimes pasticcieri do both: Gluck and Giacomo Durazzo's *L'innocenza giustificata* (1755) is an opera in which the libretto mostly consists of aria texts selected from Metastasio's various works with a new story written around them in recitative by Durazzo. The music is wholly by Gluck and consists of intensively revised aria settings he composed in the 1740s. Betzwieser describes it as a double pasticcio with both the libretto and score mostly constructed from existing material: yet he notes that the music is so changed as to beg the question whether it can also be seen as a new composition.[36] This opera, then, can be classified as both a true pasticcio and a self-pasticcio. Whether a self-pasticcio needs to be created by the composer themself, or by a pasticciere acting on their behalf, is a question begged by Rossini's *Robert Bruce* (1846), which was created under his oversight by Louis Niedermeyer. Later in the nineteenth century, Wilhelm Meyer Lutz's comic operas for London's Gaiety Theatre, such as *Cindy Ellen Up Too Late* (1891), made use of his earlier compositions, dramatic situations and comic tropes. This opera included music from many composers including Leopold Wenzel, Frank Osmond Carr, Walter Slaughter and Lionel Monckton, so this a collaborative pasticcio as well as a self-pasticcio.

Collaborations

These are operas where two or three composers or librettists each write a part of the score. Strohm proposed that although these were sometimes called pasticcio operas, they are really collaborative operas. Unlike the two previous categories, here the composers are all alive and consciously working together; an example is *La virtù trionfante* (1724), performed in Rome: Act I was by Benedetto Micheli, Act II by Antonio Vivaldi and Act III by Nicola Romaldo.[37]

Prior to the twentieth century, composers working together often reused their own earlier works so collaborations could also be self-pasticci. Francesco Bianchi and Giovanni Bertati's *La villanella rapita* (1783) is another example of a collaboration to which a number of living composers, including Mozart, contributed items, some of which they had previously used elsewhere. The Royal Welsh College of Music and Drama created an opera this way in 2009, using three interweaving musical themes each created by a different student composer.[38]

Adaptations

Changed operas bearing the name adaptation are, like pasticcio, found between the seventeenth century and today; writing of baroque opera in 1985, Strohm argued that 'in cases where an arranger modified an already existing opera by making additions that were exclusively his own, we should speak rather of an "adaptation"'.[39] He was no doubt thinking of arrangers who added a modest amount of careful parody in the style of the original. Yet into this reverential limelight crowd the numerous adaptors who added considerable material from other works by the same author and often material from other authors unconnected to the original opera except, perhaps, by contemporaneity. Nor does this definition envision the wholesale replacement of the original score, as Michael Kelly undertook routinely when adapting French operas for Drury Lane; in reference to *Raoul Barbe Bleu* he recalled:

> the music, by Grétry, was very good. But so different are the tastes of a French and English audience, that when I produced my *Blue Beard* at Drury Lane, I did not introduce a single bar from Grétry.[40]

At which point in the process of changing the original version of an opera we should speak of an adaptation and at which point a pasticcio is moot. An extensive spectrum exists of operas called adaptations, either by their adaptor or by reviewers: at one end are straightforward translations where the text is altered only to make allowances for variations in expression between the two languages, and at the other is an opera where only the story and a few key arias remain from the original. I propose then that the boundary between an adaptation and a pasticcio is polysemous, yet within the broad spectrum of its use the term 'adaptation' carries certain resonances regardless of how much change from the original has occurred. It suggests that the opera is changed from an original which was intended for other audiences at another time, city or country so that it is not a wholly new telling of the story but rather a revision of the existing telling. The purpose of adaptation is to provide accessibility; its alterations serve to make it more comprehensible to particular audiences or more in accord with contemporary mores, culture or understanding. As Christina Fuhrmann shows, the morality and behaviour inherent in continental stories were frequently altered to suit audiences who were less travelled.[41] The common denominator in the associations attached to adaptation, then, is that the original is still *supposed* to be discernible, and while this may also happen with a pasticcio opera, the associations attached to pasticcio are of a completely new story or the telling of old ones in a wholly new way.

In her study of English adaptations of continental operas Fuhrmann argues that they gradually increased in fidelity to the original between the Regency and the 1840s.[42] She views this as a stadial progression where adaptation replaces pasticcio.[43] This is discussed in detail in Chapter 4, but a problem with this interpretation is that a pasticcio opera could also be conceived as a reverential homage to a composer and their original works, as was Torribio Calzado and Arcangelo Berettoni's pasticcio of Rossini's music, *Un curioso accidente* (1859).[44] The Carltheater commissioned the aged and ailing Johann Strauss II to create a pasticcio from his earlier works in 1899. Strauss supported the project but was too ill to do the arranging and orchestration himself and it was carried out by the house poet and composer.[45] Another problem with presenting adaptations as being essentially different from pasticcio, is that variant versions of operas, with light-touch deviations from the original, can be found from the seventeenth century onwards, some of which are designated pasticci, others adaptations, others something else: they cannot all tend towards nineteenth-century fidelity. Chapter 4 argues that many light-touch pasticci of the eighteenth century made far fewer changes to the original than are seen in the adaptations of Henry Bishop, Michael Rophino Lacy and Thomas Cooke in the 1820s and 1830s.

Occasional pasticci

A type of pasticcio which usually goes unmentioned are those created to mark historic anniversaries, commemorations or national events. Such were the pasticci celebrating George III's return to health at the King's Theatre in 1789, Nelson's victory on the Nile at the Royal Circus in 1798, the re-enactment of Queen Victoria's wedding at Her Majesty's in 1840 which comprised sequences from the Cathedral service and the ball, and the masque created by Benjamin Lumley for the opening of the Great Exhibition at the same theatre in 1851. Twentieth-century pasticci of this kind can be found from the Boer War to V.E. Day. These pasticci are given varied names; some are masques, others operas, musical presentations or pageants; but they were not always grand national celebrations. William Dowton's farewell to the stage at Her Majesty's Theatre, *The Poor Gentleman* (1840), marked the retirement of an esteemed comic actor yet still included among its cast the leading singers of the day, Giulia Grisi and Julie Dorus-Gras.

Burlesques, burlettas and extravaganzas

Although the burlesque had existed in spoken theatre since the sixteenth century, burlesques of operas, such as *Hurlothrumbo* (1729) by Samuel Johnson, become more frequent in the eighteenth century. Arguably deriving from the Italian intermezzo, the burletta was an all-sung short opera, usually in one act and comic, which could begin as an original piece and become a pasticcio, or begin as a pasticcio. Examples stretch from Charles Dibdin's *The Recruiting Sergeant* and Samuel Arnold's *The Portrait*, both 1770, while William Thomas Moncrieff's *Tom and Jerry, or Life in London* (1821) marks a change, where spoken dialogue and a less operatic structure are used. Roberta Montemorra Marvin argues that the extravaganza, a genre developed by James Robinson Planché, derives from the burletta.[46] During the monopolies of London's patent theatres, the illegitimate ones – those which lacked a royal warrant – were not supposed to stage spoken plays; nevertheless burlettas were an exception, and continued evolving into plays with music, only retaining an operatic veneer to evade the proscription on unpatented theatres. After the patent system was reformed in 1843, the burletta stopped being advertised as a performance category. The extravaganza was also pasticcio in structure but featured longer performances and put greater focus on the visual components. These two genres sometimes ran alongside burlesques but, as Montemorra Marvin shows, sometimes playbills advertised burlesques *as* extravaganzas and sometimes there was little discernible difference between them.[47]

It was in the nineteenth century that the operatic burlesque came into its own. The process of parody meant burlesques necessarily shared characteristics with the operas they satirised, sometimes becoming more operatic than operas themselves, yet their pasticcio construction methods are all but identical with those used in baroque pastici. W.S. Gilbert's operatic extravaganza at The Gaiety Theatre, *Robert the Devil or The Nun, The Dun and the Son of a Gun!* (1868), was scored by M. Aloys Kettenus, who acted as pasticciere. As well as his own composition, Kettenus included fifteen 'introduced airs', of which only the opening chorus was from Giacomo Meyerbeer's *Robert le Diable*, 'Versiamo a tazza piena'. Of the rest, five were by Offenbach, two by Bellini and the rest were single items from Ferdinand Hérold,

Jean-Baptiste Arban, Marc Chautagne, Daniel Auber, Hervé, Victor Robillard and Jules Javelot.

Burlesques of Verdi began early with Leicester Silk Buckingham's *The Lady of the Cameleon* (1857) which burlesqued *La Traviata* (1853) and John Howard Tully's *The Very Earliest Edition of Il Trovatore, or, Who Killed the –?* (1861). Both retained the original story, using minimal textual parody and no real changes to narrative sequencing; nevertheless, the changes that *were* made altered the piece entirely. The characters were reclassed in the former burlesque as Londoners on the breadline and in the latter as an Irish community. Minimal changes to the libretto and textual parody of the original, which yet deliver a substantial recontextualisation, were also a characteristic of pasticcio in the late eighteenth-century, as discussed in Chapter 3.

Reconstructions of unfinished or partly lost operas

These mostly occur in the nineteenth and twentieth centuries and are usually thought of as texts, but in performance they are undoubtedly an assembly of pre-existing parts, sometimes with new material parodying the remaining parts of the original and thus a pasticcio. I propose this as a type of pasticcio caused by, not in opposition to, Romantic trends such as the elevation of certain composers, canonical hierarchy, the investment in text as embodying the work and the preservation of that work for posterity. Attempts to reconstruct Mozart's *L'oca del Cairo* (1783) began in 1860; it was staged in 1867 after restoration by Charles Constantin and Victor Wilding. Paul Griffiths's pasticcio *The Jewel Box* (1991) made use of *L'oca del Cairo* but created a different story for it; this pasticcio also incorporated music from Mozart's other unfinished works and his contributions to pasticci.

Alexander Borodin's *Prince Igor* was incomplete at the time of his death in 1887; it was resequenced, orchestrated and completed for performance by Nikolai Rimsky-Korsakov and Alexander Glazunov. They composed the missing sequences in Borodin's style and the opera premiered in 1890. In 2014, Dmitri Tcherniakov and Gianandrea Noseda created a new version of the opera for the Metropolitan Opera in New York. This removed the 1890 ending and created a new one from Borodin's surviving compositional sketches, turning a pasticcio into a self-pasticcio; the opera was also restructured. Interestingly, both versions make claims to having greater fidelity to Borodin's intentions than previous ones.

Changes to an opera might be made that still leave the original discernible so we are left with the question how much interpolation, aria substitution, transposition of roles to different vocal registers and story changes by other

hands can occur before the work is no longer the original? This question
has resurfaced intermittently and in varying forms over the last 400 years.
A famous court case of 1791 (often discussed by music historians) involved
Gertrud Mara (Madam Mara), together with some King's Theatre staff,
reworking a duet by Giovanni Paisiello into a solo aria for herself. The
court case concerned who had the right to publish it, which revolved around
the question whether the reworking made it a new aria or whether it was
still the original one. The judge lamented that there were no established
principles by which he could determine this.[48] More recently, US District
Judge Louis Stanton found in Ed Sheeran's court cases that the question of
plagiarism turned on a musicological grey area while existing laws were
predicated on a clear-cut binary.[49] Copyright and pasticcio are discussed in
detail in Chapter 5.

   Clearly these categories can be further multiplied and each category can
itself be divided into multiple sub-categories.[50] A similar set of categorisations
could perhaps be made for the range of pasticcio practices used in painting,
sculpture, wine, furniture and conservation of antiquities. What is demonstrated by the variety of methods whereby art can be created from pre-existing
parts is that the practice does not depend on the word pasticcio. Before
mass production and population growth brought new determinants to what
constituted artistic value, an assembled approach to creating things was
widespread in cultural and material life. The surprising thing revealed in
such category lists for operatic pasticcio is that the practice continued well
beyond society's transition to mass production and mass literacy and *despite*
the new determinants brought to artistic value. The survival of this inheritance
from oral culture merits enquiry.

How they came into the world

As discussed in relation to revivals with substitutions, original operas could
mutate into pasticci in a kind of solera system. Before the mechanical or
electronic reproduction of music in performance, pasticcio was an important
means of circulation for a composer's music. Music was heard more often
than read in the seventeenth and eighteenth centuries, as even those operas
where the music was published had limited print runs and circulation, as
discussed in Chapter 3. Up to the nineteenth century, composers expected
their operas to be changed, both in rehearsals and after the initial run, and
this was not the source of frustration that later musicology assumed it to
have been. Ellen Rosand gives the example of Antonio Cesti, employed in
Vienna in 1665 and unable to go to supervise the Venetian premiere of his

opera *Tito*. He deputised its management to Giovanni Battista Rovettino, requesting his deputy to 'cut, add, change or do whatever else was necessary in the music'.[51]

Rosand notes that librettists were expected to attend rehearsals and be ready to rewrite on their feet: Venetian librettists appear to have been fairly sanguine about doing so.[52] Paolo Vendramin, Giovanni Maria Milcetti and Christoforo Ivanovich all deputised their composer to make whatever changes to the text or dramatic structure they felt was required, readily acceding to the inclusion of aria texts by other librettists. Milcetti, though, asked for these to be given a star or comma, known as *virgolette*, in the margin of the printed libretto, so that he did not appear to be claiming the work of others as his own. Even when original operas were in rehearsal and the original librettist and composer were present, what they had written was usually moderated in the rehearsal process itself.[53]

Words were rewritten to take account of how they sounded when sung and to improve clarity; sometimes a vowel was wrong for the long note being sung on it, or more bars or fewer were needed to cover a costume or scenery change, for working the machinery or for a triumphal entry. When an eighteenth-century house composer prepared a score for a revival, he might replace those aria settings he expected to be problematic for the new singers, sourcing new accompaniments from other works by the same composer, or drawing them from other composers working in the same style. Alternatively, he might simply compose the new material himself, parodying the original. Curtis Price, Judith Milhous and Robert D. Hume refer to these as 'revivals with alterations'.[54] Once the score was completed and sent out, the singers themselves might tinker with their arias, even altering the accompaniment.[55] From the late seventeenth century onwards, leading singers acquired the customary right to substitute different arias of their own choosing, as might the theatre's management. In the absence of the house composer or arranger, let alone the original composer, those leading from the continuo or first violin often took the responsibility of adding to or subtracting from the score in rehearsals. Even today, a new opera score goes through many changes in the rehearsal process leading up to a premiere as it is worked on.[56]

A pasticcio could also come into the world as the by-product of a composer or librettist writing multiple versions of their operas to suit different cities and audiences. As mentioned earlier, Cesti reworked his opera *Orontea* (1656) more than thirty times for different revivals while, a century later, Gluck created different versions of *Orfeo* for Vienna and Paris, and Mozart different versions of *Don Giovanni* for Prague and Vienna. Gluck reused his arias so many times in different operas for different audiences, and adapted the same aria texts so many times, that, as Thomas Betzwieser suggests, a broad definition of pasticcio would make the majority of Gluck's oeuvre self-pasticci.[57]

As mentioned above, pasticcio was described in the twentieth century as a pragmatic response to practical difficulties in reproducing the original. I recognise that practical considerations were a factor in the mutation of an original opera into a pasticcio: new characters might be incorporated into the story simply because there were spare singers on the payroll who needed parts, the genders of the protagonists might be changed merely to accord with the pecking order of the company, or because social behaviour was gendered differently in Italy and London. For the seventeenth century, Rosand suggests geographic distance between the librettist, composer and singers, the haphazard delivery of libretto sequences and aria settings and the short rehearsal periods.[58] Yet the implication that only practical difficulties prevented reproduction of the artist's intentions carries an underlying assumption that seventeenth-century operas would be nineteenth-century ones if they could have been.

I suggest that recreating the opera was also an artistic decision: pasticcio methods offered a means of envisaging the story afresh, with new interpretations; unexplored narrative avenues could be travelled down and new drama introduced to capitalise on current affairs. Michael Rophino Lacy's *The Casket* (1829) was a comic reimagining of Mozart's tragedy *Idomeneo*, and his *Ginevra of Sicily* (c. 1835) a recomposition of Handel's *Ariodante* in a contemporary Romantic idiom.[59] Regional theatres like the Theatre Royal in Bristol, discussed in Chapter 4, took the opportunity to reshape metropolitan operas to accord with their own audiences and operatic traditions, as did theatres in Wales. Thomas Arne and Isaac Bickerstaffe's *Thomas and Sally or The Sailor's Return* (1760) became, in Wales, *The Maid of Gower or The Sailor's Return* (Swansea, 1806); new characters, Welsh songs, local settings and Welsh ballad traditions replaced the originals. By 1825 at the latest, Thomas Attwood and Thomas Dibdin's *St David's Day* (1801) was reworked in Welsh as *Cymro Cywir* (*A True Welshman*) and further variants evolved in both languages.

In the nineteenth century, one of the prerequisites for hailing an opera as a masterwork was a single 'finished' score which encapsulated the composer's 'vision', dubbed an ur-text by early-twentieth-century music scholars. This perspective ran counter to the custom of operas becoming widespread and long-lived performance traditions through their mutability, exemplified by Auletto's *Orazio*. While some original operas lasted comparatively unchanged in the repertoire for a decade or two, many outside the canon were either revised or dropped. To secure longevity in the repertoire *and* to remain unchanged, nineteenth-century opera critics had to ascribe a much greater cultural value to those operas they considered masterpieces, and to revere the composer's original conception as a portal into their genius. I suggest the formulation of a canon was both causal and the result of this reformist need. As discussed in Chapter 3, in the eighteenth century the conception of a canon existed in the form of an apostolic succession of musical genius, but in the nineteenth century reformers inched both operatic texts and performance towards the fixity of liturgy. This study argues that twentieth-century music history accorded too much influence to reformists and that the inherited system of variation and mutability lasted much longer than thought, remaining a reflex of opera as an artform. Even in instrumental genres, late-Romantic composers often failed to adhere to the finished work principle they were supposed to typify; Monroe Beardsley noted in 1958 that:

> it is not even agreed which of the widely different versions of Bruckner's C Minor Symphony (No. 8) he wanted performed: the 1887 original, the 1890 version, the 1892 version – or some compromise like that reflected in the Hass version of 1935.[60]

Attempts were sometimes made to reconcile the different versions of a composition in order to construct a single authoritative ur-text which, it was hoped, would enable performances to accord more exactly with the composer's intentions. Having such intentions was an essential criterion for a composer to be accorded the status of a genius, so notation on the score and stage directions in the libretto increased in the nineteenth century as a means of meeting this criterion. This is a considerable distance from the approach of seventeenth-century composers, for whom posterity was not numberless future generations but the next maestro to use the manuscript for putting together a performance. Chapter 2 shows that only the minimum was specified in terms of instrumentation, performance style or even tempo, as it was accepted that the next performances would have different resources, purposes and ideas.

Ironically, the principle of textual fidelity in the nineteenth century could result in attempts to blend a composer's variants of their work together so as to create what was in some ways a pasticcio ur-text. Such was Henry Rowley Bishop and Samuel Beazley's ultra-faithful version of *Don Giovanni* in 1833, called *Don Juan*, which incorporated all the known material written for this opera, as discussed in Chapter 4.

Unity

From a modern perspective, an approach where an opera is constructed using multiple authors sounds like a recipe for artistic chaos. The very interchangeability of aria texts and accompaniments during the baroque period speaks to the deeply formulaic nature of baroque opera, but pasticcieri were also acutely aware of the danger of stylistic fragmentation. Giuseppe Riva's book advising on the creation of opera, *Avviso ai compositori ed ai cantanti,* translated into English in 1727, emphasised that achieving a high standard of dramatic and musical unity was of the utmost concern. It was usually in the final rehearsal weeks that the real shape of a pasticcio performance emerged: at this point, aria selections, text, accompaniment and recitatives could all change. Musical and dramatic unity could be won or lost during the rehearsal process, as discussed in Chapter 3.

An expectation emerged in the nineteenth century and deepened in the twentieth that composers considered geniuses would have their own individual 'voice'. Their compositional styles were expected to sound different to those of other composers. Yet from the seventeenth to the nineteenth centuries, arias and even ensembles were often interchangeable because compositional styles were *not* perceived as unique to particular composers. Compositional campanalismo meant that styles were identifiable as a particular school, tradition or region – Neapolitan, Venetian and so on – but individual composers were not necessarily detectable to non-specialist listeners. To ensure unity, pasticcieri usually ironed out any personal quirks of the individual composers they included as part of the arranging process.

When opera composition became more complex in the last third of the eighteenth century and individual voices began to be identifiable, pasticcieri took pains to give their operas the feel of having a single compositional voice. When living composers were invited to contribute to a pasticcio, as Mozart, Vincenzo Federici, Giuseppe Sarti, Giovanni Paisiello and others were for *La villanella rapita* (1783), they were careful to write within a common, shared, Viennese Burgtheater idiom, happily parodying it where it differed from their own style.[61] Bianchi and Bertati's editing no doubt provided the final polish. Contrary to the stereotype of opera as a bear-pit filled with competing solipsists, this pasticcio is one example of contributors being much concerned with stylistic, thematic and narrative unity.[62] Hilary Poriss and Massimo Ziccari have shown that the same was true for substitutions or insertions by singers from Angelica Catalani (1780–1849) to Jenny Lind (1820–1887) to Adelina Patti (1843–1919); they were very much aware of the dramatic purpose it had to serve and the overall musical unity of the opera.[63]

Librettists were not the only people writing the words in eighteenth- and nineteenth-century operas; translators did so as well. When Italian opera reached Britain's largely monoglot audiences at the start of the eighteenth century, the libretto was usually, but not invariably, printed. Of those that were, a translation was always given, printed by Robert Walsh and others, ahead of the performance run. In a full-lit auditorium, audience members would glance at it, or even read the whole thing, during the performances, but some performances operated bilingually with certain arias in Italian and others in English; the language of recitatives depended on the characters. In Walsh's publications, the language being sung was printed on the top line with the translation below in smaller type.[64] These, unlike modern translations, could differ substantially from what was actually being sung, and often stood at a distance from the original libretto. Price, Milhous and Hume show that printed translations had a vital role in revising the drama and shaping how it was understood: things a London audience would have found problematic, such as Catholic religious imprecations, were altered, plot lacunae were ironed out and references adjusted.[65]

> The plot-aiding translation could also help to smooth out inconsistencies and to paper over the breaks in continuity … With the complicity of the translator, an all-purpose aria expressing anguish or joy could thus be made to seem apropos.[66]

I suggest that translation was one of the tools used in creating dramatic and literary unity in early eighteenth-century London pasticci and, as such, can be considered part of their creative process. Printed translations were another way of changing the libretto but, instead of altering what was sung, they altered what was understood.

By the late nineteenth and early twentieth centuries, most critics had fully internalised pejorative views about pasticcio so, whenever any esteemed canonical work was discovered to have been just that, they were shocked to discover how well it hung together and how much it sounded like the work of a single composer. In 1891 a reviewer of Handel's oratorio *Israel in Egypt* commented:

> Yet if the work is to be regarded as representing the united efforts of five composers, Handel occupying a kind of editorial position, it must be confessed that the existence of so successful a pasticcio is very nearly incredible. No critic, however discerning, has been able to detect any anomaly of style between the various parts, even after their sources have been named; in fact, to the ordinary hearer, the unity of the style of the whole is one of its most impressive features.[67]

Popularity

Pasticcio has always been popular. Venerated oratorios and operas often maintained their place in the British music canon only because pasticcio versions of them sustained their popularity. Fuhrmann notes of adaptations that 'they were the first and sometimes only way in which many listeners came to know foreign operas'.[68] Earlier in Britain, Shakespeare's plays survived through the Restoration period and into the eighteenth century due to pasticcio versions being made of them, as discussed in Chapter 2. Such was the popularity of opera from the late seventeenth to the nineteenth centuries that the demand for new works outstripped supply. This put pressure on theatres to find faster and cheaper ways to create new operas and the pasticcio method was both.

Property and ownership

The music chosen for a pasticcio was sometimes used with the knowledge and consent of the original composer but usually proceeded without it. The conception of musical ownership was different in the seventeenth and eighteenth centuries to that of the nineteenth and twentieth. In continuity from the oral past, performance was seen as the point at which music ceased to be the property of those playing it and became that of the listeners. In much the same way, possession of a story in predominantly oral cultures belongs with the storyteller only up to the point when it is told; after this point the listeners may retell the story to others or borrow parts of it for other stories. As discussed in Chapter 3, in constructing performances opera creators felt entitled to make use of whatever music they found, bought or heard; so long as they did not publish it: music had no effective copyright.

In the first half of the nineteenth century, copyright, or more accurately tradability in copyrights, increasingly commodified music in a new way. Publishers sought to create new streams of profit by separating the purchase of a musical text from the freedom to perform it publicly; performing rights legislation began in Britain in 1833. Expanding copyright legislation and performance licensing made pasticcio potentially expensive but, more seriously, the moral justification for the new commodification challenged the inherited consensus about musical ownership which had underpinned pasticcio. From the late nineteenth century until the commencement of the internet age, these new commodifications came to feel like natural and timeless property rights; with the older conception of musical property long out of collective memory, pasticcio's flagrant disregard of commodification appeared immoral, potentially illegal and controversial.[69]

Notes

1 Diomedes speculated in the fourth century that the word 'satire' might derive from the name of a sausage into which different minced foods were pushed. Hints in Greek theatre offer support; in his play *The Knights*, Aristophanes makes

the critic of the government a sausage-seller: Charles Witke, *Latin Satire; the Structure of Persuasion* (Leiden: Brill, 1970). Witke also speculated that farce might derive from 'farcimen', a different kind of sausage, but French scholars argue that it derives from 'farcir', which itself derives from the Roman verb 'to stuff' according to the *Oxford English Dictionary*.

2 Reinhard Strohm, *Dramma per Musica: Italian Opera Seria of the Eighteenth Century* (New Haven, CT and London: Yale University Press, 1997), pp. 1–2.

3 Examples of pastiche include Purcell's setting of the Second Dirge Anthem used in royal funerals, written in the style of the Tudor composer Thomas Morley; Mozart's fugues in the style of Bach, K426 and K546, which he composed in the baroque idiom; and Stravinsky's *The Rake's Progress*, a modern opera written in a neoclassical idiom. A pasticcio opera might also be a pastiche in the current sense but, despite being cognate, modern customary usage obliges us to understand very different things from these two words. There are certainly attempts in the *Princeton Encyclopaedia of Poetry and Poetics*, Wikipedia and other sources to portray the two words as having a greater overlap of meaning but Percy A. Scholes's definitions in the *Oxford Companion to Music* (Oxford University Press, online edition 2011) offer useful terminological distinctions.

4 Catherine, as pasticciere, shaped the plots, contributed text to the libretti and oversaw the selection of Russian folk songs and choruses together with new Italianate compositions which comprised the scores for her operas. *Novgorodskiy bogatyr' Boyeslavovich* [The Novgorod hero Boyeslavovich] (1786), *Fedul s det'mi* [Fedul and his Children] (1791), *Ivan Tsarevich* (1787) and *Gore bogatyr' Kosometovich* [The woebegone champion Kosometovich] (1789) are discussed by Inna Naroditskaya in *Bewitching Russian Opera: The Tsarina from State to Stage* (Oxford: Oxford University Press, 2011), pp. 81–112.

5 Reinhard Strohm, 'Handel's pasticci', *Essays on Handel and Italian Opera* (Cambridge: Cambridge University Press, 1985), p. 164.

6 Noted by E.J. Dent in 1945: transcript of a lecture for the Royal Musical Society, 'Italian opera in London' by Professor E.J. Dent, *Proceedings of the Royal Musical Association, 1944–1945*, 71st session (Taylor & Francis on behalf of the RMS digitised by JSTOR), p. 36.

7 Jacques-Philippe d'Orneval and Alain-René Lesage wrote these and over eighty such dialogue and music performances; the genre influenced Gay, Gluck and, eventually, Bizet (*Le docteur miracle* via Sheridan and *Carmen*).

8 Henry Davison, *Music during the Victorian Era. From Mendelssohn to Wagner: Memoirs of J.W. Davison* (London: William Reeves, 1912), p. 15. Frederick Corder, *The Works of Sir Henry Bishop* (London, 1918), various. O.G. Sonneck, 'Ciampi's *Bertoldo, Bertoldino e Cacasenno* and Favart's *Ninette à la Cour*: a contribution to the history of pasticcio', *Miscellaneous Studies in the History of Music*, ed. O.G. Sonneck (London: Macmillan, 1921). This prosopography also includes F. Walker, '*Orazio*: the history of a pasticcio', reprinted in *Music Quarterly*, vol. 38 (1952 edition), pp. 369–383. Winton Dean, *Handel and the Opera Seria* (Berkeley: University of California Press, 1969); Winton Dean and John Merrill Knapp, *Handel's Operas, 1704–1726* and Winton Dean,

Handel's Operas, 1726–1741 (Woodbridge, Suffolk: Boydell Press, 1987 and 2006 respectively). Carl Dahlhaus believed this of all genres of music; see *Analyse und Werturteil*. (Musikpädagogik Band 8, 1970), trans. Siegmund Levarie as *Analysis and Value Judgement* (New York: Pendragon Press, 1983) and *Die Musik des 19. Jahrhunderts* (Laaber: Laaber, 1980), trans. J. Bradford Robinson as *Nineteenth-Century Music* (Berkeley: University of California Press, 1989).

 9 Curtis Price, 'Unity, originality, and the London pasticcio', *Harvard Library Bulletin*, new series, vol. 2 (Cambridge, MA: Harvard University Press, 1991), esp. pp. 22–24 and 30. Jennifer Hall-Witt, *Fashionable Acts: Opera and Elite Culture in London 1780–1880* (Durham, NH: University of New Hampshire Press, 2007), compare pp. 35–37 with p. 46.

10 Dent, 'Italian opera in London', pp. 39–40.

11 Ellen Rosand, *Opera in Seventeenth-Century Venice: The Creation of a Genre* (Berkeley, Los Angeles, Oxford: University of California Press, 1991; paperback edn, 2007), pp. 22–24, 220. Robert D. Hume, 'The politics of opera in late 17th century London', *Cambridge Opera Journal*, vol. 10 no. 1 (Cambridge: Cambridge University Press, 1998), pp. 16–18, 36–38 and, arguably, 43.

12 Christine Siegert, 'Zum Pasticcio-Problem', *Opernkonzeptionen zwischen Berlin und Bayreuth: Das musikalische Theater der Markgräfin Wilhelmine*, ed. Thomas Betzwieser, vol. 31 (Würzburg: Thurnauer Schriften zum Musiktheater, Königshausen & Neumann, 2016).

13 *Operatic Pasticcios in 18th-Century Europe: Contexts, Materials and Aesthetics*, ed. Berthold Over and Gesa zur Nieden (Bielefeld: transcript Verlag, 2021), zur Nieden and Over, 'Introduction', pp. 12, 14–15 and Panja Mücke 'Epilogue', pp. 755–756. This publication was one output of the four-year international and multi-disciplinary Polish-German Pasticcio Research Project, led by Aneta Markuszewska and Gesa zur Nieden.

14 Christina Fuhrmann, *Foreign Opera at the London Playhouses: From Mozart to Bellini* (Cambridge: Cambridge University Press, 2015), p. 2.

15 Rosand, *Opera in Seventeenth Century Venice*, p. 220.

16 Madeline Smith Atkins, *The Beggar's 'Children': How John Gay Changed the Course of England's Musical Theatre* (Cambridge: Cambridge Scholars Press, 2006). Vanessa L. Rogers, 'John Gay, ballad opera and the théâtres de la foire', *Eighteenth-Century Music*, vol. 11 no. 2 (Cambridge: Cambridge University Press, published online, 2014). https://doi.org/10.1017/S1478570614000049 [accessed 3 July 2019].

17 Thomas Betzwieser, 'The world of pasticcio: reflections on pre-existing text and music', in Over and zur Nieden, *Operatic Pasticcios*, p. 33.

18 Ibid., p. 30.

19 That said, they have often been treated as such: the financial risk implicit in a new work meant that from the eighteenth to the twentieth centuries they were sparingly programmed against trusted favourites, or pasticcio revisions of those favourites.

20 Proto-literate is the term preferred by Goody and Watt to describe societies in transition: 'The consequences of literacy', p. 7. There is a disparity between

medievalists and early modernists concerning which societies are termed literate and which oral. The term 'pre-literate' was used by mid-twentieth-century ethnographic researchers, and is still used by medievalists, to describe societies with no literacy whatsoever. Medievalists regard societies with a very low proportion of literacy in the population as still being literate societies, whereas early modernists tend to consider pre-literate or proto-literate societies to be ones where the proportion of literate people within them is so low that the predominant culture is demonstrably oral. The printing press is the engine of transition for early modernists; they consider medieval societies to be proto-literate, the sixteenth and seventeenth centuries transitional, and the eighteenth and nineteenth centuries literate or mass-literate. I have used these early modernist terms for the periods covered by each chapter.

21 Paul Rodmell, *Opera in the British Isles, 1875–1918* (London: Routledge, 2016), pp. 84, 106–107, 155–162, esp. 156, 207.

22 Ibid., pp. 219–220, pp. 329–332, but 209–218 for discussion.

23 Paula McDowell, 'Ong and the concept of orality', *Religion & Literature*, vol. 44 no. 2 (South Bend, IN: The University of Notre Dame, 2012), p. 177, n. 5.

24 Price, 'Unity, originality', pp. 18–20. Donald J. Grout and Hermine Weigel Williams, *A Short History of Opera* (New York: Columbia University Press, 2003), pp. 212–213.

25 J. Peter Burkholder, 'The uses of existing music: musical borrowing as a field', *Notes*, Second Series, vol. 50 no. 3 (Middleton, WI: Music Library Association, March 1994), pp. 867–870.

26 Luigi Mancia is a possibility. He was involved in *Arione* in Milan and is known to have created pasticcio operas on other occasions. He was also instrumental in the introduction of Italian opera to London. In 1701 Mancia was in London singing at Hampton Court and Drury Lane, returning again in 1707. Claudio Sartori, '*Dori* e *Arione*, due opere ignorate di Alessandro Scarlatti', *Note d'archivo per la storia musicale*, vol. 18 (Rome, 1941), pp. 35–42.

27 Strohm, 'Handel's pasticci', pp. 164–169.

28 Price, referring to John Roberts's comments on Handel's *Giustino* (1737), 'Unity, originality', p. 30.

29 Walker, '*Orazio*'.

30 Curtis Price, Judith Milhous and Robert D. Hume, *Italian Opera in Late 18th-century London, the King's Theatre, Haymarket*, 2 vols (Oxford: Clarendon Press, 1995), vol. I, pp. 294–295.

31 Hilary Poriss, *Changing the Score: Arias, Prima Donnas, and the Authority of Performance* (Oxford: Oxford University Press, 2009), pp. 11, 103–110.

32 Examples of fragments d'opéras include *Télémaque* (1704) by Antoine Danchet and André Campra, a five-act tragédie lyrique, and *Les surprises de l'Amour* (1748, 1757) which included Jean-Philippe Rameau's one-act opera-ballets.

33 Walker, '*Orazio*', pp. 375 and 382.

34 Poriss, *Changing the Score*, pp. 83–96.

35 Ibid., Chapter 5.

36 Betzwieser, 'The world of pasticcio', pp. 32–33.

37 Strohm, 'Handel's pasticci', p. 151.

38 The student composers were Chris Fossey, Tom Floyd and Chris Petrie; they worked under the supervision of Tim Raymond, professor of composition, setting a bilingual libretto by myself based on the Welsh legend *Cantre'r Gwaelod*.

39 Strohm, 'Handel's pasticci', p. 161.

40 Michael Kelly, *Solo Recital, The Reminiscences of Michael Kelly* (London, 1826, reprinted by The Folio Society, 1972), p. 178.

41 Fuhrmann, *Foreign Opera at the London Playhouses*, pp. 161–165.

42 Ibid., pp. 2, 13–15.

43 Ibid. but also pp. 39 and 47.

44 Henry Sutherland Edwards, *Rossini and His School* (The Great Musicians Series, London 1881) p. 14. See also Annalisa Bini, '"Accidente curioso a proposito di *Un curioso accidente*", un contestato pasticcio rossiniano (Parigi, 1859)', *Ottocento e oltre. Scritti in onore di Raoul Meloncelli*, ed. Francesco Izzo and Johannes Streicher (Rome, 1993), pp. 339–353.

45 *Wiener Blut* (1899) was translated and adapted for Broadway in 1901 and filmed in 1942: Richard Traubner, *Operetta: A Theatrical History* (Oxford: Oxford University Press, 1989), p. 423.

46 Roberta Montemorra Marvin, 'Verdian opera burlesqued: a glimpse into mid-Victorian theatrical culture', *Cambridge Opera Journal*, vol. 15 no. 1 (Cambridge: Cambridge University Press, 2003), p. 41.

47 Ibid., pp. 40–42.

48 Maik Köster, 'Borrowed voices: legal ownership of insertion arias in 18th-century London', in Over and zur Nieden, *Operatic Pasticcios*, pp. 479–480.

49 Sheeran was accused of plagiarism and prosecuted for copyright infringement in two cases brought in May 2023. As under Lord Kenyon in 1791, the court nonsuited the plaintiffs and the jury found in Sheeran's favour. 'Stanton on Tuesday found that the combination of chord progression and harmonic rhythm in [Marvin] Gaye's song was a "basic musical building block" that was too common to merit copyright protection': Blake Brittain, *Reuters*, 17 May 2023.

50 The pornographic pasticcio I have not discussed, but Axel Englund notes *Lady Bumtickler's Revels* (1872), which he suggests is possibly of late eighteenth-century origin: Axel Englund, *Deviant Opera: Sex, Power and Perversion on Stage* (Berkeley: University of California Press, 2020), p. 1.

51 Rosand, *Opera in Seventeenth Century Venice*, p. 219.

52 Ibid., pp. 206–207.

53 Ibid., pp. 211–219.

54 Price, Milhous and Hume, *Italian Opera*, vol. I, p. 29.

55 As Gertrud Mara famously did with 'Anche nel petto io sento' in April 1791.

56 James MacMillan and Michael Symmons Roberts's *The Sacrifice* (2007), commissioned by Welsh National Opera, saw changes made during the rehearsal process. Similarly, changes are regularly made by Music Theatre Wales in preparing new works for performance and these are typical of the process. Corrections and

changes are also made when a new translation is tried out for the first time. During twenty-first-century forays into pasticcio, time is spent during the music calls tailoring the selected sequences to the singers and making sure the notes serve the text well. Suiting transpositions to the vocal ranges of the singers also occurs in rehearsal.

57 Betzwieser, 'The world of pasticcio', p.33.
58 Rosand, *Opera in Seventeenth Century Venice*, pp. 211–212.
59 Brian Trowell, 'Michael Rophino Lacy and *Ginevra of Sicily*: a 19th-century adaptation of Handel's *Ariodante*', *The Handel Institute Newsletter*, vol. 6 no. 1 (London: The Handel Institute, 1995). Digitised by the Handel Institute: https://handelinstitute.org/wp-content/uploads/2021/07/61.pdf [accessed 6 June 2023].
60 Monroe C. Beardsley, *Aesthetics: Problems in the Philosophy of Criticism* (New York: Harcourt, Brace and World Inc., 1958), p. 22.
61 Mozart, Vincenzo Federici, Giuseppe Sarti, Giovanni Paisiello, Pietro Guglielmi, Giacomo Ferrari and Johann Gottlieb Naumann all contributed items to this opera at some point.
62 Singers were often represented by eighteenth- and nineteenth-century opera reformers as capricious replacers of arias, egotistically motivated by what best displayed their vocal abilities and heedless of both musical or dramatic unity. This trope occurs in a letter to *The Morning Post* written by 'Marcello' on 9 December 1789 and continues in the writings of William Ayrton, J.W. Davison and others, as discussed in Chapter 4.
63 Poriss, *Changing the Score*. Massimo Zicari, 'Expressive tempo modifications in Adelina Patti's recordings: an integrated approach', *Empirical Musicology Review*, vol. 12 (Columbus, OH: Ohio State University Libraries, 2017).
64 Alison Clark de Simone, 'The myth of the diva: female opera singers and collaborative performance in early eighteenth-century London' (unpublished doctoral dissertation, University of Michigan, 2013), p. 208n.
65 Price, Milhous and Hume, *Italian Opera*, vol. I, pp. 34–40.
66 Ibid., pp. 36–37.
67 *The Times*, 27 June 1891, p. 7.
68 Fuhrmann, *Foreign Opera at the London Playhouses*, p. 2.
69 An example of this concern can be found in Price, 'Unity, originality', p. 30.

1

The creative process

We have really no patience with this spirit of *improving* the master-pieces of men of genius – who, being dead, have nothing to say in defence of their original intentions ... interpolations, omissions, transpositions, alterations and what not. And so, to keep up the character of the times, *Don Giovanni* must be mauled about, at the opera, in similar fashion.

> J.W. Davison, *The Musical Examiner*, 17 August 1844

I recently created a pasticcio opera about Casanova with the writer Stephen Pettitt. We joyfully plundered operas and oratorios from Vivaldi to Bellini, committing some glorious heresies along the way.

> Julian Perkins, Sounds Baroque, interview in *Meet the Artist*, 2018

As these quotations suggest, the criteria for selecting material for pasticci changed over four centuries as society's gradual, uneven transition from orality to literacy complicated the process of storytelling. Similarly, the reasons for disliking pasticcio changed too. Examples of transhistoricism in the practice of pasticcio are thus rare, but a summary of the few there are provides a baseline from which we can identify developments over time. In selecting music for use in pasticcio, the emotional purpose of the original, its pathos in rhetorical terms, is often the determinant as, once the original narrative is stripped away, the emotional thrust of the music remains. Presto continues to tighten the pace or convey excitement even in new contexts, adagio still provides more pensive or sorrowful moods and these break down further into the *kinds* of excitement or *kinds* of sorrow conveyed by different settings.

Yet accompaniments which are nearly right for the new context (but not quite) are rendered so by reworking and, throughout the four centuries, pasticcieri have tailored original music to fit its new dramatic moment more exactly; but wherever possible, they have made only minimal changes to the text or music. The reasons for this vary over time and from opera to opera: sometimes it is because the opera is an homage to the original creator, at others it is because the compilation time is too short for much reworking, most often it is because the revision process stops once the new dramatic purpose has been achieved. Yet however minimal the reworking, a new context can still utterly change the meaning of the music, as discussed in Chapter 3. Slight alterations to orchestration can turn an inspiring march into a menacing one, through only a slight tempo change and the addition of a contra-bassoon, for example. To make a pompous march ridiculous or a comic march majestic might require nothing more than altering the note values or adding a counter-melody. The same is true for libretti, and slight textual changes with large dramatic consequences are also discussed in Chapter 3.

Words, music and intertextuality

Libretto and score

Scholars agree that the words were the principal vehicle for telling the story in the operas of the seventeenth and most of the eighteenth centuries. Consequently, the creative process for pasticcio in these periods began with choosing a story and then selecting arias with appropriate texts to tell it. The music gave the text its emotional or dramatic power and created the immersion which characterised opera, but it was seldom the vehicle for conveying the narrative in the way it would be in melodrama or in nineteenth-century opera. Rosand and others note that music was as changeable and disposable as scenery.[1] Librettists, consequently, were senior to composers. They might direct them over how they wanted sequences to be set and, above all, they did not want the music to upstage the words. Yet no operatic trend is without counter-examples: instances can be found of a venerated or independent composer, such as Monteverdi or Cavalli in Venice or Handel in London, directing the librettist. In a later era, when the composer was senior to the librettist, similar examples of reversed seniority can be found. The 26-year-old Kurt Weill deferred to the 48-year-old established dramatist Georg Kaiser when they created *Der Protagonist* (1926). Rosand noted that in seventeenth-century Venice:

> [l]ibrettists, however inadequate, casual or amateurish they claimed to be were educated in and practiced *lettere*: they were writers whose words laid traditional claim to immortality, especially since the invention of the printing press, and whose capabilities were well judged by well-established critical criteria. Composers on the other hand, no matter how intelligent or well educated – and whatever the higher claims of music as theory – were essentially artisans, practitioners of a trade, for hire. Theirs was a service profession.[2]

Across the four centuries pasticcieri or singers endeavoured to retain the original text of an aria where they could, only changing the words when a new dramatic context or translation made it necessary; examples of this are discussed in Chapters 2 and 3. The use of common metrical formulae in seventeenth- and eighteenth-century arias allowed a text from one aria to be grafted onto the setting for another with comparative ease.

Throughout all the periods I survey, pasticcieri have had to set new words to existing notes, a much harder task than simply writing what one wants and handing it over to the composer for setting. It can be laborious work ensuring that the stressed syllable of a word sits on a pre-existing stressed note, and necessitates a flexible attitude towards phrasing and a willingness to rework lines multiple times until the right match is found. In London, John Dryden found this task a painful experience when reworking his poetry for *Albion and Albanius* with Louis Grabu in 1684–1685. In his preface he is largely complimentary about his composer colleague but there were clearly tensions, as Dryden loathed having to change his verse to fit the pre-written music. In an age where the librettist was senior to the composer, he felt the natural operatic hierarchy was being inverted:

> It is true I have not been often put to this drudgery but, where I have, the words will sufficiently show that I was then a slave to the composition, which I will never be again. It is my part to invent and the musician's part to humour that invention. I may be counselled, and will always follow my friend's advice where I find it reasonable, but will never again part with the power of the militia.[3] [My punctuation]

By contrast, the Venetian librettist Giulio Strozzi had an exceptionally generous understanding of the relationship of words to music in operatic storytelling. His prefaces show an awareness that while libretti are verse, they are not actually poetry. In *Delia* (1639), he refers to 'gorghe', usually translated as ornaments but which literally translate as eddies, a metaphoric term for what we might today call the resonances words and phrases carry in poetry. Strozzi argued that, in opera, such resonances are best expressed through the music: '[i]t is the duty of the poet to abandon his resonances [eddies, gorghe], which are his digressions and episodes, to give rise to the passaggi [shifting resonations] of the musicians' [my translation].[4] He noted that if the text and music both attempt to provide resonance at the same time, the text usually comes off worse. Aria text is at its best, he implies, when the poetic significance of a phrase is understated, thus leaving room for the music to create that significance.

From the mid- to late eighteenth century the function of music in opera changed, as it became a storyteller in its own right. Music had always been the means for progressing an audience's emotional journey through the narrative, but it developed greater interplay between instrumentation and voices during this period and described journeys or progressions beyond the text.

This occurred very gradually and examples can be found in earlier operas, but this period saw a great expansion in accompaniments making allusions to other parts of the story, signalling motives, inviting comparisons – even subliminal messaging was used, with a bar or two passing too quickly to be consciously discerned but warning audiences not to trust a character or alerting them to potential danger. A pared-down theme could be used to prefigure the dénouement, at which point that theme would be fully developed. In the early nineteenth century, music became the senior storyteller in London for those operas which were sung in a continental language.

This changed the selection criteria in borrowing arias for pasticcio. Discernible from the 1780s, pasticcieri increasingly selected arias for their congruence with each other in compositional style, as well as for expressing the right dramatic moment. Textual and compositional parody now played a bigger role than it had formerly, as seen in the London staging of Steven Storace's adaptation of Paisiello's *Le gare generose* (1787) and Filippo Livigni's *I due castellani burlati* (1790), discussed in Chapter 3.

Yet audiences and many critics only tended to notice the centrality of musical complexity to their operatic experience when it was absent. Occasionally, an opera attempted to return to a text-led approach, with a deliberately simple accompaniment: such was Charles Ambroise Thomas's *Hamlet* (1868), an unexpectedly simple, even reverential setting of his librettist's adaptation of Shakespeare. Many libretti, at this point in time, were considered to be of indifferent quality and a number of operas adapted Shakespeare to forestall such criticism. Ambroise Thomas took what was, for the time, the unusual step of forestaging the words and restraining the music to an illustrative or accompanying role. It was warmly praised by devotees of spoken theatre and attracted large audiences in its initial runs at the Paris Opéra but also met with serious critical hostility.[5] Recent revivals in London and New York also attracted large audiences but criticism, then and recently, focused on the elective subordination of the music to the text. Reviews have shared a common defensive tone, as if the pre-eminence of music within opera is being challenged or the balance between the two questioned. Perhaps this response demonstrates that there is no going back to text-led opera, either in the nineteenth century or the twenty-first.

Nineteenth-century pasticcio works that did continue to privilege text over the music tended to be demoted from the rank of serious operas. Operettas, burlettas, burlesques and Savoy operas were very successful with audiences not least because they cultivated accessibility. Operas sung in other languages, meanwhile, accrued the impression of being intellectual, formal and serious, a stereotype they went out of their way not to dispel. Elite nineteenth-century reactions against the accessible and popular would evolve into the highbrow and lowbrow categorisations of the twentieth century, examined by Chris Chowrimootoo, Kate Guthrie and Alexandra Wilson.[6]

Intertextuality

A question much discussed in modern scholarship is how far pasticcio is concerned with intertextuality: are reused sequences of music or text intended to refer, comment or contrast with their original context or, if not intended, was intertextuality perceived anyway by audience members? The Pasticcio Research Project identifies intertextuality as a core question in the study of pasticcio. Using the terminology of Gérard Genette's theory of transtextuality, Betzwieser questions whether a relationship can be posited between hypotext (pre-existing texts) and hypertext (new texts):

> The crucial point is the issue of intertextuality ... I mean an 'intentional' intertextuality, producing a deliberate correlation between texts, and eventually targeting the recipient's perspective. To put it in a nut-shell: is the borrowed music in a pasticcio primarily used as 'material', or is the selection of the music bound to specific meanings between the hypotext and the hypertext? ... Are pasticcios generally bound to a framework of (intentional) reference? Should we read the pre-existing arias in a Handel pasticcio as quotations, and should they therefore be identified as a reference? Are the Italian arias in *Love in a Village* intended as quotations?[7]

Betzwieser suggests that reading pasticcio operas in this way is problematic, noting that Genette's theory is intended for text per se rather than texts set to music, and even if music is read *as* a text the theory fits certain pasticci but not others. I agree, and to these problems suggest adding some others. As argued below, proto-literate oral culture remained influential in the reception of seventeenth- and eighteenth-century opera, the most significant feature of which was a profound immersion in the story. Musicology has often drawn attention to the talking and chatting which occurred among opera audiences prior to the rise of silent listening in the deeply literate operatic culture of the mid-nineteenth century. This quirk of past societies has meant that the intense emotional engagement of theatre audiences with storytelling has been less discussed. As a counter-quirk, I submit a performance of *Ann Bullen* in 1711, at which one of the sentries on duty before the proscenium arch was unable to restrain his tears at Piercey's protestations to be heard by Ann. His absorption in the drama divided the audience between laughter at his neglect of his duty to watch the crowd, and applause for his recognition of the power of the drama. The actor playing Piercey came out of character to give him half a crown.[8]

I propose that, in its first two centuries, the new narrative context given to pre-existing music in a pasticcio tended to drive out recollections of its previous context during performances. Only in a limited number of a diegetic comedies were audiences invited unambiguously to bring the previous contexts back to mind: Betzwieser gives Lorenzo da Ponte's *L'ape musicale* (1789, 1792, 1830) as an example that might meet Genette's definition of inter-textuality (pp. 38–41). Habitués of the King's Theatre were accustomed to hearing their favourite arias in new contexts but recalling earlier performances at the same time as being immersed in the current performance was not how societies listened, prior to mass literacy. In the seventeenth and eighteenth centuries, some pasticci used arias from the previous season, sung in the very same theatre to much the same people, yet in oral narrative tradition, discussed below, this does not weaken immersion in the new narrative.

I argue below and in Chapter 4 that intertextuality in Genette's interpreta-tion only emerged when a culture of mass-literacy brought older ways of listening and seeing to an end in the nineteenth century. Immersion in reading became a more intensive experience than listening to performances and, I propose, emerged only when audience members began to view performances as animations of a text, rather than ongoing performance traditions. Per-formances which were consciously intended to be read often made greater use of visuality in delivering their narrative, and relied on audiences possessing the skills to decode such visuality. As part of a literate culture this occurred in popular artforms, where an audience's literacy capacity might be expected to be limited; it is found from puppet shows to magic lantern shows to silent cinema. While pasticcio operas of the seventeenth and eighteenth centuries abounded in contemporary allusion, parallels, references and applications, it unlikely that audience members were intended to unpick their constituent parts in performance and mentally trace their origins to enjoy submerged layers of metatextuality. As Robert D. Hume famously pointed out with regard to applications in late seventeenth-century opera: when they *were* intended for the audience, they were a lot more likely to be flagrantly obvious than to be subtle and hidden.[9]

Handel reworked an aria by an older German colleague from his time in Brunswick, Reinhard Keiser, for Polyphemus, the lumbering comic cyclops in *Acis and Galatea* (1718). Keiser's aria 'Wann ich dich noch einst erblicke' from *Templum der Janus* (1698) was used by Handel for 'O ruddier than the cherry' and it has been suggested by Ellen T. Harris that Handel's Polyphemus may be a burlesque of Keiser himself.[10] There are reasons for doubting this. It is unlikely that Keiser was sufficiently well known in London for the audience to make the connection; if anything, they might have recalled the original aria from *Templum der Janus*, but the opera was either never or very seldom performed in London. Nevertheless, if any of

Handel's audience did know the opera – George I, for example – I doubt they would have perceived any echoes of the appalled, betrayed and suffering Vipsania Agrippina in Polyphemus. Agrippina is tormented by being allowed to see her lover/betrayer, but is forbidden to speak to him. Handel took the bass line from the orchestration of the original aria to create the new vocal line; he then changed the words and shifted the meaning from tragic to comic, even grotesque. The urgent, rapid, anxious feel of the music remains, but it no longer illustrates a love-stricken and devastated heroine in a paroxysm of rage and longing, but rather a cartoon giant in lust. Handel changed the meaning of the music without working against its musical structure. It is hard to see intertextuality being intended for the audience, which is not to say that Handel was not amusing himself.

If pasticcieri in the first two centuries *had* sought the kind of intertextualities enjoyed in nineteenth-century musical performance we might expect them to appear unrevised rather than reworked. The changes routinely made suggest more than disinterest in reminding audiences of a previous context; that context was often positively obscured by textual changes, using instrumental lines for vocal ones and vice versa, changes of character and thus the gender and vocal register of the singer and new ornamentations by singers. Pasticcieri of the seventeenth and eighteenth centuries usually intended their operas to be worlds within themselves, each opera having its own robust unity. When musical allusions to other operas were intended to be noticed, they were usually backed up by the narrative and the reference is pointed out. To *L'ape musicale*, I propose Mozart's aria from *Figaro* in *Don Giovanni* and his parody of Italian, French and English musical tropes in 'Con un vezzo all' Italiana' in *La finta giardiniera* (1775). Most examples are fleeting moments of comic or satirical effect and there are few pasticci in a sustained discourse with a single original in this period, as we find later with parody operas, such as Meyer Lutz's *Faust up to Date* (1888) or *Carmen up to Date* (1890). I suggest that the sparse examples of intertextuality in this period do not make it a hallmark of the pasticcio operas of these years.

Another characteristic of pasticcio in these centuries, indicating that remembering the original contexts of its component parts was not sought, is that many avoid well-known music. This contradicts Dent's assumption that the plums are always abstracted, based perhaps on Horace Walpole's comment that he was looking forward to tomorrow evening's pasticcio opera 'full of most of my favourite songs'.[11] Many pasticcieri preferred to present their audiences with arias of proven excellence that were unfamiliar to those listeners as a novelty. The numbers Handel selected for his pasticci were usually from composers whose work was little known in London such as Leonardo Vinci, Johann Hasse and Leonardo Leo.[12] When he reused his own arias, he certainly selected successful ones but he avoided those most recently heard, preferring to give a fresh airing to ones which were unknown in London or which had slipped in popular memory. Handel's accompaniment for his famous aria in *Rinaldo* (1711), 'Lascia ch'io pianga', had been used twice previously, once in Hamburg in his opera *Almira* (1705) and once in an oratorio, *Il trionfo del Tempo e del Disinganno* (1707). Following the performances of *Rinaldo*, Handel did not use the aria again when he revised *Il trionfo* in 1737.

Ballad opera, on the other hand, does co-opt the fame of very well-known airs as part of its storytelling: Johann Christoph Pepusch and John Gay's use of Jeremiah Clarke's famous 'March of the Prince of Denmark' (*c.* 1700) for their sequel to the *The Beggar's Opera*, *Polly* (1729), is one example, and this was retained in Samuel Arnold's 1777 revival. In ballad opera, however, the storytelling is different in form; instead of being all-sung which, as argued below, is the principal means of compelling complete immersion in the story, dialogue carries much of the narrative. Its airs were a combination of new lyrics and well-known melodies and while familiar music *could* offer tensions or ironies where the words were sung, it was not consistently used in this way: often, a well-known song tune was simply a well-known song tune, with no discernible relevance beyond expressing the right emotional register for the situation. Instead of the forms of transtextuality identified by Genette, ballad opera, ballet d'action, nineteenth-century melodrama, film accompaniments and other genres tend to use the familiarity of famous music as plot information. As in modern cartoons, where a few bars of Chopin's *marche funebre* tell us the cat has died, or Mendelssohn's wedding march suggests that the mouse is in love, the use of famous music in pasticcio is to advance the *current* story, not invite recollection of the original context, save in its loosest associations.

Once nineteenth-century London had become a city with a mass-literate culture, intertextuality became a well-attested feature of the opera texts held to embody the work itself; such were Arthur Sullivan's quotations, a practice reaching into the twentieth century. Benjamin Britten quotes the poisoning music from Richard Wagner's *Tristan* when Albert Herring drinks alcohol for the first time (*Albert Herring*, 1946). Intertextuality became a central feature of performance too, with parody operas and burlesques depending on knowledge of the original. However, Rossini's *Robert Bruce* (1846) demonstrates continuity with the former practice of giving the selected music wholly new meanings and containing them in the world of the new story. It is a serious pasticcio and was revived in 2002 at the Festival della Valle d'Itri; this opera revealed to the reviewer, Richard Osborne, that recalling the source material was something he did not particularly enjoy doing. Osborne argued that the opera worked better when the sequences from *La donna del lago* were more frequently interspersed with those from *Zelmira*, as occurred in Act III.[13] This was more satisfying for him than when the libretto was supported by long sequences from *dell lago*, as occurred in Act II, because then, memories of the source opera kept peeping through the surface, not through intertextual intention, but because the sequence was long enough for the original to come to mind and had been insufficiently reworked to disguise it. Osborne found this interrupted his immersion in the present story. Intertextuality, then, is a double-edged sword for pasticcio; it can be the guest of honour in *Die falsche Catalani* (1818) or *Carmen up to Date* but be an unwelcome intruder in *Robert Bruce*.

Lastly, nineteenth-century insertion arias are sometimes argued to have intertextual purposes as singers from Angelica Catalani to Kate Santley 'owned' what we might today call signature arias. Hilary Poriss shows that the moment in an opera when such arias were sung were as apposite as possible and complementary to dramatic context but, in many cases, this was a metatheatrical moment when the singer's metacharacter as a celebrity opera singer came to the fore and the opera's character temporarily receded. Such were 'Ah! non credea mirarti' from Bellini's *La sonnambula* (London, 1833) for singers ranging from Giuditta Pasta and Maria Malibran to Adelina Patti, who recorded it in 1906. 'The last rose of summer', used in Friedrich von Flotow's *Martha* (1847), was a signature aria for Anna Zerr and Anna Bishop and the 'Gipsy song' from Meyerbeer's *Ein Feldlager in Schlesien* (1847) likewise for Jenny Lind. I suggest these interpolations were not genuinely intertextual, as their performance was not intended to recall the original dramatic context of another opera but rather to further identify the celebrity singer with the current opera and draw lustre from the popularity of her performance of the aria.

I suggest the comparative sparsity of intertextuality in early pasticcio operas is one of the indicators that there are no specific visual images or single-purpose narratives embedded in clusters of notes; multiple visualisations or dramatic resonances are possible from each and every musical sequence. Thus, each opera score has, potentially, dozens of other operas latent within it.

Performance culture in London prior to the arrival of opera

To understand the origins of pasticcio and its continuing role in opera, we first have to recognise the centrality of storytelling in early modern society and contextualise pasticcio within Western society's communications technologies. The following discussion will be of service to the reader throughout the book as the interactions between orality and literacy allow a new understanding of pasticcio to emerge. Previously, operatic history has been explored in isolation from this ever-evolving relationship, so a thumbnail historiography and survey of current thinking is a useful preliminary.

The approach of many late-nineteenth- to mid-twentieth-century scholars of orality and literacy was to study societies which had never encountered literacy, terming them 'primary oral cultures'. These could only be found in the developing world so they took a largely ethnographic approach: one consequence of this methodology was a tendency to reinforce the perception of orality and literacy as a mutually exclusive binary. Later scholars in the 1960s to 1980s, including Walter Ong, argued that such a binary could not be applied to the late medieval and early modern periods in Europe, demonstrating that tale and text interacted substantially between the Roman Empire and the advent of the printing press (albeit the numbers of literate people were minimal). More recently, scholars have challenged both the antagonistic binary of orality *or* literacy and the progressivist conception *from* orality *to* literacy. Formerly, it had been thought that the transition from privileging speech and memory for recording and disseminating information to privileging literacy had resulted in the decline and death of oral media, leaving only vestigial remains: Ong's 'oral residue'. The late twentieth century saw a consensus emerge that these two cultures cross-pollinated and influenced each other. Far from oral transmission declining, Jack Goody and Ian Watt argue that literacy should be seen as an addition to oral transmission rather than an alternative to it.[14] Medieval oral culture did not diminish evenly and orality continued to influence texts, information systems and behaviours up to the nineteenth century; Shirley Brice Heath argues that it continues to outweigh literate culture in certain contexts today.[15] In the twenty-first century, an awareness developed that this perspective was underplaying the rise and spread of literacy in recent centuries; it was argued that more recognition was required that a transition from oral to literate culture *had* occurred, although not in the ways previously formulated. As Paula McDowell put it:

> In fact, there now appears to be so much consensus concerning the co-existence of media and the value of careful focused studies that some scholars now feel the need to remind us of the value of identifying larger patterns. The editors of a recent volume addressing 'the interfaces between orality and literacy and between the products of the pen and the press' in early modern England emphasize the 'danger ... of emphasising continuity [of oral traditions and practices]. It cannot be denied that dramatic as well as gradual shifts were taking place in the culture of communications in the four centuries under investigation.'[16]

This study aims to identify such larger patterns and, while it considers pasticcio an oral continuity, it also recognises the transition in Britain to an increasingly literate culture. The rise of literacy had a different history in the Italian peninsula to that in Britain, but storytelling changed in response to increased literacy in both regions. Spoken theatre in Britain left many oral characteristics behind in the eighteenth and nineteenth centuries, but opera, in contrast, tended to retain them. Why this should have occurred is a question considered throughout the study. Pasticcio was one of opera's most notable inheritances from oral culture.

Before the tipping point

I suggest that the frameworks, parameters and audience relationships of seventeenth-century theatre derived from oral storytelling practice and traditions as much as from the medieval precursors of theatrical artforms. Acting in British theatre and Italian opera were embedded in oral traditions that made them much closer to storytelling than to acting, as we would recognise it today. Even though literate people remained a minority in Britain throughout the seventeenth century, their overall numbers increased and a tipping point was reached at which literacy became the more prestigious method of cultural exchange.

Oral storytelling was still the most widespread artform in early modern society and the numbers of literate people were minimal so, as oral storytelling can only be studied today if it has been recorded in textual or visual form, our examples are much fewer than the totality of storytelling created. Throughout medieval Europe, spoken, chanted or sung storytelling had featured hugely in daily life, embracing all economic groups, ages and genders. Common characteristics of oral storytelling traditions – from a literate perspective – include a penchant for familiar stories and well-known narrative tropes rather than originality. The actions or emotions of characters often have little causality or motivation but repetitions and other strategies allow listeners to know, hope or fear what is coming next. Stylistically, stories show a love of listing and repeated verbal formulae and oral tradition was largely uninterested, throughout the early modern period, in obeying classical rules such as the unities. Such storytelling is also characterised by the cutting and pasting together of sequences from other stories and these characteristics remained an integral part of opera long after most of Britain's oral culture had diminished into regional subcultures.

As an oral practice, the survival of pasticcio far into an age of mass literacy is surprising and merits discussion. Arias were selected in the compilation of pasticci in much the same way that incidents, tropes and character types were in oral storytelling. Saints' lives, for example, frequently record miracles borrowed from other saints; the duplication made them *more* convincing rather than less in a storytelling environment where originality was not particularly a virtue; rather, derivation from an authority, even a fictional one, legitimised the story. Originality weakened credibility. Another reason why orality in a proto-literate society is important in understanding pasticcio, is that it allows us to relocate debates such as when performance was reoriented to text and the 'work-concept'. These can be contextualised within similar changes occurring in the same timeframe within many activities from ranging from commodity marketing to religion.

In the early modern period, literacy grew from being something used in a profoundly narrow range of contexts by a small number of people, most of whom belonged to professional groups, to becoming society's principal and most authoritative method of recording and disseminating information. This expansion was a great social divider. Those who possessed literacy skills rose economically and socially while those who did not were left lamenting the decline in status of a culture based on spoken contracts and memory skills. In calling these changes a transition, I do not wish to imply a switch-over like that of stage coaches to railways; in many cases the transition simply consisted of status changes between the two methods while both continued in use. Nevertheless, the forms and content of opera changed gradually during the seventeenth and eighteenth centuries as this transition influenced subject matter, modes of delivery, performance practices and, above all, reception.

The tipping point

Foundational work on the seventeenth-century tipping point was carried out by David Cressy in the 1970s and has been updated by Margaret Spufford, R.A. Houston, Cecile M. Jagodzinski and Adam Fox, among others. While they acknowledge that literacy rates in England can never be calculated precisely for the seventeenth century, they argue for a rise from 30 per cent of about 4 million people in 1641 to 47 per cent of roughly 4.7 million by 1696, with 90 per cent of women remaining illiterate throughout the intervening decades, though this latter statistic is open to challenge.[17] The civil wars were the key stimulus for an increase in literacy with both handwritten and printed news increasing in volume and frequency. Political propaganda, religious tracts and ballads were printed and long-distance handwritten correspondence proliferated. The teaching of literacy was felt to be a vital weapon in the ideological struggles of the period, securing people's hearts and minds towards particular politico-religious allegiances.

Growth in literacy continued upwards, by 1800 reaching 62 per cent among an English population of roughly 8 million.[18] Fox describes literate culture as discernibly replacing the features of an oral one even among non-literate groups.[19] Indeed, the non-literate remained a substantial minority in the eighteenth century: William St Clair argues that although eighteenth- and early nineteenth-century circulating libraries can be found across Britain, they never reached more than approximately 1 per cent of the population.[20] Yet there was no counter-action fought against literate culture nor any coherent movement to defend the oral one; along with pre-Reformation religious practices, professional knighthood and chivalry, its passing was more often lamented than resisted. Twentieth-century scholars may have initiated modern exploration of this subject, but seventeenth-century observers such as John Norden and John Aubrey, the antiquary and philosopher, witnessed the tipping point at first hand. Aubrey reflected in 1686–1687 on the demotion of oral culture which had occurred in his lifetime and commented:

> [b]efore printing, old wives tales were ingenious: and since printing came in fashion, till a little before the civil warres, the ordinary sort of people were not taught to reade: now-a-dayes books are common, and most of the poore people understand letters: and the many good books, and variety of turns of affaires, have put all the old fables out of dores: and the divine art of printing and gunpowder have frighted away Robin Good-fellow and the fayries.[21]

Aubrey's point, quoted more extensively later, is that the culture which literacy was replacing had been sophisticated and vibrant. The process of change fractured what had formerly been a common, if heterogeneous, culture. As the status of literacy increased, the difference between literate and non-literate people was signalled through speech. Schooling or tutoring could not be exhibited like a material object so conversation became more performative, with the conversational styles of the literate becoming more elaborate and self-consciously literary: this indicated that a person came from a family with means and cultivation.[22] Those who continued the forms and modes of oral culture were equally distinctive; an invitation to enter a house in Wales or Scotland was a formulaic declaration of hospitality and responded to by a declaration of gratitude by the visitor. This exchange could be repeated several times before the visitor actually entered the house and such repetitions could easily be elevated to a formal or even ritual level at festival times or when marriage contracts were being agreed.[23]

As scholars of orality from Milman Parry to Walter Ong to Adam Fox have noted, people in less literate families or communities were trained to listen more carefully to speech than people in literate ones, having been schooled from infancy to absorb speech attentively and for long periods so as to transmit what had been said with great accuracy.[24] Memory and speech remained the primary method of recording and transmitting information in low-status or even professional households long into the eighteenth century and mimesis was the predominant method of learning roles in plays and operas. Sensitivity to the capacity of spoken words to perform speech acts, intended or unintended, was another defining trait of the unlettered, yet all these traits would become déclassé in literate circles as time went on.[25]

Andrew Gurr detects this cultural antagonism in the divergence of repertoire between hall theatres and amphitheatres. More literate audiences attended the former and, it is thought, less literate audiences the latter.[26] Levels of neoclassical education were higher in hall theatres and, as this usually went hand-in-hand with greater means, so were the ticket prices. There were differences in plots, political sympathies, characterisation and pacing between amphitheatres and hall houses. The people who attended London's amphitheatres may or may not have been less literate or wealthy, but what evidence survives suggests amphitheatre audiences were attracted by plays reflecting traditional oral culture. These were less neoclassical and more anchored in pre-Reformation frames of reference: friars, guilds, pageantry and the tropes of Corpus Christi plays. Those fond of plays probably attended both, like Aubrey's 'ordinary sort of people', those who formerly had only listened to stories but now had the option of reading a book as well.

After the tipping point

The theatre's relationship with rhetoric is an example of how fluid the transition from orality to literacy could be. Lawyers from the Inns of Court and many other audience members whose work required public speaking took to jotting down fine phrases when they went to the theatre, for their own professional or social use later on. The Devonshire minister Thomas Trescot decried this practice of lawyers borrowing their oratory from the stage. In *The Zealous Magistrate* (1642), he argued that contemporary oratory was in terminal decline: '[b]esides the very language it selfe, what is it oft times, but a few shreds and scraps dropt from some stage-poet, at the Globe or Cock-Pit, which they have carefully bookt up to serve them for such an occasion'.[27] Writing shortly before the closure of the theatres, he had contempt for theatrical rhetoric, but the practice of scribbling down phrases shows that they could pass from the playwright's manuscript via the player's speech to the listener's notebook and back into speech again. Yet rising literacy in the seventeenth-century was no anticipation of nineteenth-century social reform: many felt that, like Latin, its use should be the preserve of the few and concern about its seemingly indiscriminate spread came not from those whose livelihoods were threatened by the devaluing of mnemonic skills, but from those who feared reading and writing would lead to insubordination. Edmund Hickeringill's Whig-leaning tract linked increased literacy with a rise in impertinence: 'I answer with a late learned author, Why may not a man be suffered to talk Impertinently now and then? 'Tis the mode, the very Gazet-mode, and the fashion of every weekly Pamphlet.'[28] The contract between performers and audience was one that opera inherited from the storyteller/listener in proto-literate society; consequently, we look next at how differently people listened and imagined in proto-literate cultures from those brought up ones with mass literacy.

Memory as a performance tool

Professional storytellers were ubiquitous in the Middle Ages, engaging audiences in all social groups from castle to cottage; those who worked in high-status contexts were usually literate but they delivered their stories from memory rather than reading them out loud, as was formerly presumed. Books were sometimes used in storytelling, but as props rather than from any want of retention by the speaker; a book signalled the learned or authoritative nature of the tales, lending prestige and auctoritas to the entertainment.[29] Court poets, minstrels, historians and high-status messengers made very different uses of their two skills. Literacy was required in preparing a performance as storytellers clearly borrowed narrative tropes from various texts, but it was their retentive skills, styles of delivery and capacity for performance that gave elite storytellers professional success.[30] The capacity to remember stories, sermons, poetry, genealogies or instructions and then repeat them verbatim was highly prized in early modern society and, I suggest, the actors and opera singers of the period could be considered, from a courtier's point of view, a type of professional storyteller. The skills required in storytelling formed the basis of Elizabethan theatre and Florentine opera: Jennifer Popple argues that when roles were learned for late sixteenth- and most seventeenth-century plays, masques, operas or other performances, mimesis was core to the process.[31] In revivals, the new performer often sought out or watched the previous player who undertook the role. If lucky, they were instructed in its performance. This is the way professional storytellers had worked when developing new repertoire or passing stories on to their children or apprentices. Learning a part orally embedded the music or words so confidently in memory that a capacity was created to make decisions during the performance of how to interact with the audience. Oral learning also meant the material was retained in the memory for long periods afterwards.

These were skills in which the audience were also trained to a degree. Children were brought up to develop extensive retention capacities: Elizabethan children from literate homes appear to have been taught oral and memory skills from four years old – the age modern societies begin teaching literacy. Teaching in literacy began only from around seven years.[32] In 1610

John Norden remarked in *The Surveyor's Dialogue*: 'I haue obserued that many vnlearned men have better and more retentiue memories than haue some schollars ... such as haue not use of the pen, must use the memory only'.[33] Learning by rote was the key tool in developing children's retentive capacities as well as adult performers' lines, accompaniments or arias.

In the same year, John Dowland recommended learning music through memory alone: 'without booke: for whilst the minde is busie searching here and there for that which is written, the hand is more unapt to performe the Note'.[34] The same might be said of the difference between singing from a text and performing it from memory: singing from memory allows for more interpretation and frees the performer's eyes to 'read' the audience. Of course, there were wide variations in retentive ability just as there are in literacy proficiency today but, because of this childhood training, proto-literate people had a greater capacity to sustain their concentration when listening to speech. Sermons, speeches and ballads could be of a longer duration in medieval and Renaissance societies than would be the case in mass-literate societies. Gurr points out that Marlowe's company, the Admiral's Men, had between twenty-seven and thirty-eight plays in its repertoire of which between seventeen and twenty-one were new each year. This means that each of the 14 or so actors in the company retained between 90 and 114 hours of speech, of which approximately 50 hours were new each year.[35] Modern literate actors usually retain a maximum of between ten and twelve hours with accuracy and a few more in approximate form.

Sets and costume were minimal in Elizabethan theatre, the blocking was extremely static and the acting so stylised as to bear analogy with Japanese Noh theatre to modern eyes. There were 168 approved poses which apprentice players had to learn, including 59 hand gestures, mostly drawn from classical oratory. Sometimes these rhetorical gestures are found in paintings, carvings or sculpture; a few examples are given in Figures 1.1 to 1.6.

Dene Barnett, Judy Tarling and others argue that this acting style was extrapolated from brief references to the gestures and expressions used in classical oratory.[36] They were taught in the schools and universities and made their way into theatre, Parliament and pulpit. According to the classical rules, such paralinguistic codes of gesture were supposed to avoid distracting the imaginative absorption of the listeners, but still underscore the key moments of the speech.

It has long been noted that the oratorical acting methods of early Italian opera, and British theatre in the 1580s to 1640s, were highly stylised; this is discussed in detail in Chapter 2 but I propose that, while storytelling could be formal or informal, experiments in the reception of told stories show that engagement is enhanced if the storyteller is expressive, but if they cross the

1.1 *Prince Henry* by Robert Peake the Elder in the pose of a man defending his honour, leaning back on his left foot.

1.2 Woodcut: Hieronymo from Thomas Kyd's *The Spanish Tragedy* (London, 1615 edition), in an aggressive pose, leaning forward on his right foot with drawn sword.

line into acting listeners usually become frustrated.[37] By acting, the teller is overriding the listeners' own imagining of the narrative and obliging them to focus on the storyteller's performance instead. Yet it would be wrong to imply that the art of storytelling is wholly inimical to the art of acting; while frustration can be prompted if storytelling is interrupted by acting, when a story is acted from the very beginning listeners are quite happy to let the actor take the lead and depict the characters and action for them.[38] When the actor or singer is 'being' a character or demonstrating the action, audiences do not envisage these things independently from the representation, becoming immersed in the performer's interpretation and depictions.

The rhetor Quintilian made the point that acting is a distraction in oratory and specifically proscribed theatricality. He argued that gesture should be subtle, merely hinting at the action described and should not attempt to

1.3 The pose of a spy or assassin from the Scuole di San Rocco in Venice carved by Francesco Pianta.
Source: Scuole di San Rocco, released under Creative Commons Licence.

1.4 The gestures and poses of cozerners depicted in *The Cheat with the Ace of Diamonds* by Georges de la Tour (1635). According to current interpretation, the expensively dressed figure on the right is being cheated. The eyes of the three other characters are turned to the viewer's left, signifying deception. The hand gesture of the courtesan in the centre is called 'invitio'; she is cueing her confederate on the left of the painting to play the winning card. He hides this cheating card behind his back with his left (sinister) hand. Examples of these gestures are found in John Bulwer's *Chirologia* (1644).
Source: The Louvre, released under Creative Commons Licence.

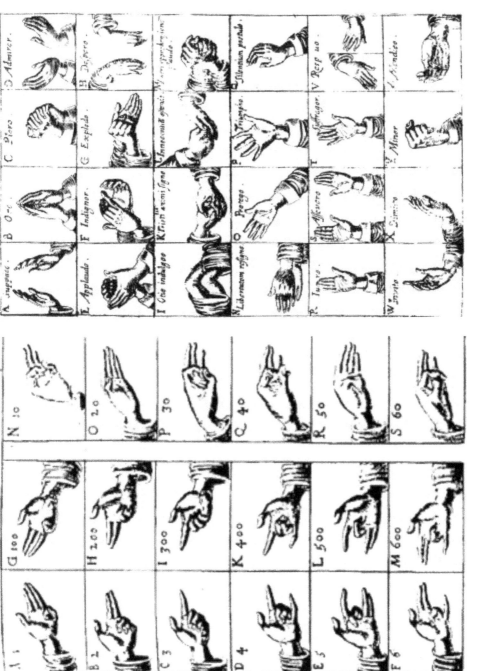

1.5 and 1.6 Hand gestures from John Bulmer's *Chirologia: or the Naturall Language of the Hand*, p. 164 (London, 1644). The 'invitio' gesture seen above is given here as I 300.

reproduce it.[39] Stylisation in acting leaves the kind of space Quintilian describes, where there remains room for audience members to retain their own imagining of the characters' motivations and actions. Audiences alternated, in early theatre and opera, between imagining some parts of the story in their own minds and giving the performers their full focus for others. This will have a bearing on attitudes towards aria and recitative.

The supernatural potential of words

Given the capacity of proto-literate people to remember what has been said, words were chosen with great care. Oral cultures retain an anxiety about supernatural potentialities of the spoken or sung word which Walter Ong and others believed to have derived from a very remote past.[40] It was believed that saying something could make it happen, echoed in vestigial form today when fearing bad weather: 'don't say that or it'll happen', 'touch wood', 'don't tempt fate' and other turns of phrase. Speech was thought capable of transforming things that lay outside of everyday control: it could bring good or bad luck, or seal someone's fate, while ritual speech could heal, absolve sins, transubstantiate or excommunicate. The ritual quality of spoken vows created much more binding obligations than written contracts.

That Elizabethans responded to theatre speech in oral ways is implied in the anecdote of Edward Alleyn wearing a clerical surplice under his clothes when he played Doctor Faustus, lest the words he spoke should actually conjure up the Evil One.[41] The anecdote has parallels elsewhere in Europe; Giovanni Paolo Marana describes a scene in a French play where a necromantic spell struck truly dead the actor playing a dead body.[42] Storytelling could be dangerous in oral cultures: the supernatural potential of speech meant that vows, imprecations to Fate, invocations of gods and conjurings of the dead occurred in a liminal space where the world of the story and the real world outside interfaced with each other.

All theatre has the potential to change the way audience members envision the world, but the supernatural potential of speech in oral cultures means that performance could have the same intensity of immersion as that which occurs in rituals and liturgies. The performance of a story thus had a transformative capacity, especially so if it was sung, and this helps to explain why authorities, and religious authorities in particular, were so keen to regulate stage performances.

Audiences in predominantly oral cultures experience full immersion in a story; their emotions and attention are wholly engaged so that they are 'transported' into the world of the story. It was only when this was changing in early modern Europe, as the literate were increasing in numbers and literacy was widening its uses, that people became conscious of theatre having this transformative power. In the seventeenth and eighteenth centuries this enhanced immersion was given the Greek term thelxis (θελξις), translated by Milton as 'enchantment' and by the Venetian librettist Gian Francesco Busanello as 'incanto'; tellingly, both English and Italian translations derive from 'song'. It was the singing of the story which wove the spell. In her study of discursive, iconic and somatic ritual, Margo Kitts notes the frequency of sung storytelling in somatic rituals; immersion is experienced by the body in a more intensive, emotional and transformative way than mere listening or comprehending.[43] A wholly sung story had the potential to change the listener's sense of self, their morality, definition of honour or what they saw as their responsibilities in life, and the formulaic structures of early opera sometimes have a consciously ritualistic feel to them, perhaps more obviously so in tragedies, where the performativity of familiar rituals is so often harnessed by the plot.

To take one example, repetition is a ritual characteristic found both in oral storytelling and seventeenth- and eighteenth-century opera. As society became more literate, musical and textual repetitions were more often cut in revivals of earlier operas. Walter Ong and Albert Lord suggested that repetition serves to heighten the significance of a phrase by giving it a ritual quality. Lord, reflecting on Ong's thoughts, considered that

> repetitions … do not, in my opinion, arise from the need to remind the audience of what has been said, but from what I would call 'ritual repetition'; … as Father Ong has indeed quite rightly seen, but it appears to me that they are not there to fill up time while the singer thinks of what comes next, or for the convenience of the audience who have to be told what happened previously in the story. The repetitions have, or once had, an important role of their own, a ritual one of great antiquity. This applies as well to those repetitions of instructions given to a messenger or to the receiver of a message. There is not only a kind of verisimilitude, … but also an emphasis on the ritual character of the communication. The original ritual function of such repetitions may in time become lost, and the repetitions may be kept as conventions of literary style which are retained as 'oral residue' in written literature. Such repetitions, by the way, are characteristic of both oral traditional verse and oral traditional prose.[44]

Lord is surely right and both the vocal and instrumental repetitions used in opera derive, ultimately, from pre- rather than proto-literate storytelling. Phrase repetitions in everyday speech are a convention in oral societies so, when they were used in spoken or sung storytelling, they would not have felt like an antique theatrical convention as they do today; their ritual resonance would have been stronger. Societies with mass literacy discontinued phrase repetitions in ordinary conversation and gradually this occurred in opera too. The repetition of four short lines of verse over a baroque aria of three or four minutes can seem tedious or mystifying.[45] Whatever the prevalent emotion being communicated in an operatic sequence, repetition intensified it. Roger North, writing in the 1680s, is quoted by Tarling; he considered that sensations of pleasure, familiarity and even safety can be enhanced by the repetitions in a fugue:

> How will people call for a tune, over and over againe; but that the repetition pleaseth them? Upon this reason it is that a fuge is agreeable, for the air after it hath been heard once or twice, comes easily upon the attention, for there is a shadow of what is to come; which the sound turns to light and this shall remain a considerable time, before satiety enters. For pleasure is not on a sudden but improves like a plant till it hath a perfection, and then declines till it is good for nothing, and comes to stink at last.[46]

To North, the repetition in a fugue suggests the organic cycle of the natural world; it is not a literary or even rhetorical device but something embedded in the make-up of human pleasure. In the early modern period, then, repetition was part of the fabric of storytelling and occurred in many contexts, of which opera was only one.

Repetition along with other ritual elements was integral to creating thelxis but a key facet of ritualisation is the conflation of time. To attend an opera was often to attend the animation of a classical myth or an episode of history; it may have been enacted in the present but it was a conjuring up of the past. In creating these demi-numinous performances, repetition was part of a spell that reified the story in similar ways to chanted repetition in liturgical narratives: it helped to present the Last Supper, Crucifixion and Resurrection as occurring in the recent past, rather than an ancient past, and in opera it allowed Orpheus, Caesar or Agrippina to come to life. Although we look on baroque and classical operas as examples of Enlightenment art and harbingers of rationalism, their ritual features are embedded in the pre-Enlightenment world.

Oral reflexes among the literate and the visualisation of stories

Before the tipping point, literacy functioned within a predominantly oral culture with literate people retaining the same profound respect for the power of the spoken or sung word as their non-literate neighbours. Documentation was often merely a confirmation or record of changes that had been created through speech acts, such as a spoken judgement, agreement made on oath or a vow sworn before witnesses, and was not the instrument of that change in itself.[47] Medieval punishments for perjury (spoken lying) had been more severe than those for forgery (written lying).[48] Political and administrative life had depended on such speech acts but, as literacy increased in the eighteenth and nineteenth centuries, this authority gradually passed to texts.[49]

Ong noted that literate people living in proto-literate societies tended to bring oral reflexes with them into their relationship with texts.[50] When a medieval person read a text they usually did so aloud. The sound of their voice saying the words on the page prompted the image in the reader's mind, rather than the sight of the letters.[51] Paul Saenger and Carmen Luke date the beginning of silent reading to the late medieval period but conclude that the majority of readers probably read aloud long into the sixteenth century.[52] William A. Graham on the other hand argues that, outside scholarly, clerical or bureaucratic contexts, individuals continued to read aloud into the eighteenth and nineteenth centuries.[53] The connection between increased literacy and intensified visuality is argued by Gunter Kress and Theo van Leeuwen to be inherent in literacy itself:

> Writing itself is of course also a form of visual communication. Indeed, and paradoxically, the sign of the fully literate social person is the ability to treat writing completely as a visual medium – for instance, not moving one's lips and not vocalizing when one is reading, not even 'subvocalizing' (a silent 'speaking aloud in the head', to bring out the full paradox of this activity). Readers who move their lips when reading, who subvocalize, are regarded as still tainted with the culturally less advanced mode of spoken language. This kind of visual literacy ... has, for centuries now, been one of the most essential achievements and values of Western culture, and one of the most essential goals of education, so much so that one major and heavily value-laden distinction made by Western cultures has been that between literate (advanced) and non-literate (oral and primitive) cultures.[54]

For a nineteenth-century advocate of the score as the work, such as J.W. Davison, reading a score would have been an internal aural experience reached through the visual one of reading. Many of his complaints about infidelity to the score stem from a clash between the private performance he had given himself when reading an opera, and the public one he saw in the opera house. Reading aloud to other people could be highly performative in proto-literate society but Jagodzinski notes that, as literacy increased, such performativity declined.[55]

The practice of silent reading steadily eroded performativity in vocalising text to other people, yet in an age before the widespread use of spectacles, people from their mid-40s onwards required text to be read to them, as their vision worsened. Text thus remained an oral experience for many recipients well into the nineteenth century.

Audiences for proto-literate storytelling were listeners but also imaginers. They were not though, viewers, at least not in Britain. As a story is told, the listener imagines the location, characters and actions as the teller is

1.7 *Rhetoricians at the Window* by Jan Steen, *c.*1658-1665. Steen depicted
Chambers of Rhetoric, where members met to hear arguments.
Source: Philadelphia Museum of Art, released under Creative Commons
Licence.

1.8 *The Rhetoricians*, *c.*1655 by Jan Steen.
Source: Bredius Museum, The Hague, released under Creative Commons
Licence.

speaking. Despite the use of repeated phrases, storytelling is fast and there is not much time to imagine complex images or create original visualisations, still less ones outside the listener's experience. In consequence, it has been argued, people relied on a mental bank of stock images when listening to stories in oral or proto-literate societies.[56] In psychological terms, the images conjured are heuristic rather than systematic. Bruno Bettelheim, speaking of fairy stories, writes '[t]he fairy tale simplifies all situations. Its figures are clearly drawn; and details, unless very important, are eliminated. All characters are typical rather than unique.'[57] Each listener visualises the story differently so listeners have individual reception experiences. Sixteenth- and early seventeenth-century performances tended to describe in speeches or arias the actions they could not depict effectively on stage, or activities it was taboo to stage, such as religious services. Extended narratives carried listeners' imaginations to exotic places; Faustus travels through Europe with Mephistopheles by description, for instance, rather than depiction. The exordium in *Henry V* (*c.*1599) asks the audience to let the actors work on their imaginations and bids them conjure the scene; this is followed by two scenes consisting of a very long story, told largely by the Archbishop of Canterbury, setting out Henry's claim to the throne of France. The back-story at the start of *The Tempest* (1611) is an adventure tale of treachery that introduces the key characters. The recitative operas of early seventeenth-century Italy were similar; Tragedy's extensive opening recitative and the pastoral chorus at the beginning of Giulio Caccini's *Euridice* (1602), and Arianna's lament in Monteverdi's *L'Arianna* (1608), both offer vivid imagery for the audience to imagine, but with music to create emotional engagement, guiding the audience in how they should feel about what they are visualising. That early staging in Britain was, physically, fairly static, does not mean it lacked drama: wars, shipwrecks and the conjuring of mythological creatures abounded, though the number of times such events were intended to be coloured in by the audience's imaginations is likely to have been vastly greater than the number of times actual depiction was attempted.

Descriptions of plays by theatre-goers from this period, quoted by Andrew Gurr and Tiffany Stern, often contain such different accounts of known works as to suggest that companies delivered very different versions of the same play on different occasions.[58] There is certainly evidence that alterations were made when performing at court or for touring outside London, but an alternative explanation might be that with so much of the narrative being imagined in the audience's minds, variations in the written descriptions of plays were inevitable.

Written stories, by contrast, have more room for descriptive detail because the reader can go at their own pace, reading or rereading sequences and taking the time to visualise each event in greater detail. Stage performance remained an essentially oral artform but, by the late seventeenth century, writers were developing their own storytelling form in the novel. The novel offered an opportunity for writers to control how the story was being imagined: through detailed visual descriptions novelists could create common visualisations among their readership, instead of multiple individual ones. Eventually, the novel would become a governing influence on opera and theatre, but the process was gradual. The early novels of Aphra Behn are closer to the tales of Petrarch and Boccaccio in that they feel like spoken tales written down, rather than stories conceived as a read experience. The following sequence is from *The Unfortunate Happy Lady*, written in 1698; Philadephia's brother, Sir William, is selling his sister into prostitution, while deceiving her that she is becoming the companion of a virtuous older lady.

> The young Lady was very joyfully and respectfully received by her Brother's venerable Acquaintance, who was mightily charm'd with her Youth and Beauty. A Bottle of the Best was then strait brought in, and not long after a very splendid Entertainment for Breakfast: The Furniture was all very modish and rich, and the Attendance was suitable. Nor was the Lady *Beldam's* Conversation less obliging and modest, than Sir *William's* Discourse had given *Philadelphia* occasion to expect. After they had eaten and drank what they thought Convenient, the reverend old Lady led 'em out of the Parlour to shew 'em the House, every Room of which they found answerably furnish'd to that whence they came.[59]

While we may imagine the modish and rich furniture in detail if we wish, we are not really invited to. Nor is there space to imagine the madam's conversation; Behn simply assumes we know the kind of thing and moves the story on at a cracking pace. When we compare this with Maria Edgeworth's descriptive detail for Lady Clonbrony's gala in *The Absentee* (1812), we see the writer *designing* the mise-en-scène and how we *see* Lady Clonbrony, who is oblivious of the ruin her extravagance is wreaking on the family's estates back home in Ireland:

> The opening of her gala, the display of her splendid reception-rooms, the Turkish tent, the Alhambra, the pagoda, formed a proud moment to Lady Clonbrony ...
>
> With well-practised dignity, and half-subdued self-complacency of aspect, her ladyship went gliding about – most importantly busy, introducing my lady THIS to the sphynx candelabra, and my lady THAT to the Trebisond trellice; placing some delightfully for the perspective of the Alhambra; establishing others quite to her satisfaction on seraglio ottomans; and honouring others with a seat under the statira canopy. Receiving and answering compliments from successive crowds of select friends, imagining herself the mirror of fashion, and the admiration of the whole world, Lady Clonbrony was, for her hour, as happy certainly as ever woman was in similar circumstances.[60]

The details are not just aids to the imaginer, they are an attempt to immerse the reader in Clonbrony's own visualisation; Edgeworth is keen to ensure that what she is imagining as she writes is exactly what her readers are imagining as they read. Written storytelling became less dependent on collective stock visual traditions and more dependent on personal experience. Inevitably, the more detailed visuality of literature would influence opera design. Opera still relied on the audience's capacity to imagine the more visual parts of the drama into the final third of the eighteenth century, after that, verisimilitude was sought in opera, in its staging, sets and acting. Novels increasingly became the basis for opera plots from the late eighteenth century onwards and pasticcio, though an oral practice, was of great service in shaping operas to the visualisations expected by deeply literate novel-reading audiences.

The arc of both plays and operas from the seventeenth to late eighteenth centuries would be to increase the depiction of the story onstage and steadily to relieve audiences of the need to imagine parts of it themselves.[61] After 1660 London theatres assumed literate, classical education in their audiences and aimed to depict narratives in full, pre-imagined, with spectacle, scenery and costuming. New styles of acting replaced the older stylised formalism that had been in use before the civil wars. The history of opera now begins to depart from that of spoken theatre in Britain, and continues to separate over the course of the eighteenth century. The stylisations of operatic acting multiplied and varied but did not move closer to real life in the way that those of spoken theatre did. Pasticcio would remain common to opera into the twentieth century, showing that some oral inheritances survived the transition to mass literacy while others, such as protracted repetition, did not.

Motivation

Weak or unexplained motivation for a character's behaviour is a much-noted feature of medieval and proto-literate storytelling, one inherited by early theatre and opera. Reasons for the hostility of villains are seldom given and their penitence often appears out of nowhere; why fathers agree to the murder or abandonment of their children is not explained and the reasons for intense love are often specious. In *A Winter's Tale* we are never given a motivation for Leontes' jealousy that is convincing for post-Enlightenment audiences; indeed, to ask what it is that underlies it and why Leontes is so consumed by it are very modern questions. Jacobean audiences were satisfied that the play was a study *in* jealousy as a human quality and answered the question 'why' theologically rather than psychologically: Leontes is a victim of original sin like all humanity, and jealousy is his defining sin as Herod's was wrath.

For seventeenth-century audiences the play explored the consequences of this sin for Leontes' own life, his family and his court. His jealousy was part of a tradition of stage jealousy going back to medieval plays such as *Joseph's Jalousie* and *The Trial of Mary*.[62] In art, too, St Joseph was usually represented as an older man jealous of his younger wife, fearing that he has been cuckolded by someone other than God. As society's explanations for causality became less theological, the perceived motivational weakness in this and other seventeenth-century plays and operas was often resolved through pasticcio practices: plots and characterisations were changed. Macnamara Morgan's pasticcio *The Sheep-Shearing* (1754) cut out the Leontes and Hermione narrative altogether while David Garrick's *Florizel and Perdita* (1756) condensed the narrative of the first three acts into a briefing given by Camillo to another courtier. Avoiding depiction allowed the jealousy to appear more credible. Pasticcio practices, aria substitution especially, would also be used in the first third of the nineteenth century to realign operatic characterisation with new expectations of gender identities, as discussed in Chapter 4. The capacity of pasticcio to renovate operas so they better accord with the times is a key reason for its surviving society's transition from orality to literacy.

1.9 St Joseph contemplating divorce, Tuscan terracotta statue c.1475–1500.
Source: The Walters Art Museum.

1.10 Henry Daniell as Leontes, 1946.
Source: Museum of the city of New York.

Rhetoric

Neoclassical rhetoric not only accommodated pasticcio but was one of the factors giving the practice classical validation.[63] Both rhetoric and opera had sub-structures deriving from oral culture: public speaking, the verbal performance of an argument and the use of emotion for engagement, immersion and persuasion. Quintilian noticed the relationship of rhetorical structures with pre-literate speech and storytelling, commenting that the same structures reappeared even in the speeches of the 'unlettered, barbarians and slaves'.[64] He concluded they were natural. Arguably, eighteenth-century society's investment in rhetoric was one of the reasons why opera's oral inheritances continued so long in the face of an increasingly literate culture. Neoclassical rhetoric and theatrical storytelling informed each other and pasticcio was germane to both.

The very formalisation of argument structures tended to facilitate exchange and borrowing between them with the reuse of known arguments, familiar metaphors, analogies and repeated narrative tropes being recommended by Greek and Roman authors. Pasticcio borrowings and interpolations in theatre and opera were thus complemented, indeed derived authority from Renaissance respect for same practices in classical rhetoric. As well as being a continuity from Britain's oral culture, pasticcio was thus part of a current literate society's reinvention of an ancient classical oral code.

Many neoclassical humanists treated classical texts with the same selective fundamentalism which reformers brought to the Bible. Lacking a conception of the scale of difference between Greek or Roman societies and their own, the applicability of ancient rules appeared unproblematic, yet neoclassical oratory owed more to early modern interpretation than to any accurate reconstruction of Cicero, Quintilian and others. The reinvention of rhetoric influenced pleas in law courts, addresses to public figures, sermons, speeches in Parliament and stage performances. We therefore have the paradox of increasingly literate societies reinventing an ancient oral tradition within which to perform new and more literate forms of music and theatre.

Operatic structures as a whole, as well as their constituent arias, often follow a rhetorical pattern. Neoclassical drama moved from exordium (welcoming the audience and exhorting their attention) to narratio (exposition) to partitio (revealing the things of concern) to confirmatio (proof that the concerns are grave and justified) to confutatio (the solution or resolution of the problems) and finally conclusio (an emotional peroration, invoking joy, relief or reflection as we emerge from the experience). Speeches or extended arias could be rhetorical journeys in themselves, combining various figures, affects and modes of delivery as they worked through the stages of

1.11 *St Paul preaching in Athens* by Raphael, 1515, demonstrates the use of
gesture in oratory during the Renaissance.
Source: Sistine Chapel, released under Creative Commons Licence.

argument. Composition itself was conditioned by rhetorical theory in both
Italian and English operas, as shown in contemporary writing. As early as
1577, Henry Peacham the Elder in *The Garden of Eloquence* argued for
the extension of the principles of rhetoric to music.[65] His son, Henry Peacham
the Younger, wrote in 1622:

> Hath not music her figures, the same with rhetoric? What is a revert but her
> antistrophe? her reports, but sweet anaphoras? her counterchange of points,
> antimetaboles? her passionate airs but prosopopoeias? with infinite other of
> the same nature.[66]

This perspective lasted long into the eighteenth century: Johann Mattheson
in 1739 and Johann Joachim Quantz in 1752 both argued that musical
performance ought to follow the persuasive strategies of rhetoric and their
writings offer determined attempts to synthesise the grammar of music with
that of oratory.[67] In giving examples of this integration of rhetoric and
music, Judy Tarling notes that Joachim Burmeister, in his *Musica Poetica*
(1606), used the rhetorical term 'hyperbole' to describe pushing a melody

above or below its natural (usually middle) range.[68] Quantz, over a century later, wrote:

> The orator and musician have, at bottom, the same aim in regard to both the preparation and the final execution of their productions, namely to make themselves masters of the hearts of their listeners, to arouse or still their passions, and to transport them now to this sentiment, now to that. Thus it is advantageous to both if each has some knowledge of the duties of the other.[69]

Music was to persuade the listener, to depict incidents, to sway their mood, engage their feelings and lead them on a journey of progressive revelation. We think of rhetorical persuasion as concerned with political or legal arguments but in music and storytelling, when the aim was thelxis, the art of persuading was the art of immersing.

There were other, more political, reasons for marrying music and rhetoric. The massive authority accorded classical civilisation by Renaissance societies was driven, in northern Europe at least, by the need to escape the cultural carnage caused by endemic religious conflict. Art that was safely pre-Christian and classical occupied a heterotopic space as it evaded the scrutiny and judgement of contemporary sectarian policing, and artists and the consumers of art sought such cultural space. Neoclassical art, albeit pagan, was less likely to come unstuck during sectarian power shifts than art which was more obviously aligned to one particular Christian tradition.[70] Turning music into a branch of rhetoric gave it a classical sanction, so that it could evade conflict with all but the most musically suspicious of denominations.

* * *

To fully evidence my argument that the contract between performers and audiences in opera remained an oral one, Chapter 2 explores the path taken by opera in Italy and compares it with that of spoken theatre in Britain. In the latter, a common oral heritage shared by both was gradually severed, yet when Italian opera made its début in London at the start of the eighteenth century it was received warmly, and especially so by women. While greeted as a novelty, opera offered a reconnection with a lost storytelling experience, restoring the kind of emotional investment that was increasingly absent from London's male literate culture.

Notes

1 Ellen Rosand, *Opera in Seventeenth-Century Venice: The Creation of a Genre* (Berkeley, Los Angeles, Oxford: University of California Press, 1991; paperback edn, 2007), p. 220.

2 Ibid., p. 209.

3 John Dryden, *Albion and Albanius* (London, 1691), reprinted in The Mermaid Series, *The Best Plays of John Dryden*, ed. George Saintsbury, vol. 2 (London: Ernest Benn Ltd, 1950), p. 229.

4 Giulio Strozzi, *Delia* (Venice: Pinelli, 1639), p. 80, quoted in Rosand, *Opera in Seventeenth-Century Venice*, p. 208. Original Italian text Appendix I, 15j, p. 414.

5 Michel Carré and Jules Barbier created the libretto from an adaptation in French by Alexander Dumas the Elder and Paul Meurice.

6 Christopher Chowrimootoo, *Middlebrow Modernism: Britten's Operas and the Great Divide* (Berkeley: University of California Press, 2018), pp. 1–30. Christopher Chowrimootoo and Kate Guthrie, 'Colloquy: musicology and the middlebrow', *Journal of the American Musicological Society*, vol. 73 no. 2 (Berkeley: University of California Press, 2020), pp. 327–334. Alexandra Wilson, 'Opera for the "country lout": Italian opera, national identity and the middlebrow in interwar Britain', *Journal of Modern Italian Studies*, vol. 26 no. 1: 'Italian musical migration to London' (Abingdon: Taylor & Francis, 2021), pp. 54–69.

7 Thomas Betzwieser, 'The world of pasticcio: reflections on pre-existing text and music', *Operatic Pasticcios in 18th-Century Europe: Contexts, Materials and Aesthetics*, ed. Berthold Over and Gesa zur Nieden (Bielefeld: transcript Verlag, 2021), p. 34.

8 *The Guardian*, no. 19, 2 March 1714, p. 78.

9 Robert D. Hume, 'Politics of opera in late 17th century London', *Cambridge Opera Journal*, vol. 10 no. 1 (Cambridge: Cambridge University Press, 1998), p. 43.

10 Ellen T. Harris, *Handel as Orpheus: Voice and Desire in the Chamber Cantatas* (Cambridge, MA: Harvard University Press, 2001), pp. 225–226. N.M. Murray, 'Handel and music borrowing' (unpublished doctoral thesis, Massachusetts: Wheaton College, 2009), pp. 5–6.

11 Letter, 1 November 1742, *Horace Walpole's Correspondence with Horace Mann*, edited by W.S. Lewis, Warren Hunting Smith and George L. Lam, vol. 2 (New Haven, CT: Yale University Press, 1960), p. 96. Quoted by Curtis Price, 'Unity, originality and the London pasticcio', *Harvard Library Bulletin*, new series, vol. 2 (Cambridge, MA: Harvard University Press, 1991), p. 20.

12 Reinhard Strohm, 'Handel's pasticci', *Journal of Ancient Music*, no. 14 (1974), p. 167.

13 Richard Osborne, 'Recycled Rossini receives a lively presentation at this Italian festival', *Gramophone Magazine* (2002). https://www.gramophone.co.uk/review/rossini-robert-bruce [accessed 19 October 2021].

14 Jack Goody and Ian Watt, 'The consequences of literacy', *Perspectives on Literacy*, ed. Eugene R. Kintgen, Barry M. Kroll and Mike Rose (Carbondale, IL: Southern Illinois University Press, 1963, this edn 1988), p. 27.

15 Shirley Brice Heath, 'Protean shapes in literacy events: ever-shifting oral and literate traditions', *Perspectives on Literacy*, ed. Kintgen et al., pp. 350–351.

16 Paula McDowell, 'Ong and the concept of orality', *Religion & Literature*, vol. 44 no. 2 (South Bend, IN: The University of Notre Dame, 2012), p. 176. The

volume quoted is *The Uses of Script and Print, 1300—1700*, ed. Julia Crick and Alexandra Walsham (Cambridge: Cambridge University Press, 2004), pp. 4 and 20.

17 Statistics taken from David Cressy's *Literacy and the Social Order: Reading and Writing in Tudor and Stuart England* (Cambridge: Cambridge University Press, 1980), pp. 72–74, 150–151 and 176–177. Cressy, 'Literacy in seventeenth-century England: more evidence', *The Journal of Interdisciplinary History*, vol. 8 no. 1 (Cambridge, MA: The MIT Press, 1977), pp. 141–150 and Cressy, 'Literacy in context: meaning and measurement in early modern England', *Consumption and the World of Goods*, ed. John Brewer and Roy Porter (London: Routledge, 1993), pp. 305–319. Margaret Spufford, 'First steps in literacy: the reading and writing experiences of the humblest seventeenth-century autobiographers', *Social History*, vol. 4 (Oxford: Oxford University Press, 1979), pp. 407–435. Cecile M. Jagodzinski, *Privacy and Print: Reading and Writing in Seventeenth-Century England* (Charlottesville, VA: University of Virginia Press, 1999), pp. 8–9. Adam Fox, *Oral and Literate Culture in England, 1500–1700* (Oxford: Clarendon Press, 2000), p. 18.

18 Cressy, *Literacy and the Social Order*, p. 128. Conversely, David Vincent argues this figure was reached by 1840: 'The invention of counting: the statistical measurement of literacy in nineteenth-century England', *Comparative Education*, vol. 50 no. 3 (Abingdon: Taylor & Francis, 2014), p. iii. Digitised by Taylor & Francis, 2014. https://www.tandfonline.com/doi/full/10.1080/03050068.2014.921372 [accessed 6 February 2023].

19 Fox, *Oral and Literate Culture*, throughout.

20 William St Clair, *The Reading Nation in the Romantic Period* (Cambridge: Cambridge University Press, 2004), p. 241.

21 'Remaines of gentilisme and Judaisme in 1686–7', printed in *John Aubrey: Three Prose Works*, ed. John Buchanan-Brown (Carbondale, IL: Carbondale Press, 1972), p. 290.

22 Katie Halsey and Jane Slinn (eds), *The Concept and Practice of Conversation in the Long Eighteenth Century 1688–1848* (Cambridge: Cambridge Scholars Publishing, 2008), throughout.

23 The Caseg fedi and Mari Lwyd traditions are famous examples in Wales; for Scotland, Neill Martin, 'The Gaelic rèiteach: symbolism and practice', *Scottish Studies*, vol. 34 (Edinburgh: Edinburgh University Press, 2006), pp. 103–104, 107, 136.

24 Adam Parry, *The Making of Homeric Verse: The Collected Papers of Milman Parry* (Oxford: Oxford University Press, 1971). Albert B. Lord collaborated with Parry and their methodology is known as the Parry/Lord method. Walter J. Ong, *The Presence of the Word: some Prolegomena for Cultural and Religious History* (New Haven, CT, London: Yale University Press, 1967), *Orality and Literacy: The Technologizing of the Word* (London: Methuen, 1982), and 'Writing is a technology that restructures thought', *The Written Word: Literacy in Transition*, ed. Gerd Baumann (Oxford: Clarendon Press, 1986). Fox, *Oral and Literate Culture*. Thomas J. Farrell and Paul Soukup, *An Ong Reader: Challenges for further inquiry* (Cresskill, NJ: Hampton Press, 2002).

25 Brice Heath, 'Protean shapes', p. 348, referring to Lord's research, writes 'research which examined oral performance in particular groups is said to support the notion that as members of a society increasingly participate in literacy, they lose habits associated with the oral tradition'.

26 Gurr demonstrates that hall theatres drew in law students from the nearby Inns of Court and more clerks and merchants whereas amphitheatres drew in more apprentices and craftsmen: Andrew Gurr, *Playgoing in Shakespeare's London* (Cambridge: Cambridge University Press, 1996), pp. 73–80.

27 Thomas Trescot, *The Zealous Magistrate* (London, 1642), p. 14, quoted in Fox, *Oral and Literate Culture*, p. 132.

28 Edmund Hickeringill, *The Black Non-Conformist* (London, printed by George Larkin, 1682), p. 20. Luther, ironically, considered the spread of literacy to be potentially dangerous. In 1718, Francis Hutchison blamed the spread of literacy for the continuing belief in witchcraft and other superstitions in *An Historical Essay Concerning Witchcraft* (London, 1718). He noted the number of books on the subject since 1660, observing '[t]hese books are in tradesmen's shops and farmer's houses, and are read with great eagerness and are constantly levening the minds of youth who delight in such subjects'.

29 The illustrated frontispiece to Chaucer's *Troilus and Criseyde* was traditionally described as the poet reading to the court of Richard II yet, as scholarship from the 1970s has pointed out, no book is shown: Derek Pearsall, 'The *Troilus* frontispiece and Chaucer's audience', *The Yearbook of English Studies*, vol. 7 (Cambridge: Modern Humanities Research Association, 1977), pp. 70–71.

30 As seen in the training of court poets in Wales and Ireland. Dafydd Jenkins, 'Bardd Teulu and Pencerdd', *The Welsh King and his Court*, ed. Thomas Charles-Edwards, Morfydd Owen and Paul Russell (Cardiff: University of Wales Press, 2002), pp. 153 and 155. Katherine Simms, 'Literacy and the Irish bards', *Literacy in Medieval Celtic Societies*, ed. Huw Pryce (Cambridge: Cambridge University Press, 1998), pp. 238–253: this describes the different grades of Irish poet including the filid and the bard; the status of each depended on their retentive capacity as much as their creative faculties but the filid were possibly literate while the bards operated in a predominantly oral milieu. A description of how the oral training of Gaelic bards intersected with literacy is given in the preface to the *Memoirs of the Marquess of Clanricard* (1641–1643), probably written by Thomas O' Sullivane in 1722 but drawing on earlier material.

31 Jennifer Elizabeth Popple, *The Restoration Actress in Her Seventeenth-Century Social, Political, and Artistic Context: Nell Gwyn, Elizabeth Barry, and Anne Bracegirdle* (New York: Edwin Mellen Press, 2015), Chapter 4.

32 Richard L. de Molen, 'Ages of admission to educational institutions in Tudor and Stuart England', *History of Education*, vol. 5 no. 3 (London: Routledge, 1976), pp. 207–219; de Molen points out that petty schools or dame schools began teaching handwriting at 7. In grammar schools, pupils began study at 7 years of age and were taught by ushers until they were 10; de Molen quotes Francis Clement, the 1587 author of *The Petie Schole*, who says he found very few grammar school boys under the age of 8 who could read or write: p. 207.

33 John Norden, *The Surveyor's Dialogue* (London, 1610), p. 173. Quoted in Fox, *Oral and Literate Culture*, p. 22.

34 John Dowland, *Varietie of Lute-Lessons* (London, 1610), p. 6, quoted in Judy Tarling, *The Weapons of Rhetoric* (St Albans: Corda Publishing, 2004), p. 130.

35 Andrew Gurr, 'Runs of plays in early modern London', *Notes & Queries*, vol. 68 (Oxford: Oxford University Press, 2016), pp. 28–33 (p. 28). Speaking of the company, 'Henslowe registered them staging a different play every day, through years of six-day weeks. Each afternoon the same players had to recall a different part. The Admiral's Men, through their first year at the Rose playhouse, starting in May 1594, staged thirty-eight plays, twenty-one of them completely new. No play appeared on successive days. The same team of eight or later ten sharers, along with various hired men and boys, learned and played them all. For modern actors, memorizing so many different parts and performing them week after week would be unbelievably demanding.'

36 Dene Barnett, *The Art of Gesture: The Practices and Principles of 18th Century Acting* (Heidelberg: Carl Winter Universität Verlag, 1987), p. 27. Tarling, *The Weapons of Rhetoric*, various.

37 I carried out practical experiments in this for the South Eastern Education and Library Board (SEELB) in Northern Ireland between 1994 and 1998: Peter Morgan Barnes, 'Shakespeare in schools: understanding the oral imagination', *SEELB Educational Resources for English Literature* (Belfast: EDCO, 1998).

38 Ibid.

39 Quintilian, *Institutio Oratoria*, book XI, chapter III, quoted in Tarling, *The Weapons of Rhetoric*, pp. 130–131.

40 Walter Ong, 'Some pschodynamics of orality' reprinted in *Perspectives on Literacy*, ed. Kintgen et al., pp. 29–31 and Albert B. Lord, 'Characteristics of orality', *A Festschrift for Walter J. Ong, Oral Tradition*, vol. 2 no. 1 (Bloomington, IN: Slavica Publishers, 1987), pp. 54–72, especially pp. 57–59. Fox, *Oral and Literate Culture*, pp. 179–180.

41 The anecdote originates with a verse by Samuel Rowlands, 'When Knaves Meete' written in 1600. Significantly, surplices – and this one was stitched with a black cross – were considered a Catholic vestment and proscribed by the Established Church at the time. The anecdote indicates perhaps that the supernatural force of the old religion could still command belief within the playhouse profession, at least when people felt threatened.

42 Giovanni Paolo Marana, *Letters Writ by Turkish Spy*, vol. 6, book II, letter X, 1662 (trans. William Bradshaw, London, 1694), p. 80.

43 Margo Kitts, 'Discursive, iconic, and somatic perspectives on ritual', *Journal of Ritual Studies*, vol. 31 no. 1 (privately published, 2017), pp. 18–20.

44 Lord, 'Characteristics of orality', pp. 57–58.

45 For a detailed discussion of the emergence of the da capo aria, see Rosand, *Opera in Seventeenth-Century Venice*, pp. 281–321.

46 J. Wilson (ed.), *Roger North on Music, being a selection of his essays from the years 1695–1728* (London: Novello, 1959), pp. 69 and 209, quoted in Tarling, *The Weapons of Rhetoric*, p. 236.

47 Being written down bolstered the authority of information but was no more trustworthy a recording method than memory, as the vast quantity of forged, revised or otherwise tampered-with medieval documents show. Anthony Welch, *The Renaissance Epic and the Oral Past* (New Haven, CT: Yale University Press, 2012), p. 6. M.T. Clanchy, 'Hearing and seeing *and* trusting writing', *Perspectives on Literacy*, ed. Kintgen et al., p. 140, points also made by Thomas Charles-Edwards in *Wales and the Britons 350–1064* (Oxford: Oxford University Press, 2013), pp. 247–251.

48 Clanchy, 'Hearing and seeing *and* trusting', p. 142.

49 The key moment in the granting of a charter was the spoken ritual of swearing the terms on relics or before the altar, rather than the writing, signing or sealing of the text, practices which continued down to the Reformation. Charles-Edwards, *Wales and the Britons*, pp. 247–251.

50 Secondary orality and oral residue are discussed by Walter J. Ong in 'Oral residue in Tudor prose style', *Publication of the Modern Language Association of America*, vol. 80 no. 3 (New York: PMLA, 1965), pp. 145–155. Lord, 'Characteristics of orality', pp. 65–71, discusses stability in the oral tradition.

51 This is one of the reasons the orthographies of the medieval period did not need to be tightly defined; as long as the sound produced from saying the word aloud produced the image of a door, it did not matter whether it was spelt 'dore', 'dor' or 'door'.

52 Paul Saenger, *Space Between Words: The Origins of Silent Reading* (Palo Alto, CA: Stanford University Press, 1997), p. 276. Carmen Luke, *Pedagogy, Printing and Protestantism: The Discourse on Childhood* (New York: State University Press, 1989), p. 77.

53 William A. and Albert Graham, *Beyond the Written Word: Oral Aspects of Scripture in the History of Religion* (Cambridge: Cambridge University Press, 1993), p. 41.

54 Gunter Kress and Theo van Leeuwen, *Reading Images: The Grammar of Visual Design* (London: Routledge, 1996), pp. 15–16.

55 Jagodzinski, *Privacy and Print*, pp. 10 and 54.

56 Alastair Minnis, 'Medieval imagination and memory', *The Cambridge History of Literary Criticism*, vol. II, part III, 'Textual psychologies: imagination, memory, pleasure' (Cambridge: Cambridge University Press, 2008), pp. 241–242, 254, esp. 260–262. This is discussed again in Chapter 4. Minnis shows that medieval and proto-literate imagery often derived from localised ecclesiastical art, but interpretations of the imagination itself were shaped by classical writers from Plato to St Augustine. As society became more literate imagery prompted by storytelling became more complex, but several scholars argue that stock imagery is still what children visualise: Rebecca Isbell, Joseph Sobol, Liane Lindauer and April Lowrance, 'The effects of storytelling and story reading on the oral language complexity and story comprehension of young children', *Early Childhood Education Journal*, vol. 32 (Cham, Switzerland: Springer International, 2004), pp. 158–159. The comparative study by Isbell et al. compared children who

were read stories with those who were told them orally, and their conclusions were shared by Brice Heath in her work with schoolchildren in Trackton: Shirley Brice Heath, 'What no bedtime story means: narrative skills at home and school', *Language in Society*, vol. 11 no. 1 (Cambridge: Cambridge University Press, 1982), pp. 49–76, also 'Protean shapes', pp. 352–354.

57 Bruno Bettelheim, *The Uses of Enchantment: The Meaning and Importance of Fairy Tales* (New York: Vintage Books, 2010), p. 9.

58 Such as Simon Foreman's account of *The Winter's Tale*, where the statue scene is unmentioned. Gurr, *Playgoing in Shakespeare's London*, pp. 11–112. Tiffany Stern, *Documents of Performance in Early Modern England* (Cambridge: Cambridge University Press, 2009), pp. 82–85.

59 Aphra Behn, *The Unfortunate Happy Lady, A True History*, (London, 1698), p. 25.

60 Maria Edgeworth, 'The Absentee' in *Tales of Fashionable Life*, series 2 (London: J. Johnson, 1812), Chapter III.

61 As discussed in Chapter 5, the importance of staging the visual dimension of a story rather than requiring individual visualisations increased as literacy increased.

62 *Joseph's Jalousie* and *The Trial of Mary* were performed in many medieval play cycles including that of Coventry. William Marriott (ed.), *A Collection of English Miracle and Mystery Plays* (Basel: Schweighauser and Co., 1838), pp. 41–55. Digitised by Internet Archive. https://archive.org/details/collectionofengl00marruoft/page/40 [accessed 27 January 2019].

63 To disambiguate rhetoric and oratory, it might be said that rhetoric is the theory of persuasion while oratory is its techniques. Rhetoric is concerned with the purpose of a public speech, its structure, rationale and methodology. Oratory is concerned with its practical delivery: the gestures, vocal dynamics, pauses, choice of metaphor and so on.

64 Quintilian, book II, chapter XVII, quoted in Tarling, *The Weapons of Rhetoric*, p. 153.

65 Oliver Strunk, *Source Readings in Music History: The Renaissance*, 4 vols (London: Norton Press, 1998), vol. III, p. 17. Strunk says that examples of this view can be found as early as the fifteenth century.

66 Henry Peacham the Younger, *The Compleat Gentleman* (London, 1622) reprinted in Strunk, *Source Readings*, vol. III, p. 73. Quoted in Tarling, *The Weapons of Rhetoric*, p. 47.

67 Johann Mattheson, *'Der vollkommene Capellmeister' (Hamburg 1739): a revised translation with critical Commentary*, trans. Ernest C. Harris, (Ann Arbor, MI: University of Michigan Research Press, 1981), chapter 10, p. 13. Johann Joachim Quantz, *Versuch einer Anweisung die Flöte traversiere zu spielen* (Berlin, 1752), trans. Edward J. Reilly, *On Playing the Flute*, (London: Faber and Faber, 1966), chapter 11, p. 1.

68 Joachim Burmeister, *Musica Poetica* (1606), trans. Benito V. Rivera (New Haven, CT: Yale University Press, 1993), p. 183. Quoted in Tarling, *The Weapons of Rhetoric*, p. 75.

69 Quantz, *Versuch einer Anweisung die Flöte*, chapter 11, p. 1. Quoted in Tarling, *The Weapons of Rhetoric*, p. 47.

70 The English Commonwealth's destruction of the Rubens altarpiece in Queen Henriette Marie's chapel – along with many other artworks – is a northern European example of art losing its protectors during a sectarian power shift but, in the south, Veronese's *Feast at the House of Levi* (1570) is another example. Originally titled *The Last Supper*, it fell foul of religious scrutiny and the Inquisition demanded the painting be changed or destroyed, but Veronese checkmated the inquisitors by simply retitling it *Feast at the House of Levi*.

2

Origins and development

In its earliest days Tragedy was recited by the poet alone, his face tinted by the dregs of crushed grapes. Later, characters were introduced and masks; and then choruses were added, and music, and sound effects, and scene-changes, and dances replaced the choruses; and perhaps in future, as times change, our descendants will witness the introduction of still other forms.[1]
                                Giacomo Badoaro, 1644. Prologue to *L'Ulisse errante*

The Venetian librettist Giacomo Badoaro believed, along with his colleagues, that opera was not a new artform but a revival of the ancient performance traditions of Greece and Rome. Yet he believed it was necessary to make accommodation for the passing of time and that opera should not be restricted to replicating ancient traditions. Like many scholars of his time and city, Badoaro was a 'Modern' and his libretti sometimes depart strikingly from the classical rules. Today, we can recognise his historical narrative as self-serving: he is offering us a view of classical performance as constantly evolving because this allowed him to innovate while still claiming classical precedent. I suggest, however, that although Badoaro had nothing resembling the evidence required by modern historians, his narrative may not have been so wide of the mark, at least in broad terms. Narratives, tragic and comic, gradually evolve away from their originator; parts of them are used in other stories; while singing new words to existing music is probably as old as singing itself. The chapter's introduction argues that pasticcio had a long history before opera emerged around 1600; it existed in many forms and had as respected a role in Greek and Roman culture as it did in Badoaro's.

The cento was a Roman genre of poetry which created new poems from existing lines of verse, frequently those of Homer and Virgil, with examples of the latter surviving from the third and fourth centuries AD. A cento of Faltonia Betitia Proba, the only extant work of this politically important noblewoman, is known from the mid-fourth century. Her *Cento Vergilianus de laudibus Christi* is a repositioning of 694 lines from the *Aeneid*, to tell the story of Jesus. The prestige of Virgil and the endemic religious controversies of the period suggest that Proba's work had very serious purposes. Her poem transforms the revered, but pagan, lines of Rome's national poet into a new work that is Christian as well as Roman. Like the city authorities, she was dismantling a temple and reusing the dressed stone to build a church.

Ausonius, writing in Gaul in the same century, was commissioned by the Emperor Valentinian to write the *Cento Nuptialis*. Sending the poem to his friend the rhetor Axius Paulus for criticism, Ausonius gave his own thoughts on the genre. He compared it to a Greek game in which fourteen pieces of bone carved into various geometric shapes can be used to create a variety of objects or images (like Lego in the modern age). He considered a good cento to be constructed so as to

> make different meanings correspond, make adopted lines naturally relate, let interpolations show no chink of light between themselves and the originals; prevent disparate parts from appearing to be forced together, prevent the closely packed thoughts from sticking out and the loose ones from gaping. If you find all these conditions duly fulfilled according to these rules, you can say that I have compiled a cento.[2]

A more perfect description of the requirements for a pasticcio opera would be hard to find. There is no sense that the cento was considered a secondary genre of poetry because the lines were not original; if anything its potential to subvert respected texts gave church fathers some anxiety over the following centuries.

The cento never entirely disappeared from Europe in the following thousand years but its practice resumed more detectably among Renaissance lettere in the fifteenth and especially the sixteenth centuries. This genre would provide seventeenth- and eighteenth-century pasticcieri with a classical example, and thus a justification, for their practice.[3] Compilator (compiler) was the term most frequently used for the creator of a cento and, interestingly, eighteenth-century English commentators on opera, such as 'Marcello' who wrote to *The Times* in 1789, used this term, probably in conscious recognition of affinity between the cento and the pasticcio.

In 1545 Bartolomeo Ricci published *De imitatione*, a text which would be republished throughout the century, in which he defended the cento and the practices of parody, imitation and borrowing. This highly influential text offers a window into the early modern perception of borrowing as virtuous and laudable, in contrast to later modern conceptions of it as a failure of originality at best or theft at worst. The *Centones ex Virgilio* by Lelio Capilupi (1497–1560) was published in 1555–1556 at Mantua and, in 1589, the Dutch humanist Joest Lips published a collection of centone, *Politicorum sive Civilis Doctrinae Libri Sex* at Leiden. In the following century the French scholar Andreas Fabri Wethulensis (Andre Le Fevre de

Vetheuil) published *Centones, cum Diana, et iuvenilibus* in Paris in 1609 and Etienne de Pleure, *Sacra Aeneis* in 1618, respectively. That the Renaissance cento reached Britain is evidenced by the Scottish poet Alexander Ross publishing *Virgilii Evangelisantis Christiados* in 1634. These texts and others like them testify to the conceptualisation of pasticcio having already been well established in both literate and oral culture prior to the emergence of opera. Pasticcio not only had the authority of classical precedent but was a ubiquitous practice in other artforms including poetry. These texts were composed and published in towns where pasticcio operas would also be created or performed.

In its early modern form the cento could be in prose or verse, but stylistic unity was as important in the cento as it would be in pasticcio opera. In his study of the cento, George Hugo Tucker notes that scholars such as Ricci and Vetheuil argued that the lines used should come from a single source, such as Cicero, rather than multiple sources as allowed by Ausonius.[4] He also notes that many advocates of the early modern cento were at pains to differentiate it from plagiarism. Imitatio, as Vetheuil defines it, is not the attempt to pass off the master's text as one's own, but to create new works from it, as if the great master were living in the present and writing works apposite to the times.[5] I suggest this perspective lies behind the printing of the names of composers whose music was borrowed for a pasticcio opera and argue later that it is more likely to have been a declaration of imitatio than any acknowledgement of ownership by the composer of the material used. In his preface 'Benigno proboque lectori' Vetheuil noted that the cento has its parallel in music, and argues that imitatio of composers such as Adriaan Willaert would be to the artform's benefit.[6]

> But he who has seen our little work which is not ours [i.e. centones] will speak of us as if we had followed Ausonius as the imitator, but Virgil as the author, from whose works (as from music) can be drawn certain compositions which, periodically, do not coincide with that author's meaning or which, for the most part, respect the author's intention almost amazingly, beyond most people's conception.[7]

Vetheuil recognises that the original meaning of a reused line might sometimes be apposite in its new context and, also, that sometimes the new context alone changes its meaning. That he could confidently state that this has a parallel in music suggests that the practice was more widespread than just the imitation of Willaert's Low Countries style by Venetian musicians.

The very name 'cento' was, like pasticcio, a metaphor for the creative process. Tucker notes that the Latin word was thought to derive from the Greek κεντρόνη (kentróni), meaning a patchwork textile, such as a quilt or blanket stitched together from textile fragments of varied colours; such was Isidore of Seville's understanding in the seventh century.[8] Yet Tucker suggests that a different derivation had emerged by the later Middle Ages, with a more literary flavour. Giovanni Marchesini (c.1300) and Lilio Gregorio Giraldi (1479–1552) thought the derivation might be from κέντρωνος (kéntronos), 'I ingraft', or κεντρίζω (kentrízo), meaning a point or needle, a term also used for a stylus. They argued that it derived from the process of combing a Virgilian or Homeric text and underlining or pricking the text selected for use.[9] These are evocative, if invented, derivations which hint at the compilation process at the time the derivation was current. Tucker notes that writers earlier than Marchesini imply that the compiler drew their Homeric or Virgilian lines from memory in the oral manner rather than from using a text. The process of creating of poetry from pre-existing parts was, then, an interplay between literary and oral methods over many centuries. The story providing the source material may have shifted between text and memory over time, and the compilation could have been made from either, although the final outcome of a cento was not a text for reading, but its performance. We might then ask what the relationship was understood as being between the performer, the compiler of the cento, and the original poem. Tucker argues for intertextuality being a feature of the Renaissance cento:

> As a literary form, the cento encapsulated the marginalisation or absence of an authorial 'voice' or 'subject' characteristic of Early Modern textuality ... Moreover, this depended as much upon any reader's (or listener/beholder's) ability to read and decode such a cento, as it did upon an author's (or artist's) technical abilities and powers of memory to compose or 'compile' it. The cento form could thus be viewed as an Early Modern precursor of intertextuality, of which it is an extreme illustration in that it overtly patches together fragments of still recognisable canonical texts so as to form new text, whose radically different meanings ... are informed by an implicit dialogue with the original contexts and meanings of those lifted fragments.[10]

As discussed in Chapter 1, the original dramatic context of a piece of music can be stripped away when it is reused in a pasticcio, but its emotional thrust remains. With text, I suggest the option is open for intertextuality when *reading* a cento as Tucker identifies, but one questions whether there is time when hearing a performance of the poem to identify and consider the interplay between what one is hearing and its source material. The lines are often far removed from their original context and it would be a very fast thinker who could follow the new story, imagining it as the teller speaks, and not just recognise the original lines as Homer's but reflect on their interplay. Performance conditions, I propose, are inhospitable for intertextuality, though a reader in their closet would have time to uncover or project intertextuality onto the poem. A more common purpose, I suggest, was to enlist the authority of the original author and their work for a new poem, rather than engage in discourse between the two. The cento offered a new originality or, as Ausonius himself expressed it, *de alieno nostrum*, from another's but our own.[11]

Practices later termed pasticcio in opera are not only prefigured in literary genres like the cento, but in late medieval and early modern musical practices such as contrafacta, quodlibet and the widespread borrowing of refrains between polyphonic motets and chansons from the thirteenth century onwards. Mark Everist argues that while no genuine 'refrain centos' can be found, as once thought, French-text motets demonstrate substantial borrowings both in text and setting.[12] He notes that such borrowings are seldom cut and pasted intact, and usually show some reworking to ensure verbal and musical unity.[13] I suggest that pasticcio practices not only preceded the emergence of opera but continued in parallel with opera, throughout the first century of its development. In assessing motets with borrowed material, Everist concludes:

> What survives here is not a genre along the same lines as the motet enté or the rondeau motet – or even the less easily defined motet with terminal refrain. What survives is a technique which could possibly appear in various genres … The … pieces discussed are radically different in so many of their musical characteristics that this musical phenomenon needs to be considered a technique and not a genre.[14]

I argue the same for pasticcio in opera. It was the continuing interaction between literary genres, vocal music and oral storytelling traditions that allowed pasticcio practices to be normal in all three during the seventeenth and eighteenth centuries. The histories of music and literature have generally been studied with little reference to the oral cultures out of which they emerged but with which they are still, in many ways, symbiotically linked. The following section traces this interconnection between oral storytelling and the emergence of opera.

Orality and early Italian opera

Unlike Britain, storytelling in Italy had an external visual dimension from the beginning. Cantastori were the professional singer-storytellers of the Italian Middle Ages, performing both spoken and sung stories at inns, festivals, baptisms, weddings and popular gatherings. Their title was sometimes changed to trovatori when they appeared in more elite households. They illustrated their tales with a large banner or billboard on which the key dramatic moments were stitched or painted in a series of panels to help with the visualising process. These visual aids to storytelling were also

popular in Germany but never became widespread in Britain, where purely
mental imaging was expected of listeners.[15]

2.1 *Il cantastorie* by Gian Domenico Tiepolo, *c.1765.*
Source: Dickenson Gallery, in public domain

Telling a story through music *and* visual display established an expectation
which influenced Italy's theatre genres including commedia dell'arte, commedia
erudita, intermedi and opera. Visuality was a core part of the storytelling
in these performances, an expectation of this having been created from the
medieval period onwards by cantastori. Such expectation was not present
in British storytelling tradition and thus a visual dimension took longer to
develop in British theatre. Nor were Italian oral traditions demoted by rising
literacy as they were in Britain: cantastori continued into the nineteenth
century and were revived in the twentieth.

Cantastorie repertoire and traditions varied in each region of Italy as did
theatre traditions; their repertoire in general was largely historical, some of
it was spoken, some cantillated and some sung. When sections of the story
were sung, simple monodies were used and narratives were taken from
strombotti and ballads such as 'Rinaldo', 'La donna Lombardo' and 'La pesca
dell' ancello'. They contained more detailed visual description than stories
usually did in Britain; this could be afforded as illustrations were on hand
to guide listeners in imagining them. Given that most cantastorie listeners
would not have been literate, it can be shown that narrative enhancement
through depiction, scenery and visuality in the seventeenth century did not

2.2 *Bänkelsänger* by Hieronymous Hess, *c.*1830–1840, depicting the German
tradition of storytelling with imagery and music.
Source: Released under Creative Commons Licence.

have to be linked to rising literacy as I argue below that it was in Britain.
Literate and oral cultures were interwoven in noble environments: houses
such as the Medici in Florence, the Visconti in Milan or the Barberini in
Rome had libraries of printed books which were often read silently and
in private, in the modern literate fashion, yet these same households also
retained professional trovatori and sometimes received itinerant cantastori,
who performed tales to assembled courtiers in continuity from medieval
practice.[16] The one culture did not demote the other.

When opera began to emerge at the very end of the sixteenth century, it was naturally conditioned by these highly visual performance genres and stage design, especially, was central to the conception of opera. Trompe l'œil scenery was used to create illusions of distance, perspective and grandeur, increasingly sophisticated stage machinery was invented and so were mechanisms enabling the larger, purpose-built theatres, such as those of Venice, to move flats efficiently in all directions. Ways were found to oscillate low flats painted with seas and to recreate the sound as well as the sight of waves. When storms were recreated, they consisted of thunder *and* lightning; not only were people flown on wires but whole chariots, ensembles on clouds or gods seated on thrones were lowered from above; tableaux were also lifted up from below the stage. Yet not all Italian performance genres placed visual representation at their core. One genre which did not, relying instead on the audience's imagination, was madrigal comedy. This genre developed at the same time as opera in the 1590s and declined when Italian opera consolidated its popularity in the 1630s and 1640s.

2.3 Italian wave machine installed at Drottningholms Royal Opera House in 1766.
Source: Drottningholms Slottsteater.

Madrigal comedy

This genre consisted of a sung story told through choruses, brief connecting instrumental sequences and well-known songs, all punctuated by a declaimed narrative. They were semi-staged with a strictly limited theatricality and their stories often derived from commedia dell'arte plots. This genre dispensed with dramatising its narratives and remained rooted in storytelling to foreground the musical experience. This is explicitly stated by the composer of the first published madrigal comedy, Orazio Vecchi, in his 1597 preface to *L'Amfiparnasso*:

> The music is not interspersed with such pleasures for the sight as might relieve the one sense by the attentiveness of the other. However, those desirous of more action may refer every want to what is presupposed and inwardly expressed, and thus will they be able to form a complete idea [mental vision] of the play.[17]

Vecchio is saying that the usual expectation of seeing the drama in action, as when attending a commedia dell'arte performance, should not apply when attending this kind of performance. Rather, one should listen and imagine the staging from memories of having seen the story performed; one should imagine the action 'inwardly' as it is 'expressed' or described through the singing. This point is reinforced in the prologue spoken by Lelio:

> But meanwhile, I know
> That the Spectacle of which I speak
> Is beheld by the imagination
> Which it penetrates through the ear,
> Not through the eye.
> Therefore, be silent!
> And instead of seeing, listen![18]

Despite the absence of spectacle and design, madrigal comedy was a successful and popular artform precisely because it made use of the oral storytelling contract between teller and listener; the imagination was specifically required in this kind of musical storytelling, and was thus closer to British spoken performance of the same period. The Italian composer Adriano Banchieri followed Vecchi very closely when he created his own madrigal comedies, basing five of them on commedia dell'arte stories and his texts even contain stage directions. These misled an earlier generation of scholars into believing the works were staged like plays or operas, but scholars including Alfred Einstein, Nino Pirrotta and Martha Farahat argued that these stage directions are principally intended to aid the imagining of a theatrical setting by those reading the comedy in book form. Farahat concludes by suggesting that by the 1620s madrigal comedies had developed to the point where there was an itch to cross the line into dramatic representation.

Banchieri veiled his instrumentalists and chorus behind a curtain and allowed these singers to use their scores; the 'recitanti' or 'aperatanti' stood in front of the curtain and sang the characters' roles off the score.[19] It is hard to imagine that these aperatanti never interacted with each other dramatically, even if not in the physical commedia fashion. Perhaps operatic acting before Monteverdi was not that much different. Visuality and hints of theatricality emerge in this decade as the genre began to make use of modest sets and costumes, although the movement still remained static. A number of madrigal comedies might be considered to be pasticci as items included in them were originally free-standing and their narratives were borrowed. The significance of this short-lived artform is that it demonstrates how literate Italian audiences still sought pleasure from proto-literate storytelling traditions, as British audiences would later do with opera. Opera, then, emerged among a rich variety of dramatic traditions; some, such as commedia erudita, leaned towards literate culture while others, such as madrigal comedy, testified to the continuing appeal of oral culture.

The origins of recitative

What Badoaro probably meant by 'recite' (recitata) in the epigraph, was the kind of cantillation he was familiar with: recitative. He knew that poetry was often sung aloud in both Greek and Roman society and was projecting the sound of his own seventeenth-century recitative back into the classical past. Opera's recitative did not, of course, derive in any linear way from ancient Greece, but many cultures make use of sung speech and in a wide variety of contexts. I suggest that operatic recitative derived from a broad range of cantillations in daily use during sixteenth-century Italian life.

Medievalists have explored the different types of sung speech used to perform metrical tales in secular courts across Europe, finding a wide range that were cantillated rather than either spoken or fully sung.[20] As early as 1200, the French chantefable was a sung prose genre though unfortunately only one example remains extant that has a reconstructable musical character, *Aucassin et Nicolette*. John Stevens, writing the *Grove* entry on the piece describes it thus: 'interspersed in the narrative are verse sections (laisses) written in lines with equal numbers of syllables, all sung to the same double phrase of melody'.[21] Stevens sees this as deriving from Chansons de Geste, but court poets would have been familiar with many kinds of sung speech, both liturgical and secular. For the chantefable, narrative seems to have been more important than the musicality of the cantillation and this was probably also true for the cantillations of cantastori. The chanting of liturgy will be discussed as one influence on recitative but examples of low-status, non-narrative uses of cantillation abound. In Britain, auctioneering is still sometimes performed with a sing-song voice which the eighteenth century called 'selling by public cant'. Dairymen called in the cattle, huntsmen encouraged their hounds, nightwatchmen intoned the hours and the cries of market sellers were so musical that secular choral works were created out of them by Orlando Gibbons and others. This canting is a very different kind of sung speech to that used in religious liturgy, though canting, chanting, cantillation, chauntering and sauntering all derive from the Latin for singing.

I do not believe that there was one type of cantillation from which operatic recitative derived: many would have been similar in sound even though they evolved independently from each other in very different times and places. Evidence for similarities has emerged recently, discussed below, as textual scholars have developed methods for extrapolating the intended vocalisation of sung speech from historic texts. In cases where texts contain indications for performance, reconstructions have been attempted, each with greater or lesser levels of proof or interpretation. Among the many interesting results is the striking similarities many reveal with operatic recitative. The evidence suggests similar tonal inflections may have been widely used across different languages, contexts and periods. The significance of this in understanding operatic recitative is its derivation from earlier storytelling performances. Storytellers freely adapted the tellings of their stories to particular audiences and to the occasion: cuts, borrowings and rearrangements were part of the process. I propose that recitative was thought of in this way, as something which the performer might themselves adapt as occasion offered, so long as the overall conception of the story was served.

The methodologies developed by Armand d'Angour and David Creese to reconstruct the performance sound of ancient Greek verse have been highly influential.[22] Their reconstruction technique involved extrapolating sound patterns from the prosody and scansion of poems, then utilising a vocal notation system for intervals, introduced into texts and inscriptions from c.450 BC onwards. This consisted of alphabetic letters and signs placed above the vowels in each word which indicated pitch rather than stress.[23] They set their findings to strings, flutes or percussion known to be in use at the time of the poem from contemporary illustrations and archaeology. Not all were songs and, sometimes, a stringed instrument merely provided chords at certain points, with the singer's voice alone ornamenting the line.

A similar reconstructive approach was taken in Italy to Matteo Maria Boiardo's epic poem *Orlando innamorato*, written in the 1480s, and argued by Jo Ann Cavallo and Blake Wilson, on the basis of its prologue, to have been sung or cantillated at the court of Ferrara. Experiments in reconstruction began with Gianni Celati in 1996, but in 2014 students from the Universities of Colombia, working in an exchange project with the town of Scandiano, attempted a reconstruction.[24] Wilson shows that fifteenth-century teachers like Vittorino da Feltre encouraged their students in the Studia Humanitatis to see classical texts as essentially scripts for oral performance. Feltre recommended the singing of verse to the accompaniment of stringed instruments as the continuation of classical practice as well as a form of recreation.

Sioned Hughes at Cardiff University led the way in seeing written Welsh narratives, such as the prose work *Culhwch ac Olwen,* as intended for oral performance rather than as literature in the modern sense.[25] This assisted the Centre for the Ancient Music of Wales at Bangor University in examining the performance of verse at fourteenth- and fifteenth-century Welsh courts; reconstructions showed that in some performances lines of verse or prose were improvised on a single note for each sentence, changing only on words of emphasis, as with sung liturgy. In these kinds of performance, a stringed instrument such as a harp was probably used to give the note.[26] In reconstructions of English poems, New York University's *The Weddyng of Sir Gawen and Dame Ragnell* found ornamentations illustrating the key parts of a sung line and several instruments forming the accompaniment.[27] This not only prefigures recitativo secco, but recitativo accompagnato. Even the use of the operatic melisma is known from the medieval period in Italy and France.

I am not arguing for long transhistorical continuities or transmission of cantillations from region to region, merely that when societies create sung speech for different purposes, some of the forms generated are likely to be similar in sound. What can be said with confidence is that the sound of recitative would have seemed traditional, perhaps even antique at the new artform's inception in 1600, especially given that the Camerata's new monody was intended to be a reconstruction of the singing in ancient Greek tragedy.[28]

Recitative conveyed expositional information, prosaic but necessary plot details, rapid-fire comic routines and, crucially, allowed the key to change between arias as well as giving the singer their note. Very seldom is a passage of recitativo secco borrowed in a pasticcio and given new words; they tended to be written afresh each time or improvised orally. Trying to set new words to an existing pattern of speech is a much harder task than composing it afresh. Recitativo accompagnato performs the same tasks but is accompanied by more instrumentation; these are sometimes reused in a pasticcio but, mostly, they too are written afresh.[29] Scholarship has tended to focus on arias as the locus for pasticcio, but recitative is also the site for changing the telling of a story, and one with a very long provenance.

The emergence of opera in Italy

The first opera for which the music is extant is usually considered to be *Euridice*, composed in Florence in 1600 by Jacopo Peri and Giulio Caccini to a libretto by Ottavio Rinuccini and performed at the Palazzo Pitti. Caccini scored it again, alone, in 1602. Extant in different versions, it is mainly sung speech with an instrumental support, prefiguring recitative rather than aria. This choice, I suggest, indicates its affinity with court storytelling traditions. A recent recording of *Euridice* with the title role sung by Gloria Banditelli reveals how much the role of the music was to help create emotional investment *in* the story rather than help *tell* the story.[30] Earlier operas, such as Peri's *Dafne* (*c*.1597) and the pastorales of Emilio de Cavalieri (1590s) are described by Caccini as consisting of songs rather than recitative, but the music has not survived. Music does survive for Cavalieri's *Rappresentatione di anima e di corpo* (1600), performed in Rome; Cavalieri claimed in letters that this made him the first modern artist to revive the sung acting of ancient Greece, a claim admitted by Peri in his preface to the 1601 publication of *Euridice*.[31] All four artists – Cavalieri, Peri, Caccini and Rinuccini – had worked closely together at the Medici court since the late 1580s – not always harmoniously – and had collaborated on *La pellegrina* which, while technically being an intermedi, was arguably another staging post on the road towards opera.

Giulio Caccini wrote about how he had evolved his ideas for musical storytelling in the prologue to *Le nuove musiche* (1602). He looks fondly back to the aristocratic camerata in Florence which flourished in the 1570s and 1580s, where he claims to have learned more about musical storytelling than in thirty years of studying counterpoint.

> I say this because these insightful gentlemen [the camerata] always encouraged me and convinced me with the clearest reasoning not to value the kind of music that prevents the words from being well understood and thus spoils the sense and the form of the poetry. I refer to the kind of music that elongates a syllable here and shortens one there to accommodate the counterpoint, turning the poetry to shreds. Instead, they urged me to adhere to the manner [of composition] praised by Plato and the other philosophers who affirm that music is nothing but speech, rhythm, and harmony.[32]

In arguing that counterpoint should be discreet and that storytelling through words should be the governing aim, Caccini's prologue did not advocate the reduction of music to mere cantillation, he was no Crescimbeni; rather, he saw music as a tool supporting traditional storytelling, along with other tools such as metre. Caccini was well aware of the capacity of monodies to deliver drama if carefully scored; the prologue reveals that he viewed the work as an exciting development within court storytelling traditions rather than an entirely new genre; it was thus both original and ancient: the authority of Plato is invoked to reaffirm music's role as a branch of rhetoric. Similarly, Cavalieri's performance instructions in the published score show concern that the music does not overshadow the words, and he counselled against ornamentation except where specifically scored.[33] Early operas were classical in narrative, literary in structure but oral in their construction techniques: mimesis was used in the rehearsal process, the audience's imagination was required for the story to be visualised, rhetorical principles governed the composition and pre-existing texts and music were borrowed. These early operas were commissions from royal or aristocratic households and mostly new material, but pasticcio was an embedded practice in oral storytelling tradition and soon becomes detectable in early operas.

2.4 Cameo engraving of Francesca Caccini, artist unknown, *c.*1630s.
Source: Conservatorio di Firenze.

The operas of Claudio Monteverdi began in Mantua with *La favola d'Orfeo* in 1607 and *L'Arianna* in 1608. It is hard to overstate Monteverdi's influence on the artform; he helped give opera the shape it would retain throughout the seventeenth century and long into the next. His style of composition was followed by Stefano Landi in *La morte d'Orfeo* in 1618, and by Marco Marazzoli and Virgilio and Marco Marazocchi, who composed in the 1630s.[34] Francesca Caccini, Giulio's daughter, was the first woman to write an opera: *La liberazione di Ruggiero dall' isola d'Alcina*, written in 1625, is the only opera of hers to survive.[35] While Francesca Caccini used Monteverdi's flexible approach to recitatives, canzonetti and ensembles, the two composers have different styles. She departs from her father, Peri and Monteverdi by gendering the different keys, using flat keys for the feminine and sharp for the masculine; this gendering of the music is echoed in the drama but given greater complexity as the characters also cross-dress. She used a distinctive accompagnato style lying between recitative and aria, whereas later composers employed a crisper separation.

Monteverdi's storytelling

Monteverdi was credited by twentieth-century musicology with introducing the twofold system of recitative and aria; more recent scholarship views this system as pre-existing; but the types of aria he included in his operas are more diverse than they would become in opera seria. The demarcation

2.5 Portrait of a young man argued to be Monteverdi, by a Cremonese artist, *c.*1597.
Source: Ashmolean Museum, Oxford

between aria and recitative was also more permeable in this early phase of opera than it would later become and Monteverdi's recitatives could be tuneful and evocative, even conveying the emotional or intimate parts of the story, while his arias could advance the plot, provide exposition or supply narrative detail.

Innovative though his settings were, telling the story still came first; in 1607 he published *Scherzi musicale* which contains a defence, written by his brother, of the new compositional style. His brother quotes Monteverdi as declaring the text to be the governor (padrona) of the music, not the reverse.[36] Monteverdi thus affirmed Caccini's principle that the first concern of opera was storytelling.

I suggest that underlying Monteverdi's approach to opera composition are two earlier traditions for setting music to liturgy: these demonstrate the intersectionality between textual and oral inheritances in early operatic storytelling and explain how the space for pasticcio was created. Settings for liturgical narratives which had declaratory or pedagogic purposes, such as the Credo or the chanting of the gospel, usually privileged the text over the music so the musical element was simple. Settings for speech acts, on the other hand, where the sung words played a locutionary or operative role in the sacrament, interacting directly with God or invoking the intercession of saints, did not have to privilege the text over the music and could be more complex. Similarly, the words of the Kyrie, Agnus Dei and Sanctus did not have to be decipherable to the human ear because God was the listener and he already knew what was being communicated. Consequently, these settings could be more musically complex with polytextual motets, melismatic expansion of words, increased numbers of independent vocal lines and ritornelli, as seen in Alessandro Striggio the Elder's *Missa sopra Ecco sì beato giorno* (1565). An analogy is the way the names of the departed were written into medieval gospel books for the good of their souls. These names were often cut very lightly into the vellum and are undetectable to the naked eye: it was not necessary for the writing to be legible or even visible as it was not the human reading of the name that benefited the soul but the *act* of writing itself, the dry-point glosses in the Gospel of Chad being an example.[37]

Monteverdi's Credo in his *Missa in illo tempore* (1610) is simple and written in an antique style borrowed from Nicholas Gombert; it focuses on the storytelling while his Sanctus and Benedictus, which occur in the consecration of the host, are more ethereal. The dramatic intention in his composition for these speech acts is to transport the listener into the divine presence; it is not the relation of a past event as is the Credo but something occurring 'on stage' at that precise temporal moment. This dramatic immediacy can also be found in the Magnificat of Monteverdi's *Vespers* (1610).

I propose that these two contrasting approaches to setting liturgy are reflected in early opera. Monteverdi used simplistic settings for arias conveying narratives such as the Messenger's tale of Euridice's death by snake bite in *L'Orfeo*, 'Ahi, caso acerbo, ahi, fato empio e crudele … In un fiorito prato', which is a simply scored, plaintive lament. The settings for locutionary speech acts were more musically sophisticated, such as Pluto's granting of Prospina's suit to rescue Euridice from death, 'Benché severo ed immutabil fato'. Several other speech acts in *L'Orfeo* are also set in ways reminiscent of direct addresses to the deity: the Kyrie and Gloria are echoed in the beginning of Orfeo's 'Qual onor di te fia degno', where he praises his lyre for effecting the rescue of Euridice from death. Resonances of the Sanctus and Benedictus, responses in the Consecration, can be heard in Proserpina's 'Quali grazie ti rendo' and 'Pietade, oggi, e Amore' by the Chorus of Spirits. The supplication for absolution in the Agnus Dei is echoed in Orfeo's supplication to Caronte, 'Possente spirito'. By this, I do not mean that Monteverdi's liturgical and operatic settings are similar in sound but rather that the composer's understanding of operatic drama is conditioned by his sense of liturgical drama, that he was composing within liturgical paradigms when setting operas, probably unconsciously.

In this balancing of musically simple and musically complex settings, Monteverdi created a subtle interplay of private and public moments in the audience's experience. Simple settings of narrative allowed listeners to withdraw their focus temporarily from the stage, the social context and the hurly-burly of the auditorium, to visualise a narrative as it was sung. Applauding at the end of these items brought listeners out of themselves and they would come back together as an audience. Examples include Ottone's 'I miei subiti sdegni', in *L'incoronazione di Poppea* (1643), which clearly relies on interior imagining. These short spaces of individual thelxis did not recreate the long-sustained imaginings of proto-literate storytelling, but are, perhaps, an operatic development from it. Moments of action on the other hand were set so as to compel attention to the stage and involve the audience in more collective responses of joy, suspense or horror. Monteverdi scored such arias in a fast, punchy way, pulling the audience's focus out of themselves and back onto the stage, as with Ottone's attempt to murder Poppea at the end of Act II Scene XIV (though the Ottone sequences were probably not composed by Monteverdi personally, as discussed below).

This rhythm, whereby audience members repeatedly move between their own private imagination, memory and emotions before rejoining the communality of the audience to focus on the stage, is the same as the rhythm of church ritual, but liturgy did not usually seek dramatic tensions or changes of pace during its progression.[38] Monteverdi, I suggest, reached beyond liturgy and borrowed techniques used in contemporary theatre to create changes of pace and dramatic tensions. He liked to interrupt contemplative sequences with bursts of action or urgency. The soldiers' recitative 'Chi parla? Chi parla?' in Act I is dramatically urgent; the recitatives and aria for Seneca and Ottavia in Scenes VI and VII, 'Ecco la sconsolata Donna', are not really an interaction between them but rather a succession of rhetorical discourses on the miseries of unhappy queens. These sung orations are interrupted by the valet, who is outraged by Ottavia's treatment, but even this story of Nerone's misdeeds is a catalogue redolent of oral epic, rather than a plot recapitulation. Once the others have gone, Seneca delivers a final peroration – 'Le porpore regali e imperatrici' – for which private imagination is required rather than attention to staged action. Yet later, the same character's musing on his forthcoming death – 'Amici, è giunta' – is punctured by his friends' vibrant 'Non morir, Seneca!' Most compelling is Nerone's rejoicing in Seneca's death, 'Hor che Seneca è morto, cantiam', pinning our attention on the performer and his drinking companion.

The anonymous librettist of Monteverdi's *Le nozze d'Ennea e Lavinia* (1640), in defending his practice of dividing his operas into five acts, explains that his principal reason was to rest the concentration: 'although the modern practice is to divide even spoken plays into three acts, I have preferred to divide mine into five, so that with more pauses the audience might rest from the mental effort of following a series of depicted events'.[39] Depicted in the imagination, rather than on stage. Musical pictoriality offers further evidence of this desire to stimulate mental imagery; in Act III of *L'Orfeo*, a Chorus of Infernal Spirits describes how nature succumbs to Man's determination in 'Nulla impresa per uom si tenta invano':

> No enterprise by man is undertaken in vain,
> nor can Nature further defend herself against him.
> He has ploughed the waving fields
> of the uneven plain and scattered the seed
> of his labour, whence he has reaped golden harvests.
> Wherefore, so that the memory
> of his glory shall live,
> Fame has loosened her tongue to speak of him
> who tamed the sea with fragile barque
> and mocked the fury of the winds of the north and south.

The brass illustrates Man doggedly pushing a plough, multiple voices illustrate the scattering of seeds, a more piano unison portrays the taming of the seas while the voices then divide again into separate catcalls to mock the fury of the winds. The new artform thus made use of long-standing traditions to create its new kind of musical drama. Neither recitative nor the aesthetics behind aria scoring were innovations in the early seventeenth century, and pasticcio was not, either. It was as much received inheritance in opera as the cento was in poetry.

Contrafacta, the reuse of a musical setting to support a new or different text, were a common part of the musical environment and a medieval tradition ancestral to pasticcio. In a prefiguring of the self-pasticcio, the masses of Josquin des Prez (1455–1521), Antoine Brumel (1460–1512) and Giovanni Palestrina (1525–1594) all contain settings which the composers had used many times before.[40] As mentioned above, Monteverdi himself borrowed Nicolas Gombert's 1538 motet setting for his *Missa in illo tempore*, and his madrigals, published in five books before 1605, were reused by his friend Aquilino Coppini as settings for sacred texts. Dedicated to Cardinal Borromeo, these were published in 1607, 1608 and 1609, with the title pages specifically stating that Monteverdi's madrigals formed the settings.[41] Coppini's placing of new text on Monteverdi's notes is a masterpiece of pasticcio writing and Agnieszka Budzinska-Bennett points out its skill:

> First, his Latin contrafacta are creative re-textings in which he reproduces the metric structure and the sound quality of Guarini's [Monteverdi's original lyricist] original Italian texts through the careful placement of phonemes, vowels and consonants. Second, he transforms them into madrigali spirituali, always following their original affetti, creating strong associations and often profound intertextual relationships among the original and the new texts, in which he elevates the profane situations from Guarini's texts to the spiritual level of the Gospel teachings. In this respect, Coppini's work remains a fascinating contribution to the enduring discussion on the thin line between the sacred and the profane.[42]

The reuse and repurposing of both settings and texts was normal practice in other musical genres before opera emerged; pasticcio practices were emerging naturally in Italian opera along with other oral characteristics. Alessandro Striggio the Younger borrowed text from Rinuccini's libretto for *Euridice* (1600) when writing the libretto for Monteverdi's *La favola d'Orfeo* (1607). Yet pasticcio opera as the eighteenth century would understand it only really begins in the 1630s and 1640s. It has long been argued that the extant scores of *L'incoronazione di Poppea* (1643) contain music by hands other than Monteverdi's: Francesco Sacrati is a strong contender as are Benedetto Farrari and Filiberto Laurenzi for the final duet in *Poppea*, 'Pur ti miro'.

Mark Ringer has suggested that a studio system might explain the composite nature of the surviving scores, arguing that Monteverdi had younger composers studying with him to whom he deputised parts of the work.[43] Yet the pasticcio approach to creating large-scale performances was already embedded in genres from masses to madrigal comedies and was emerging in opera, too, as Giulio Strozzi's operas show. Ways of telling classical stories set patterns, narrative tropes were shared and dramatic structures, texts and tunes were copied. A formal business or employment relationship between Monteverdi and those whose music was incorporated into his operas, while feasible, is still an explanation which projects backwards modern needs for single authorship, ownership of the work and canonical integrity. Multiple explanations are possible for the presence of material not written by Monteverdi or his librettist Giovanni Francesco Busanello, but simple borrowing, amendments made after the initial run of performances or even after Monteverdi's death are, I suggest, the most likely. As Rosand says, 'nearly every work that was revived, either in Venice or elsewhere, in the original composer's absence or after his death, was a pasticcio'.[44] Similarly, Francesco Cavalli's contract with the Teatro San Cassiano required him to 'be present at all the rehearsals that are needed and also to change parts, alter, cut and add whatever is necessary in the music in the service of the opera'.[45] There is insufficient evidence to claim that *L'incoronazione di Poppea* was *conceived* as a pasticcio but it clearly became one fairly soon after 1643.

Suggestions that early opera composers sought any kind of fixed reproducibility of their scores are undermined by the looseness with which they sketched their intentions into them. Monteverdi's published score for *L'Orfeo* shows that he had a detailed and ambitious musical schema for the opera, intending very different instrumental sounds for the pastoral world from that of the underworld and using different instruments for different dramatic moments. But, as Mark Ringer and many others have noted, he left the question of which instruments should play which parts up to whoever was organising the performances, and scored only five parts.[46] The orchestra parts for *Poppea* are similarly open: three parts were written in the Venetian score and four in the Neapolitan score but, again, it is left it to those staging the opera to choose which instruments use which parts. Several other scores survive which are written in this way: composers were aware that the accompaniment depended on what instruments were available at the time of performance, the proficiency of individual players and the rehearsal time available. Each opera was expected to evolve between conception and performance, but also between performance run and revival. The mutating traditions of storytelling rather than the text-governed fixity of liturgy characterised early opera; its creators possessed only a contingent ownership.

The court context for opera changed irreversibly when the Republic of Venice embraced the artform in the 1630s. Opera moved for the first time from the households of princes into public theatres. Commercial success began to become as important as patronage in the funding of opera; publishing their libretti became an important source of income for poets rather than their being court-produced souvenirs of a court event. Venice saw the opening of a number of public theatres which staged operas; the first, the Teatro San Cassiano, opened in 1637, the Teatro Santi Giovanni e Paolo followed in 1638, the Teatro San Moisè in 1639/40 and from 1641 the Teatro Novissimo, which operated only to 1645. At least one new opera house opened later still, the Teatro San Giovanni Grisostomo in 1678.

Monteverdi, remarkably, managed to span both worlds: *L'Orfeo* (1607) and *L'Arianna* (1608) had been court entertainments for the Duke of Mantua but, in 1613, he moved to Venice to become maestro di cappella at St Mark's Basilica. In the 1630s Monteverdi saw Benedetto Ferrari and Madalena Manelli's new operas at the Teatro San Cassiano. Initially he kept his distance from this new phase of development but, slowly, a growing chorus of flattery bore fruit and the elderly maestro re-engaged with the artform he had helped originate.

2.6 Monteverdi in the late 1630s by Bernardo Strozzi.
Source: Gallerie dall'Accademia, Venice, released under Creative Commons Licence.

At the age of 70 Monteverdi reworked *L'Arianna* for the 1640 carnival to make it more appealing to the citizens of the Republic, adapting it to the new performance conditions. He then agreed to set a libretto by his friend Giacomo Badoaro. Appropriately, it was called *Il ritorno d'Ulisse in patria*. This was a new work written for a new age and Monteverdi showed he was more than capable of adapting his compositional style. He set another, *Le nozze d'Enea e Lavinia*, in 1640 and, in 1642, *L'incoronazione di Poppea*. Monteverdi was held in high regard in Venice, despite which his music seems not to have been systematically collated, archived or published. Venetian theatre managers usually printed a scenario, so that audience members could glance down to follow what was going on; this is the only document which definitely survives from the first production of *Poppea*, yet Monteverdi is not mentioned in it. The libretto was published twice, once by Busanello himself, and seven manuscripts are still extant which give parts of it. In only one, the Udine manuscript, is Monteverdi mentioned and that is thought to have been scribbled down during one of the first performances.[47] Only two contemporary scores survive, both manuscripts: one from Venice owned by Cavalli, and one from *Poppea's* 1651 revival in Naples. These are working documents which survive by chance, probably preserved in case of further revival, rather than archived because of their intrinsic value. They show considerable reworking, with sequences cut and pasted, rearrangements and transpositions. That they contain music not by Monteverdi suggested to Rosand 'that music per se had no practical value except as a basis for further performance'.[48]

In a performance-centred environment, music was considered to be over once it was no longer being heard, like a spent firework. Libretti may have had an earlier and closer relationship with printing than did scores but any textual record of an opera, libretto or score, printed or in manuscript, was assumed to carry with it the right to perform it, or to use parts of it for other performances. Therein lies an oral continuity; vocalising a story in public released it, without caveats, into the wider world; circulating it through text in these early days of printing was thought to have the same freedom.

Pasticcio and early modern conceptions of musical ownership

No sooner did public opera houses open in Venice than the true pasticcio began. *La finta savia* (1643), which appeared the same year as *Poppea*, made a selling point of having no fewer than four separate composers, Filiberti Laurenzi, Benedetto Ferrari, Tarquinia Merula and Giovanni Battista Crivelli. *Argiope* (1649), *Giasonne* (1649) and *Il novello Giasone* (1671), along with many others, were also advertised as having multiple composers.

The word pasticcio was not yet used and no term comparable to the compiler of centone appears but, perhaps, for so ubiquitous a method, it was too normal to require one; 'opera' covered it.

The conception of opera music as property and the parameters of its ownership are discernible in Venice between the 1630s and 1660s. It was a conception shared by other parts of Italy too, but it is in Venice that it is most visible. These conceptions and parameters would travel with opera as the artform spread across Europe and would last into the nineteenth century, at which point new conceptions and parameters drove out the old. Its profile can be seen in Giulio Strozzi's relationship with pasticcio.

As librettist of *La finta pazza* (1641), Strozzi had rejoiced in its success at the Teatro Novissimo and had it published twice. He was then disturbed to find that when touring companies and accademici restaged it in other cities outside the Veneto, or even outside Italy, they were amending it drastically. These other companies removed the specifically Venetian elements of the libretto to make it more relevant to their own localities, then published these variant libretti, sometimes acknowledging Strozzi's authorship and sometimes not.[49]

In response, he printed fresh editions of his libretto, motivated, I suggest, by two anxieties: firstly, that the alterations might not be very good but his name would still be attached to the operas; secondly, that if they were good, these foreign pasticcieri might be credited with improving his work.[50] That Strozzi did not think opera libretti should be as unchangeable as liturgy is demonstrated by his own creation of pasticcio versions of the sequel, *La finta savia*, (1643), in future years.

In his preface, he explained that by republishing the original he was providing readers with an opportunity to compare his work with what he considered to be feeble variants:

> I willingly undertook this third printing of the true *finta pazza* because I saw some wandering musicians have had it reprinted elsewhere in various ways, and that they go around performing it as if it were their own. The author takes little notice and would be able to thank God had his [work] been improved for him. Hence you will be the judge by reading the one and the other, and if you should not discover any improvement, you will say, if it was such a success altered, what must it have inspired in its original form: ... it stupefied Venice herself.[51]

Strozzi clearly felt himself to be owner of his story and, to modern eyes, his problems might appear to be caused by the absence of copyright, but this is to view copyright the wrong way round. As discussed in Chapters 4 and 5, it is not that without legal protection there is no textual stability and so no 'finished' definitive work to own; rather, there can be no effective legislation to create ownership if works remain mutable and exist in variant versions. Strozzi lost control of 'his' story the moment he published it, but he knew this and so, I propose, his motives in trying to reclaim it were much less modern.

2.7 *Giulio Strozzi* by Tiberio Tinelli, *c.*1620s.
Source: Uffizi Gallery, Florence.

Strozzi desired the reputational enhancement and increased commissions which widespread revivals of *La finta pazza* gave him; consequently, he did not feel he could complain about his work being restaged per se, as that was the only form of dissemination possible beyond the small print runs of his book. He 'takes little notice' of the reworking and restaging of his opera and, indeed, the very republishing of *La finta pazza* was an invitation for people to continue staging it. What irked him was the impression given by some adaptors, notably those of the Piacenza version, that they had originated the opera. The offence was thus plagiarism rather than pasticcio per se. That said, he certainly took umbrage at the changes made to the opera, but he saw this as an insult to his skill as an artist rather than the theft of his property. While he may have been piqued by rival accademici gaining financial advantage from his work, he had too much noblesse to complain of this; he resented only the arrogance of the rewriters in assuming their versions would be better. The dissemination which pasticcio facilitated was eagerly sought and Strozzi accepted it as the way of his world but, like a modern composer signing away their copyright to a music corporation, it was a queasy moment.

Another reason Strozzi did not mind, or pretended not to mind, the reworking of *La finta pazza* was because an unconscious parameter was in place, deriving from oral culture. As discussed, ownership was accepted as ending at the point of transmission, but printing complicated this conception of ownership. On one level it could simply be the recording of a performance in text but, on another, printing could be a claim to authorship of the story itself. While reiterating a story in a changed form, even without crediting the known author, was normal in early modern society, plagiarism – claiming to author a story that was already well known or demonstrably authored by someone else – was strongly disapproved of. As Strozzi's fears show, printing could thus be a highly authoritative kind of plagiarism but it could also offer storytellers a means of retaining control of a story, or at least of their particular telling of it.

The variant forms of his opera also caused Strozzi political problems; his opera was for the glory of Venice so when the Codogno version stripped out the Venetian slant of his opera, he found his work being used to promote rival cities, such as Bologna. This diminished Strozzi's own standing as a successful advocate for his city; his competitive stance towards these 'foreign' pasticcieri is thus political as well as artistic. Reprinting his original was a lost cause, however. Unable to see beyond his own campanilismo, Strozzi failed to recognise that the success of the work outside Venice *depended* on its being amended. Genoa, Milan, Florence, Bologna, Naples, Paris and the wider world had no interest in listening to Venice talk to herself. The themes and concerns of Strozzi's opera were universal and this is what attracted other companies to stage it. Strozzi's response was the natural feeling of a storyteller hearing their story in the mouth of another, but it was these changes which ensured the opera's fame beyond the Veneto and which secured its continuity in the repertoire. As opera continued to develop, librettists, including Strozzi himself, became more sanguine about pasticcio and, by 1652, he was amending Giulio Cicognini's libretto *Veremonda* in precisely the way he had so bitterly complained of when it had been his turn.

My argument in this section condenses to this: pasticcio was essential for operas to spread and survive. It was core to making opera revivals work but, beyond this, the survival of instrumental music, church music, dances and tavern songs also depended on being changed to fit different contexts and resources. In an age without mechanical or electronic reproducibility and where pen written scores were rare and printed ones rarer still, it was changeability which secured the continuity of a composition or text beyond its initial use. Posterity held no substance for librettists, composers, impresarios and managers: today's audience was their only reality.

The oral to literate transition in Britain

Britain's spoken theatre, like the performance genres of Italy, was greatly conditioned by oral storytelling. Britain, however, has longer winters with fewer daylight hours, leaving rural workers with more time on their hands after dark, when little manual labour could be achieved and artificial lighting was minimal. Winter was, consequently, the storytelling season. In low-status communities and families, brewing ale and telling stories were largely feminine skills and possibly interconnected, the one being a draw for selling the other. Alewives are frequently mentioned and in pastoral plays 'the wisest aunt telling the saddest tale' appears in numerous guises. In higher-status contexts, storytellers were male and literate. The most distinctive difference from Italian storytelling is the absence of a visual dimension in either context. Given the visual vibrancy of Britain's medieval country churches, and the tapestry tradition in castles, tower-houses and mansions, it is tempting to think this dimension was lost rather than absent, an unrecorded victim perhaps of Reformation iconoclasm. But, so far, no evidence has emerged for storytelling in Britain having ever made use of banners or painted panels as a matter of course. Elizabethan theatre, as a result, felt no expectation that its plays would be illustrated throughout by scenery, though medieval plays and masques often had been. When we do encounter the likelihood of scenery being necessary, such as a bush for the comic characters to hide behind in *Twelfth Night*, or an arras to conceal Polonius in *Hamlet*, critics have detected overseas influence. This is not to say that the early shoots of spectacle and theatrical visuality cannot be discerned in this period, but the absence or comparative rarity of such continental-style visuality is seldom discussed.

I suggest that acting styles between the 1570s and 1630s took the form they did to continue the familiar relationships of storyteller to listeners, rather than prefiguring later seventeenth- and eighteenth-century conceptions of verisimilitude, despite the occasional use of the word. Players did not seek to impersonate people realistically; rather they represented them emblematically with emotions such as envy expressed through pose and gesture.[52] An Elizabethan representation of envy did not frustrate the internal imagining process of audience members because it bore the same relationship to that emotion 'in the life' as heraldic lions bore to the real lions kept in the Tower of London. Stylised acting created a space for each audience member to draw on their own emotional memories and, consciously or unconsciously, embroider what they were seeing in their own imagination. This allowed the personal investment in the story being performed, described by so many theatre commentators. To create this immersion the actor made no attempt to 'be' the character but, rather, to tell the story of the character. Thus, a man in a dress was sufficient to tell the story of Hermione in *A Winter's Tale* and, while the reference to the witches having beards in *Macbeth* could be a moment of meta-comedy, it might suggest that players did not always need to shave their beards off to play women. They were not depicting them but telling their story; a character's reality, so to speak, was in the listener's mind not on the stage and so the performer was only the initiator of their creation. Later in the century, this would not be enough and audiences came to dislike having to do so much imaginative work; real women were required, costumed to depict their characters and with scenery to illustrate their location.

In this early period, though, modes of speech were heightened to create a formal distance between theatre dialogue and real-life speech. Such artificiality is a natural choice for a storytelling kind of theatre which requires the audience to invest the performance with their own imagined design. Theatre-going was thus a private catharsis, as well as participation in a public event, and the relationship of this acting style to that of opera need not be stressed. The artificiality of singing about grief, envy, fear or joy, rather than expressing it realistically, provides the same space. Music facilitated the inward journey, allowing the Italian audiences of early opera to find their own personal emotional response in ways similar to the stylised acting of early British plays.

It might be thought that stylised acting techniques, whether in early British theatre or Italian opera, would distance the audience from personally engaging with the story; one might expect that the artificiality would inhibit empathy with characters or situations. However, contemporary accounts show that, far from being disengaged, audience members responded with full emotional investment, sometimes completely losing the boundary between stage and self: shouting, hissing, heckling, challenging, sometimes storming the acting area or even rioting; some members showed genuine fear at stage ghosts. The 'explanation' for this from Walter Ong and Albert Lord down to, more recently, John Astington and Matthew Steggle has been that audiences frame their emotional responses in emulation of those expressed by the actors.[53] From the *Ars poetica* onwards those who have written about oratory and acting have assumed that an audience will weep if the speaker weeps, that a speaker's laughter is contagious and that for fear to spread to the listeners the storyteller must perform first. In the middle of the twentieth century, scholars of orality and literacy agreed with classical writers that this was how emotion is inspired in an audience. They argued that listeners identify the storyteller with the protagonist so, if the storyteller emulates the protagonist's likely emotions, the listeners then experience them too. This argument certainly has a venerable history but, I suggest, that does not make it true.

It has been axiomatic among actors and storytellers, for perhaps an equally long period of time, that to raise an audience to large and vocal laughter it is more effective if the performers do not laugh at their own jokes. Similarly, if a performer is recognised by an audience as soliciting their tears they usually withhold them; we naturally resist having our emotions manipulated. This is not to say that Renaissance writers did not themselves believe that the way to stimulate tears or laughter was to have the actors express these emotions themselves; Steggle brings ample evidence that writers from Horace to Ben Jonson thought this, but Peter Hall, reflecting on a lifetime of directing theatre and opera, especially Greek and Renaissance drama, argues differently:

> Here is an interesting paradox. Any actor will tell you that if you wish to move an audience, you must not cry. Do not cry. If you cry, the audience will not. The actor must exercise restraint. It is made easier for him if the form provides a mask – the emotion can then be expressed without indulgence. Ophelia's outburst 'Oh what a noble mind is here o'erthrown' after the nunnery scene expresses the girl's complete breakdown. The level of tearful emotion is such that if the actress allows it to be 'real', the speech is incomprehensible. It is also impossible to believe that a girl gripped by such hysteria would invent the rhetorical cadences that balance so perfectly, and express her regrets in what is in effect a sonnet. The verse is here indeed a kind of mask. It enables Ophelia to contain and govern her emotions, so that she can describe the consequences of them rather than indulge them. The form is the conductor of her emotions; and for the actress, it both induces [them] and disciplines [them] … The paradox is that drama deals with huge emotions; but if it displays them in a hugely emotional way … the audience is liable to reject them. They are unpleasant, unbelievable, even repulsive. To be acceptable on the stage they must be stage real – which means transformed, shaped and contained.[54]

I propose that the ritualistic acting style in London's theatres created such a mask, as does the singing in opera. It allows a space between the performer's stylised depiction of an emotion and each individual audience member's reception of it. In this space individuals can colour the face behind the mask from their own memories, visualisations and experiences, triggering their own emotional response. Hall believed that the purpose of theatrical 'form, language, action and presentation' was to provide that space. My own projects with Belfast school children in the 1990s echo this: I learned that storytellers do not need to emote themselves in order to inspire strong emotion in their listeners.[55] The study found that when a storyteller described a gross injustice or something to be feared, listeners responded more emotionally if the teller understated their own emotion. When a storyteller expressed their own emotion strongly the listeners emoted less, because the speaker was emoting *for* them. Instead of emotional emulation what occurred was vicarious emoting. Another way of looking at this is to say that when the storyteller emotes strongly, they take up all the available space for emotional reaction, leaving little room for the listeners to react.[56] The emotional tenor of Elizabethan audiences was thus a consequence of the formalised, artificial style of performing the story rather than simulation of the actors' emotions and, I suggest, this is true of the emotion inspired by opera.

Another oral trait, mimesis, can be found in the rehearsal process. Though comparatively little was written about rehearsals or how lines were learned, an outline can be extrapolated from hints in plays and from attempts during the early Restoration period to recreate the process. As Jennifer Popple identifies, mimesis was core to the approach; players copied the performance of the player who previously undertook the role.[57] The previous performer tutored the new one in the gestures and delivery style traditional to the part; the new performer may well have learned the lines this way too. The actor thus studied a performance rather than a text. This is implicit in John Downes's description of Thomas Betterton being 'instructed' in his role by Sir William Davenant, for Henry VIII: '[t]he part of the King was so right and justly done by Mr Betterton, he being instructed in it by Sir William, who had it from Old Mr Lowen, that had his Instructions from Mr Shakespear himself'.[58] Betterton's Hamlet was similarly derived from Shakespeare through a Mr Taylor.[59] The performance of roles was thus conceived as essentially fixed; there might be a little room for reinterpretation by new performers but only within the tightly defined tradition of the role. This conception of performing a role would gradually disappear from spoken theatre but it remained a feature of opera long into the nineteenth century; singers were often judged by how well they reproduced the traditional interpretation of a role in comparison with the previous performer. In 1836 The *Musical World* and *The Times* discussed Giulia Grisi's acting in Bellini's *Norma*:

Norma was revived this week ... Grisi did more than justify our highest
expectations; if she was not equal to Pasta in majesty of demeanor — if some
of her attitudes were angular, and some of her motions a little too much
hurried for the dignity which tragedy demands, she approached nearer to her
predecessor than any other actress of the day could do — with the superior
advantage, a voice altogether unrivalled in force, clearness and abandon of
execution.[60]

The other oral characteristic which Jacobean theatre shared with Italy
was pasticcio. Pasticcio was in use in Elizabethan and Jacobean playwrighting,
especially collaborative authorship; nor do all collaborations fit into the
studio model of a master and apprentices. John Fletcher collaborated with
Francis Beaumont, Shakespeare, Ben Jonson, William Rowley, Thomas
Middleton and Phillip Massinger among many others over the course of a
long career from the late 1590s to late 1620s. Of the forty extant plays for
which his authorship is reasonably certain, sixteen are collaborations. Thomas
Dekker was another, with thirty-five out of fifty of his known works being
collaborations. Dekker's more famous ones include *The Mad Man's Morris*
(*c.*1599) in collaboration with Robert Wilson, Henry Chettle and Michael
Drayton; *The Roaring Girl* (1611) in collaboration with Thomas Middleton;
and *Keep the Widow Waking* (1624) in collaboration with John Ford, John
Webster and William Rowley. As well as a frequent collaborator, Dekker
appears to have been a reviser who updated once-popular plays which had
fallen out of the repertoire. Ben Jonson, one of Dekker's many collaborators,
was on the opposite side to him during the war of the theatres and described
him as a 'dresser of plays about town'. Among the more famous plays
Dekker is known to have revised are *Sir John Oldcastle* (Part II) in 1602,
Sir Thomas Wyatt, 1602–1606 and *Guy of Warwick* in 1620. There is a
consensus that this last play emerged in the early 1590s and may have been
an earlier work by Dekker himself. It was reworked for the stage in 1618
before Dekker and John Day published this version of it in 1620.[61] When
opera began in Britain in the second half of the seventeenth century, many
of its oral traits, pasticcio especially, were thus already familiar from
indigenous spoken theatre. The main absence was onstage visualisation.

Depicting the visual on stage

As the anonymous librettist of Monteverdi's *Le nozze d'Ennea e Lavinia*
noted in 1640, continuous envisioning is tiring; his answer was breaks
between the acts for social interaction and, probably, instrumental sequences.
Moments of action, clowning or dances in Elizabethan plays provided points
of mental relief during which the listeners could relax their imaginations
and switch their focus wholly to the stage. These relief valves were carefully

placed in play narratives but, in the late Jacobean and Caroline period, these breaks in the imagining process grew in length and frequency. Much of the documentation surviving from audience members demonstrates that, up until *c.*1610, people principally went to hear a play. They judged it on the spoken poetry rather than its visual effects.[62] Serious attention to visual display can occasionally be found, such as in the pageants of George Peele, but by and large, it was not until the masques of the 1610s and onwards that visualisation became an expectation for plays in London's theatres.

Visual experimentation was key to masques and this genre influenced plays. Some masques had strong narratives, others simply made the same point repeatedly through a mixture of forms; *The Masque of Augurs* (1622) is a mini-play whereas *Hymenaei* (1606) by Jonson and Inigo Jones contains only seven lines of verse but is filled with scenery, allegory, dances and the bearing of emblematic artefacts. Masques began to be incorporated into, or between, the acts of plays and by the 1620s and 1630s the simple approach of comparatively unadorned storytelling seemed stale without such exciting visual diversions scattered throughout. Plays increasingly borrowed stage effects such as ropes or wires for flying people, fireworks, masque costumes and special effects such as, possibly, a bear.

Masques, fantasy sequences and dumb shows incorporated into plays depicted a moment in the narrative visually, instead of requiring audiences to imagine it, yet their integration into the narrative was in its infancy during the Jacobean period. The story was virtually halted during spectacles as they tended to convey a single dramatic point each time; for example, the sequence where harpies accost the courtiers in *The Tempest* is a terrifying visitation conjured by Prospero. The harpies probably appeared in elaborate costumes and possibly flew in or emerged through trapdoors. They chant a conscience-provoking list of the wrongs the courtiers had perpetrated against Prospero but this spectacle is a sealed-off event. The harpies startle people and declaim or chant unpleasant truths but the courtiers do not interact with them, nor do the harpies interact with each other. The visitation is intended to make the courtiers suitably penitent, but it is only in the dialogue after the spectacle that the penitence emerges and moves the story on. Similarly, the parade of Banquo's royal descendants in *Macbeth* shows that, although Divine Providence permits Macbeth to carry out his atrocities at this point in history, it will not allow his evil to prosper over time. This is made in an entirely visual statement, a double-layered one admittedly, with its message of divine favour for the virtuous Stuarts, Banquo's alleged descendants. However this sequence is without dialogue or song; the future kings do not interact with Macbeth or Banquo and there is no interaction with the witches; the sequence makes this one dramatic point and is less assimilated into the drama than even the Hecate sequences.[63] By contrast, the dumb show in *Hamlet* is very carefully woven into the drama as a whole and, though Shakespeare could not have known it in 1601, this more integrated approach to visual sequences pointed the way to the future. Britain's theatre in this period did not conceive of visuality as a medium through which a whole narrative might be conveyed, as medieval frescos or stained-glass clerestories had done. In Italy, by contrast, painters were fully confident of their capacity to convey complete narratives through a single static composition: Tintoretto's epic canvas of St Mark freeing a slave (1548) being one example, and Veronese's *Wedding at Cana* (1563) being another.

I propose that the reason why visual and auditory experiences took decades to integrate successfully in Britain's theatre was that the traditional oral contract between storyteller and listeners was too deeply embedded to change quickly; nonetheless, despite the slow and uneven pace of change, it can be discerned. The oratorical style of late-sixteenth- and early-seventeenth-century acting gave way to a more visually arresting approach. A performance of *Othello* at Oxford in 1610 was described as particularly moving in a letter by Henry Jackson:

> In the last few days the King's actors have been here. They performed, with the greatest applause, ... tragedies which they performed with decorum and skill. In them, not just in their speaking, but also in their action, they moved tears ... Desdemona, when dead, was even more moving than when alive, lying on the bed imploring the pity of the spectators even with her expression.[64]

Jackson thought the visual side of acting, when performed with verisimilitude, could provoke as much emotion as the words. A new kind of immersion was being created, where the story's visualisation occurred increasingly on the stage and hardly at all in the private imagination. Increased literacy brought with it an increased awareness of the power of the visual and the Puritan preoccupation with iconoclasm indicates this new awareness. Visuality in theatre had just as much capacity to change the way the world was seen as did cartography or models of the solar system.

Caroline drama became increasingly successful at telling stories where the audience's focus remained on the stage throughout. By the time we reach plays like *The Picture* by Phillip Massinger (1630), *The Antiquary* by Shackerley Marmion (1631) or *The Antipodes* by Richard Broome (1640), visuality was almost as much a vehicle for the story as the words. The earlier oral requirement that large sections of the story be imagined in an audience's mind was disappearing when the theatres closed in 1642. I suggest that the appeal of opera in Britain lies, partly at least, in its being a revivification of this lost kind of immersion.

The closure had more complex and less conscious motives than Puritan joylessness. It was not just the theatre's transparent – though not uncritical – royalism or even the number of Catholics it employed; a sizeable body of male citizens disliked plays as relics from a bygone age. Martin Wiggins points out that the majority of plays leading up to the closure were not controversial in religious or political terms, rather their plots felt childish in the midst of grave religious and political controversies.[65] A new generation sensed an older society's disregard for what was now felt to be extremely important; Henry Jackson, quoted above, felt Jonson's *The Alchemist* treated biblical texts with a cavalier disrespect, for example.[66] The acting styles, fantastical plots and fascination with Italy; the friars, popish oaths, jesting and dancing, characterised a society against which the current generation were reacting. Plays belonged to the world of Corpus Christi pageants, Church Ales and highly staged jousting matches rather than the sequestration of the clergy, political pamphlets and civil war. Wiggins finds little evidence, proportionally, for the Puritan hostility towards the theatre so beloved by theatrical tradition; instead, he argues, the theatre was not seen as a huge danger by its enemies, merely an unprogressive influence. Theatre simply lost status and importance, at the same time as other expressions of oral culture.

The closure of the theatres in England did not, as we know, end theatre itself but it did perhaps sever the theatre's continuities with proto-literate storytelling. When theatre recommenced in the 1660s, it would be an artform for the literate exclusively; it would be expensive to attend and its characters would mirror genteel metropolitan life in comedy and neoclassical ideals in tragedy. Theatre's oral heritage is mostly found only in vestigial form in the 1660s, when attempts to revive pre-closure practices were attempted. Elizabeth Barry's early career on the stage was hindered by Davenant's considering her to have a 'bad ear', meaning that he felt she could not mimic the performances of other female players. This is an indication that roles may still have been learned orally and thus mimetic ability was still important. Performance tradition rather than textual examination was still the principal means of constructing a role, as discussed earlier.[67] But the discontinuities from the oral past gradually outnumbered the continuities; verisimilitude and visuality rose in concert during the last third of the century, but one key characteristic of oral storytelling tradition not only continued but flourished in the Restoration period: pasticcio. Indeed, these decades were something of a golden age for pasticcio in spoken theatre.

The rise of literacy and devaluation of orality

The research of Gunter Kress and Theo van Leeuwen shows that, across Europe between the fifteenth and seventeenth centuries, rises in literacy were usually accompanied by a desire for greater visual detail.[68] Everything from paintings to performances grew in visual complexity during the later seventeenth century and the simple stock images required by oral storytelling traditions were gradually discarded. The common bank of images in urban minds was increasingly homogenised by printed woodblock illustrations on pamphlets, tracts, magazines, ballads and the frontispieces of books. The 1674 text of Thomas Shadwell's pasticcio opera *The Enchanted Isle*, a retelling of *The Tempest*, gives his design ideas for the opening:

> The Front of the Stage is open'd, and the Band of 24 Violins, with the Harpsicals and Theorbo's which accompany the Voices, plac'd between the Pit and the Stage. While the Overture is playing, the Curtain rises, and discovers a new Frontispiece, joyn'd to the great Pylasters on each side of the Stage. This Frontispiece is a noble Arch, supported by large wreathed Columns of the Corinthian Order; the wreathings of the Columns are beautifi'd with Roses wound round them, and several Cupids flying about them. On the Cornice, just over the Capitals, sits on either side a Figure, with a Trumpet in one hand, and a Palm in the other, representing Fame ... In the middle of the Arch are several Angels holding the King's Arms, as if they were placing them in the midst of that Compass-Pediment. Behind this is the Scene, which represents a thick, cloudy Sky, a very rocky Coast, and a Tempestuous Sea in perpetual Agitation. This Tempest (suppos'd to be rais'd by Magick) has many dreadfull Objects in it, as several Spirits in horrid shapes flying down among the Sailors, then rising and crossing in the air. And when the Ship is sinking, the whole House is darken'd, and a shower of Fire falls upon 'em. This is accompanied with Lightening, and several Claps of Thunder, to the end of the Storm.[69]

This suggests that, behind the frontispiece, a mechanised depiction of the storm is shown with moving waves, a ship and flying machines for the spirits. To this, lighting effects, pyrotechnics and sound effects are added. This is little short of cinematic and shows that, long before the twentieth century provided the technology, the desire to animate a story in ways which matched the human imagination already existed. Shadwell sought to amaze his audience with a visual experience equal to, and hopefully beyond, what they could visualise for themselves in response to spoken or read description. This tempest had been conveyed by spoken description alone in Shakespeare's performances of 1611 but, by 1674, it was fully depicted.

John Aubrey, writing in the 1680s, reveals that the status of oral traditions, methods and practices was consciously, even programmatically, devalued in the middle decades of the century. As Adam Fox demonstrates, oral culture was gendered as female and literate culture as male. Narratives preserved by memory were reclassed as 'old wives' tales' while written ones were upgraded to 'records'.[70] There was certainly hostility to the education of women amongst Puritan groups but Cressy's low estimate of female literacy throughout the century may reflect something other than entrenched discrimination. It is possible that women did not accept male characterisation of oral methods and culture as having less value than literacy; their continued use of speech and memory as a technology for recording and transmitting information may have been a conscious expression of female identity. Judith Butler and others have taught us that gender is performative and evidence that seventeenth-century women embraced a role as curators of oral heritage is plentiful.[71] Aubrey's childhood nurse Katherine Bushell passed on oral versions of English history: she was 'excellent at these stories and had the history from the Conquest down to Carl. I in ballad'. Aubrey notes that it was the custom for 'maydes to sitt-up late by the fire, tell old romantique stories of the old time, handed downe to them with a great deal of alteration … In the old ignorant times before women were readers, the history was handed down from mother to daughter.'[72]

Elite women took a curatorial role in the continuation of theatre and opera in both this and the following century. Queen Henriette Marie continued to commission plays, masques and semi-operas prior to and during the dynasty's period of exile as well as after the Restoration between 1645 and 1665. Female influence in opera remained dominant throughout the eighteenth century. Thomas McGeary brings ample evidence that it was women who were considered the gender most attracted to Italian opera in the early decades of the century and that critics of the artform saw it as intrinsically feminine and feminising.[73] Ilias Chrissochoidis notes that a committee of 'twenty ladies of the first distinction' managed the opera season of 1738–1739 and were probably emulating the Shakespeare Ladies Club that had been very successful the preceding year.[74] Frances Brooke and Mary Ann Yates managed the King's Theatre from 1773 to 1778. The oral characteristics of operatic storytelling may have had an unconscious appeal for women, these being consonant with inherited female traditions but, in itself, this became another reason for hostility to opera by male critics.

Orality is not among the things directly identified in turn-of-the-century male polemics about the dangers of female attraction to Italian opera, but its potential to lead women into Catholicism certainly was and, for the sectarian, orality and popery went hand in hand. Orality was not only gendered as female but associated with a discredited Catholic past rather than a text-based, bible-focused Protestant future.[75] Indeed, as Paula McDowell shows, the first discussions in text which conceive orality and literacy as antagonistic to each other occur in religious debates in the 1660s.[76] Anglican divines argued that the textual transmission of scripture was a surer foundation for Christianity, while the Catholic divine John Sergeant argued for 'the Orality of the Rule of Faith, its Uninterruptedness, and Assistance of God'.[77] John Dryden argued for text when he was a Protestant and for orality when he became a Catholic showing, perhaps, that the interconnected nature of both in reality could be lost in theory during polemical discussion.

Late-seventeenth- and eighteenth-century elite women were highly literate, neoclassical in their tastes and thus able to participate in masculine elite culture, yet such participation did not inhibit them from continuing to engage with activities which relied on oral practices and traditions. The characterisation of literacy as masculine was accompanied by male abandonment of their formerly leading roles in oral culture. The male storyteller lost his status in much of urban society, while opportunities for women to lead in cultural practices which relied on speech and memory thus opened up. Learning and education were redefined as synonymous with literacy and numeracy so elite women who had both these skills and facility with oral culture were very well placed.

Aubrey clearly regrets the passing of oral culture and looks wistfully back at the capacity of oral storytelling traditions to engage the imagination. By contrast Daniel Defoe, during his tour through Britain between 1724 and 1727, was both fascinated and annoyed by female curation of local history. In Radnorshire he noted '[t]he stories of Vortigern and Roger Mortimer are in every old woman's mouth here', and in Cumberland

> [t]he cape or head land of St Bees, (derived from St Bega, an Irish female saint) still preserves its name; as for the lady, like that of St Tabbs beyond Berwick, the story is become fabulous, viz. about her procuring, by her prayers, a deep snow on Midsummer Day, her taming a wild bull that did great damage in the country; these, and the like tales, I leave where I found them, (viz.) among the rubbish of the old women and the Romish priests.[78]

For Defoe and other harbingers of Enlightenment rationalism, the rhyming contests, proverbs, saws, 'sooth' poems, adult storytelling, pre-Reformation rituals and pre-war theatre were all of a piece: embarrassing, superstitious, infantilising and déclassé. The transition to a literate culture within Britain and Ireland was inextricably bound up with the formation of politico-religious identities; Defoe relishes the demise of oral culture as an unprogressive force, while Aubrey laments it. These attitudes would later underlie hostility to, or acceptance of, recitative.

As literacy rose in Britain, another rapid change was a dramatic shift in personal privacies. Scholars including Cecile M. Jagodzinski argue that new privacies came into being over the course of the century as old ones were discontinued.[79] Privacy, too, was intimately bound up with increasing literacy:

> Private, silent reading encourages the discovery of individuality but also, eventually, creates a nation of strangers ... Walter Ong observes that that a roomful of people sharing in an oral/aural presentation ... establishes a community in a way which a roomful of readers does not. As reading became less a communal activity, it also became associated with the private spaces being created in seventeenth-century homes.[80]

It used to be argued that privacy and the conception of the individual self barely existed before the seventeenth century but modern scholarship argues that previous conceptions of the self were different rather than absent. Frank Ebjy Poulsen has argued against an essentialist conception of privacy as too broad a brushstroke.[81] In Britain, the use of reflexive pronouns – 'myself', 'ourselves', 'oneself' and so on – increased exponentially in discourse and texts from the Reformation onwards. Anni Haahr Henriksen shows that homilies printed in 1547, 1563 and 1570, which were read out in church services on most Sundays, use proportionately more reflexive pronouns than do pre-Reformation English homilies or sermons. Printed homiletic texts thus promoted both reading and, unconsciously, a conception of the self. Henriksen shows that usage of the word 'privacy' also spikes dramatically in European texts in the middle of the seventeenth century.[82]

Peter Clark points out that whereas a Protestant family's bible had formerly been left in a public room such as the hall, to testify to the family's identity and loyalty, it now migrated to the bedchambers and closets. The closet was itself a new private space in many houses, these rooms having previously been found only in palaces and castles.[83] Silent, private reading of scripture in the closet gradually replaced the custom of the paterfamilias reading it aloud to the assembled household in the hall.

Literacy and privacy appear on the surface to have fostered a distinction between stories told through text and those told orally in the form of opera and theatre but, in looking at the storytelling of literature, we are reminded of Jack Goody and Ian Watt's conclusion that literacy is a component of orality rather than an alternative to it. Individual visualisation, which was essential for listening to stories, is also needed when reading them. The increased spectacles, sets, scenography, props and costumes of seventeenth-century theatre rendered the individual imagination less necessary for enjoying a performance, but envisaging the characters, actions, environments and matériel in a written story remained essential to the experience. Closet drama emerged along with the printing press, but became increasingly popular in Britain during and after literacy's tipping point in the mid-seventeenth-century. These were plays or libretti for reading, aloud or silently, alone in a private space. The motivations for creating them were various; as Catherine Burroughs points out, Margaret Cavendish's epistle to the reader in her *Plays Never Before Printed* (1668) states that her reason for printing them, rather than having them staged, was to evade the marble grip of neoclassical rules.[84] Closet drama was thus felt to be a heterotopia over which purist critics held no sway, a space also claimed by opera, as discussed below. While staged drama now preferred to show rather than describe its mise-en-scène, closet drama remained a form in which long descriptive speeches could still hold the imagination and Burroughs shows that long Prospero-like speeches remained characteristic of closet drama well into the nineteenth century.[85] The inherent orality of storytelling through text was not confined to closet drama, of course, it was also seen in epic verse such as Milton's *Paradise Lost* (1667) and, later, the novels of Aphra Behn.

What then was gained and lost in this transposition within storytelling from hearing speech and imagining to seeing text and imagining? The rise in literacy reduced people's willingness to concentrate on speech for long periods, so it was literature rather than performance which now offered free rein to the imagination. Through description, literature could conjure small and subtle narrative moments with greater verisimilitude than scenography could at this point in time: it could take the reader through a rapid series of very different locations for fleeting moments, for instance, or create very small and intimate spaces such as carriage interiors. After the 1770s, scenography began to find new technologies for spectacles that rivalled the reader's imagination. Above all, the soliloquy could be dispensed with in literature as readers were not just taken into the internal monologues of characters, but into their unconscious motivations, their dreams and fantasies. Literature, too, had stricter parameters: the sexual candour of Restoration comedy is much more muted in closet drama and visual gags are not nearly as funny in text as they are on the stage. Paratextual communication too is unavailable to the reader in the way audiences experience it. In Behn's *The Lucky Chance* (1686), Sir Cautious Fulbank, a notorious miser, owes £300 to a rakish gallant who offers to set the debt aside in exchange for permission to sleep with his wife. Fulbank's response is outrage at the very suggestion: 'What! Set it against my wife?' In itself, the bare text does not convey the opportunity for an ambiguous tone in this outrage. When vocalised, an actor can reveal that Sir Cautious might actually be considering the offer. Comedic opportunities are not necessarily obvious when read.[86]

Aubrey and Defoe may have seen orality and literacy as a binary but, with long hindsight, we can see that oral storytelling accommodated itself to literate audiences rather than disappearing. Some of its methods continued in literature and others in theatre, some were germane to both but, I suggest, one reason why a society which had abandoned theatre altogether in 1642 should resume it so readily less than two decades later is that there was only so much that reading stories could do in the way of thelxis. It was opera, beginning in London in 1658, which provided the one continuity from oral storytelling that neither books nor spoken plays could: enchantment, in its literal sense.

Privacy, self-consciousness, literacy and increased visuality rose in concert with each other, yet opera stood in stark opposition to much of this emergent culture and this, of course, was a major part of its appeal. Instead of reporting the emotions, opera laid them bare in song, giving no rationalist expositions on human longing, sorrow, joy or malevolence. Stylised though it might have been, Dido's sorrow, the Witches' sinister cackling, Venus's patriotism and the threats of hell in the Masque of Devils carried immediate conviction and emotional resonances for the audience. The stylisation of operatic acting and its use of singing to tell its stories re-established the thelxis of teller and listener as experienced before the civil wars, though in new ways. This capacity of opera was one reason those critical of the artform feared it; the next century would see repeated concerns that opera might cast spells over its audience, as Richard Steele, though prejudiced, observed:

> Long, ah! too long the Enchantment reign'd
> Seduc'd the Wise, and ev'n the brave enchain'd
> Hence with thy Curst deluding Song! away![87]

Just as John Aubrey missed the storytelling of his youth, the later seventeenth century welcomed opera as something exotic but also deeply familiar. Opera may have filled a vacuum left by the ending of oral storytelling traditions in spoken theatre, but it was by no means a return to Jacobean performance techniques. Born out of Italy's deeply visual storytelling culture, opera provided the richly painted sets, flamboyant costumes and special effects to which seventeenth-century audiences had gradually become accustomed; it was also highly neoclassical in structure and content, thus appealing to the scholarly. Opera was a hybrid of the ancient and modern, of female-gendered oral culture and masculine learning, of high-status public grandeur and the thelxis of the fireside tale. The seventeenth century had seen binaries imposed on cultural identities of all sorts: Roundhead and Cavalier, Whig and Tory, Protestant and Catholic, Puritan and Anglican, town and country, oral and literate; but opera stood outside these divisions. I suggest that opera's popularity was due, in large measure, to its capacity to dispel for a few hours the solipsism of the private, silently reading, silently praying, sectarian self, and release people from the allegiances they found themselves locked into outside the theatre.

Opera begins in Britain

The earliest performances: Davenant

The first opera to be performed in Britain that was described as such was William Davenant's *The Siege of Rhodes* (Part I), sung at Rutland House in 1656. It was a collaborative pasticcio with five or six composers and, although the score is lost, it is believed to have consisted entirely of recitative and instrumental sequences. Henry Lawes, Matthew Locke and Henry Cooke composed the vocal music and Charles Coleman, who composed for the theorbo, lute and other strings along with George Hudson, wrote the instrumental music. Steven Watkins also identifies John Bannister as contributing.[88] Lawes and Locke had worked on court masques in the Caroline era and Cooke had worked with the singers at the Chapel Royal so there were strong links with Britain's former musical performance traditions.

Rutland House was a dilapidated town house leased from the Rutlands by Davenant, former poet laureate to the former King. Located in an enclave of London noted for its royalist sympathies, he and his fellow writers used it to share their works and even attempt tentative stagings.[89] It had a long salon, much like a Venetian piano nobile, which was turned into a basic studio theatre. It had a tiny acting area, fifteen feet deep, with the audience crowded onto benches. The instrumentalists were likewise bunched together at a large, slatted, ventilation window overlooking the stage. In further evidence of the experimental or studio theatre feel to this production, the composers not only acted as instrumentalists but also took roles: Henry Cooke sang Solyman the Magnificent, Edward Coleman sang Alphonso, the heroine's jealous husband, and Matthew Locke the Admiral.[90]

Despite the conditions, *The Siege of Rhodes* was innovative, using perspective scenery with three pairs of shutters and no less than five 'Scenes of Relieve' occurring in a room which, Davenant notes, had only eleven feet available in height. The scenery was designed by John Webb, who had learned the art from Inigo Jones and was later the architect's son-in-law. In another innovation, Britain's first professional female stage performer was cast, Catherine Coleman. Although she had married into the Coleman family of English musicians, Catherine was the daughter of Alphonso Ferrabosco the Younger, son of an Italian family of professional musicians, who had been employed at English courts from Elizabeth I onwards. They remained bilingual and retained their connections with Bologna. The Colemans and Ferraboscos may possibly have provided a link with Italian opera for this production but not a contemporary one, given that Davenant described it as being wholly in recitative, a style suggesting the early operas of the 1600s in Florence and Mantua. Another route for the transmission of very early opera into London may have been through Angelo Notari (1565–1663), an elderly Venetian musician at the Stuart courts who is known to have composed adaptations of Monteverdi and would have been known to Davenant and the Colemans.

Strohm reminds us that in seventeenth-century Italy the word 'opera' was an informal, even slang, term, literally meaning 'a work' but analogous today to 'show' or 'gig' rather than 'work of art'. In formal contexts, such as court commissions or publishing, performances were usually designated 'dramma per musica' if they were serious and 'dramma giacosa per musica' if they were comic. All the early mentions in Britain, however, refer to the artform as 'opera' which suggests that Britain's earliest links with it were through practitioners rather than commissioners. London's Italian community had other musical families who would have been familiar with opera beside the Ferraboscos, including the Bassano, Lupo and others.

This group of Rutland House ci-devants had previously collaborated in court entertainments and, in the case of the Colemans and possibly others, there were family connections between them. These interconnections are reminiscent of the Florentine Camerata which led to the creation of *Euridice*; the production may even have had a camerata feel to it, given that Catherine and Edward Coleman were married in real life as well as in the story. Yet this production was deliberately distanced from the royal masques of the past. For one thing, given the known backgrounds and presumed political allegiance of the participants, staging something as royalist as a masque would have been a flagrant provocation to the regime. Davenant had put a considerable amount of effort into courting toleration for stage performance from important Commonwealth officials; it is unlikely that he would have jeopardised these tenuous relationships by performing something so controversial. In the current scholarly debate about the nature of this performance, I believe *The Siege of Rhodes* to have been an opera, albeit an antique one by Italian standards, rather than a republican-friendly type of masque.

Davenant was a permanent thorn in the side of Cromwell's regime. Having been paroled from prison in 1652 and pardoned in 1654 for playing an active role in royalist insurrections, he would be back in prison in 1659. Despite this track record, Watkins shows that he tried ceaselessly to persuade the regime to revise their views on theatre, with mixed success.[91] To John Thurloe, Cromwell's secretary of state, Rutland House was a potential hotbed of anti-regime sentiment and he sent a government agent to the first known performance there in May 1656, *The First Day's Entertainment*.[92] The agent was impressed as the performance had prudently ended with a paean of praise to the Lord Protector.[93] As it was technically Davenant's home, he evaded the laws proscribing public theatres but was still careful to avoid staging a dialogue play, which was more heavily prohibited than musical performance. Britain's first opera was granted a special permit as such, and probably only then because Davenant represented the work as an anti-Spanish broadside to support Cromwell's flagging war with Spain. This is apparent from his application letter to Thurloe where he described the piece not as an opera but as a 'moral representation'.[94] This demurely costumed, unflamboyant experiment forms a striking contrast with the state-supported, publicly accessible, well-funded operas of Cromwell's allied republic, Venice. Yet some of Davenant's lobbying of the regime may have borne fruit; in 1659, Richard Cromwell permitted a masque, *Cupid and Death*, to be performed for the Portuguese Ambassador.

Moving from Rutland House to the Cockpit in 1657 or 1658 (another royalist enclave according to Christopher Matusiak), Davenant created two more operas, *The Cruelty of the Spaniards in Peru* and *The History of Sir Francis Drake*, in 1658.[95] Both attempted to persuade the regime that the propaganda value of theatre outweighed its supposed immorality. After the fall of the Commonwealth in 1660, Davenant restaged *The Siege of Rhodes* as a spoken play, an action argued by Robert D. Hume to show that 'the default setting in England at this time was always dialogue theatre'.[96] Against this, Watkins argues that Davenant was an enthusiastic creator of recitative operas and continued to create others after the Restoration.

Continental influence on opera in Britain

All-sung operas were very sparse in Britain until Vanburgh's Italian project began at the end of the seventeenth century; Hume observes that of the twenty English operas performed between 1660 and 1700 that were published, seventeen contained spoken dialogue and musical sequences with only three being all-sung. Of these, two were imported from Paris: *Ariane* (1674) and *Rare en tout* (1677); Purcell's *Dido and Aeneas* (1689) was the third.[97] The identification of operatic influences is complicated by the restoration of the court masque at the same time as spoken plays, both following hard on the heels of restored monarchy. Yet spoken theatre was influenced by opera in a number of ways: the adoption of continental singing techniques, concepts such as period costume and trompe l'œil scenography all appear in Restoration theatre. To these I propose that indigenous methods of assembling theatre from pre-existing parts were greatly emboldened by a new approach which derived from operatic pasticci, though not always received first-hand from Italian librettists themselves, but transmitted through France.

Below are three examples of how pasticcio is interwoven with the acknowledged continental influences on Britain's theatre. Firstly staging became increasingly important in a theatre that was now serving a more literate culture, and continental techniques increased the capacity of scenography, using ingenious stage machinery to depict not just locations but events. Formerly undepictable events were now staged and, to augment their impact, new roles were found for instrumental music. Such music reused existing melodies, was often created collaboratively and, like the melodrama it sometimes anticipated, was used to sustain immersion while scenery was being moved or candle wicks trimmed. Secondly, I argue that Italian pasticcio was sometimes the model for recreations of Shakespeare's plays; again, Davenant provides the link and these new pasticcio techniques were grafted onto older Jacobean and Caroline practices. Lastly, the early interest in recitative operas did not last and despite recitative being a form of great service to Italian pasticcio, less use of it was made in British operas, and the reasons for this anomaly are considered. Taken together, these three examples show how continental influence helped to restore thelxis to theatre in Britain: oral culture's experience of full imaginative engagement was renovated for a new literate culture and, I suggest, pasticcio was a key method in achieving this.

In his reminiscences, John Downes noted the relationship of Davenant and Dryden's 1664 version of *Macbeth* with opera and his comment identifies both visuality and pasticcio as integral to that relationship:

> *The Tragedy of Macbeth*, alter'd by Sir William Davenant; being drest in all its Finery, as new Cloath's, new Scenes, Machines, as flyings for the Witches; with all the Singing and Dancing in it: The first Compos'd by Mr. Lock, the other by Mr. Channell and Mr. Joseph Priest; it being all Excellently perform'd, being in the nature of an Opera, it Recompenc'd double the Expence; it proves still a lasting Play.[98]

London's dramatists had the opportunity to see continental opera at the Cockpit at the very beginning of the new reign. Two companies of French performers came to London between August 1661 and January 1662, the first under the patronage of the Duchess of York and the second under that of the King's niece, Mademoiselle d'Orléans. They performed Gabriel Gilbert's *L'amours de Diane et L'Endimion* (1657), Chapoton's *La Descente d'Orphée* (1640) and Corneille's *Andromède* (1650), publishing the dessein (an illustrated scenario) in English and French. These performances belong to the genre of tragédie à machines; they were declaimed rather than sung in recitative but were interspersed with arias, as *The First Day's Entertainment* had been in Rutland House. Andrew Walkling discusses these French performances, the first two of which were adapted from the Paris performances of two Italian operas, Strozzi's *La finta pazza*, and Francesco Buti and Luigi Rossi's *Orfeo* (1647). The machines and scenography for both were designed by Giacomo Torelli. The ambitious design for these performances were its most operatic feature. The dessein emphasised these special effects, from which Walkling lists a flying dragon, a serpent 'which by an admirable machine creeps over the Theatre', and a floating boat for Charon. Animals, trees and rocks closed in to 'incompass' Orpheus, and Bacchanal dancers metamorphosed into trees.[99] Walkling argues that the primary dramatic function of the instrumental music which accompanied these effects was to:

> create an audible approximation of divine or celestial harmony, and thus to increase the sense of otherworldliness that was the machine play's stock in trade. Indeed, it might be argued that the same principle can be applied to the vocal music.[100]

This description of the aim of machine operas – to dissolve the solid world in the audience's imagination and transform the theatre into a mediate space where the impossibilities of storytelling could be realised – suggests that thelxis was a consciously sought aim. Many kinds of Restoration performance in Britain sought to recover such immersion and operatic approaches were more successful than most. Yet Samuel Pepys was critical of these operas performed at the Cockpit, complaining that it was 'so ill done and the Scenes and company and everything else so nasty and out of order and poor, that I was sick all the while in my mind to be there'.[101] His disappointment may indicate that the underground studio feel of Rutland House was still very much in evidence during these early days at the Cockpit and either the mechanics or the execution may not have realised the grand claims made in the dessein. But it is also possible that Pepys typified highly literate men of his generation, and actively resisted immersing himself in oral tropes which he had learned to see as valueless. Charles II and his entourage nevertheless attended these operas and both Davenant and Dryden absorbed this Italian influence, as is discernible in their operatic *Macbeth* of 1664.

This time Pepys was impressed and willing to allow the operatic form to engage him; he saw performances in 1664, 1666 and again in 1667: 'most excellently acted, and a most excellent play for variety', and of the later staging: 'a most excellent play in all respects, but especially in divertisement [*sic*], though it be a deep tragedy; which is a strange perfection in a tragedy, it being most proper here, and suitable'.[102] Barbara Murray suggests that *Macbeth* had at least three scene settings depicting grim castles and wild scenery. To the songs and dances interpolated in Shakespeare's day, more were added; as well as music; the piece also included sound effects such as screeching owls, thunder and sounding bells. The machinery included wires for flying the witches in and out, their entries being accompanied by sinister fanfares; small traps in the forestage saw the rising of ghosts and a large trap upstage was used to allow the witches' cave to sink.[103] In revising the dramaturgy, Davenant removed nearly everything in the plot that relied on the audience imagining it. That said, as Murray points out, he made considerable use of 'depictive images' in the dialogue itself to press home his rhetorical points. The explanation for this paradox might be that, while he wanted to restore the paradigms of pre-civil war royalist drama, the hallmark of which was poetic imagery, he nevertheless wanted the story to be told visually with sufficiently compelling staging to pin the audience's attention on the stage throughout. It was thus a balance between Shakespearean hommage in the language and a pre-constructed visuality which alleviated imagining by the audience.

Little alteration was made to the core narrative but continental pasticcio practice is discernible in Davenant's willingness to depart from his model to augment those parts of the plot of greater interest to contemporary audiences. He reworked the relationship between the Macbeths and Macduffs, with the two ladies discussing their respective marriages during an exchange in Act I. Lady Macbeth's guilt is expanded on with Duncan's ghost returning as an hallucination, nor does she simply peter out as she does in the latter part of Shakespeare's play: Davenant interpolates further husband and wife dialogue to show the disintegration of the Macbeths' marriage into recrimination and guilt.

The Italian operatic conception of theatre as an essentially visual experience can be seen in other Shakespearean pasticci: Shadwell's 1674 pasticcio opera of Davenant and Dryden's pasticcio play of *The Tempest* (1667) discussed above, for one.[104] While visuality had been integral to continental storytelling, from cantastorie banners to opera scenery, it was now adopted by a society that had, within the preceding twenty years, consigned much of what remained of its religious visual art to destruction. In part, perhaps, as a reaction against iconoclasm, Restoration society felt a thirst for vibrant and animated imagery; operatic scenography showed how this might be introduced into spoken theatre.

Examples of literati marrying the older indigenous tradition of Thomas Dekker's 'dressing' with newer, bolder, continental-style pasticcio reinventions can be found, I suggest, in the Shakespearean plays of Davenant, Dryden, Nahum Tate, Thomas Shadwell and later Colley Cibber. Older methods are found, such as multiple authorship in both the composition and text; collaborative composition occurred in *The Siege of Rhodes*, Shadwell's *The Tempest* had at least three composers and *Oedipus, King of Thebes* (1678–1679) had its first two acts written by John Dryden and the last by Nathaniel Lee.[105] Yet Restoration dramatists went beyond this pre-civil wars tradition to create something closer in structure to the true pasticcio. Davenant's *The Law against Lovers* (1661) is one such, and although it is a stage play rather than an opera, close reading reveals a close resemblance to Italian pasticcio practice: I suggest he anticipates Nicholas Haym and Peter Motteux more than he shows continuity from Thomas Dekker.

Eight months after staging his dialogue version of *The Siege of Rhodes*, Davenant created *The Law against Lovers* by integrating *Much Ado about Nothing* with *Measure for Measure*. He also interpolated his own material, adding the political revolution and siege sequence from his former opera. He told his new story by weaving together the serviceable plot strands from all three, redrawing the characters and adding new ones. It is very much Davenant's story and Shakespeare's is only discernible as a palimpsest. It concerns two brothers, Angelo who governs repressively and hypocritically, and Benedick who raises an armed revolt against him, egged on by Beatrice. There is a discernible increase in the pacing from pre-civil war theatre and Shakespeare's speeches and dialogues are trimmed to facilitate this; Davenant also made use of textual parody to give the work stylistic unity.

The source play examined a fault line running through early modern society, that law codes – the principal means of enforcing order, protection and justice – work to an extent when enforced by those in power, but when this system is applied to moral codes, catastrophe ensues. *Measure for Measure* hints that perhaps governance and moral enforcement are better uncoupled and this political question was reconsidered by Davenant. The question was all the more resonant after twenty years of Puritan control of the legislature, but Davenant took it further to ask whether one should overthrow magistrates who try to enforce laws which run counter to nature. This in turn begs the question, what is the moral status of a law if more injustice, repression and cruelty are caused by its enforcement than in breaking it? Davenant also revisited another of Shakespeare's questions: what role does individual conscience have when morality is enforced by state violence? In returning to questions asked sixty years previously he found himself confronting how different the plays and society of his godfather's time were from his own.

Davenant could put these questions more bluntly than Shakespeare could in 1604; Shakespeare had written under an absolute monarchy served by rigorous censorship in a city filled with competitive theatres and equally competitive playwrights. It was an environment where rival companies would have liked nothing more than to see the Lord Chamberlain's Men fall from favour through staging too controversial a play. Davenant, on the other hand, wrote when a new and insecure royalist regime needed the theatre to characterise it as the bringer of liberty. He worked in a city with only two licensed theatres, both monopolies, and with few real rivals to his position. He could afford to strip away Shakespeare's diplomatic multivalences and punishment-avoiding ambivalences and confront these political questions head on.

Davenant's approach to pasticcio certainly owes something to his earlier experience of libretto-writing but, I suggest, he also drew on what he knew of Italian operas. The insistence, expressed in the prefaces of Badoaro, Busanello and other librettists, on their right to accommodate their classical source material, or even history itself, to their narratives and not the other way round, established a new parameter which Davenant embraced. Baroque pasticcio was not a return to Renaissance *imitatio* as Vetheuil had defined it: the creation of fresh works from old ones, as if the master who had written the originals was alive, well, and writing in the present. Davenant, Dryden and Shadwell were as radical in their departures from Shakespeare as Italian librettists were from Homer and Virgil. Yet, also like Italian librettists, Davenant did not want to originate from scratch or depart entirely from inherited masterworks.

His bold revision of the source material presented the temptation to make allusions to or draw parallels with, recent history. Applications of Angelo to Cromwell and his Puritan minions, with Benedick's rebels signifying as cavaliers, were an option in the new narrative, especially as Cromwell's law of 1650 actually did impose a death sentence for adultery. But Davenant seems to have made a latitudinarian decision to rise above easy sectarian applications and avoid royalist triumphalism: a subtlety of approach that allowed him to maintain the universality of his story's questions. Instead of making the play's questions specific to Britain, the story is located in a distant, fictionalised Turin at some unspecified point in the past, rather as Shakespeare had used Vienna. These timeless settings, lacking any of the known Italian or Austrian cultures or customs, derive from storytelling tradition: they are the Hamelin, Illyria or Carthage of tales. *The Law against Lovers* also retained the soft unrealities of blank verse, a technique which, in the 1660s, must have evoked the almost-lost storytelling world recalled by Aubrey. Davenant's approach thus separated the core political questions from both their original Jacobean context and his own society, isolating them in a heterotopic test tube, as it were, for closer examination. Such ambitious pasticcio skills allowed Shakespeare's godson to act as Schrödinger's playwright, inhabiting both past and present simultaneously. Why Turin in particular was chosen may have been for a practical reason, such as the company already having scenery depicting an Italian city; but to dramatise the social and political fractures in the story, the city had to be no-state and any-state. Davenant left it to his audiences to create connections with contemporary politics if they so desired: he provided the dots and left his audience to join them or not as they wished.

To the puzzlement of nineteenth- and twentieth-century scholars, contemporary commentators on *The Law against Lovers* made no mention of Shakespeare at all and offered no comparison with the source texts. Recognition of intertextuality was thus absent and, as argued in Chapter 1, this was the hallmark of a successful pasticcio. The storylines used in *Measure for Measure* do not even begin with Shakespeare; this narrative extends from George Whetstone's 1578 play *Patmos and Cassandra*, where the plot thread of Angelo and Isabella can be found, and do not end with Davenant. His pasticcio was reworked by Charles Gildon in 1699 as *Measure for Measure or Beauty the Best Advocate*. This was a revival with substitutions – Gildon's own interpolations – but his choice of Shakespeare's title rather than Davenant's is an indicator of how much successful revision had boosted Shakespeare's reputation over the intervening forty years. Long after Gildon, a version was created by Mr Younger, the prompter at Covent Garden, in 1771. This story, and others like it, can be seen as an ongoing, evolving, performance tradition rather than a series of textual adaptations from what was once a fixed original. During the course of its evolution, the political arguments were redrawn successively to resonate with the times in which the story was being reworked. The pasticcio approaches taken by Davenant show transnational influence appearing in this particular performance tradition, one which helped to draw Britain's theatre further into international neoclassical culture.

Pasticcio practices, then, can be found in the conceptualisation of dramatic narratives, in the spoken text where interpolations by the pasticciere were common and more than one text combined, and in the arias and choruses which often existed before the operas in which they were incorporated. Recitatives on the other hand were less frequently used or reused. When opera began in Britain it made great use of recitative but, despite this early enthusiasm, recitative did not become a central feature of either dramatick opera or, later, ballad opera. Certainly, recitative was used in the musical sequences, but spoken dialogue was usually the medium for moving the plots. Dryden was insistent that English operas should follow Italian models, and rewriting the recitatives was a method used by Italian pasticcieri to create new narratives, scenes or to introduce new characters.[106] The comparative disinterest in recitative thus merits discussion.

Michael Burden, discussing the nineteenth-century tendency to replace operatic recitative with speech outside the King's Theatre, comments that the English had always detested it.[107] I suggest that the origin of this dislike lies in an ambivalence towards sung speech itself which arose during the long Reformation. In Catholic Italy, which had no such complications, sung speech and thus recitative were uncontentious but in Britain, the practice of chanting the liturgy was challenged persistently in anti-Catholic discourse.[108]

Chanting, though not necessarily singing, were felt by the more Protestant reformers to be superfluous to worship; they agitated for its discontinuation along with the use of Latin and the symbolic gestures performed during key parts of the Mass. This hostility to cantillation spilled over into secular life, creating negative associations for chanting in non-religious contexts: the word 'cant' was applied to dishonest speech, where the speaker sought to impose on the listener. It also described the jargon used by the underclass, especially thieves, vagrants, false beggars and various kinds of criminal, even though this was not sung or chanted.

A further explanation may lie in a gender metaphor Dryden used when discussing recitative and airs in his preface to *Albion and Albanius*:

> The recitative part of an opera requires a more masculine beauty of expression and sound. The other, which, for want of a proper English word, I must call the *songish part*, must abound in the softness and variety of numbers; its principal intention being to please the hearing rather than to gratify understanding.[109]

We can recognise here the same gender projections onto operatic musical forms as those superimposed onto literacy and orality: whereas the feminine airs give pleasure and diversion they cannot be expected to meet male expectations of reason and clarity of argument. This is only a metaphor of course, and Dryden is not imagining all melodies as sung by women and recitatives by men. Yet if recitative is more masculine than airs, then speech is thus more masculine still, which offers another reason for the privileging of speech over recitative in English operas: it carried literate, masculine, Protestant authority whereas recitative had resonances of the oral, the Catholic and the feminine.

Baroque operas: a hybrid of oral storytelling tradition and literate neoclassicism

This section locates the argument for pasticcio as an oral survival within late seventeenth-century debates occasioned by an increasingly literate culture. Opera creators were negotiating an increasingly fundamentalist attitude taken by scholars towards classical texts, while recognising the necessity of making changes to deeply revered stories in order to stage them effectively. Walter Ong defined secondary orality as oral characteristics co-existing and interacting with literate culture; as we have seen, pasticcio opera, both in Italy and Britain, exemplify this.[110] Anthony Welch observed, when writing about the demise of epic poetry in the last decades of the seventeenth century, that '[i]n several respects, it was in early opera that the epic tradition returned at last to an oral idiom, but one transformed by centuries of literate cultural history'.[111] While I quibble that, for most families, literate culture was less than a century old and, even at this point, accessible to only 5 per cent of women, Welch's recognition of opera's oral idiom is a recognition of its running counter to the prevailing literate tilt. Busenello and Cavalli's *La Didone* (1641) and Purcell and Nahum Tate's *Dido and Aeneas* (1689) both bristle with secondary oral characteristics and a comparison shows how fidelity towards source material was balanced by oral approaches to storytelling.

Dido and Aeneas was not only a conscious emulation of continental practice, but also an enthusiastic entry into a Europe-wide contention between the Ancients and Moderns. This *querelle* used to be portrayed as a predominantly French literary contention but examples of the dispute can be found in most European societies and *Dido and Aeneas* is one expression of it. The Ancients argued that art, and indeed society, should follow the precepts laid down by Greco-Roman authors, and groups such as the Accademia dell'Arcadia in Rome took a fundamentalist approach to doing so. Such attitudes led to 'reform-opera' in the later decades of the seventeenth century.[112]

This school sought a stricter adherence to the unities of time and place as outlined by Aristotle. Domenico David, Apostelo Zeno, Girolamo Frigimelica-Roberti, Antonio Salvi, Ludovico Antonio Muratori and Pietro Ottoboni all advocated such reforms; they wished to see less artifice, less musical ornamentation and more verisimilitude in the staging.[113] What they meant by verisimilitude was not greater likeness to contemporary life as it was currently experienced, but greater likeness to what classical authors had laid down as being eternal verities in human behaviour. They sought to anchor operatic dialogue in patterns used by spoken theatre, especially French spoken theatre. The school's advocates could be extreme; Giovanni Mario Crescimbeni suggested that in setting texts for *drammi per musica*, the music should be confined to illustrating the cadences of speech alone.[114] Crescimbeni was something of an extremist among the reformers and it can be argued that he totemises rather than typifies the movement, as J.W. Davison would later do for the nineteenth-century's opera reformers in London.

The Moderns on the other hand argued that undeviating subservience to Greco-Roman rules in contemporary art inhibited the creation of art relevant to the times; parts of Badoaro's prefaces read like a manifesto for the Moderns. The Ancients responded that modern art failed not because adherence to ancient rules was fettering it, but because it was not adhering to them tightly enough.

Welch shows that Virgil's *Aeneid* was often the ground on which this contention was fought out. The Moderns noted the yawning gulf between Virgil's imperial propaganda — in which the Queen of Carthage is all too easily seduced by the founder of Rome — and his fellow historians' portrayal of Dido as a chaste woman who sacrificed herself for her country rather than surrender to foreign suitors. Seventeenth-century scholars were aware that Virgil's portrayal of Dido had been criticised in the Roman period by Servius and Macrobius as a libel on a virtuous woman. Moderns preferred an honourable Dido while the Ancients defended the Virgilian.[115]

La Didone and *Dido and Aeneas* are examples of the virtuous Dido of the Moderns. As in Venice, Britain's Cavalier-scholars were keen to look beyond the Ancients' unhesitating veneration of Virgil and make a chivalrous restoration of Dido's reputation. Welch argues:

> Taking up the chaste Dido tradition, *Dido and Aeneas* explores the Virgilian epic's lost voices. It exposes the mechanics of political myths, the process by which both artists and their political masters recast history in their own ideological image. It finds charismatic authority not in the figure of the ancient bard but in a heroine whose good name has been suppressed by Virgil's imperial fiction. But in transferring the ancient mystique of the epic poet's voice to that of his slandered queen, *Dido* struggles to come to grips with the meaning of this shadowy figure from the past and her enigmatic vocality.[116]

2.8 Virgil's Dido from a mosaic at Low Ham Roman villa, 4th century AD.
Source: Museum of Somerset.

2.9 The virtuous Dido of the Moderns by Rutilo Manetti, *Dido and Aeneas*,
c.1630.
Source: Los Angeles County Museum of Art.

Cause-and-effect and rational motivations still had little influence on
character construction for the operas of this century and oral paradigms
could still be the denominating factor. I suggest that, rather than struggling
to create a unified meaning for Dido, Tate and Purcell aligned their character
with the wronged heroines of storytelling tradition: they did not see the
creation of unified meaning as an imperative so their Dido was as composite
a character as Shakespeare's Cleopatra or Hermione. Dido's deeply moving
aria 'When I am laid in earth' inspires sorrow and sympathy in listeners by

evoking their own personal griefs, yet its repeated phrase 'Remember me' was also the final plea of Charles I on the scaffold.[117] A strong royalist association with a wronged sovereign was thus evoked for contemporary audiences. The anniversary of the king's death was commemorated in public prayers in every church throughout the three kingdoms and these words appear on mourning rings, etched glass and funerary monuments. The narrative of martyrdom, that Charles had shed his blood out of love for his country, the worst of whom had deserted him, was propagated at every opportunity. I suggest Tate and Purcell's final aria references these themes, combining the personal and the political. The opera is not, then, merely a correction of Roman history but the reworking of a very ancient story to make it relevant to the writers' own generation, and within a cultural framework they would understand. Interpolations, updated tropes and changes to previous versions were a matter of course; pasticcio practices in opera were the method whereby a story remained relevant and valuable.

In Tate's libretto, very English seventeenth-century witches appear, rather than ancient Carthaginian *streghe*, who, for no more specific reason than general hatred for human happiness, destroy the love between Dido and Aeneas. There is no interaction between the lovers and the witches, who operate in separate environments; there is not even indirect contact between the court and the witches through intermediaries.[118] This narrative structure derives from a received oral system rather than the rational motivations increasingly required by spoken theatre and early novels. This suggests Tate felt that opera was a form where the pressure for correct adherence to Greco-Roman models was lighter than for spoken theatre or poetry and interpolations from English storytelling into classical myths permissible. I am not suggesting that, in making such deliberate departures from Virgil, Tate and Purcell were consciously choosing oral characteristics; these were almost certainly residual, imbibed unaware from traditions that were still embedded in their transitional culture.

A comparison with Cavalli and Busanello's telling of this story is instructive. Both operas applied the wronged queen topos and both operas display weak or absent motivations for key actions by their characters. Just as the cause of Leontes's jealousy in *The Winter's Tale* is only very lightly sketched in, the motivation for Dido's love for Aeneas remains largely unexplored in both operas. *La Didone* also dispenses with the Virgilian ending of this story. Early on, Dido rejects the advances of Iorbas, a neighbouring king, when she is swept off her feet by Aeneas, a rejection which drives Iorbas mad. When Mercury orders Aeneas back to Rome to fulfil his destiny, the god also relieves Iorbas of his madness; Iorbas then renews his suit to Dido and she marries him instead of committing suicide as Virgil describes.[119] Busanello thus reversed the famous ending, but the narrative supplies no emotional rationale for this new resolution to the story. Busanello makes no attempt to explain Dido's change of heart and acceptance of Iorbas – there is no earlier flirtation between them, no sense that she is a broken-hearted person settling for second best, nor any sense that it is a political marriage of convenience. The weakness or absence of motivation in oral storytelling is partly due to pre-rationalist conceptions of cause and effect, but also when stories are told they occur in a continuous, protracted, present moment. What is happening in the story right now holds the audience's attention rather than the distant past of a few minutes ago. There is literally no time to ask why, unlike written stories which go at the pace of the reader.

Traditionally, the wrapping up of a spoken or sung story relied on the storyteller distancing the listeners from the main characters' fate, prising the audience off their immersion by reminding them that this was a long time ago and in another land. Busanello's ending probably relied on the audience's willingness to leave the story in this way. As with Patient Griselda and Cinderella, once the trauma is over, the heroine resumes or begins married life without any emotional scars. Suicide was too dark an ending for Busanello's purpose but the remarriage of widows was ordinary: marriage to Iorbas dissolved the audience's care and interest in Dido's life, disengaging them from the story and returning them to the light of common day. Both Busanello and Tate put the storytelling tropes familiar to their own generation before any adherence to neoclassical rules. The libretti of *La Didone* and *Dido and Aeneas* feel much closer to *A Winter's Tale* than they do to Handel's *Giulio Cesare* or Gluck's *Orfeo*.

As ever, we must treat binaries with caution; the problem with identifying seventeenth-century librettists such as Busanello and Tate as card-carrying Moderns is that they were also neoclassical scholars wedded to most of the neoclassical rules. Busanello and Tate could argue that they were no more departing from Virgil's epic than he had himself departed from his historical sources. Rosand gives many examples from the published prefaces prefaces to Venetian libretti of Modern-leaning authors refusing to apologise for their departures from rules, yet they seldom argued that the rules themselves had no validity (Badoaro excepted).[120] The same librettists could be neoclassical enough in other contexts: when Tate revised *King Lear* in 1681 he removed the death of Cordelia to bring the play's conclusion more into line with neoclassical rules, making him an Ancient in plays and a Modern in opera.

An inherent tension lay between the simplicities of storytelling, which theatre sought to emulate, and neoclassical restrictions imposed on theatre such as observing the unities. The tendency of epic stories to move from Rome to Egypt, or from Greece to India or Persia, was unproblematic in storytelling, but in staging such narratives this was deeply problematic if one also had to obey unities of place, time and plot. To set the opera in one location alone usually meant having to tell just one episode in a much longer story. It was possible in *Dido and Aeneas*, which is set in Carthage alone, but not in Badoaro's *Giulio Cesare* (1646) which staged episodes in Rome, Egypt and Greece. Breaching the unity of place necessarily damaged the unity of time: ellipses in time occur either side of scenes depicting sea-journeys in operas; kings assemble an army of thousands by the following day and the carrying of messages across half the world takes no time at all. Venetian librettists employed a number of apologia to forestall censure by Ancient fundamentalists. Badoaro is the least apologetic; indeed, making a virtue of breaking the unities, he gives Time the following speech in his prologue to *Giulio Cesare*:

> Here you will see years
> Epitomised in hours ...
> Who could ever object
> If one melodious night reveals to you
> The happenings and deeds of a thousand days
> ... And I, in order to delight you
> Disciples, or rather teachers, of Alcydes
> With flattering art,
> Have enclosed more than a year in an evening:
> Without using either couriers or ships.
> Without changing your seats you will discover
> Thessaly, Lesbos, the Lighthouse, Egypt and Rome.[121]

Librettists often tried to argue that they *had* followed the unities in some abstruse technical sense. Busanello defends himself (unconvincingly) against damaging the unity of plot in his preface to *Gli amori d'Apollo e di Dafne* (1640), thus:

> The other things in the present play are episodes interwoven in the manner that you will see, and if perchance someone should judge that the unity of the plot is broken by the multiplicity of love stories (that is, of Apollo and Daphne, of Tithonus and Aurora, of Cephalis and Procris), let him be reassured by remembering that these interweavings do not destroy the unity, but rather embellish it. Let him remember that the Cavalier Guarino, in his *Pastor Fido*, did not intend a multiplicity of loves (that is between Myrtillus and Amaryllis, and between Sylvius and Dorinda), but rather used the love story of Dorinda and Sylvius to adorn his tale.[122]

As well as criticism for proliferating sub-plots, librettists also faced censure over structure: drama was supposed to have five acts but opera usually reduced them to three. Instead of a consistent metrical form, interpolations and pasticcio meant that libretti often skipped about between different metres. Right up to the end of the seventeenth century, many Venetian librettists blended tragedy and comedy to allow high- and low-status characters to interact with each other in flagrant disregard of Aristotle. There was plenty to appal an Ancient, and Rosand notes that apologia tended to argue the unique requirements of setting a story to music, but also obligations to friends and the pressure of popular taste.[123] The assembling of an opera, or parts of an opera, from pre-existing materials might have many motivations, but in the seventeenth century, the method was often used to preserve the tropes of storytelling at the expense of fidelity to an ancient text. In the nineteenth century, ironically, pasticcio would be used to help *ensure* fidelity to a cherished text, as discussed in Chapter 4.

Verisimilitude and its alternatives in Britain's emergent operatic tradition

Opera first appeared in Britain some fourteen years after the closure of the theatres and became progressively more popular and influential over the rest of the seventeenth century, but there is a paradox in this. Opera embraced nearly everything spoken theatre had deliberately abandoned by 1642; opera singers remained largely static save for occasional bursts of comic physicality during the recitatives. Plays had become more interested in depicting the real world while most operas displayed a spectacular disregard for it: Purcell's *King Arthur* abounds in sprites, gods, fantasy and magic while the witches in *Dido and Aeneas* are counter-rationalism personified. Opera had fantastical plots with motivations as weak as those of fairy stories. The narratives which opera offered were of a kind that Restoration audiences usually rejected as being steeped in a discredited oral culture. Verisimilitude had become increasingly important in spoken plays and Restoration acting rejected the misericord poses of Elizabethan theatre and moved instead towards personation. Yet, being sung, operatic acting could not follow suit; verisimilitude in opera thus had to be constructed in a different way. Badoaro, in his preface to *Ulisse errante* (1644), shows that librettists had long been aware of the incompatibility of opera and verisimilitude but also with classical rules of drama:

> It is nothing if, to increase the pleasure of the spectators in the present moment, I give permission for something unlikely. We see that it does not weaken the action if, to give more time to scene changes, we introduce music; we cannot avoid the implausible, namely, that men should carry on their most important transactions while singing. Moreover, in order to enjoy variety in the theatre, we are used to music for two, three and more voices, which causes another unlikelihood: that several people conversing together should suddenly find themselves saying the same thing simultaneously. It is not a dazzling marvel

if we adapt ourselves to the delight of the spirit of the age; we are rightly distanced from the ancient rules.[124]

Opera had to evolve its own strategies for being true to life and, though these were different to those of spoken theatre, they were not absent. Handel's soprano aria 'Lascia ch'io pianga' is a haunting plea for liberty and release which continues to be emotionally true to life. Had this been spoken as part of a play, the heightened speech and artificiality of contemporary theatrical delivery would have reduced its impact on the audience. Nonetheless, its dramatic context within the opera is profoundly anti-realistic: the Queen of Damascus, an Amazonian sorceress who appears in a chariot drawn by dragons, invokes the Furies to help her and, later, abducts the heroine in a black cloud, imprisoning her in an enchanted palace guarded by monsters. Opera's approach to verisimilitude was to touch the private memory and unconscious emotional make-up of the individual listener; this mattered more than the likelihood of the story occurring in real life. Dryden and Purcell's *King Arthur* (1691) is offered as an example later in this section but first, a consideration of how audiences conceived verisimilitude in spoken theatre allows us to understand the paradox of opera's appeal.

Restoration actors no longer represented characters emblematically, but 'personated' them. The word derived from the Greek, prosopon, πρόσωπον, meaning a mask but also 'to sound through something', a mask or a flute; personation was thus the *animation* of the mask. The actor's voice and body created the character's 'likeness'. Such verisimilitude was praised when it was achieved and was a widely approved approach to acting, being sanctioned by Greek and Roman aesthetics. Recalling Thomas Betterton's acting, Colley Cibber, in later life, praised his capacity to personate with verisimilitude:

> The most that a Vandyke can arrive at, is to make his Portraits of great Persons seem to think; a Shakespear goes farther yet, and tells you what his Pictures thought; a Betterton steps beyond 'em both, and calls them from the Grave to breathe and be themselves again in Feature, Speech, and Motion. When the skilful Actor shews you all these Powers at once united, and gratifies at once your Eye, your Ear, your Understanding: To conceive the Pleasure rising from such Harmony, you must have been present at it! 'tis not to be told you![125]

What most delighted Cibber was Betterton's capacity to reanimate famous figures 'in the life', to make the audience feel they were witnessing an historical event as it must have happened, making the stage match the private imagination. To modern sensibilities this is closer to historical re-enactment than acting, and *im*personation, which is recorded in the *Oxford English Dictionary* in a transitive sense from 1715, conveys a shift which had occurred in the sense of the term. Instead of animating the mask itself, the term (by this point) conveyed the performer revealing the man or woman *behind* the mask. In spoken theatre, this meaning came into its own with Garrick. Personation was the kind of verisimilitude sought in Restoration acting; it was an expectation in Paris too, as described in Giovanni Paolo Marana's contemporary account of plays at Versailles. Recommending plays, he wrote:

> a man, ... cannot better pass away his time, than in being present at these entertainments; where all that he has read, either in ancient or modern history, deserving remark, shall be successively presented to his view, as efficaciously as if the persons were now living and in presence, whose actions each play describes ... all the ingenious fictions of Orpheus, Homer, Hesiod, Ovid, and the rest of the Greek and Roman poets, are here translated, not so much from one language to another, as from words to actions, and from dead, inanimate characters, to living figures of the things themselves.[126]

Opera's capacity to reanimate the past with this kind of verisimilitude was curtailed by its sung medium, yet singing allowed the audience to look beyond the ethos and logos to the pathos. Dryden and Purcell's *King Arthur* of 1691 is an example of an opera in Britain attempting to find a space, in terms of form, narrative and legitimacy, that was outside the Ancient/Modern querelle and beyond the reproaches of neoclassical purism; one that would also appease the new whiggish suspicion of continental influence following 1688. *King Arthur*, a dramatick opera like Shadwell's, was not a classical story nor did it aim at the verisimilitude of spoken plays.

Dryden and Purcell confidently disregarded all previous narratives of the Matter of Britain: instead of Malory's medieval English court, they set their story in fifth-century Britain, amidst a struggle for control of the island by Britons and Saxons. They sought to depict Dark Age Britain as authentically as scholarship then allowed, including a depiction of sacrifices to Saxon gods. Lyrics even referred to recently found archaeological artefacts such as Romano-British drinking bowls. No doubt those well read in Geoffrey of Monmouth and other texts would have baulked at Dryden's many departures from tradition but this was not as hot a contention and legitimacy was sought not from fidelity to medieval texts but from current historical research. The fantastical and meandering plot certainly reflects oral storytelling but here, I suggest, it was a conscious choice: the opera was thus a synthesis of indigenous storytelling paradigms and antiquarianism.

At the time this opera was being created, Edward Lluyd was collecting Welsh and Cornish material for his *Archaeologia Britannica* and Edmund Gibson was completing the first printed edition of the *Anglo-Saxon Chronicle*. Dryden admits to studying Bede, and Andrew Pinnock shows he also drew on Aylett Sammes's *Britannia Antiqua Illustrata*. But the plot of the opera deliberately avoids all known historical accounts; Oswald, Grimbald and the others are Saxonesque rather than Saxon and the Britons are Cavalier English gentlemen rather than the Cymry. It is an artistic response to the fragmentary texts and artefacts surviving from what was seen as the dawn of a recognisable Britain. Given the amount of anachronism in the opera – Comus's song about cheating the parson of his tithes, references to the British wool trade, and 'foreign Kings adopted here' – almost certainly William III – the audience were in no doubt that parallels were intended to be drawn between ancient and contemporary Britain. Yet these playful applications were not intended to disrupt or subvert the historicism; one could have both.

As in Davenant's revisitation of Shakespeare's questions, a latitudinarian invitation to reflect on how far society had come since the civil wars runs through 'How blest are shepherds', 'Fairest isle' and the ensemble with Aeolus, the Nereid and Pan. Intertextuality in this opera is thus between the island's ancient past and its recent past. Its verisimilitude is based neither on a programmatic adherence to ancient texts nor true-to-life depictions of society; rather, the story is loosely based on indigenous history, exploiting textual lacunae to invent a new Arthurian narrative, while references to recent events promote a conception of Britain's woes and joys as timeless. There have always been periods of endemic division and internecine war, Britain has always adopted foreign kings and, though unpalatable at first, if this had not happened the English would never have become the predominant nation in the island (the consequences for the Britons goes unmentioned). The Comus scenes depict an unchanging agricultural class.

It is not a pasticcio as all the music was original and all composed by Purcell, as was Dryden's text with the exception of Howe's duet. *King Arthur* may not have begun as a pasticcio but it became one in the following century; it continued in the repertoire in various forms, sustained, like Shakespeare's plays, by substantial amendments over time. The original version survived until 1736, probably altering a little with each revival but, after this date, it was altered substantially both dramatically and textually. Retitled *Arthur and Emmeline* it became an after-piece, before being reworked again by David Garrick in 1776, with arias interpolated by Thomas Arne. Garrick explained his reasons for the changes in his advertisement:

THE Names of *Dryden* and *Purcel* have made the following Performance hitherto regarded as one the best calculated to show the Effects of Poetry, Action, and Music. Yet the want of a Plot sufficiently interesting and varied, has prevented it keeping its Rank on the Stage, as a first Piece. This it is hoped will excuse the present alteration, by which, the whole of the Story, with the most approved Parts of the Music and Machinery are compressed into two Acts, leaving the beautiful Scenes of Emmeline almost wholly untouched.[127]

It was still playing in the 1780s under this title and only in 1842 was an attempt made to restage the original version. William Charles Macready was a great restorer of Shakespeare's original texts and he revived *King Arthur* in as close to its original form as was felt possible. It received a mixed response for complex reasons discussed in Chapter 4. Purcell's opera indicates that Britain's emergent indigenous opera tradition was evolving on very different lines to those of its spoken theatre tradition.

Reshaped by continental influence though it was, pasticcio as a construction method was only one of a number of continuities from the oral past, and seen across many performance genres. Opera displayed this and other oral characteristics and, in doing so, embodied everything the country was supposed to dislike, yet was evidently popular. When Italian performers arrived at the beginning of the next century there were, once again, unambiguously Catholic people on the stage, being fêted and applauded. Addison remained sceptical of Italian opera and argued that its departures from the verisimilitude familiar in spoken plays made the artform irrational. He consciously represented the expectations of literate male culture in Britain and his criticisms reveal his underlying association of opera with oral culture, the female world and Catholicism. Orality might have been a discredited heritage in Britain but not all of the elite desired to be entertained rationally every time they went to the theatre. Another reason for opera's popularity, I suggest, is that it offered a respite not just from the narrow and constrictive identities brought into being by the seventeenth century's endemic religio-political divisions, but from the rise and gendering of literacy and the demotion and feminising of oral culture.

Italian opera arrives in London

It was not until the turn of the century that Italian opera found its feet in London and it was the pasticcio method on which companies mostly relied when creating performances. In 1705 the first opera staged at Vanbrugh's new theatre was Jakob Greber's *Gli Amore di Ergasto*; it was poorly received by an audience familiar with English operas while Drury Lane's *Arsinoe*, a pasticcio arranged by Thomas Clayton, met with greater success.[128] Eight out of the twelve operas performed between 1705 and 1711 were pasticci.[129] Audiences in Britain were already familiar with the pasticcio approach from their own plays and operas, so this facet of Italian opera was neither strange nor new. These operas were judged on their immediate performance and it was only after travel to Italy had increased over the course of the eighteenth century that King's Theatre operas would be judged on how authentically they reflected the artform in Italy itself.

By telling its stories through music, opera recreated a lost imaginative space; it was art for the highly literate but mediated through oral frameworks.

The return of thelxis was greatly welcomed and opera, for half a guinea a seat, could provide elite audiences with the same immersion and emotional connection to a story that could still be had in an illiterate cottage for nothing. I suggest that opera's way of telling a story arrived in London at a key moment in the oral to literate transition: the thelxis provided by storytelling had long left the theatre, but the desire for it had not yet left society.

Notes

1 Ellen Rosand, *Opera in Seventeenth Century Venice: The Creation of a Genre* (Berkeley, Los Angeles, Oxford: University of California Press, 1991, paperback edn, 2007), p. 49, the original Italian in Appendix 1/8h, p. 410.

2 'Decimus Magnus Ausonius, Cento Nuptialis', in R.P.H. Green, *Ausonii Opera* (Oxford: Oxford Classical Texts, 1999), p. 151. My translation.

3 Ingeborg Hoesterey points out that twentieth-century musicologists have also used the term cento as a synonym for pasticcio, often to describe a libretto the lines of which are drawn from famous novels or plays. Such was Hofmannstahl's libretto for *Der Rosenkavalier*. Ulrich Weisstein, 'Farce oder wienerische Maskerade? Dir Französischen quellen des *Rosenkavalier*', *Hofmannstahl-Forschungen*, ed. Wolfram Mauser, vol. 9 (Freiburg im Breslau: Mauser, 1987), pp. 105–141, quoted in Ingeborg Hoesterey, *Pastiche: Cultural Memory in Art, Film, Literature* (Indianapolis: Indiana University Press, 2001), pp. 9, 80, 95, 96.

4 Benedetto Ricci, *De imitatione*, Book 3 (Venice: Aldi filii, 1545), fols 75–77. Andreas Fabri Wethulensis (Andre Le Fevre de Vetheuil), *Centones, cum Diana, et iuvenilibus* (1589, reprinted Paris: D. Douceur, 1609), pp. 3–7 (p. 6), quoted in George Hugo Tucker, 'From rags to riches: the early modern cento form', *Journal of Neo-Latin Studies*, vol. 62 (Leuven: University of Leuven Press, 2013), pp. 7–22.

5 Advocates such as Fabri Wethulensis in his preface, 'Benigno proboque lectori', to *Centones, cum Diana, et iuvenilibus*, pp. 3–7.

6 Ibid., p. 6.

7 Ibid. My translation and punctuation is a slight amendment of Tucker's, 'From rags to riches', pp. 9–10.

8 *Isidori Hispalensis episcopi Etymologiarum sive Originum*, libri XX, ed. W.M. Lindsay, Oxford Classical Texts, vol. 1 (Oxford: Clarendon Press, 1911), pp. 39–40, quoted by Tucker, 'From rags to riches', p. 23.

9 Giovanni Marchesini, *Mammotrectus super Bibliam* (*c*.1300); Lilio Gregorio Giraldi, *De Historia poetarum tam Graecorum quam Latinorum dialogi decern* (first edn, *Historice poetarum* ..., Basle: 104 Isingrinius, 1545), both quoted by Tucker, 'From rags to riches', p. 23.

10 Tucker, 'From rags to riches', p. 14.

11 Preface to Ausonius, *Cento Nuptialis*.

12 Mark Everist, 'The refrain cento: myth or motet?', *Journal of the Royal Musical Association*, vol. 114 no. 2 (Cambridge: Cambridge University Press, 1989), pp. 164–188. Everist debunked an earlier view that a musical equivalent of the cento existed, showing instead that, while refrains were swapped and exchanged freely between motets and chansons, none were deliberately emulative of the cento method.

13 Ibid., pp. 176–181.

14 Ibid., pp. 187–188.

15 Peter Burke, 'Oral culture and print culture in Renaissance Italy', *ARV: Nordic Yearbook of Folklore*, vol. 54 (Uppsala: Royal Gustavus Adolphus Academy, 1998), pp. 7–18. Cantastorie were known under different names across Europe and were also a strong feature of German storytelling culture. Mauro Geraci 'The poetic-musical reflection of Sicilian storytellers', *Le letterature popolari. Prospettive di ricerca e nuovi orizzonti teorico-metodologici*, ed. D. Scafoglio, vol. 60 s. 4 (Naples: Edizione scientifiche Italiane, 2002), pp. 509–520. Mauro Geraci writes regularly about the cantastorie in a journal dedicated to the subject, *Il Cantastorie*.

16 F. Alberto Gallo, *Music in the Castle: Troubadours, Books and Orators in Italian Courts of the Thirteenth, Fourteenth, and Fifteenth Centuries*, trans. Anna Herklotz (Chicago: University of Chicago Press, 1995), pp. 51–53 for reception by the Visconti of both the cantastorie Dolcibene, and the littérateur Petrarch, with frequent reference to the assembly of libraries and retention of entertainers throughout. Hans-Erich Keller, 'Italian troubadors', *A Handbook of the Troubadours*, ed. F.R.P. Akehurst and Judith M. Davis (Berkeley: University of California Press, 1995), pp. 295–307.

17 *L'Amfiparnasso* by Orazio Vecchi was first performed in 1594 and published in 1597. The modern score is translated and transcribed by Cecil Adkins in *Early Musical Masterworks*, vol. 1 (Chapel Hill: University of North Carolina, 1977), p. 15. This interpretation is supported by Nino Pirrotta, *Music and Theatre from Poliziano to Monteverdi* (Cambridge: Cambridge University Press, 1982), p. 115.

18 Adkins, *Early Musical Masterworks*, p. 17.

19 Martha Farahat, 'On the staging of madrigal comedies', *Early Music History*, vol. 10 (Cambridge: Cambridge University Press, 1991), pp. 123–143.

20 Sioned Davies, 'Performing *Culhwch ac Olwen*', *Arthurian Literature XXI: Celtic Arthurian Material*, ed. Ceridwen Lloyd-Morgan (Cambridge: D.S. Brewer, 2004), pp. 29–51. Lifris, in his late eleventh-century *Vitae Cadoci* (Life of St Cadog) uses metrical sections which suggest cantillation of at least part of the text. A.W. Wade Evans, *Vitae Sanctorum Britanniae et Genealogiae*, Life of St Padarn (originally published 1944, new edn Scott Lloyd) (Cardiff: Welsh Academic Press, 2013), pp. 25–141.

21 John Stevens, *Grove Music Online*, digitised January 2001. *Aucassin et Nicolette* is held at the Bibliothèque Nationale (F-Pn fr.2168). For a reconstruction of a performance excerpt see Alana Bennett, '"Performance of excerpt from *Aucassin et Nicolette*", medievalism in Australian cultural memory', (honours dissertation,

Medieval and Early Modern Studies, University of Western Australia, 2012). http://www.youtube.com/watch?v=Dcqd9j3EhZY&feature=relmfu [accessed 10 January 2019].

22 Armand d'Angour, 'Sense and sensation in music', *Companion to Ancient Aesthetics,* ed. Pierre Destrée and Penelope Murray (Oxford: Wiley Black-well, 2015), pp. 188–204. David Creese, *The Monochord in Ancient Greek Harmonic Science* (Cambridge: Cambridge University Press, 2010). Armand d'Angour is associate professor of classics at Oxford and David Creese is head of classics and ancient history at Newcastle University at the time of writing; examples of their reconstruction techniques can be found on the following links: Armand d'Angour, 'How did ancient Greek music sound?' BBC website, 2013. http://www.bbc.co.uk/news/business-24611454 [accessed 21 May 2018]; David Creese, eight-string tetrachord, YouTube, uploaded by Babette Babich, 2012. https://youtube.com/ZV6QDQOw4S4 [accessed 21 May 2018].

23 Armand d'Angour, 'The sound of mousike: reflections on aural change in ancient Greece', *Debating the Athenian Cultural Revolution*, ed. R. Osborne (Cambridge: Cambridge University Press, 2007), pp. 296–297.

24 Jo Ann Cavallo has written on Boiardo's *Orlando innamorato* throughout her career; '*L' Orlando innamorato*: un romanzo per la corte Ferrarese', *L'Enigma Boiardo*, ed. Silvano Vinceti (Rome: Armando Press, 2003), pp. 15–29. Blake Wilson, '*Cantorini* and *improvisore*: oral poetry and performance', *The Cambridge History of Fifteenth-Century Music*, ed. Anna Maria Busse Berger and Jesse Rodin (Cambridge: Cambridge University Press, 2015), pp. 298–299. Gianni Celati argues in 'Le posizione narrative rispetto all'altro', *Cahiers de littérature et civilisation Romanes,* vol. 3 (Caen: University of Caen Press, 1996), pp. 33–45, that the work has to be seen as storytelling first and literature second.

25 Davies, 'Performing *Culhwch ac Olwen*', pp. 29–51.

26 Below is a link to a reconstruction of a fifteenth-century Welsh stick chant by Dafydd ap Gwylim performed by Dr Peter Greenhill as part of the Centre for the Ancient Music of Wales's project 'Voicing the verse: Y Gerdd ar Gan' at Bangor University. The second link is a poem by Gruffydd ap Dafydd ap Howell from the early sixteenth century accompanied by crwth; this reconstruction drew the music from 'Kaniad y Gwynn Bibydd' in the Robert ap Huw Manuscript, and is performed by Bragod, a duo consisting of Robert Evans and Mary Ann Roberts. https://youtu.be/ZP5IDCRjOm8; http://www.bragod.com/bragodvideo.html [both accessed 23 January 2018].

27 The link that follows is a reconstruction with accompaniment of the English medieval poem *The Weddyng of Sir Gawen and Dame Ragnell*, made by New York University and performed by Linda Marie Zaerrin, 2012. https://vimeo.com/48847736 [accessed 23 January 2018].

28 Strohm describes the doubters and defenders of the founding myth: Reinhard Strohm, *Dramma per Musica: Italian Opera Seria of the Eighteenth Century* (New Haven, CT and London: Yale University Press, 1997), p. 24.

29 John K. Andrews, 'The historical context of Handel's *Semele*' (unpublished doctoral thesis, Queen's College, Cambridge, 2007), p. 227. Andrews shows Handel's tendency to derive those recitatives that lead to an arioso from English operatic tradition, e.g. 'Daughter, obey, hear and obey' in *Semele*, Act I, Sc. I is perhaps from John Eccles's earlier setting of this opera. Andrews also discusses others from Scarlatti's *Il Pompeo*: pp. 238–240.

30 *Euridice* composed by Jacopo Peri and Giulio Caccini to a libretto by Ottavio Rinuccini, conducted by Riccado Farolfi with the title role sung by Gloria Banditelli, posted online at YouTube by 'La Pellegrina 1589' in February 2015. https://youtu.be/wNIv0gQMLQA [accessed 13 September 2016].

31 This was formerly deemed an early oratorio but is considered by its most recent conductor, René Jacobs, to be an early opera. See René Jacobs and Achim Freyer's programme note for performances at the Berlin Staatsoper, June 2012, by the Akademie für Alte Musik. Andrew Clements' review of the CD of these performances in *The Guardian*, 20 February 2015, concurs in seeing it as an opera. Cavalieri's claim to have preceded Caccini in restoring the sung drama of ancient Greece was given in the published preface to *di anima e di corpo* (3 September 1600) by Alessandro Guidotti and reiterated by Cavalieri in a letter to Marcello Accolti dated 10 November 1600. Claude V. Palisca, 'Cavalieri, Emilio de', *Grove Music Online* (2001).

32 Prologue to *Le nuove musiche* by Giulio Caccini (printed in Florence, 1602, trans. Zachariah Victor for the facsimile edn, New York: Broude Brothers, 1973), p. 1.

33 Emilio de Cavalieri, 'Avvertimenti per la presente *Rappresentatione*, à chi volesse farla recitar cantando', *Rappresentatione di anima e di corpo* (Rome: Nicolò Mutij, 1600), trans. and digitised, Lorenzo Girodo, 1986.

34 Rosand, *Opera in Seventeenth Century Venice,* pp. 10–11. Strohm, too, cautions against assuming an overly rigid division of function between recitative and aria in *Dramma per Musica,* pp. 11–13.

35 Ronald James Alexander and Richard Savino, *Francesca Caccini the secular songs from 'il libro primo delle musiche', 1618* (Bloomington, IN: Indiana University Press, 2004), p. 4. For an example of her work, Mathew Reed sings Nettuno in a student production of Caccini's *La liberazione di Ruggiero* by the Cornish College of Arts, 2012: https://vimeo.com/39074777 [accessed 2 October 2016].

36 Claudio Monteverdi, *Scherzi musicali a tre voce* (Venice, 1607) reprinted in *Tutte le opera di Claudio Monteverdi*, ed. G.F. Malipiero, vol. 10 (Vienna, trans. Zachariah Victor, 1968), pp. 69–72.

37 Gifford Charles-Edwards and Helen McKee, 'Lost voices from Anglo-Saxon Lichfield', *Anglo-Saxon England*, vol. 37 (Cambridge: Cambridge University Press, 2008), pp. 80–83, 86–87.

38 At least at this point in time. Later composers such as Vivaldi, Mozart, Walton and Bernstein regularly brought these things to mass settings.

39 Rosand, *Opera in Seventeenth Century Venice,* p. 48. Original text in Appendix I/9j, p. 411.

40 Palestrina used a contrafactum in at least fifty masses and motets, while the *Missa malheur me bat, Missa Mater Patris* and *Missa fortuna desperata* of Josquin des Prez and the *Missa de Dringhs* by Antoine Brumel also use contrafacta. These are sometimes called parody masses or imitation masses. Robert Falck and Martin Picker, *Grove Dictionary Online*: https://doi.org/10.1093/gmo/9781561592630.article.06361 [accessed 19 August 2020].

41 Margaret Ann Rorke, 'Sacred contrafacta of Monteverdi madrigals and Cardinal Borromeo's Milan', *Music & Letters*, vol. 65 no. 2 (Oxford: Oxford University Press, 1984), pp. 168–175.

42 Agnieszka Budzinska-Bennett, 'Musica fatta spirituale. Aquilino Coppini's contrafacta of Monteverdi's *Fifth Book of Madrigals*', *Interdisciplinary Studies in Musicology* (Poznań: PTPN and Wydawnictwo Naukowe UAM, 2012), p. 273.

43 Mark Ringer, *Opera's First Master: The Musical Dramas of Claudio Monteverdi* (Lanham, MD: Amadeus Press, 2006), pp. 218–219.

44 Rosand, *Opera in Seventeenth Century Venice,* p. 220.

45 Ibid., p. 210.

46 Ringer, *Opera's First Master*, pp. 27–28.

47 Paolo Fabbri, *Monteverdi* (Turin, 1985, trans. Tim Carter 1994, reprinted Cambridge University Press, 2018) quoted in Ellen Rosand, *Monteverdi's Last Operas: a Venetian trilogy* (Los Angeles: University of California Press, 2007), pp. 61–65.

48 Rosand, *Opera in Seventeenth Century Venice*, pp. 22–24.

49 Ibid., pp. 110–111.

50 Giulio Strozzi, *La finta pazza* (Venice: Surian, 1641) quoted in ibid., p.111, original Italian text Appendix I 16e, p. 415.

51 Ibid., p.111, original Italian text Appendix I 16e, p. 415.

52 Andrew Gurr and Mariko Ichikawa, *Staging in Shakespeare's Theatre* (Oxford: Oxford University Press, 2000) p. 22; also John Astington, *Actors and Acting in Shakespeare's Time: The Art of Stage Playing* (Cambridge: Cambridge University Press, 2010), pp. 17–24, but note p. 16 where Astington warns against assuming the actor is unaffected emotionally by what he is saying; he cites the player in *Hamlet* who weeps with genuine emotion at the fate of Hecuba.

53 Walter Ong, 'Some psychodynamics of orality', reprinted in *Perspectives on Literacy*, ed. Eugene R. Kintgen, Barry M. Kroll and Mike Rose (Carbondale, IL: Southern Illinois University Press, 1988), p 38. Astington, *Actors and Acting,* throughout; Matthew Steggle, *Laughing and Weeping in Early Modern Theatres* (Aldershot: Ashgate, 2007), pp. 6–8.

54 Peter Hall, *Exposed by the Mask: Form and Language in Drama* (London, Oberon Books, 2000), pp. 6–7.

55 Peter Morgan Barnes, 'Shakespeare in schools: understanding the oral imagination', *SEELB Educational Resources for English Literature* (Belfast: EDCO, 1998).

56 As illustrated in Cathy Coulter, Charles Michael and Leslie Poynor's 'Storytelling as pedagogy: an unexpected outcome of narrative inquiry', *Curriculum Inquiry*, vol. 37 (Abingdon: Routledge, 2007), pp. 111–114.

57 Jennifer Elizabeth Popple, *The Restoration Actress in Her Seventeenth-Century Social, Political, and Artistic Context: Nell Gwyn, Elizabeth Barry, and Anne Bracegirdle* (New York: Edwin Mellen Press, 2015), Chapter Four.

58 John Downes, *Roscius Anglicanus, or, an Historical Review of the Stage From 1660 to 1706* (London, 1708), p. 24. Internet Archive. https://archive.org/details/rosciusanglicanu00downrich/page/32 [accessed 27 January 2019].

59 Ibid., p. 21.

60 *The Athenaeum*, April 1836, quoted by Tom Kaufman, 'A fresh look at Giulia Grisi', *Opera Today* (8 December 2005). https://operatoday.com/2005/12/a_fresh_look_at_giulia_grisi/ [accessed 10 January 2024].

61 Helen Moore (ed.), *Guy of Warwick, 1661*, The Malone Society Reprints (Manchester: Manchester University Press, 2007), Introduction, p. xiii.

62 However, the dislike expressed by playwrights – especially Ben Jonson – for those audience members with poor concentration, who went merely to spectate rather than listen, occasioned an academic debate at the end of the twentieth century about spectators versus listeners, as discussed by Andrew Gurr, *Playgoing in Shakespeare's London* (Cambridge: Cambridge University Press, 1996), pp. 86–98.

63 Another explanation for the lack of interaction with the characters is that the harpy sequence in *The Tempest* might have been sung and Banquo's line of descent, depicted in *Macbeth*, accompanied by music. There is no evidence either way of course, but interaction with singing harpies or singing witches would not have necessitated the main characters singing back to them; the final masque in *The Tempest* is a mixture of speech and singing. Music could still have allowed Macbeth to speak over the procession of Banquo's descendants.

64 Gāmini Salgādo, *Eyewitnesses of Shakespeare*, trans. Matthew Steggle (London: Sussex University Press, 1975), p. 30.

65 Martin Wiggins, *Drama and the Transfer of Power in Renaissance England* (Oxford: Oxford University Press, 2012), pp. 93–105.

66 Salgādo, *Eyewitnesses of Shakespeare*, pp. 112–113.

67 Popple, *The Restoration Actress*.

68 Gunther Kress and Theo van Leeuwen, *Reading Images: The Grammar of Visual Design* (London: Routledge, 1996), pp. 16, 19–21, 24–26, 119–159.

69 *The Tempest or The Enchanted Island, a Comedy, as it now Acted at His Highness the Duke of York's Theatre* (London: 1674), p. 1. Digitised by the Internet Archive. https://archive.org/details/tempestorenchant00shad/page/n15 [accessed 26 January 2019].

70 Adam Fox, *Oral and Literate Culture in England, 1500–1700*, Chapter Three, 'Old wives' tales and nursery lore' (Oxford: Clarendon Press, 2000), pp. 173–212.

71 Judith Butler, from 'Performative acts and gender constitution: an essay in phenomenology and feminist theory', *Theatre Journal*, vol. 40 no. 4 (Baltimore,

MD: Johns Hopkins University Press, 1988), pp. 519–531, to *Notes Toward a Performative Theory of Assembly* (Cambridge, MA: Harvard University Press, 2015).

72 John Aubrey, 'Remaines of gentilisme and Judaisme in 1686–7', printed in *John Aubrey: Three Prose Works*, ed. John Buchanan-Brown (Illinois: Carbondale Press 1972), pp. 287, 289.

73 Thomas McGeary, '"Warbling eunachs": opera, gender and sexuality on the London stage', *Restoration and 18th Century Theatre Research*, vol. 7 no. 1 (University Park, PA: Penn State University Press, 1992), various.

74 Ilias Chrissochoidis, 'Handel at a crossroads: his 1737–1738 and 1738–1739 seasons re-examined', *Music and Letters*, vol. 90 no. 4 (Oxford: Oxford University Press, 2009), pp. 600–601, n. 8.

75 Fox, *Oral and Literate Culture*, pp. 173–212.

76 Paula McDowell, 'Ong and the concept of orality', *Religion & Literature*, vol. 44 no. 2 (South Bend, IN: The University of Notre Dame, 2012), pp. 171–172.

77 John Sergeant, Letter of Thanks from the Author of *Sure-Footing* to his Mr. J.T. [John Tillotson] (Paris, 1666), p. 108, quoted in ibid., p. 172.

78 Daniel Defoe, *A Tour through the Whole Island of Great Britain* (London 1724–1727), vols II and III respectively, quoted in Fox, *Oral and Literate Culture*, p. 191.

79 Cecile M. Jagodzinski, *Privacy and Print: Reading and Writing in Seventeenth-Century England* (Charlottesville, VA: University of Virginia Press, 1999), p. 7. Significant recent scholarship on the topic includes A. Goldhammer, 'Histoire de la vie privée', *De la Renaissance aux lumières*, ed. Philippe Ariès, Georges Duby and Roger Chartier, vol. III (Paris: Seuil, 1985–1987); Mary Trull, *Performing Privacy and Gender in Early Modern Literature* (London: Palgrave Macmillan, 2003); Corinne S. Abate, *Privacy, Domesticity, and Women in Early Modern England* (Aldershot: Ashgate 2003); Michael McKeon, *The Secret History of Domesticity: Public, Private, and the Division of Knowledge* (Baltimore, MD: Johns Hopkins University Press, 2005); *Private and Domestic Devotion in Early Modern Britain*, ed. Jessica Martin and Alec Ryrie (Farnham: Ashgate, 2012); *Religion and the Household*, ed. Alexandra Walsham, Charlotte Methuen and John Doran, Studies in Church History vol. 50 (London: Boydell and Brewer and The Ecclesiastical History Society, 2014); and Ronald Huebert, *Privacy in the Age of Shakespeare* (Toronto: Toronto University Press, 2016).

The Danish National Research Foundation Centre for Privacy Research, founded in 2019 at the University of Copenhagen, includes Anni Haahr Henriksen, Frank Ejby Poulsen, Natalie P. Koerner and many other scholars to whom this sub-section is indebted.

80 Jagodzinski, *Privacy and Print*, p. 12.

81 Frank Ebjy Poulsen, 'Towards a history of privacy: conceptual and methodological considerations', The Danish National Research Foundation Centre for Privacy Research, University of Copenhagen, digitised on 25 October

2019. https://privacy.hypotheses.org/author/privacystudies [accessed 25 August 2020].

82 Anni Haahr Henriksen, 'Roads not taken and the reflexive pronoun in the Edwardian homilies (1547)', The Danish National Research Foundation Centre for Privacy Research, University of Copenhagen, digitised on 18 May 2020. https://privacy.hypotheses.org/author/ahhenriksen [accessed 25 August 2020].

83 Peter Clark, 'The ownership of books in England, 1560–1640: the example of some Kentish townsfolk', *Schooling and Society*, ed. Laurence Stone (Baltimore, MD: Baltimore University Press, 1976), pp. 95–111.

84 Catherine Burroughs, 'The stages of closet drama', *The Oxford Handbook of Georgian Theatre 1737–1832*, ed. Julia Swindells and David Francis Taylor (Oxford: Oxford University Press, 2014), p. 455.

85 Ibid., pp. 447–448.

86 Aphra Behn, *The Lucky Chance*, ed. Fidelis Morgan (1686, London: Virago Press, 1981), Act IV Sc. I. During its first performance in nearly 300 years by the Women's Playhouse Trust at the Royal Court, on this line Paul Bacon, playing Sir Cautious, flicked his eyes from the rake's face to the purse he was holding up. The house convulsed.

87 Richard Steele, 'On Nicolini's leaving the stage', *Poetical Miscellanies* (London, 1714), quoted by McGeary, "Warbling eunachs"', p. 4.

88 Stephen Watkins, 'The Protectorate playhouse: William Davenant's Cockpit in the 1650s', *Shakespeare Bulletin*, vol. XXXVII no. 1 (Baltimore, MD: Johns Hopkins University Press, 2019), p. 18.

89 Rutland House was in Aldersgate Street. Its environs were a safe district for royalists with both the Fortune and Red Bull theatres having been nearby. The former was only finally destroyed by Commonwealth troops in 1649. A number of grand royalist families owned houses in the street and ousted bishops retired there in the 1650s including Robert Sanderson, former Bishop of Lincoln, and Brian Walton, former Bishop of Chester. It was popular with littérateurs including Milton and Thomas Flatman. Christopher Matusiak has shown that the Cockpit, where Davenant moved next, was also a district noted as sympathetic to royalist activism and hostile to the government: Christopher Matusiak, 'Elizabeth Beeston, Sir Lewis Kirke, and the Cockpit's management during the English civil wars', *Medieval and Renaissance Drama in England*, vol. 27 (Hamilton, NY: Rosemont Publishing, 2014), pp. 181–182.

90 Watkins, 'The Protectorate playhouse', p. 18.

91 Ibid., pp. 4, 9–10, 13, 21. *Pace* Watkins, I do not think the Protectorate government ever saw Davenant as one of their own, despite his success at sustaining friendships with those well placed in the regime.

92 The agent's report is in the National Archives SP18/128, no. 108.

93 Watkins, 'The Protectorate playhouse', p. 26, n. 10.

94 C.H. Firth, 'Sir William Davenant and the revival of the drama during the Protectorate', *English Historical Review*, vol. 18 no. 70 (Oxford: Oxford University Press, 1903), p. 319, quoted in Watkins, 'The Protectorate playhouse', pp. 92–93.

95 Matusiak, 'Elizabeth Beeston, Sir Lewis Kirke', pp. 181–182.

96 Robert D. Hume, 'The politics of opera in late seventeenth century London', *Cambridge Opera Journal*, vol. 10 no. 1 (Cambridge: Cambridge University Press, 1998), p. 20.

97 Ibid., p. 17.

98 Downes, *Roscius Anglicanus*, p. 33.

99 Andrew R. Walkling, *English Dramatick Opera, 1661–1706* (Oxford: Routledge, 2019), pp. 41–52. Watkins, 'The Protectorate playhouse', pp. 22–23. Both reference Colin Visser, '*The Descent of Orpheus* at the Cockpit, Drury Lane', *Theatre Survey*, vol. 24 (Cambridge: Cambridge University Press, 1983), pp. 46–49 and John Orrell, 'Scenes and machines at the Cockpit, Drury Lane', *Theatre Survey*, vol. 26 (Cambridge: Cambridge University Press, 1985), pp. 104–111.

100 Walkling, *English Dramatick Opera*, p. 45.

101 Samuel Pepys, *The Diary of Samuel Pepys*, ed. Robert Latham and William Matthews, vol. 2 (Berkeley: University of California Press, 1971), p. 165.

102 *Memoirs of Samuel Pepys Esq, FRS*, ed. Lord Braybrook, 2 vols (London: Henry Colburn, 1825), quoted by Barbara A. Murray, *Restoration Shakespeare: Viewing the Voice* (Madison, NJ: Fairleigh Dickinson University Press, 2001), p. 51.

103 Murray, *Restoration Shakespeare*, pp. 50–63.

104 In our own century this pasticcio was the inspiration for Jeremy Sams's pasticcio opera at the New York Met, *The Enchanted Island* (2011).

105 Downes, *Roscius Anglicanus*, p. 37.

106 John Dryden, *Albion and Albanius*, The Mermaid Series, *The Best Plays of John Dryden*, ed. George Saintsbury, vol. 2 (London: Ernest Benn Ltd, 1950), p. 224.

107 Michael Burden, 'The writing and staging of Georgian romantic opera', *The Oxford Handbook of Georgian Theatre 1732–1832*, ed. Swindells and Francis Taylor, p. 425.

108 Sonja G. Wermager, '"That hart may sing in corde:" defense of church music in the psalm paraphrases of Matthew Parker', *Yale Journal of Music & Religion*, vol. 6 no. 1 (New Haven, CT: Yale University Press, 2020), pp. 43–44, see note 49 for primary sources. Bernard Capp, *England's Culture Wars: Puritan Reformation and its Enemies in the Interregnum, 1649–1660* (Oxford: Oxford University Press, 2012), pp. 178–179.

109 Dryden, *Albion and Albanius*, p. 224.

110 Walter J. Ong, *Orality and Literacy, the Technologizing of the Word* (London: Methuen, 1982), p. 11.

111 Anthony Welch, *The Renaissance Epic and the Oral Past* (New Haven, CT: Yale University Press, 2012), p. 176.

112 The Academy reformers should be distinguished from the reform movement later in the century, typified by Gluck. The early century reformers wanted to guard the oratorical framework of opera, privilege text over music and prevent opera's drift towards entertainment. The later reformers wanted to

shake up the formulaic structures of opera seria, making it more musical and more entertaining rather than less. They introduced more ensemble pieces and choruses, increased the orchestral complexity and brought the singers closer to the score, allowing less room for improvisation.

113 Strohm, *Dramma per Musica*, pp. 11–12, 23–24.
114 Giovanni Mario Crescimbeni, *La bellezza della volgar poesia* (Rome, 1700) quoted by Robert S. Freeman, *Opera without Drama: Currents of Change in Italian Opera, 1675–1725* (Ann Arbor, MI: UMI Research Press, 1981), pp. 13–14. Strohm, *Dramma per Musica*, p. 123.
115 Welch, *The Renaissance Epic and the Oral Past*, pp. 175–177.
116 Ibid., p. 176.
117 Musically, it is an air on a ground bass, drawing attention to its own technicality; a stepping stone towards the instrumentation itself being the storyteller.
118 Modern directors of *A Winter's Tale*, *Dido and Aeneas* and *La Didone* confront the problem that modern audiences understand the self in psychological terms. Decisions have to be made about whether Leontes is jealous before the play begins or whether something in Hermione and Polixenes' conversation prompts his jealousy. Conservatoire productions of Purcell and Tate's *Dido and Aeneas* regularly explore the possibility that Dido's court *are* the witches; she is thus betrayed by her friends and confidants rather than people with whom she has no connection. William Christie and Clément Hervieu-Léger's production for Les Arts Florissant in Paris in 2012 depicted a blood-stained, emotionally drained Dido who no longer has the strength of will to shape her own future.
119 Rosand, *Opera in Seventeenth Century Venice*, pp. 122–123.
120 Ibid., pp. 47–49.
121 Ibid., p. 51 with original text in Appendix I/12d, p. 412.
122 Ibid. with original text in Appendix I/10, pp. 411–412.
123 Ibid., pp. 45–51.
124 Ibid., p. 44, original text, appendix I/8j, p. 410.
125 Colley Cibber, *An Apology for the Life of Mr. Colley Cibber, Written by Himself* (London, 1740, republished by John C. Nimmo, ed. Robert W. Lowe, 1889), pp. 99–105.
126 *Letters Writ by Turkish Spy* (Giovanni Paolo Marana), vol. 6, book II, letter X, 1662, trans. William Bradshaw (London, 1694), pp. 77–78. Marana wrote under the persona of an Ottoman spy writing home to Constantinople from Paris.
127 *King Arthur: or, the British worthy: A masque. By Mr. Dryden. As it is performed at the Theatre-Royal in Drury-Lane, … the music by Purcell and Dr. Arne* (London: printed for W. Strahan, L. Hawes and Co., T. Davies, T. Lownds, T. Becket and W. Griffin, 1770), p. 2.
128 Curtis Price, Judith Milhous and Robert D. Hume, *Italian Opera in Late 18th-century London, the King's Theatre, Haymarket* (Oxford: Clarendon Press, 1995), vol. I, pp. 2–4. Thomas McGeary, 'Thomas Clayton and the introduction of Italian opera to England', *Philological Quarterly*, vol. 77 no. 2 (Iowa City:

University of Iowa, 1998), pp. 171–186 and Alison Clark de Simone, 'The myth of the diva: female opera singers and collaborative performance in early eighteenth-century London' (unpublished doctoral dissertation, University of Michigan, 2013), pp. 48–67 and 194–210.

129 These were *Arsinoe* (1705), *Thomyris* (1707), *Love's Triumph* (1708), *Pyrrhus and Demetrius* (1708), *Clothilda* (1709), *Almahide* (1710), *Hydaspes* (1710) and *Etearco* (1711).

3

Pasticcio opera: the golden age

The self can act as/in another, the social or transindividual self is a rôle or set of rôles. Symbolic and reflective behaviour is the hardening into theatre of social, religious, aesthetic, medical and educational process. Performance means: never for the first time. It means for the second to nth time.

Robert Schechner, 'Restoration of behaviour', *Between Theatre and Anthropology*, 1984.[1]

The skills of the pasticciere rose in status during the eighteenth century; indeed, this could be argued to be a golden age for pasticcio as the practice produced more artistically complex operas and saw greater technical refinement across all its varied expressions. In this chapter I argue that the reason pasticcio was so widely embraced in this period was that it reflected the way in which people understood the self and that it complemented other elite practices such as collecting. Pasticcio was the preferred method of tailoring Italian art to meet Britain's new political and cultural needs, being used in neoclassical sculpture, painting and commodities as well as opera. Yet pasticcio was not just a method for tailoring art to recipients, it was also the method for constructing personal performances of civility, gender, class and culture. Since 1976 there has been a consensus that the eighteenth century's conception of the self was a performative one.[2] As Robert Schechner argued in the 1980s, people's behaviour in public could harden into theatre: iterations of the rites of civility accrued ever more formality and, like the arias of opera seria, tropes could be borrowed from one context and applied to another.

More recently, Judith Butler has argued that identity is not a natural thing revealed but a performance, sometimes consciously so, at other times unconscious; although her analysis concerns gender, it is, I believe, applicable to other fields of identity construction. Consequently, I adopt her use of performative 'in the sense of a dramatic and contingent construction of meaning'.[3] Neither Schechner nor Butler were writing about specific historic periods; the principal difference between eighteenth-century performances of the self and those described by Butler as a feature of modern society are that the former were profoundly self-conscious performances. The self-conscious performance of identity was an inheritance from the religious conflicts of the previous age but Georgian civility was a very different kind of performance to that of factional allegiance.[4] A considerable amount of Britain's art during the eighteenth century was focused on the need for national unity and reconciliation though advocations of civility and what might be called model personalities.

The second argument notes that eighteenth-century elites collected everything from antiquities to art, wine, animals, books and plants, and I propose that the ethos behind this spilled over into their attitudes towards performed art. From the point of view of its patrons, Italian opera was collected at the King's Theatre in ways that reflected on national prestige and an increasingly travelled elite. Successive managers of the opera house adopted methods, approaches and assumptions common to the collection of Italian art of all sorts. This chapter will also look sideways, observing the practice of pasticcio in other artforms such as sculpture, and discuss how pasticcio was affected by the increasing complexity of music.

Late-seventeenth- and early-eighteenth-century society in Britain was shaped by a reaction against the factionalism and conflicts which had characterised most of the earlier century. I argue that neoclassicism, a cult of civility and the quest for national unity were motivated and propelled by a need to counter ongoing legacies from the bitter divisions of the past; these three politico-cultural forces are written into artforms of all kinds up to the last decades of the century. The chapter also explores the increasing role of music in telling the story: it gradually rose to become an equal means of conveying the drama with the words and, by the century's end, became a greater means of telling the story. By the end of this arc, the psychological insights formerly conveyed by poetry and acting in spoken theatre were conveyed by music in opera. A slow transition can thus be discerned from music illustrating an operatic narrative, to becoming the medium of that narrative in itself.[5] The goal of replicating, in performance, the visual capacity of the human imagination went through a series of lulls and accelerations in this period. Innovations in visual depiction in both pictorial music and scenography gradually changed the relationship between staging and the audience's imagination.

1660s–1780s: Italian opera, English nationalism and the cult of civility

Reaction against the past

As an eighteenth-century ideal, a civil person belonging to the elite was formal in their manners, exercised careful judgement before committing to an opinion, was moderate and judicious in conversation, highly literate, well travelled and classically educated: an ideal code of behaviour subscribed to by most European countries. In theory, such codes were the spontaneous result of good breeding rather than forced study, ambitious emulation, or spur-of-the-moment performance, but they were framed in opposition to earlier, more profoundly sectarian, religio-political identities. These had originated in the Reformation and crystallised during the religious wars in Britain, Ireland, France, Germany, the Netherlands, Scandinavia and eastern Europe. Endemic sectarian wrangling had characterised many seventeenth-century societies, complicating transnational exchanges such as royal marriages and leading religious and political discourses to become emotionally charged very quickly. Some examples are given below.

Seventeenth-century ideologues did not merely hold an intellectual position, they expressed it performatively through personal identity: black clothing announced a person's Protestantism and David Trotter suggests that swearing became a social signifier of cavalier identity in the civil wars, a deliberate provocation to the biblical speech of Puritans.[6] What one called things, how one ate, what one wore all proclaimed one's ideological allegiance and eighteenth-century writers were very sure that the bloodshed, prejudice and endemic factionalism of their forefathers was due to such constructed identities. *The Spectator*, in 1711, has Sir Roger de Coverley look back at the society of his childhood as one so divided by sectarianism that civil life was all but impossible:

> My worthy friend Sir Roger, when we are talking of the malice of parties, very frequently tells us of an accident that happened to him when he was a school-boy, which was at the time when the feuds ran high between the Round-Heads and Cavaliers. This worthy knight, being then but a stripling, had occasion to enquire which was the way to St Anne's Lane, upon which the person whom he spoke to, instead of answering his question, called him a young Popish cur and asked him who had made Anne a saint? The boy, being in some confusion, inquired of the next he met which was the way to Anne's Lane, but was called a prick-eared cur for his pains, and, instead of being shown the way was told that she had been a saint before he was born and would be one after he was hanged ... Sir Roger generally closes this narrative with reflections on the mischief such parties do in the country.[7]

Between the 1660s and 1720s codes of civility were active challenges to the sectarianism of preceding generations. Before the civil wars, Roman Catholics, Church Catholicks,[8] low-church Episcopalians and Puritan groups of multiple shades made alliances with each other or developed implacable differences until, gradually, they coalesced into the two umbrella groups who fought those wars. During the long protectorate, royalists and Parliamentarians unravelled again into separate, competing groups.[9] New religio-political factions were formed such as the Presbyterians, Independents, Quakers, Levellers, Fifth Monarchy Men, Sealed Knot and still others in Scotland and Ireland.[10] When the Whig and Tory parties emerged in the Restoration period, they were also composed of smaller factions and were also frequently on the brink of balkanising, a pattern which continued long into the eighteenth century.[11] The one common feature of all seventeenth-century identity groups was a desire for hegemony. Despite their ideological heterogeneity the *ambition* of each religious faction was remarkably homogeneous in that they all sought to proscribe rival ideologies and establish a monopoly for their own. The hubris felt by each faction was more than matched by their paranoia about the others and mutual toleration was all but unthinkable.[12] This was the poisonous and checkmated climate against which the generation at the turn of the eighteenth-century reacted: the new generation's cult of civility was thus a containment strategy and one which would make great use of artforms such as opera.

After 1660, a new generation of scholars understood that their bitterly fragmented society could not be healed by the victory of one faction over another, but only by the creation of a common, shared culture in which people of all factions felt they had a stake. The promotion of an English national identity was one strand of this. The Latitude-Men were an influential group leading this reaction against factionalism; they included scientists, writers, clerics and thinkers such as John Tillotson, John Wilkins, Joseph Glanvill, Robert Boyle, Thomas Sprat and Edward Stillingfleet. Charles II was an active advocate. This broad network shared what might be termed neocavalier identities and were far from free of sectarianism themselves, but they sought to bury divisions and effect social reconciliation through religious and intellectual consensus. Factionalism was to be contained not by suppressing particular factions but by tolerating them and toleration was to be achieved through a more secular culture which prized commonality over factional allegiance. Latitudinarians recognised that the containment had to begin with changes in social behaviour.

Charles's court held plenty of factionalists but its culture of hostility to religious fanaticism and support for latitudinarian thinking spread through London and beyond. Speeches, sermons, newspaper articles, plays and, later, operas, were agents in recasting factionalism as a malign force. Instead, nationhood was promoted as something which demanded greater loyalty than any religious, political, economic or regional allegiance. Emergent nationalism underlies *King Arthur* and, perhaps, the interpolation of English storytelling tropes such as the witches, into *Dido and Aeneas*. Many artforms show a desire to write England (though seldom Britain as a whole) into the classical past, a desire still seen at the end of the century in the commissioning of new neoclassical sculpture, discussed later in this chapter.

For Parliamentary or Puritanical households, speaking as conscience dictated and acting spontaneously had been approved behaviour; the less a person governed their own tongue the more this allowed God to govern it instead and use the speaker as his conduit. The incomprehensibility of some of Cromwell's speeches may have been due to their being deliberately unprepared.[13] Rude speech had thus carried a sanction that dissenter groups inherited in the Restoration period and early eighteenth century, but new codes of civility gradually overcame this sanction. This can be seen by comparing two dinners, the first described by the first Lord Shaftesbury in his memoirs, and the second a generation or two later. It was customary at civic and state dinners to allow spectators to stand behind the diners and follow the conversation; travelling to just such a dinner in Tewkesbury with the town's bailiffs, Shaftesbury recalled that:

> part of our discourse had been of an old knight in the field, a crafty perverse rich man, in power as being of the Queen's Privy Council, a bitter enemy of the town and Puritans as rather inclined the Popish way. This man's character and all his story I had learnt of them. At dinner, the Bailiffs sat at the table's end; Sir Harry Spiller [the knight in question] and myself, opposite to one another, sat near them, but one betwixt. Sir Harry began the dinner with all the affronts and dislikes he could put on the Bailiffs or their entertainment, which enraged and discountenanced them and the rest of the town that stood behind us; and the more, it being in the face of the best gentlemen in the country, and when they resolved to appear in their best colours. When the first course was spent, and he continued his rough raillery, I thought it my duty, eating their bread, to defend their cause the best I could, which I did with so good success, not sparing the bitterest retorts I could make him, which his way in the world afforded matter for, that I had a perfect victory over him.[14]

This dinner is a performance arena where a wider politico-cultural dispute is acted before an audience of local notables. This was conversation as factional competition with statements of allegiance characterising the discourse; codes of hospitality or gentility fail utterly to contain the participants' antagonism. By contrast, in 1714 Nestor Ironside, the persona of *The Guardian*, gives seventeen rules for conversation in a programme of advice to a young man about how to conduct himself at a dinner.

> THOUGH good humour, Sense and Discretion can seldom fail to make a Man agreeable, it may be no ill Policy sometimes to prepare yourself in a particular manner for Conversation, by looking a little farther than your Neighbours into whatever is become a reigning Subject ... NOTHING is more silly than the Pleasure some People take in what they call *speaking their minds*. A Man of this Make will say a rude thing for the meer Pleasure of saying it, when an opposite behaviour, full as Innocent, might have preserved his friend or made his Fortune.[15]

This is also conversation as performance but the difference in behavioural codes is stark. Prepping for table discussions and exercising self-restraint were part of the new civility, which, if not entirely absent from the seventeenth century, came into its own in the eighteenth. For this period, social or economic goals were the aim and civility the method: it is the self which was displayed to advantage at a dinner, rather than the faction one supported. In 1733, *The Craftsman's* editor, discussing non-conformists and Church Whigs, noted how far society had come in realising latitudinarian ideals:

> Most men in the Kingdom are so far improved in their judgments, as to believe that *Heaven* is not so entailed upon any particular Opinion in Religion, as to sacrifice the *Liberties of their Country* in defence of them. The State of things in the Nation is greatly altered from what it was *forty years ago.* The *Dissenters* have neither that Rigidness among Them as formerly, nor the *Low-Churchmen* their ill-will to Them, as *neighbours* and *Englishmen.*[16]

A person's identity was not considered natural to them or ordained by God, as it had been in the Renaissance, and was unconfined by the nineteenth century's conception of a core personality or inner self. For eighteenth-century people the self was an elected choice, a matter of will: they were free to invent and reinvent themselves according to their milieu. This is not to say there were no negative sides to the self-consciously performed self: people often forced themselves to express the emotions appropriate to their constructed persona. Frightened men forced themselves to show courage and fight duels, women in arranged marriages forced themselves to love their husbands. Through elaborate performances these constructed selves were felt to become real and concrete. Behavioural codes varied in their specifics according to region, context, class and gender but the themes, parameters and content of what constituted 'polite conversation' became surprisingly homogeneous across the three kingdoms.[17] Opera, indeed theatre of all kinds, both reflected this culture of performativity and helped to create it.

A self constructed from a range of pre-existing manners, gestures, beliefs and conversation, where people's performances of their identity were consciously borrowed from each other to suit the occasion and changed when necessary, was refracted in the extensive use of pasticcio in eighteenth-century art. Pasticcio operas were not unchangeable canonical works, they were revised extensively at each revival and personal performances were similarly reconstructed to suit different social contexts: both were temporary and contingent. Flexibility was a virtue and social mobility commendable, thus it was considered admirable for a person to adapt their manners and conversation to very different types of company, as it was for operas to be adapted for different audiences.[18] The same distinction between similitude and plagiarism in pasticcio existed in social behaviour, and detecting someone copying the behaviour of others and passing it off as their own was cause for hilarity.

Restoration and early eighteenth-century Britain was a postconflict society and all artforms, including opera, were expected to highlight the message that toleration and flexibility were virtues and rigidity a vice. Depictions of unity feature large in both the visual and performed art of the period with consensus, harmony, love and civil peace being depicted repeatedly; neoclassical architecture and music both emphasised resolutions. Narrative art iterated these themes stylistically as much as in their plots and pasticci such as *Thomyris* (1707) are an example. This pasticcio showed the damage caused by two sides fighting each other and lauded the virtues of reconciliation, remorse and unity; its plot thus shows the latitudinarian message in action. The pasticciere of *Thomyris* was Peter Motteux; he based the libretto on a story in Herodotus and selected the arias with Johann Jacob Heidegger, who arranged them. They are from Scarlatti and Bononcini with new recitatives written by Johann Pepusch.

There are two sides in a brutal war: the freedom-loving Scythians led by Queen Thomyris, and the Persians – the bad side – led by the tyrannical Cyrus. Thomyris has won the war but the Scythian victory is not secure: the Persians still occupy Scythia and outnumber her forces. Her son, Orontes, who is also her general, falls in love with Cyrus's niece Cleora, who is one of their prisoners. Cleora also loves Orontes. Thus, an ideal and obvious solution to the feud is presented early on, but the thinking bred by endemic war and factionalism is presented as the obstacle to their marriage. The love story is complicated by Tigranes, a Persian ally of Cyrus who is also in love with Cleora and who is Cyrus's designated choice as her husband.

Despite the temptation to see the opera as having application to England and France, England and Scotland, or Stuart family politics, I suggest it is about the resolution of conflict in the abstract. Love, mutual respect, honourable behaviour and parental generosity are Motteux's panacea for bitter conflict, yet the opera is not so naïve as to suggest conflict can be resolved without straining those same family ties and factional allegiances beyond their breaking point.

The desired peace between Scythians and Persians is endangered by interloping factionalists, Tigranes on the Persian side, but also by Thomyris herself, who considers marrying Orontes off to the daughter of one of her own allies, in exchange for more troops. The allies of sovereigns at war are thus presented as the enablers of continued conflict and division; uniting Orontes and Cleora may offer the only sure path to peace, but the lovers themselves are torn between love and loyalty to their respective families and nations. At its crisis, when the conflict seems irredeemable, Tigranes rejects Reason itself which, given the age, is tantamount to losing his wits:

> Oh! Reason, leave me
> Life with thee is but a pain
> And will but grieve me.

Factionalists and disruptors of peace were seen as enemies to Reason in much eighteenth-century discourse and war, Motteux suggests, is where unreason leads. Tigranes notes that the external war he had been fighting has now become an internal one with his own senses. Cleora also couples falling for Orontes with falling captive in war; love is feared as a kind of defeat by those wedded to their faction:

> First by war, and you undone,
> Greater Dangers yet I shun.
> Cruel Prince, while you pursue me,
> Love, and you, may more undo me.

When Orontes believes he has lost Cleora, he determines to throw himself back into war and pursue it to the death. At this point, then, endangered sanity, defeat and despair have been visited on the lovers in direct consequence of loyalty to parents, family and faction. Thomyris herself equates her son's falling for Cleora with his army falling to the Persians. Among the libretto's many subtleties is the military language all the characters use to describe love, frequently terming it an invasion, a victory or a defeat. The world depicted is thus one where war has saturated the language of everything else; there is no civil society, nothing exists outside the war. The opera thus offered a stark message to its audiences: political peace comes at a price, loss of family identity, weakening of parental control and family dissension might be necessary. This would have resonated with many in the audience as marrying children into families from a different denomination or political faction was common. Marrying 'out' could be a battlefield and Motteux's narrative held a mirror to the fissures in a postconflict society, but he had solutions to advocate too. The turning point in the story is caused by a latitudinarian change of heart in the queen:

> Awhile tho' Conquest charms me,
> Compassion soon disarms me,
> And melts my tender heart.
> Let Pity do her Part
> The greatest Joy
> We have
> Is when we kindly save
> Those whom we may destroy.

Thereafter, Tigranes and Orontes become friends, respecting and honouring each other, even though they are still rivals in love, and still on different sides in the war. In essence, they become gentlemen who rise above their differences. Later the war goes against the Scythians and Orontes becomes a prisoner of Tigranes, who promptly frees him in an act of noblesse oblige. Neither wishes the other's death yet neither, with honour, can lose the war they are sworn to fight.

A party of Scythians attack Tigranes at the end of his aria and he is badly injured, but Orontes arrives to rescue him. The three lovers are reunited and Tigranes, as a wounded man, nobly gives up his claim to Cleora, who pities him. Codes of civil behaviour triumph and the latitudinarian message is underlined. Thomryris agrees to let Orontes marry Cleora and, at this moment, we might expect a straightforward joyful finale; but there is a hiccup: Cleora is still a Persian and, though she wants to comply, she doubts she can betray her people so easily:

> Oh! Ask no more what Fate's denying.
> Let me rather share the Ruin,
> All my Persian Friends pursuing,
> Than blush at my complying.

Orontes stomps off, saying he will sue no more, but Cleora calls him back and asks only for more time to dry her tears. Motteux's meditation on factional conflict is too sincere for him to suggest that entrenched loyalties can be abruptly cancelled by dynastic marriage. In a moment of verisimilitude, it is recognised that the ending of factionalism takes time. The final chorus trumpets the virtue of unity:

> Love and Vertue the Conquest obtain.
> Peace shall last;
> Freedom by Union shall gain:
> All Danger is Past.
> Victorious,
> And Glorious,
> Astrea's Reign
> The Blessings shall maintain.

Astrea is Queen Anne, Thomyris being too bloodthirsty a character for that role to apply to her throughout. Although the union referred to might well glance at Scotland and England's, signed the same year as the opera, it is, I think, unity itself being promoted as a virtue and a source of civil freedom.

That operas of this kind were recognised as potentially subversive is demonstrated by John Dennis in *An Essay on the Opera's after the Italian Manner, Which Are About to Be Establish'd on the English Stage: With*

Some Reflections on the Damage Which They May Bring to the Publick (1706). In 1709, Steele, later quoted by Bickerstaff, describes a critic, who, attending *Pyrrhus and Demetrius*, expressed his concern, given Britain was at war, that Italian operas 'have already inclined us to Thoughts of Peace, and if tolerated, must infallibly dispirit us from carrying on the War'.[19] He might not have been directly referring to *Thomyris*, but he may as well have been. Suzanne Aspden notes that the verb from 'luxury', strictly used, means to dissipate, to expend, to disperse, and that the critic John Brown, saw luxury as leading the nation back to 'an Infinity of Factions'.[20] When the Scythians drive off the Persians in *Thomyris*, they capture Cyrus's tent, loaded with wines, drugs and other luxuries (in the modern sense). Once the Scythians are utterly enervated after sating themselves, the Persians come back and kill them all. Given the accusation that Italian opera was just such an enervating luxury, the irony was unlikely to have been lost on the audience. Motteux was attempting to have his cake and eat it by joining in the condemnation of luxury while still creating an opera, one he carefully distanced from the charge of being foreign.

The presence of Italian art itself prompted debate about how the newly united kingdom should interact with 'the other' discussed below, and Motteux was concerned to present pasticcio opera as reconciliatory in its very form. In his preface to the printed libretto, he argues that it marries the best in the British theatre tradition with the beauties of the Italian musical one.

> Though all the Airs of this Opera are by the famous *Scarlatti* and *Buononcini*, except a few by other great masters, neither the Words, the Thoughts, nor the Design owe anything to *Italy*, except the Advantage of the Musick; to which, with more Pleasure yet than Pain, I have endeavoured to make 'em subservient. I hope those who would not have Sense sacrificed to Sound, nor the Mind displeased while the Ears are entertain'd, will consider the Difficulties in working so many Airs of different Kinds into one Subject, and in putting Words wholly different from the *Italian*, to Songs … in a language perhaps too Manly for such Composures, if not managed with the utmost Art.

In trying to appeal to both opera sceptics and aficionados, Motteux assures the audience that, while the music is authentically Italian, the drama is not (thus allaying the anxieties of the xenophobic). Yet the drama is still subservient to the music (thus allaying the fears of aficionados that it might not be a proper opera). Motteux claims that the pasticcio process nativises Italian opera by allowing the expectations of spoken British theatre to still be met. Italian music might be superior in an effeminate sort of way, but the opera's use of the English language masculinises it and renders it fit for English audiences. How far Motteux himself bought into such chauvinism is open to question, but he recognised that many in his audience did and sought to reconcile them to the artform.

Civil society and the performed self is reflected in pasticcio

This sub-section explores how pasticcio practices in art reflected the pasticcio practices used in the construction of social identities and civil society. The performance of one's identity in the eighteenth century, perhaps more than in any other period, required considerable rehearsal and costuming. Necessarily then, there had to be a backstage area where the self was not being *consciously* performed, an area peopled by servants, apprentices, employees or close family members, who laced the stays, fixed and powdered the wigs, attached the mouse-fur eyebrows, tested the conversation, critiqued the attitudes and arranged the props. A person's conduct might differ greatly between onstage and offstage environments, as Boswell's journal shows:

> I went to St James's Church and heard service and a good sermon on 'By what means shall a young man learn to order his ways' ... What a curious inconsistent thing is the mind of a man! In the midst of divine service I was laying plans for having women, and yet I had the most sincere feelings of religion ... I am therefore given to love, and also to piety or gratitude to GOD and to the most brilliant and showy method of public worship.[21]

Boswell, talking to Johnson about his father, said 'I never believed what my father said. I always thought that he spoke *ex officio*, as a priest does', meaning that he thought his father's advice was the performance of a paterfamilial role rather than taking his son into his confidence.[22] The wealthier a family was, the more its servants conducted the backstage work so that family members could perform their identities to each other; such performances were given a neoclassical sheen with 'mater' and 'pater' being used as forms of address into the twentieth century and children being dressed as muses or classical characters. For those less well off, it was family members themselves who had to undertake these backstage offices so the performances of these families tended to be of the collective family identity and directed towards those outside. Novelists from Smollett to Edgeworth had much fun with this kind of performance; the preparations made by genteel families in straitened circumstances for visits by those wealthier than themselves was a standing comic trope in novels.

Just as the backstage area for a person's or family's public performances was something private, even secret, the construction processes for operas, sculpture and other arts were also hidden from public view. The unseemly haggling over contracts, budgets and publishing rights, the sometimes tense relationship between the librettist and the composer/arranger, the determinants of aria selection and the mistakes made in rehearsals were firmly hidden from all but insiders. That the Burney family were sometimes admitted to King's Theatre rehearsals shows how much they were considered to be insiders. Even today, casts often dislike strangers attending rehearsals: singing flat, missing entries and getting used to the set has to be corrected within the temporary family that is that season's company and outsiders are usually only admitted once the performance has reached a certain level of polish. That the creative process should be private was thoroughly accepted in a society where individuals also required such spaces for preparing their public self. Indeed, if by one accident or other this private space was suddenly laid public, or the method for constructing a personal identity or artwork abruptly exposed, the response was scandal, shock, laughter or pity.

In Frances Burney's *Evelina*, such an exposure befalls Madame Duval, a refined kind of pantomime dame. She is tied up in a ditch when their coach is attacked by highwaymen and she suffers the loss of her wig, revealing a bald head.

> Her dress was in such disorder, that I was quite sorry to have her figure exposed to the servants, ... however the disgrace was unavoidable ... Her head-dress had fallen off; her linen was torn; her negligee had not a pin left in it: her petticoats she was obliged to hold on; and her shoes were perpetually slipping off. She was covered with dirt, weeds and filth, and her face was really horrible, for the pomatum and powder from her head and the dust from the road were quite *pasted* on her skin by her tears, which, with her *rouge* made so frightful a mixture, that she hardly looked human.[23]

This is the comeuppance of an infuriating character, but her humiliation is horrifying and compels sympathy more than laughter, especially to twenty-first-century readers. Burney is acutely aware that the stripping away of the performed self and revelation of the unpolished, unprepared self was not just breaking a taboo, but a violation of the person so exposed. Exposing the method by which a restored antiquity or a pasticcio opera had been constructed was not quite such a violation, but still an impertinence. To dissect a pasticcio in order to identify its constituent parts ran counter to a social pattern in which the division between construction and performance was also between private and public. This is another reason, I suggest, why intertextuality was seldom something expected or desired in the reception of pasticcio operas: it was rude. This is not to say it did not happen, of course, and examples can be found of intertextuality intended to be noticed by the audience, but, proportionately, the methods used to construct them were no more public than those of original operas.

Between the 1790s and 1830s the performed self was gradually rejected as outdated and socially unreliable. The civil wars, by then, were far out of living memory and the behavioural codes forged in reaction to them were now subject to a reaction themselves. Hall-Witt quotes Judith Lewis: '[t]he social role, so important to the polite world, was now regarded as a mask of artifice'.[24] The nineteenth century was a time of inveterate examination of backstage areas, in politics, theatre and in the human character. These areas lost their privacy and, as ways of constructing the self changed, so pasticcio practices in art also found themselves exposed, questioned and challenged, as we discuss in Chapter 4.

English nationalism and Italian opera

As Suzanne Aspden, Linda Colley and others have noted, Englishness became a self-conscious performance whenever the 'other' was encountered; Colley argued that 'Britishness was superimposed over an array of internal differences in response to contact with the Other'.[25] Yet the potential for nationality to be a unifying force was compromised from the beginning as the qualifications for belonging to the nation were defined very narrowly. To be British was to be pro-Hanoverian, English-speaking, English in culture and Anglican. Those who did not express all of these characteristics were left in no doubt that they possessed only a contingent membership of the nation. The cultures of Scotland, Ireland and Wales were viewed as just another kind of potentially destabilising faction, along with non-Anglican denominations.[26] Such identities were to be firmly contained, and Catholics and Dissenters remained disenfranchised by the Test Acts until the nineteenth century while intermittent, underfunded and thus unenforceable legislation for anglicisation was periodically introduced into the non-English countries within the islands. The presence of a rival dynasty over the water offered a focal point for the discontent of those who did not fit the approved national identity. In consequence, unity remained fragile: the Jacobite rebellions were instances of how suddenly discontent might flare into armed conflict, so the possibility of factionalised disintegration felt very real up until the last third of the century.

Colley and Aspden argue that it was antipathy to the foreign Other, France in particular, that defined Britishness.[27] I suggest that Englishness was defined by antipathy to the internal Other. Britishness was more reluctantly invoked in England, being more a diplomatic civility towards the other peoples in the islands than a new, unified identity for the three kingdoms. London's Italian operas could promote national unity through their plots, as we have seen, but the metaperformance of going to the opera in itself helped to define the relationship between Englishness and the wider world. Like military reviews, royal festivals and state occasions, the opening of the opera season was an event at which those who felt themselves to embody the best of the nation could perform its newfound unity and confidence. A principal purpose of this performance was for the nation-in-microcosm to display itself to each part of itself, as Hall-Witt has demonstrated, but also to the wider world which was present in the form of the opera itself. Italian opera was beautiful but extraneous, a foreign artform in which Catholic people performed in Italian. The audience met it by performing their Englishness back in response.

Those who embraced Italian opera did not see their attendance as compromising their patriotism; they parried accusations of unpatriotic conduct through a useful narrative: the outside world had come to lay its artistic riches at the feet of a resurgent England. The presence of Italian opera in London was thus presented as an act of tribute to a nation which had come of age, which tribute they were gracefully accepting. This narrative was promoted in a variety of media and discourses including poetry. In May 1740 'G.O.', on hearing *Alexander's Feast* and *L'Allegro, il penseroso ed il moderato* addresses Handel in *The Gentleman's Magazine* as the Britannia of Music:

> ... uncontested is in song thy sway
> Thee, all nations, where 'tis known, obey:
> E'en Italy, who long usurp'd the lyre
> Is proud to learn thy precepts and admire.
> What harmony she had thou thence didst bring
> And imp'd thy genius with a stronger wing;
> To form thee, talent, travel, art combine
> And all the powers of music now are thine.[28]

Despite stretching the point by claiming Italy now learns how to make opera from Handel, the poet sees him as embodying British music and triumphing over other nations, as he felt Britain was doing economically and militarily. Handel collects Italy's harmony and brings this spoil home to Britain; this strengthens him and, to his own and Britain's talents, travel and foreign art bring Prospero-like powers. Those less cosmopolitan, and who definitely did feel threatened by Italian opera, thought the whole thing was dangerously un-English. Joseph Addison, Richard Steele and especially John Dennis typify this stance. They feared the popish luxuriousness of Italian art would sap the manliness of an unwary ruling class and even undermine the new unity which was putting nation before faction.

Tim Neufeldt has argued that Italian opera's insistence on Greco-Roman representations of Arcadia was another irritation for such opera sceptics, most of whom were invested in anglifying classical locations.[29] We have already discussed Dryden and Purcell's drawing on English folklore traditions for the witches in the Carthaginian location of *Dido and Aeneas*. Aspden shows that anxiety about Italian opera offering different norms for gender and sexuality was linked closely to fears that domestic stability, that ongoing work of common endeavour, might disintegrate.[30] Opera sceptics also used poetry, but to affirm the purpose of England's theatres as being the confirmation and celebration of approved versions of English identity. In the same month as G.O.'s poem, a 'gentleman of Oxford' wrote about Italian opera singers:

> Britons! Away with the degenerate pack!
> Waft, Western Winds, the foreign spoilers back!
> Enough has been in wild amusements spent,
> Let *British* verse and harmony content!
> No musick once could charm you like your own,
> Then tuneful *Robinson*, and *Tofts* were known;
> Then *Purcell* touch'd the strings, while numbers hung
> Attentive to the sounds – and blest the song!
> Even gentle *Weldon* taught us manly notes
> Beyond the enervate thrills of Roman throats!
> Notes foreign luxury could ne'er inspire
> That animate the soul and swell the Lyre
> That mend and not emasculate our hearts,
> And teach the love of Freedom and of Arts.[31]

This poet had undoubtedly heard of Handel but probably did not count him as British. The underlying political purpose he believed music should serve lies in the penultimate line: music was to mend our hearts, an admission that even by 1740 it was felt the healing of the nation was not yet complete. Ironically, both Robinson and Tofts had sung in Italian in their opera performances and Purcell was a conscious imitator of Italian practice. I suggest that both these attitudes, though apparently inimical, are rooted in the same desire: to promote national unity. Underneath this desire, anxiety forms a subtext in both poems, that there should be no return to a past where Britain was three weak, riven and unstable kingdoms.

The conception of Italian opera as tribute laid at the feet of the British aristocracy can be seen in discourses surrounding the collection of other kinds of Italian art. The vast sums spent on sculpture, paintings and antiquities were justified in the same way but, while these could be privately owned, opera had to be enjoyed publicly. Nevertheless, I suggest Italian opera was collected by the King's Theatre, its trustees and patrons, on behalf of the British elite in much the same way that art and antiquities were collected by private families. In some ways, then, the opera house served the same function as national collections would; it testified to the long reach of a powerful nation who could extract continental art through its strong currency and international standing.[32]

Italian opera and British collecting

The supporters of opera in Britain take a collector's approach

While a collection is an assemblage of pre-existing objects, it is not necessarily narrative and not an artform in itself. Nonetheless, I propose that eighteenth-century pasticcio approaches to creating opera complemented the period's approach to collecting in a number of ways. Collections that were displayed often did have narrative purposes. Sometimes they used classiccal antiquities to reify neoclassical interpretations of the past, to portray certain gender or sexual behaviours as timeless, to create material depictions of a family's heritage or to write Britain more visibly into classical history. Choices of what was displayed and what was stored away, where each part of the collection was placed in relation to the others, and changes made to the objects themselves in preparing them for display are all techniques shared with pasticcio opera. Like the eighteenth century's construction of the self, collecting is an example of how pasticcio methods were embedded in the period.

Italian art and antiquities were acquired on a vast scale by the British elite in this period with collectors exulting in the high purchasing power of sterling.[33] The enjoyment derived from Italian opera by the Beckfords, Legges, Grosvenors, Hamiltons, Townleys, Butes and Walpoles closely resembled that derived from their material collections of Italian art. Both served as portals through which imagined classical otherworlds could be touched or animated. Tellingly, the processes for acquiring art and opera were almost identical. Private collectors and the King's Theatre both had agents in Italy who were authorised to keep their patrons informed of what was coming onto the market. These agents were commissioned to purchase objects or hire singers by drawing money from Italian banks at which their patrons held accounts. The King's Theatre held its account with the Orsi banking house in Florence for over thirty years but this house was also used extensively by Britain's sculpture, painting and antiquities collectors.[34]

In her study of one such agent, Francesco de' Ficoroni, Tamara Griggs argues that agents were mainly Italian in the first half of the century but gave way to British dealers in the second half, men like Thomas Jenkins, Richard Wilson and, later, Richard Dalton and James Adam whose clients included George III, James Byres and Gavin Hamilton.[35] Apart from dealers, those with official diplomatic positions in Italy or who were wealthy residents often acted as ad hoc agents for friends and relatives. Such were Lord

3.1 Francesco de'Ficoroni, contemporary caricature by Pier Leone Ghezzi, undated.
Source: Congresso di archeologi di Roma, Biblioteca Apostolica Vaticana, Ott. Lat. 3116 fol. 191.

Cowper and Sir Horace Mann in Tuscany, and Sir William Hamilton in Naples.

Griggs emphasises that Italian agents like Ficoroni were published scholars, archaeologists and respected conservators as well as dealers. They were called antiquari, distinguishing them from the local guides, the ciceroni, whose status was lower. Antiquari were often collectors in their own right; this was true of Ficoroni and Giuseppe Bartoli, the professor of Greek at the University of Turin, and antiquaro to the King of Sardinia. Ficoroni had no prince or pope as a regular patron; instead, he made his fortune from, and trusted his protection to, the French, German, and British tourists who came to Italy to collect. Despite retaining the terminology of patronage when dealing with collectors, Griggs points out that Ficoroni's relations with them were thoroughly commercial. She argues that Ficoroni is one instance of an international trade in art and antiquities outdistancing the power of princely treasure-trove laws. That said, Ficoroni and other agents periodically faced vicious attacks on their reputations by the defenders of princely prerogatives; Ludovico Muratoni insisted that antiquities unearthed in the Papal States should automatically be the property of the pope.[36]

Many agents were both recruiters of opera singers and traders in art, a combination which continued into the nineteenth century. Owen Swiney, an escaped bankrupt and formerly successful opera impresario, recruited singers for Handel as did Francis Colman the Elder, British Resident at the court of Tuscany. Swiney also sourced art for his patron the Duke of Richmond and Colman for his brother-in-law William Pulteney, Lord Bath and others.[37] From the 1760s, as more French, German, eastern European and British agents joined the market, greater specialisation occurred. In the 1780s, King's Theatre staff including Peter Crawford and Leopoldo de Michele travelled in Italy on a recruiting visit, but we do not find them dealing in art and antiquities at the same time, nor did Gavin Hamilton recruit opera singers.[38] Michael Kelly remarked of his time in Italy from the late 1770s to the 1780s, 'I never had any taste for antiques'.[39]

The exception to this trend was Lord Cowper, who retained a close involvement in the art trade while continuing to act as an agent for Giovanni Gallini, who managed the King's Theatre during the 1780s. Cowper recommended both opera house staff and singers, and advised on new operas and on which scores to purchase. He was well aware that considerable alterations would be needed to reshape the operas he was sending and sometimes recommended detached arias either as concert pieces or for interpolation. As well as his agency in opera he still obliged aristocratic visitors who were collecting art, introducing Allan and John Ramsay, father and son, to the artists Giuseppe Fabrini, Vicenzo Giannini and another named Pascinio.[40] At the same time that he was acquiring the *Holy Family* by Fra Bartolomeo from the Salviati family, through the agency of Vincenzo Gotti, Cowper helped John Udny, the English consul at Livorno, acquire the *Adoration* from them.[41] Udny also recruited singers for the King's Theatre in the early 1770s and late 1780s.[42] John Ramsay's diary shows that they all attended the opera in Florence together, along with Donato Orsi of the banking family who provided the liquidity.[43] It was a small world.

The patriotic fig leaf of art-rendered-as-tribute coloured the language of purchasing, which often sounded more appropriate for prizes taken at war than for shopping. In 1726 Conyers Middleton wrote to Ficoroni, ostensibly to compliment him on the large showroom of antiquities he stocked at his home:

> I intend among other things to utterly despoil you – strip you of all your possessions – and I know what reinforcements would be needed to carry off such an assault. That house of yours is so stuffed with riches, so heavily defended by battle hardened troops, that I realise it can hardly be taken without a great onslaught of money.[44]

3.2 Gentlemen at the house of Sir Horace Mann, a caricature by Thomas Patch,
c.1765.
Source: Currently at the Yale Center for British Art, Paul Mellon Collection.
Released under Creative Commons Licence.

Griggs notes the aggressive undertone to Middleton's humour, the language
of piracy, raiding and sacking but with money rather than troops. Outbidding
a continental rival for an art purchase was considered patriotic, but the sale
did not always go Britain's way. France captured *The Westmoreland* in
1778, a 300-ton merchant ship which was packed with art, antiquities and
Italian luxury goods which young men on the Grand Tour were sending
home. The cargo ended up in Spain and was never returned.[45] There was
little sense on either side that Italian art or antiquities 'belonged' in Italy.
Despite reactive legislative action by Italian states to update their treasure-
trove laws and retain newly unearthed antiquities, these measures had little
effect and were weakly enforced. The Townley Marbles were officially
contraband when Charles Townley bought them from Gavin Hamilton in
the 1770s.[46]

   Another similarity between collecting art and collecting opera singers
can be found in the pricing. Charles Townley paid £700 for his statue of

3.3 The Townley Venus.
Source: British Museum, released under Creative Commons Licence.

Venus and £300 for his Thalia in 1777; Thomas Nugent's mid-century rates of exchange put the scudo at five shillings, so 2,800 and 1,200 scudi respectively.[47] This was a fortune in Italy; the annual salary of the Venetian army's chief of staff was 3,000 scudi.[48] It paid to work in Britain and Griggs describes the dealer Bernardo Sterbini trading regularly in England; on one visit, he brought 4,000 scudi worth of art and antiquities from Ficoroni's stock (equivalent to £1,000 sterling) but the profit margin would have been much greater.[49] When we consider the fees paid to Italian opera singers in

London, they correspond to the sums paid at this end of the art and antiquities market. Senesino's fee per season in 1720 was around £1,500 (6,000 scudi) while seven secondary singers received between £300 (1,200 scudi) and £1,100 (4,400 scudi).[50] The dancer Charles Le Picq was paid 1,700 guineas in 1782–1783, but that may have been for both seasons, and Madam Mara turned down £1,200 in 1786–1787, as she felt the workload demanded for it was too great.[51]

As Robert D. Hume points out, figures are effectively meaningless without knowing their spending power, and he argues that for most of the century 83 per cent of Britain's population earned less than £50 per annum, 94 per cent earned less than £100 per annum, while available figures suggest those who had the resources to attend the opera regularly were about 0.8 per cent.[52] When compared to the fees earned by actors or instrumentalists, those paid to Italian opera singers are exorbitant indeed but, to understand the willingness to pay such sums, Italian singers should be bracketed amongst other, more material, kinds of Italian acquisition. National pride in having an Italian opera house in London was an echo of the pride felt by having a Roman bust in the hall or a Titian in the drawing room.

Given that objects and people were collected using much the same process and for similar sums, it is not surprising that the difference between them could sometimes be forgotten. William Beckford of Fonthill Abbey was both an art collector and an opera enthusiast; a friend of Pacchierotti, he also commissioned chamber operas for his private musical events, hiring his own singers through the same contacts that he used to buy art, including Sir William Hamilton and Lord Mount Edgcumbe.[53] The Beckford fortune had been founded on slave labour in the West Indies and the family remained pro-slavery throughout the century. William's cousin Peter Beckford also took a commodified approach to people in his relationship with Italy and, in an act of consummate objectification, he purchased outright the young musical prodigy Muzio Clementi from his father in 1766.[54] That this was a purchase not an adoption, fostering, pupillage or any kind of articling is demonstrated not only by the purchase agreement but by Clementi's treatment. He was taken to Fonthill, received virtually no training and was essentially kept as a possession. Nevertheless, he developed into a fine composer and musician. Singers were bargained over and competed for but engagements could be cancelled at the last minute leaving them without work for months to come. Their payments could be delayed, extra work could be demanded from them within the same fee and their freedom to sing outside their contracts was severely controlled.[55] Julius Bryant describes similar treatment meted out to sculptors by their commissioners and emphasises the toll that cancelled, unpaid or uncollected commissions had on their mental health.[56]

The most significant overlap between collecting and opera was that pasticcio was also widely practised in preparing individual sculptures, paintings and antiquities for display. They were often restored using pre-existing parts; interpolations were made and sections were substituted for others; reinterpretations and shifts in meaning were common; and the resulting display was thus a kind of performance. This is also found in furniture, architecture and wine making: opera was not unique. While the techniques themselves necessarily differ from artform to artform, common purposes, methodologies, aesthetics and ethical parameters are discernible. The reconstruction process for damaged statuary, for example, had little to do with recovering a statue's original meaning or purpose in the way modern archaeology understands such recovery; statues were, effectively, constructed anew and purposed towards contemporary interpretations of the classical past. The repairs were sometimes left deliberately visible so that viewers knew they were looking at a pasticcio not an attempt to forge an intact sculpture, or an idealised copy. An innovative use of pasticcio in one artform was soon taken up by the others: when the acceptability of certain gender behaviours changed, pasticcio methods were used to bring art objects into line with new expectations. The use of pasticcio in sculpture is another indicator of its being a widespread method rather than a discrete genre within opera.

Pasticcio in other artforms

Joseph Nollekens began his career in 1761 by combining authentic fragments into complete sculptures and by making marble copies of antique originals, copies which could show considerable amendment as Julius Bryant notes. Piranesi created torchères and other furniture out of architectural salvage.[57] The Cavaceppi studio were expert in refinishing the entire surface of statues so that new heads or limbs were undistinguishable from antique bodies. Surfaces were given the perfect finish of freshly created works and Carlo Albacini, their star pupil, was particularly expert. The Venus Kallipyge was a Roman statue of the late first century rediscovered in Rome in the late sixteenth century. Missing its head, it was first restored about the time it was found and then again by Albacini in 1786. He replaced the head, arms and one leg, so this might be considered a pasticcio sculpture.[58]

In fitting the heads and limbs of one or more statues onto the torso of another, a new story was being told with pre-existing materials. The sixteenth-century restorer of the Venus Kallipyge recreated the figure as looking over her shoulder, a decision which greatly influenced later interpretations. In the

3.4 Venus Kallipyge.
Source: Museo archeologico nazionale di Napoli, released under Creative
Commons Licence.

eighteenth-century these ranged from Venus arising from her bath to the
foundation legend of her temple at Syracuse. It may be, of course, that
the original head had a different gaze, expression or hair and thus was
referencing a very different narrative. The parallel between such restored
sculptures and pasticcio opera are clear, but again, intertextuality was clearly
unintended in the reception: no one was invited to imagine the original
sculpture from which a section was taken to become Venus's new leg.

Venus's gaze is directed to her buttocks which, if this *is* what the original head was doing, may have had a narrative purpose, since the exposure of sexual body parts in Greek statuary, anasyrma (ἀνάσυρμα), is a comedic trope in a narrative where the leading character's mourning, distress or fear is broken by a lower-status figure exposing themselves out of pique at an assumed insult. In its more heroic register, warriors perform the act in scorn of their opponents. For early-modern male gazers, however, the need to dissociate the appreciation of art from erotic pleasure, to peek but not to sin, was an imperative. The restored figure glances at her buttocks with an expression suggesting she is in a private context, dressing, bathing, or alone, and unconscious of the viewer; the statue was thus brought into line with the eighteenth century's conception of a backstage area for the preparation of the public self: a private space it was taboo to enter. The original, if the anasyrma theory is correct, may have a had a more directly erotic, comedic or combative expression, consciously directed at the viewer. None of this would have been acceptable for display in the sixteenth to eighteenth centuries; definitions of female virtue and the parameters clamped onto permitted behaviour proscribed the depiction of female sexual agency in iconography, especially if used to challenge, jeer or insult.

Pasticcio in opera performed similar tasks; many of the gender behaviours permissible in Italian stage conventions were problematic or unacceptable in Britain. House poets laboured to put operas into a shape that would pass through the Lord Chamberlain's office uncensored and meet the audience's codes of acceptability. An aria listing sexual conquests by the Marchese Calandrano was cut from *Il curioso indiscreto* (1785) and throughout the century different kinds of swearing were cut. What went far beyond the pale for British audiences, and which pasticcio practices were used to remedy, was any suggestion of how Britain itself was seen on the continent. Domenico Cimerosa and Giuseppe Petrosellini's *L'Italiana in Londra* (1778) was performed widely across Europe and contained fairly mild mockery of British behaviour and preoccupations. Yet the London staging in 1788 renamed it *La Locandiera* and relocated it in Holland; stripping out any references to Britain whatsoever. The vaunted national characteristic of the British as able to laugh at themselves was not something the Italian staff at the King's Theatre felt they could rely on in practice. The overlap with sculpture is the need to remould operas to accord with the cultural parameters of the present; a visit to the museum they most definitely were not.

If a statue was discovered during an excavation, first came identification. Neoclassical expectations played a role in this, with a Hermes, Cleopatra or Venus being declared on the basis of the figure's 'attitude'. What may have been the original gesture or pose was identified by relying on eighteenth-century interpretations of oratorical gestures described in classical texts, or seen on more complete statues. The statue was then restored to demonstrate this presumed pose using fragments from other sculptures. Not every pose was oratorical; statues were also restored so as to hint at or even directly illustrate a narrative which attached to that deity or historical figure. The process in both operatic adaptation and sculptural restoration thus involved parody of the original to create an overall unity of style. Christian Heyne, in an unconscious echo what Ausonius had said about the cento, wrote in 1779 '[r]estorations must be so skilfully made that the eyes will not be disturbed but deceived'.[59]

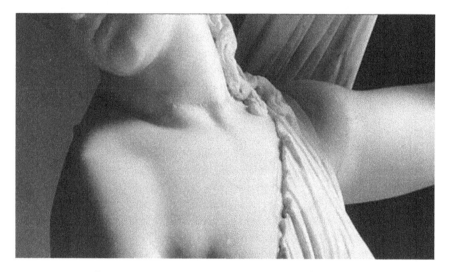

3.5 Venus Kallipyge, detail of Albacini's discreetly exposed suture between the head and torso.
Source: Museo archeologico nazionale di Napoli, released under Creative Commons Licence.

Restorers like Albacini certainly had the skill to disguise the outlines between the restored and original sections but they sometimes left them visible. The reason, perhaps, was that restoration was freely admitted. Despite Heyne's recommendation, eighteenth-century collectors felt no need to deceive the viewer about the work being a pasticcio; restoration was an homage to the original sculptor, in the Renaissance manner, and similitude was the aim, not plagiarism. The restorer's skill was thus something to display rather than hide. Those operas where changes and revisions are clearly apparent, such as the French fragments d'opéras and pasticci such as Bertoni's *Cimene* at the King's Theatre in 1783, perhaps have a similar motivation. Albacini was more than capable of using finely powdered marble to make his sutures invisible, just as Haym, Handel, Cherubini and Bianchi were capable of parodic composition or text when they needed it. Reconstructed statues and operas reflected their purchasers' requirements or audience's expectations, not the intentions of the original sculptor or composer. It was only in the last two decades of the century that operatic performances grew closer to how they were staged in their place of origin, and much longer before they were staged according to the original intentions.

The display of statuary and paintings in aristocratic households was performative: beholders were invited to associate their current owners, and Britain's current empire, with ancient oligarchies and empires. Applications and parallels were enhanced when busts of the collector, dressed in Roman senatorial garb, were placed among genuinely Roman ones in the entrance hall, in imitation of those in Roman villae suburbani. Britain's sculpture halls were emulations of those in Italian palaces, as David Adshead shows, and their theatricality is demonstrated by the care taken over spacing, grouping, the tincture of the paint on surrounding walls and, above all, the lighting; this was both natural and artificial, and use was made of large mirrors and torchlight.[60] In 1766, William Patoun recommended:

> Go to the Belvedere at Night and see the Apollo and Laocoon by torch Light … You may by this means throw what masses of Light and shadow you please and see a thousand delicacies that are unobservable in the Open Air in broad daylight.[61]

Groupings could be based on genre, but they could also relate mythological or historical narratives. While statuary formed what might be called a tableau mortant, paintings of action sequences relating to the same narrative hung on the walls. Reconstructed statuary and operas both aimed at the animation of the classical past, but through very different media; both sought a profound immersion in their beholders or audiences. Opera's myth that it was a recovery of the singing of ancient classical tragedies was balanced by sculpture's revivification of authentic but long-buried fragments. The imaginative fervently wanted to enter the classical world and neoclassical art created a conflation of time which allowed them to make that journey. Pasticcio was a necessary tool in both artforms, and critical in realising neoclassical aims.

Music becomes a storyteller in its own right

While storytelling remained the core purpose of opera throughout the century, music gradually rose from subservience to the words to become a narrative medium in itself. This is most detectable over the last three decades, but instances of this trend can be found from much earlier on.

In the nineteenth century, critics would perceive music as the predominant storyteller in serious operas, although a harmonious balance between words, music and design was considered the optimum operatic achievement by the majority of reviewers. This transition from verbal to musical prominence is inextricably linked to the establishment of a culture based on literacy. This sub-section traces the movement of opera music from being the magical ingredient which empowered the words and aided thelxis, to creating its own narrative tropes through specifically musical idioms. This process necessarily shifted the aesthetics and practice of pasticcio. As orchestral scoring and aria settings became less formulaic, the easy swapping of musical sequences became more problematic. Stylistic unity became more important, so it took more time to create musical and literary homogeneity; this meant a greater reliance on parody, and *La villanella rapita* (1784) will be explored as a case study. On one hand, pasticcio operas became much more sophisticated as a result but, on the other, they were becoming more expensive to create.

Early stirrings

A snapshot of the beginning of the process can be seen in Apostolo Zeno's 1706 libretto *Teuzzone*, originally set by Antonio Lotti in 1708 and reworked as a pasticcio by Vivaldi in 1719. Zeno's *Teuzzone* is an example of a 'reform' libretto which followed the strict Aristotelian models of French spoken theatre, in this case Racine's *Bajazet* and Thomas Corneille's *Le Comte d'Essex*. Libretti of the reform movement followed the metre and content of spoken verse theatre as closely as an opera libretto can, even drawing on the pauses and stresses of spoken verse.[62] Music's role in reform opera, as with French tragédie lyrique, was confined to revealing and enhancing the rhetorical structures of the libretto, essentially to display its oratorical correctness.[63] The words were to carry the story and the music was merely to ornament the telling. Strohm discusses how both Zeno and, later, Vivaldi departed from the reform models of the Accademia.[64] While Zeno aimed for maximum fidelity to his French models, he sometimes consciously departed from them, not just to take account of the different pacing which occurs when dialogue is sung, but because he was aware that music can bring its own emotional colouring to the story. He trimmed Racine and Corneille's alexandrines to increase the pace of the drama and streamlined the narrative by reducing the number of dramatic incidents. It is truly a libretto, rather than a verse play.

When Vivaldi used Zeno's libretto to create his pasticcio ten years later, Lowell Lindgren shows that he used his own previous aria settings, so his *Teuzzone* is an autopasticcio.[65] Vivaldi made a number of changes to Zeno's text, partly to ensure the words sat well with the notes and partly to reflect operatic tastes in 1719, but, in the process, Strohm points out that he severed the last links between the libretto and the French spoken-verse models.[66] Instead of merely ornamenting the dialogue, Vivaldi used his music to dramatise the emotions, depict the metaphors and point up the key narrative moments in arias. Strohm's analysis provides numerous examples of how Vivaldi's scoring is faithful to the dramatic *intentions* of both Racine and Corneille, as well as those of Zeno, but uses music to convey them rather than relying on the cadences of speech, in this and in his other operas. Strohm's final assessment of *Teuzzone* is:

> It is rather an as yet immature attempt to 'musicalize' the drama as a whole: to seize responsibility for drama from the poet. The 'immaturity' of the attempt can be felt in the rather chaotic result for characters and affections in this opera. Music still needed to grow with the new challenge: the ability to express the whole of the drama could not be acquired overnight.[67]

In Britain, we encounter a similar transition from the distanced, austere dissertation on war, peace, honour and love driven by the libretto in *Thomyris* (1705), to the more affect-driven, emotional aria texts which Haym and others wrote for Handel, creating space for the music to tell the story.

Pictorialism

Eighteenth-century audiences showed great enthusiasm for pictorial music and Vivaldi is known today for the pictorialism of his best-known composition. In an article on Handel's opera seasons of 1737–1739, Ilias Chrissochoidis shows that this composer was moving in a similar direction and, when he created pasticcio operas, preferred to use music from composers who also sought to seize a dramatic role for their opera music.[68] Whether it was Vivaldi's sauntering bee in *The Four Seasons* or Handel's terrifying plague of flies in *Israel in Egypt*, eighteenth-century music 'painted'. Certainly, there are examples of the musicalisation of visual events long before this: Clement Jannequin's *La Chasse* (1541) is a choral work which includes mimicry of hounds on the scent, and both Jannequin and Gibbons scored the cries of street markets. Musicalisations of cantering horses, animal cries, thunder and lightning, battle sounds, rivers or streams were common and have continued as a practice, in varying forms, down to the present.[69] As discussed earlier, increased literacy brought with it greater imaginative complexity in the visualisation of stories. While this can be traced in novels, increasing sophistication in pictorial music during the eighteenth century is another of its facets; like enhanced scenography and costuming, it became a component of the visual experience of opera.

In *Saul* Handel introduced a carillon, a new machine to convey the sound of a city's pealing bells heard from far off. The city's celebratory peal for David's military victories is high-pitched and insistent, the bells' sound driving King Saul mad with envy. Handel also made an innovative use of trombones in this oratorio to signify the commands of God and borrowed the kettledrums used by the Tower of London for state ceremonies and executions.[70] These monumental sounds of church and state added to the pictorialism and are perhaps analogous to the use of cannons in nineteenth-century works celebrating military victories.[71] A second, contrasting, example is the concluding aria of his pastoral opera *Acis and Galatea* (1739 version), where the pulsing melisma over four bars given to the word 'glide' suggests both a heartbeat and a brook (No. 28).

> Heart, the seat of soft delight,
> Be thou now a fountain bright!
> Purple be no more thy blood,
> Glide thou like a crystal flood.

3.6 *Handel's Acis and Galatea, a Mask, as it was Originally Composed ... by Mr Handel*, (London: I. Walsh, before 1743), p. 81.
Source: Digitised by Petrucci Music Library (IMSLP), 2014; in public domain.

But eighteenth-century composers went further; the best pictorial music was considered to be that which succeeded at 'imitation', by which was meant the vivification of something which only existed in narrative.[72] As discussed in Chapter 2 and earlier in this one, this was something sought in neoclassical plays and sculpture as well as music. In his analysis of *Israel in Egypt*, Chrissochoidis describes Handel's highly innovative oratorio as

[p]ushing musical pictorialism to the edge[;] the orchestra often dissociates itself from the narrative chorus and becomes the action described. For example, the unisons in 'He spake the word' are followed by the mighty discharge of a thrice-repeated triad by three trombones (doubling the oboes); a clear reference to the Trinity … this instrumental signal, not the narrating chorus, instantly releases swarms of buzzing sounds in the auditorium that move faster than the chorus describing them as flies. Similarly, the chord pounding in 'He smote all the first-born of Egypt' is obsessive enough to cancel its function as accompaniment, leading us to feel these chords as the actual thrusts. The veil between representation and presence, between music standing for something else and embodying it becomes even thinner.[73]

Music was becoming a storyteller, rather than a tool in storytelling. Chrissochoidis shows how redundant the reform movement's strict tenets had become for composers like Handel: music now presented an image to which the words gave a name. Pictorialism now meant more than creating soundscapes or reproducing real-life events vocally or instrumentally, as Jannequin and Gibbons had done; it did not just tell audiences what something looked or sounded like but how they should feel about it. The best imitation *commented* on what it was conjuring rather than just depicting it literally. When Handel scored the plague of flies, he recreated the sound of a buzzing swarm of insects by using the strings in a highly literal way, but when he came to score the plague of darkness there was no sound to imitate. Instead of resorting to owls hooting and the cries of night-watchmen, the music conveys how menacing darkness can feel. The music evokes in the memory feelings about darkness and silence to conjure emotion and sympathy. That Handel consciously intended to provoke emotional responses to imitations is evidenced in his advertising and salon conversation. His conversations sometimes found their way into correspondence, such as that between Katherine Knatchbull and James Harris which refers to his depiction of darkness: 'the storm of thunder is to be bold and fine, & the thick silent darkness is to be expressed in a very particular piece of musick'.[74] In the oratorio *Samson*, how the audience should empathise with the protagonist's sudden blindness is conveyed in the aria 'Total eclipse' by musical idiom rather than by text alone. The music depicts something's absence through a bold use of rests to create moments of silence, silences which provide space to imagine the loss of sight; no one specific image is prompted. This kind of pictorialism was a further advance for music as a storyteller.

That pasticcio operas borrowed from oratorios is well known – they would also borrow from symphonies in the nineteenth century – and oratorios could themselves be a pasticcio. Handel recognised the failings in drama of *Israel in Egypt* in 1739 and rebalanced the oratorio using pasticcio methods, altering it again substantially in 1756. Yet there is a tension between oratorio and opera. Oratorio tapped into proto-literate storytelling in similar ways to madrigal comedies a century earlier, as the imagery occurred wholly in the audience's imagination rather than being depicted on a stage. One might then expect it to be difficult to incorporate pictorial music into operas which sought to pin the audience's attention on the stage and depict things scenographically or through action. But the popularity of pictorial music and its capacity to engage and immerse an audience made it irresistible: when the moment was right, Handel imbued arias with a pictorialism that turned the singer back into a storyteller. One example is the writhing snakes and furies in Dejanira's accompagnato in *Hercules*, Act III Scene III (1744). This is happening in Dejanira's mind so it is unlikely that scenery or dancers depicted any of the imagery.

> Chain me, ye Furies, to your iron beds,
> And lash my guilty ghost with whips of scorpions!
> See, see, they come! Alecto with her snakes,
> Megaera fell, and black Tisiphone!
> See the dreadful sisters rise,
> Their baneful presence taints the skies!
> See the snaky whips they bear!
> What yellings rend my tortur'd ear!
> Hide me from their hated sight,
> Friendly shades of blackest night!
> Alas, no rest the guilty find
> From the pursuing furies of the mind!

Moments of pictoriality, then, preserved within eighteenth-century opera, and within music generally, an older storytelling approach which relied on audiences imagining the musical imitation. The theatrical nature of much of the period's instrumental music was not monocausal, but pictoriality made a contribution in keeping music within a storytelling rather than a textual culture. This is not to say the textual framing of music did not increase during the eighteenth century, but long-standing, orally derived performance traditions were not discontinued as music developed.

Pasticcio, the use of instrumentation and parody

One of the changes detectable in the last third of the century is that pasticcio operas show an increased tendency to borrow from instrumental music as well as vocal. Nor was this just for overtures, entr'actes or ballets. While concerti had been reworked earlier in the century for use in cantatas such as J.S. Bach's Concerto No 1 was reused in Cantata 207.1, and No 3 revised for Cantata BWV 174, a discernible increase in the repurposing of instrumental music for vocal narratives can detected from the 1770s onwards. Repurposing of instrumental compositions was not confined to opera, it occurred in sacred music too: the minuet at the end of Thomas Arne's overture for *Artaxerxes* (1762) later appeared in Scottish psalmodies and by 1820 had been appropriated by St George's, Edinburgh under the name 'Princes Street'.[75] Vocal music was also repurposed as sacred instrumental music: Alina Madry notes the reworking of Mozart's aria 'Non piu andrai farfallone amoroso' from *Figaro*, as a symphony in C for performance in church services in Grodzisk Wielkopolski. This occurred within a few years of the first Polish performance.[76] In 1777, Samuel Arnold revised Gay's ballad opera *Polly* (1729), setting words to Jeremiah Clarke's 'March for the Prince of Denmark' (*c.*1700). In 1829, Nicholas Charles Bochsa would create ballet-opera from Beethoven's sixth symphony. Partly, this was a continuation of the baroque contrafactum but such borrowings were also a new response to the growing dramatic power of instrumental music itself.

This development was not without its critics: it transgressed against the classification systems so beloved of the period. Opera purists preferred to compartmentalise the uses of music very strictly and the pseudonymous 'Marcello,' in a letter to *The Morning Post* in December 1789, expressed his dislike of what he saw as blurring the line between vocal and instrumental. He accepted that opera was created in two ways – compilation (pasticcio) and composition – but objected to the new practice:

> A blemish, highly deserving of rebuke has lately crept into the English Opera. The music of a piece is said to be *composed* and *compiled*; but, on examination, airs are found referable neither to the class of composition or compilation but exhibiting an uncouth mixture of both.
>
> The manner of fabricating those strains of equivocal gender is, to select a melody from Haydn, his pupil Pleyel, or some other *instrumental* composer of eminence, and by much cobbling and botching, substitution of octaves, and inversion of chords, to bring it within the *vocal* compass.
>
> Such an operation, however, argues both poverty of invention and depravity of taste in the workman. Airs written for instruments *da prima intenzione*, can never be perfectly adapted to voices. Between these two species there is, and ought to be, a marked distinction, each possess its appropriate excellence and expression.

> On this subject, censure is the more necessary, as the vicious practice flies
> like contagion from the composer to the performer; and the human voice,
> instead of being considered as the most delightful found in nature, and its
> unforced inflexions only cultivated, is assiduously strained and tortured to
> imitate the fiddle and the hautboy.[77]

He backed up his objection that the practice damaged singer's voices by
two examples: Elizabeth Billington and Cecilia Young. These suggest that
the composer he had in mind as exemplifying the fault was Samuel Arnold.
Billington had recently sung in Arnold's English operas; according to the
European Magazine she sang Polly in a March production of either *The
Beggar's Opera* or Arnold's arrangement of *Polly*; probably the latter as
Macheath is described as being sung by a Miss Fontantelle. In June, Billington
sang Yarico in Arnold's revival of *Inkle and Yarico* in Drury Lane; certainly,
Arnold included sections which were difficult to sing in *Inkle and Yarico*
and he repeated instrumental introductions within the vocal lines, as Joice
Waterhouse Gibson discusses.[78] She also notes that additional verses were
added in the printed scores, *c.*1790.[79] Robert Hoskins describes Arnold's
creation of fine coloratura arias with flute obbligato but also his use of
woodwind and interest in using more complex instrumentation within opera
generally.[80] This may be what 'Marcello' is referring to, though his objection
was not truly a singer's objection since their issue with an instrumental
approach to scoring arias appears to be that it restricted the interpolation
of ornamentations rather than doing any vocal damage. Angelica Catalani's
hostility to this restriction was noted by Lord Mount Edgcumbe.[81]

Cecilia Young, Thomas Arne's wife, had died in the October of that year,
having not performed a role since 1774 (so far as is known). She had reduced
her performing career after the late 1740s through poor health which, it is
thought, affected her vocally. There is no evidence that her voice was ruined
through singing vocal music adapted from instrumental, but it is conceivable
that a rumour to that effect may have been current.

The incorporation of pre-existing instrumental sequences into operas
would increase and evolve in the next century; they would be used in operatic
melodrama to accompany action sequences and were already being used
to accompany visual spectacles such as magic lantern sequences, discussed
in Chapter 4. It was not all one-way traffic though, and the tropes and
structures of opera, oratorio and other dramatic vocal music also influenced
instrumental music as Charles Burney (1726–1814), Auguste Frederick Chris-
tophe Kollmann (1756–1829) and Heinrich Christoph Koch (1749–1816)
show.[82] Modern scholars including Nancy November, Michael Lively, Suzanne
Anita Bratt, Michelle Elizabeth Ayres and others have traced and discussed
the cross-pollination.[83] A requirement for a more unified musical prosody
was the gradually evolving consequence for pasticcio operas from the late

eighteenth century onwards. The requirement was met, largely, through a greater use of parody than earlier in the century. I propose that this particular technique was chosen because one by-product of the increasing complexity of music was that individual composers cultivated their own, distinctive, compositional style, what the twentieth-century would term a 'voice'.

Formerly, composers had written within the collegial style of particular courts, theatres, cities or regions. As discussed in Chapter 2, music could be intended to represent a region such as Venice or Naples over the course of its dissemination and Strozzi expressed irritation at variant versions of *La finta pazza* losing their Venetian character. London theatres had their own kind of campanilismo and in his memoirs Michael Kelly, as house composer at Drury Lane, was adamant that any music borrowed for use by his employer had to be reworked to suit that theatre. The growing individuality of compositional styles caused complications for pasticcio: the assembled parts could now be very different to each other stylistically and require reworking to reinstate a single collegial style. *La villanella rapita* (1783), discussed in the next sub-section, is an example of this with the pasticciere Francesco Bianchi giving the contributions of six composers the style of the Viennese Burgtheater. In later pasticci, such as those of Rossini, parody was used to give the whole opera the style of its principal contributor. Parody consequently required subtlety and greater attention to musical and literary detail than formerly; the lighter touch associated with nineteenth-century adaptations can be first detected in the 1780s. Pasticcio methods were thus a key tool in opera's acculturation to the narrative potential of instrumentation, yet the gravitational shift towards music as a storyteller should not be seen as a linear development.

When Luigi Cherubini composed *Giulio Sabino* for the King's Theatre in March 1786, it ran for only one performance. Price, Milhous and Hume conclude that Cherubini lacked the literary skills to identify the nodal points in the narrative, so his music did not compel attention to them.[84] Like many composers he was not working alongside a living librettist who could have identified the significant points in the drama for him. Even Mozart sometimes failed to mark central dramatic moments musically. There is not so much as a pause or crescendo in *Così fan tutte* to mark Dorabella's and Fiordiligi's shock when Ferrando and Guglielmo remove their disguises and reveal themselves as the pair's original fiancés. There is no allowance for a reaction of shock or surprise by the women in the score; instead, they jump straight to indignation.

If opera's progression towards musical storytelling is judged only from works which succeeded in their aims, then an artificial impression is created of a smooth linear progression in music's attempt to seize responsibility for drama from the poet, to use Strohm's words: it is presented as a bloodless revolution. The reality was that a sizeable number of composed operas failed to seize the drama. Music may have become a storyteller by the 1780s but could still, sometimes, be an inexperienced and clumsy one.

La villanella rapita

La villanelle rapita (1783) provides an example of how pasticcio operas remained au courant with music's new equality with the words, and of how additional compositional work was needed to create stylistic coherence. The opera also shows how new, contemporary, political and literary trends could be incorporated as an opera was changed from revival to revival.

Originally conceived as a pasticcio by the composer Francesco Bianchi in Venice in 1783, the music was assembled to serve a libretto by Giovanni Bertati. Leaving Bianchi aside, contributors included Sarti, Mozart, Naumann, Guglielmi, Paisiello and Ferrari. It was performed at the Teatro S Moisè in Venice, at the Eszterháza in 1784 and in Vienna in 1785, with two ensemble items contributed by Mozart: the finale of Act I and a quintet in Act II. The opera evolved again when it was performed in Paris in 1789 and in the year after that when it was staged at the King's Theatre, rearranged by Vincenzo Federici, who had only just joined the staff as house composer. Price, Milhous and Hume argue that Nancy Storace was the driving force behind this production, having played the lead, Mandina, in Vienna.[85] She was a friend and zealous supporter of Mozart and is known to have taken especial care with his arias and ensembles.

The methodology by which Bianchi initially created stylistic unity in the overall musical prosody is currently unknown. Contributors to *La villanella rapita* may have consciously toned down their own compositional idiosyncrasies, or Bianchi may have selected and then refined their contributions to achieve a required level of stylistic unity. Such unity, however, was not stylistic homogeneity and it would be a mistake to assume that a single, distinctive compositional voice was considered essential at this point in time: for audiences in 1780s Venice, Vienna, Paris and London, the general Viennese flavour of the music may have been unity enough. When played to people who are not music specialists today, the whole opera is easily misidentified as a composition by Mozart alone; indeed, Mandina's aria 'Bella rosa porporina' was thought at the time to have been written by Mozart, at least by the *Morning Herald*.[86] The selective nature of the canon, the nineteenth- and twentieth-century cult of Mozart and the modern accessibility of his music compared to that of many of his contemporaries have made him the most frequently heard composer from that period; consequently, to non-specialists, most other Viennese composers in this period also sound like Mozart. The aria changes made in Paris and London added non-Viennese arias to the performances, such as the duet by Martin y Solar discussed later in this sub-section, but as the piece evolved in successive revivals the underlying style of the Burgtheater remained.

The plot of *La villanella rapita* is pacy, dramatic and highly political.[87] Bertati explored the same themes as Pierre Beaumarchais's *Figaro*, pre-empting Mozart and da Ponte's opera of 1786, which *La villanella rapita* probably influenced. An imperious but louche count takes advantage of the innocence of a country family who are his tenants. They fawn on him and offer their loyalty at the beginning, but it is clear to the audience that he intends to seduce Mandina, one of the daughters. This is also clear to Mandina's fiancé Pippo who, in many ways, prefigures both Figaro and Gaetano Donizetti's Nemorino; Pippo struggles to convince the family of the count's real intentions. Much of the comedy derives from Mandina's excessive innocence which, at times, borders on idiocy. This allows for numerous double entendres and yet the politics has a decidedly sharper edge than in *Figaro*. The count grooms Mandina and, at the end of Act I, drugs her family, then, when they are too ill to see what is happening, abducts the daughter. 'Rapita', while literally translatable as kidnapped or abducted, implies abduction for sexual exploitation. He takes her to his town residence and Act II opens with her asleep, drugged, but wearing new clothes, presumably those appropriate for a mistress. This count is a darker figure than Almaviva: he is obsessed with Mandina and, in his determination to thwart her wedding to Pippo, uses his rank to force her compliance to his will. His failure to live up to the conduct expected of his rank is repeatedly emphasised and his obsession with control alienates even his best friend. The count is only brought to heel when Mandina's father reports him to a more senior noble within his family. Any possible recourse to the laws of the land is conspicuous by its absence. In the finale, the count is menaced into climbing down when the whole ensemble openly stand as one to oppose him and sing a resounding 'Signor, no!' Resolution through resistance rather than trickery gives Bertati's narrative a starker, more direct hostility to the ancien régime than that of da Ponte.[88]

I propose that as operatic accompaniments grew in sophistication, the skill of pasticcieri lay in recognising the characteristics that made the original scoring and dramatisation effective and capturing those characteristics in the new context. Consequently, parody of aria texts or settings leaned towards minimum amendment; this had many practical advantages: it preserved what made a sequence popular, saved the pasticciere's time in the amount of revising needed and that of the singer in learning new versions, especially if they knew the original one. Its principal advantage was artistic, however: the London version of *La villanella rapita* creates a different kind of comedy by altering the *context* alone as discussed later in two examples. It might be thought that this shows the beginnings of a concern for fidelity to the original work, but such an argument implies that pasticcieri had previously felt no respect for the original but were now beginning to find it. As we have seen, respect for the original artistry and its creator was a principal motivation for pasticcio in both classical and neoclassical cultures.

In the French version of 1789, a duet written by Bianchi occurs in Act II but, for the London version, Federici, Storace or both changed this to 'Occhietto furbetto', a duet by da Ponte set by Martin y Soler. This duet had originally been created for their 1787 opera *L'arbore di Diana*, where it was placed at the end of Act I. The duet is a fast-moving comic sequence in which Doristo declares love, or at least lust, for Amore. In its original context, the insistent music conjures sexual urgency as two people stand on the brink of consummating their passion there and then: the rhythm almost prefigures that of the waltz. The text in *L'arbore di Diana* runs as follows:

Amore:	*Amore:*
Occhietto furbetto,	Wicked eyes,
che cosa m'hai detto	what do you mean
bagiando mi qui?	by kissing me thus?
Doristo:	*Doristo:*
Se furba tu sei	If you are clever,
capira lo dei.	you will know.
Amore:	*Amore:*
Capisco, capisco, capisco, si, si.	I know, I know, I know, yes, yes.
Doristo:	*Doristo:*
Ebben che diss'io?	Well, what do I mean?
Amore:	*Amore:*
Che sei l'idol mio?	That you idolise me?
Doristo:	*Doristo:*
E poi?	And then?
Amore:	*Amore:*
Che vorresti ...	That you would like to ...
Doristo:	*Doristo:*
E poi?	And then?
Amore:	*Amore:*
Che faresti, che faresti,	That you want to, that you want to,
che faresti, che faresti, ah!	that you want to, that you want to, ah!
Taci, mio bene, ah, basta così.	Quiet, my precious, ah, that's enough.
Doristo:	*Doristo:*
Ah! Taci così la mano gradita	Ah! I also want to give you my
anch'io ti vo dar.	hand.
Amore:	*Amore:*
Fa presto, mia vita,	Hurry, my life,
che anch' io vo baciar	I also want to kiss you.

Doristo:	*Doristo:*
Ah, come tu tremi!	Ah, you're trembling!
Amore:	*Amore:*
Cor mio, di che tremi?	My heart, for what do you tremble?
Doristo:	*Doristo:*
Che caldo, che caldo!	Such heat, such heat!
Amore:	*Amore:*
Stà saldo, stà saldo,	Steady, steady,
e lasciami far.	I'll take care of everything.
(Parte.)	*(They leave.)*

London's *La villanella rapita* deftly reused this duet to lead into the finale for Act II, the dénouement for the whole opera. Although the words are virtually unchanged the dramatic context is shifted and, with it, the imagery suggested by the music. Mandina and Pippo declare their love for each other as Amore and Doristo had done, but in this opera they are reconciling after a terrible row. Pippo had rejected Mandina, believing her to have willingly become the mistress of the count; Mandina was hurt by this rejection as she did not understand that the count intended to seduce her. She was mystified by her family's and Pippo's horror at finding her in his house, dressed as his concubine, on her wedding day. But Pippo establishes the truth: she was abducted while everyone was drugged, given a sleeping drug herself and, even though her clothes were changed, to everyone's huge relief she has not been raped. The emotional state of the lovers is thus penitence on Pippo's part and relief on Mandina's that he still loves her; consequently, this is now a reconciliation duet with the sexual urgency changed to a mounting hope that their marriage is back on. The rhythmical insistence in the music now suggests Mandina's beating heart. The English translation below was printed in the published libretto accompanying the London performances in 1790.[89]

Mandina: What said those roguish eyes as you kissed me?
Pippo: If you are sly you must understand them.
Mandina: Yes, yes, I understand them.
Pippo: What did they say?
Mandina: That you are my love.
Pippo: Well!
Mandina: That you –
Pippo: Well!
Mandina: That you'll –
A2 [meaning both together]: Hush, my love, you've said enough.
Pippo: My hand, my heart is yours
Mandina: Give me that dear hand to kiss

Pippo: How you tremble! My life, what do you fear?
Mandina: My heart's on fire.
Pippo: Your lover will ease that pain.

It is likely that what Mandina is looking for in Pippo's roguish eyes is an apology, or confirmation of his love; however, given her English characterisation, it is possible she asks because she has literally no idea what the roguish look means but, anxious to be thought knowing or sly, pretends she does. Her hesitant 'That you – that you'll …' now means asking whether or not he will go through with their wedding. The loving but decorous hand-kissing contrasts with Mandina's kissing of the count's hand at the beginning of the opera: formal but affectionate on her part, lascivious on his. This short duet was sung through twice and the orchestration was slightly amended, presumably to help alter the imagery suggested. It was also given a more comic ending, finishing with repeats of the line 'ah basta, basta, così!'[90]

One of the things which may have brought Soler's duet to the minds of Federici or Storace is the repeated phrase 'che caldo', which occurs again in other parts of the finale. By keeping the original words, they not only saved learning time, they helped the literary unity of the finale; indeed, a care for both literary and musical unity runs through the opera. As the century neared its close we can see that pasticcio and fidelity were not the opponents later reformers would represent them as being.

The second example is Vincenzo Fabrizi's and Filippo Livigne's comic opera *I due castellani burlati*. This was staged as a pasticcio by the previous house composer Felice Giardini in 1790, shortly before *La villanella rapita*. Although Mozart's *Don Giovanni* would not be staged at the King's Theatre for another twenty-seven years, this pasticcio made use of Zerlina's aria 'Batti, batti, o bel Masetto':[91]

Don Giovanni	*I due castellani burlati*
Batti, batti, o bel Masetto	Pace, pace, bel mostaccio
La tua povere Zerlina	Non piu guerra, Spagnoletto
Staro qui come agnellina	Un di voi mi stagia in petto
Le tue botte ad aspettar	Questo core a pizzicar.

It exemplifies the capacity of light-touch textual revision to capture the aural success of the original by altering the meaning but not the structure: minimum change is made to the dramatic thrust of the rhythm and the stresses, rhymes and even the asonances are retained, but a substantial change in meaning was created by the words themselves. The new text told a different story and, musically, it was performed as a trio not a solo. The same aria, 'Batti, batti', was also parodied in *La villanella rapita* and Price, Milhous and Hume propose that some of the parodic text used might be Nancy Storace's work.[92] Again, the same lightness of alteration in no way hampers a change of meaning:

La villanella rapita:
Batti, batti o bel Pippetto
La tua povera Mandina:
Staro qui come angnellina
Le tue botte ad aspettar

The pasticci of composers like Giardini and Federici, and the reorientations of arias created by singers like Storace and Mara, an obvious example of whose approach is her revision of 'Anche nel petto io sento' in 1791, discussed later in this chapter, show how pasticcio techniques changed to embrace the new musical complexity and the enhanced role of composition itself within opera. I propose that the narrativity of operatic music and that of instrumental music cross-pollinated each other in the last third of the century; yet the narrativity of both contained underlying derivations from oral tradition and carried many ingrained tropes from storytelling.

Opera as property in the eighteenth century

Modern society largely believes that composers and librettists have a natural right to own the music and words they write. This subchapter argues that the view of pasticcio as an infringement on a composer's 'natural' right of ownership over their music only begins with the commodification of music, and the shaping of copyright legislation to serve that commodification, in the nineteenth century. Prior to that, both theatres and composers saw opera music as property only in those limited areas where a profit was realistically achievable. In an age where printed music was comparatively rare, print runs short and mimesis still played a substantial role in learning and disseminating music, composers had no interest in limiting the dissemination of their music. Any copyright system which prevented the free reuse of music would have restricted dissemination, thus impeding the fame of a composer and reducing their chances of new commissions. Pasticcio was a key part of the dissemination system. In both the eighteenth and nineteenth centuries, copyright legislation was more likely to deliver a profit for the commissioner of the music than the composer, so while dissemination was of value to the composer, legislation was less so. The eighteenth century, therefore, offers a view of pre-commodification conceptions of property in operatic music.

The composer is the commodity rather than their music

I suggest that, through fame, eighteenth-century composers became the commodity themselves, rather than the commodity being their music. Music was fluid and ever-changing whereas the capacity and skill of the artist was thought to remain fixed, unless a scandal or catastrophe damaged their reputation. Singers also perceived themselves as having a personal market value; when they accepted less payment than formerly from a theatre, their agreements often stipulated that the lower sum was to be kept secret so that the public perception of their status and ranking within the profession remained unaffected.[93]

Fame was important in the eighteenth century and a person's public reputation was not just something they went to court over but for which they were willing to risk death by duelling. As with storytellers' reputations in oral culture, fame led directly to an increase in a composer's market value; it allowed better fees from commissioners and greater social capital. Composers recognised their public reputation was a form of property but, in order to grow that reputation they needed widespread performances of their music regardless of whether a monetary reward was received each time and regardless of whether changes were made to their music. Pasticcio, I suggest, was an integral part of the cultivation of fame. Before the phonograph and gramophone, the principal means of disseminating music was performance. Music was printed to aid performances of various kinds rather than as a capture of the work itself in textual form. Scores were expensive and had small print runs compared with those of the following century; only a very limited number of people experienced music through text in the eighteenth century compared to those who experienced it through performance. For their compositions to be the vehicle whereby composers' fame spread, it was important that reworkings of their music reflected well on their abilities; composers accepted that this was not something they could always control, but it was more important that the performance was a success than that their music was performed as written.

Inclusion in pasticci was only a good method of growing one's fame, of course, if the composer's name was associated with the music. Consequently, an increase in the attribution of music to individual composers can be discerned in the later eighteenth century; more frequently than formerly they were named in playbills and private correspondence, but fame also spread through word of mouth in coffee-houses, at social occasions or benefits, and the reliance of managers on trusted opinion. Michael Kelly describes the role of conversation in the interplay of reputation, work and financial reward throughout his memoirs.[94] This increase in attribution was unmethodical and haphazard, so it could be a double-edged sword: it could certainly add to the reputation of a composer or librettist but false attributions, which were all too easy to make, could destroy one.

A conception of intellectual property did exist in the eighteenth century, even though it went largely unrecognised in copyright law, based on neoclassical interpretations of similitude and plagiarism; a boundary was drawn between declared derivation from an original – which the eighteenth century called similitude – and the surreptitious parody of an unacknowledged original, called plagiarism. Similitude was a re-expression of the Renaissance concept of imitation; it was the emulation of previously created art in an open and obvious manner; plagiarism was when that emulation was concealed and a claim to original authorship was made or implied. When pasticcieri interpolated their own material into an opera presented as original, they were not attempting to deceive the audience that it was hearing a previously undiscovered version of the original opera, or trying to pass their own music off as the original composer's; rather, the audience were invited to admire the pasticciere's skill in parody and similitude. A pasticcio would have carried no reputational benefits for an eighteenth-century pasticciere if their work was thought to be wholly that of the original creator.

To have an aria or ensemble included in a pasticcio was a compliment to the original composer. When printed, pasticcio opera texts were usually careful to name the composers who had sequences incorporated into the opera on the title page and sometimes in the advertising too, as a declaration of similitude was often a selling point. Naming the composers was not to demonstrate their permission but as a mark of admiration and serious pasticcieri strove to follow this; in his letter to the Théâtre Italien of 1859 Rossini still proclaimed this the right way to proceed, but mistakes were easy to make.

3.7 *Giovanni Bononcini* by Bartholomew Dandridge (1728–1732).
Source: Royal College of Music, released by Google Arts and Culture.

Price, Milhous and Hume list several key scandals in the eighteenth century in which composers' reputations were damaged. One example, in 1731, concerned a madrigal thought of as having been composed by Giovanni Bononcini, because Maurice Greene, his friend and fellow composer, had attributed it to him. It later resurfaced and was shown to be by Antonio Lotti, who confirmed that it was indeed his composition. Not only did Greene's reputation collapse, obliging him to resign from the Academy of Ancient Music, but Bononcini himself was engulfed in the disgrace. He left London, where his reputation never quite recovered.[95] While this was accidental damage, in 1782 Venanzio Rauzzini deliberately sought to damage the reputation of his colleague Antonio Sacchini, the house composer at the King's Theatre. He either instigated or gave his tacit consent to stories in *The Morning Herald* and *Morning Post*, suggesting that he was the real power behind Sacchini's work, and that it was he who had really written most of Sacchini's operas.[96] That Rauzzini chose not to go to court on the matter, preferring to inflict reputational damage, is, I suggest, indicative of the continuing importance of reputation as property and the comparative weakness of copyright laws as commodifiers of musical authorship.

3.8 *Venanzio Rauzzini*, engraving by Robert Hancock.
Source: New York Public Library, released under Creative Commons Licence.

* * *

These allegations of plagiarism show that the issue at stake is reputational rather than any prefiguring of modern conceptions of musical property or copyright. Plagiarism was not the use of someone else's music per se, even when the originator's name was not fully acknowledged, it was the acquisition of fame through claiming to have written their music, or even being perceived to have done so. There was no accusation in the newspapers that Rauzzini was owed money by Sacchini for his contributions; it was not the *use* of someone else's music that was seen as taboo, that was a thing too normal to be controversial and an essential component of the dissemination process.

3.9 *Antonio Sacchini*, engraving by Augustin de Saint Aubin, 1786, after a drawing by Charles-Nicholas Cochin.
Source: Released under Creative Commons Licence.

Conceptions of music as property

From the early nineteenth century onwards, composers were no longer expected to gift their music to the world merely because they were well paid for creating it at the outset. Today, state-funded art in the UK, along with the internet, have, in certain contexts, reinstated this older conception of already-paid-for musdic as free but, between the performance licensing act of 1833 and the advent of the internet, the artist's right to continued profit from their work became a normal assumption. It was not always so: a debate surfaced in eighteenth-century Britain about whether an author, librettist or composer owned their works as natural property under common law, or whether those works only had a legal reality if the copyright was registered, or the work was assigned and printed. Creative works were never recognised as, or legislated to become, the natural or absolute property of their creator. In 1817 Francis Hargrave discovered that even after the copyright span permissible at the time – twenty-eight years – had expired on one of his books, he had no right to reassign the work to a different publisher.[97] The 1709 Statute of Anne, so often held as a breakthrough law which made copyright a great advantage to the author, was bitterly lamented by Sharon Turner in a tract of 1813, as the very thing that prevented authors holding their works as absolute property:

> authors before the [Statute of Anne] had the same perpetual right of property in their works as in their money. [The Statute] instead of being a boon and a benefit to authors, has operated to their injury, since it has been found to curtail their natural and legal right to their intellectual property. If this Act had not been passed, they would not only have had no copies to deliver [i.e. to copyright libraries], but their Copyright would have been perpetual. Why should not an author be entitled to his Copyright as free and as permanently as the humblest individual is to his freehold, his furniture, or his money? What right, in reason, distinct from verbal subtleties, can we allege for the one, which is not applicable to the other?[98]

Turner was specifically lamenting the terminations placed on copyright and his view of how copyright functioned prior to the Statute of Anne is undoubtedly romantic; nevertheless, his argument that absolute ownership should be invested in the creator of a work was repeatedly made in the eighteenth century and continued to be raised as an alternative to ever-expanding copyright laws into the twentieth century. It was a free market to trade in the ownership of a composer's music which was created by Britain's copyright legislation in the eighteenth and nineteenth centuries, rather than anything approaching modern conceptions of intellectual property. An artist's ownership of their work as their own inalienable intellectual property was not established in UK law until 1988.[99]

Copyright laws needed to create a quantifiable commodity so that it could be tradable; music which was partly one composer's, partly another's and both remarkably similar to other music was hard to quantify. In this free market of copyright trading, the composer was only one of a number of competing interests. From the eighteenth through to much of the twentieth century, music publishers, booksellers, theatres who commissioned operas and, later, record companies, cinemas and broadcasters were largely successful in defining copyright in terms favouring the disseminator over the creator. For example, the third clause in the 1808 Copyright Bill, which would have granted authors the right to withdraw, cancel or nullify contracts with their publishers, printers or assignees, was quietly dropped from the Bill during the committee stage.[100]

It would be wrong, however, to portray the creators and disseminators of music as having consistently opposed interests during these centuries. In calling for artistic works to be recognised as natural property, Turner recognised the dependence of artists on disseminators but did not foresee the potentially drastic imbalances in rewards between creator and disseminator. Chapter Five discusses how this became very much the case over the nineteenth and twentieth centuries, resulting in rifts between consumers of music and disseminators, as well as between creators and disseminators. The conceptualisation of copyright itself faced substantial resistance in both Britain and the United States. Yet far from being a perversion of the original intentions of copyright legislation, I propose that this weighting in favour of disseminators over creators was a direct continuity from early modern copyrighting intentions and an intrinsic part of the legislation governing printing.

Conceptions of musical property inherited by the eighteenth century

In the eighteenth century, conceptions of musical property which preceded the copyright systems of mass-literacy were still widely held. I propose that these earlier conceptions offer another reason for this century's enthusiasm for pasticcio. The earlier conception of music as property facilitated borrowing and exchange while the later property definitions needed by copyright militated against them. The property relationship of the storyteller to their story, which had long obtained in oral culture, was still reflected in the relationship of eighteenth-century theatres, composers, librettists and singers to their performances. So long as a story was unperformed it was perceived as 'belonging' to the speaker, singer or instrument player who created it, even if they were beholden to a commissioner for the money to create it. The point of transference came when it was performed; at this point de facto ownership moved to the listeners. Attending a performance brought with it the right to retell the story or play the music to others. This was true regardless of whether the listeners had paid or whether the performance was given gratis: ownership transferred at the point of telling. Storytelling material itself had little reality outside of its performance and this kind of dissemination was something early modern storytellers and musicians expected and were flattered by.

This transference of ownership was not one of commodification: listeners did not feel they now owned the story in the way they owned a field or a horse after paying for it; rather, the listening experience conferred a freedom to make whatever use of the story they would, more like commoners' rights. Members of the audience for Jacobean plays felt free to scribble down pithy or lyrical phrases for their own reuse in speeches or sermons, having paid the entrance fee, and composers from Bach to Beethoven felt free to reuse folk or hymn tunes after hearing them in taverns, churches, fairs or country dances. Telling jokes still works this way, even after more than a century of mass literacy.

This is not to say that stories had a negligible market value in oral culture and there are numerous examples of professional storytellers buying stories from each other, but the real commodification was the right to *be* the storyteller, a right bound up with personal status. Only certain court poets could tell certain stories, much as only ordained clergy could read the gospel during Mass. The right to read eulogies to the sovereign, relay a message from the battlefield, present an address, or perform a welcome ode or valediction was a jealously guarded privilege in court contexts. Similarly, in village contexts, David Thomson tells of an elderly master storyteller in Ballinskelligs Bay, Ireland, who refused to tell his best story in front of an up-and-coming rival because the storyteller was 'jealous of it': he wanted to retain sole possession of it.[101] Hearing the story would have entitled the rival to add it to his own repertoire; but further, the right to be its only teller, on which the master storyteller's pre-eminence in the village depended, would have been compromised. The right to perform and the status it brought was thus the commodity rather than the story itself in oral cultures. The status of the story and that of the storyteller were interlinked: a local person telling a new story, which they had freely 'made up' themself, robbed it of interconnection with the wider world and thus of its status. If, on the other hand it was an ancient tale of classical provenance or packed with learned allusion as Chaucer's tended to be, the story itself lent status to its teller. Wendy Welch notes that many stories began with a flat denial of ownership by the storyteller and their ascription to someone the listeners knew or had heard of.[102] Again, these were not necessarily ancient authorities but someone the listeners knew personally, and gossip still works this way today. George Tucker also notes this tendency to marginalise the authorial voice, or sometimes avoid it altogether, in early modern narratives.[103] This tendency continued into printed early-modern texts: anonymity was often accompanied by a rumour of celebrity authorship.

The rise in literacy during the sixteenth and seventeenth centuries complicated these oral conceptions of stories and music as property. A written text, be it manuscript or print, was a tangible material commodity unlike a performed event. There were profits to be made out of republishing an existing book which had not existed when a story was retold orally and this, in itself, was a motivation for printers to apply the traditional freedom of listeners to printing material that had already been printed by others. Content from other books was regularly reprinted in the sixteenth and seventeenth centuries: the printer felt free to do so as they had bought and read the original; the liberty obtaining for listeners was felt to automatically encompass readers. The only check on doing so was whether another printer had acquired an exclusive licence or if reprinting infringed a monopoly.

This oral residue was restricted in France, England and many European countries by a system of privileges under which princes or their governments granted a monopoly on publishing to a particular company within their jurisdiction. In France, the company Le Roy et Ballard enjoyed such a monopoly, printing all music between 1551 and 1713; between 1713 and 1790 they still enjoyed a partial monopoly shared with the engravers they used. In England, Mary I granted a similar monopoly to the London Stationers' Company in 1557, which operated until 1695. This system, like the patent system for theatres, made all printing outside the monopoly illegal unless it was given special licence or permission (though this did not prevent it happening). Early modern laws about printing were concerned firstly with the relationship between printers and the state and secondly with that between printer and printer; their concerns were who had the right to be a printer and what they could print. The relationship between printer and writer went largely undefined in law and early modern copyright legislation was framed around the competing needs of printers rather than those of writers.

Oral storytelling practices thus continued into eighteenth-century printing practices, another demonstration of the non-binary nature of orality and literacy. Nonetheless, published content could not be a stable commodity, nor could publishers reliably estimate their profits unless they owned the content in some legally defined way. After the Stationers' monopoly came to an end in 1695, publishers and printers pressed governments for copyright legislation and the Statute of Anne began the process of vesting ownership in the disseminator rather than the creator. Certainly, from the creator's point of view, registering their copyright allowed them to negotiate with publishers, printers and booksellers on a more tangible basis so, to begin with at least, creators were on the same side as disseminators in welcoming commodification. Yet commodification was slow to take root; even after the end of the century, Lewis Lavenu felt completely at liberty to produce instrumental reductions of Beethoven's symphonies, without any authorisation from Beethoven himself or his German publishers, Breitkopf and Härtel.[104]

The right of theatres, companies and academies in the eighteenth century to own the music or text which they had commissioned or which had been created by staff contracted to them also derived from early modern conceptions of musical property. When an opera was commissioned by an Italian prince in the early seventeenth century there was no doubt that the product belonged to him. He might order the libretto to be published, bearing the costs arising and receiving any profits, and the librettist might publish it later on with the prince's permission (or in a different jurisdiction without it), and these commissioning prerogatives were inherited by theatres, companies and academies. Theatres in London, as in Venice, who had paid fees to contracted creators of opera, or employed them on salary, held the right to publish any music or libretti they might create without any obligation to pay the creators anything further, especially if the work had already been performed. King's Theatre contracts stipulated that new music created while under contract to the theatre belonged to it, thus the publishing rights lay with them.

Unlike France, there were no sums paid from a successful run of performances to the composer and librettist in Britain, so commissioning fees were more generous than they would become in the age of expanded copyright. It would be wrong, however, to portray eighteenth-century composers as people who gifted their music to the world in a proto-socialistic spirit. Strozzi, as we have seen, republished his libretto to reassert his authorship and Vivaldi made concerted efforts to retain control of his opera music and, where possible, prevent it ending up in other people's pasticci. In doing so he was not an early copyright pioneer, he merely wished to finish disseminating his music himself, and enjoy the profits therefrom, before allowing it to be disseminated by others.[105]

There was no conception of separating the purchase of printed music from the right to perform it. When King's Theatre managers instructed their agents in Italy to buy opera scores, they sometimes received a printed vocal score along with the unpublished orchestral parts in manuscript, or rehearsal libretti with any changes scribbled in; the price for the whole package of documents thus contained the right to perform the opera. When agents sent just the printed score and libretto, bought at the bookseller's price, it was still taken for granted that the right to stage the opera came along with the books. Commodifying the right to perform an opera separately from the right to read a text of it did not emerge until the nineteenth century.

Nineteenth- and twentieth-century arguments in favour of ever-tighter copyright legislation usually argued that this would preserve the integrity of original works. This was an argument predicated on Romantic definitions of originality, but the autopasticcio stands at odds with this definition. Composers did not feel themselves to be cheating their commissioners by reusing existing material in a 'new' opera. Despite having been paid previously for composing the material used, if a particular audience had not heard the music before it was considered new to them and so advertised as such. The oral derivation of this perspective is self-evident and I propose in the following discussion about presentism that the nineteenth century's conception of absolute originality did not have its beginnings in this period as is sometimes argued. Absolutely original music was seldom stipulated in eighteenth-century contracts; it was sometimes required for royal commissions, for which a generous length of composing time was allowed, yet the King's Theatre commissioned these less frequently than Paris or Vienna.[106] This attitude lasted a long time: Rossini's 1824 commission in London was very definitely for a new opera, *Ugo re d'Italia*, yet he was very open about intending to rework one of his existing ones, probably *Adelaide di Borgogne* (1817), with music also borrowed from *Ermione* (1819).[107]

Presentism in musicological interpretations of eighteenth-century court cases

Twentieth-century music historians believed that conceptions of musical and narrative property in opera *had* moved towards the modern position during the eighteenth century. The several court cases concerning the ownership and printing of operatic material were argued to be staging posts on the road towards modern copyright. This sub-section disagrees with this perspective, arguing that twentieth-century musicologists joined the dots of these court rulings to construct a linear development towards copyright – a development in which the principle of copyright is invariably presented as desired and beneficial, despite the refusal to vest absolute ownership in the artist. I propose this is to project the justifications needed by a later music industry backwards into the eighteenth century.

Frederick Scherer, Curtis Price, Jennifer Hall-Witt, Gillen d'Arcy Wood and others view the copyright journey as beginning with the Statute of Anne, which saw copyright enacted for the writers of books not just commissioners or printers. This granted those authors registering their own copyright the exclusive right to sell the permission to print their work, for fourteen years. This act certainly covered literature, writing and 'books' but music was not specifically included. In a suit brought by Johann Christian Bach against

Longman and Lukey in 1777, the judge decided that printed music *was* covered by the Statute of Anne. This meant that simply getting hold of an existing composition, printed or in manuscript, no longer entitled one to publish it; publishers and printers had to have the consent of the owner of the copyright; although, as discussed earlier, this was not necessarily the composer.

Registrations of music copyrights steadily increased over the 1780s, rising to 1,828 by 1790. Registrations were made by publishers, aristocratic commissioners and sometimes incorporated bodies such as music academies, theatres and cathedral chapters, as well as by composers.

The role of the music copyist within opera houses is key to understanding eighteenth-century conceptions of operatic music as property. These officers received the handwritten score from the composer if it was a new commission, or sometimes a printed one if the opera had already been published. They passed this to the house poet and house composer for revision, then the copyist and his staff wrote out the vocal and orchestral parts. They provided copies for the theatre manager, the singers and the stage manager, and a fair copy was sent to the Lord Chamberlain. All except the Lord Chamberlain's copy were carefully collected after the performances and archived by the music librarian, who supervised their storage. Even today, opera houses collect their scores back from the singers and orchestra involved, although some allow performers to buy their scores from the house. Music copyists across Europe acquired the perquisite of selling a score or popular arias therefrom to a publisher. Leopold Mozart wrote in 1770:

> The copyist is full of joy, which in Italy is a very good omen, since, when the music pleases, the copyist can sometimes make more money sending out and selling the arias than the composer received for his composition.[108]

Copyists did not sell only to publishers; to those anxious for a copy well ahead of the performance, the copyist would sell handwritten versions of the score, as Scherer points out.[109] Curtis Price reveals his neoromantic perspective in his hostility to copyists:

> The house music copyist ... controlled the rights to all music performed in the theater. This perquisite, which gave the copyist power far beyond his immediate duties and which stifled original opera composition in London for decades, lies at the center of two important Chancery lawsuits.[110]

Three cases involving Bach, Stephen Storace and Gertrud Mara are accordingly linked by Price to illustrate a move in the direction of composers claiming their fair dues. I propose, instead, that these cases illustrate a robust defence of a profoundly eighteenth-century concept: the perquisite. In modern employment practice expenses incurred through carrying out one's work are usually borne by the employer but, in the eighteenth century, holding a post could mean that some (or all) of the associated costs were borne by the post holder. Such positions were often a kind of freehold living, similar to that of a vicar, where the holder was entitled to certain revenues and perquisites but also liable for certain expenses. Leopoldo de Michele, the King's Theatre copyist, received an income of £150 per annum (the same as the house treasurer, composer, poet and leader of the band) but engaged a number of musically literate copying clerks to assist with writing out the parts; he paid them himself and billed the theatre. He also billed the King's Theatre separately for stationery costs and undoubtedly had other day-to-day costs and he relied on being reimbursed by the house fairly promptly.

Under William Taylor's management the Theatre suffered grave cash flow problems and de Michele went unpaid for long periods; the amount owing to him exceeded £500 by the time he took the King's Theatre to court in 1788.[111] The additional income brought in from his perquisite of selling to publishers was, no doubt, vital in defraying slow payments. Income from such perquisites was often the difference between a job returning a living and costing more to carry out than one received from doing it. Courts took the entitlement to perquisites very seriously, even in contexts where the perquisite itself appears corrupt to modern eyes. As late as 1838 Disraeli's electors at Maidstone took him to court over unpaid election bribes on the grounds that these were binding promises made to the voters.[112]

The case of *Stephen Storace v. Longman and Broderip* was heard in 1787 and has been argued by a number of music historians to have been a victory for composers in securing ownership of their work through the medium of copyright, and the wresting of publishing rights away from the copyist, a move portrayed as beneficial for the artform. Recently, doubt has been expressed by Maik Köster, a doubt with which I very much concur. Storace had written an aria for his sister Nancy, 'Care donne che bramate', which was inserted into Paisiello's opera *Il re Teodoro in Venezia*. Storace had the aria printed, as it had been extremely popular, and kept the profits arising from doing so. In a foreshadowing of the Mara case discussed next, the copyist, de Michele, sold the complete score, which included Storace's aria, to Longman and Broderip according to the theatre's usual practice. As far as de Michele and Longmans were concerned, all music written for the house belonged to the house, and de Michele said so in his testimony.

The inherited rule of thumb in opera houses had been that while any new music created by the house's contracted musicians belonged to the house, anything pre-existing was considered to have no de facto owner and was thus available for use. Despite his sister giving the aria to de Michele for publishing according to normal practice, Storace argued that de Michele had no right to publish this aria as it was not new and he had not been under contract to the King's Theatre at the time it was created or sung. Lord Kenyon, the Master of the Rolls, ruled in the composer's favour but, significantly, awarded him only one shilling in damages. As Price, Milhous and Hume admit, Kenyon saw it as a victory which turned on a legal nicety and he clearly did not consider that the King's Theatre had committed a serious infringement of another man's rights.[113]

A clash of interests had occurred in an area which exposed the lack of definition about what kind of property an opera aria was. Storace had composed the music, and the house poet had written the words. As the house poet was very definitely under contract to the King's Theatre, the theatre very definitely owned the words and had formally registered copyright in them. Moreover, they had not borrowed Storace's setting without his knowledge; Nancy Storace had specifically requested to replace an unsuitable aria in *Teodora* with one composed by her brother and the house had consented. From the King's Theatre's point of view, they had given a platform to Storace's aria but, instead of gratitude, he had sought to poach the publishing income from the copyist.

The traditional approach to aria reuse assumed the original creator of an aria was either employed in the staging, dead or very far away, but Storace was none of these things and this allowed him to challenge the traditional conception that pre-existing music was ownerless. Because he was uncontracted to the theatre at the time he wrote the aria, this gave him the loophole he needed and there is little evidence that he was pioneering a natural right to his work out of principle; there is rather more that he was making a challenge only in this one specific instance. Making money on his aria appears to have been his sole motivation. As an international performer and composer, Storace was well aware that the conception that pre-existing music was free for use was common in opera houses across Europe, that his librettist also had claims and, similarly, that the copyists enjoyed a long-standing perquisite. Without this freedom, suitcase arias became untenable along with pasticcio practices of all sorts. Yet this case has been hailed by Price, Milhous, Hume, Scherer, Hall-Witt and others as a landmark, whereby composers secured a kind of 'moral' ownership of their work in the face of the commissioners who had paid for its creation and performance.[114] As Köster writes:

> Price interprets *Storace*'s outcome as an emphatic affirmation of musical authorship, going so far as to conclude that later contractual agreements over copyright were now 'technically illegal', because they did not account for the author's right to his or her composition.[115]

This is to build quite a lot on very slender foundations. I suggest these cases were selected by musicologists to create a linear, pro-copyright narrative while other cases have been ignored because they complicate such a narrative. *Tonson v. Collins* prompted the anonymous pamphlet *An Enquiry into the Nature and Origin of Literary Property* (1762). This tract repudiated the concept of a natural authorial property right existing at common law; it was met by a counter-tract, *A Vindication of the Exclusive Rights of Authors to their own Work* (1762), arguing the reverse.[116] Significantly, both sides in the debate saw publication as the end of an author's ownership and control over their work; thereafter the publisher or even the bookseller might make changes to the text in further editions, edit it for inclusion in an anthology, or even commission revisions or variations of the work by other people. It could certainly be changed for performance. In sum, they saw ownership as ending at the point of transmission. Alteration thereafter was normal and seen in operatic practice throughout the century. Both sides in this debate were aware that a wholly new law would be required to invest authors with absolute property rights in their work.

3.10 *Gertrud Elisabeth Mara* (Madam Mara), by Elisabeth Vigée-Lebrun, *c.*1786.
Source: Released under Creative Commons Licence.

Storace's case and Mara's shortly after offer valuable insights into the late eighteenth-century creative process but, in terms of what they reveal about property conceptions in opera, I suggest they demonstrate how removed eighteenth-century conceptions still were from those of the nineteenth and twentieth centuries. I argue that it is the collaborative nature of aria shaping which is revealed in the 1791 court case involving the prima donna Gertrud Mara (usually referred to as Madam Mara), rather than any stepping stone in the development of copyright. The case was fought between two firms of publishers, Mara's being Longman and Broderip, and the King's Theatre's being Skillern and Goulding. Price tells the story:

> In April 1791 Madam Mara introduced the aria 'Anche nel petto io sento' into her benefit performance of Sarti's *Idalide* at the King's Theatre in the Pantheon. Anticipating the popularity of the catchy tune, she asked the music librarian to bring the orchestra parts to her dressing room immediately after it had been sung, even before the opera was over. She then quickly sold the aria to Longman and Broderip. In the meantime, de Michele acquired an illicit copy which he sold to the rival firm Skillern and Goulding; hence the lawsuit.[117]

Hardly an illicit copy one might think, given that it was de Michele's job to collect the scores and his right to publish them. The aria itself was revealed to be an adaptation of a duet in Paisiello's opera *La Mollinarella*, 'Nel cor più non mi sento'. This duet had been performed the previous year and Skillern and Goulding had already published it as Paisiello's work; they argued that the reworking of the duet meant it counted as new music, which meant it was owned by the King's Theatre and thus theirs to publish. Longman and Broderip argued it was old music, owned in theory by Paisiello, but in practice by anyone, and thus Madam Mara had every right to sell it to them to publish. As Köster shows, Skillern and Goulding's argument put Madam Mara in a position where she had to downplay her revision of the aria.[118] Tellingly, the process of reshaping the aria was so collegial that it proved almost impossible to identify a single person responsible for its composition. Madam Mara admitted to being one of those involved and thus a co-author of the aria as it was actually sung. Price describes her evidence:

> She recalled inviting several members of the King's Theatre orchestra to her home to run through the piece; she had sketched out a distinctive accompaniment for two flutes, two French horns, bassoon and harp. Dissatisfied with the instrumentation, she asked the house composer, Mazzinghi to take her rough score away for adjustments …[119]

I suggest the significance of Mara's testimony for musicology is that it demonstrates that a prima donna could involve herself so minutely in the compositional process. She also says that she went as far as she could with her own ideas before passing the accompaniment over to the house composer. There is no sense here that composition is a jealously guarded creative role, reserved to the house composer alone. Indeed, Madam Mara's account suggests an emotionally uncharged coming together of musicians, at her home, to improve a piece of music; instrumentalists, Mazzinghi, Madam Mara and her husband were all in her drawing room seeking a common goal. This is not to overstate the collegiality of this creative process; I am not suggesting it resembled co-operative theatre in the 1960s; eighteenth-century creative processes were intensely hierarchical, but the hierarchy was fluid. Often it was force of personality or musical ability which dictated who was the driving force in refining a score. While collegiality seems inescapable, Price identifies the core of the case thus: '[t]he serious crux of this tawdry little squabble was whether the beguiling accompaniment was the work of Mazzinghi ... or Madam Mara'.[120] In other words, who was the author? Price interprets this as the crux, to further his presentation of the case as a staging post on the road to an artist owning their own work. This assumes a work has to have a single artist who creates it and thereafter owns it. I suggest that what the interrogatories reveal is a very different, pre-Romantic, landscape. What began as an existing duet saw collaborative work undertaken, on the instrumentation, the vocal line and the words; these changes blurred the line between an old aria and a new one. As Lord Kenyon, who also presided over this case, was all too aware, there was no law, principle or tradition to offer parameters on how much change to a piece of music might be considered minimal and how much substantial enough to make it a new work. In the absence of such parameters, counsel on both sides were left resorting to analogies.

Instead of highlighting the desire for copyright laws, at no point in the trial did anyone suggest Paisiello was owed anything for what had begun as his duet, not even the shilling Storace had been awarded. Nor was there any suggestion that Guiseppe Sarti's authorship of *Idalide* had been compromised as a result of inserting the aria. Significantly, the collaboration only turned sour when Madam Mara sought to turn the company's joint efforts into her personal gain by appropriating the aria as hers alone.

It is also important to note the gender implications of this collaborative approach; it clearly allowed female singers to have an extensive and acknowledged input into the compositional process in a way that would be drastically curtailed in the nineteenth century. Fifty years after this case, the perceived masculinity of a compositional style was a criterion for its value; involvement by the prima donna in the compositional process would be seen as unconscionable meddling and potentially unfeminine. The singer was employed to give voice to the male composer's genius, not participate in that genius herself, as George Eliot sardonically depicts in her dramatic poem *Armgart* (1870). Yet the *Mara* case shows an eighteenth-century prima donna not only had the right to substitute arias but to amend them; not simply to bring them within her vocal capability, but to improve them musically and dramatically. The number of aria compositions and recompositions by eighteenth-century women is now recognised to be substantial.[121]

In these court cases, inherited oral conceptions, where music was uncommodified, bumped up against emergent music literacy, and increased profits in music publishing. The cases show a scramble by different opera practitioners to gain access to the income streams offered by music publishing, but neither the claimants, the defendants nor the courts were interested in limiting the *uses* that could be made of music once it was in the public domain. Storace and Mara must have expected their new arias to be sung by those purchasing the book and often sung for money. They would have expected changes to be made to those arias by the new singers to suit their voices, the instrumentation available or the occasion. They were not interested in the future life of their arias, merely in cashing in on their popularity during the season in which they were popular. It was not until the nineteenth century that opera composers began to restrain the free dissemination of their arias through performance and rely instead on copyright and their publishers to gain them a reputation. New ways of thinking about music as property lay in the future; maybe not far in the future, but far enough for it not to be a factor in 1791.

Kenyon found for the singer's publishers again in *Madam Mara* and nonsuited those of the opera house, allowing both published copies to stand. Köster shows that Kenyon, once more, felt unable to penalise either side in a case where it was impossible to draw clear lines between authorship, property and ownership.[122] This is Price's thought after recounting the trial:

> The law is an ass, you will say. The court was in effect upholding the right of a performer to introduce arias and then sell them, even when authorship was uncertain or, as in this case, plagiarism had been admitted. But there was a larger consequence: this lawsuit, however untidy, finally broke the stranglehold which the King's Theatre had on its composers: a great hindrance to the development of opera in late eighteenth-century England had been removed.[123]

I take issue with this interpretation on a number of accounts: firstly, Madam Mara did not admit plagiarism. As discussed, the reuse of existing material was understood at the time to be quite distinct from plagiarism. She may have posed as the sole creator of the aria in her transaction with her publishers, but could not have done so with her colleagues. When she passed the piece on to Mazzinghi she did not initially mention to him that it had begun as a Paisiello duet but, most probably, he would have recognised it as such, it being fairly well known and recently performed. In any case, by this time the duet would have been considered common property. Nor was the 'stranglehold', if such it was, 'finally broken' by this case; business resumed as normal with the copyists' right to publish the theatre's music continuing unchanged and the theatre's right to any new music remaining a feature of artist's contracts, as Köster argues.[124]

The word 'finally' is revealing. Price's deterministic narrative relies on presentism – in the literary sense – by assuming that modern forms of copyright were a consciously desired goal for composers in the eighteenth century. He sees the *Madam Mara* case as part of opera's journey towards setting composers in what the nineteenth century would consider their rightful place. The case is a step to removing 'a great hindrance to the development of opera in England'. In this narrative, the granting of operatic authorship to the composer alone is presented as an unassailably progressive step, while the advantages of any collegial endeavour are downplayed. The nineteenth-century *Harmonicon* would no doubt have agreed and, although this is not explicitly stated by Price, the underlying implication is that nineteenth-century operatic practice is the apogee of the artform and the preceding periods are merely leading up to it. The theatre's ownership of the operas it commissioned would not have seemed like a 'stranglehold' to Leopoldo de Michele, his wife or his children. To see an exceptionally well-paid performer capture an income stream belonging to another member of staff who earned a tenth of her fee would hardly have seemed a progressive development, even at the time. The theatre manager and the house committee were, perhaps for once, on the side of their copyist in this case: they did not wish to see publishing fees swell the already scandalously high rewards of the leading singers.

The beginning of new thinking on musical ownership for composers

Chapter Five will pick up the thread of copyright development in the nineteenth century, but I suggest that the idea of paying composers *after* the first run evolved out of the radical idea of paying them *for* the first run. In France, instead of money only being paid at the commissioning stage or on submission of the written work, Scherer notes that

> [e]ven before a copyright law existed, there was a long-standing tradition that opera composers received fees for subsequent performances. By a 1776 decree, this compensation scheme held for the first 40 performances, declining from 200 livres for the first 20 performances to 100 for iterations 21–40. Because of this provision, Paris was a special magnet to would-be opera composers.[125]

This rewarded opera composers for success with the public and thus involved them financially in the postcommission fate of their music. In Paris, a long run meant not merely reputational gain, but hard cash. In London, this practice was much slower in coming, although a discernible rise in commissioning fees to composers, in certain contexts, began in the 1780s. The trustees of the King's Theatre were shocked to learn the manager, Gallini, had paid Samuel Arnold £80 for his Handelian pasticcio *Giulio Cesare*, commissioned for the centenary celebrations. It is not until Rossini that we find a composer enjoying sufficient reputational muscle to consistently dictate high fees for subsequent performances of his operas, both in London and abroad. Between 1816 and 1823, Rossini wrested the right to publish his operas away from the copyists, selected his own publishers and actively preserved their exclusive rights to print his music. His agents and publishers, such as Antonio Pacini, were active in registering copyright in different jurisdictions and demanding additional payments for staging the composer's works, once the scores had been bought. He thus controlled his music's dissemination through a successful partnership with his publishers, one in which he was the senior partner in that he retained ownership of his copyrights.

To achieve this, Rossini acted as a kind of composer-impresario who entered into contracts with opera houses on his own terms, only becoming an employee or entering a patron/client relationship in a nominal sense. As one of Europe's few celebrity composers he was not dependent for his financial security on holding posts such as house composer.[126] Even though composers like Rossini held their copyrights in their own hands, they were still happy for their music to be used in pasticci, so long as the proper fees were paid and credit given. Rossini himself created autopasticci during the first third of the nineteenth century.

A slow transition away from the earlier conceptions of musical property occurred between the early and the middle nineteenth century. By the end of this period operatic music no longer changed ownership at the point of transmission. New legislation was passed in Britain over the course of the nineteenth century, the benefits of which were principally reaped by international celebrity composers such as Rossini and Verdi; less well-resourced, less famous composers or those lacking a wealthy patron were not necessarily able to access this income stream.

So long as the creators of operas retained their copyright, they could potentially benefit from both publication and performance rights within nineteenth-century Britain. It was not long, however, before commissioners, companies and opera houses wrested this income from most composers and librettists by requiring the surrender of their copyright as a condition of their contract. Reputation, therefore, really did have a relationship to hard cash; those with sufficient reputation could retain their copyrights and bargain their terms with publishers and theatres advantageously. For composers who were still building their fame, copyright laws did not automatically place them favourably in such negotiations. Significantly, throughout the nineteenth century both the famous and the less well known continued to allow and sometimes encourage pasticcio versions of their works as an inexpensive means of dissemination. Only the mechanical and electronic reproducibility of opera music would rival pasticcio as a means of dissemination, and that lay eighty years in the future.

Notes

1 Robert Schechner, 'Restoration of behaviour', *Between Theatre and Anthropology* (Philadelphia: University of Pennsylvania Press, 1984), p. 36.
2 Richard Sennett, *The Fall of Public Man* (New York: Norton, 1976). E.J. Hundert, 'The European Enlightenment and the history of the self', *Rewriting the Self: Histories from the Renaissance to the Present*, ed. Roy Porter (London: Routledge, 1997). Dror Wahrman, *The Making of the Modern Self: Identity and Culture in Eighteenth-Century England* (New Haven, CT: Yale University Press, 2004).
3 Judith Butler, *Gender Trouble* (New York: Routledge, 1990, 2008 edn), p. 190.
4 Late-twentieth-century developments from semiotic theory led to new ways of interpreting sign and signifier; performance theory is one such offshoot. Ibid., p. 25. Also, Marvin Carlson, 'Theorizing the performative event', *The Oxford Handbook of Georgian Theatre 1737–1832*, ed. Julia Swindells and David Francis Taylor (Oxford: Oxford University Press, 2014), pp. 60–64.
5 Strohm's studies of Vivaldi illumined the beginnings of this transition within Italian opera, while Handel scholars demonstrated the same ambition for opera music in Britain. Reinhard Strohm, *Essays on Handel and Italian Opera* (Cambridge: Cambridge University Press, 1985), but also *Dramma per Musica: Italian Opera Seria of the Eighteenth Century* (New Haven, CT and London: Yale University Press, 1997). Gordana Lazarevich, 'Eighteenth-century pasticcio: the historian's Gordian knot', *Studien zur Italienisch-Deutschen Musikgeschichte*, ed. Friedrich Lippmann, Silke Leopold, Volker Scherliess and Wolfgang Witzenmann, vol. 11 (Böhlau: A. Volk Verlag, 1976), pp. 121–145. Recent scholars include Ilias Chrissochoidis, 'Handel at a crossroads: his 1737–1738 and 1738–1739 seasons re-examined', *Music and Letters*, vol. 90 no. 4 (Oxford: Oxford University Press, 2009). Sir John Eliot Gardiner's essay on Gluck in *The Guardian*, 12 September 2015, also discusses the transition: https://www.theguardian.com/music/2015/sep/12/john-eliot-gardiner-gluck-orphee-et-eurydice-opera [accessed 12 August 2018].
6 David Trotter 'Wanton expressions', *Spirit of Wit*, ed. Jeremy Treglowan (Oxford: Basil Blackwell, 1982), p. 115.

7 *The Spectator*, No. 125, Tuesday 24 July 1711.

8 Church Catholicks, also known as Church Papists, supported the sacraments, Latin mass, the apostolic succession, transubstantiation and other tenets of Catholicism but attended the services of the Established Church as the laws required, thus avoiding recognition as recusants.

9 The Levellers, Diggers and the slightly longer lived Fifth Monarchy Men were sub-groups within the Parliamentary faction composed mainly of working men. It is often forgotten that some individual Puritans were royalist and Charles II's court-in-exile included disenchanted Presbyterians as well as Anglicans and Catholics.

10 In 1650, for example, Calvinist Scottish nobles, especially the Argyll family, offered the exiled Charles II the crown of Scotland and an army to reclaim his English one, if he would embrace the covenanter identity, make a full profession of Calvinist faith and promise to enforce it as the state religion across his three kingdoms. Charles made the promises, but his sincerity was highly questionable. At the same period in England the Levellers were an emergent group within the Parliamentary faction, unifying themselves with branding such as rosemary sprigs in their hats and sea-green ribbons on their doublets. They had a newspaper, an internal organisation and a manifesto. Rebuffed by Cromwell and his army leaders in 1647, by 1650 they were making overtures to the royalist court-in-exile.

11 The Whigs were divided into court and country parties, with both sub-groups containing Church Whigs and Dissenters, while the Independent Whigs were opposed to the leadership. After 1688 the Tories were likewise divided into Jacobites and those content with William III, along with other sub-groups.

12 The Fanatics or Phanaticks were actually a discrete group collected around John Lambert, but during the Restoration the term broadened. The court preferred the term 'saints' to describe religious extremists and among the defining characteristics of these groups was an insistence on pushing their demands to a point beyond any practical possibility of delivery. They could vary from the opportunists who fomented the Popish Plot, such as Titus Oates and Israel Tonge, to those who exploited the paranoia the opportunists created, such as the first Lord Shaftesbury. In Scotland, extremist dissenters such as Richard Cameron publicly supported the sectarian murder of Archbishop Sharp while on the Catholic side polemicists such as Jacques-Bénigne Bossuet demanded Catholic toleration in Britain while refusing Protestant toleration in France. Other examples of Catholic extremism might be argued to include James II himself, at least in the opinion of Innocent XI.

13 Antonia Fraser, quoting Clement Walker, *The Compleat History of Independency 1640–1660* (London, 1660), p. 153, suggests that one reason why many of Oliver Cromwell's speeches were repetitive, tautological or intractable in meaning, was that he consciously refrained from planning or practising them, so as to open himself to God's direction. Antonia Fraser, *Cromwell, Our Chief of Men* (London: Phoenix Press, reprinted 1997), p. 265.

14 William Dougal Christie, *A Life of Anthony Ashley Cooper, first Earl of Shaftesbury, 1621–1683* (London: Macmillan 1871), Appendix 1, p. xxii.

15 *The Guardian*, No. 24, 9 April 1714.

16 *The Craftsman*, 6 October 1733, No. 379, quoted in *The Gentleman's Magazine*, October 1733, p. 519.

17 Historians from Harold Perkin to Dror Wahrman have argued that this period saw a remarkably unified culture emerge among the English elite. Harold Perkin, *The Origins of Modern English Society* (London: Routledge, 1969), pp. 51, 55–56, 62. Wahrman, *The Making of the Modern Self*, pp. 166–198.

18 That said, the love of incognito by royalty was more praised than the adoption of gentrified ways by yeoman farmers. Condescension became an accepted term, 'conascension' not.

19 Richard Steele, *The Tatler*, 19 April 1709.

20 Suzanne Aspden, '"An infinity of factions": opera in eighteenth-century London and the undoing of society', *Cambridge Opera Journal*, vol. 9 (Cambridge: Cambridge University Press, 1997), p. 13.

21 *The Journals of James Boswell*, November 1762, edited by John Wain (London: Mandarin Press, 1990), p. 17.

22 Ibid., June 1763, p. 71.

23 Frances Burney, *Evelina*, Letter XXXIII (London, 1778, republished by Norton Press, 1965), p. 134.

24 Judith S. Lewis, *Sacred to Female Patriotism: Gender, Class and Politics in Late Georgian Britain* (New York: Routledge, 2003), p. 171.

25 Linda Colley, *Britons: Forging the Nation, 1707–1837* (New Haven, CT and London: Yale University Press, 1992), pp. 6 and 11, quoted by Suzanne Aspden, 'Opera and national identity', *The Cambridge Companion to Opera Studies*, ed. Nicholas Till (Cambridge: Cambridge University Press, 2012), p. 280.

26 The word 'patriotism' was used at the time rather than 'nationalism'. Despite attempts to define the union of Scotland and England as a partnership of equals within the new state of Great Britain, it was soon clear that in reality the smaller polity had been absorbed into the larger. The failure to create a more inclusive identity covering all the peoples of the British Isles meant that Great Britain and England became interchangeable terms. This, together with much-resented programmes of anglicisation, intensified already existing antagonisms rather than achieving the desired unity. Conflicts with Scotland loomed large in the eighteenth century and conflicts in Ireland continued into the twentieth century.

27 Colley, *Britons*, Aspden, 'Opera and national identity'.

28 'To Mr Handel' by G.O., *The Gentleman's Magazine*, May 1740, vol. 10, p. 254. 'Imp'd' meant engrafting, and derived from the practice of adding feathers to birds in falconry.

29 Tim Neufeldt, 'Italian pastoral opera and pastoral politics in England, 1705–1712', *Discourses in Music*, vol. 5 no. 2 (Toronto: University of Toronto,

2004). Digitised by the University of Toronto. http://library.music.utoronto.ca/discourses-in-music/v5n2a2.html#link1 [accessed 2021].

30 Aspden, 'An infinity of factions', various but esp. pp. 11–13.

31 'On our late Taste in Musick' by a Gentleman of Oxford, *The Gentleman's Magazine*, May 1740, vol. 10, p. 520.

32 The very wealthy could afford to stage their own private operas, oratorios and concerts, as the Beckfords and Dukes of Chandos did, but attendance at the communally owned opera was important; here it was that talented musicians could be sourced and changing tastes among fellow aficionados gauged; also, attendance at the opera house was important in displaying a family's standing and continuity.

33 Robert D. Hume, 'The value of money in eighteenth-century England: incomes, prices, buying power – and some problems in cultural economics', *Huntington Library Quarterly*, vol. 77 no. 4 (Philadelphia: University of Pennsylvania Press, 2014), p. 377. Hume calculates that £1.00 sterling had a present-day spending power of between £200 and £300 for some goods such as bread or gold (at least for most of the eighteenth century; there was considerable inflation towards the end), but counsels against assuming similar equivalences exist between past and present, or between Britain and Italy. Food was cheaper in Italy than Britain, but tolls and taxes greater and housing more expensive.

34 Curtis Price, Judith Milhous and Robert D. Hume, *Italian Opera in Late 18th-century London, the King's Theatre, Haymarket* (Oxford: Clarendon Press, 1995), vol. I, p. 125.

35 Tamara Griggs, 'The local antiquary in eighteenth-century Rome', *The Princeton University Library Chronicle*, vol. 69 no. 2 (Princeton, NJ: Princeton University Library, 2008), pp. 312–313.

36 Ibid., p. 283.

37 Elizabeth Gibson, 'Owen Swiney and the Italian opera in London', *The Musical Times*, vol. 125 no. 1692 (London: *Musical Times Publications*, 1984), pp. 82–86. For Swiney's art dealings see Elizabeth Gibson's entry on him in the *Oxford Dictionary of National Biography*, 2008. Swiney was active in introducing Canaletto to England. For Francis Colman see Richard Brinsley Peake, 'Memoirs of the Colman family including their correspondence with the most distinguished personages of their time', *Edinburgh Review*, vol. 72 (London, 1841), pp. 209–212.

38 At least I have not found any evidence that he did. Crawford and de Michele made their recruiting trip from 11 August to 29 October 1783. Price, Milhous and Hume, *Italian Opera in Late 18th-century London*, vol. I, p. 304.

39 Michael Kelly, *Solo Recital, The Reminiscences of Michael Kelly* (London, 1826, reprinted by The Folio Society, 1972), p. 34.

40 John Ingamells, 'John Ramsay's Italian diary, 1782–84', *The Volume of the Walpole Society*, vol. 65 (London: The Walpole Society, 2003), p. 142, entry for Saturday 8 November.

41 Ibid. The Ramsays were visited by John Udny on 4, 10 and 11 December when he was also visiting Lord Cowper: pp. 145–146. Charles S. Ellis, 'Documentation

for paintings by Fra Bartholomeo in the Salviati Collection in Florence', *Mitteilungen des Kunsthistorischen Institutes in Florenz*, vol. 54 (Florence: Max Planck Institute, 2008), pp. 381–383.

42 Elizabeth Gibson, 'Italian opera in London, 1750–1775', *Early Music,* vol. 18 (Oxford: Oxford University Press, 1990), p. 50.
43 Ingamells, 'John Ramsay's diary', pp. 138–147.
44 Griggs, 'The local antiquary in eighteenth-century Rome', p. 301.
45 Victoria Donnelan, 'The English prize: the capture of the *Westmoreland*', exhibition catalogue (Oxford: Ashmolean Museum, 2018). DOI: http://dx.doi.org/10.5334/pia.419 [accessed 30 November 2018].
46 The British Museum, Collection Online, the Townley Venus. Curator's comments. https://www.britishmuseum.org/research/collection_online/collection_object_details.aspx?objectId=460007&partId=1 [accessed 29 November 2018].
47 Ibid. Thomas Nugent, *The Grand Tour*, vol. 2 (London: 1756), digitised by Pablo Günther, 'The Casanova tour', part XVI, https://www.giacomo-casanova.de/catour16.htm#ITALY [accessed 29 November 2018], p. 30.
48 Nugent, *The Grand Tour*.
49 Griggs, 'The local antiquary in eighteenth-century Rome', p. 302. In June 1731 Francesco Valesio (1670–1742) recorded in his diary that 'a certain Sterbini has left Rome, a priest, but [also] a public dealer [pubblico negoziante] of antiquities. He's been many times in England and he has carried with him many things to sell: 800 rings [and] 4,000 scudi worth of stuff from Ficoroni, and many marbles, inscriptions, statues and busts from Cardinal Albani.'
50 Hume, 'The value of money in eighteenth-century England', p. 389.
51 Price, Milhous and Hume, *Italian Opera in Late 18th-century London*, vol. I, pp. 128–129.
52 Hume, 'The value of money in eighteenth-century England', p. 377. He argues that an annual income of £200 left only around 27s. per month spare for cultural products (£16 a year) and a season ticket to the opera was £21; of the few families wealthy enough to muster such money, only around 150 did so.
53 Beckford hired Pacchierotti to perform at the celebrations for his majority in 1781, and again at Christmas; Beckford also arranged his grand tour around Pacchierotti's performances in Lucca and Venice. The chamber opera or cantata commissioned for the celebrations from Rauzzini was the appropriately named *Il tributo*. D. Landry, 'William Beckford's *Vathek* and the uses of Oriental re-enactment', *The Arabian Nights in Historical Context: between East and West*, ed. S. Makdisi and F. Nussbaum (Oxford: Oxford University Press, 2008), pp. 167–194; I. McCalman, 'The virtual infernal: Philippe de Loutherbourg, William Beckford and the spectacle of the sublime', *Romantic Spectacle*, no. 46 (Montreal: University of Montreal, 2007), digitised by Romanticism and Victorianism on the Net, pp. 1–14, DOI 10.7202/016129ar [accessed 15 July 2017].
54 Peter Beckford, *Familiar letters from Italy to a friend in England*, vol. 2 (Salisbury, 1805), p. 228.

55 In a letter quoted in Price, Milhous and Hume, *Italian Opera in Late 18th-century London*, vol. I, p. 302, Gertrud Mara lost her engagement in Turin while waiting for confirmation of an engagement by Karl Friedrich Abel. They also point out that under Sheridan's management, the King's Theatre, unable to pay the singers' fees in full, extended the season and scheduled more performances until enough box office had been gathered to pay them: ibid., pp. 248–249. Gallini's contracts tied singers to performing at his own concerts in Hanover Square, but as well as the box office he took half their fees, and seems to have taken half again for benefits at the King's Theatre: ibid., p. 409.

56 Julius Bryant, 'Eccentric pioneers? Patrons of modern sculpture for Britain *c.*1790', *Burning Bright: Essays in Honour of David Bindman*, ed. Diana Dethloff, Caroline Elam, Tessa Murdoch and Kim Sloan (London: University College London Press, 2015), pp. 67–72.

57 Ibid., pp. 72–73.

58 Ibid., pp. 74–75.

59 C.G. Heyne, *Sammlung antiquarischer Aufsädtze* (Leipzig, 1779).

60 David Adshead, 'The architectural evolution of picture and sculpture galleries in British country houses', *Art & the Country House*, ed. Martin Postle (New Haven, CT: Paul Mellon Centre digital publications, 2020).

61 William Patoun, 'Advice on Travel in Italy', MS, *c.*1766, Exeter Archives, Burghley House, pp. xxxix–lii, quoted by Adshead, ibid.

62 Strohm, *Dramma per Musica*, p. 125.

63 Ibid., pp. 125–133.

64 Ibid., pp. 125–165.

65 Lowell Lindgren, 'Venice, Vivaldi, Vico and opera in London, 1705–17: Venetian ingredients in English pasticci', *Nuovi studi Vivaldiani*, ed. Antonio Fanna and Giovanni Morelli (Florence: Olschki Press, 1987), pp. 633–666.

66 Strohm, *Dramma per Musica*, p. 138.

67 Ibid., p. 164.

68 Such as Leonardo Vinci, Johann Hasse, Leonardo Leo. Reinhard Strohm, 'Handel's pasticci', *Journal of Ancient Music*, no. 14 (1974), p. 167. Chrissochoidis, 'Handel at a crossroads'.

69 Schubert depicted gusts of wind in *Winterreise* (1827) and Benjamin Britten depicted wolf whistles on a violin for *Albert Herring* (1947) and train sounds in *Midnight on the Great Western* (1953).

70 Chrissochoidis, 'Handel at the crossroads', pp. 610–612, p. 611 for kettledrums.

71 *Wellingtonsieg* by Beethoven (opus 91) was to include muskets and artillery; it was arranged to include cannons by Antal Dorati in 2013. *The 1812 Overture* by Tchaikovsky (opus 49) has cannons and cathedral bells while Franz Liszt's *Hunnenschlach* (opus 105) is a battle symphony but, although the instrumentation is idiosyncratic, it is a pre-cannon battle being depicted.

72 Walter Rex, 'Apropos of the figure of music in the frontispiece of the *Encyclopédie*: theories of musical imitation in d'Alembert, Rousseau and Diderot', *International Musicology Society: Report of the Twelfth Congress*

(Berkeley: University of California Press, 1981), throughout but especially p. 220.

73 Chrissochoidis, 'Handel at the crossroads', p. 612.

74 Correspondence between Katherine Knatchbull and James Harris on 5 December 1738, discussed in Donald Burrows and Rosemary Dunhill, *Music and Theatre in Handel's World: The Family Papers of James Harris 1732–1780* (Oxford: Oxford University Press, 2002), quoted by Chrissochoidis, 'Handel at the crossroads', p. 612.

75 James Love, *Scottish Church Music, its Composers and Sources* (London and Edinburgh: Blackwood and Sons, 1891), p. 65.

76 Alina Madry, 'The use of extracts of Mozart's operas in Polish sacred music', *Operatic Pasticcios in 18th-Century Europe: Contexts, Materials and Aesthetics*, ed. Berthold Over and Gesa zur Nieden (Bielefeld: transcript Verlag, 2021), pp. 591–593.

77 *The Morning Post*, 3 December 1789.

78 Joice Waterhouse Gibson, 'A musical and cultural analysis of *Inkle and Yarico* from England to America, 1787–1844' (unpublished doctoral thesis, University of Colorado, 2011), pp. 140–141, 146–158.

79 Ibid., p. 192.

80 Robert Hoskins, 'Samuel Arnold', *Grove Dictionary Online* (updated 30 March 2020). https://www.oxfordmusiconline.com/grovemusic/view/10.1093/gmo/9781561592630.001.0001/omo-9781561592630-e-0000041499 [accessed 21 September 2021].

81 'She detested Mozart's music which keeps the singer too much under the control of the orchestra, and too strictly confined to time, which she is apt to violate.' Richard, Earl of Mount Edgcumbe, *Musical Reminiscences of the Earl of Mount Edgcumbe; Containing an Account of the Italian Opera in England from 1773 to 1834* (London, 1834), quoted by Jennifer Hall-Witt, *Fashionable Acts: Opera and Elite Culture in London 1780–1880* (Durham, NH: New Hampshire Press, 2007), p. 51.

82 Charles Burney, *A General History of Music from the Earliest Period to the Present Age*, vol. 5 (London, 1789) p. 226. A.F.C. Kollmann, *Essay on Practical Musical Composition* (London: self-published, 1799), pp. 15–16. Heinrich Christoph Koch, *Versuch einer Anleitung zur Composition*, vol. 3 (Leipzig: Bohme, 1793) quoted by Janet M. Levy, 'Contexts and experience: problems and issues', *Mozart's Piano Concertos: Text, Context, Interpretation*, ed. Neal Zaslaw (Ann Arbor, MI: University of Michigan Press, 1996), p. 142.

83 Nancy November, 'Instrumental arias or sonic tableaux: "voice" in Haydn's String Quartets Opp. 9 and 17', *Music and Letters*, vol. 89 no. 3 (Oxford: Oxford University Press, 2008), pp. 346–372, but esp. p. 363. Michael Lively, 'The narrative persona and the nineteenth-century solo concerto: an analytical study of stylistic competency and the troping of temporality', unpublished paper given at the American Musicological Society Conference 2013 (Houston: Texas Women's University, 2013), pp. 1–3, 6. Suzanne Anita Bratt, 'Obligato/obligé:

a musical etymology' (unpublished doctoral thesis, University of Pennsylvania, 2017), p. 180. Michelle Elizabeth Ayres, 'Crossover genres, syncretic form: understanding Mozart's concert aria "Ch'io mi scordi di te", K. 505, as a link between piano concerto and opera' (unpublished doctoral thesis, University of North Carolina, 2018), pp. 61–62.

84 Price, Milhous and Hume, *Italian Opera in Late 18th-century London*, vol. I, pp. 347–351.

85 Ibid., p. 431.

86 The Paris score of *La villanelle rapita* gives a Signor Ferazzi as the composer of this aria on page 34 – presumably Ferrari. The score of the French production is online at the Petruccio Music Library (IMSLP) site: http://hz.imslp.info/files/imglnks/usimg/e/ea/IMSLP408527-PMLP661645-BnF_bpt6k1168470k_-_VM5-78_-_—_La_villanella_rapita_(1789).pdf [accessed 29 October 2018].

87 The critic in the *Morning Herald* was less impressed, but his mistakes about the origins of some of the items suggest he was not a perspicacious critic. His unstinted praise of Mozart also suggests his aim was to encourage the house to stage a Mozart opera. *Morning Herald*, 1 March 1790.

88 In reading it this way I find myself disagreeing with *Italian Opera in Late 18th-Century London*, vol. I, p. 431; Price, Milhous and Hume argue that Bertati himself undermines his opera's 'serious attack on arbitrary aristocratic behaviour' for the sake of a happy ending. There are many possible readings of the finale, but to me the count's backing down seems a direct response to the entire ensemble rounding on him with a powerful 'No, signor!'

89 *La Villanella Rapita; A Comic Opera in two acts, as performed at the Theatre Royal in the Hay-Market* (London: H. Reynell, 1790), pp. 64–67. Reprinted by Ecco Print Editions, 2010.

90 *The Favourite Duett sung by Sig*[ra] *Storace and Sig*[r] *Buselli in the opera La Villenella Rapita* (London: Longman and Broderip, 1790) p. 9. Digitised by the University of Western Ontario https://archive.org/details/lavillanellarapi00mart [accessed 29 October 2018].

91 Price, Milhous and Hume, *Italian Opera in Late 18th-Century London*, vol. I, p. 429.

92 Ibid., pp. 430–431.

93 Examples in 1783–1784 include Pachierotti, Dauberval and Madame Theodore: ibid., p. 128. The evidence mentioning padded contracts is in a Chancery report concerning the King's Theatre finances, Public Record Office, C38/715 Hett's third master's report, 12 November 1784.

94 Michael Kelly also describes appointing singers based on the opinion of other opera practitioners, in *Solo Recital*, pp. 168–169, 230–231.

95 Price, Milhous and Hume, *Italian Opera in Late 18th-century London*, vol. I, p. 266.

96 Ibid., pp. 264–266.

97 Ronan Deazley, 'Commentary on Copyright Act 1814', *Primary Sources on Copyright (1450–1900)*, ed. L. Bently and M. Kretschmer (Cambridge: Cambridge University Press, 2008), n. 130. From 1814 copyright reverted to the author after twenty-eight years, but this Act did not operate retrospectively,

so the right in works published prior to 1814 did not revert. This meant the Act did not cover all authors until 1842.

98 Sharon Turner, 'Reasons for a modification of the Act of Anne, respecting the delivery of books and copyright' (London: Nichols and Son and Bentley, 1813), pp. 24, 26, quoted in Deazley, ibid., '8. The Copyright Bill 1814 and the author's voice'.

99 The Copyright, Designs and Patents Act 1988 created moral rights for creators for the first time; this initiated further legislation over the next thirty years protecting artists in contexts extraneous to copyright registration and establishing intellectual property rights.

100 Deazley, 'Commentary on Copyright Act 1814', '5. The 1808 Copyright Bill'.

101 David Thomson, *The People of the Sea* (Edinburgh: Canongate Press, 1954), pp. 48–49, quoted in Wendy Welsh, 'Identity authority, artistic authority, markets and meaning: contemporary English-language storytellers examined' (doctoral thesis, Memorial University of Newfoundland, 2006), p. 299.

102 Welsh, 'Identity authority', pp. 305–308.

103 G.H. Tucker, 'From rags to riches, the early modern cento form', *Journal of Neo-Latin Studies*, vol. 62 (Leuven: University of Leuven Press, 2013), p. 5.

104 Alfred W. Pollard proposed in *Shakespeare's Fight with the Pirates and the Problems of the Transmission of his Texts* (London, 1915) that some of Shakespeare's quartos were printed illegitimately. For Lewis Lavenu see James Q. Davies, 'Dancing the symphonic: Beethoven-Bochsa's Symphonie Pastorale, 1829', *19th-Century Music*, vol. 27 (Berkeley: University of California Press, 2003), pp. 31–32.

105 Strohm, *Essays on Handel and Italian Opera*, pp. 123–124.

106 Ellen Rosand, *Opera in Seventeenth Century Venice: the Creation of a Genre* (Berkeley, Los Angeles, Oxford: University of California Press, 1991), pp. 219–220. Strohm, *Dramma per Musica*, pp. 37–60.

107 Richard Osborne, *Rossini* (Oxford: Oxford University Press, 2009), p. 90.

108 Quoted by F.M. Scherer, 'The emergence of musical copyright in Europe, from 1709 to 1850', Faculty Research Working Papers Series (Cambridge, MA: Harvard Kennedy School, 2008), p. 5.

109 Ibid., pp. 6–7.

110 Curtis Price, 'Unity, originality, and the London pasticcio', *Harvard Library Bulletin*, new series, vol. 2 (Cambridge, MA: Harvard University Press, 1991), p. 25.

111 Price, Milhous and Hume, *Italian Opera in Late 18th-century London*, vol. I, p. 130. The figures are drawn from the interrogatories of the court of Chancery, 20 October 1788, C24/1929 in the Public Record Office.

112 Charles Austen, a Maidstone lawyer, brought an action against the new MP for financial promises contingent on votes in his interest, which were still considered binding in law: Stanley Weintraub, *Disraeli, a Biography* (London: Hamish Hamilton, 1993), p. 181.

113 Price, Milhous and Hume, *Italian Opera in Late 18th-century London*, vol. I, p. 389; also Price, 'Unity, originality, and the London pasticcio', p. 27, n. 33.

114 Price comments in 'Unity, originality and the London pasticcio', p.27, '*Storace v. Longman and Broderip* is a landmark case in the history of British music copyright, but the judgment left several important questions unanswered'. See also Price, Milhous and Hume, *Italian Opera in Late 18th-century London*, vol. I, p. 393. Scherer, 'The emergence of musical copyright', p. 8. Robert P. Merges, *Justifying Intellectual Property* (Cambridge, MA: Harvard University Press, 2011), pp. 198–202. Hall-Witt, *Fashionable Acts*, pp. 39–40 and 249–250. Hall-Witt does not hail the judgment as a landmark so much as accept the underlying significance routinely placed on it.

115 Maik Köster, 'Borrowed voices: legal ownership of insertion arias in 18th-century London', Over and zur Nieden (eds), *Operatic Pasticcios in 18th-Century Europe*, p. 471, quoting Curtis Price, 'Italian opera and arson in late eighteenth-century London', *Journal of the American Musicological Society*, vol. 42 (Berkeley: University of California Press, 1989), p. 94.

116 Anon., 'Commentary on *An Enquiry into the Nature and Origin of Literary Property* (1762)', critical edn by Ronan Deazley in Bently and Kretschmer (eds), *Primary Sources on Copyright (1450–1900)*.

117 Price, 'Unity, originality, and the London pasticcio', pp. 17–30 (p. 27).

118 Köster, 'Borrowed voices', pp. 472–474.

119 Price, 'Unity, originality, and the London pasticcio', p. 28.

120 Ibid., p. 28.

121 Corona Schröter (1751–1802) in Germany, the Portuguese singer and opera composer Luísa Todi (1753–1833) in Italy and Russia, and Harriett Abrams (1758–1821) in Britain, to name but three. The list continues to grow. Hilary Poriss, *Changing the Score: Arias, Prima Donnas, and the Authority of Performance* (Oxford: Oxford University Press, 2009) shows that compositional choices were still being made by prima donnas until at least the First World War.

122 Köster, 'Borrowed voices', pp. 479–480.

123 Price, 'Unity, originality, and the London pasticcio', p. 30.

124 Köster, 'Borrowed voices', p. 471.

125 Scherer, 'The emergence of musical copyright', p. 5.

126 Osborne, *Rossini*, pp. 92–110 (esp. 92–93, 108–109).

4

Rumours of death greatly exaggerated: 1780s to 1870s

'I hope you have preserved the unities, sir?' said Mr Curdle.

'The original piece is a French one,' said Nicholas. 'There is abundance of incident, sprightly dialogue, strongly-marked characters —'

'— All unavailing without a strict observance of the unities, sir,' returned Mr Curdle. 'The unities of the drama, before everything.'

'Might I ask you,' said Nicholas, hesitating between the respect he ought to assume, and his love of the whimsical, 'might I ask you what the unities are?'

Mr Curdle coughed and considered. 'The unities, sir,' he said, 'are a completeness — a kind of universal dovetailedness with regard to place and time — a sort of a general oneness, if I may be allowed to use so strong an expression. I take those to be the dramatic unities, so far as I have been enabled to bestow attention upon them, and I have read much upon the subject, and thought much. I find, running through the performances of this child,' said Mr Curdle, turning to the Infant phenomenon, 'a unity of feeling, a breadth, a light and shade, a warmth of colouring, a tone, a harmony, a glow, an artistical development of original conceptions, which I look for, in vain, among older performers — I don't know whether I make myself understood?'

'Perfectly,' replied Nicholas.

'Just so,' said Mr Curdle, pulling up his neckcloth. 'That is my definition of the unities of the drama.'

Nicholas Nickleby, Charles Dickens, Chapter 24, 1838–1839.

Mr Curdle's woeful interpretation of the unities gives us a snapshot of the twilight of neoclassicism. His neoclassical vision of drama, as his name implies, has gone sour and the purposes the unities once served are imperfectly remembered; the narrowly defined, Aristotelian rules of art had given way to expectations later classed as Romantic. The benefits the unities were supposed to bring are not those Mr Curdle actually seeks from the drama, 'an artistical development of *original* conceptions' (my italics). Curdle appreciates the feeling, originality, warmth and passion he perceives in the Infant Phenomenon and does not really want the older generation's marble stylisations. His call for 'a completeness', a 'general oneness' recall the now faded socio-political aims of national and cultural unity that eighteenth-century drama was supposed to serve, and even his pseudo-connoisseur bluffing has an eighteenth-century performativity to it. By the time Dickens was writing *Nicholas Nickleby*, calls for national unity seemed unnecessary; patriotism was sufficiently entrenched as to require no advocation but its purposes no longer went unquestioned. To radical audience members such as Leigh Hunt and William Hazlitt calls to patriotism seemed the self-serving propaganda of a closed aristocracy.

In tracing the evolution of pasticcio in the nineteenth century, this chapter finds no discontinuation as was once argued. Weariness with the grand manner and Georgian neoclassicism in general brought certain styles of pasticcio to end, such as the grand neoclassical tragic pasticcio, while other eighteenth-century styles, such as the comic true pasticcio, continued to develop at both metropolitan and regional theatres throughout the century. When a pasticcio style ended, it was more usually because its subject matter or operatic format appeared antiquated, than because the way it had been constructed worked against it. In this, pasticcio was no different to original operas. Operas which designated themselves as a pasticcio continued up to the 1870s, after which it became rarer for reasons discussed in Chapter 5: as the operatic repertoire contracted the word became more associated with other artforms and took on a metaphoric quality, being used for many things constructed out of pre-existing parts. This century also saw an intense hostility develop among connoisseurs, the press and scholarship towards the *practice* of art or commodities being compiled from pre-existing parts, regardless of whether the result was designated pasticcio or not; this is seen in sculpture, wine making and many other activities as well as opera. Undoubtedly, this pressure acted as a deterrent to commissioners and pasticcieri in labelling their works as pasticci but, as discussed in this book's introduction, self-designation had never been a rule for pasticcio operas in the eighteenth century. As argued in the introduction, pasticcio was not, strictly speaking, a genre but a construction method so adaptations and extravaganzas felt no need to advertise this so much as characteristics which described the story. Nineteenth-century pasticcio methods were mostly identical with those used in the eighteenth century and reformists in the press delighted in rooting out pasticcio practices and sneering at them. The *Musical Standard* dismissed James Robinson Planché's *King Christmas*, arranged by J.W. Eliot in 1872, as a 'mere pasticcio of English airs'.[1]

Adaptation is, of course, a spectrum and it is impossible to formulate a universally applicable measure that pinpoints when an opera ceases to be the original work and becomes that of its adaptors. The *expectation* that operas, ballet scores and the accompaniments for fantoccini, spectacles and historical re-enactments would be compiled from pre-existing music, with textual and narrative interpolations from elsewhere, obtained throughout the nineteenth century. This did not necessitate advertising such performances as unoriginal: in the nineteenth century's elastic use of this term, a new compilation was as original as a new composition. In this chapter, I have called an opera a pasticcio when its construction method is identical with traditional pasticcio practice, but identify whether it called itself a pasticcio, was branded as such by critics, or called itself something else. Adaptations which were close to the original opera but still contained some aria substitutions, plot or textual changes, or interpolations, I have referred to as having some pasticcio practices.

The first section looks at the vexed relationship between pasticcio and a society which increasingly privileged (and redefined) authenticity and originality. I suggest that pasticcio was used to further an opera's authenticity and originality and was not uniformly seen as compromising it. One example is its use in revising the gender characteristics of operatic characters and the vocal types and ranges thought appropriate. The second and third sections offer case studies from London and Bristol that demonstrate the continuation of pasticcio operas of all kinds, from grand operas to one-act farces, in a wide range of theatres and, in so doing, counter assumptions that pasticcio became extinct in the nineteenth century.

The concluding section argues that pasticcio's continuation and evolution was connected to the development of mass literacy. Although many oral characteristics survived in opera, mass literacy shaped the context in which they functioned – pasticcio is one example. Novels were increasingly the source material for new operas, as were contemporary events such as the pasticcio depicting Queen Victoria's marriage which drew on both oral and newspaper accounts. Another noticeable impact of mass literacy on nineteenth-century opera was an intensification of the visual experience it offered. As Michael Burden and others have noted, design, special effects and credibility when representing the gothic or fantastical all increased in sophistication from the late Georgian period onwards.[2] Pasticcio was a preferred method of creating musical accompaniments both for wholly visual performances and for visual sequences within performances. The evolving concept of authenticity is traced throughout these sections and, while this put pasticcio under pressure as a practice in many artforms, I propose that it was not until the financial and legal constraints of the performing rights system that pasticcio became marginalised in opera, a discussion reserved for Chapter 5.

Pasticcio and society from the 1780s to 1830s

Authenticity and originality

The Stuart dynasty, the great rivals of the reigning Hanoverians, was politically defunct by 1807. While the threat it represented came to an end politically in that year, the earlier sense of urgency for national unity had long been replaced by other anxieties.[3] The civil wars and their aftermath had been so long out of living memory that the combatants' strategies for containing sectarian divisions were no longer understood, or deemed unnecessary.[4] Along with other artforms, operatic narratives reflected new concerns such as civil liberties, personal freedoms and personal identity. Operas now questioned the legitimacy of authority, probed different fault lines in morality from those examined in the eighteenth century and kept pace with changing expressions of gender, class and what might constitute honour, vice and virtue.[5] Most noticeably, opera was deeply influenced by a new value placed on authenticity and originality, a preoccupation which affected much of elite life in nineteenth-century Britain.

Industrialised mass production increased exponentially in Britain and this changed people's relationship with the material world. Goods which had formerly been affordable only by the elite, or been rare, treasured possessions among the poor, such as dinner services, carpets, wallpaper, books, guns and ornamental lighting, gradually became cheaper and affordable through mass production. In reaction to this, an insistence by the elite that their own goods be handcrafted and unique pervaded the luxury goods market; the status of the artisan producer of such goods rose in consequence. The Pugin family, James Purdey and William Morris were considered to be artists as much as craftsmen and their designs for furniture, candelabra, guns and wallpaper were equated with artforms. Critical reviews and the opinion of connoisseurs thus protected the status and price of luxury goods by downgrading the social status of factory-produced goods. Outside the luxury market the status and income of artisans of all kinds sank. There was nothing organised or deterministic in this and exceptions can be found, but in a society where a famous painting had hundreds of copies or variations and where statuary could be reproduced in miniature as household ornaments, possession of the original and evidence of its authenticity conveyed wealth and status.[6] The originality and authenticity which elite society sought from goods and material art were also sought from the performing arts: an opera created by a single artist, canonised as an acknowledged master of the form, became more valued than an assembled one, created collaboratively.

Authenticity became something of a fetish. Critics began to demand authentic stagings of operas, which could mean authentic representations of the country it was set in, as much as a reproduction of the composer's intentions. At Covent Garden in 1801, the playbill for Mazzinghi and Reeve's opera *The Blind Girl*, 'set in the country surrounding Lima', assures audiences that the dresses were 'entirely NEW and Fashioned in exact Conformity to the Costume of the Country'.[7] The concept of a 'national song' emerged: an opera set in Scotland, Poland or Germany would contain a typical song from that country, often a folk song, interpolated into a scene to enhance the authenticity of the location. *The Illustrated London News* saw 'The Last Rose of Summer' in Flotow's *Martha* as exemplifying this: '[t]he composer introduced it as a national air, taking it for granted that it would be understood as such'.[8] Playbills in regional theatres began to advertise their staging of an opera as authentically the London staging, while metropolitan operas claimed to be authentically those of the continent, even though both seldom were.[9]

Authenticity might include fidelity to the original intentions of the composer and librettist but this was not the only or the most obvious interpretation. Opera performances were often caught between competing kinds of fidelity: being true to the original source material, especially if that was a famous play or novel, counted for more with many audience members than whether the performance was faithful to the texts of the composer or librettist. Regardless, James William Davison claimed that absolute fidelity to the texts mattered more to his 'Musical Public' than any fidelity to the original story.[10] To those invested in traditional interpretations of leading roles, fidelity to an interpretative apostolic succession by succeeding divas was more important than either of the previous fidelities. A nineteenth-century opera often served one kind of fidelity at the expense of others, drawing sharp criticism from reviewers invested in those others. Fromental Halévy and Eugène Scribe's *La Tempesta* (1850) was an original opera, that departed substantially from Shakespeare's story, giving scenes to Sycorax (Sicorace in Italian) who sows discord between the lovers Miranda and Ferdinand up to the point that Miranda is ready to murder Ferdinand. There are also new scenes for Caliban, who imprisons Ariel in a pine instead of his mother, while the plot to overthrow Prospero is wholly excised. *Punch*, *The Musical World*, Henry Chorley and others were deeply critical of the opera's departures from Shakespeare's story, feeling that the continental artists had not understood it properly.[11] Conversely, Ambroise Thomas's *Hamlet* (1868) was criticised for being insufficiently operatic. I propose that overlapping, competing and contradictory fidelities characterise nineteenth-century opera and, as discussed in Chapter 5, twentieth-century musicologists from Oscar Sonneck in the 1920s to Carl Dahlhaus in the 1980s extrapolated just one fidelity over the others – fidelity to the score – a perspective that influenced opera studies up to the end of the century.[12] For nineteenth-century audiences, all kinds of fidelity were production values, to use that term anachronistically, goals which made an opera performance authentic and pointed up its originality.

William Macready stripped from Shakespeare's plays the accretions and interpolations of a century and a half, returning to the dialogue given in the First Folio (1623). Nineteenth-century scholars were determined to excavate the original and authentic Shakespeare, but Macready's motivation in his stagings was as much to augment the playwright's premier status as it was an act of antiquarianism. He did the same with Purcell's *King Arthur* and, while many lauded these restorations as bringing greater authenticity, others lamented his departure from the traditional stagings they knew and understood. For these audience members it was this new fidelity to an all-but-unknown, crude, original, often full of plot imbalances, which rendered the performances inauthentic. Unexpectedly perhaps, these critics included Davison, an otherwise arch-advocate for fidelity to the composer's intentions: he castigated Purcell's opera as profoundly dull and disappointing before lamenting that

> the admiration, so generally professed, by non-professors, for the music of *King Arthur* must remain a mystery. To us, the entire performance at Drury Lane Theatre wears the atmosphere of a gorgeous pantomime – a pantomime rejoicing in every desirable characteristic but that of *good pantomime music* – in which latter characteristic it is totally and lamentably deficient ... And this pantomimic display – this miserable handle for the machinist, the decoratist, and the scene-painter, is thrown at our heads by Mr Macready, and the *Spectator*, as a noble specimen of British musical genius, and as a guarantee and a sign, how much that excellent actor, but very ignorant musician, has the interest of native composers at heart![13]

Davison was angered by a fidelity which he thought did not show indigenous English music in a good light and was caustic about the Antiquarian Society (the non-professors of music) who had commissioned this restoration. Not only did he dislike experts from outside his coterie, but he felt that fidelity to the intentions of the composer and poet in what he saw as weak operas undermined his arguments for absolute fidelity to the scores and libretti of great ones.[14] In contrast to his stereotype, I suggest that Davison preferred a strong pasticcio to a weak original.

Originality did not solely mean something that had not been done before; its earlier resonances were of a story, event or object the origin of which was discernible and respected. An original opera could thus be one based on classical myths, a novel or a famous play; it did not have to offer an entirely new story to be original. An artwork created by a single canonical genius had a clear and laudable origin whereas an artwork created by people who were unaware of each other's contributions, compiled by an editor whose process was not obvious, or artworks which had changed radically over time, had no clear origin. If such an opera was good, on whom did one lay the laurels? Pasticcio art, like illegitimate children in novels, were mysterious in their histories. In oral cultures, storytellers had downplayed claims to authorship, as we have seen, and neoclassical opera had inherited this passivity; authorship was displaced from the storyteller or librettist to ancient or semi-mythic figures like Virgil or Homer and this gave the story's origination fame and antiquity. Yet between the 1780s and 1830s this changed in many performance genres and opera began to prefer stories where a named, canonical and *relatable* originator could be identified: new works by the unknown could still be met with suspicion. Only a comparatively small number of new operas stayed in the repertoire for more than few seasons, and fewer still achieved canonical status, as Frederick Curtis Petty has shown and Paul Rodmell discussed.[15] In tune with this trend, in the nineteenth century comparatively few true pasticcio operas were created with an entirely new story; most retold or burlesqued existing ones. Pasticci that did create new stories were often responding to contemporary events – such as coronations, military victories, royal marriages or the Great Exhibition – their origination thus carried the authority of a national event. Origination in pre-existing continental operas also provided acceptable provenance but it was not until the twentieth century that confidence in using pasticcio to create wholly new narratives re-emerged.

Nineteenth-century definitions of what constituted authenticity or originality could be at odds with each other, but adverse attitudes towards assembled goods, art and performances can be found in writers and critics of all kinds. Composite classical sculptures and blended wines came under much the same pressure as pasticcio operas, with critics using much the same quasi-religious language. A common pool of metaphors was used to elevate products felt to demonstrate authenticity and originality – 'purity' and 'immortality' being common – while products felt to be inauthentic or unoriginal were castigated as 'blasphemous', 'sacrilegious' or a form of apostasy. Advocations of fidelity in all artforms, I suggest, used such language to create an unchanging fixity in value, and the common, though unacknowledged, result of this connoisseurial stance was protection of the socio-economic value and prices of artistic luxury goods and experiences. Rejecting the plentiful and the easily accessible as artistically unequal to the handcrafted and expensive was part of professional criticism's service in the nineteenth century. Even so, this and Chapter 5 argue that critical hostility was not as synoptic as has been claimed, nor did it extinguish pasticcio within the artform. Consequently, I propose that the demotion of pasticcio in the nineteenth century was socio-economic in motivation rather than due to any intrinsic deterioration in the artistic quality of pasticcio art during this period; very fine pasticcio operas, sculptures and wines were still created.

While pasticcio operas may not have been mass produced, they did proliferate in the nineteenth century. They occur regularly at Her Majesty's Theatre and Covent Garden up to the 1870s, and formed a substantial part of the programming in London's new theatres and that of new regional theatres across the country. As in the eighteenth century, some were designated pasticcio, others not, but those that were not now had a new motivation for not doing so in critical hostility. Yet, ironically, it was during this period of critical hostility that pasticcio operas became most ubiquitous and their very proliferation may have been a causal factor sustaining the critical hostility. The next sub-sections examine how advocations of fidelity and hostility to pasticcio affected other artforms and commodities such as sculpture and wine making.

Pasticcio practices in sculpture change

From the turn of the nineteenth century, the practice of creating pasticcio statues and antiquities through interpretative restorations began to be discontinued. A new value was given to the incomplete, the damaged and the fragmentary as these became an expression of the object's authenticity. So rooted did this new perspective become in the world of antiquities that, by the twentieth century, eighteenth-century interpolations would be removed from many statues so as to recover the sculptor's original intentions. The additions of later periods were considered to have no value in themselves as they provided no insights into the original conception. Yet from the late twentieth to the twenty-first centuries a renewed interest in seeing the journey of a work of art over time has meant that often, now, a statue's commercial value is higher with later-period restorations than without.[16] This coincides with the rehabilitation of pasticcio opera both in scholarship and in practice.

Modern neoclassical or 'ideal' sculpture established itself between the 1780s and the 1830s in response to the new premium on originality; these works dispensed with the antique fragment around which an essentially modern sculpture was created. Modern neoclassical sculptures were created by British artists working in Italy, including Thomas Banks, John Deare, John Flaxman and Joseph Nollekens, and by Italians serving the British market, such as Antonio Canova and others. Their 'new' Greek or Roman sculptures were made out of white marble or plaster but remained firmly within the classical idiom. Sculptures salvaged from the classical past had never quite delivered what the neoclassical present had wanted that past to be: they seldom tallied with the texts, had variant styles and were damaged. Creating classical statues from scratch meant that sculptors could now match the classical past more exactly to neoclassical desires.

4.1 *Caesar invading Britain* by John Deare, *c*.1791–1796.
Source: Victoria & Albert Museum, released under Creative Commons Licence.

An example is John Deare's marble frieze *Julius Caesar invading Britain* (1791–1796). The British empire was keen to write itself into the past, much of the island having been part of the Roman one which so fascinated it. No surviving sculpture from the Roman period that specifically referenced Britannia existed in the form of great statues: there was no equivalent of *The Dying Gaul*, for instance, only references on tombstones, altars to British gods and mosaics which may or may not have depicted scenes relevant to Britain. Deare's frieze is one of a number of examples of patriotic presentism, works that corrected Rome's puzzling omission of Britain; such works supported an origin story and even provided a template for British imperialism. Such works provided patrons with sculpture that perfectly reified their fictive world and this sculptural genre moved steadily from pasticcio to pastiche.

Initially patrons and collectors were hesitant to accord modern sculptures the same status as genuine antiquities.[17] In an indicator not so much of desirability but status, modern statuary was priced beneath the best examples from antiquity as a matter of course. Julius Bryant notes that in 1774 George Grenville bought an antique statue, *Meleager*, for £450 from Thomas Jenkins, heavily restored by Carlo Albacini. Yet in 1778, he refused to pay £200 for a bas-relief he had commissioned from Thomas Banks in Rome; according to Mrs Banks '[h]e has Protested Mr Banks Bill for two Hundred Pounds, being one Hundred more than his due ... for he never intended to give so much for Modern work'.[18] Even so, the last two decades of the century saw opinion gradually change and prices for modern sculpture grew closer to those for antique works. Increasingly, sculptors themselves preferred to create originals rather than copy or restore antiquities. In 1780–1781, an original sculpture by Antonio Canova, *Theseus and the Minotaur*, was commissioned by the Venetian Ambassador in Rome, a commission given only after the artist had refused to carve marble copies of antique originals.[19]

4.2 Reclining figure from the East Pediment of the Parthenon, identified in the early nineteenth century as Theseus, the statue to which Hazlitt refers. *Source:* British Museum, released under Creative Commons Licence.

A counter-genre emerged in reaction to modern neoclassical sculpture: collectors who had invested heavily in antique statuary fought a rearguard action against any notion of parity in cultural value between ancient and modern. Faced with astonishing similitude in modern sculpture, they did not want new artistic criteria applied when comparing the two. Canova and others had been advocating exactly that, a reform of the criteria for judging sculpture based not on age or even authenticity but on aesthetics alone. The new, pristine, modern works had the advantage of providing the subject matter collectors wanted, in the style they wanted and in a state of perfection so, to retain the status and value of their antiquities, collectors had to compete on different grounds, ones where authenticity was pointed up. As part of this reaction, restorations were gradually rejected in favour of displaying broken and fragmented statues; a new approach which saw patinas left alone, lost arms and noses unreplaced, and worn inscriptions unrechiselled. Writing of Hazlitt's response to the Greek sculptures shipped to England by Lord Elgin between 1802 and 1812, Orietta Rossi Pinelli says:

> Hazlitt judged the Parthenon statues as richer with life than the ancient statues known up to then, precisely because they were fragments. The fact that the work of art had lost its completeness meant it could be imagined to be of another realm where it acquired the force and integrity of a natural phenomenon. The marbles were impregnated with an historical aura that no complete work, even antique, could achieve: 'Ruins are grand and more venerable than any other modern structure can be, or than the oldest could be if kept in their most entire preservation ... So, the Elgin marbles are more impressive from their mouldering, imperfect state. They transport us to the Parthenon, and old Greece. The Theseus is of the age of Theseus; while the Apollo Belvedere is a modern fine gentleman, and we think of this last figure only as an ornament to the room where it happens to be placed.'[20]

Susan Walker of the British Museum, along with most specialists in classical sculpture, also see the Elgin marbles as leading this reaction against pasticcio sculpture and in favour of unrestored antiquities.[21]

Gallini's policy at the King's Theatre in the 1780s chimes in with these changes in sculpture. He too, was concerned to provide an authentic experience, but of modern Italian opera rather than ancient Greece and Rome. Unamended Italian operas were now allowed to be unfamiliar, odd, or to reveal different behavioural codes, just as the imperfections caused to antique art by nearly two millennia in soil or water were increasingly allowed to testify to their authenticity. The King's Theatre distanced its operas from those of its rivals by performing wholly in Italian, preserving recitative and offering genuinely continental operas and performers. Unlike sculpture however, authenticity in opera did not militate against the use of pasticcio, which could be a method of enhancing the authentic: the interpolation of national songs to create a greater sense of locale, aria substitution to make characters' behaviour accord with what were felt to be timeless values, both gave greater authenticity. But while a desire for the authentic did not always go hand in hand with originality during the nineteenth century, pasticcio came under pressure in most artforms through the privileging of these two requirements.

Pasticcio loses status in wine making

For centuries, ordinary claret had been a blended wine created from the wines of various vineyards stretching across the Bordeaux region and sometimes far beyond.[22] The skills involved in blending wines were no less than those required for pasticcio statues or operas but blenders of wine also found their skills declining in prestige from the late eighteenth century onwards. Wine blending faced similar criticisms, couched in similar language and underpinned by the same imperatives as pasticcio in opera and restoration in antiquities. Nineteenth-century wine connoisseurs perceived blending as a failure to respect the original character of a wine from a discrete commune or estate. Wine writers proposed that a particular terroir or grape variety had an intrinsic flavour that it was the wine maker's duty to reveal; in other words, an inner self. Such a narrative inevitably cast blending as a violation but its devaluation began earlier in wine than it did in opera or sculpture.

Charles Luddington describes how the 'new French claret' arrived in Britain in the same decade as Italian opera, 1700–1710.[23] Casks of Châteaux Haut Brion, Margaux, Latour and Lafitte [*sic*] consisted of wine supposedly made from grapes grown on these respective estates alone. Along with similar château-bottled wines, they were presented as superior to all blended claret and priced accordingly; the blends that had previously led the market continued to be sold alongside them with prices indicating the standard of the constituent wines and the skill of the master blender.[24] The gradual price discrimination between what one might call pasticcio wines and new château-bottled originals occurred from the eighteenth into the nineteenth centuries. To take the 1740s as a baseline, of the wines sold by Tastet and Lawton Château Haut Brion was the most expensive at 1,458 livres tournais per tonneau (£60 15s. according to Thomas Nugent's conversion tables), making a hogshead (roughly a quarter of a tonneau), around £15, while you could get very good blended claret for 450 livres, £18 5s., per hogshead (Sir Robert Walpole paid this). Walpole usually preferred exceptionally good blended claret and Nigel Surrey notes £36 as the usual price he paid for a hogshead (*c.*£146 per tonneau), more than twice what he paid for Haut Brion.[25] By 1803, however, Priddy's Foreign Warehouse and Vaults gives the price of first-growth clarets as £3 3s. per dozen bottles while the price of blended claret was 12s. 6d. per dozen: prices of blends had fallen to almost a sixth of those for château-bottled wine.[26]

The conceptualisation behind blended wine production was that there was a distinctive character to be maintained for each commune; wines from Margaux, for example, were supposed to be 'feminine' and evoke violets. Rather than not declare a vintage when the harvest was not quite as typical as hoped for, when the grapes were insufficiently ripened or diminished by disease, a supposedly single-estate wine was topped up with additions from other estates to preserve its typicity: it was a practice called 'équivalance'. A tonneau of blended Margaux might contain wines from outside Margaux, chosen because they displayed the femininity and violet tones required. Château Lascombes, for example, owed Château Margaux two tonneau annually, as a latter-day feudal due, used for topping up that year's vintage. The parallel with aria substitution is inescapable: arias were interpolated not as stylistic interruptions or dilutions but to ensure the high standard of a sung performance. As discussed in Chapter 2, the regional styles of Italian opera meant that aria selection had to preserve the Venetian, or Neapolitan, character of the opera being staged, so were carefully chosen. Équivalence was practised with the similar aim of preserving a wine's high standard; it created a stable product that offered a recognisable and expected expression of the wine.

The faith in vineyards having an inner self led to wines being marketed as typifying not just a single estate but even specific parts of an estate, or specific harvestings. Château d'Yquem sold separate wines from each trie, this being a passing of the pickers through the vineyards. Marketed as 'tête', 'centre' and 'queue', they were different wines as each had different levels of botrytis or noble rot in the grapes. More noble rot set in with each trie so they increased in sweetness and complexity from tête to queue. In reality, not all bunches did rot with equal nobility at each trie, so the three were blended to create the three distinct identities. Château-bottled wines that were as authentic as they claimed to be only emerged slowly out of a centuries-long heritage of blending. As with pasticcio opera, the practice continued for longer and was more prolific than the châteaux marketing suggests. Château-bottled wines continued to use wines extraneous to the estate in this period. Yet as a Romantic ethos influenced nineteenth-century wine writing, knowing how a wine had been made became as much a part of the overall experience as its taste, so équivalence was put under critical pressure.

Mid-nineteenth-century wine writers used remarkably similar language in condemning blended wines to that used to condemn pasticcio in the arts. Music critics like J.W. Davison were greatly concerned to know how true a performance was to the composer's original intention as this affected how much he enjoyed it; William Hazlitt felt the same about sculpture, Cyrus Redding and George Saintsbury the same about wine. Rod Phillips notes that Redding deplored the continuation of équivalence in the 1850s:

The influential English wine writer Cyrus Redding ... noted all Bordeaux wines destined for the English market were 'worked' in some way; they were blended with wines from Spain and Hermitage, and some alcohol was added:

'Orris root is employed to give the perfume taken away by mixing, and sometimes a small quantity of raspberry brandy is introduced, two ounces to a cask, in order to flavour factitiously and replace the natural flavour it has lost'.[27]

Redding regarded blending as an imposition on the public rather than a skill in itself, dismissing the product as an indiscriminate mixture concocted for the merchant's profit. Yet when his hostility to blending is stripped away, he reveals that unity of style was of great concern to blenders. They were conscious that intermixing wines lost distinctive elements of character and took steps to prevent this happening. We see a similar care taken to ensure that substitute arias or pasticcio sequences preserved the dramatic unity and, often, the Italian flavour of an opera, rather than allowing weak original sequences to lower the whole. Reconstructed antiquities, similarly, sought to match the neoclassical expectations of art collectors.

Due to blending, vintages before the 1780s were remarkably like each other, but for those vineyards in the following century, after the practice was discontinued, vintages were more variable. In some years, a wine could be terrible, in much the same way that originality in an opera composition is no guarantee of its quality. The question has to be asked, then, whether original operas, the new classical sculpture or single-estate wines were the progression Romantic and neoromantic writers have claimed. Christina Fuhrmann demonstrates that absolute fidelity in an opera did not always go down well in nineteenth-century London.[28] If one included everything that had been written for an opera, as happened with Samuel Beazley and Henry Bishop's *Don Giovanni* in 1833, an interminable performance could ensue which lacked pace. The originality of an original composition was often disappointing (critics found that Rossini's new operas often sounded remarkably similar to his previous ones). Not every year could be a vintage one for château-bottled wines, unless a degree of blending took place or the definition of a vintage was broadened to include sub-standard years. Blended clarets continued to be sold and pasticcio operas continued to be programmed throughout the century, but often in less exclusive markets. Some wine blends have remained highly prized up to the present, including those of burgundy and port; moreover, current French law only requires 75 to 80 per cent of a wine to be that stated on the label. The capacity to go outside the appellation, if not the region or country, is still considered essential for product stability.

Pasticcio might have been under pressure from reformers but it remained the core method of making the product meet the expectations of the consumer and survived the century in both arts and commodities. Leaving economics aside, why did critical hostility to pasticcio intensify so emotionally in the mid-nineteenth century? I propose that attitudes were influenced by a new conception of personal identity which emerged between the 1780s and 1830s and which greatly impacted on society in Britain.

The decline of the performed self and the rise of the inner self

In a reaction against the self as a polished performance, a new preoccupation with the 'inner self' began to influence artforms; it embedded itself between the 1790s and the 1830s and remained throughout the century. Civility and formality were still core to elite social interaction but, within these parameters, sincerity became a defining virtue.[29] Sincerity was revealed rather than chosen and this influenced how people were portrayed in novels, plays and operas. Characters who gave self-conscious performances of themselves were now received as liable to be deceptive and artificial, rather than being judged approvingly on their polish. The inner self, almost a secular form of the soul, was held to be a person's true character, their real nature, which could not be changed, or changed only very slowly and by bitter experience. Novels, ranging from 'Monk' Lewis's gothic exposé of clerical hypocrisy in 1796 to Dickens's *Pickwick Papers* in 1836, reveal a deepening anxiety that people might not be what they seemed.[30] Ambrosio the lecherous monk, Matilda his mistress and Alfred Jingle the plausible swindler conceal their real characters behind a mask of virtue and this distrust of the performed self characterised narratives up to the 1880s. George Gissing's character Osmond Waymark, in *The Unclassed* (1888), scrutinises his fiancée's account of her upbringing for traces of performance, knowing that he would have performed if called upon to do the same:

> His relation, he knew, would have been a piece of more or less clever acting, howsoever true ... How far was this the case with Maud Enderby? Could he have surprised the faintest touch of insincerity in look or accent, it would have made a world of difference in his position towards her. His instinct was unfailing in the detection of the note of affected feeling ... That all was sincere he could have no doubt.[31]

As well as those of individuals, the public persona displayed by institutions became increasingly distrusted; many offices of state, churches, courts of law and parish organisations prided themselves on ancient custom and conducted their business with great ceremony, but nineteenth-century reformers often felt ceremonial to be a concealment of failings and incompetence.[32] A new generation of fictional heroes, typified by Nicholas Nickleby, Martin Chuzzlewit and David Copperfield along with their creator, wanted to peep into the hidden workings of government, suspecting that they would find a mass of rottenness and corruption. Exhumations, to open the coffins of long-dead kings and saints when any building work was needed on cathedrals and churches, changed from being a mere curiosity, as it was in the eighteenth century, to an antiquarian and scientific determination to test the authenticity of received history.[33] A political speech now had greater effect if it was perceived as coming 'from the heart' rather than being a highly polished recreation of classical oratory. The nineteenth century would want to know what precisely went into its food, whether its antiques were genuine and if its wines really consisted of what was said on the label.

The artistic process, that private, backstage area in which art was constructed, was no longer a reserved space for insiders alone; consumers now wanted to check that their art conformed to the new parameters of a luxury product and process was now a matter of critical discussion. So far as possible, operas were to be the work of a solo author, grand in their origination and quite unlike the more accessible kinds of performance. These criteria militated against pasticcio and yet, I suggest, the number of opera performances in nineteenth-century Britain which successfully met all the requirements for fidelity, originality and authenticity were proportionally very few. Evidence that pasticcio and fidelity were not an opposing binary is revealed by the use of pasticcio practices to bring an original opera more into line with the need for 'authenticity'. When eighteenth- or early nineteenth-century operas were revived later in the century, pasticcio tools such as aria substitution, interpolation and transposition were used to create inner selves for characters that had originally been conceived without them, and to provide credible motivations for characters when these had been lightly sketched in, or absent. Yet at the same time that pasticcio practices were used to bring greater credibility to the setting, the period or to move an opera closer to its original narrative, this was also departing from the composer's score or the libretto. Moreover, operatic practices such as cross-dressing, gender parody and, given a mass literate society's tendency to read art as texts, intertextuality, were positively disruptive of authenticity and originality as we conceive these concepts today. I propose that these three operatic traits feature more noticeably in pasticcio than in new canonical works.

Musicology's older narrative, that fidelity simply drove out pasticcio, is too stadial. While current scholarship argues that nineteenth-century opera changed unevenly and inconsistently, twentieth-century musicology, until its last decades, subscribed to the Romantic concept of eternal verities. Music writers tended to depict changes as stadial and coherent, with absolute fidelity being a principle sought by all serious musicians.[34] I suggest that nineteenth-century music writing could be apophenic: the same critic who deplored departures from the score in one opera could accept them in another. A critic appalled by a singer's failure to perform an eighteenth-century Italian character in a manner acceptable to nineteenth-century British expectations could also be appalled if doing so required changing the text. Such critical contradictions are explored in detail below.

The Romantic inner self was still a world away from the psychological self of the twentieth century and, viewed from a modern perspective, it was just as much a social construct as the openly performed self it sought to replace. Judith Butler's writings about gender construction are not specific to any particular period, and tend to describe modern rather than historic gender formulations; nevertheless, I suggest her arguments are relevant to gender construction in the early nineteenth century as this period saw the formulation of much that constitutes modern conceptions of the inner, gendered self. Noting of the 'psychic space or soul' that its 'primary mode of signification is through its very absence, its potent invisibility' Butler argues that the inner self is 'a figure of interior psychic space inscribed *on* the body as a social signification that renounces itself as such'.[35]

> In other words, acts, gestures, enactments and desire produce the effect of an internal core or substance, but produce this *on the surface* of the body, through the play of signifying absences that suggest, but never reveal, the organising principle of identity as a cause.[36]

The inner self is performed through bodily behaviours which deny the constructed nature *of* those behaviours, invoking the very absence of any other evidence for an inner self as proof of its existence and character. The collection of behaviours, parameters and types of appearance that constituted masculinity and femininity were held to be natural and timeless, rather than recent constructs, and integral to the true or inner self. Although Butler is writing about gender identities specifically, her point holds good for performances of class, virtue, learning, maturity, ingenuousness, competence and other things. This change in the perception of the self was causal in changes of attitude towards pasticcio in all its many expressions. The transformation of maquillage between 1789 and the 1820s offers an encapsulation of how the new inner self was inscribed on the body and performed. This in turn allows us to see how this new understanding of the self affected operatic characterisation and how the climate for pasticcio became more emotional as a result.

Stylisation in maquillage had been entirely acceptable up to 1795 but, thereafter, it was increasingly decried as unnatural and artificial in women's journals such as *La Belle Assemblée* and books on female conduct including *The Mirror of Graces: Or, The English Lady's Costume*.[37] Patches, white face paint, the delicate painting in of veins, the shaving of eyebrows to paste on softer ones made of mouse fur and even the whitening of natural hair to counterfeit wigs were all discontinued by the young and fashionable. By 1806, eighteenth-century styles were considered passé except among ci-devants.[38] The concept of natural beauty which replaced it put great value on a seemingly undisguised countenance.

4.3a *Countess de Bavière-Grosberg* by
Alexander Roslin, 1780.
Source: Auktions verket Stockholm,
released under Creative Commons
Licence.

4.3b *Grace Dalrymple Elliott* by
Thomas Gainsborough, *c.*1778.
Source: The Frick Collection, released
under Creative Commons Licence.

4.3c *Virvara Ivanovna Ladomirsky* by
Élisabeth Vigée Le Brun, 1800.
Source: Columbus Museum of Art,
released under Creative Commons
Licence.

4.3d *Mrs Harrison Gray Otis* by
Gilbert Stuart, 1809.
Source: Reynolda House, Museum of
American Art, released under Creative
Commons Licence.

The use of rouge survived the make-up cull, though its new purpose was to create a rosy glow, to convey a bloom in the cheeks, whereas formerly it had stylised the shadow cast by high cheekbones. It had also contrasted the whiteness of the foundation with a vibrant red, a contrast now felt to be too stark and artificial. The simplicity of directoire gowns replaced the stiff paniers and panels of high Georgian fashion; hair was still elaborately dressed but given the appearance of being unstyled. Free-flowing, 'natural' locks conformed to Regency ideas of femininity yet probably took longer than attaching a wig, while corsets were still worn underneath the Empire dresses.[39] As the misogynist cartoons of the day pointed out, this natural simplicity took a lot of artifice to create, but in this period true déshabillé was still unthinkable. In these decades society was much attracted to the *idea* of a woman appearing without maquillage, wigs, and with her 'true' figure undisguised but, in reality, it was by no means ready to accept a woman appearing in public with her hair and face just as it was, or wearing practical clothing. Such styles did exist but they were considered statements of extreme political affiliation and thus a fringe identity for many women.[40] Cropped hair à la Titus was a statement of radicalism and sympathy for the Revolution, consequently it was considered to be going too far in all but the most radical of circles. Coiffure à la victime was almost identical but expressed the reverse: solidarity with the executed enemies of the Revolution and was thus a statement of ultra-royalism.[41]

The maquillage of eighteenth-century men, in many instances, had been indistinguishable from that of women; both had borrowed styles from each other, and books such as Pierre-Joseph Buc'hoz's *The Toilet of Flora* (1772) contained receipts for pomades, face paint, toothpastes, perfumes and beauty regimes, which were written without discrimination of sex.[42] But male use was not uncontested. Much the same charges levelled at opera were levelled at male 'face-painting', that it was foppish, continental, unpatriotic and tending towards luxury and dissolution.[43] In the 1820s and 1830s, hostility to male maquillage became acute as the male inner self was required to reveal a tightly defined and socially approved masculinity with an obvious heteronormative sexuality. Maquillage formerly common to both sexes was now gendered as one or the other, and books on appearance and conduct were increasingly written for men *or* women. Fixity and clarity in what constituted masculinity and femininity were major desiderata in the early nineteenth century and male maquillage was disruptive of these new, tighter parameters.

Changes such as these prompted similar gender delineations in the construction, or reconstruction, of operatic characters. Vocal casting for masculine heroism in the 1790s still preferred higher-register voices – castrati, female musicos and tenors – but over the next forty years high-register heroism

4.4a Coiffure à la Titus (or à la Victime), *Madame Arnault de Gors* by Louis-Léopold Boilly, *c.*1807.
Source: The Louvre, released under Creative Commons Licence.

4.4b Portrait of an unknown lady by Louis-Léopold Boilly, *c.*1807.
Source: The Louvre, released under Creative Commons Licence.

gave way to lower-register masculinity sung by baritones and tenors – the latter succeeded in spanning the shift. The musico had originally referred to a castrato but in the early decades of the nineteenth century they tended to be female contraltos.[44] In a study of the early nineteenth-century tenor Nicola Tacchinardi, Parkorn Wangpaiboonkit discusses the singer's criticisms of female musicos.[45] To modern eyes, Tacchinardi's criticisms suggest that musicos struggled to negotiate between performance of their own female identity as 'inscribed on their bodies' (their hair, carriage, physique and gestures), their metacharacter as a famous female singer (the deportment, modesty and manners of a lady) and the masculinity of their stage character. Tacchinardi describes them as refusing to wear swords and opting for female clothing and appearance where they could:

> The fit of her dress and the style of her hair are always that of a lady. Her helmet is worn at an angle in order to show off her lavish curls, which are parted at the front to descend across her cheeks, always in the feminine manner. How could we ever deceive ourselves that this figure represents a conquistador, a fearsome warrior, a husband already a father, a rival for kings and for queens.[46]

Wangpaiboonkit argues that Tacchinardi felt his own masculinity slighted by this femininised performance of heroic male roles: a performance of masculinity so unreverential made the very concept absurd for the tenor.[47] This suggests a new anxiety in opera about cross-dressing which was largely absent in earlier generations.

Pasticcio's multiple practices were agents of disruption to these newly solidifying gender boundaries but also provided the tools whereby they happened. Wangpaiboonkit shows how Tacchinardi used aria substitutions to reframe the masculinity of his characters so that they accorded more with the new gender parameters. His substitutions heightened their physical activity, their willingness to engage in confrontation and highlighted the character's emotional profile rather than their breeding: status was now qualified by gender.[48] As Uberto in Rossini's *La Donna del lago* (1819) he departed from the composer's highly traditional construction of the character as august and disengaged. Traditionally, Uberto was performed as one who orders others into action while remaining static himself, a character type inherited from opera seria and not very far removed from Queen Thomyris, but Tacchinardi replaced 'O fiamma soave' with Giovanni Pacini's more impassioned 'Essa il mio cor rapi' in his performances throughout Italy and subsequent tenors singing the role followed suit.[49] When contraltos sang this role many of them did so too: the former aria was omitted in the London performance of 1823 and replaced by the latter in the 1829 performance by the contralto Rosamunda Pisaroni.[50]

The scene following this was frequently replaced with one depicting a confrontation between the different male suitors, as Wangpaiboonkit demonstrates. In a production in Paris in 1824, Rossini himself got involved and created a confrontation quartet, for which he reworked a sequence from *Bianca e Falliero* (1819), and other substitute scenes were staged across Europe over the succeeding decades.[51] Only a handful of substitutions were made to Rossini's *La Donna del lago*, compared to full pasticcio operas, yet considerable changes to the characterisation resulted. Singers, then, were not just responding to changes in gender performance, they were themselves active participants in creating that change.

The sound of a singer's voice was surely integral to such identity construction but Wangpaiboonkit does not see the tenor's vocal characteristics as integral to the display of his gendered inner self:

> The tenor during Tacchinardi's career could not claim his place in the masculine-heroic roster by privileging the gendered timbral quality of his voice: his singing was more an emitted 'representation' of fixed mimetic states, not an extracted 'presentation' of inner life, a physiological presence from deep within. To be 'as a man' on stage in the 1820s, then, was not determined by an ontologically male voice of particular timbre, but rather was an aesthetic register codified in the performer's visual presentation and decisiveness of action.[52]

He claims that prior to the development of the heroic tenor chest voice in the late 1830s, singing was not yet understood 'as a "grainy" expression of an individual's natural interiority'.[53] Rather, he sees Tacchinardi's interiorising of a new conception of the gendered inner self as occurring in the field of acting and visual appearance alone.[54] I question whether the timbre and qualities of tenors' voices at this time could form *no* part in their performance of an inner self. Tacchinardi's sensitivity towards the portrayal of masculinity did not occur in a vacuum: criticism of all high-register male singing was mounting in the press, who portrayed it as essentially feminine and feminising.

In his studies of Velluti, the last known castrato on the London stage, and of falsetto singing in early-nineteenth-century German opera, Robert Crowe examines critical hostility to higher-register male singing by castrati, counter-tenors and tenors, as well as falsetto singing in all its forms.[55] The use of falsetto (voce finta), called the feigned voice in English, was an integral part of tenor singing and used in various ways and contexts by all vocal registers. Yet falsetto faced pressure in these decades with critics portraying it as an inauthentic type of singing.[56] As the century went on, acceptable uses of falsetto narrowed to certain specific circumstances such as parodic or comedic impersonation, or church choral music where female singers were not permitted. Joseph Corfe, principally a church musician but intimately acquainted with Italian opera, wrote *A Treatise on Singing* in 1799.[57] His turn-of-the-century comments show that falsetto was still ubiquitous at this point on the operatic stage and he praises the skills involved in producing it:

It has always been a matter, not to be accounted for by Professors of Music, why the deepest Bass Voices should, in general, sing in a Falsetto, and with greater taste than in their natural voices and that the contr'alto should have the least Falsetto of either of the other voices. The fact is however certain, if a Treble part is wanted in a Quartetto, and there is no Soprano Voice, the Bass is generally called to sing it.[58]

In the twenty years between falsetto being one of the regular skills employed in opera, as Corfe describes, and Giambattista Velluti's arrival in 1825, enthusiasm for falsetto, castrato singing and counter-tenor singing chilled considerably. Crowe gives Richard Mackenzie Bacon as an example of a critic who castigated such singing as unmasculine in his treatise on singing in 1823:

Of the artificial falsette I do not speak. It is now, happily for humanity, unknown in England; nor, I do hope and believe, will my countrymen ever again endure such a degradation of their species.[59]

Bacon's 'countrymen' and 'species' are masks for 'men' and 'masculinity', offended nationalism being a displacement of his disquiet at the ambivalence implied by men singing in a register increasingly gendered as female.[60] Tenors were implicated in this hostility because, as well as having a high vocal timbre, falsetto was a normal part of their singing. I suggest that Tacchinardi, and tenors like him, felt a need to combat this growing identification of their vocal timbre with femininity, passivity or want of virility. Tacchinardi's voice was thus the window through which he invited listeners to view his inner self; what they perceived when they looked through that window had already been shaped as masculine by his visual appearance, his action and acting, but the artistic and personal aim of these displays was, I suggest, to perceive his *voice* as masculine. I agree that visual presentation, action and aria substitutions were the weapons used, but the wider fight was for the meaning of the tenor voice; Tacchinardi wanted his vocality to reflect his own masculinity as well as that of his characters. That vocality *could* be perceived as revealing the inner self is evidenced in George Eliot's dramatic poem *Armgart* (1870); the central character is a prima donna who

> ... often wonders what her life had been
> Without that voice for channel to her soul.[61]

Aria substitution may have been of service in bringing operas into accord with new gender definitions but many operatic practices undermined the conception of gender as an immutable essence. Cross-dressing was one such; not only did it complicate gender, but it usually necessitated departures from the original texts to greater or lesser extents. When older tragedies were updated and former castrato roles adapted for contraltos, as in Gluck's

Orfeo, or male parodies of female characters were created, as in *Die falsche Catalani* (1818), transpositions, substitutions, recompositions and parody were often required. Gender disruption and textual disruption went hand in hand.

Cross-dressing continued throughout the century in serious operas as much as comic and in pasticci in particular. They often delight in the sexual frissons they created: Eugène Scribe's libretto for *Gustave III* (1833) was the basis for a range of operas on this story; not only does it make the king's page Oscar a travesti role, but the libretto hints at a liaison between page and king. This controversial feature was part of Auber's original setting and the pasticcio version created by Thomas Cooke and James Robinson Planché for Covent Garden in the same year.[62] It was retained in Mercadante's setting in 1843, but when Verdi and his librettist Antonio Somma were writing their several versions of the opera between 1857 and 1859, they redacted from the libretto anything likely to stir controversy, especially the implied liaison between Oscar and Gustav.[63]

Pasticcio versions of Gluck's *Orfeo* had been staged in London and Dublin with a male Orfeo so long as castrati could be found; after that, male falsetto singers and female musicos were used until Berlioz's *Orphée* of 1859. This adaptation made Orpheus definitively a contralto role and subsequent variations by Alfred Dörffel (1866), and others at Riccordi & Co. (1889) and Novello & Co (1890), followed suit. Eliot's prima donna in *Armgart* sings Berlioz's Orpheus, and this offers a snapshot of how departures from the score, gender construction and cross-dressing intersected in problematic ways for the nineteenth century. There is tension between Armgart and her vocal coach Leo, an elderly composer, over absolute fidelity to Gluck's vocal scoring. Armgart introduces a trill, unscored by Gluck, for which act Leo is critical. The prima donna's defence is not only the audience's enjoyment of it, but that in some sense she *is* Gluck:

> ... Tell them, Leo, tell them
> How I outsang your hope and made you cry
> Because Gluck could not hear me. That was folly!
> He [Gluck] sang, not listened: every linkèd note
> Was his immortal pulse that stirred in mine,
> And all my gladness is but part of him.[64]

Leo, however, refuses to accept that she could embody Gluck and thus gain the authority to alter his score. If the singer is an 'artist', Leo implies, she makes herself the docile channel for the perfect animation of texts left by the dead male god that is Gluck. He rejects the notion of the singer as Gluck's successor through a kind of apostolic succession; for him, a woman's attempt to usurp Gluck's authority is an insulting transgression, which not only downgrades the kind of singer she is but the kind of woman she is:

... quit your *Orpheus* then,
And sing in farces grown to operas
Where all the prurience of the full-fed mob
Is tickled with melodic impudence:
Jerk forth burlesque bravuras, square your arms
Akimbo with a tavern wench's grace,
And set the splendid compass of your voice
To lyric jigs.[65]

For Leo, there is nothing between absolute fidelity and a roaring Italianate pasticcio for the mob. In identifying departures from the score with low-status women and pasticcio, there is more than an echo of Davison and similar critics, and one proposes that Leo contains an element of satire by Eliot. Yet the biggest departure from Gluck is the one Leo fails to mention: that a male lead is sung by a woman; it is Armgart who points this out, noting that no one in the audience missed having Orpheus played by a man.[66] Having the authority to change the score is thus inextricably connected in this poem to ever-tightening gender constructions, a process Armgart is well aware of when refusing marriage: 'I need not crush myself within a mould of theory called nature'.[67] The two divide on this question, but when a departure from the original is needed to save a male genius's work from disappearing, such as changing the sex of the lead singer, then even Leo's fidelity must give way.

Butler notices the capacity of cross-dressing or gender parody to disturb the conception of masculinity and femininity as unchanging, inherited human characteristics:

In imitating gender, drag implicitly reveals the imitative structure of gender itself – as well as its contingency ... Parodic proliferation deprives hegemonic culture and its critics of the claim to naturalized or essentialist gender identities.[68]

While pasticcio practices facilitated gender disruption in serious operas, it is in comic pasticcio operas that we find direct challenges to naturalised or essentialist gender identities. Cross-dressing was often used for gender parody, sometimes in very sophisticated ways, which directly addressed questions of whether the parameters of gender actually lay where they were thought to. Crowe describes pasticci which had male singers performing a female prima donna singing the male lead. In Germany, Ignaz Schuster performed Gentile Borgondio's performance of Tancred in 1817, but did so reverentially rather than mockingly, recreating her performance with perfect mimesis.[69] Yet, following Schuster, the title role in this pasticcio was performed by women as the 1820s went on, bringing one less layer of fluidity to the gendering.[70]

Pasticci which offered not just cross-dressing but gender parody ran throughout the period. Drury Lane's *The Son in Law*, originally by Samuel

Arnold in 1779, was reworked in 1825, when James Russell parodied Velluti. In the famous German parody opera *Die falsche Catalani*, Crowe shows that Catalani's performances were recreated by Schuster, then Karl Blumenfeld, Friedrich Kirschner and others, into the 1860s. Catalani had attended a performance and enjoyed it but, when she had passed from living memory, the piece became a portrait of a generic prima donna. Female roles written for men also continued such as the Witch in *Hansel and Gretel* (1893), but most frequently in operatic burlesques which also saw most of the male roles sung by women. Comic operas could afford to expose fault lines and contradictions in the grand claims made for gender that would have been unacceptable in a serious opera. In all of these examples, cross-dressing, gender parody and pasticcio practices go together.

It is hardly coincidental that critics such as Barnes, Alsager, Bacon and others who were markedly hostile to departures from the original texts were also deeply invested in tight definitions of gender, perceiving German music as masculine and Italian as feminine. The one concern could often act as a mask for the other, as we have seen in Bacon's hostility to falsetto: criticisms of infidelity to the score masked another discomfort over gender disruption. In 1857, Benjamin Lumley commissioned an updated staging of *Don Giovanni* for Her Majesty's Theatre. Reviewing its revival for *The Times* in 1858, Davison was challenged by Marietta Piccolomini's performance of Zerlina as a woman of sexual agency and decision and, like Bacon, he couches his objection as a breach of Mozart's intentions:

> Mademoiselle Piccolomini's Zerlina is bustling, eager and vivacious, but hardly the Zerlina with whom 'Mozart seemed to have fallen in love as Pygmalion with his statue'. We fail to recognise in her 'the soul, the mind', and even the 'much vanity' which the young peasant-bride of whom Don Giovanni becomes suddenly enamoured is supposed to possess. Nevertheless, if Mademoiselle Piccolomini would not always be striving to appear *the* most prominent figure on the stage she might do much more with this part – histrionically at least.[71]

Davison's quotations are probably from Alexander Dmitryevich Ulybyshev's 1843 biography of Mozart which turned both the composer and his characters into nineteenth-century Romantics, complete with inner selves.[72] Davison's criticisms of female singers usually focus on problems in singing techniques, breathing or departures from the vocal score, but here he finds little to criticise musically in Piccolomini's performance. His discomfort is the distance between her arguably more authentic portrayal of Zerlina (without an inner self), and the nineteenth century's need for gender to be a natural, timeless and unchanging essence.

As Annika Bautz has shown, defences of fidelity to mask gender discomfort can also be found in critical reactions to Henry Bishop and Daniel Terry's

Guy Mannering (1816). Sir Walter Scott himself had co-operated with the adaptors and Terry faced high expectations of literary fidelity in his libretto, yet Terry represented Lucy Bertram, Flora and Julia Mannering as more submissive than they were in Scott's novel.[73] Later female performers experienced criticism if they departed from this chaste and passive characterisation, even though they may have been more in line with Scott's original intentions.[74] As Bautz argues:

> Terry's adaptation renders the novel more conservative, for example in its representation of issues relating to gender. Lucy Bertram is passive in Scott's novel, too, but this is intensified in the play and reviewers expected actresses to present the character in 'chaste' ways.[75]

In other words, fidelity to Scott's novel was less important than fidelity to contemporary conceptions of the feminine ideal. A certain Mrs Gibbs was castigated as Flora because her costume was felt to be insufficiently demure for the character, while Maria Tree, Catherine Stephens and Miss Carew were praised for their 'modest propriety', 'sweetness and simplicity' and 'chaste acting'.[76] As with Tacchinardi's aria substitutions, Bautz notes that insertion arias were 'the means for the actor to render his or her version of the character distinct'.[77] Feistier Victorian heroines followed and, by 1847, Julia Mannering was singing 'I'll be no submissive wife'.[78]

The need for an inner self to be inscribed on the (sounding) body is also apparent in the change in attitudes to vocal ornamentation. Opera singers still created their own ornamentation and fioritura during the early decades of the nineteenth century, but musicologists from John Rosselli in the 1990s to Sean M. Parr in 2016 have noted that as the composer's status within opera creation rose, they increasingly felt that they should be the ones to compose any such ornamentations.[79] Critics who advocated what was later called the work-concept thought so too, and both parties felt that too much floridity militated against a character's emotional sincerity. The melismas given to Miranda in Fromental Halévy's *La Tempesta* (1850) were criticised by the *Daily News* as 'too florid and ornate for the simplicity of the character'.[80] Emotion, it was argued, was conveyed in the voice more realistically through clear vocal lines, than in the stylised trills, cadenzas and extended melismas that characterised coloratura singing. Rosselli considers 'Dormono entrambi' sung by Bellini's Norma and Rigoletto's 'Pari siamo' as instances of the new approach; Rossini's tomb scenes in *Semiramide* (1823) and the Israelites' Prayer by the Red Sea in *Mosè in Egitto* (1818) he sees as examples of vocal simplicity in ensembles.[81] Despite male critical disapproval however, singers did continue to add their own ornamentations, as Poriss and others show, and as Eliot's Armgart portrays.[82]

Although the condemnation of flamboyant ornamentations was a conventional admonition to singers, it gained new traction as verisimilitude and textual fidelity rose in importance for critics and connoisseurs.[83] High coloratura had been written for all vocal types in the eighteenth century and used in a wide variety of dramatic contexts but Parr shows that composers increasingly confined it to female roles during the middle decades of the nineteenth century.[84] It was increasingly reserved for contexts where elaborate coloratura was congruent with a character's inner self or emotional state, being often used to suggest a giddy, overexcited or vengeful state, such as in Violetta's 'Sempra libera' in Verdi's *La Traviata* or Abigaille's 'Anch'io dischiuso' and 'Salgo gia' in *Nabucco*. Parr argues that high coloratura had largely disappeared from Italian operas for female mad scenes by the 1840s, but it had a final flourishing in French opera in the 1850s and 1860s. After this, mental illness was scored and staged differently and singers found different ways of performing the coloratura scored in earlier operas.[85]

This section has argued that pasticcio practices, being simply techniques for altering the artwork, were in themselves ideologically neutral. They were tools which could be used to promote authenticity but could equally be used to undermine it and, unlike the varying kinds of fidelity, no ideological programme was attached to them. The exact proportion of pasticcio practices needed before an opera can be declared a pasticcio is a question for Lord Kenyon or, more recently, the judges in Ed Sheeran's court cases, but not only were these practices required for maintaining a canonical repertoire and for balancing competing fidelities, they created a substantial number of operas constructed wholly through pasticcio methods. Indeed, pasticcio operas were ubiquitous throughout the nineteenth century, as discussed next, and were arguably more plentiful than in its supposed golden age.

Pasticcio opera continues throughout the nineteenth century

Pasticcio and the old musicology

Scholarly tradition, until the relatively recent New Musicology, saw pasticcio operas of all kinds, as well as pasticcio practices such as substitutions, interpolations, changed plots or libretti, as stuttering to an end during the first thirty years of the nineteenth century. After the 1830s, scholars considered the moral argument for fidelity to have outdistanced justifications for changing scores or libretti for performance. Opera performances that failed to reproduce the original authors' intentions, as these were envisioned in their original texts, were thought to have been obstructed from achieving this in some way, by a lack of resources or other problems rather than by the performers or theatre making a deliberate artistic decision to. Commissions to a famous composer and librettist were seen as the only legitimate means of creating a new opera with any claim to authenticity. This perspective is reflected in the writings of Oscar Sonneck, Theodor Adorno, Stanley Sadie, Winton Dean, Carl Dahlhaus and others.[86] In reaction to this, the musicology of recent decades has challenged such stadial or determinist perspectives on music history, arguing that performance history (as distinct from the history of musical texts) show that metanarratives and stadialism tend to crumble on closer inspection.[87] I agree, but suggest that modern attitudes towards pasticcio have remained, in many ways, within the frameworks created by the older musicology: mid-twentieth-century conceptions of pasticcio seep into the writings of otherwise modern scholars.[88] Jennifer Hall-Witt and Theodore Jenner considered Bochsa's *I Messicani* of 1829 to be the last pasticcio at the King's Theatre, though John Goulden's study of Michael Costa pushed the terminus of the approach to the mid-1830s, with *L'esule di Roma* (1832) and *Mathilde de Shabran* (1833).[89]

The bracket of operas which were neither true pasticci nor original compositions – those which had been changed to greater or lesser extents for performance – and often labelled adaptations, are argued by Fuhrmann to have steadily accorded more closely with the intentions of their original authors over the course of the century.[90] She proposes that pasticcio was steadily replaced by adaptations of continental operas between the 1820s and 1840s, arguing that these formed a transitional stage between the eighteenth-century pasticcio and an absolute fidelity located later in the nineteenth century.[91] As suggested in Chapter 1, light-touch adaptations that retained as much of the original opera as was serviceable can be found throughout the eighteenth century as well as the nineteenth. André Grétry's *Zémira e Azore* (1771), staged at the King's Theatre in 1779 using the Italian translation by Mattia Verazi, was more faithful than the Drury Lane adaptation by Thomas Linley, which was still being programmed in 1813.[92] Similarly, the London version of Paisiello's *Il barbiere di Siviglia* in 1789 was a substantially faithful staging, with the revivals of 1793, 1798 and 1807 becoming gradually less so, as one might expect. By comparison, Bishop's adaptation of Rossini's version of the story from 1818 and onwards, as described by Fuhrmann, showed a greater quantity of changes and interpolations.[93] This does not discount her argument that many nineteenth-century adaptations showed an increased concern for fidelity towards the original, yet these were contemporaneous with operas showing little or no textual fidelity. Some of these proudly designated themselves a pasticcio in demonstrable continuity from eighteenth-century practice, such as *Il Ritorno di Columella* (performed in London 1857); others were new nineteenth-century genres and include burlesques which parodied operas, such as Meyer Lutz's

Faust Up to Date (1888). New descriptors were found for operatic pasticci such as the extravaganza and, taken together, these suggest that the nineteenth-century continental adaptation was not necessarily a stadial evolution *from* pasticcio but one of its many expressions, one shade in a broad spectrum.[94]

Secondly, I propose that the absolute fidelity presumed to lie somewhere later in the nineteenth century, and to which Fuhrmann argues the continental adaptation leans, never quite emerged.[95] A reformist network of critics, writers and music scholars, as discussed in Chapter 5, are represented in twentieth-century narratives of opera history as the agents who achieved a uniform textual fidelity in opera; however, their battle cries span a suspiciously long time. The Handel Society's performance of *Israel in Egypt* at the Crystal Palace on 26 July 1891 was lauded in *The Times*, the reviewer assuring readers that no one in the audience felt the piece was the least diminished by Handel's borrowings from Stradella, Kerl and Erba. Yet, rather inconsistently, he deplored the use of Costa's arrangement because it was not the composer's original score:

> The highest credit is due to Mr Manns the conductor who, however, missed one or two opportunities of making the bicentenary of Handel's birth as memorable as it might have been. Such an occasion should have been used for producing a short choral work or a selection from one of the oratorios exactly as Handel wrote it and instrumented it. Or if this was impossible, Mr Manns might at least have amended some of the more glaring acts of violence inflicted on Handel's scores by the late Sir Michael Costa.[96]

This is one of many reviews suggesting that nineteenth-century reformers did not succeed in banishing pasticcio from the stage. Music writers, especially professional critics, could be much more vitriolic than this reviewer, and their venom was seldom deflected when a theatre marketed a pasticcio as an adaptation; they named such operas pasticci because that is what they felt these were, Planché's *King Christmas* (1872) being an example mentioned earlier.[97] Despite their pejorative value judgements, I suggest such identifications were accurate.

The evidence presented below and in Chapter 5 shows that there is no ultimate terminus for pasticcio, even in leading opera houses. Not only do pasticcio operas designated as such continue into the twentieth century, but pasticcio operas that are labelled something else proliferate. Different styles, dramatic genres and formats constantly emerge but the practice of assembling operas from pre-existing material continued. Reformist critics were often less invested in absolute fidelity than later musicology presented them as being: both William Ayrton and Davison could take an adaptation to task if it had not gone far enough in remodelling the opera for London audiences, as discussed below.

The assumption that pasticcio ended was a consequence of the contraction in its definition, discussed in Chapter 1. Only true pasticci which designated themselves as such were considered to *be* pasticcio operas; the vast numbers that did not were excluded from the definition however much they were assembled from pre-existing material. To have included them would have disturbed the entrenched metanarrative normalising textual fidelity and projecting it backwards. In an age when F.R. Leavis found widespread acceptance for the concept of a deserving literary immortality for a small canon of greats, any recognition of the sheer quantity of composite works would have presented fidelity as time-contingent rather than transhistorical; yet, following Strohm's reassessment of Handel's pasticci in 1974, the definition began, slowly, to broaden once again.[98]

Another strand of evidence running counter to the traditional metanarrative concerns the geographic parameters of the discussion. Most analysis in the twentieth century was metropolis-centred, the assumption being that what was true for theatres in the capital must hold true for the country as a whole. This section offers evidence for the continuation of pasticcio in regional opera and the influence of this continuity on metropolitan practice: it was two-way traffic. What follows is a survey demonstrating the wide range of pasticcio operas performed in nineteenth-century London before moving the discussion out of London to the Theatre Royal, Bristol.

Pasticcio continues in London

The King's Theatre became Her Majesty's following Victoria's accession in 1837 and Covent Garden became the home of the new Royal Italian Opera Company in 1847. Alfred Bunn established a German Opera Company, named for Prince Albert, at St James's Theatre in 1840. Michael Burden notes that until Lumley's management of Her Majesty's, French and German opera tended to appear first at the two patent theatres, then the new minor theatres, while the former King's Theatre staunchly continued all-sung Italian programming, translating Austro-German operas into Italian where necessary.[99] A great number of new theatres had sprung up between the 1770s and 1830s, not just in London but in towns and cities across Britain and Ireland. The Restoration period's system of licenced monopolies came to an end and a comparatively free market in performance genres took its place. Censorship still existed and even became more exacting but the multiplication of theatres was caused by, and was causal in generating, more socially and economically diverse audiences. What had been called the illegitimate or minor theatres grew in stature over the course of the century and the range of performance genres went far beyond those available in the eighteenth century. The 'mixed bills' that 'had something for everyone' now included reduced versions of operas, parodies of operas, burlesques and new types of short opera amongst the exotica, acrobatics, patriotic addresses, illusionists and farces. The mixed bill was the perfect environment not only for pasticcio opera to thrive but for artistic cross-pollination between it and the city's opera houses.

Striking examples of ambitious, true pasticcio operas which are so named can be found throughout the century and a contemporary Neapolitan one, *Il ritorno di Columella*, was given at St James's Theatre in 1857. Originally *Il ritorno di Pulcinella*, it was composed by Vincenzo Fioravanti in 1837 but, becoming *Columella* in 1842, this opera buffa was performed in the Neapolitan dialect and acted in that style. The piece had accrued arias and new sequences in the meantime from Saverio Mercadante and others and the music had been further modernised by the conductor, Alberto Randegger. It was reviewed with unexpected warmth in *The Times*; the authenticity of the piece was acknowledged but the reviewer thought the acting, at least, should have been adapted to suit English tastes. *The Times* admitted the pasticcio was hugely popular with the audience, who laughed throughout, and suggested a bit less fidelity might improve it.[100] This moderation seems hard to square with Davison's usual snarling hostility towards pasticcio. He may have been ill and delegated to a stand-in with diametrically opposed views, or perhaps unseen influence was brought to bear by the newspaper, but a more likely explanation is that Davison was not as absolute in his views as he is sometimes represented as being. There are several instances of Davison evading his stereotype by advocating changes to an original text; he argued the acceptability of transposing Don Giovanni to a tenor when reviewing an adaptation of the piece at Covent Garden in 1858.[101] Davison or his deputy also offer a snapshot of how intertextuality, as experienced in a mass-literate society rather than a proto-literate one, began to factor in audience 'readings' of pasticcio operas. He described the music thus:

> The serious portion is very much in the style of Verdi; the comic part is better, because it contains many pleasant reminiscences of Rossini. The trio, in particular, between the doctor and the two valets in the third act, by far the best thing in the piece, brings at one to mind the famous 'Papataci'.[102]

Unscrambling the omelette to identify its constituent eggs during the performance itself was not a feature of storytelling reception in orally conditioned cultures. Reference, allusion and parody were frequently present and intended to be noticed, but mentally disassembling a pasticcio to observe its origins and thus test its authenticity belongs to the nineteenth century.[103] Pasticci which advertised themselves as such were staged into the 1870s at the Royal Gallery of Illustration, including *Baden Baden* created by Corney Grain in 1871 and others by James Robinson Planché.[104]

Among pasticci which called themselves something else was Milton's *The Masque of Comus*, given at Covent Garden in March 1842 and reviewed in the *Morning Chronicle*.[105] Performances of this story were, by tradition, pasticcio in form, incorporating ballets, text and characters from Milton's other poems and ever-changing selections of music. The closest it got to an original setting was Thomas Arne's *Comus: A Masque Alter'd from Milton* (1738). Since then, it had been a performance tradition to base the music on Arne's score but also include items from Purcell's *King Arthur* and Handel's *L'Allegro*. As a genre term, 'masque' carried resonances for nineteenth-century audiences of a courtly English form and of English history; pasticcio, by contrast, carried Italian connotations, but nineteenth-century audiences still expected a masque would be a mixture of good things and that single authorship was not to be expected. Madame Vestris's visually extravagant 1842 production was typical of an antiquarian pasticcio, displaying the music of the past to inspire pride in that past as Arnold's *Cesare in Egitto* had done, but reshaping it to the needs of 1842, rather than exhibiting it in the manner of a museum piece. The *Chronicle's* reviewer praised it, noting its success with the audience, but in the manner of reformist reviewers, he was not entirely satisfied as to the 'propriety' of replacing some of Arne's music or changing some of Handel's words, but reveals an understanding of why this was done. In *The Times*, Davison traced the lineage of the component parts, praised the performances but was also uncomfortable with the assembled format. The following year William Macready responded at Drury Lane with a version claiming to be closer to Milton textually (although only half the lines appear to be so), and with only one of Henry Lawes's original airs restored; the pasticciere was Thomas Cooke.[106] Madame Vestris's pasticciere so far remains anonymous; like Cooke, however, he or she was probably someone relied on by Covent Garden to create pasticci, such as Michael Raphino Lacy or Henry Bishop.[107]

One indicator of how far the value of music had risen over the libretto in this period was that the latter could sometimes be changed completely without the opera being castigated as a pasticcio. Sweeping though such a change was to an opera, the relative stability of the score meant the work was still felt to be within the bracket of the authentic and original. In deference to lobbying by religious groups, Rossini's *Mosè in Egitto* was adapted as *Pietro L'Eremita* in 1822, the lobbyists having objected to the staging of biblical narratives as a frivolous use of holy text. Through similar deference, Verdi's *Nabucco* became *Nino, Rè d'Assyria* in 1846. On one hand, the replacement of the *Mosè* narrative with Peter the Hermit's medieval crusade fitted the music well: peasant crusaders are taken prisoner by Noraddin, Sultan of Egypt, who refuses to let them go until Peter's miraculous proofs of divine favour compel him to. On the other hand, the manager John Ebers still found himself apologising to much the same lobby in his foreword to the printed libretto, this time for stretching the audience's capacity to believe in popish miracles, the opera having now become a very unProtestant story: '[t]his may serve as an apology for the marvellous which it was found necessary to introduce in this Drama'.[108] The transformation of Verdi's Children of Israel into Babylonians was equally controversial, though here the religious lobby shot themselves in the foot by performing the music, unacted, at Exeter Hall. Both operas saw new words fitted to adapted existing scores. These pasticci remained the form in which these operas were known to much of the anglophone world until at least the 1860s.

The Olympic Theatre staged a pasticcio of *John of Paris* in 1869; this was originally a composition by François Adrien Boieldieu, set to a libretto of Claude St Just in 1812. It was first reworked in England by Henry Bishop and Isaac Pocock in 1814 and staged intermittently throughout the century, being reworked each time. Mostly these are described as adaptations of Boieldieu, but fidelity to the story greatly outweighs fidelity to the texts of Boieldieu and St Just, demonstrating how the material distinction between a pasticcio and an adaptation could become overstrained. In evading press hostility to the word pasticcio, those staging this opera had no qualms about using pasticcio methods to create the performances, yet were sincerely concerned with fidelity when it came to representing the story. The Olympic's 1869 revival was directed by the principal singer and manager Constance Roden, with new interpolations written by Thomas Taylor, the theatre's musical director. Taylor's contributions to the piece were greatly applauded by the audience; it was widely popular and staged across the country.[109] Hariel Becker's touring company revived it with Anne Lapommeraie (Rose Bell) and Henry Hallam in the leads in 1877 and it was staged again at the Theatre Royal, Dublin in 1880.[110] It was still being included in Charles Annesley's *The Standard Opera Glass, containing the Detailed Plots of 158 Celebrated Operas* in 1915, prefaced by references to a recent revival. Like Auletto's *Orazio* in the eighteenth century, this is an example of an opera remaining in the repertoire for a long time but evolving over that period. I suggest that *John of Paris* could thus be seen as a performance tradition, like *Orazio*, rather than a fixed 'work', despite retaining the original authors' names.

Unfinished or fragmentary opera texts by composers considered great geniuses in the Romantic period were completed by other hands and marketed as restorations of forgotten masterpieces, in much the same way that eighteenth-century sculpture studios had repaired the damage to recently excavated Greek and Roman statues. Both artforms created fully restored, pristine works which were composites of the original and the new. The restored sections of both reflect perceptions, prevalent at the time of restoration, about the period to which the original belonged. While eighteenth-century restorers were careful and scholarly in their pastiches of original sculpture, nineteenth-century opera restoration was more concerned to make the original match the composer's reputation. In 1870, *L'Oca de Cairo* was staged at

Her Majesty's Theatre in April and then again in May at Drury Lane as part of the latter's Italian opera programme. This was an opera begun by Mozart and then abandoned; it was completed in Paris by Charles Constantin in 1867 using music from Mozart's other operas, although Constantin also interpolated his own music and wrote the required recitatives. This French pasticcio was reworked in Italian for London audiences by Giuseppe Zaffira and given a new ending by Victor Wilding.[111]

Chabrier's *L'étoile*, like *John of Paris*, demonstrates that canonical operas could still last for decades in the repertoire as a pasticcio performance tradition, even though the original score was published and available. Unlike *John of Paris*, however, *L'étoile* lasted long into the twentieth century. The opera was successful when it first appeared in Paris, Berlin and Budapest in 1877–1879, but the 1890s, English-language versions of the opera were pasticci. John Cheever Goodwin severely adapted the libretto in 1890, replacing much of the original music with that of Henry Woolton Morse and retitling it, for the New York production, *The Merry Monarch*.

4.5 King Ouf I (Walter Passmore), Lazuli (Emmie Owen) and Siroco (Sydney Paxton), in *The Lucky Star*, 1899.
Source: The Gilbert and Sullivan Archive.

In 1899, Ivan Caryll did the same to this pasticcio, reworking Goodwin and Morse's score and interpolating his own music; this production at the Savoy Theatre, London was titled *The Lucky Star*.[112] It was revived in New York in 1910, possibly after Caryll moved there that year.[113] Very little of Chabrier's original music survived in the score by this point and the gradual replacing of the original music over the course of successive revivals makes it a striking analogue to *Orazio*, which evolved in the same way between 1738 and 1760. Chabrier's original score was revived in Brussels in 1909 but not in Paris until 1925 and only securely in 1941. Caryll (1861–1921) was a noted pasticciere of opéra-comique, interpolating his own music into an English language adaptation of Edmond Audran's *La Cigale et la Fourmi* (1886) in 1890 for the Lyric Theatre. The libretto was similarly changed by Sir Francis Burnand and Gilbert à Beckett. It won high praise from *The Theatre* reviewers, Bernard Capes and Charles Eglinton, who commended the unity achieved in the piece through Caryll sublimating his own compositional style to Audran's:

> Audran's music pleased every one, it was so bright and melodious, and the considerable portion of the opera, for which Mr Ivan Caryll is responsible, gave equal satisfaction. The hand of M. Audran is audible all through it … Where Mr Ivan Caryll's co-operation comes in, is not easily detected (though most of the first night critics seemed to be very *cognoscenti*).[114]

4.6 Ivan Caryll, pasticciere of *La Cigale* (1890) and *The Lucky Star* (1899).
Source: Gallery of History Inc.

In addition to these operas, which were programmed among the main events in a theatre's season, venues as varied as Drury Lane, Covent Garden, the New Theatre Royal or English Opera, Sadler's Wells, the Surrey Theatre, the Lyceum, the Royal West London Theatre, St James's, the Olympic and the Royal Victoria, even the Royal Circus regularly placed adverts in newspapers or playbills listing a 'musical pasticcio' or just a 'pasticcio' as part of a mixed bill, up to the 1870s and sometimes beyond. These could be a warm-up, a one-act interlude or the final farce of the evening. There is often no other title, as if the name 'pasticcio' was itself explanatory, but when titles are given, they convey the comic style of the piece clearly: *Black Spirits and White or The Haunted Chamber*, *T.T.S. or The Bar and the Stage* and so on.[115] They are mostly advertised between the 1820s and the 1870s; dialogue was almost certainly used where necessary rather than recitative but the numbers tended to roll into each other, thus obviating the need for either. They were usually in English and included popular songs, ballads, airs and glees as well as operatic arias.[116]

A little-discussed type of pasticcio opera which continued through the century was the masque-like entertainment marking specific occasions. What might be termed occasional pasticci are found in the eighteenth century, being created for the Handel Centenary, the King's return to health in 1789 and so on. *Nelson – A Match for Bonaparte* was staged at the Royal Circus in 1798 to celebrate or re-enact Nelson's victory on the Nile.[117] Others were created to celebrate the victory at Waterloo in 1815. Lucia Vestris commissioned Henry Bishop to create an 'allegorical and national masque' *The Fortunate Isles, or, The Triumphs of Britannia*, performed on 12 February 1840 to celebrate Queen Victoria's marriage.[118] In June that year, Her Majesty's staged a farewell benefit performance for the veteran actor William Dowton. This operatic version of Colman's pasticcio *The Poor Gentleman* was created and directed by Thomas Cooke, a colleague of Bishop's. The cast included the prima donna Giulia Grisi who, along with Julie Dorus-Gras, joined a mixed British cast including Miss Delcy, the daughter of the noted pasticciere Michael Rophino Lacy, Elizabeth Rainforth, Mr Braham, Mr H. Phillipe and the German Chorus borrowed from St James's.[119] This and similar events defy the portrayal of London's musical world as riven by Stildualismus; the image of two mutually hostile factions seems unreal when the German opera chorus appears in the former King's Theatre along with Grisi, Dorus-Gras and others, being directed by Tom Cooke, Drury Lane's principal pasticciere and musical director.

The word pasticcio retained its currency as a generic descriptor for musical storytelling compiled from pre-existing music and sometimes text, up to the 1870s. Yet in the last two decades of the nineteenth century the number of self-describing pasticci diminished. It would be tempting to suggest that the reformists carried their point and the term itself sunk under negative associations but the continued usage of the word pasticcio outside of musical contexts casts doubt on this as an explanation: it enjoyed currency in painting, arts journalism and even political diplomacy beyond the end of the century. Art reviewers took to using the term at least as early as 1842 to describe a painting where the composition or characterisation of the figures were drawn from other paintings depicting similar scenes.[120] Christie's advertised paintings coming up for auction as pasticcio works up to 1912 with no suggestion that they were second-rate pieces in consequence.[121] The word was used in political journalism, too, with some exactness, to describe a new policy which contained reworked facets of earlier policies; *The Times*'s discussion of French politics in 1873 used it in this way.[122] By 1900 the word had broadened still to include French usages of 'pastiche' to describe a comic imitation of a particular style.[123] Yet the decline of the self-describing pasticcio was temporary; in the years after 1918, it was revived as discussed in Chapter 5.

The pasticcio method of creating performances continued evolving into the twentieth century even without the word as its descriptor: the parody opera, the operetta and the musical comedy among other terms came into use. In a study of the many German operettas translated, reworked and staged in London and the United States in the early twentieth century, Derek Scott notes the centrality of drastic deviation from the original in creating and sustaining their popularity for anglophone audiences.[124] In London, this was a continuity from late nineteenth-century practice, as Scott acknowledges.[125]

Wilhelm Meyer Lutz (1829–1903) became musical director and, effectively, composer-in-residence at the Gaiety Theatre from 1869 onwards. Between 1869 and 1885 he compiled comic pasticcio operas which influenced, and were influenced by, the Savoy operas of Gilbert and Sullivan. From the mid-1880s the Gaiety turned to burlesques, revues and operatic parodies which in some ways prefigured the musical comedies of the early twentieth century. These were his own original compositions and were often complex satires of serious operas; Meyer Lutz used the opportunity to parody a grand opera as a chance to recreate them afresh. His 1888 burlesque, *Pas de Quatre or Faust up to Date*, was written to a libretto by his usual collaborators George Sims and Henry Pettitt. Gounod's *Faust* had first been performed in London in 1863 but in 1855 the composer had himself written a serious three-act opera, based more closely on Goethe's play, called *Faust and Marguerite*. Lutz's satire is thus a kind of intertextual discussion between Goethe as the source, Gounod's *Faust* and his own views on how to approach the story. Lutz and his team wrote a similar burlesque, *Carmen up to Date*, in 1890. The burlesque had evolved from the one-act parody seen earlier in the century into a three-act operetta; it could be argued that by the 1880s the burlesque had subverted its own subversion, becoming an excuse to smuggle serious operatic singing styles and intertextual commentary into light entertainment. The change to this more complex kind of comedy reflected the changing audience at the Gaiety; those who were moved by grand opera in prestigious theatres also wanted to laugh at them, and at themselves, in less august settings. Meyer Lutz was also the pasticciere of *Cindy Ellen Up Too Late*, created in 1891; this included music from many composers including Leopold Wenzel, Frank Osmond Carr, Walter Slaughter and Lionel Monckton. Monckton would go on to create his own pasticcio musicals up to the First World War. This pasticcio pointed towards one of the many avenues pasticcio would take in the twentieth century. That operettas and musicals did not call themselves pasticci may have been due to unwelcome resonances of antiquated high and grand opera, and one-act after-pieces in Victorian mixed bills but, I suggest, it is another example of the generic descriptor being the chosen identifier rather than the construction method. As Scott notes, the term operetta would itself acquire an antiquated resonance as the twentieth century went on.[126]

Pasticcio in the regions: further evidence of continuity

Bristol's Theatre Royal in context

Most of what has been written in this chapter so far concerns London, but when the rest of Britain and Ireland are factored in, we can see that textual fidelity was even less of a concern in the rest of the British Isles. This sub-section focuses on the Theatre Royal, Bristol and demonstrates that pasticcio characterised this theatre's operatic content throughout the nineteenth century, demonstrated in the rich quantity of surviving data for it.[127] Such data demonstrates even more clearly than those of London theatres how ubiquitous pasticcio was as a construction method throughout the nineteenth century. Pasticcio works – whether explicitly labelled or not – formed the backbone of this theatre's operatic repertory and its techniques enabled an agile adaptation of operas to local resources and tastes.

To contextualise the Theatre Royal in Bristol, its origin lay in the population increase and the rise in disposable income seen in many regional towns between the 1770s and the 1830s. This led to a demand for new or refurbished public theatres in many towns and cities across the islands and was accompanied by a greater diversification in the types of theatre staged. James Winston's *The Theatric Tourist*, published in 1805, gives details of twenty-three new regional theatres built in the Regency period alone. Operas were performed in places as far apart as Dublin, Belfast, York, Edinburgh,

4.7 Theatre Royal, Bristol, 1778–1904.
Source: Bristol Old Vic, released under Creative Commons Licence

Newcastle, Durham, Oxford, Cambridge, Norwich, Canterbury, Bury St Edmonds, Bath, Bristol, Chepstow, Cardiff, Swansea and smaller cities and towns. By the 1850s town theatres were no longer the small 200-seat affairs they had been at the turn of the century; a mid-century spate of rebuilding and enhancement across Britain testifies to a determination to stage entertainments on a larger scale. Theatres were often constructed out of civic pride but usually run as commercial ventures. The landowner on whose ground the theatre stood was often focused on ground rents rather than investing in the theatre as a business.[128] Theatres were leased to people who intended to develop them as such but, all too often, they failed financially and most regional theatres went through periods of disuse. After going dark, they were usually neglected or even used for vegetable storage, leaving them damp, mildewed and malodorous. Reopening a theatre meant considerable outlay in refurbishment. Even between seasons it was necessary to inform the public that fires had been lit in every fireplace for days beforehand to dry the place out and warm it up.[129]

In the regions, relations between theatres and local newspapers were usually better than in London and regional reviewers consistently encouraged the public to support their local theatre. The wholly eulogistic review, which continues in some towns to this day, originated in response to these periods of financial anxiety, when sustaining a town's theatre looked precarious. Failure of a local theatre brought discredit to a town's claims to cultivation.[130]

Operas were expensive to stage regardless of whether theatres created them themselves using their own stock companies or booked them from touring companies, so although they usually filled the house, profit was not assured. In modern terms, operas in regional theatres might be seen as loss-leaders: they brought affluent and discerning people into the theatre in the hope they would return for other repertoire.[131] Until the 1830s, operas were special events programmed at certain times of the year such as race week, hunt week or the local assizes, when towns had more affluent or well-travelled visitors than usual. Michael Kelly describes Tate Wilkinson, a York-based impresario, arranging singing fixtures across the north during these occasions for opera singers including Madam Mara, himself and others.[132] Prior to the large-scale productions created for regional touring by London-based companies like the Carl Rosa and the Moody-Manners, which emerged in the 1870s, regional opera depended on pasticcio. Famous operas were reworked to suit local resources and audience expectations, both by stock companies and by small- or middle-scale touring companies. This was often a deliberate artistic approach rather than one necessitated by circumstances and, consequently, continued into the period when Bristol also received productions of canonical repertoire offering what was claimed as absolute fidelity to the original.

Regional relationships with London

Two kinds of operatic experience were provided by the stock or resident company at the Theatre Royal: Bristol's own indigenous operas and, up to the 1870s, emulations of operas performed in London. Small touring companies like the South Wales Company or impresarios such as Andrew Cherry, William M'Cready and James Woulds, like Tate Wilkinson in the north-east, hired cast members from the London season, along with instrumentalists and, as the century progressed, machinists, scenographers and costumiers. The resident company were frequently added to the London cast, stage crew and orchestra. From the 1870s onwards, however, when London theatres were able to tour their performances regionally, Bristol formed part of the western circuit for companies like the Carl Rosa and Her Majesty's. The house continued to stage Bristol-focused operas periodically but mainly booked in the large-scale canonical works offered by the London touring companies. Bristol's outline is shared in many ways with the theatres studied by Paul Rodmell in Birmingham, Dublin, Huddersfield and Norwich, although Bristol also deviated from them in some interesting ways.[133]

The house had regularly staged its own operas since the 1790s and probably earlier still, continuing to do so into the twentieth century. Bath had also staged its own operas since 1781 or earlier.[134] While these stagings were often regional adaptations of what was being performed in London, some were created independently, in the Bristol Theatre Royal house style and based on Bristol's own heritage and culture. These included *Lundy in the Olden Times* and *The Bristol Apprentice* (both 1840). Cornelius Bryan, the organist at St Mary Redcliffe, set *Lundy in the Olden Times* to a libretto by his daughter based on a traditional Bristol story. It was scheduled for performance on 27 March but, tragically, Bryan died a few days before the performance and it was postponed.[135] *The Bristol Apprentice* was advertised in the *Bristol Times* and *Bath Advocate* for 25 April 1840.[136] New plays telling local stories had always been written for spoken drama in regional theatres and the same happened for opera. As late as 1924, the then lessee, Douglas Millar, staged an opera, *False Dawn*, written by local solicitor F.E.C. Habgood.[137] As well as operas touring westwards from London, those created in Ireland or Wales were staged in Bristol on their route eastwards towards London, ranging from John Stevenson's *The Patriot* (1810) to Joseph Parry's *Blodwen* (1878).

Highly distinctive, localised operatic traditions influenced the way London's operas were staged regionally; operas were transposed from their metropolitan idiom to accord with local narratives, moralities, a different language in Wales, as well as political and cultural concerns. This occurred in a number of ways: towns and regional cities were keen to write themselves into an opera, for example, in much the same way that British neoclassical collectors wanted to write Britannia into Roman antiquity. A striking number of insertion arias in Theatre Royal operas refer to Bristol: the theatre's 1808 production of O'Keefe's *Fontainebleau* was copied from the production at Bath but amended to contain 'Rambles to Bristol' by a Mr Evans. It also contained a sequence sung by the pupils of a local school.[138]

The Theatre Royal also produced its own pasticcio operas based on novels. James Henry Chute, Sarah Macready's son-in-law, was periodically an actor, singer, stage manager and manager of the theatre. He was also a pasticciere; he not only reworked many of the plays and operas staged at Bristol (and presumably Bath) but created a number of operettas from current popular fiction. *Gold* was a staging of Charles Reade's *It's Never Too Late to Mend* and he created an occasional pasticcio to mark a victory in the Crimean War, *The Fall of Sebastopol*, in 1856. Chute also opened the New Royal Theatre in 1867 with a Shadwellian pasticcio of *The Tempest*, probably the work of a number of hands, but under Chute's editorial control.[139] Another way in which local concerns influenced operatic amendment was the expectation that its narrative would relate to contemporary discussions and issues. London audiences wanted operas to be applicable to metropolitan or national discussions and the connection between Verdi's *La Traviata* (1853) and ongoing concerns about prostitution at every level in society is an example.

THE GREAT SOCIAL EVIL.

TIME:—Midnight. A Sketch not a Hundred Miles from the Haymarket.

Bella. "AH ! FANNY ! HOW LONG HAVE YOU BEEN *GAY !*"

4.8 *Punch* cartoon by John Leech, 1857. The cartoon points up the perceived hypocrisy of the ruling classes in approving of an opera deploring society's double standards towards courtesans. While they sympathised with a courtesan in an Italian opera, they condemned women in straitened circumstances resorting to sex work in their own city every day. Gay, at this point, meant willingness to engage in an illicit sexual life.
Source: Punch, released under Creative Commons Licence.

Regional audiences wanted the same but in a more local context. In Bristol, discussions about slavery are reflected in Theatre Royal programming beginning with *Inkle and Yarico* in 1792. Ira Aldridge performed regularly at Bristol from 1826 onwards, staging his operatic adaptation of *The Padlock* and other pieces. *The Padlock* was originally a two-act after-piece of 1768 with Charles Dibdin's music to a text by Isaac Bickerstaffe; it was a standard commedia dell'arte story of the jealous husband who locks up his wife. In neoclassical fashion, the comedy was provided by a household slave but Bickerstaff departed from Greco-Roman templates by making the slave a West Indian, Mungo. Beyond a West Indian accent, Mungo was merely a combination of Plautus's slaves and Pantaloon from the commedia. Aldridge changed all this dramatically, making the operetta a discourse on slavery without losing the comedy. At the end of the story, Aldridge gave a short oration to enforce its abolitionist message. *Othello* and its photographic negative, *The Revenge*, were, in a Bristol context and with Aldridge in the title roles, part of a discussion on race in a way they were not in other cities. While he clearly made use of pasticcio practices to attune his plays and operas to these discussions, neither Aldridge nor the Theatre advertised his performances as being politically revised. Bristol audiences were clearly not averse to pasticcio, declared or otherwise, so the reason may have been to avoid alerting potential audience members who would not have attended had they suspected the subtle insertion of political persuasion. While the Theatre Royal's stance appears to have been largely abolitionist, the majority of its portrayals of black people on stage still depended on blacking up and racial stereotyping: such were *Jim Crow* in 1838 and Chute's adaptation of *Uncle Tom's Cabin* in 1855. Aldridge's performances stand apart from this.

Musical amendments were also the result of local traditions asserting themselves. A substantial number of operas at Bristol were pasticci of operas by Henry Bishop, his pupil George Rodwell and the Loder family. A pre-Romantic Italianate style characterise these compositions and this late classical style remained the lodestone when adapting operas into the 1880s and beyond. In western Britain, substitutions were not only intended to make the opera Bristol's own but seem intended to preserve and develop a distinctive early-century conception of operatic music; this is true for Wales, too, Parry's *Blodwen* (1878) being the obvious example.

Bristol's second kind of operatic experience was very much the reverse; these were still local adaptations but intended to provide as authentic a London experience as possible. In much the same way that the habitués of the King's and later Her Majesty's Theatre wanted to experience the best of current Italian opera without the bother of going to Italy, audiences for regional opera wanted to hear the best Italian operas current in London, but at home and mostly not in Italian. Adaptations of continental operas for London audiences saw further amending for regional touring by London-based impresarios, or touring companies.[140] Up to the 1830s, regional theatre managers like Sarah Macready travelled to London to study its opera performances with the aim of reproducing them as closely as possible with her own company back home. Her models tended to be the operas at Drury

Lane and Covent Garden rather than Her Majesty's; they were shorn of any metropolitan jokes and references that were not already well known, but were still marketed as embodying the latest metropolitan trends, the strapline in playbills being 'as now performing in London'.[141] Bristol's *John of Paris* in 1814 was an emulation of Covent Garden's and, later that year, some of the King's Theatre cast toured Bishop's pasticcio of *Love in a Village* together with his original opera, *Aladdin*, to Bristol. The playbill proclaimed they had come

> [w]ith entire new Scenes, Machinery, Dresses and Decorations, which have been in preparation during the whole of last Summer, under the immediate direction of the Principal Artists of the Opera House, and of the Theatre Royal, Covent Garden, upon a scale of Expence equal to its original production in London, and superior to any efforts in Spectacle ever yet attempted on the Bristol Stage.[142]

The strapline of George Rodwell's *The White Maid* (1827) reads '[a]s Performed and now Performing at the Theatre Royal, Covent Garden, with Unprecedented Attraction and Applause'.[143] While the *aim* was to reproduce a London experience, until the 1870s it was almost impossible to do so with anything like exactitude. Stagings had to be scaled down for regional tours and thus lacked many of the things that had made the opera successful, such as the full set, stage machinery, a professional chorus and an expert orchestra. To counter this, regional theatre companies met touring operas half-way. The key performers and the conductor came from London, as did the more transportable scenery such as the canvas drops, costumes and props, but the regional theatre supplied most of the instrumentalists, filled the smaller solo roles and sometimes recruited a local amateur chorus. When a tour from Her Majesty's Theatre visited Bristol in December 1877, the playbill announced 'band from Her Majesty's Theatre assisted by the resident local staff'.[144] As the opera could not be staged with absolute fidelity to the original staging, these collaborations could be highly creative: a touring opera was an evolving one, changed not just to get over the practical difficulties of reproduction but to take advantage of artistic opportunities that amendment offered, as I discuss below.

Regional touring companies

Regional touring companies feature regularly in Bristol's operatic programming and their reshaping of London operas for Bristol reveals much about what they considered regional audience expectations to be. Bristol was a wealthy city with many well-travelled residents, so arias which had been sung in English in London were often sung in Italian in Bristol. Italian arias reaffirmed that it *was* an opera and sometimes recitative replaced spoken dialogue, presumably in imitation of Frederick Gye's operas at Covent Garden. When Mrs Dickens was 'released from the Theatre Royal, Covent Garden' to sing the lead in *Love in a Village* in 1809, she introduced a bravura aria by Giordani.[145] 'Bravi Bravi!' was sung as a trio in an otherwise English-language staging of Auber's *Fra Diaviolo* in 1841 and Mrs Woods sang 'Di piacer'.[146] Italian suitcase arias can be found in Bristol performances between 1809 and 1914 along with the signature arias associated with famous singers. These were inserted whatever the opera and many other pasticcio practices such as the insertion of action scenes from similar operas, dances, visual spectacles and even animal acts testified to a determination to counter the prejudice that opera was staid, static or stuffy.

Troupes who toured to Bristol were often small-scale companies run by singer-managers. They could even be a duo such as Mr and Mrs Woods. Mary Ann Paton and Joseph Woods, soprano and tenor, were a husband-and-wife team active between 1824 and 1843. They sang the lead roles in the operas they toured to theatres in the south-west, singing *Love in a Village*, *Clari*, *Fra Diavolo* and *Norma* at Bristol in September 1841 alone.[147] The Woods visited the Theatre Royal over a number of years but relied on considerable support from the venue itself: the resident company played all the supporting roles apart from a Mr Brough, who was perhaps a protégé of theirs.[148] For operas created in-house by the resident company, Sarah Macready sometimes hired the couple to sing the lead roles, as in *The Quaker* of 21 April 1831, and *Guy Mannering* in 1841.[149]

4.9a Rebecca Isaacs, coloured etching of the 1840s or 1850s.
Source: Released under Creative Commons Licence.

4.9b Kate Santley in a photograph of the 1870s.
Source: Released under Creative Commons Licence.

Female singer-managers with a metropolitan base are a striking feature of regional opera touring throughout the century and these were larger companies. Rebecca Isaacs sang many leading roles in English operas in London during the 1840s and became 'Directress of Operas' at the Strand Theatre; during the 1850s she included Bristol in her tours, naming her company London Grand Opera. The insertion arias she regularly used and which might be considered her signature arias were sufficiently broad in their lyrics to be dropped into many operas without violating the narrative. She had two especially composed for her, 'There's somebody waiting for me' by Edward J. Loder and 'What love' by Meyer Lutz. These were used in her English adaptation of *Il Trovatore*, performed at Bristol in September 1856, which nevertheless advertised in the playbill 'the Whole of the Music by the Celebrated Verdi'. Isaacs sang Leonora and the piece was conducted by Loder himself.[150] In her earlier tour to Bristol in March that year, Isaacs and her company gave *The Village Nightingale* by Sidney Nelson and Thomas Craven.[151] This had been a new commission by the Strand Theatre in 1851, with Craven and Nelson's daughter in the cast, but by 1856 this couple had emigrated to Australia and Isaacs herself took the lead role. That this was a collaborative staging with Bristol is shown by John Chute playing the male lead. She interpolated three of her signature arias and the characters also seem to have changed. The opera was also probably contracted to make space for the burlesque which followed it, one of the earliest satires on electricity:[152]

A 'New Electro-Biological Burlesque' written expressly for Miss Isaacs entitled: *Alonzo the Brave and the Fair Imogene*, in which she plays a Victim of Electro-Biology.[153]

Kate Santley, a singer and actor who became the manager of the Royalty Theatre in 1877 and collaborated with the D'Oyly Carte Opera company, also toured comic operas regionally. She performed an English-language version of Offenbach's *Orphée aux enfers* at Bristol in a double bill with Gilbert and Sullivan's *Trial by Jury* in May 1877, having managed a revival of the latter in 1876. An indication of the increasing influence of the music hall can be seen in the introduction of her 'Celebrated new song, Awfully Awful' into *Orphée aux enfers*.[154] Miss May Bulmer, the manager of the Garrick Opera Company, toured their English translation of François Bazin's *Le Voyage en Chine* to Bristol in 1879, translated as *A Cruise to China*.[155] Among the men are Bochsa's casually assembled corps, who gave concerts in Bristol during the 1830s and Richard W. South's Comic Opera Company in the 1870s.[156]

Although based in London, regional touring was central to the revenue of these companies as Paul Rodmell points out; this also sustained a nationwide rather than just metropolitan profile for their leading singers.[157] Nineteenth-century touring companies reworked metropolitan operas 'for the provinces' yet, as argued in the next sub-section, there was something more than metropolitan arrogance here; reshaping gave artistic opportunities, allowing an opera staging to change, evolve and even improve in dramatic structure. Prior to the large touring companies of the 1870s and later, such as the Carl Rosa and Moody Manners, regional touring companies brought considerable variation to well-known operas, experimenting with them as well as tailoring them to the region.

Experimentation in regional opera

In addition to the excisions and interpolations made in London for revivals of Thomas Arne's *Love in a Village* (originally 1762), Bristol added more. The *Bristol Gazette* reviewer noted that the singer performing Young Meadows in the 1838 revival, Mr Granville, had added 'Away ye gay landscapes', composed by himself, along with two or three 'introduced songs'. The part of Hawthorn was transposed and adapted for the tenor Mr Gerald, some Handel had been introduced along with 'What is this spell' from a recent revival of William Rooke's Irish opera *Amilie* (Dublin 1818, London revival 1838). *Love in a Village* was given at Bristol in October 1814, January 1838, September 1841, afterwards and probably in between; the 1841 playbill describes it as 'the national Opera'. As with *Orazio*, new arias were inserted and others dropped out at each revival, but the reworkings indicate a freedom to play with the opera in ways diametrically opposed to reformist fidelity principles.

In Rebecca Isaacs's 1847 revival of Terry and Bishop's *Guy Mannering* (1816), performed at Bristol that year, the manager introduced into Julia Mannering's role, sung by Miss Poole, 'I'll be no submissive wife', an aria (*c.*1835) by Thomas Haynes Bayley and Alexander Lee.[158] Earlier in this chapter it was discussed how Terry had shaped the female roles rather more submissively than Scott had done in his novel. In 1847, with the Married Woman's Property Act less than ten years away, the female manager used substitution to reshape the role into a form more suitable to changing gender identities. Her development of the opera's characterisation can be seen in her other insertions, including Bishop's 'Echo duet' from *Brother and Sister* sung by Mr Rafter as Guy and Miss Poole, and 'Safely follow him' sung by Mr S. Jones as Gabriel. Some of these may predate Isaacs's revival, but the playbill also announces that she 'will introduce one of her most popular ballads'; this was presumably undecided when the playbill went to press but indicates that audiences in Bristol would have accepted the fluidity in the operatic numbers and not have been appalled by a want of fidelity.[159] Bishop's original scoring had been a pasticcio with contributions from John Whitaker and Thomas Attwood (a former pupil of Mozart) and the opera was still evolving in Bristol's programmes in the 1860s.[160] Frederick Corder, Bishop's biographer writing in 1918, noted that it was still customary, even at that time, to replace four of Bishop's original ballads.

This opera also shows how the Theatre Royal participated in operatic transnationalism. Rodwell's *The White Maid* (1827) was an adaptation of Boieldieu's *La Dame Blanche* (1825) which, in itself, had been drawn from Bishop and Terry's *Guy Mannering* (1816). Dramatic treatments of the story thus travel from Scott in Scotland to Terry and Bishop in London, then to Boieldieu in France before returning to London to be redramatised by Bishop's pupil Rodwell for performances in London, Bristol, Wales and elsewhere. As in the eighteenth century, there is often no mention of the composer on the playbills and this was the case with the 1847 *Guy Mannering*, suggesting that it was still the story that counted rather than the artist. Nor was Bishop mentioned on a bill for *Clari* in 1841, arguably his most famous opera, yet Bishop was the composer of choice for Bristol and enjoyed regular programming.

Opera within a mixed bill

Until the 1870s, filling the house was thought to be best achieved in regional theatres and many metropolitan ones by satisfying as many tastes as possible in one evening, so variety was central in programming. Operas, in consequence, were often presented in a mixed bill among very eclectic acts. The quantity of operas on many bills would have necessitated condensing drastically. If unedited, Bristol's 1847 offering of Donizetti's *The Daughter of the Regiment* followed by three acts of *Guy Mannering* would have had a running time of over five hours.[161] Bills with fewer items and more intact operas begin at Bristol in the late 1870s and 1880s. In October 1877, Offenbach's *Blind Beggars* is only half an hour and Procida Buccalossi's *Monsieur Pom*, which followed it, was approximately two; this was the premiere of this opera in Bristol so there were probably fewer cuts.[162]

At the end of Bristol's spring season in 1827, George Rodwell's adaptation of Boieldieu, *The White Maid*, was followed by a farce called *Tit for Tat*, possibly an updated pasticcio of the Crow Street Irish ballad opera *Tit for Tat or The Cadi gull'd* (1766). This was followed by tightrope walking, performed by a Monsieur Lalanne and an Infant Phenomenon aged 5 who also danced a pas seul, then an 'Ode to Chatterton', more acrobatics by Monsieur Lalanne and a farce to conclude the evening, translated from the French.[163] The mixed bill was not just a calculated list-ticking of different age groups, tastes and markets; nor was it as haphazard as it seems to modern eyes. Rather, I suggest, the positioning of acts involved careful artistic choices intended to create an evening not just of contrasting genres but a coherent progression of emotional reactions. High-stakes combat between good and evil is followed by comedy; suspense and tension were provided by trapeze and tightrope walking, charm and delight by the dancing child who followed, then a sense of grief and loss at the brilliant Chatterton's tragic death at 17, more stirring heroism follows and, finally, comedy once again. Certainly, practical considerations were also a governing factor in billing: different timeslots were required for the previous sets to be struck and new ones to be rigged between plays, operas and farces and for the company to change costumes; these needed short acts in front of the curtain or music to cover the changes but, I suggest, the art of mixed-bill programming also lay in creating an experiential journey for the audience over the course of the evening.

Examination of two mixed bills, 25 March 1833 and 21 September 1841, show how operas functioned in this capriccio context. Bishop's adaptation of *The Marriage of Figaro* was given in March 1833, presumably much reduced, followed by a masque celebrating the genius of Sir Walter Scott, who had died the year before, written by Sheridan Knowles and set by Bishop, Lee and Stansbury. This incorporated a long series of tableaux vivant from the Waverley novels, an '[a]ssemblage of Characters intended as a Jubilee ... in commemoration of Scotia's Minstrel'. After that there was a farce called *Mr and Mrs Pringle*.[164] Henry Bishop's music runs through the evening, while Joaquín Telesforo de Trueba y Cosío's comic interlude *Mr and Mrs Pringle* satirises the pretensions of an amateur musical family. The evening thus begins with a comic opera before moving into the bitter-sweet event that memorialises the departed Scott before returning to the comic vein once again but, underlying the variety and contrast is a thematic discourse on genius and patriotism.

Mozart was the great continental genius, yet Count Almaviva exemplifies what was wrong with the ancien régime, a refined but morally bankrupt and, crucially in this context, foreign aristocracy. Scott the North Briton was the great British genius and *his* heroes, by contrast, embody a rugged, spartan, Scottish virtue. Comparisons are thus invited. Scott himself is heavily romanticised in the following masque: the first part is called 'Vision of the Bard', followed by 'The Poet's Tomb', leading on to 'The Bard's Vision'. The first two parts may have consisted of musical accompaniments to visual sequences such as magic lantern projections or scenographic reconstructions of his intended tomb. The third sequence, where the tableaux and succession of characters remind everyone of Scott's works, probably involved the characters laying tributes at their creator's tomb. In this obituary masque, Scott is deified as much as canonised, with grief at his passing mixed with pride in his genius. Many of the contemporary illustrations of Dickens, surrounded by the characters he had conjured into being, echo this kind of masque. The farce is interesting in that it reinforces the conception of genius by inviting the audience to laugh at those who pretend to it but have no genius. The pomposity of those with pretensions contrasts with the modesty assumed to belong to those who genuinely possess this numinous quality.

In September 1841, Bellini's *Norma* was followed by Auber's *Fra Diavolo* and finally Richard Brinsley Peake's operatic farce *Master's Rival or a Day in Boulogne*.[165] This offered a similar journey; the world of pre-Christian Celtic druids facing a Roman invasion in *Norma* is succeeded by a southern Italian community preyed upon by a diabolical bandit; comedy succeeds tragedy, but in both there is the danger that the central character will end up with the wrong person. Norma fails to stop Pollione pursuing Adalgisa and Lorenzo nearly fails to stop Zerline marrying the elderly miser, Francesco. The farce continues this exploration of the triangular theme with a thieving servant dressed as his master winning the affections of his master's intended. The whole evening is, in addition, a meditation on criminality. Both the Celtic Norma and the Roman Pollione are burned to death by the druids for committing religious sacrilege. These are criminals with whom we sympathise, while the predatory Fra Diavolo, by contrast, is a curse to society, a bandit whose thefts of people's fortunes nearly leads to both romantic and financial disaster for the people on whom he preys. In *Master's Rival*, the two brothers are both thieves and they are treated by Peake as loveable rogues. By showing criminality in highly contrasting periods and places, we move from thinking some laws absurd and sorrowing with those trapped by them, to viewing law as an essential bulwark against chaos and lawbreakers as a social menace. Finally, our sympathy returns to the criminal, or Peake intends it to, and we recognise that even criminals are human beings. *The New Monthly Magazine* found this positive depiction of criminality insufferable and thought the ending would have been improved if they had been transported.[166] The bill as a whole thus connected with contemporary discussions of law and order.

The happy endings of comedy and farce can also produce tears, as the psychologists Panksepp and Bernatzky have noted.[167] So, in an evening's final catharsis offered by the farces, we see the end of a progression that is not quite a narrative, but more than a random assemblage. The positioning of acts was thus intended to serve what appear to be contradictory aims: variety and unity. Variety was achieved through form with each item contrasting with the preceding one, with highly active events following static ones and so on. Unity was achieved through content, with each item commenting on or developing the themes underlying the bill as a whole.

Stability and family connection

Managers like Sarah Macready usually recruited their performers in London, as the local press described her doing in the 1820s and 1830s.[168] They also recruited local performers and, as the playbills and Kathleen Barker's transcripts show, local families retained livelihoods and involvement with the theatre throughout the century. Transgenerational continuity within a regional theatre is an important factor in understanding the continuity of pasticcio in regional opera. As well as the passing on of pasticcio skills and techniques, the *acceptability* of changing music and text was passed on. The Macready and Chute families are only one example: the Macreadys had interests in the Theatre Royal from 1799 and were managers or lessees between 1819 and 1853 when Sarah Macready died. The Chutes appear regularly in playbills and correspondence from 1841 onwards, when James Henry Chute joined the company to sing Lord Allcash in *Fra Diavolo*; his brother John sang the smaller role of Carlo and, later that year, Eustace, in *Love in a Village*.[169] Sarah Macready's daughter Mazzerina married James Henry Chute in 1844 and, in 1846, he appears as stage manager in a mixed bill including *The Beggar's Opera* and other items by the visiting Ethiopian Serenaders.[170] Barker notes that he became the manager of the Theatre Royal in 1852 having acted in that capacity for a number of years previously and, following Sarah Macready's death in 1853, the lessee. He occupied the same positions at Bath but still found time to write plays and entertainments and act in performances.[171] John Chute also remained in the company, playing Mr Blewitt in *Uncle Tom's Cabin* and, in 1856, he was the leading man, Sam Copybrief, in Rebecca Isaacs's visiting opera, *Village Nightingale*.[172] During the summer of 1853 James Henry, as lessee, had the theatre thoroughly refurbished and in 1867 he was responsible for building the New Theatre Royal at Clifton. What might be his final appearance in a playbill is dated 1877, where he is described as having negotiated the inclusion of Bristol in a tour by Her Majesty's Theatre of three Italian operas.[173] James Henry Chute died in 1878 but his and Mazarina's children continued to manage the New Theatre Royal in Clifton into the twentieth century, when it was renamed the Prince's Theatre.[174]

Other families who span decades include the Norman, Powell and Lodge families; the latter, mother and son, are included on playbills from 1814 to 1846. John Gover Powell was an actor in the company during the 1850s and his sister married the repetiteur F. Merry. His brother G.F. Powell also acted and wrote Chute's patriotic address during the Crimean War; his son, G. Rennee Powell joined the company in 1866 and published a history of the Theatre Royal in 1919. Even a family who sold apples, oranges and lemonade between the acts went through three generations.[175] These families had long memories of pasticcio and other traditions including mimesis in learning roles from other performers, and thus form a counterweight to metropolitan preoccupations with fidelity. Chapter 5 discusses how positive attitudes to pasticcio in regional theatres left a legacy in the twentieth century when cinema accompaniments also took a pasticcio form.

The uncoupling of the mixed bill and the beginning of fidelity

In 1859, possibly for the first time, two operas were given at the Theatre Royal wholly in Italian and with all the original London cast. The Drury Lane productions of Verdi's *Il Trovatore* and Donizetti's *Lucrezia Borgia* were performed that September with a cast including Tietjens, Giuglini, Badiali, Borchardt, Vialetti and others – enough in fact for cover singers to be on hand. Chute refurbished the theatre, creating extra boxes and the *Bristol Mercury* confirms that the visit was a great success.[176] Over the next twenty years the programming of intact opera productions from London remained an occasional treat; operas such as Bishop's adaptation of Bellini's *La sonnambula*, performed on 20 December 1877, remained the norm in programming.[177] Local productions of English operas by the company continued as did pasticcio operas of all sorts including celebrations of national events and burlesques.

From the late 1870s onwards, however, the provision of performance in the city of Bristol changed, as it did in London. Instead of a broad range of performance genres being concentrated into a single mixed bill, they began to diffuse themselves across the city, settling into separate venues. At first, the Theatre Royal offered genre-specific nights, opera night being one, but gradually single-genre venues replaced this. A snapshot can be seen on 2 October 1883, when the Theatre Royal, now under the management of Arthur Melville, hosted *The Black Flag* by Henry Pettitt, a melodrama about an escaped convict being toured by Fred Gould's company. The New Theatre Royal in Clifton, managed by George and James Macready Chute hosted the Carl Rosa Opera Company which performed *Esmeralda* by A. Goring Thomas; their forthcoming operas included Bizet's *Carmen*, Balfe's *Bohemian Girl*, Gounod's *Faust* and Verdi's *Il Trovatore*. The Colston Hall, which stood near some dissenting chapels, advertised two 'Grand Concerts' for later in the month, modelled on Exeter Hall. Charles Halle was the orchestra conductor, Madame Albani the lead soloist among a group of six which included Charles Santley. The programme included Felicien David's ode symphony *The Desert*, followed by Gounod's oratorio *Redemption* and the event was managed by the Bristol Musical Festival Society. Meanwhile, in the Drill Hall at Queen's Road, Hengler's Grand Cirque announced an 'entire Change of Entertainments with New Acts of Equestrianism – New Examples of Horse Training – New Acrobatic Exploits – New Scenes of Merriment'. These included the Gregory Troupe giving gymnastic performances on three silver bars and 'marvellous Aerial Flights and Mid-Air Gyrations'. A play or an opera now tended to form the bulk of the evening with just a short after-piece surviving, and even this was dropped as the century neared its end.

In his analysis of regional touring companies in the last quarter of the nineteenth and first two decades of the twentieth centuries, Paul Rodmell concludes:

> As the touring system bedded down and stock companies closed[, d]edicated opera troupes expanded in number and activity, bringing performances to a greater number of people than ever before – and, quite possibly, ever since ... their appearances were anticipated positively up and down the country, and opera as a genre came nearer at this time in the United Kingdom to being a mass entertainment than at any other.[178]

As we have seen, the presence of a stock company continued at Bristol throughout the century and thus lasted longer than those of Dublin, Birmingham, Huddersfield and Norwich. The large touring companies still relied occasionally on local instrumentalists but less on local singers; London productions were now able to tour virtually intact and yet in 1893 Verdi's *Otello* was sung in English, but not translated very well, according to the *Bristol Mercury*, and 'freedoms' were taken with the meaning and drama.[179] Instances of substantial divergence from the original can still be found in other kinds of opera. Bristol staged several Savoy operas from the 1880s onwards, but felt free to cut and interpolate numbers from other Gilbert and Sullivan operas as they chose. A reviewer in May 1893 noted that the operas were being tailored to the available cast rather than the cast to the operas.[180] Arthur Sullivan and Basil Hood's *The Rose of Persia* was staged on 23 April 1900 with a number of arias substituted from other Savoy operas.[181] The Bristol Amateur Operatic Society began in 1894 and it was a testimony to the sustained success of opera programming at Bristol's theatres for over a century, that more than seventy participants involved themselves in the new society as cast, orchestra and chorus. The Society had its favourites, including *Erminie* by Edward Jakobowski and Harry Paulton; the leading role was sung by Edith Evans in 1899.[182] Though set in France, it was written in English and used dialogue instead of recitative in the English tradition; of the twenty-one numbers, at least four were adaptations from Mozart's *Così fan tutte* and they substituted six other numbers to avoid paying the copyright price for the full score. Pasticcio was thus an enduring tradition in Bristol and remained part of their conception of stage performance throughout the century.

Rises in literacy create a new relationship between pasticcio and visual experience

The influence of mass literacy on opera

As discussed in Chapter 1, the relationship between rises in literacy and the intensification of visual culture has been well documented. The chapter discussed novelists moving from the orally derived practice of leaving the visualisation of a story up to the reader, to a practice of tightly controlling the reader's visualisation through detailed description, and how musical performance became much more depictional in Britain following the tipping point towards literacy in the seventeenth century. Sophisticated scenery, properties, costumes, machinery and staging continued to evolve steadily along with literacy between the 1660s and 1770s, but between the 1780s and 1870s an exponential intensification of the visual experience within theatre occurred, precipitated, I suggest, by incremental rises in literacy in the same period. The orally derived practice of pasticcio thrived during this century not despite increasing literacy, but because of it. This section will firstly explore how the visual experience in opera intensified as a result of increased literacy and, secondly, how pasticcio methods were adapted to serve the musical accompaniment of new, intensified visual sequences. Lastly, the significance of this change is discussed when musical storytelling is viewed over a long timeframe.

David Vincent argues that, over the nineteenth century, each generation of children tended to be approximately 20 per cent more literate than their parents and that even middle-class families only seem to have achieved complete literacy throughout all their immediate members by the middle of the century.[183] Approximately two-thirds of men and half the women in England and Wales are thought to have been taught to read and write in childhood in the 1820s, based on their marriage licence signatures recorded by the General Register Office in 1841 but, by the introduction of compulsory education in the 1870s, literacy was around 95 per cent. By 1914 only one person in forty was, by this measurement, non-literate.[184]

The significance of these statistics for opera studies lies less in celebrating the numbers acquiring this communication skill, and more in contextualising the centrality of text for nineteenth-century society. The democratisation of literacy was pursued with fervour and a by-product of this campaign was an excessive value, even fetishisation, placed on text of all sorts. Textual evidence became the most credible type of evidence in academic, legal and religious spheres, at the expense of oral evidence such as viva examinations, witness testimonies and liturgical traditions. For twentieth-century musicologists, this was reflected in the relocation of the intention, outcome or identity of a composition from its performance to its text.[185] As argued earlier however, oral and literate cultural practices are interwoven rather than being the binary that nineteenth-century literacy campaigns perceived them as being. Consequently, the habit of understanding an opera as a performance tradition continued alongside the insistence by some music writers that the 'work' was a timeless text and its performance merely a time-limited animation of that text. Current musicology argues that one did not extinguish the other; the arguments by earlier generations of music historians in the twentieth century, that it did, relied heavily, I suggest in Chapter 5, on writings by nineteenth-century reformers which presented themselves as both evidential and authoritative.[186]

In our earlier discussion of the relationship between rising literacy and enhanced visualisation, it was noted that, unlike reading a text, oral storytelling goes at the pace of the speaker not the listener so there is little time for listeners to invent complex visualisations. Before the seventeenth-century tipping point, the images conjured during story reception in Britain, where there were no cantastorie banners to guide the visualisation, were often simple and stylised. The figures and actions conjured in medieval minds as they listened to stories, gospel readings or narrative poems appear to have been connected to real-life experience but mediated by whatever imagery they had encountered in art; thus stained glass, friezes or misericords in churches, shop or inn signs, festival plays and, for the well off, manuscript illuminations, paintings, tapestries and carvings.[187] John Lydgate (*c.*1370–1451) has an illustration of Christ in a book address the reader:

> Set this lyknesse in your remembraunce,
> Enprenteth it in your Inward sight.

In another poem, Alistair Minnis quotes Lydgate expressing the hope that images created in art (fygur) come to mind during wholesome storytelling and remain embedded in the memory:

> That holsom storyes thus swewyd in fygur
> May rest with ws with dewe remembraunce.[188]

The imagery prompted in listeners' minds by storytelling was thus highly stylised and theatre scenography remained so until Renaissance perspective, trompe-l'œil and increased description within eighteenth-century textual narratives prompted greater verisimilitude.[189] Mass literacy in the nineteenth century created the more sophisticated kind of reading described by Gunter Kress and Theo van Leeuwen. This level of proficiency though, where the words on the page stimulate images in the mind without the mediation of an internal voice 'speaking' the words, would still have been proportionally rare. Nevertheless, opera and theatre practitioners and their audiences were highly literate and, I propose, this kind of hyperliteracy can be discerned in a gradual shift to displace text with music and visuality between the 1770s and 1900s. The shift was hesitant in late eighteenth- and early nineteenth-century theatres, but as the shift towards mass literacy intensified in the middle decades, the symbiotic relationship between music and visual experience became an entrenched part of theatrical storytelling in many performance genres. Examples are discussed later in this subsection. Pasticcio might have been an inheritance from oral culture, but in multiple nineteenth-century performance genres we see it continuing, not as an antique vestige, but as tool of mass literacy. It furthered this type of literacy where 'reading' the performance came second to comprehending it visually.

Stage design is an example. Up to the 1770s, and often beyond, stylisation continued to characterise theatrical scenography: waves, clouds, forests and buildings were depicted as they were seen in artistic tradition rather than in life, in derivation from proto-literate practice. Staging and scenography moved closer to real-life experience, not just through increased naturalism, but also by depicting landscapes, buildings, interiors and exteriors as they were refracted in dreams and fears.[190] This was another expression of the requirement for authenticity and there was a growing expectation among audiences that they would not have to stretch their imaginations too far to be able to believe in the locations, spectacles or effects they were looking at. Reduced credibility among audiences might be counted as a diminishing oral reflex in a culture of mass literacy.

Withholding of credibility is seen in the hilarity caused by props that were recognisably something other than what they purported to be. George Colman the Elder describes a rolling pin used for Macbeth's truncheon, the Ghost in *Hamlet* who wore a postillion's leather jacket in place of chainmail and a Cupid who used a violin case as a quiver for his arrows, as all arousing the audience's mirth.[191] I suggest that unconvincing props disrupted immersion only because there was less and less room for suspending disbelief in a literate culture. Ironically, as silent reverential listening became the norm in theatres, the characteristics of thelxis – credibility, emotional engagement and rapt immersion – were becoming more difficult to inspire.[192] Nineteenth-century innovations in visual appeal were thus prompted by a recognition that theatre now had to match the expectations of people used to imagining the more complex visual imagery found in textual literature.

From the late eighteenth century onwards, the capacity to immerse audiences completely in the world of a story was widely acknowledged to depend on more physically active blocking and on scenography and spectacles that transformed the space from the social environment of the theatre to the private world of the imagination. Michael Kelly's staging preferences exemplify this awareness; in the 1770s, Kelly noticed how a ballet of *Artaxerxes* in Naples had been staged with greater dramatic credibility than in the opera in London:

> On our stage, in the scene where Artabanes makes Arbaces exchange swords with him, and receives the bloody one, he comes on at the side scene, which is very poor. In the ballet, the scene is placed in the middle of the stage – the galleries over each other, with apartments opening into them, are before you; you see Artabanes rush out of the chamber of Artaxerxes, having murdered him, and fly across the different galleries pursued by the guards of Artaxerxes, with lighted torches; here he makes his escape into the royal gardens, where he meets Arbaces.[193]

This is a much more visually exciting, even cinematic, staging but derives from action scenes in novels.[194] Michael Burden notes that Philippe de Loutherbourg's mechanism for changing the leaves on trees from green to autumn colours in 1773 was a harbinger of ever-more ambitious machinery for producing spectacle.[195] By 1794 castles burning to the ground and magic lantern scenes were incorporated into operas; by the 1820s there were gas-lit dioramas which effected cinematic dissolves. Novel readers, by this time, were used to imagining Frankenstein's monster in the frozen wastes and Raymond de las Cisternas in a carriage crash with the Ghost of the Bleeding Nun, so composers like Carl Maria von Weber and Heinrich Marschner needed sets and staging that reflected their musical depictions of the Wolf's Glen or Lord Ruthven being struck by lightning and descending into hell. To achieve the kind of thelxis provided by novels, visual events had to be presented as if viewers had somehow entered their own imagination, the stage thus had to be a realm where the impossible was somehow possible and where the social environment of the theatre was superseded by immersion in the story.

The names of scenographers, machinists and costume makers began to appear in playbills for the first time but it was not their technical wizardry that was praised; rather, the effects they created were described as if they were real. For *Don Juan* in 1809 the playbill advertised 'to conclude with: A View of the Infernal Regions and a Shower of Fire'.[196] The phrasing

4.10 *Tales of Wonder*, caricature by James Gillray of ladies reading a gothic novel, 1802.
Source: Released under Creative Commons Licence.

suggests a view of the real thing rather an image of it; it was a glimpse of hell in a contingent reality that the playbill was marketing. While early opera had depended on the words to carry the storytelling, and music had gradually risen to become an equal or sometimes greater storyteller in operas, the nineteenth century saw the visual dimension move from providing context and exposition to helping conduct the narrative in its own right.

Initially, enhancement of the visual experience relied on built constructions; these were elaborate, expensive and, by modern standards, dangerous. Storace's pasticcio *Lodoiska* (1794) had, as a coup de théâtre, a rescue scene from a burning tower which then collapses. This construction and its conflagration appear to have been intended to match the imagery conjured in the novel from which the opera was taken.[197] Even today, setting fire to the set on a nightly basis could have unexpected consequences and, during one performance, both Kelly and Mrs Crouch were nearly killed. The technologies for projected imagery would advance faster over the nineteenth century than those for built sets, and magic lanterns displaying moving images had developed considerably in the preceding century.

Magic lanterns could even provide three-dimensional imagery, as techniques for projecting onto smoke to create apparitions evolved along with techniques for enlarging or diminishing the image.[198] Even moving different sections of an image became possible as lanterns acquired more sophistication: slipper slides, lever slides, masked slides, pulley slides and rack and pinion slides all created the effects of motion.[199] Although they had been used in opera scenography earlier in the century, projections were incorporated more frequently into operas between the 1780s and the 1830s. By the 1850s photographs on glass plates were used as well as paintings; these projections used 'biunial' lanterns which allowed dissolves from one photograph to another to be used as stage effects. Limelight replaced candles or oil lamps, giving greater strength and a larger image.[200]

The role played by pasticcio operas in the nineteenth century's expansion of visual technologies was often one of experimental space. It was easier in a pasticcio opera to find and tailor pre-existing music to ambitious visual techniques such as moving sets, new lighting effects or projection machinery than to tailor the visuals tightly to an original score. Even when stage designs were described or implied in the libretto, sets were never built ahead of the composition and composers seldom consulted stage managers about how long effects or movements might take to realise on stage. The more ambitious the scenography was, the more likely the opera was to be at least partly a pasticcio. Stephen Storace not only experimented with built sets but with projections too: in his autopasticcio *The Pirates* (1792) he offered a whole projected divertissement of *Hero and Leander* and the association of this opera with magic lanterns continued into the next century. Two arias from the opera were printed by J.B. Cramer in a booklet *La Lanterna Magica, Divertimento for the piano forte and flute ad lib, on Two Favourite Airs from the Opera of The Pirates, composed and dedicated to Miss Moore,* (1826).[201] Henry Langdon Childe (1781–1874) became a specialist in magic lantern projections within plays and operas and created a phantasmagoria for *The Pirates* in 1828. In the gothic melodrama *The Castle Spectre* by 'Monk' Lewis, staged at Drury Lane in 1797, most of the music was composed by Michael Kelly but, for the ghost sequences, he selected a chaconne by Niccolò Jomelli. This was considered a controversial decision but he writes 'the effect which it produced warranted the experiment'.[202] Gabriela Cruz discusses how *Der Freischütz*, at the English Opera House in 1824, staged the phantasmagoria in the Act II finale, setting a pattern for London performances throughout the century.[203]

Projection not only allowed visual effects to be tailored more easily to the score but it substantially reduced the costs. Edward Fitzball's pasticcio burletta *The Flying Dutchman* (1826 at the Adelphi) and Wagner's music drama are an example of the relationship between experimental pasticcio and new compositions by a single composer. Cruz argues that Fitzball's opera was a precursor, in design terms, of Wagner's opera.[204] There is no evidence that Wagner ever saw a version of the burletta but Cruz demonstrates that when he was working on *Der fliegende Holländer* between 1840 and 1843, projections of the ghost ship were already a stage convention in both spoken plays and musical pasticci.[205] She shows that operatic composition itself altered to tell sections of the story through visual effects and, in his remarks to Liszt, Wagner was confident that the projections, physical action and even the facial expressions of Vanderdecken could be tailored to specific bars in the score.[206]

Cruz argues they were adopted in original compositions throughout the century. She cites the London performances of Meyerbeer's *Robert le Diable* (1832 in the Little Theatre, Haymarket) and *L'Africaine* (1865 at Covent Garden), Wagner's *Der fliegende Holländer* (1870 in Drury Lane as *L'Olandese Dannato*), Verdi's *Aïda* (1876 at Covent Garden) along with many others as examples.[207] Magic lantern sequences in operas and even their stand-alone performances often dispensed with text altogether and were accompanied instrumentally.[208] As Kelly intuited, music that differed from the rest of the score was required for these moments of non-textual storytelling as the instrumentation was serving imagery not sung text. By the end of the nineteenth century, these proto-cinematic experiences were so embedded in performance culture that they were influencing the depictional structures of novels. Joss Marsh has shown how much Dickens's visual effects are drawn from magic lantern shows and vignettes in operas and other genres.[209]

When opera sang its narratives in seventeenth-century Britain, it recovered thelxis for its audiences at a time when society was losing the oral relationship between teller, tale and listener. Again, in the nineteenth century, we can see that as communication media shifted towards a society of mass literacy, narrative artforms shifted again so as to retain thelxis, this time from text to image. The combination of visual and musical storytelling created an emotional engagement with the narrative in ways which words themselves, spoken or sung, were no longer achieving for all audience members. This combination took the viewer out of the present moment and transformed the space to one in which credibility in the story was possible. Melodrama illustrates the trend; its technique of using instrumental music to heighten emotions by playing beneath dialogue or action was incorporated by opera, as Fuhrmann discusses.[210]

In the Wolf's Glen scene in *Der Freischütz* (1821), Weber gives almost a full minute of ominous introductory music for the audience to take in the scenery. Distant church bells chime in warning before Kaspar's summoning of the demon Samiel. A minute and a half of tense and anxious instrumentation accompanies Kaspar's fretful wait for the arrival of Max, his dupe, interrupted only by two lines of recitative. Finally, four minutes of instrumental music accompany the special effects surrounding the moulding of the seven bullets, punctuated only by Kaspar counting to seven. Thus, a total of seven minutes of instrumental music accompany visual effects in a seventeen-minute sequence. This contrasts substantially with the operatic compositions of a generation before, where key moments were verbalised in singing. I suggest that the deeply cinematic approach to opera taken in the late twentieth and twenty-first centuries has its roots in this enhanced visuality of a society moving towards mass literacy in the nineteenth century. Operatic approaches to displacing text influenced other performance genres, indicating how much nineteenth-century opera was part the period's general cultural trends.

Mass literacy sees a displacement of text by visuality

As well as operas themselves, between the 1770s and the 1920s a range of deeply visual performance genres made use of operatic music, narratives and texts to accompany the imagery they created. Ballet is the most obvious but the list also includes professional and amateur tableaux vivant, fantoccini and other puppet shows, magic lantern shows, pre- and post-photography cinema and melodrama. These genres could form parts of operas of course, but their performances could also stand alone, with specialist companies giving performances at their own discrete venue. They could also form items in mixed bills or occur as private entertainments. Their musical component tended to be assembled using pasticcio methods rather than being especially composed so, I propose, pasticcio techniques were used in the service of enhanced visuality for a mass-literate culture. A change can be detected from the continuity of eighteenth-century uses of pasticcio, seen in the first half of the nineteenth century to these new usages in the second half.

In the first half of the nineteenth century, performances of fantoccini, ballet and tableaux vivant depended on being 'read' as a kind of text with a symbiotic interplay of text, visual and musical experience creating the narrative. Audiences for these genres responded to interpretation clues in the instrumentation and words. Later in the century, words were no longer the storyteller around which everything moved; they tended to be relegated to exposition, programme notes or relief *from* the plot, while interactive dialogue between the characters was staged differently. Kress and Leeuwen's hypertextuality was, I suggest, echoed by the reduction in verbalisation seen in these para-operatic genres.[211] Of course, there had been performance genres going back to the medieval period which had done this, puppet shows and clockwork automata especially, but, I propose, the proportion of such performances spiked in the nineteenth century. Modern anxieties about the decline in reading capacity as a result of the enhanced visuality provided by information technology can thus be seen as part of a very long arc, one concomitant with mass literacy itself.

Looked at with hindsight, it is tempting to see these trends in dance, puppetry, kinetic sculptures, tableaux vivant and magic lanterns as all leading to cinema. We should be wary of determinism, however; Christopher Baugh argues that cinematic ways of performing a narrative existed long before celluloid technology became available.[212] Henry V. Hopwood, writing advice on the projection of moving images in 1899, clearly viewed cinema as the extension of long-standing techniques.[213] Nor is cinema the end of the arc; indeed, we know that the displacement of text in musical and visual storytelling did not stop with cinema and television, it continues into animation, three-dimensional films, computer-generated imagery and virtual reality. To place nineteenth-century opera and genres making use of operatic components within Britain's four-century transition from oral to literate to visual culture, a brief summary of that transition may be useful.

In 1600, listeners still visualised much of a performed narrative in their imaginations, yet as staging, scenery and visual effects became more sophisticated, audiences imagined less and watched more, allowing theatres to express more of the story by visual means over the course of the next two centuries. This gradual change was motivated in part by rising numbers of literate people, but more by a distinctly literate culture becoming dominant among the theatre-goers. This created ever-increasing expectations in the depiction of stories, not all of which were for greater verisimilitude or realism. Rather, expectations rose for greater thelxis, for deeper submersion in the story of each individual audience member; thus, for both opera- and, later, cinema-goers, the performance not only had to match but to exceed the audience's imaginative capacities. Audience members no longer participated in shaping the world of the story in their own imaginations; instead they internalised a pre-constructed world pre-imagined for them by submerging themselves in it. This implies passivity, as Baugh said of Loutherbourg's advancements in scenography:

> An additional effect was that, although the technology was not available during the eighteenth century, theatre would become a place where spectators might be rendered passive and quiescent in darkened anonymity as they were presented with authoritative images on the stage.[214]

Even so, I suggest that audience members' *interpretation* of imagery, or 'worlding' in Rachel Hann's term, and their emotional reactions to it, remain individual to each audience member.[215] Nor is this the end of the journey: twentieth- and twenty-first-century participative techniques place the audience member *physically* in the pre-imagined story. Site-specific opera, and opera en promenade aim for this as much as virtual reality does in cinema. Hann notes that Adolphe Appia identified this part of the arc as early as 1921, stating that the theatre of the future will be the difference between watching a young girl running across a field, and running hand in hand with her.[216] Computer-generated imagery, the electronic remastering of singing and other techniques yet to come continue the aim of complete immersion in a story or other process.

In this summary we can see that many musicological debates often discussed as binaries, such as text versus event and fidelity versus pasticcio, are part of wider societal developments conditioning how opera was made and received. Locating them in larger contexts does not minimise the importance of these debates, but it does suggest that binaries are too reductive to capture how the determinants of what is marginal and mainstream change over time.

The practice of constructing opera from pre-existing parts is a visible method throughout this arc of change and played a key role in advancing those changes. In the seventeenth century, making changes allowed operas to be performable outside their original location and context, while in the eighteenth pasticcio was the means whereby Italian opera negotiated the socio-political needs of very different societies. Pasticcio acculturated opera to greater musical sophistication in this period, and as verisimilitude and personation gave way to concepts of authenticity and realism, pasticcio practices were key to bringing narrative and characterisation into accord with these new requirements. Similarly, during the shift towards mass literacy pasticcio, in all its diverse expressions, facilitated the greater visual complexity towards which narrativity now leaned. In the nineteenth century, I suggest pasticcio proliferated rather than terminating. Chapter 5 follows its evolutions in the twentieth century when it acquired new enemies but, ironically, became even more widely practised.

Notes

1 Examples can be found in the *Musical Standard*, 7 January 1871, p. 8 and 6 January 1872, p. 8.
2 Michael Burden, 'The writing and staging of Georgian Romantic opera', *The Oxford Handbook of The Georgian Theatre*, 1737–1832, ed. Julia Swindells and David Francis Taylor (Oxford: Oxford University Press, 2014), pp. 427–441 and 'The lure of aria, process and spectacle: opera in 18th-century London', *The Cambridge History of Eighteenth-Century Music*, ed. Simon Keefe (Cambridge: Cambridge University Press, 2009), pp. 385–401. Christopher Baugh, 'Philippe de Loutherbourg: technology-driven entertainment and spectacle in the late eighteenth century', *Huntington Library Quarterly*, vol. 70 no. 2 (Philadelphia: University of Pennsylvania Press, 2007), pp. 251–286. This development was noted as early as 1831 in 'Historical sketch of the rise and

progress of scene-painting in England', in the four-volume *Library of the Fine Arts, or, Repertory of Painting, Sculpture, Architecture and Engraving*, vol. 1 (London: Arnold, 1831), p. 328.

3 Though as ever with the dating parameters for social change, examples can always be found of the new concerns predating the earliest boundary and old concerns lasting into and beyond the later one; periodisation can seldom be absolute.

4 Opposition to the Test Acts had grown extensive long before they were repealed in 1828 and 1829. The 1798 rebellion in Ireland was not between Catholic and Protestant, still less between those who identified as British and those identifying as Irish, but between tenant farmers and landlords, townsmen and civic authorities. The rebels called themselves United Irishmen to underline that the identity divisions of the past played no role in their socio-economic uprising.

5 While Motteux's *Thomyris* (1707) had promoted friendship, civility and respect between rivals in love and probed the parameters of parental control and obedience, Rossini's *La Donna del lago* (1819) was altered to enhance the confrontation between male rivals, as discussed later, which accorded better with nineteenth-century constructions of masculinity.

6 David Wilkie's painting *The Blind Fiddler* (1806) was one among many famous paintings reproduced across Britain and Ireland in the nineteenth century, mostly by individual painters copying copies. For nineteenth-century mass production of statuary, see Trevor Fawcett, 'Plane surfaces and solid bodies: reproducing three-dimensional art in the nineteenth century', *Visual Resources*, vol. 4 no. 1 (London: Routledge, 1987), pp. 1–23.

7 *The Blind Girl*, 1801, Covent Garden playbill, S.695: 16–1997, Theatre and Performance Collection, Victoria & Albert Museum.

8 *The Illustrated London News*, 20 July 1861, bound edition, vol. 39, p. 53.

9 For more on opera and conceptions of authenticity and originality see Christina Fuhrmann, *Foreign Opera at the London Playhouses: From Mozart to Bellini* (Cambridge: Cambridge University Press, 2015).

10 Jennifer Hall-Witt, *Fashionable Acts: Opera and Elite Culture in London 1780–1880* (Durham, NH: New Hampshire Press, 2007), pp. 244, 229–231, 234–235.

11 Christopher Hendley, 'Fromental Halévy's *La Tempesta*: a study in the negotiation of cultural differences' (doctoral thesis, University of Georgia, 2005), pp. 67–77.

12 See Introduction, note 8, and this chapter, note 34, for some of this criticism.

13 *The Musical Examiner*, 3 November 1842, p. 21.

14 Literature on J.W. Davison includes Charles Reid, *The Music Monster* (New York: Quartet Books, 1984), Leanne Langley, 'The musical press in 19th-century England', *Notes*, vol. 46 (Middleton, WI: Music Library Association, 1990), pp. 583–592 and Meirion Hughes, *The English Musical Renaissance and the Press 1850–1914: Watchmen of Music* (Aldershot: Ashgate, 2002). Davison is discussed in greater detail in Chapter 5.

15 Frederick Curtis Petty, *Italian Opera in London 1760–1800* (Ann Arbor, MI: UMI Research Press, 1980), p. 38. Paul Rodmell, *Opera in the British Isles, 1875–1918* (London: Routledge, 2016), pp. 84, 155–162, 336.

16 Christie's antiquities expert Judith Nugee on the sale of the last Smith Barry marbles, quoted in Rita Reif, 'Auctions; classical sculpture', *New York Times,* 10 July 1987.

17 Julius Bryant, 'Eccentric pioneers? Patrons of modern sculpture for Britain *c.*1790', *Burning Bright: Essays in Honour of David Bindman,* ed. Diana Dethloff, Caroline Elam, Tessa Murdoch and Kim Sloan (London: University College London Press, 2015), pp. 73–74.

18 Elizabeth Banks to Ozias Humphry, 1 April 1778, Royal Academy of Arts, Upcott MSS 11, 67, quoted in ibid., p. 68.

19 Ibid., pp. 71–72.

20 Orietta Rossi Pinelli, 'From the need for completion to the cult of the fragment', *History of the Restoration of Ancient Stone Sculptures; Papers from a Symposium,* ed. Janet Burnett Grossman, Jerry Podany and Marion True (Los Angeles: Getty Publications, 2003), pp. 66–67.

21 Susan Walker quoted in Reif, 'Auctions; classical sculpture'.

22 Bordeaux wines delineated by district or commune (identified today as appellations) began to emerge only in the late seventeenth century and were few in number, Haut Brion, owned by Arnaud de Pontac, being the principal example.

23 Charles Ludington, 'Walpole, Whigs and wine', *History Today,* vol. 63 no. 7 (London: Andy Patterson Press, July 2013), pp. 47–48, from Charles Ludington, *The Politics of Wine in Britain: A New Cultural History* (London: Palgrave Macmillan, 2013).

24 Edmund Penning-Rowsell, 'Christie's wine auctions in the 18th century', *Christie's Wine Review* (London: Christie's, 1972), pp. 11–14.

25 Clive Coates, *The Wines of Bordeaux* (Berkeley: University of California Press, 2004), p. 43. For Sir Robert Walpole's blends see his cellar accounts for Houghton Hall, M23, record of wine at Houghton Hall 1750, estate papers of the Cholmondley family, Houghton Hall, listed by A. Smith, February 1994, Historical Manuscripts Commission. Nigel Surry, 'Two early Georgian wine merchants: the correspondence of James Brydges, first Duke of Chandos with Edward Hooker and Gilbert Wavell, 1720–*c.*1730', *Proceedings of the Hampshire Field Club & Archaeological Society,* vol. 40 (Winchester: HFC&AS, 1984), p. 95.

26 Advertisement in *The Morning Post,* Thursday 12 May 1803, p. 2.

27 Rod Phillips, *Wine: A Social and Cultural History of the Drink that Changed our Lives* (Oxford: Infinite Ideas, 2018), p. 233. 'Hermitage claret' was, in fact, an expensive, popular and respected blend in France and the United States as well as in Britain; it featured on the wine lists of Berry Brothers and Rudd in St James's, Priddy's of Poland Street, the Vauxhall Gardens wine list, The Franklin Wine Store in Washington DC and the Hôtel des Princes et de la Paix in Paris. Anon., catalogue of old wines, part of the estate of Thos. B. Adair, 3 December 1845, David M. Rubenstein Rare Book & Manuscript Library, Duke

University Libraries (Durham, NC: Duke University). http://library.duke.edu/digitalcollections/broadsides_bdsmd30948/ [accessed 11 February 2019]. *The World*, Tuesday, 5 January 1790; Burney Collection Newspapers. *Times-Picayune*, Saturday, 24 August 1878 (New Orleans), p. 2.

28 Fuhrmann, *Foreign Opera at the London Playhouses*, pp. 47–48 for dissatisfaction with gender portrayal, 68–70, 173–176, 180–182.

29 Patrick Joyce discusses this requirement in *Democratic Subjects: The Self and the Social in Nineteenth-Century England* (Cambridge: Cambridge University Press, 1994), pp. 46–48, 54, 116–117, 140; and, more recently, Jason Camlot, *Style and the Nineteenth-Century British Critic: Sincere Mannerisms* (London: Ashgate, 2008), pp. 3–6. Paul Rodmell quotes *The Musical Times* as praising sincerity or deploring its absence in different performances: *Opera in the British Isles*, pp. 20, 228, 28. The same insistence can be found in *The Harmonicon*, *Musical World*, *Monthly Musical Record* and others.

30 Matthew Lewis, *The Monk, a Romance* (Waterford: J. Saunders, 1796). Charles Dickens, *The Pickwick Papers* (London: Chapman and Hall, 1836).

31 George Gissing, *The Unclassed* (Teddington, Middlesex: The Echo Library, 2006), Chapter 27, p. 177.

32 See, for example, reformist arguments for the abolition of Doctor's Commons, the Court of Common Pleas, the Poor Laws and the reform of the patent system. These were echoed in Dickens's novels such as *David Copperfield* and *Little Dorrit*. The Lord Chamberlain's office regularly demanded the removal of satire or criticism of institutions from stage performances: British Library, *Register of the Lord Chamberlain's Plays*, vols I, II and III (Supplementary Papers, 1840–1873), ADD MS 42865–43038 and ADD MS 53702–53708. For a useful survey of institutional reforms, *Studies in the Growth of Nineteenth Century Government*, ed. Gillian Sutherland (London: Routledge, 1972).

33 Michael L. Nash, *The History and Politics of Exhumation: Royal Bodies and Lesser Mortals* (London: Palgrave Macmillan, 2020), various but esp. Chapter 6, pp. 137, 143–144, 149, 156–160.

34 I would include among these writers Oscar Sonneck, *Miscellaneous Studies in the History of Music* (New York: Macmillan, 1921), Theodor Adorno, *Night Music: Essays on Music 1928–1962*, trans. Wieland Hoban (Chicago: University of Chicago Press, 2009) and *Philosophy of New Music*, trans. Robert Hullot-Kentor (originally published 1949, University of Minnesota, 2006). Stanley Sadie (ed.), *The New Grove Dictionary of Music and Musicians* (Basingstoke: Macmillan Reference, 1980–2001); editor, *Man and Music*, 8 vols (Basingstoke: Macmillan, 1989–1993). Carl Dahlhaus, *Analyse und Werturteil* (Musikpädagogik Band 8, 1970), *Die Musik des 19. Jahrhunderts* (Laaber: Laaber, 1980). Unconscious echoes of this generation's thinking can still be found occasionally in turn of the century scholarship including that of Curtis Price, 'Unity, originality, and the London pasticcio', *Harvard Library Bulletin*, new series, vol. 2 (Cambridge, MA: Harvard University Press, 1991), even Hall-Witt, *Fashionable Acts* and, no doubt, my own.

35 Judith Butler, *Gender Trouble* (New York: Routledge, 1990, 2008 edn), p. 184.

36 Ibid., p. 185.

37 *La Belle Assemblée*, 1806, pp. 79–80, 298–300; compare with *The Ladies Magazine*, 1775, pp. 316, 351–2, 482 and 660. Anon., *The Mirror of Graces: Or, The English Lady's Costume* (London: Crosby, 1811).

38 A term used for aristocratic émigrés from the French Revolution; they deliberately dressed in antique styles to signal their high position in the ancien régime prior to their current embarrassments.

39 *The Lady's Magazine, The Gallery of Fashion, Ackerman's Repository* and *La Belle Assemblée*.

40 Jessica Larson, 'Usurping masculinity: the gender dynamics of the coiffure à la Titus in revolutionary France' (unpublished thesis, University of Michigan, 2013), pp. 8–11. E. Claire Cage, 'The sartorial self: neoclassical fashion and gender identity in France, 1797–1804', *Eighteenth-Century Studies*, vol. 42 no. 2 (Baltimore, MD: Johns Hopkins University Press, 2009), pp. 194, 203–205.

41 Larson, 'Usurping masculinity', various but esp. pp. 32–34, 36, 38.

42 Kirstin Olsen, *Daily Life in 18th Century England* (London: Greenwood Press, 1999), p. 106.

43 Amelia Rauser, 'Hair, authenticity, and the self-made macaroni', *Eighteenth-Century Studies*, vol. 38 no. 1 (Baltimore, MD: Johns Hopkins University Press, 2004), p. 107. Shearer West, 'The Darly macaroni prints and the politics of "private man"', *Eighteenth-Century Life*, vol. 25 no. 2, (Durham, NC: Duke University Press, 2001), p. 174. Olsen, *Daily Life in 18th Century England*, p. 107.

44 Naomi André, *Voicing Gender: Castrati, Travesti, and the Second Woman in Early-Nineteenth-Century Italian Opera* (Bloomington, IN: Indiana University Press, 2006).

45 Parkorn Wangpaiboonkit, 'Rethinking operatic masculinity: Nicola Tacchinardi's aria substitutions and the heroic archetype in early nineteenth-century Italy', *Cambridge Opera Journal* (Cambridge: Cambridge University Press, 2020).

46 Nicola Tacchinardi, *Dell'opera in musica sul teatro Italiano* (Modena: Mucchi, 1955), pp. 41–42, quoted in Wangpaiboonkit, 'Rethinking operatic masculinity', p. 3.

47 Ibid., pp. 1–3.

48 Ibid., pp. 7–10, 12–19.

49 Ibid., pp. 14–17.

50 Ibid., p. 17.

51 Ibid., pp. 17–18.

52 Ibid., p. 3.

53 Ibid.

54 Wangpaiboonkit thinks too much significance has been placed on the change in tenorial vocal technique which occurred in 1837 with Gilbert Duprez, at the expense of the broader context of considerable change in reception of

the whole practice of higher-register male singing between the 1790s and the 1830s: ibid., pp. 5–6.

55 Robert Crowe, 'Giambattista Velluti in London (1825–1829): literary constructions of the last operatic castrato' (unpublished doctoral thesis, Boston University,
2017), throughout. '"He was unable to set aside the effeminate, and so was
forgotten": masculinity, its fears, and the uses of falsetto in the early nineteenth
century', *19th Century Music*, vol 3. no. 1 (Berkeley: University of California
Press, 2019), pp. 34–35. See also Heather Hadlock, 'Different masculinities:
androgyny, effeminacy and sentiment in Rossini's *La Donna del lago*', *Rethinking
Difference in Music Scholarship*, ed. Olivia Bloechl, Melanie Lowe and Jeffrey
Kallberg (New York: Cambridge University Press, 2015), pp. 170–213, 202
and 209, and 'Women playing men in Italian opera, 1810–1835', *Women's
Voices across Musical Worlds*, ed. Jane Bernstein (Boston, MA: Northeastern
University Press, 2004), pp. 289–290, 296.

56 Crowe, '"He was unable to set aside the effeminate"', various.

57 Joseph Corfe, *A Treatise on Singing, Explaining in the most simple manner,
etc.* (London, 1799).

58 Ibid., p. 9.

59 Richard Mackenzie Bacon, 'Elements of vocal science: being a philosophical
enquiry into some of the principles of singing' quoted in Crowe, '"He was
unable to set aside the effeminate"', p. 22.

60 Ibid.

61 George Eliot, *Armgart* (London and Edinburgh: William Blackwood and Sons,
1878, cabinet edn), p. 75. Digitised by the George Eliot Archive, ed. Beverley
Park Rilett. http://GeorgeEliotArchive.org [accessed 23 January 2023].

62 Cover page of sheet music, the Gabrielle Enthoven Collection, Accession No.
S.57–2014. Theatre and Performance Collection, Victoria & Albert Museum,
https://collections.vam.ac.uk/item/O1277982/gustavus-the-third-sheet-music-
auber/ [accessed 22 May 2023].

63 Verdi and Somma created several versions of their opera, largely in responses
to censorship; these made substantial changes to location, character names
and plot details. Mapleson's version of Verdi's final recension, which set the
story in colonial-era Boston, was performed at the Lyceum in June 1861 with
Covent Garden following shortly after. The original Swedish setting was not
restored until the twentieth century.

64 Eliot, *Armgart*, p. 77.

65 Ibid., p.80.

66 Ibid., p. 96.

67 Ibid., p. 98.

68 Butler, *Gender Trouble*, pp. 187–188.

69 Crowe, '"He was unable to set aside the effeminate"', p. 24.

70 Ibid., pp. 25–26.

71 *The Times*, 17 May 1858, p. 9.

72 Alexandre Oulibicheff (Alexander Dmitryevich Ulybyshev), *Nouvelle biographie
de Mozart* (Dresden, 1843), trans. and serialised in *Dwight's Journal of Music*,

vol. 8 (Boston: Edward L. Balch, 1855–1856), beginning 2 February 1856 and concluding 29 March 1856.

73 Annika Bautz, 'The "universal favourite": Daniel Terry's *Guy Mannering; or, The Gipsey's Prophecy* (1816)', *The Yearbook of English Studies*, vol. 47, *Walter Scott: New Interpretations* (University of Plymouth, 2017), p. 57.

74 Ibid., p. 56

75 Ibid., p. 57.

76 Ibid., p. 56. Bautz is quoting *The Ladies' Monthly Museum*, October 1819, p. 227, *The Theatrical Inquisitor and Monthly Mirror*, 11 September 1817, p. 229, *The Observer*, 11 October 1819, p. 3 and *La Belle Assemblee*, 1 March 1817.

77 Ibid., p. 55

78 Bristol Theatre Collection, Playbills, TC/PB 000318.

79 John Rosselli, 'Italy: the centrality of opera', *The Early Romantic Era between Revolutions, 1789 and 1848*, ed. Alexander Ringer (Basingstoke: Palgrave Macmillan, 1990), pp. 166, 170–172, 186. For Rosselli this was an acceptance by Italian opera of northern Romantic ideas, though the conception of operatic ideas as having national or regional characters has been displaced in recent decades by the weight of evidence for transnationalism. Sean M. Parr, 'Coloratura and technology in the mid-nineteenth century mad scene', *Technology and the Diva: Sopranos, Opera and Media, from Romanticism to the Digital Age*, ed. Karen Henson (Cambridge: Cambridge University Press, 2016), pp. 37–49.

80 The *Daily News* critic was quoted by the *Musical World*, 15 June 1850, and more recently by Hendley, 'Fromental Halévy's *La Tempesta*', p. 174.

81 Rosselli, 'Italy: the centrality of opera', pp. 171–172.

82 Hilary Poriss, *Changing the Score: Arias, Prima Donnas, and the Authority of Performance* (Oxford: Oxford University Press, 2009), various.

83 Treatises on singing including Corfe's *A Treatise on Singing*, p. 8 and Mackenzie Bacon, *Elements of Vocal Science*, pp. 58, 104, among many others. Among connoisseurs, Lord Mount Edgcumbe's famous criticism of Catalani is quoted by Hall-Witt, *Fashionable Acts*, p. 51.

84 Parr, 'Coloratura and technology', pp. 37–38, and *Vocal Virtuosity: The Origins of the Coloratura Soprano in Nineteenth-Century Opera* (Oxford: Oxford University Press, 2021), p. 2.

85 Parr, 'Coloratura and technology', pp. 37–39, 47–49.

86 See note 34.

87 William Weber, 'The history of the musical canon', *Rethinking Music*, ed. Nicholas Cook and Mark Everist (Oxford: Oxford University Press, 1999). Nicholas Matthew, 'History under erasure: "Wellingtons Sieg", the Congress of Vienna, and the ruination of Beethoven's heroic style', *The Musical Quarterly*, vol. 89 no. 1 (Oxford: University Press, 2006), pp. 17–61. Sarah Hibberd, *French Grand Opera and the Historical Imagination* (Cambridge: Cambridge University Press, 2009). Carolyn Abbate, Roger Parker, *A History of Opera: The Last Four Hundred Years*, (London: Allen Lane, 2012). *The Invention of Beethoven and Rossini*, ed. Benjamin Walton and Nicholas Matthew (Cambridge:

Cambridge University Press, 2013). Clair Rowden (ed.), *Performing Salome, revealing stories* (Aldershot: Ashgate, 2013). Roger Parker (principal investigator), *Music in London 1800–1851* (research project with multiple outputs including over twenty publications, 2013–2018). James Q. Davies, *Romantic Anatomies of Performance* (Berkeley: University of California Press, 2014). Gianmario Borio, Giovanni Giuriati, Alessandro Cecchi and Marco Lutzu (eds), *Investigating Musical Performance: Theoretical Models and Intersections* (Abingdon: Routledge, 2020). Sarah Hibberd and Miranda Stanyon (eds), *Music and the Sonorous Sublime in European Culture, 1680–1880* (Cambridge: Cambridge University Press, 2020), and many others.

88 An example is Price's 'Unity, originality, and the London pasticcio'. Although Price queries neoromantic assumptions of what has always constituted a great opera, he discusses the eighteenth-century true pasticcio as if it is the only kind. See also discussion in *Operatic Pasticcios* in *18th-Century Europe: Contexts, Materials and Aesthetics*, ed. Berthold Over and Gesa zur Nieden (Bielefeld: transcript Verlag, 2021) discussed in Chapter 1.

89 Scholars writing within inherited conceptions of pasticcio include Hall-Witt, *Fashionable Acts*, p. 46; Rachel Cowgill, 'Mozart productions and the emergence of the *Werktreue* at London's Italian Opera House, 1780–1830', *Operatic Migrations: Transforming Works and Crossing Boundaries*, ed. Roberta Montemorra Marvin and Downing A. Thomas (Aldershot: Ashgate, 2006), p. 148. Theodore Fenner, *Opera in London; Views of the Press* (London: SIU Press, 1994), pp. 276–301. John Goulden, 'Michael Costa, England's first conductor, 1830–1880' (doctoral thesis, Durham University, 2012), pp. 310–311. Goulden notes that Costa continued to sanction aria substitutions, interpolations, cuts and transpositions until at least 1850, though in increasingly defined contexts, and continued to reorchestrate operas throughout his career: pp. 312–314. https://core.ac.uk/download/pdf/9641057.pdf [accessed 28 March 2019].

90 Fuhrmann, *Foreign Opera at the London Playhouses*, pp. 2, 13–15, 170–171.

91 Ibid., pp. 15–16, 22, 39, 47.

92 For the fidelity to *Zémira e Azore* in the King's Theatre adaptation of 1789: Curtis Price, Judith Milhous and Robert D. Hume, *Italian Opera in Late 18th-century London, the King's Theatre, Haymarket*, 2 vols (Oxford: Clarendon Press, 1995), vol. I, pp. 212–213 and 214–215. For the Covent Garden performance of Linley's 1784 adaptation on 5 October 1813: J and J Lubrano Music Antiquarian Archive, University of Illinois, digitised in 2016, p. 9. https://www.library.illinois.edu/mpal/wp-content/uploads/sites/17/2016/11/Bishop-Lubrano_Description_of_Archive.pdf [accessed 21 April 2022].

93 For the fidelity of *Il barbiere di Siviglia* in London, see Price, Milhous and Hume, *Italian Opera in Late 18th-century London*, vol. I, pp. 415–416; also Alfred Loewenberg, 'Paisiello's and Rossini's *Barbiere di Siviglia*', *Music & Letters*, vol. 20 no. 2 (Oxford: Oxford University Press, 1939), p. 160. For Bishop's 1818 adaptation: Fuhrmann, *Foreign Opera at the London Playhouses*, pp. 47–49.

 94 See Introduction for terminological parameters.

 95 Fuhrmann, *Foreign Opera at the London Playhouses*, pp. 173, 193.

 96 *The Times*, 26 July 1891, p. 10.

 97 *Musical Standard*, 6 January 1872, p. 8.

 98 Frederick Corder, *The Works of Sir Henry Bishop* (London, 1918). Reinhard
     Strohm, 'Handel's pasticci', *Journal of Ancient Music*, no. 14 (1974), pp.
     208–267. For authors in between see Introduction, note 8 and this chapter,
     note 34.

 99 Burden, 'Georgian Romantic opera', pp. 425–426.

100 *The Times*, 11 November 1857, p. 12. The opera was popular enough for the
     libretto to be translated and printed: *Il Ritorno di Columella*, trans. Thomas
     Williams (Printed by T. Brettell and to be had at The Box Office, St James's
     Theatre, Haymarket, 1857).

101 *The Times*, 2 August, 1858, p. 12.

102 Ibid.

103 See 'Intertextuality' in Chapter 1.

104 *Musical Standard*, 7 January 1871, p. 8, and 6 January 1872, p. 8, respectively.

105 *Morning Chronicle*, 3 March 1842, p. 3; also Jan Piggott, 'Milton's *Comus*:
     from text to stage, the fine arts, and book illustration, *c*.1750–1850', *British
     Art Journal*, vol. 15 no. 2 (London: BAJ Press, 2014). Charles H. Shattuck,
     'Macready's *Comus*: a prompt-book study', *The Journal of English and Germanic
     Philology*, vol. 60 no. 4, *Milton Studies in Honor of Harris Francis Fletcher*
     (Champaign: University of Illinois Press, 1961), pp. 732–735.

106 Shattuck, 'Macready's *Comus*', p. 734.

107 Kevin Pask, *The Fairy Way of Writing: Shakespeare to Tolkien* (Baltimore,
     MD: Johns Hopkins University Press, 2013), p. 83. Bishop's wife Anna was
     in the cast as was Mrs W. Lacy.

108 *Pietro L'Eremita or Peter the Hermit. A Serious Opera in Three Acts, Adapted
     to the Music of 'Mosi' Composed by Rossini* (London: Printed for John Ebers,
     1822).

109 *Pall Mall Gazette*, 16 August, 1869, p. 11.

110 Belknap Playbills and Programmes Collection, George A. Smathers Libraries,
     University of Florida.

111 *Morning Post*, 14 May, 1870, p. 5.

112 Mary Helen Still, 'The artist and the entertainers: Emmanuel Chabrier and
     his imitators' (unpublished masters thesis, University of Georgia, 2013), pp.
     53–58, quoting Roger Delage, *Emmanuel Chabrier* (Paris: Fayard, 1999).

113 Frank Cullen, Florence Hackman and Donald McNeilly, *Vaudeville Old and
     New: an Encyclopedia of Variety Performances in America*, vol. 1 (New York:
     Routledge, 2007), p. 249.

114 *The Theatre*, 1 November 1890, vol. 16 (London: Eglinton and Co, 1890),
     pp. 241, 245.

115 Examples of pasticci designated as such staged as part of mixed bills in various
     theatres in the 1830s and 1840s, advertised in newspapers:

The Times	Black Spirits and White or The Haunted Chamber	Sadler's Wells 13 February 1826, p. 2.
		Surrey Theatre, 11 December 1828, p. 2.
		Royal West London, 22 January 1829, p. 2.
		Surrey Theatre, 8 June 1831, p. 2.
	T.T.S. or The Bar and the Stage	Royal Victoria Theatre, 17 September 1833, p. 2.
		Drury Lane, 3 May 1835, p. 1.
		Drury Lane, 20 April 1838, p. 4.
		Her Majesty's Theatre, 6 June 1840, p. 4.
Morning Chronicle	Here we are or The Old Ship New Timbered	Sadler's Wells, 31 March 1825, p. 3.
	Cousin Joseph	New Theatre Royal or English Opera House, 29 May 1835.
	Comus	Drury Lane, 3 March 1842, p. 3.
John Bull	Turning the Tables	Drury Lane, 1 April 1838, p. 1.
Morning Post	The Princess who was Turned into a Deer	Drury Lane, 4 November 1845, p. 5.
The Standard	'Pasticcio'	Lyceum, 4 June 1847, p. 2.

From 1856 onwards German Reed and his family advertised pasticci at the Gallery of Illustration, the most famous of which were those of Richard Corney Grain from 1870 to 1895.

116 British Library, Register of the Lord Chamberlain's Plays and the Lord Chamberlain's Plays and Day Books.

117 *The Times*, 18 October 1798, p.1.

118 Clive Brown, 'Sir Henry Rowley Bishop', *Oxford Dictionary of National Biography*, published online 23 September 2004, https://doi.org/10.1093/ref:odnb/2470 [accessed 5 June 2019].

119 *The Times*, 6 June 1840, p. 4.

120 *Morning Post*, 20 May, 1842, p. 6. Henry Melling's *Battle of Agincourt* exhibited by the Society of Arts in the Great Room at the Adelphi on 20 May 1842 was one such; the *Morning Post's* art critic described it as a pasticcio, noting that it was drawn from other battle paintings including De Keyser's *Flight from the Field of Spurs*.

121 *Morning Post*, 24 March 1851, p. 1. For its longevity of use see also 'Concerning expertise' by C. Collins Baker, *The Saturday Review*, 10 February 1912.

122 *The Times*, 15 May 1873, p. 10.

123 *Morning Post* 15 February 1900, p. 3.

124 Derek B. Scott, *German Operetta in the West End and on Broadway, 1900–1940* (Cambridge: Cambridge University Press, 2014), pp. 12–13.

125 Ibid., pp. 7–9.

126 Ibid., pp. 14–15.

127 The Kathleen Barker archive at the University of Bristol's Theatre Collection is a mechanically typed corpus, sadly unpaginated, but running to eighty stout lever-arch ring-bound folders. It consists of all documentation relating to Bristol's Theatre Royal between 1766 and 1966. Dr Barker's material, collated mainly between the 1960s and 1980s, is complemented by a collection of playbills, mostly from the Theatre Royal in Bristol, with a few from London, Bath and elsewhere. Bristol City Library's Local Studies Collection includes playbills as does the Bath Central Library Theatrical Collection and the Evanion Collection of Ephemera at the British Library Theatrical Records.

128 The Theatre in the Regency Era Conference, held by The Society for Theatre Research in July 2016, contained the following talks: Jean Baker, 'Life's troubled waves': Sarah Baker, '"Great grand" Kentish theatres and the Napoleonic wars, 1793–1815', Hannah Manktelow, '"Country acting is at a very low ebb at present": perceptions and realities of provincial performance in the Regency era', David Wilmore, 'In Winston's footsteps: the next three guides to provincial theatre – 1827, 1833 and 1864', Judith Hawley, 'Blowing up the pic nics: private theatricals in the Regency era'.

129 Peter Davey, *The Theatrical History of Wales 1748–1857* (typewritten manuscript, 1945, Swansea University Library), pp. 18, 28(a), 30, 31–32, 39, 61, 78, 106.

130 Ibid., pp. 86–88.

131 Innumerable local reviews lament the meagre houses which leading performers of Shakespeare and Mozart drew, though the houses even for pantomimes and farces could be too thin to save a theatre from ruin.

132 Michael Kelly, *Solo Recital, The Reminiscences of Michael Kelly* (London, 1826, reprinted by The Folio Society, 1972), pp. 163–165, 180–181, 202–203.

133 Rodmell, *Opera in the British Isles*, pp. 130–183.

134 *The Lord of the Manor* was performed at Bath and *The Deserter* at Bristol, 28 July 1794. The former was an English opera performed the previous year at Drury Lane. The latter was an English pasticcio by Charles Dibden of a French opera by Pierre-Alexandre Monsigny. TC/PB 000264.

135 *Bristol Journal*, 21 March 1840, quoted in Kathleen Barker Archive KB/4/8.

136 KB/4/8, 25 April 1840.

137 Kathleen Barker, *The Theatre Royal Bristol, Decline and Rebirth 1834–1943* (the Bristol Branch of The Historical Association, Bristol University, 1966), p. 21.

138 TC/PB 000272, 4 July 1808, Theatre Royal Archive, University of Bristol Theatre Collection.

139 G. Rennee Powell, *The Bristol Stage: Its Story* (Bristol: Bristol Printing and Publishing Co. Ltd, 1919), p. 43 (*Gold*), p. 47 (*Sebastopol*), pp. 76–78 (*Tempest*). Chute's other adaptations for the stage include Harriet Beecher Stowe's *Dred, A Tale of the Swamp* (1856), though this seems to have been a dialogue play as was *Caste and Colour*, an adaptation of Auguste Anicet-Bourgeois and Philippe Dumanoir's *Le Docteur Noir*. *Gizelle – the Phantom Night Dancers* (1860) was a true pasticcio as was *The Bottle* (1876), based on Cruikshank's picture.

140 Playbills and Posters, Theatre Collection, Core Collection, Theatre Royal Archive, University of Bristol Theatre Collection. Examples include those listed in these notes, but many more besides.

141 Bristol Theatre Collection, Playbills, TC/PB 000285.

142 TC/PB 000283.

143 TC/PB 000036.

144 TC/PB 000626. Her Majesty's Theatre company performed Bellini's *La Sonnambula*, Verdi's *Il Trovatore* and Gounod's *Faust* for three nights, 20, 21 and 22 December 1877, at the Theatre Royal, Bristol, conducted by Joseph Li Calsi.

145 TC/PB 000282. The opera was performed on 2 January 1809, followed by a melodrama, *Ella Rosenberg*. It is unknown if the supporting cast were from the Theatre Royal or brought by Mrs Dickens.

146 Sarah Macready is recorded as recruiting Italian singers in London in August 1835, to stage operas at the time of the Fortnight Fair. *The Theatrical Observer*, 10 August 1835, p. 2.

147 TC/PB 000326, TC/PB 000333 respectively.

148 TC/PB 000318. Conceivably this could have been a young William Brough or another member of his family.

149 TC/PB 000310 and TC/PB 000318.

150 TR/Pub/1/1486, see also TC/PB 000025. 10/11 March 1856.

151 TC/PB 000025.

152 Kathleen Barker Archive KB/4/8. 2 March 1840.

153 Bristol Theatre Collection, Playbills, TC/PB/000025.

154 TC/PB 000645. 8, 9 and 10 May 1877. Kate Santley's company was that of the Royalty Theatre, London. *Trial by Jury* was reworked as 'a novel and original cantata'.

155 TC/PB 000622.

156 TC/PB 000644.

157 Rodmell, *Opera in the British Isles*, pp. 130–137.

158 Bristol Theatre Collection, Playbills, TC/PB 000318.

159 TC/PB 000318.

160 John Dicks produced an illustrated one-penny edition of the opera *Guy Mannering* as part of The British Drama series in 1864. Walter Henry Fisher played the lead in Bristol's 1866 staging.

161 Bristol Theatre Collection, Playbills, TC/PB 000318.

162 TC/PB 000644.

163 TC/PB 000036. By Monsieur Lalanne's daughter.

164 TC/PB 000314.

165 TC/PB 000333.

166 *The New Monthly Magazine*, 1 March 1829.

167 J. Panksepp and G. Bernatzky, 'Emotional sounds and the brain: the neuroaffective foundations of musical appreciation', *Behavioural Processes*, vol. 60 (Leiden: Elsevier, 2002), p. 144.

168 Kathleen Barker Archive. KB/4/8.

169 Bristol Theatre Collection, Playbills, TC/PB 000333 for James Henry, contra Powell who gives 1843 as the date Chute joined the Bristol company. TC/PB 000326 for John Chute.

170 TC/PB 000070.

171 Kathleen Barker Archive (unpaginated).

172 Bristol Archives, ref: 26404 (documents relating to James Henry Chute and theatres in Bristol and Bath 1845–1909), digitised at Bristol Old Vic archives website, https://bristololdvic.org.uk/archive/james-chute [accessed 16 June 2019]. For Chute in *Village Nightingale* see Bristol Theatre Collection, Playbills, TC/PB 000025.

173 TC/PB 000626 and Bristol Archives, ref: 26404 (documents relating to James Henry Chute and theatres in Bristol and Bath 1845–1909).

174 Ibid.

175 Powell, *The Bristol Stage*, pp. 73–74.

176 *Bristol Mercury*, 24 September 1859, p. 6.

177 Bristol Theatre Collection, Playbills, TC/PB 000626.

178 Rodmell, *Opera in the British Isles*, p. 183.

179 *Bristol Mercury*, 14 October 1893, p. 8.

180 *Bristol Mercury,* 12 May 1893, p. 8.

181 *Bristol Mercury*, 24 April, 1900, p. 8.

182 *Bristol Mercury*, 3 February 1899.

183 David Vincent, *Literacy and Popular Culture: England 1750–1914* (Cambridge: Cambridge University Press, 1989), pp. 23, 26–28.

184 David Vincent, 'The invention of counting: the statistical measurement of literacy in nineteenth-century England', *Comparative Education*, vol. 50 no. 3 (Abingdon: Taylor and Francis, 2014), p. iii and iv. Digitised by Taylor and Francis https://www.tandfonline.com/doi/full/10.1080/03050068.2014.921372 [accessed 6 February 2023]. Signing one's name does not imply full literacy of course, as Vincent discusses. The bar on what constituted literacy was set very low in the nineteenth century compared with modern definitions, nor did everyone classed as literate read for pleasure or information: usage could be confined to reading and signing a handful of legal documents throughout a person's life. Dyslexia also went unrecognised in this century.

185 Lydia Goehr, *The Imaginary Museum of Musical Works: An Essay in the Philosophy of Music* (Oxford: Clarendon Press, 1992). This was an influential and ground-breaking book which still causes controversy. Many criticisms were made of Goehr's temporal framework by Reinhard Strohm and others. In 2000, Michael Talbot edited *The Musical Work, Reality or Invention?* (Cambridge:

Cambridge University Press, 2000) to widen the debate. Essays included Strohm's 'Looking back at ourselves: the problem with the musical work-concept', pp. 128–152, arguing for a longer timespan in assessing ontological changes in music. Goehr responded with 'On the problems of dating or looking backward and forward with Strohm', pp. 231–246. Gavin Steingo's 2014 assessment of the initial critical response found that Goehr's thesis had more defenders than detractors by that point and a recognition existed that her timeframes were not written as absolutes. Steingo found a consensus that, while examples of the perceived changes can be found over a longer timeframe, occur they did, and with a demonstrably higher proportionality in the nineteenth century. Gavin Steingo, 'The musical work reconsidered, in hindsight', *Current Musicology*, vol. 97 (New York: Columbia University, 2014), pp. 81–112.

186 George Hogarth is one example, a committed ideologue in the cause of textual fidelity whose books were intended to be evidential and authoritative: *Musical History, Biography, and Criticism: being a general survey of music, from the earliest period to the present time* (London: J.W. Parker, 1835), *Musical History, Biography, and Criticism*, 2 vols (New York: Da Capo Press, 1838) and *Memoirs of the Opera in Italy, France, Germany and England*, 2nd edn, 2 vols (London, 1851). Frederick Corder's 1918 biography of Henry Bishop, O.G. Sonneck's essay of 1921 'Ciampi's *Bertoldo, Bertoldino e Cacasenno* and Favart's *Ninette à la Cour*: a contribution to the history of pasticcio', *Miscellaneous Studies in the History of Music* (New York: Macmillan, 1921) and Robert Newton's *Peter Anthony Motteux 1663–1718* (Oxford: Blackwells, 1933) continued Hogarth's disquiet over pasticcio, seeing it as a pre-fidelity curiosity which showed how much opera had advanced in the meantime. These studies influenced Winton Dean and John Merrill Knapp's *Handel's Operas, 1704–1726* (Woodbridge, Suffolk: Boydell Press, 1987) and *Handel's Operas, 1726–1741* (Woodbridge, Suffolk: Boydell Press, 2006). Their perspectives find echoes in Price's 'Unity, originality and the London pasticcio', as well as Hall-Witt's *Fashionable Acts*.

187 Alastair Minnis, 'Medieval imagination and memory', *The Cambridge History of Literary Criticism*, vol. II, part III: *Textual Psychologies: Imagination, Memory, Pleasure* (Cambridge: Cambridge University Press, 2008), pp. 241–242, 254, esp. 260–262. In pp. 256–257, Minnis discusses Richard of St Victor's *Benjamin Minor* (before 1162), a text which discusses not only how people imagined biblical or poetic descriptions from their depictions in art, but how they should interpret such art-derived images as Christians. Later, Angela of Foligno's *Memorial* (*c.*1449) describes her emotional responses to paintings of the passion, stained glass windows and statuary, highlighting the permanent impression these made on her memory.

188 John Lydgate, 'The minor poems of Lydgate, part I', ed. Henry Noble Mac-Cracken, Early English Text Society, Extra Series 107 (Oxford: Oxford University Press, 1911), pp. 250 and 290 respectively. Quoted in Minnis, 'Medieval imagination and memory', pp. 260–261.

189 Christopher Baugh, 'Stage design from Loutherbourg to Poel', *The Cambridge History of British Theatre*, vol. 2 *1660–1895* (Cambridge: Cambridge University

Press, 2004), pp. 310–314. More recently, Rachel Hann has provided a new theoretical basis for understanding the mise-en-scène of performance: Rachel Hann, *Beyond Scenography* (Oxford: Routledge, 2019).

190 Gunter Kress and Theo van Leeuwen, *Reading Images: The Grammar of Visual Design* (London: Routledge, 1996), pp. 15–16. Most writers on literacy make this point about the literate imagination leaning more towards naturalism. Ian Watt, *The Rise of the Novel* (London: Penguin, 1963), p. 32. J.J. Mooij, *Fictional Realities: The Uses of the Literate Imagination* (Utrecht: Utrecht Publications in General and Comparative Literature, 1993), pp. 125–149.

191 George Colman the Elder, *The Connoisseur*, vol. 1, pp. 135–136, quoted by Shearer West in 'Manufacturing spectacle', *The Oxford Handbook of Georgian Theatre 1732–1832*, ed. Swindells and Francis Taylor, p. 289.

192 For silent listening: James Johnson, *Listening in Paris: A Cultural History* (Cambridge: Cambridge University Press, 1996).

193 Kelly, *Solo Recital*, pp. 40–41.

194 Such as Charlotte Lennox's *The Female Quixote* (1752), Hugh Kelly's *Memoirs of a Magdalen* (1767) and Voltaire's *The White Bull* (1772); later examples of novels influencing theatrical action scenes include Rudolf Erich Raspe's *Baron Munchausen* (1785), William Beckford's *Vathek* (1786) and Ann Radcliffe's *The Castles of Athlin and Dunbayne* (1789).

195 Burden, 'Georgian Romantic opera', pp. 427–429, effect described on p. 428.

196 *Don Juan* playbill, 1809, Eddison Collection, Accession no: S.695:15–1997. V & A, Theatre and Performance Collection, https://collections.vam.ac.uk/ item/O1170989/eddison-collection-playbill-unknown/ [accessed 5 November 2022].

197 Michael Burden notes that this opera's story derives from a 1787 French novel, *Les amours du Chevalier de France* by Louvret de Couvrai. The pasticcio was compiled from two other settings of the story, Cherubini's and Rudolphe Kreutzer's, both in 1791. It had a new libretto, however, by John Phillip Kemble who drew heavily on the Kreutzer version's libretto by Jean-Élie Bédéno Dejaure: Burden, 'Georgian Romantic opera', p. 429.

198 Deac Rossell, 'The magic lantern and moving images before 1800', *Barockberichte*, vols 40–41, (Salzburg: Salzburg Baroque Museum, 2005), pp. 686–693.

199 Ibid.

200 Kirsten Treen, 'Stereopticon', *Writing, Medium, Machine: Modern Technographies*, ed. S. Pryor and D. Trotter (London: Open Humanities Press, London, 2016), p. 36. See also p. 109.

201 Stephen Bottomore and Minici Zotti identified this publication in the British Library.

202 Kelly, *Solo Recital*, p. 221.

203 Although Cruz thinks this may have been a diorama, as it appears to have been in continental stagings. Gabriela Cruz, *Grand Illusion: Phantasmagoria in Nineteenth-century Opera* (Oxford: Oxford University Press, 2020), p. 43.

204 Ibid., pp. 117–122.

205 Ibid., pp. 104–109.

206 Wagner's remarks to Liszt, quoted in ibid., p. 126.

207 Cruz, *Grand Illusion,* pp. 43–84.

208 Slide shows even accompanied religious services; one was given at Toxteth Workhouse: *Liverpool Mercury*, 8 January 1896. Item 7006247, Lucerna Magic Lantern Web Resource, Lucerna CIC, hosted by the University of Exeter. lucerna. exeter.ac.uk [accessed 15 March 2023]. The Magic Lantern Society also holds a substantial collection of sheet music that accompanied performances.

209 Joss Marsh, 'Dickensian "dissolving views": the magic lantern, visual story-telling, and the Victorian technological imagination', *Comparative Critical Studies*, vol. 6 no. 3 (Edinburgh: Edinburgh University Press, 2009).

210 Fuhrmann, *Foreign Opera at the London Playhouses*, pp. 40–47.

211 Kress and van Leeuwen, *Reading Images*, pp. 15–16

212 Baugh, 'Stage design from Loutherbourg to Poel', p. 309.

213 Henry V. Hopwood, *Living Pictures: Their History, Photoduplication, and Practical Working* (London: The Optician and Photographic Trades Review, 1899), p. 188.

214 Baugh, 'Stage design from Loutherbourg to Poel', pp. 309–310.

215 Hann, *Beyond Scenography*, various.

216 Adolphe Appia, *L'oeuvre d'Art Vivant* (Geneva and Paris: Edition Atar, 1921) quoted by Rachel Hann, 'Notes on *Beyond Scenography*', *Revista Cena*, no. 31 (Porto Alegre, 2020), p. 30.

5

Survival and revival

> [Pasticcio] still persists in the theatre: the recipe is too useful to have dropped out of the entertainment promoter's cookery book, but it is a tricky dish to serve ... Expert dramatists like Miss Eleanor and Mr Herbert Farjeon can sometimes supply sufficient unity. *Elephant in Arcady* was one of the best pasticcios of modern times. It owed its unity to the fact that it started definitely on an operatic basis. The play was musical in conception and the songs culled from a dozen composers were no decorations but elements in the dramatic structure. Within the music there was a surprising unity of style – personal idioms were hardly discernible within the eighteenth-century Italian convention. To a sufficiently well-founded musical unity, the satire on Arcadian pretensions added unity of subject; witty dialogue and amusing situation provided the flavour for a theatrical success.
>
> Review of a pasticcio opera in *The Times*, 6 January 1940.[1]

By 'personal idioms' the reviewer meant what is currently termed the composer's 'voice', an individual style that romantic tradition believed to reveal the composer's inner self. That the absence of such individualities is lauded suggests that even in 1940 the techniques required for a good pasticcio were still remembered: the unity that made *La villanella rapita* a success in the 1780s could still be achieved in the 1930s. This review in *The Times* discusses several more contemporary pasticcio operas but *An Elephant in Arcady* is of particular interest: unlike the extravaganzas and burlesques of the previous age, it designated itself as a pasticcio and offers an example of continuity from baroque practice on the British stage. It was compiled in 1938 by Eleanor Farjeon (1881–1965) and her brother Herbert (1887–1945), arranged musically by Ernest Irving (1878–1953) and published that year, having premiered at the Kingsway Theatre on 5 October. This was also the first pasticcio opera to be broadcast on television, being transmitted on 28 November that year. A satire on eighteenth-century neoclassicism, it used music by Mozart, Scarlatti, Paisiello, Pergolesi, Vinci, Sarti, Ariosti, Durante, Galuppi, Bononcini, Piccinni and Cimarosa to tell its story. *The Times* summarised the plot thus:

Florinda [is] the daughter of a count who devotes to his menagerie the money that should buy her dresses. She is a star of the Arcadian Academy of Pisa but is deaf to the love-making of an honest gentleman. It is not until he has passed himself off as her father's mahout and loosed a fictitious elephant among the earnest but timorous Arcadians that she is brought to a knowledge of true love.

What is significant about this twentieth-century pasticcio is that its emulation of earlier practice was deliberate and clearly visible, having an impeccably Georgian structure. As discussed later, the Farjeons were the end of a line of teacher/pupil descent going back to Giovanni Bianchi in the 1780s. Whether the Farjeons saw their opera as a rediscovery of an all-but-forgotten method or part of a continuity is the key question, yet these are not mutually exclusive possibilities. Those with specialist knowledge of pasticcio, such as the Farjeons or Beatrice Saxon Snell, might create them consciously and designate them as pasticci, but others using the same method might call them something else, such as an operetta. Similarly, Ryan Ross shows that Julius Bürger designated his radio compositions as 'musical potpourri' but sees his method as deriving from pasticcio.[2] Yet Bürger would never have used the word pasticcio for his compositions as, by then, it was tightly defined as an eighteenth-century operatic genre. Pasticcio was periodically rediscovered by theatres, companies or managers who had no previous knowledge of its long history or techniques, such was Heinrich Berté. Richard Traubner shows that Berté created his pasticcio *Dreimäderlhaus* (1916) through personal discovery.

Commissioned to set a libretto about the life of Schubert, based on a novel by Rudolf Hans Bartsch, the composer intended to create an original score with just one insertion aria from Schubert himself. After discussion with his brother and others he created a pasticcio instead. He learned to do this as he went along, selecting appropriate music from across Schubert's oeuvre to serve dramatic sequences for which they had not originally been intended and using his own composition only to bridge the figures; even in this he parodied Schubert's style to preserve the unity of the piece. It cannot be proved that Berté had no previous knowledge at all of pasticcio opera but it shows that a lineage of tuition was not essential to picking up the necessary skills. His operetta was a great success leading to 650 performances.[3]

I propose that the first half of the twentieth century was an arena for both continuity *and* rediscovery of pasticcio and suggest that if the principle of absolute fidelity to original scores really had been universally supported by musicians and audiences alike in the nineteenth century, and applied across the board, then the twentieth century's pasticcio operas, operettas, film scores, and radio and television medleys would all have been rediscoveries of the method. Yet the reader will by now be wondering: if pasticcio operas did not terminate in the nineteenth century and if the advocates in the press for textual fidelity were not all as hostile or did not have the influence claimed, then why did pasticcio opera disappear from leading opera house repertoires? This chapter argues that a combination of factors were causal.

The commodification of music through the process of performance licensing in the nineteenth-century was followed by a dramatic expansion of rights legislation in the early decades of the twentieth century. The advocacy of textual fidelity in music was intended to enhance respect for the composer and protect their works for posterity: this goal was the justification for the legislative structures introduced at the Berne Convention in 1886; nevertheless, this section argues that in the majority of instances the consequence of these structures was the transfer of profit *from* composers to disseminators. I argue later that national and international music companies made selective use of nineteenth-century arguments for textual fidelity to justify the exclusion from copyright or licensing of variant versions of compositions, those where ownership was shared, complex or open to contest. The legislative structure insisted on by a nascent music industry worked best if compositions were works with a tradable copyright, written by a single author, existing in one version and unchanging over successive reproductions.[4] Companies were highly active on an ideological level and promoted absolute textual fidelity in music as, if not exactly a timeless norm, then certainly a timeless desideratum rather than a comparatively recent demand. This contributed to modern perceptions of pasticcio as historically marginal during this period, but another result was the prolonging of Romantic tenets and priorities in high-end opera creation.

Paul Rodmell shows that between 1875 and 1918 attempts to establish an indigenous English-language operatic repertoire failed and this was felt to be due to the lack of a national opera house or state funding.[5] But when these came into existence in the period after the Second World War and an English-only policy was put in place, with translations of continental works and new English-language commissions, Covent Garden's own reports show that audiences stayed away in droves. Indeed, Harold Rosenthal declared that during the years between the First and Second World Wars the theatre was only open six months in the year.[6] In the eighteenth century, pasticci had balanced new commissions in King's Theatre programming with known repertoire, but throughout the twentieth century old favourites from the continent were preferred and a narrowing nineteenth-century canon was augmented more by eighteenth-century rediscoveries than contemporary operas. In the twentieth century, pasticcio was not among the resuscitation strategies of national opera companies. What led to, and what might cure, an ever-contracting operatic canon for leading opera houses continues to be debated. All agree that audiences are aging, that funding is uncertain and the artform itself is experiencing a marginalisation it did not experience in previous centuries, a malaise which metropolitan houses and national opera companies strive constantly to resolve.

But this picture focuses too much on leading houses: outside this, pasticcio operas can be found across Britain in festivals from Haddo to Glyndebourne, in metropolitan and regional theatres and on television and radio. Pasticcio operas drew strength from the popularity of pasticcio in cinema, radio and television music. Opera intersected with cinema and television in many ways throughout the twentieth century, as it had done with the novel in the eighteenth and nineteenth centuries; the use of pasticcio in cinema helped to legitimise it in opera and vice versa. The chapter finally surveys the tentative revival of pasticcio opera in the twenty-first century, and the potential it can offer in resisting repertoire contraction.

Copyright, performance licensing and the commodification of music

This section begins by arguing that the politics and mechanics of performance licensing had a greater influence in tilting large-scale opera companies in the direction of textual fidelity and away from pasticcio than reformist pressure from sections of the press. It is not a new argument: Matthew Ringel, Gabriella Diderikson and Jennifer Hall-Witt all identified copyright and performance licensing as one of the factors causing the adoption of textual fidelity.[7] To this argument, I propose that it was also causal in the marginalisation of pasticcio. These scholars also argue that copyright and licensing structures were a factor in the contraction of the operatic repertoire, an argument which has been explored more recently by Rodmell, who demonstrates that licences to perform famous continental operas saw hot competition among Britain's opera companies and, consequently, these operas tended to be staged repeatedly and in much the same form. In comparison with this, relatively few original or rediscovered operas attained a permanent place in company repertoires.[8] I propose that the expansion, tightening and enforcement of copyright legislation in the 1920s and 1930s contributed further to this contraction and also made pasticcio a risky business. These chains of causality achieved virtually no recognition in twentieth-century music history as anything challenging textual fidelity became virtually taboo, a discussion of which is also given.

The 1833 Dramatic Literary Property Act, and another specifically encompassing musical performances in 1842, created a new commodity: the performance licence. Simply purchasing the published text of an opera or play no longer entitled one to perform it; a licence to stage an opera now had to be purchased from the copyright owner who, as we have seen, might not have been the composer or librettist; even so, these early acts were worded carefully to allow pasticcio practices to continue. Opera companies who purchased performance licences arranged for the copyright to be assigned to them or even re-registered the copyright themselves; they used this ownership as a guarantee to the public that their productions were a true record of the composers' original intentions, and advertised them as such. As Ringel and Diderikson discuss, Frederick Gye negotiated carefully and for quite some time with Meyerbeer in 1855 to purchase exclusive rights for the Royal Italian Opera Company at Covent Garden to perform *L'Étoile du Nord* (1854). During these negotiations, Drury Lane pipped Gye to the post by bringing out their own, variant version. Gye salvaged the situation by inviting Meyerbeer to superintend Covent Garden's production and offering him what we would today call artistic control: his choice of singers, six weeks' rehearsal and even his choice of dates in the programming.[9] This allowed Gye to present his production as the most unassailably authentic version of the opera in London.

Gye at Covent Garden, his rival Mapleson at Her Majesty's and many other managers and impresarios, both in Britain and the continent, found they could spend considerable sums acquiring the rights to an opera only to find the composer had sold a variant form of it to a rival. Sometimes a rival company simply poached an opera and the courts declared that, as much of music was already in the public domain, the exclusivity clause was unenforceable. An example is described by Diderikson and Ringel, where Lumley bested Gye over Auber's *L'Enfant prodigue* (1850) in 1851:

> Gye had been in Paris in January and agreed with Brandus [the copyright administrator] to pay £300, ... Gye paid the first installment but refused payment of the second one on the grounds that the 'music was in London, long before I had it'; Gye himself had heard some of the ballet music performed at Drury Lane in March. A more severe discovery was that Lumley also planned to stage *L'Enfant* ... Lumley may have acquired the music to *L'Enfant* by legal means, though Gye's explicit contract with Brandus suggests not. Illegal copying of music was not uncommon in Continental or London theaters – the performances at Drury Lane indicate as much – and performance rights were no guarantee against such behavior.[10]

Licensing had made opera performance a commodity but an unreliable one in terms of tradability. The Drury Lane version had been a pasticcio created by Edward Fitzball and Henri Laurent; it had used only selected sequences from Auber's score but borrowed heavily from Scribe's narrative. Even though Meyerbeer's involvement in Covent Garden's *L'Étoile du Nord* gave it the stamp of authenticity he recognised that, for Covent Garden, it needed to be in Italian and have recitatives rather than dialogue, so he revised it to meet the grand opéra style of the RIO. I suggest that these were tacit admissions that, for composers, there could be no single version of an opera if they wanted it performed widely by different companies with different audiences, each with their own expectations. Verdi, as we saw in Chapter 4, had acceded to a complete change of narrative for *Nabucco* in London. While many composers obliged managers by writing variant versions, Wagner resisted creating a London variant of *Lohengrin* in 1872; he also refused to have the work sung in Italian, though he recognised the necessity of doing so for Covent Garden as much of the opera was already in the public domain.[11]

Courts found themselves once again in Lord Kenyon's position in 1791, trying to establish how much change from an original opera constituted a new opera. Given the high prices being paid for performamnce licenses, the question arose whether opera managers could afford so unreliable a system to endure in the long term. For performance licensing to function as they needed, managers and their lawyers recognised the advantage in securing rights only for those operas which were fixed and stable products with a single, published ur-text, and licensing for which admitted no variations. Between the 1870s and 1918, Rodmell shows that metropolitan opera companies, especially those that toured regionally, acquired a stock of licences which allowed them a limited but legally secure repertoire; in 1887, the Carl Rosa Company owned twenty-five such licences.[12] Some companies held the same licences throughout their existence and the same comparatively small number of operas remained central to their programming for decades: licences for Balfe's *Bohemian Girl*, Gounod's *Faust* and Verdi's *Il Trovatore* were held by the Carl Rosa Company from 1876 to 1916. Other companies licensed to perform these same operas included the Blanche-Cole, Telma-Walsham, Charles Durand and Mapleson at Her Majesty's.[13] Rodmell shows that companies profitably sub-licensed their operas to each other, allowing the works to be performed when they themselves were not touring them, noting that James Turner acknowledged Carl Rosa's generosity in allowing his company to stage several operas for which Rosa held exclusive performing rights.[14] The company was not always so generous, however, and it jealously guarded its right to English-language stagings of Bizet's *Carmen* up to 1900.[15]

A small canonical repertoire emerged in consequence, centred around mid-century operas. Anxieties surrounding this were felt at the time by opera practitioners of all kinds, including the company managers; the press, too, feared that the repertoire was contracting and stagnation setting in.

Companies responded to this by taking the risk, when they could afford it, of securing the rights to new operas or English translations of unfamiliar continental ones.[16] Yet, as Rodmell's tables indicate, the majority of these remained in a company's repertoire for only a few years and seldom joined the British, let alone continental, canon. Audiences became used to a static, predominantly continental repertoire and the economics of opera staging meant that these productions were staged largely unchanged, year after year. Rodmell quotes Turner in an article for *The Era* in 1892:

> Sometimes critics will complain that our repertory contains too large a proportion of hackneyed old favourites. The fact is, that to obtain novelties worthy of our efforts, or even to obtain permission to perform some well-known masterpieces, would be so costly as to be prohibitive. It is an essential condition of the existence of my company that it must pay.[17]

A tighter copyright and licensing system, one which added to the expense of staging operas, thus brought unforeseen problems for the artform itself across Europe and the United States. Necessity was made a virtue as the limitation of a company's repertoire was spun as a greater commitment to its audiences: only the best composers and only the best of works was provided. Consequently, newspaper advertisements and handbills for operas no longer needed to announce productions as being the original or a window into the composer's original vision: there was only one *Carmen* and every *Don Giovanni* resembled the others, so authenticity was taken for granted.[18] The more this continued into the twentieth century the stranger this dependence on nineteenth-century repertoire seemed; it was termed 'the operatic problem' but, as Rodmell points out, that all involved were aware of it did not make solving it any easier.[19] Radical reinterpretations of an opera and its frequent revisualisation, which occurred later in the century, were simply too expensive for the precarious profit margins at the turn of the century, when companies worked without subsidy of any kind.

A tightening up of legislation occurred in the 1880s to give managers greater security in purchasing licences, but if rights had to be bought for each component part of an opera this made pasticcio potentially very expensive. That said, variant versions, burlesques or parodies were far from stifled by the legislation, as examples cited in Chapter 4 show. Yet before the Second World War a substantial number of twentieth-century pasticcio operas tended to use music that was safely out of copyright. These pasticci were often staged in an antiquarian spirit with audiences invited to visit an operatic museum. *An Elephant is Arcady* has this feel; the structure emphasised its curiosity value, thus playing down the opera as a potential challenge to Romantic values such as the necessity for originality. This approach to presenting pasticcio operas was no doubt intended to deflect those who policed breaches of copyright as well as those reviewers who still policed fidelity.

Nineteenth-century reformists and fidelity

For many in present-day society, the requirement for fidelity seems natural and obvious but how this principle came to gain such widespread traction requires discussion. Twentieth-century music histories played an important role in creating this modern perception: they were often highly deterministic, representing absolute fidelity to operatic texts as being universally desired by composers and librettists but a hard-won battle fought against philistinism and vested interests. It was presented as a wholly progressive advance, of much the same order as the achievement of mass literacy. In constructing this eternal verity, music historians drew on a prosopography of nineteenth-century reformists. In the 1920s, for example, Oscar Sonneck's music writing juggled to explain the prevalence of pasticcio if the desire for absolute textual fidelity was purportedly timeless; he resolved his dilemma by presenting all composers as advocates for fidelity but as suppressed by the tyranny of singers, impresarios and 'the system', a trope of some antiquity. He even back-projects Wagnerian music drama to argue that, from the inception of the artform, all composers and librettists had sought to achieve music drama.[20] Monroe Beardsley's writings on music in his promulgation of aesthetic theory in the 1950s seeks to locate all art within the progressive evolution of human freedom.[21]

The great and good of the Romantic movement were presented as driving musical reform.[22] Indeed, they were often presented as advocating precisely the kinds of fidelity demanded by twentieth-century purism, as discussed later in this chapter. While no one has proposed that musical reformer networks acted in concert or with a co-ordinated agenda, the implication has been that like-minded and well-known people with public influence achieved a uniform artistic change. The evidence for this argument appears strong when the interconnections, sympathies and mutual support of the nineteenth-century reformist network are pointed up.

D'Arcy Wood notes that Charles Lamb was a close friend of William Ayrton and attended Ayrton's staging of the British premiere of *Don Giovanni* in 1817, as did Percy Bysshe Shelley and Thomas Love Peacock.[23] Bennett Zon has shown how effectively the reform network sustained each other in print.[24] George Macfarren the elder was a friend and tutor of J.W. Davison and edited *The Musical World*, while Davison enthusiastically reviewed the compositions of his friend's son, George Macfarren the younger, in his own journal, *The Musical Examiner*. The publishers of both these journals, Wessel and Stapleton, were also musicians and part of the same circle. The compositions of Henry Smart, the organist at St Luke's, Old Street, were passionately supported by these journals while Smart himself was a music critic for *The Atlas* as was Edward Holmes, a schoolfriend of John Keats. Charles Cowden Clarke was friends with Keats and an editor of *The Musical World* while his wife, Mary, the daughter of Vincent Novello, was a music writer, and a close friend of and collaborator with Leigh Hunt. Samuel Sebastian Wesley, William Sterndale Bennett and Lovell Phillips were also part of the circle. Zon points out that eleven members of the circle had been at the Royal Academy of Music together and ten of them were members of The Society of British Musicians.[25]

When the succeeding generation wrote about how music had changed in their lifetime, it was these earlier reformist luminaries who were awarded the laurels. Charles Villers Stanford's article 'Some aspects of musical criticism in England' (1894), Hermann Klein's *Thirty Years of Musical Life in London, 1870–1900* (1903), Henry Davison's biography of his father J.W. Davison (1912) and Frederick Corder's biography of Henry Bishop (1918) are prime examples.[26] Written at a time when large-scale opera companies such as the Moody-Manners and Carl Rosa opera companies practised (mostly) textual fidelity, the laurels for this were accorded not to mundane performance licensing systems but to reformers of an earlier generation. Corder denigrated Bishop's pasticcio work to contrast it with the enlightened fidelity of the biographer's own day. Taken together, these writings appeared an evidential and authoritative prosopography to twentieth-century music historians. However, I suggest these writings tended to be consciously directed at posterity and intended to give permanence to the previous generation's contribution to opera. That contemporary human agency is the driving force behind social change is a more comforting explanation than such change being the result of longer, wider, societal shifts which began outside the UK and were launched by people long dead before the reformers were born. Alison Booth, in her essay on Victorian prosopography, notes that 'far from establishing a representative biographical history, prosopography always reveals the incoherence and exclusivity in what Raymond Williams calls "selective traditions", or what Benedict Anderson conceives as "imagined communities"'.[27] Another writer on prosopography, Donna Loftus, notes the tendency of nineteenth-century life writing to back-project intentions and coherent plans onto the early lives of reformers so that changes which are clearly manifest later, at the time of writing, can be ascribed to the reformer's agency. Writing about the autobiography of the industrialist, Samuel Smith, Loftus notes:

> by the end of the century he had moved far from his roots and early associations. He had, like others, helped to build a world he no longer understood. Smith's

life writing then, like others of his generation and class, was a way of under-standing how the present had arrived and what had happened to the future they had imagined.[28]

Twentieth-century opera scholarship fits the pattern Loftus describes, being highly selective in which writings were admitted to the prosopography. Sources that were not congruent with the narrative – such as Benjamin Lumley's *Reminiscences*, the memoirs of Alfred Bunn, Gye's diaries, which provide ample evidence that deviations from the original texts remained ubiquitous – were simply ignored. James Hepokoski observes that as late as 1980 Carl Dahlhaus, in his advocation of Stildualismus, offered contemporary texts such as those of Raphael G. Kiesewetter in the 1830s, quite uncritically, to support his view of nineteenth-century music as locked into a binary divide.[29] Hepokoski notes that Dahlhaus did not identify his contemporary sources as part of a faction, nor even as one side in the binary he was seeking to establish, but offered his writing as unbiased reportage from the period. I suggest that Dahlhaus's trust in texts which self-identified as evidence was characteristic of the century's text-focused academia, where only texts were permitted as evidence in an argument for the centrality of text, itself perhaps characteristic of a mass-literate culture. Current scholarship considers Stildualismus to have existed more in texts than in lived experience.[30]

That opera history continued to make positivist arguments up to the 1980s and beyond had, I propose, two unconscious motivations. Firstly, the democratisation of literacy had been pursued with fervour in the nineteenth century and British academia had been a driving force in campaigns to increase literacy. One of the by-products of this was that textual evidence became the most credible type of evidence and there was a tendency to accord authority and objectivity to contemporary writings that had been consciously constructed *as* authoritative historical evidence. Biographies, encyclopaedias, dictionaries, histories and treatises formed the most reliable sources for nineteenth-century opera, while other writings about performances such as journalism, correspondence and ephemera such as programmes and playbills did not.[31]

The second reason is thus the comparatively low value placed, for much of the twentieth century, on performance data as evidence. As suggested in Chapter 1, only in recent decades has the study of performance gained sufficient standing within the humanities to rebalance histories based on *intentionally* evidential textual sources.[32] Performance history complicates the formerly accepted binary of Dahlhaus, which had composers and opera reformers on one side and aria-substituting singers and pasticcieri on the other, frustrating the great advance that is the musical 'work'. Performance histories recoverable from sources *not* intended to be historically evidential, such as reviews, playbills, correspondence, the Lord Chamberlain's revisions, books providing the plots of popular operas and material ephemera such as photographs and gramophone recordings were, for much of the twentieth century, considered lesser sources of evidence. Leanne Langley has described the dismissive attitude to professional reviewing which obtained among earlier generations of music scholars.[33]

Restoring performance to academic understandings of nineteenth-century opera, shows not only that pasticcio and pasticcio practices ran alongside the work concept but that they intersected with each other in a variety of ways, as Chapter 4 argued. Based on performance evidence, reviewing especially, the fidelities sought by nineteenth-century reformers were various, competing and differed from twentieth-century purism in many ways. Fidelity to the operatic text occurred in a haphazard way, being adopted in certain contexts but not in others, and critical demands for the continuity of performance traditions featured as much as demands for textual fidelity; indeed, the same critic could demand both at different times, unconscious of any inconsistency.[34] By limiting its definition solely to a reproduction of the artists' original intentions, early twentieth-century opera historians such as Sonneck and Edward J. Dent curtailed the concept in a way which modern opera historians such as Hilary Poriss, Massimo Zicari and Christina Fuhrmann are careful to avoid.[35]

A key musicological discussion, initiated by Lydia Goehr at the end of the twentieth century, recognised that a relocation of the intention, outcome or identity of a composition from its performance to its text occurred in the nineteenth century although the precise dating of the process has been disputed.[36] Current musicology argues that, alongside the insistence by reformers that the 'work' was a timeless text and its performance merely a time-limited animation of that text, the habit of understanding an opera as a performance tradition continued: the one did not extinguish the other. For much of the twentieth century, however, a deterministic and stadial narrative that it did held the field. This narrative supplied a music industry seeking further expansions of copyright and performance right legislation with academic justifications in defining operas as single- or dual-authored works, each with an ur-text, for which a strict copyright system was wholly beneficial.

Corporate advocates of such legislation in the nineteenth and twentieth centuries did not base their arguments as simply being to their own economic advantage, but on claims of protecting the authors of creative works from exploitation. As early as 1813, London's booksellers and publishers petitioned the House of Commons against a judgment which upheld the right of certain universities and libraries to receive a copy of each book printed within the

United Kingdom. Unable to argue that being compelled to submit eleven copies of each book would ruin them, they argued it would discourage authors from writing books in the first place. In giving evidence to the select committee, one publisher, Joseph Mawman, declared:

> [a]n author has declared, though he has a work already in press, and which he prints with a view to profit, if this legislative regulation should take place for the eleven copies, he will destroy what he has already printed, and suppress the work altogether.[37]

This argument continued in various forms long into the twentieth century. Expansions of copyright law and performance licensing were argued not just as essential for protecting the practice of composition itself, but to defend the original vision of the composer; an adroit dissection of such claims has made been made by Edwin Hettinger.[38] Making changes to an opera was nearly always portrayed negatively in copyright and licensing advocation: they were not seen as saving the work from atrophy as times changed, or from neglect in the repertoire, but as the desecration of a timeless masterpiece and betrayal of the genius who wrote it.[39]

The cultural overheads incurred by expanding copyright and performance licensing

This sub-section demonstrates the tight economic parameters within which pasticcio operas functioned in the twentieth century. Although, as shown next, pasticcio operas continued, the legislative context greatly influenced both their forms and the selection of material. As mentioned in Chapter 3, even before the eighteenth century and certainly from that century onwards copyright legislation had aimed to make copyrights a tradable commodity rather than vest absolute ownership in the artist. Graham P. Cornish shows that, in UK law, commissioning bodies which had funded an artist's work or disseminators who acquired the artist's rights through assignment were in most cases the de facto owner of that work up to 1989.[40] That tradability could be detrimental to the artist was exposed very early on: Parliament's attention was called to the unscrupulous practices of Harry Wall, a racketeer operating from a cellar in the East End of London during the 1870s. Wall bought up copyrights from indigent composers, or pre-empted those who were slow in registering their work themselves, threatening to prosecute any accidental users of the music he now owned, including its composers, unless they paid him damages. The Copyright Acts of 1882 and 1888 were intended to quash this practice though, as we shall see, this abuse returned in other guises throughout the twentieth century.

As the previous discussion shows, performing rights licences increased the value of copyrights. For nineteenth-century opera companies, purchasing rights over a new, untried work from a composer was a financial risk, so the price for such rights was much lower than for the rights to a tried and tested opera, purchased from another opera company or theatre. The need to make a sufficient return made opera companies risk-averse, with record companies and music publishers adopting the same caution. Consequently, arguments that the rights system protected operatic authors from financial disadvantage did not hold water when applied to new operas. Only famous composers enjoying international reputations managed to retain control of their copyrights and thus the right to license performances; even then, they often found managers suspicious of untested works and many were still dependent on a wealthy patron to support them while writing new operas.[41] The majority of composers had little negotiating power; for every Rossini, Verdi or Wagner there were many such as Ruggero Leoncavallo, Camille Saint-Saëns, Ethel Smyth and Charles Villers Stanford who struggled to get their works staged, and found them dropped from the repertoire in place of old, commercially safe favourites all too soon.[42] While this was a problem that European operatic practitioners in the late nineteenth and early twentieth centuries were highly aware of, it was difficult to resolve without one sector or another in the production chain making a loss.

Rodmell shows that late nineteenth- and early twentieth-century discussions of opera's problems in Britain recognised that the want of commissioning fees to the creators of opera led to a dearth of new operas in the repertoire and a marked absence of native operas.[43] Royalties paid after the opera's first run and in proportion to its success did not entice composers or librettists to undertake the substantial quantity of work which writing an opera entails. Given that opera companies were usually adamant that they could not bear the risk of funding commissioning costs realistically, Rodmell argues that the solution to the problem was thought to lie in the establishment of a national opera house or company.[44] Whether this would encourage the creation of new operas if government subsidies paid the commissioning fees was hotly debated.[45] There was an element of Whiggish nationalism in these proposals, as Rodmell notes that the aim was not just to broaden the repertoire or create a support system for opera creation but to secure a specifically English-language operatic repertoire, one that would join the European canon and place English music alongside that of Germany, France and Italy. It was also hoped that such an institution would develop a distinctive, insular operatic style as well as providing opportunities for native artists; accessibility arguments were made for the first time with discussions about widening access to the artform to other social classes, and expanding the repertoire for educative purposes.[46] Decommodifying music formed no part of these discussions, although public demand for that very thing would grow in the 1920s and 1930s.

When writers such as Corder looked back to the early part of the twentieth century, prior to the rights system, he failed to see the breadth of the repertoire and noticed only the violations of fidelity. Any solution to the contracting repertoire would require a philosophical shift; as Rodmell concludes, 'the desire to find an easy and quick solution to the "operatic problem" was perhaps the single greatest reason for its remaining'.[47] I propose that while the twentieth century preserved an apparent elevation of the composer, librettist and singers, they grew more financially squeezed as the commodification structures favoured disseminators over artists. Certainly, from the seventeenth to the nineteenth centuries public theatres had needed to make a profit, but the late nineteenth and early twentieth centuries saw the emergence of what the press came to call 'the music industry'. This included publishers, agencies representing artists, broadcasters and recording companies such as the Columbia Phonograph Company (1889), the Gramophone Company (HMV, 1898), Decca (1929) and Electric and Musical Industries (EMI, 1931). While these companies were ostensibly in competition with each other, they could come together and act in concert, when necessary, to protect and develop the commodification of music, even restricting tradability when their profits were threatened.[48] When early-twentieth-century opera companies, music publishers and record companies entered into contract with a composer or librettist they sought to own the licensing for both live *and* recorded forms of the work.

In the beginning a composer such as William Walton was able to play different record companies off against each other. His breakthrough piece, *Façade*, had acquired a degree of attention, some laudatory some hostile, between 1923 and 1929 when Decca recorded the piece; he later recorded these orchestral suites again with HMV at a higher price before having his other works recorded by EMI. The work was not actually published in print until 1951, nearly thirty years after its composition, by which time it was well known through records and performance.[49] Yet the freedom of composers like Walton to sell their copyrights for the best price did not last; the record industry realised the commercial advantage of adding clauses to their contracts giving companies the first option over all music produced by a particular artist (exclusivity clauses). This prevented the artists from selling more famous and thus profitable compositions to rival record companies. Clauses of this kind appear in Sergei Rachmaninov's contracts from 1920–1942 and Arturo Toscanini's from 1920 to 1954 with the Victor Talking Machine Company.[50] In opera, record companies found that a small, tight number of famous arias and celebrity singers was more profitable than a profuse network of niche markets; the companies often protected the fame of their celebrity singers and songwriters by buying up the copyrights of rivals and suppressing their work.[51] Operatic recording was even more risk-averse than theatre programming, so the number of known operas and arias contracted further. Now, in theory, pasticcieri had the scope to create operas from a great number of unknown, unrecorded or forgotten works, which the majority of the public had not previously heard. That this did not happen is probably due to the difficulty in establishing who owned the copyright in these works hovering on the margins of the canon. To use without permission was now to risk legal penalties where, previously, none had existed.

The Copyright Act 1911 provided that copyright holders did not own just the rights to license a work but also those to mechanically produce recordings of any performance of that work. Reproduction rights thus expanded in ways which had not been envisaged by earlier legislation, yet in their desire to incorporate the making of records within one commodity – the initial copyright – legislators actually created a new commodity. Record companies demanded that the law recognise any playing of music on a gramophone in a public place to be, essentially, a public performance. This included contexts where listening was not specifically charged for. A licence was now required from the copyright holder for recorded music to be played in cafes, barbers and hairdressers, or workplaces just as if the work was being physically staged there. This was not represented as creating a new commodity; rather, it was argued to be a mere updating of the 1908 Copyright Act to take account of new technology; it was thus presented as within long-accepted copyright principles.

This was not quite the case. Nineteenth-century performance right legislation had been largely concerned to end the practice whereby musicians could perform a work so long as they had purchased the score and prevent piracy in publishing; it had never been intended to broaden the definition of a performance to include sharing music in non-commercial, non-professional contexts, where no money changed hands. An industry body emerged determined to create a second income stream out of recategorising listening to records as a performance. Eric Gilder and Mervyn Haggar describe the origins of this body, the International Federation of the Phonographic Industry:

> Mussolini hosted the Confederazione Generale Fascista dell' Industria Italiana which was held in Rome from the 10th to the 14th of November, 1933. At its conclusion the International Federation of the Phonographic Industry was born. IFPI opened its first headquarters in the EMI offices at Hayes, just outside of London, … The idea behind IFPI was to make record sales in Europe conditional and for personal use only. If there was to be any form of public 'audience', then the manufacturer could charge a licensing fee for public performance of the manufactured recording.[52]

In 1914, a group of visionary music publishers got together to devise a sustainable future for both music creators and music lovers alike.

5.1 From the Performing Rights Society centenary celebration video, 1914–2014. *Source:* Performing Right Society, www.prsformusic.com.

Record companies recognised that these legislative provisions would not be enforced by the police and sought to safeguard their new commodity by founding societies to act in their stead. In 1911 the Mechanical Copyright Protection Society was established and soon merged with the Performing Right Society, founded in 1914. These and other societies such as Phonographic Performance Ltd, formed in the United States in 1934, argued that their purpose was to increase the profitability of composition in a new age of mass-dissemination technology. Record companies and the artists whose copyrights they had bought were portrayed as being united in the demand that public listening be understood as legally the same as attending the theatre in real life. It would not be an alliance that lasted. Many of these policing societies were led, supported or funded by large-scale music companies: EMI joined Decca, for example, to found Phonographic Performance Ltd. Record companies argued that, as their own profits were increased by the policing of copyrights by their societies, so they increased the income of composers: a symbiotic relationship. However, the proportionality of profit distribution makes this claim questionable: Phonographic Performance Ltd awarded 80 per cent of its income, after running costs, to its membership (effectively its shareholders, among which EMI and Decca were prominent) and only 20 per cent to its featured artists.[53]

Over the course of the century new technologies for recording and playing music – the phonograph, gramophone, radio, cinema, jukebox, television, cassette recorder and eventually the internet – all precipitated additional

5.2 Newspaper advertisement, May 1905 in *The Cornell Countryman*.
Source: The Cornell Countryman, released under Creative Commons Licence.

copyright legislation. The argument used to justify such legislation remained consistent: it was essential to allow composers to keep control of their music. Record companies quickly developed the practice of purchasing rights of reproduction from artists at the beginning of their careers, often in ways which would today constitute mis-selling.[54] As the advertisement in Figure 5.2 shows, registering one's own patent was represented as more onerous, expensive and bureaucratic than it actually was. Hostility to copyright and licensing systems is often thought of as a modern reaction against corporate power, but it was present almost from the beginning, when opera companies, record manufactures and publishers could hardly be described as multi-national.

Resistance to the commodification of music

The intensifying commodification of music was fiercely resisted in a high-profile but little-remembered struggle in the 1920s and 1930s. This struggle over how far rights over music should extend cracked the earlier alliance between composers and disseminators if, indeed, complete unanimity had ever existed. Few composers or recorded singers were disposed to rally around those who made more money out of their music than they did. Pasticcio operas, along with capriccio performances of all kinds from mixed bills to village concerts, were now part of the pushback against the new commodifications of performance led by large-scale music publishers, recording companies and performing right societies. This opposition reopened a space in which pasticcio was seen as harmless and its operas entertaining and also opened a discussion space in which conceptions of musical property beyond copyright became thinkable.[55] Resistance to copyright in the 1920s was not a challenge to Romantic interpretations of music history per se but, later in the century, when such challenges did emerge, there was already a tradition of scepticism towards the Romantic tenets proclaimed by music companies. Their arguments and justifications were already seen as self-serving and cynical when musicological revisions of Romanticism began in the last decades of the century.

A raft of prosecutions followed each expansion of musical copyright, beginning with the 1911 Act and intensifying after 1918. Soon amateur operatic societies, pub entertainers and radio clubs were obliged to accept the new licensing rules but, when confronted with unfeasibly high charges for some copyrighted music, many simply gambled on not being caught. A grey area was detected over the point at which private listening became public listening. It was asked: if one person listened to music on their radio for their own entertainment in the workplace, but others overheard it, did this fact make the radio a public performance?[56] The debate in the press, both in Europe and the United States, repeatedly asked whether a person whistling a tune while walking down a street was amusing themself or giving a public performance and, if the latter, did the whistler need a licence? These absurdities were supposed to be offset by the concept of 'fair use', which recognised certain contexts in which the insistence on a licence was considered unreasonable.[57] Nevertheless, women's suffrage societies existed in most towns and cities before the First World War and local societies often listened to speeches and messages from the movement's leaders at their weekly or monthly meetings on a gramophone.[58] When the meeting took a break for tea, music was often played. Suffrage societies found themselves prosecuted for doing this and some complained that this was a politically motivated manoeuvre by anti-suffragists in performing right societies.

Another important motivation for resistance was that gramophone recordings were made of political speeches, sermons, court cases, poetry recitations and as the equivalent of voicemails. People recorded messages, often in a photographer's studio or a post office, and mailed them in a protective box to family and friends: it was a popular method of keeping in touch at a time of high emigration. People feared that expanding copyright might mean that their private family conversations would soon be owned in law by the record companies and it was strongly felt that paying to make a gramophone record should include complete ownership of what was recorded on it.

5.3 Lady Denman.
Source: The Women's Institute.

For the most part, rights societies enforcing copyright ownership presented their artists as financially vulnerable underdogs and those who made free use of their works as greedy and powerful exploiters. A developing counter-narrative saw the ever-expanding reach of music companies as predators on the public; the old reflex from earlier, more oral, times, that music should be free for reuse once it had already been performed, resurfaced in public discourse. Music companies' objections that they took all the financial risk and that disseminators should not be able to siphon off their profits were very seldom denied; however, their opponents pointed out that newspapers had long accepted that their 'readership' was greater than their actual sales and that it was common practice for a literate workman to read a newspaper out loud to a group of others. A consensus existed in newspaper publishing that one paid for the product only once and any reading or reciting of the news contained in it could not be charged for a second time. Lady Gertrude Denman, the chair of the Federation of Women's Institutes (and a former suffragist), wondered why the music industry could not accept the same. She complained in *The Times* in December 1929 that:

> [a]n author only receives a few pence on each copy of his book sold, and for that it may be read aloud any number of times to any audience; villages wonder why copyright fees cannot be added to the price of a song or simple instrumental work [i.e. the published sheet music], so that people may know where they are.[59]

In 1924, the House of Commons debated whether a limit should be placed on copyright. James Burney, MP for Bootle, described an amateur band in his constituency which included unemployed workmen. They played in a public park, without charging for their performance, but were given a penalty of £50 though no indication was given on the sheet music they had bought, or by the music vendor, that they required a performance licence.[60] Another abuse cited by Lady Denman was the refusal of the Performing Right Society to quote licence costs for individual items in concerts and quote only for the whole programme. It was this practice which had made pasticcio operas potentially expensive to create, and single-item licensing would have been a boon. Radios, both crystal sets and amplified sets, were household goods by the 1920s and 1930s, and broadcasting became an opportunity to create a further musical commodity. In a critical review of copyright expansion in August 1933, *The Times* observed that a charge for collective listening was now being applied to the wireless:

> The rediffusion of broadcast programmes to the public by loud-speaker or other means became the next most important subject requiring a legal ruling following the definition of broadcasting as a public performance … The licence

held by the BBC confined the use of this repertoire to reception by listeners for private and domestic use, and the society contended that rediffusion constituted further public performance necessitating separate licensing.[61]

The core of the objection was that radio broadcasters had already paid performance fees to music companies in order to play a record on air, but the radio-set owner was then charged again if the record was listened to by a group of people. The commodification of collective listening was a step which the BBC was not prepared to accept.[62]

5.4a Frank Gray, MP for Oxford, 1923, by Alexander Bassano. *Source:* National Portrait Gallery.

5.4b William Murdoch Adamson, MP for Cannock, 1924, by Alexander Bassano. *Source:* National Portrait Gallery.

Among many objections to the practices of the Performing Right Society was that it preferred the threat of prosecution to going to court. Frank Gray, MP for Oxford, at another stage of the same Parliamentary debate in 1924, gave a fictional example demonstrating why the Society's practices were being stigmatised as blackmail:

Some amateur gets up at, perhaps, a village concert, and sings a song in all good faith; and this society, [The Performing Right Society] which takes in every local paper, large and small, to get accounts of these concerts, sees that Mary Jones sang very nicely 'Tit Willow' or something of that sort, and they write to her and say, 'Do you know the gravity of what you have done?' The poor girl, of course, does not know, and they then proceed, not to take proceedings, but to state the sum they require *without* taking proceedings. The Judge, therefore, never has the opportunity of exercising any discretion whatsoever ... What would the average man do if he were threatened with proceedings which might involve him in a lawsuit for £200 or £300? If his position had been found out in advance, as it would be, and his powers and resources sized up and it was said that he could square his illegality for £50? Would he risk the proceedings and claim the discretion of the Judge or would he pay the £50?[63]

Pressure to decommodify mounted: in 1929 a collection of small-business owners who identified themselves as 'music users' persuaded the Labour government to bring in a bill limiting the fee for performing music to 2d. per work, payable to the copyright holder.

The Music Copyright Bill was introduced as a private member's bill by W.M. Adamson. As a head-on attempt to curtail the commodification of music it was met with a howl of protest from the music companies and those few composers who were making satisfactory profits from their copyrights. Among those who supported the second reading were many former women's suffragists including Margaret Bondfield, Eleanor Rathbone, Edith Picton Turberville and, in the vanguard, Lady Denman. Bodies holding composer's copyrights or their assigns, such as record companies, music publishers, together with their performing right societies, had the sense to stay out of the headlines themselves and put their artists up to make their arguments for them. As ever, the justification was that composers would be reduced to poverty if published or recorded music ever became cheap. Chief among the apologists was George Bernard Shaw, who had formerly been a music critic. On 2 December he wrote to *The Times*:

Now it is extremely hard to make people understand that they have no more right to perform the work of a composer without contributing to his support than they have to pick his pocket. They annex his property without permission or payment by singing his songs at concerts, especially at the friendly smoking concerts and the like got up by the Labour organisations from which Parliament is now recruited. When they have broken the law, they are appalled to find some person, not perhaps the composer, but some petty trafficker in copyrights, who has bought the composer's rights for a trifle, turning up demanding a fee, which is limited only by the ability of the offender to pay. There is a wave of sympathy with the popular singer and of indignation against the copyright proprietor. He is classed as an infamous blackmailer; and all the incipient Labour MPs in the society resolve that if they ever make the House of Commons, they will make an end of what seems to them a monstrous abuse.[64]

5.5a George Bernard Shaw, *c.*1924, by Lafayette Ltd. *Source:* National Portrait Gallery.

5.5b Ralph Vaughan Williams, 1921, by Emil Otto Hoppé. *Source:* National Portrait Gallery.

Shaw goes on to argue that Adamson's bill was breathtakingly naïve and profoundly damaging to composers. He was wrong in suggesting that support for the bill emerged from left-wing circles alone. Indeed, the issue did not fall neatly into left- or right-wing brackets and the protagonists formed unexpected alliances: the struggling artists backed large-scale corporate powers, while small businesses supported the Labour Party's bill. The reference to petty traffickers in copyrights might sound like a minimisation of the corporate bodies behind the performing rights societies but, almost certainly, Shaw is referring to the prosecution of Harry Wall in the 1880s (see earlier in this chapter), during which he had already been in his 30s; this case had featured large in the Parliamentary debate. The supporters of the 1929 bill argued in the House that Wall's abuses of copyright legislation had returned with the performing rights societies taking his place. Despite Shaw's characterisation of composers as well served by the existing system, a number chose to side with the Musicians Union, who supported the bill: they included Alan Bush, Gustav Holst and Benjamin Britten. On 10 December, Ralph Vaughan Williams waded into the dispute in a letter arguing that composers had to accept that there was a genuine public grievance, even if the bill in its current form was wrongly framed:

We composers must make sure that our own house is in order. We must see to it that our agents do not use the power given them by law for the purposes of tyranny and intimidation. Let us frankly admit that the law needs amendment, though not on the lines laid down in this bill; we can then press our claims with clear consciences.[65]

Vaughan Williams correctly noted that the dispute was not a party question and even less one of class. The unexpected appearance of so distinguished a composer on the side of those who wished to restrain their profits so alarmed two music publishers that they responded the following day. Humphrey Sumner Milford of the Oxford University Press praised Vaughan Williams for his measured stance but thought cheap performance rights would discourage serious composition, concluding in shocked tones in his letter of 11 December that '[t]he bill as it stands would clearly enact that the users would make more out of music than the providers, which is contrary to our accepted system of economics'.[66]

5.6 Humphrey Sumner Milford, 1928, at Oxford Encaenia ceremony.
Source: Oxford English Dictionary Archives.

Clearly an amateur in a village hall singing a song gratis would not be making more profit out of a song than its publisher so, presumably, Sumner Milford meant that the aggregate sum realised from all performances of a particular piece, both professional and amateur, would be greater than the totality of profits achieved by the company publishing it. Even this is doubtful, but Sumner Milford declared that the proposed legislation would turn published or recorded music into a wholesale product rather than a retail one, the retailers being those staging or playing the music.

Long before the internet would make musical copyright all but unenforceable, this groundswell of opposition threatened to undermine not just the music companies' economic case but the ethical arguments used by music companies to underpin it.

Eventually, of course, the vested interests got their way and the bill was shelved. For a year or two the music companies and their rights societies were sufficiently chastened by the scale of public hostility to proceed more cautiously in issuing penalties for unlicensed performing but, before long, they sensed their power and were back to their old ways. A widely reported case was the successful prosecution in 1933, by a company that formed part of EMI, of a small coffee shop in Bristol for playing a record of Auber's overture to *Le Domino noir*. The prosecution was supported by the Performing Right Society.

Following the Gregory Report of 1952, the Copyright Act 1956 established the Performing Right Tribunal. This was intended to bring a measure of balance to the situation, ensuring that the music industry received its profits without undue predation of the public, yet the Tribunal's decisions mainly safeguarded hefty licence fees. In October 1960, it rejected an argument by Barrington Electronics that public performance licence fees for jukeboxes should be nominal as a licence had already been purchased to play records publicly. The Tribunal sided with the record companies and created a further commodity by ruling that separate permission was needed to play them in a jukebox, the fee for which should be sizeable.[67] Licence income consequently soared in the 1950s and resistance dwindled.

Resistance resurfaced again in the 1960s and again during the first decade of the twenty-first century, implying a generational dimension to the antagonism. One could peg this to technological innovations but I propose that these nodal points were reached when contradictions and failures in the philosophy underlying musical commodification were suddenly exposed. Arguments that commodification protected composers or recording artists' interests manifestly crumbled when artists and music companies went to court. Disputes in opera began as early as 1905 when Emma Eames was dissatisfied with the quality of recordings made by the Victor Talking Machine

Company. Up to the 1950s such disputes had been fought largely behind closed doors: when Renata Tebaldi and Regina Resnik found their performances pirated by Royale and Gramophone, comparative discretion was observed. Yet change was coming and the 1960s saw a new kind of popular musician emerge, whose confidence and financial success meant such disputes were now fought in public. Johnny Cash's dispute with Columbia Records in 1964, The Who's dispute with Polydor Records in 1966 and The Beatles' dispute with EMI from the 1960s to the 1980s offered examples which influenced opera. Lesley Garrett sued Silva Screen records in 1998 and, most recently, Russell Watson has sued Decca. Such cases publicly exposed the tensions between composers, performers and the disseminators of their music. Music companies began to lose control of the narrative they had traditionally used to justify commodification. Instead of protecting downtrodden composers from exploitative users who wished to play a radio in their shops without paying, a potent new narrative proposed that music companies made fortunes out of the downtrodden composers while paying them the barest minimum in royalties they could get away with. The public were off the hook.

This, then, was the legal and economic background against which the pasticcio operas of the twentieth century were created. It can be readily seen that in the context of this dispute, creating a pasticcio opera was a controversial act, and the pasticci of this period are discernibly affected by the dispute: some exhibit avoidance of confrontation with prevailing laws and principles while others offer deliberate challenges. A sizeable number of the century's pasticci were in direct descent from baroque practice, continuing up to at least 1940, while others emerged when theatres, companies, managers or composers discovered the method afresh; having no knowledge of its long history. These discoverers often imagined they were the first to undertake the practice; both are explored next.

Twentieth-century pasticcio operas

Ironically, the one arena in which pasticcio no longer had a presence in the twentieth century was in the repertoires of national opera companies in metropolitan opera houses. Grand opera refused to recognise as a proper opera anything that did not purport to be the all-sung original work of a single composer and librettist. Exceptions can be found, but attempts to challenge the Romantic parameters were swiftly attacked by reviewers and discouraged by the legal structures of the rights system. This began to change in the twenty-first century but, outside Covent Garden new pasticcio operas can be found in many theatres, festivals and in regional touring. Pasticcio continued to be used in ballet scoring and was used extensively in film, radio and television music, as I will go on to discuss. This sub-section also shows how the skills needed to create pasticci were passed on through teacher/pupil relationships, allowing a plentiful generation of musicians to emerge to create the pasticcio scores required for cinema, radio and television.

Antiquarians and radicals

In Britain, determination to extend the operatic canon tended to go in two directions: in England, new operas were commissioned in English and set in England but they often faced critical hostility because of their musical modernism or theatrical experimentation.[68] The other direction sought to extend the canon by reviving operas from earlier centuries, prompted by the success of the early music movement. Most of the twentieth century's true pasticcio operas also tend to fall into these two brackets, being either experimental or antiquarian. Taking the latter first, fear of predatory and unexpected visitation by performing right societies was one reason why music of the distant past was preferred, being safely out of copyright. Such pasticci tended to depict earlier societies and use earlier music to do so. Those mounting a pasticcio needed to convince the commissioner, venue or funder that it would not embroil them in litigation, penalties or fines. Even in the twenty-first century, the pasticci of Opera Feroce or Sounds Baroque prefer to draw from the baroque or classical periods rather than from contemporary operas and one suspects a desire to avoid copyright controversy is one of the motivations. I have found no pasticcio staged in Britain using the music of Elgar or Vaughan Williams while they were still alive to tell a contemporary story, but living composers did create autopasticci for film and television.

Another reason for the self-consciously antique pasticcio was stadialism in operatic history, as discussed in Chapter 1. Whereas the eighteenth and nineteenth centuries had recognised their pasticci as having a wide variety of methods and forms, twentieth-century historical narratives held pasticcio to be typified by examples which were at the furthest end of the spectrum from fidelity. The sheer strangeness of operas drawn from over a dozen composers, where a musical capriccio was sought rather than stylistic unity, made pasticcio a 'quirk' in the phrasing of Nicholas Matthew and Mary Ann Smart.[69] This was what fidelity was held to have replaced. Consequently, those creating pasticcio operas consciously adopted these structures, rather than more familiar ones. This preference for constructing an antique curiosity to avoid serious challenges to the Romantic conceptualisation of music, is, I suggest, an example of how the rights system impacted on pasticcio opera.

To give some examples of what might be called the antiquarian pasticcio, Alfred Reynolds's adaptations of Charles Dibdin's *Lionel and Clarissa* (1925) and Arne's *Love in a Village* (1928) were staged at the Lyric Theatre, Hammersmith. Among the new true pasticci were Dora Bright's *The Waltz King*, written in 1926 using Johann II's music and her own, set to a libretto by Frank Stayton. This was performed at the Ambassador's Theatre London in 1935 and later ran at the Webber Doublas Theatre in South Kensington.[70] Bright's piece was part of a vogue for pasticcio operettas using Strauss's music, which began in Vienna at the turn of the century and moved rapidly to France, Britain and the United States. A pasticcio of 1939 was *Georgian Springtime* by Beatrice Saxon Snell; this was performed at the Embassy Theatre in December and composed of eighteenth-century ballads and folk music.[71] According to the reviewer, the plot concerned Sheridan's elopement with Elizabeth Linley; he thought it was not a particularly strong opera and contrasted it with its ancestor, *The Beggar's Opera*, which had been revived at Glyndebourne that year. Jrene Eisinger, an opera singer who, like Julius Bürger, had escaped Nazi Germany, sang the lead in both these pasticci. As well as *An Elephant in Arcady*, the Farjeons created *The Two Bouquets* in 1939, which drew on nineteenth-century music. This was a farce, contrasting the primness of Victorian people with their boundless social vitality. *L'Oca del Cairo* was once again completed, this time in 1940 by Hans Ferdinand Redlich (1903–1968), and performed in a one-act version.

Pasticcio was also embraced by the avant garde and the experimentally inclined, precisely because it crossed so many red lines. The French composer and librettist Claude Prey created a range of new opera genres between the 1960s and 1990s and his experimental productions prefigured many opera developments of the twenty-first century. Prey insulated himself against conservative criticism by accepting, even embracing, the experimental niche in which his work was placed. This can be seen in the names he invented for his new opera genres: opéra cruciverbal, mono-mimo-mélodrame, mélo-cycle, opéra-opéra en 2 actes, among others. Prey used pasticcio in a number of ways: he used extracts of Fauré's music as part of the drama in some of these operas, while *Lettres perdues* (1961) contains pastiches of Milhaud, Hindemith and Schoenberg, and *On veut la lumière? Allons-y!* (1968) explores the Dreyfus affair by reworking music from the turn of the twentieth century.[72] Paul Griffiths's pasticci, *The Jewel Box (1991)* and *Aeneas in Hell* (1994), perhaps span these two brackets, using music from Mozart and Purcell respectively, but with an avant garde narrative.

5.7a and b Chorus sequences from Dumestre and Lazar's *Cadmus et Hermione*, 2008, an archetypical HIP production; note the orchestra below.
Source: Opéra Comique.

A movement to stage early operas or masques in their original performance conditions also began in the 1960s and these were later given the title Historically Informed Performance (HIP); they aimed to stage period operas with museum-standard accuracy. Unlike purist productions they aimed to demonstrate the scale of the differences between the society and theatre of an opera's creation point and those of today. Vincent Dumestre and Benjamin Lazar's 2008 production of Lully's *Cadmus et Hermione* (1673) used baroque pitch, baroque gestures, candlelight, sliding wing-flats and recreated period machinery. Reconstructions of pasticcio operas were part of the HIP movement and the restoration of Handel's *Giove in Argo* (1739) in 1960 and 2002–2004 were important points in reviving acceptability for pasticcio. Yet HIP did not have an easy path in Britain. Raymond Leppard reconstructed Cavalli's *L'Ormindo* (1644) for Glyndebourne in 1967, the first staging in 300 years. Writing in the festival book, Leppard emphasises that seventeenth-century scoring deliberately left much of the orchestration up to the maestro staging the opera, stating that he had used his own judgement, legitimately, in parodying Cavalli's style. Purists in the press were alarmed:

> Raymond Leppard … is commonly reproached for splashing on the colour too gaudily, for editing up something to near the point of recomposition. With no knowledge of the original, I was sometimes disturbed by flashy orchestration … Twice I wondered in my ignorance if Cavalli really meant such jolting modulations.[73]
>
> Yet anyone with a sense of period is bound to have reservations about what we actually heard. Did Cavalli really want such consistently rich string textures, even for accompanying the voices? … Did he want such eccentrically striking key changes or were these the results of cuts and transpositions in Raymond Leppard's edition?[74]

Of course, by 1967 Cavalli himself did not want anything at all. The critics, John Warrack and Stanley Sadie, failed to see the full implications of early Venetian scoring: that the text was not a set of instructions to posterity; instead, the directions they did give for future performance assumed change and further creative input by whoever was staging the piece next. The texts from past performances were of only limited help in creating new ones: creating music to suit the present performance was what Leppard was *supposed* to do if he was to stay true to the Venetian approach at that period. Both Prey's *Lettres perdues* and Leppard's *L'Ormindo* are examples of the rediscovery of pasticcio rather than its continuity, although they were very different in motivation. The former was driven by a desire to unlock the radical potential of pasticcio while the latter aimed to reconstruct, interpretatively, the original *experience* rather than the original text.

Lines of descent

While the skills to create pasticcio operas did not continue from baroque practice *exclusively* through tutor/pupil transmission, lines of descent can be traced which offer insight into how the skillsets required could be transmitted into the twentieth century. Teaching, family connections and traditions, collaborations and social interaction are the likely medium: that tutors sat their pupils down and gave structured lessons on how to compile a pasticcio opera is likely in the eighteenth and early nineteenth centuries but not in the late nineteenth or twentieth. In these later periods what I suggest was passed on was a positive attitude towards changing music to better serve a performance, a sense that textual fidelity was not the ultimate purpose of performance. The most significant thing about tutor/pupil lines, circles of collaboration and friendships is, perhaps, the insight they provide into the diversity of music as profession, in terms of fame, income and gender. Beyond the handful of celebrities and the musical in the lines of descent, we have Italian migrants, regional concert singers who advertise for pupils and opera singers who seldom sing the lead or even achieve discussion in the reviews. When the diversity of all those who interacted with pasticcio operas is recognised, we can readily perceive how cinemas found the vast number of musicians required to invent accompaniments for silent films in the first thirty years of the twentieth century. Pasticcio was not a niche skill of the antiquarian but an approach undertaken by many across the whole practice of music.

Francesco Bianchi (1752–1810), the pasticciere of *La villanella rapita* in the 1780s, taught Henry Rowley Bishop (1787–1855). Bishop's wide number of pupils and collaborators included the Loder family of Bath and Bristol. Bishop knew John David Loder (1788–1846) as early as 1822 when he conducted concerts at the Bath Assembly Rooms. The Loders were a musical family of composers and performers and John David led the house orchestra at Bristol's Theatre Royal in the 1830s and 1840s; he was probably responsible for adapting the many operas by Bishop performed there. John David and Bishop also worked together on the Concerts of Antient Music which the former conducted from 1844 and on whose committee the latter served, and at the Philharmonic Society. John David's son Edward James Loder (1809–1865) also worked on Bishop's operas, writing the suitcase aria which Rebecca Isaacs interpolated into *Village Nightingale* in 1856, mentioned in Chapter 4. He published an arrangement of Bishop's duets in the form of 'Favourite Songs', in 1838 wrote a pasticcio opera – *Francis the First* – for Drury Lane and revised the *Beggar's Opera*. As another indicator of the absence of Stildualismus, Edward James Loder was a friend of J.W. Davidson and dedicated *The Overture to the Opera of The Foresters, Arranged for the Piano Forte* to 'his friend', this being Loder's contribution to that pasticcio.

John David's niece Kate Loder (1825–1904) became the first female professor of harmony at the Royal Academy of Music in 1844. There is no known tutor/pupil connection between Bishop and Kate Loder but their social familiarity is evidenced: Bishop knew Cipriani Potter (1792–1871), her head of school at the Royal Academy, and her piano teacher Lucy

Anderson (1795–1878). Both Potter and Anderson had been taught by pupils of Mozart: Thomas Attwood and Joseph Wölfl, who were better disposed to altering music for performance than her composition tutor, George Macfarren, who loathed Bishop.[75] Kate Loder created what seems to have been a pasticcio version of Donizetti's *L'elisir d'amore* in 1855 and Kate and Bishop lived near each other in Wimpole Street and Albion Street, Hyde Park, respectively.

In the 1880s, Kate Loder taught the future Sir Landon Ronald (1873–1938). This music teacher, répétiteur and conductor, later a principal of the Guildhall School of Music, taught the Farjeon family in the late 1890s and early 1900s. Ronald was the répétiteur at Covent Garden and conducted his first opera there, Gounod's *Faust*, in 1896; he conducted others at the Theatre Royal, Drury Lane. He became the conductor of the London Symphony Orchestra in 1904, and while his approach to instrumental scores was one of strict fidelity, when he worked on opera and operetta he felt it permissible to take a pasticcio approach. Gramophone recordings of Nellie Melba and Adelina Patti accompanied by Ronald show that they interpreted their arias to best express the pieces' drama rather than adhering exactly to the original scoring. He revised operettas between 1898 and 1902, including *The Silver Slipper* (1901) where he collaborated with Ivan Caryll and Arthur Weld in adapting the American version. Transgenerational interaction can thus be shown between Bianchi and the Farjeons.

Other such lines are easily found. Tomaso Giordani (*c.*1730–1806), who came from a long line of Neapolitan musicians, worked in both London and Dublin before settling at the latter city in 1783. He taught Tom Cooke (1787–1848) and was known to, and collaborated with, Michael Kelly (1762–1826), both of whom created numerous pasticci for Drury Lane and other theatres. Cooke was a prolific pasticciere and one of the leading tenors at Drury Lane from 1815 to the 1830s. Among his pupils was the singer John Sims Reeve (1821–1900), who turned his hand to pasticcio when he had to: when performing in Birmingham in 1871 he adapted *Rob Roy*, itself a pasticcio by Bishop and Isaac Pocock, into a form suitable for that cast and orchestra.[76] Another of Cooke's pupils, Elizabeth Rainforth (1814–1877), sang in operas and concerts and taught singing. She took the management of Sadlers Wells in 1847, adapting the operas herself, and was one of the committee members for the projected Society of Female Musicians.[77] Like Sims Reeve, she adapted and arranged arias where this was necessary, famously arranging 'The Ould House' from *The Lays of Strathearn* by Lady Nairn. The pupils of Rainforth and Sims Reeve included Rachael Gray and Otto Dene respectively, whose careers want study, but show a continuity in pasticcio skills into the twentieth century.[78] A sketch of Gray's career in the Midlands shows pasticcio's extension as a practice, from operatic adaptation to cinema accompaniment.

Pasticcio opera in Britain

Originally from Leamington, Gray sang in a concert programme at the Theatre Royal, Windsor in 1860; in 1866 she was involved in adapting *Acis and Galatea* for a performance in her home town, conducted by a Mr Ward with two other singers, Mr R. Mason and the baritone Frederic Penna. By the following year she had returned to Leamington and was advertising for pupils.[79] In 1877, she toured the midlands with Penna singing Henry Smart's duet 'When the wind blows in from the sea'.[80] She may have been the 'Madame' Gray who was a singing and piano teacher in Hull in the 1880s.[81] By 1890 she had an all-female singing class in Leamington and, in June 1891, a cantata was especially written for her group by Emma Mundella, *The Victory of Song*. Gray arranged and conducted a performance of it herself at Shrewsbury's Music Hall, accompanied by Mundella.[82] A further adaptation occurred in 1906, for 200 voices at Nottingham University Choir, and this work was still being performed in the 1930s. The proprietor of Leamington's Theatre Royal, Charles Watson Mill, had his own stock company into the 1920s and the theatre was also used for early cinema showings with 'Madame Gray' as the accompanist.[83] These connections over time form a context for the continuity of pasticcio and the transmission of alternative views about music to those presented as characterising Romanticism in music.

Pasticcio in other media: cinema, radio and television

This sub-section traces the development of pasticcio in artforms specific to these media and their intersection with opera. Epic narratives occurring in fictive worlds were germane to both film and opera and each inspired the other. Cecil B. de Mille's *The Ten Commandments* (1923) influenced Schoenberg's opera *Moses und Aron* (1932); Prokofiev's work on Eisenstein's *Ivan the Terrible* (1944) and the influence of Abel Gance's *Napoléon* (1927) fed into his 1946 opera *War and Peace* (*Voyna i mir*). Franco Zefferelli's staging of Samuel Barber's *Antony and Cleopatra* (1966) was clearly influenced by Mankiewicz's film of 1963.[84] Influence worked both ways and opera also influenced film: verismo, the operatic opposite of the heroic epic, helped shape cinema's exploration of the gritty real world. Charpentier's *Louise* (1900) was made into a film by Abel Gance in 1939, assisted by Charpentier himself. Silent film music took a pasticcio approach from the beginning and this gave encouragement to the practice in opera.

Between the 1890s and the 1930s, the music staff of cinemas ranged from a full orchestra, to a string quartet or local brass band, to a single pianist with an upright piano. Instruction manuals and booklets were widely published, offering musicians advice on how to assemble ad hoc film accompaniments.

Even early 'talking films' took a pasticcio approach to musical accompaniments initially, as seen in the Marx Brothers comedies. Cinematic music selected from a wide range of musical genres; operatic music formed a substantial part but popular songs, hymns, famous instrumental pieces and sound effects could all be used in the same film accompaniment. Serving the narrative was more important than maintaining the boundaries between music genres. James Wierzbicki shows that for grander film-showings with an orchestra, there was usually a rehearsal beforehand at which the film was screened for them so that the accompaniment could be shaped around the film and the conductor could practise cueing the musical changes to fit the exact moment on screen.[85] In smaller cinemas, which might only employ a single pianist or organist, there was often no rehearsal and the accompanist improvised, keeping an eye on the screen and pulling melodies out of his or her memory as the action changed.[86] It was a considerable skill, requiring quick thinking and a wide command of repertoire. Cinema thus brought a new kind of pasticciere into being.

Early cinema spread throughout Western society with great rapidity between 1895 and 1925. Dennis Sharp calculated that by 1915 the United States had 25,000 cinemas and a daily audience of 6 million people.[87] The ease with which large numbers of accompanists could be found across Western society with the skills to create pasticcio scores at very short notice demonstrates not only the ubiquity of the required skills but that pasticcio scoring could not have been a new or wholly rediscovered phenomenon. More than any other evidence, perhaps, it shows that pasticcio skills remained deeply embedded at all levels of musicianship in the late nineteenth and early twentieth centuries, skills which could be readily drawn on when new opportunities for their employment emerged. This casts further doubt on the replacement of pasticcio practices by the work-concept or the ubiquity of adherence to textual fidelity in the nineteenth century.

The reason why cinema took this approach, I suggest, is because pasticcio had long been the method for providing accompaniments to deeply visual performance genres such as magic lantern shows, fantoccini, the Eidophusikon and shadow boxes, ballet and tableaux vivant, as argued in Chapter 4. In the 1890s, cinema was not seen so much as a new artform but as a new technology which continued the pre-existing paradigms of visual performance genres. The tendency in twentieth-century cinema analysis was to look forward, focusing on how early cinema prefigured later cinema, but up to the First World War many films demonstrate skeuomorphism in reproducing the tropes, spectacles and paradigms of pre-cinematic visual genres. This sub-section argues that the aesthetic parameters of Loutherbourg's Eidophusikon in the 1780s and 1790s were still conditioning early cinema a century later.

The Eidophusikon's name approximates to 'nature's phantom image' and this proto-cinema is first recorded as showing moving pictures to an audience of 130 in 1781. Ann Bermingham describes it as a miniature stage, six feet wide and three feet high, but ten feet in depth. It used coloured lighting, created by argand lamps, gauze and stained glass. The scenery and characters were painted; some were two-dimensional but others three; they were moved mechanically using a number of devices, including concealed strings and pulleys.[88]

> The moving clouds that played an important part in the effect were images imprinted in semi-transparent colours on a long linen strip some twenty times the span of the stage. The strip was gradually unrolled by a winding machine, with backlighting arranged so that the images cast drifting shadows over the landscape.[89]

Helene Furján notes that it was a concentration of techniques which Loutherbourg had brought to Drury Lane inspired by the mechanical illusions of Giovanni Niccolò Servandoni.[90] The Eidophusikon inspired Gainsborough's Shadow Box and these performances, together with those of succeeding panoramas, dioramas and other devices, form a tradition continued by early cinema. Filmed landscapes offered an intensive immersion in views of nature, cityscapes and seascapes; like their predecessors, they were still but not static.

The playbill for 1781 lists the scenes depicted as including dawn over London from Greenwich Park, enemy ships being brought into Plymouth Harbour at noon, sunset over Naples and a rising moon over the Mediterranean with a distant prospect of fire. Four 'Transparent Pictures' succeeded which were short narratives of characters in motion such as a magical incantation, sailors of different nations in conversation, a woodcutter attacked by wolves and a gentle pastoral scene. The whole concluded with a storm and a shipwreck.[91]

The music provided the immersion and no less a person than Charles Burney composed the music for the 1781 and 1782 performances and performed it from the harpsichord. The playbill specifically tells us that the music accompanied the scenes, with the 'vocal part' being sung by Sophia Baddely (1745–1786), presumably running underneath the visual experience in a prefiguration of melodrama. The arias presumably, as with tableaux vivant and ballet, coloured in the locale and scenic context. Prior to the shipwreck finale, Burney played a sonata which probably covered the rigging required for the new scene; I suggest the finale was probably accompanied by a soundscape rather than music, with a copper thunderplate and boxes of pebbles and gravel, though both this and the harpsichord are possible.[92] At Christmas in 1781, Loutherbourg showed scenes from Milton's *Paradise Lost* for his patrons at Fonthill, the occasion being the

5.8a *The Eidophusikon* by Francis Burney, 1781, watercolour.
Source: British Museum.

5.8b Robert Poulter's reconstruction of Loutherbourg's Eidophusikon for the
Musée Nationale de Monaco, 2006. Quarter of original size.
Source: Robert Poulter, New Model Theatre.

21st birthday of William Beckford. Oratorio music accompanied the rise of Pandemonium and it is likely that the oratorio texts were contrafacted to serve the story. This sequence formed the finale for a new season in London which commenced in January 1782 with a musical structure the same as for the Fonthill performances.[93] Given the use of well-known arias to cue audiences in location and context, I think it is unlikely that the arias sung were wholly new ones, although the accompaniment as a whole was clearly arranged by Burney.

At the turn of the twentieth century, a kinema was an event rather than a designated space and so film-showings could also form part of a mixed bill at a theatre. Mitchell and Kenyon's films, filmed around Britain and Ireland between 1897 and 1909, also featured city centres and nature scenes; they were short in duration with songs performed between them while the reels were changed on the projector. They were watched by workers who saw themselves taking trams, arriving at or leaving work, shopping at markets and enjoying days out.[94] Although Mitchell and Kenyon's films were urban and industrial as well as rural, Tom Gunning notes the centrality of landscape representation to the development of cinema and traces the origin of the cinematic panorama to eighteenth-century ways of seeing: formerly, the static viewer moved their gaze over a landscape where changing features were contained within the frame, but in both the Eidophusikon and early cinema the viewer travelled through a shifting landscape of changing light and moving features.[95] As Gunning pinpoints:

> New technologies in the representation of landscape, from the panorama to the motion pictures endeavoured to increase the sensation of immersion into a represented space, pursuing an almost obsessive goal of total spectator involvement.[96]

This desire for thelxis had its roots in oral storytelling, as discussed in Chapter 1, but the deeply visual culture of a mass literate society sought participatory immersion. Whether this was in a landscape or story, technological means were sought to facilitate participation and this characterised visual storytelling between the Eidophusikon and silent cinema, with the panorama in between. Gunning cites one noted response to a painting in 1763 as expressing this desire for participatory immersion:

> Denis Diderot in his description of the Salon of 1763 had first verbalized this fantasy of entering into a landscape in response to a painting by Philippe-Jacques de Loutherbourg, imagining lingering among grazing herds and then wandering into the distance … More than any previous form, the panorama realized Diderot's fantasy of the viewer's entrance into a fictive world.[97]

This is an anticipation of Adolphe Appia's 1921 trope – entering a story to run hand in hand through the fields with the character, as mentioned in

Chapter 4. Music was an essential vehicle for such immersion, but it required tailoring to the visual experience not the other way around: shaping pre-existing music, whether familiar or seldom heard, offered the surest way to achieve this. While the animation of landscapes was initially a thing of wonder, audiences soon required the medium to tell stories, both in the eighteenth and the twentieth centuries.[98]

When it became possible to copy films for commercial distribution, the cue-books often published by film companies offered guidelines and compilation scores for accompanists. Advice on creating a pasticcio accompaniment also appeared as a discrete column in cinema magazines, such as Clarence E. Sinn's 'Music for the Picture' in *Moving Picture World*, discussed by Wierzbicki.[99] Cue-books often contained no more than four pages listing the visual cues at which the music needed to change; they gave the title and composer of an appropriate piece, and sometimes how many bars or seconds to play it for.[100] Vocal lines of arias were converted to instrumental sequences or sections were abstracted from overtures; often, specific items were not selected, merely their effect, 'moderato', 'andante' or 'martial music' and so on. The choice of selection was thus left to the accompanists, making pasticcieri of tens of thousands of cinema accompanists.

5.9 Charles Stanton Ogle as the monster in Thomas Edison's *Frankenstein*, 1910.
Source: Edison Company, released under Creative Commons Licence.

These scores are similar in many ways to those created for ballets d'action in the nineteenth century, where the associations or resonances of familiar instrumental sequences offer interpretative clues to the narrative. Thomas Edison's film of Mary Shelley's *Frankenstein*, released in 1910, was accompanied by such a compilation: it included 'dramatic music' from Weber's *Der Freischütz*, repeatedly intercut with 'Annie Laurie', a Scottish song set by Alicia Scott in 1834–1835 and made famous by Jenny Lind. Also recommended for use was Balfe's aria 'Then you'll remember me' from *The Bohemian Girl*, Anton Rubenstein's Melody in F and Wagner's bridal chorus from *Lohengrin*, to cover the leaving of the wedding guests on Dr Frankenstein's wedding night.[101] The operatic quality was enhanced by the sequences where Dr Frankenstein is alone; he frequently apostrophises before the camera without any intertitles; at the slower rate of projection used at the time, he appears to be singing rather than speaking.

On 23 September 1911, Clarence Sinns prepared a cue chart for the accompaniment to Edwin Thanhouser's *Romeo and Juliet*. Although the film appears to draw principally on Gounod's opera, Sinns does not mention the opera as a potential source for the film score; instead, he suggests moods such as 'agitato', religioso' and 'pathetic'; the only pieces he specifically recommends are Jean Gabriel-Marie's *La Cinquantaine* (1887), for Juliet enquiring who Romeo is at the ball, and the intermezzo from Mascagni's *Cavalleria rusticana* (1890), to run from 'But Soft, what light through yonder window breaks' until 'Romeo entreats the Good Friar'.[102] These scores involved a considerable amount of editing and the creation of bars to facilitate key changes but the principal challenge was reducing well-known music to the much shorter timeframes of cinema. *Frankenstein* had a running time of only twelve to fifteen minutes, while *Romeo and Juliet* had two reels and lasted twenty minutes. Even so, these were longer than earlier operatic films; Georges Méliès created many films on the story of Faust beginning in 1897; his 1903 version, *Faust aux enfers*, drew on Berlioz's cantata but was only six minutes long. In 1904, his *Faust and Marguerite* was drawn from Gounod's opera and the score was edited by his brother Gaston; this ran for fifteen minutes.[103] Fidelity to the original work was thus the least concern, yet some cinematic versions of operas did attempt to engage with the concept.

Edison's *Faust*, released in 1909, was advertised as a film *of* Gounod's opera rather than one telling the story of Faust which happened to use Gounod's music. All the cue-books and publicity stated that the music accompanying the showing was to be drawn exclusively from the opera.[104] Even so, the short duration meant that intensive editing was still unavoidable. Film versions of operas were popular and cinematic pasticcieri emerged, such as Charles P. Muller, who created the score for Pathé's colour version of *Il trovatore* in 1911, and for Albert Capellani's 1916 *La vie de bohème*, one of several films of Verdi's opera.[105]

In what is, perhaps, a neoromantic reflex, twentieth-century film historians have tended to search for the first original film score, rather than discuss the artistic merits or demerits of pasticcio scoring. Studios commissioned single-authored original film scores in the middle decades of the century for serious films, but pasticcio continued in comedies and cartoons. Original scores only began to become important, I suggest, from the 'talkies' in the 1930s, and peaked in the 1960s, after which pasticcio gradually returned to serious film scoring. Curiously, this pattern coincides with expansions of, and resistance to, copyright and performance licensing. Resistance was at its height in the 1920s and 1930s, in which climate pasticcio is frequent in both opera and cinema, but as enforcement intensified in the 1940s, 1950s and 1960s, a rise in original commissioning and fidelity to the score is detectable along with a contraction of pasticcio in both artforms. As resistance to the rights system gradually returned between the 1980s and 2020, to 2020 pasticcio did too, but, in both film and opera scoring, it was initially in an experimental context or used for period films.

Examples illustrating the first phase of this arc include Joseph Carl Breil's score for D.W. Griffith's *The Birth of a Nation* (1915). Although this used to be hailed as an original score because it was commissioned to align specifically with the film, compositionally it was a classic instrumental pasticcio. Breil's score included sequences from von Suppé's *Light Cavalry Overture*, Wagner's 'Ride of the Valkyries', Beethoven's symphonies and Weber's *Der Freischütz*. The score did contain original composition by Breil himself as well as adaptations of American folk music, but it did not prefigure the later film scores of Prokofiev, Nino Rota or Carl Davis. In the mid-century serious, specially-composed film scores were thought to elevate a film from entertainment to art and many directors thought this approach brought a greater unity to the story's emotional progression. Original film scores were commissioned in these decades from recognised composers such as Max Steiner, Bernard Herrmann and Ennio Morricone.[106] Earlier in their careers Steiner and Herrmann had written pasticcio film scores – Herrmann as late as 1938 – yet these composers readily collaborated with directors who wanted to elevate the standing of their films.

From the 1960s onwards pasticcio returned to serious film scoring as it did in opera. Stanley Kubrick's *2001: A Space Odyssey* (1968) made use of Richard Strauss's *Also sprach Zarathustra*, as well as more modern compositions by György Ligeti. Roman Polanski's composer Phillipe Sarde made surreptitious use of Vaughan Williams in his score for *Tess* (1979) and, in the same year, Francis Ford Coppola placed the 'Ride of the Valkyries', as what might be considered the cinematic equivalent of an insertion aria, into his father Carmine Coppola's score for *Apocalypse Now*. Cinema became comfortable again with pasticcio film scores in the later twentieth century, and Coppola's conclusion to his *Godfather* trilogy (1990) merges the dénouement of the third film with the finale of *Cavalleria rusticana*.

This argument holds good for feature films, but not all kinds of film eschewed pasticcio scoring in the mid-century: public information films, documentaries and films of plays or books continued to take this approach. Unexpectedly, perhaps, composers including Benjamin Britten – who later wrote through-composed operas which are resistant to cuts let along pasticcio practices – took a pasticcio approach to his film music. Britten's *Men behind the Meters* (1935) for the British Commercial Gas Association contains an arrangement of Balfe's 'I dreamed I dwelt in Marble Halls', while his score for *Love from a Stranger* (1936) integrated sequences from Grieg's *Peer Gynt*. *The Tocher* by Lotte Reiniger (1938) contains borrowings from, and variations on, Rossini. William Walton incorporated arrangements of melodies from the Fitzwilliam Virginal Book and Joseph Canteloube's *Chants d'Auvergne* into his score for Olivier's *Henry V* (1944) and Gerald Tyrwhitt, Lord Berners, borrowed from the music hall to balance his austere modernism in *Champagne Charlie* (1944) and *Nicholas Nickleby* (1947). Film scoring is thus another indicator that professional musicians took different approaches depending on the task; sometimes fidelity was called for, sometimes pasticcio. Walton, Britten and Constant Lambert would never have permitted substitutions or interpolations by other composers into their operas, choral works or suites but they were completely at ease with this approach in their film music.

Serious or epic mid-century films may have felt that raiding the classical canon was beneath their dignity, but early television embraced the practice with alacrity. The BBC even went so far as to avoid paying copyright fees by commissioning 'library music'. These were pastiche compositions which imitated well-known works or identifiable periods or genres; programme makers and editors could thus source baroque chamber music, romantic piano sonatas, waltzes or Elizabethan madrigals without any liability for copyright. Library music was written by modern composers, who were paid at the beginning and then signed their copyright over to the BBC.[107]

In radio composition, Ryan Ross shows that the music created by the exiled Viennese composer Julius Bürger for the BBC Variety Department in Britain between 1934 and 1945 was described in programming as a 'musical potpourri'. He demonstrates that this genre was originally conceived as a short composition lasting around seven to ten minutes which reflected well-known styles. Bürger expanded these to hour-long works of musical meditation and exegesis on received musical heritage and, Ross argues, the radio form he created lay in descent from the operatic pasticcio.[108] Significantly, Bürger had been a silent-cinema pianist earlier in the century and Ross shows that he honed his skills as a pasticciere in this work. These developments in film and radio suggest a confidence that mid-twentieth-century audiences were sophisticated enough to tell the difference between plagiarism, intended to deceive, and quotation, where the incorporation of music from exterior sources served intertextual purposes.

Pasticcio approaches were taken towards television music throughout the twentieth century and its intersection with opera equals that of cinema. Steven Martin notes that forty opera programmes were broadcast on early television between 1936 and 1939 alone.[109] The pasticcio operas discussed earlier were not only staged but interacted with television on many levels. Ernest Irvine, who arranged the Farjeons' two most famous pasticci, was also a film and television composer and wrote the scores for *Whiskey Galore* and *Kind Hearts and Coronets* in 1949. Stephen Thomas (1897–1961), the producer for *An Elephant in Arcady,* was also a BBC television producer. He was instrumental in organising pasticcio operas for television including Frederic Austin's adaptation of *The Beggar's Opera* and Arne's *Thomas and Sally,* both of which were pasticci to begin with.[110] Mussorgsky's *The Fair at Sorochinsk* (*c.*1880), an autopasticcio uncompleted at the composer's death, was arranged and completed four times by different composers between the 1920s and the 1940s and these were among the many broadcast on early television.[111]

A dramatic expansion in the ownership of television sets from the 1960s onwards made television more culturally influential, and its acceptance of pasticcio in many forms made the practice itself more widely acceptable. The number of channels remained limited until the end of the century so that popular programmes gained audiences of many millions, some with viewing figures of over half the population: a pasticcio approach to music was thus normalised for millions. Twentieth-century people were surrounded by pasticcio music, in cinema, radio and television, yet Davison's model of absolute fidelity to the composer's intentions remained the entrenched approach of 'classical music'. The isolation of 'classical music' from society's mainstream is a vast subject, and its failure to utilise pasticcio as the previous 300 years had done was only one factor in causing this isolation. Nevertheless, the canonical repertoire became familiar to millions through the pasticcio approach of commercial advertisements. Bach's air on a G string, used for Hamlet cigars from the 1960s to the 1990s, created an association between contemplation and smoking. Dvořák's ninth symphony (the New World symphony), in Hovis bread commercials, fitted a new narrative onto the music, conjuring a vanished prewar working class. TV advertising might be theorised as a new kind of pasticcio, where origination in the canonical repertoire provided authority, but new meanings were created through mini-narratives whose durations were shorter even than those of early cinema.

Arguments for intertextuality might be argued to weaken in the context of television programmes. The film and television editor Ian Merrylees has used Janáček's first string quartet, the Kreutzer Sonata, originally inspired by a Tolstoy novella, to illustrate the gargoyles on Lincoln Cathedral in a children's documentary. Merrylees commented that the strength of the cinematic imagery cancelled any previous associations of the music, but the drama inherent in the composition accorded well with the visual images of aggression and strangeness in the gargoyles.[112] Continued interaction between artforms where pasticcio was acceptable and opera where, according to critics, it was not supposed to be, meant that periodic re-engagements occurred throughout the twentieth century.

The twenty-first century

Resistance to copyright and licensing in the age of the internet

The twenty-first century has so far seen a resistance to musical rehabilitation, which has coincided with an academic rehabilitation of pasticcio (discussed below), its tentative return to leading opera houses, and the arival of the internet. For the first time, the rights system faced resistance not just on economic and ideological grounds, but from a dissemination technology which was, in itself, an agent for decommodification. Digital technology sped up the practice of creating pasticcio operas but also provided a means of freeing them from legal restraints.

Despite the ease with which music could be accessed free of charge and the impossibility of creating a global jurisdiction to police the internet, music companies did not revise their justification for extending rights legislation nor did they update their strategy when creating new commodities. In 2001, the *Daily Mirror* reported that Phonographic Performance Ltd had threatened to prosecute pubs running quizzes in which a burst of music was played during a question. The organisation insisted that a separate licence was required for such quiz questions in addition to any licence the pub might already possess for playing music on other devices.[113] Yet even as copyright enforcement societies clung to their traditional strategy, websites such as Spotify, YouTube, Bebo and Facebook were providing open forums in which individuals could exchange music without any licence whatsoever. The anonymity of the poster, the lack of legislative clarity about what posting on the internet actually meant (was it a private letter, an open letter, or a kind of broadcast?), together with its transnational nature, all made prosecution extremely difficult for music companies and their rights societies.

From the 1990s onwards, the music industry put the governments of the UK, the United States and the European Union under intense pressure to revise copyright law for the digital age and, once again, sought to shape the revision in such a way as to create a new commodity. They insisted that transferring music from a compact disc (CD) to a computer or other device should be illegal unless a licence was obtained. The industry successfully lobbied the UK government to pass the Digital Economies Act in 2010, which categorised almost any free use of music on the internet as piracy. Companies holding highly profitable copyrights also successfully persuaded governments to raise the copyright span from fifty to seventy years; this occurred first in the European Union in 1993, then in the United States in 1998; however, attempts to head off resistance were made through accompanying measures to protect small businesses and non-commercial events from being charged, through Directive 2001/29/EC in the EU and the Fairness in Music Licensing Act in the USA.[114]

But the tide was turning against commodification. In the UK, the Gower Review of 2006 and the Hargreaves Review of 2010/11 collected evidence from both the music industry and the information technology (IT) sector. The IT sector's case proved stronger and the Hargreaves Review advised that transferring music from CDs should be decriminalised, which it duly was in 2011. Regarding copyright extension, Gower concluded that it 'is not clear that extension of the term would benefit musicians and performers very much in practice'.[115] Both reviews took account of academic research which questioned the music companies' arguments that copyright extensions encouraged creativity, protected artists' financial interests and made professional careers in composition possible.

5.10a and b 2000s pro- and anti-music industry slogan stamps.
Source: (a) Sony and EMI, 2010; (b) Andy Wardley 1995–2009.

The work of Martin Kretschmer, Philip Hardwicke and others refuted these claims, showing from rigorously gathered data that commodifying collective listening through copyright laws tended to have exactly the reverse effects.[116] Proposed alternatives took notice that commissioning fees for theatre works were substantially higher in the eighteenth and nineteenth centuries than was customary in the twentieth. Royalty payments, dwindling gradually over many years, were not as beneficial to composers as a handsome payment covering the creation stage, as nineteenth-century arguments for state funding had recognised. Even Frederick Scherer, assessing the claims made for copyright in a working paper for the John G. Kennedy School of Government at Harvard – hardly a bastion of anti-business sentiment – observed:

> We conclude that the absence of effective copyright certainly did not cause creative musical output to be stalemated. There is reason to believe that copyright systems made a positive contribution to the economic success achieved by some composers. But copyright was by no means the only operative stimulus. The world would be full of glorious music even if copyright laws had not come into being.[117]

Further damage to the traditional justifications for the rights system began in 2009. Artists in the United States who had signed away their copyrights to recording companies decades earlier identified limitation clauses in their contracts stating that the copyright would be returned to them after thirty-five years. The larger music companies sought to wriggle out of this obligation and tried to retain both the rights and the profits. These attempts were much publicised as wealthier artists launched a series of high-profile challenges in the courts to wrest their copyrights back.[118] This happened at a time when the same music companies were justifying a demand to expand the copyright period to seventy years by arguing it was needed to protect their artists' financial interests; widespread cynicism was the result.[119]

5.11 Shutterstock anti-copyright sticker, which, ironically, has itself been copyrighted.
Source: Shutterstock.

In a distant echo of the 'music-users' lobby of the 1920s, anti-copyright organisations began to spring up across the globe: the Association des Audionautes in France, The Pirate Bay in Sweden, Creative Commons License in the United States and many others. Occasionally, mass infringements of copyright, called 'electronic civil disobedience', were staged to demonstrate against corporate control of music. From the 1990s to the present day, academia has played an increasing role in the debate. Kretschmer, Hardwicke, Deazley, Gilder, Hagger, Lawrence Liang and others deconstructed the copyright industry's moral justifications and provided challengers with new, alternative, ethical practices to propose.[120] These scholars argued that the moral argument for commodification depended on the assumption of a fixed, unchanging artistic economy, despite a constantly changing society with changing technologies.

Needless to say, music corporations did not respond warmly to having their moral justification reinterpreted as a construct rooted in nineteenth-century Romanticism. Liang's work was often denounced as Marxist propaganda in industry publications.[121] Yet *The Daily Telegraph*, which can hardly be accused of publishing Marxist propaganda, ran a number of articles in 2011 by Shane Richmond, the paper's IT editor, which directly attacked the traditional justification:

> Copyright extensions are bad for innovation, bad for the economy and bad for our culture. The only people they are good for are those who collect the royalties and according to research that's far more likely to be record labels and already-rich stars than it is to be struggling musicians.[122]
>
> Today's arguments, whether in favour of copyright extensions or against 'piracy', are always couched in the same terms: it's about protecting artists and creators. But copyrights are now increasingly likely to be owned by corporations, not by individuals. These companies will argue that they have invested in creativity, even if they didn't do the creating themselves. But very often, they simply bought the rights from a company that once invested in some long-dead artist, or from that artist's relatives. It's not about creativity, it's about revenue – which is perhaps why, in the US, copyright extensions have tended to happen whenever Disney is about to lose their exclusive rights to Mickey Mouse. As it stands, the true purpose of copyright has been subverted. In fact, it's now an active disincentive to create.[123]

Richmond was reflecting a widespread perception that music corporations created a small number of millionaire superstars, but left the vast majority of composers, songwriters and singers substantially underrewarded.

Fidelity to the score had gone hand in hand with performance licensing but scholarship began a reassessment of the value systems applied to music from the past. Opera scholarship questioned the received definition of an opera as a text, and undermined industry insistence on an ur-text existing for each canonical work. Progressive determinism in music, which portrayed the work-concept as a cultural advance, faced critical scrutiny and the very definition of a musical work, the definition on which modern copyright and performance licensing had been built, was shown to be far from timeless. Faith in one true and indivisible *Don Giovanni* wavered before evidence that there were many. Variants of canonical works were unearthed, composers not included in the canon were reinstalled and undervalued operas reha-bilitated. This operatic spring may not appear to have much connection with those critiquing commodifications by the music industry in law and sociology but, I suggest, opera research over the last thirty years, and research in musicology generally, have fed more into the arguments against com-modification than into those justifying it. The revival of pasticcio in the twenty-first century can be seen as part of this.

Academic rehabilitation

As well as coinciding with enforcements and resistance to the rights system, engagement with pasticcio also coincides with generational shifts among pasticcieri themselves. Up to the 1940s composers in both artforms reflect a continuing tradition from baroque practice: the Farjeons, Steiner and Herrmann inherited their attitudes to reusing existing music. Following a mid-century dearth, the method was then rediscovered rather than inherited, as exemplified by Claude Prey, Paul Griffiths and Jeremy Sams. This latter phase also coincided with a rehabilitation of pasticcio academically.

The knee-jerk antipathy towards pasticcio expressed by Corder, Sonneck and others earlier in the twentieth century gave way to a less stadial view of music history in its last third; challenges to the concept of eternal veri-ties which underlied so much literary and musicological writing allowed a new generation of music historians to view the music of the past on its own terms. Writers such as Reinhard Strohm, Ellen Rosand, Curtis Price, Robert D. Hume, Judith Milhous, Donald Burrows and Lydia Goehr treated pasticcio opera without feeling the need to judge it adversely against fidelity. A snapshot of the re-evaluation of pasticcio can be seen in the career of Winton Dean (1916–2013). The last castrato died when Dean was 6, and he was 95 when the premier of Mark-Antony Turnage's *Anna Nicole* (2011) was given. During the 1950s, he began restoring the known fragments of Handel's last pasticcio opera, *Giove in Argo*, which had been largely lost, reconstructing the available sequences in 1960. His willingness to see the artistic merit in pasticcio was balanced, inevitably perhaps, by a legacy of pejorative attitudes deriving from nineteenth-century hostility.[124] Despite putting tremendous work into reconstructing *Giove in Argo*, he could be dismissive of its form:

The process often involved transposition, shuffling around of arias from one act or singer to another, and parodying of new texts. The results did not always make perfect sense; the object was to show off the singers rather than to produce a coherent drama.[125]

Yet Dean advanced the understanding of pasticcio and played a substantial role in getting Handel's operas back into the repertoires of major houses. John H. Roberts found other missing parts of the opera in 2002–2004 and completed the reconstruction so, in 2009, Dean discussed Handel's pasticcio afresh in the light of Roberts's work. David Hunter showed that though he could still dismiss the opera – 'an unsatisfactory hotchpotch. But a pasticcio is seldom anything else' – Dean nevertheless softened his position sufficiently to recognise pasticcio as the means whereby the Neapolitan style made its way into Handel's compositional style, blending it with his usual contrapuntal approach.[126] Positivist though Dean's approach was, the approach taken by Oscar Sonneck and Frank Walker had restricted itself to tracing the different arias, identifying their composer and considering possible methods of transmission. From the 1990s to 2020, as Werktreue orthodoxies were more thoroughly interrogated, new theorisations of pasticcio began to emerge; those of Berthold Over and Gesa zur Nieden with their essayists are the most recent example.[127] The rehabilitation of pasticcio, along with new perceptions of canons and canon formation, together with greater value being placed on performance studies, has influenced critiques of copyright and performance licensing systems. Together with new technologies, the twenty-first-century environment made it possible to consider commissioning pasticcio operas once again. Jeremy Sams's pasticcio at the Met in 2011, the varied works of Opera Feroce, Barbara Landis, Kombat Opera, Sounds Baroque, Victorian Opera, Opera Settecento and others should, perhaps, be contextualised within this academic rehabilitation and the collapse of the moral arguments for the rights system.

Pasticcio and the press

A tentative revival of pasticcio opera has occurred in the twenty-first century and, so far, has encountered detectably less critical hostility than regie operas. This sub-section examines critical reactions to some of the pasticci staged as, I suggest, they reveal opera criticism to be at a crossroads. For most of the twentieth century, the received framework for reviewing operas had been to measure new productions against an agreed set of Romantic eternal verities. This measurement system does not apply to pasticcio so critics found themselves confronted by good productions of operas constructed using methods traditionally considered illegitimate. Pasticcio thus forced reviewers to show their hand over where they stood in current musicological debates; many wanted to keep their cards close to their chests: they praised performances but reserved judgement on the form. Reactions to regie Oper have been, perhaps, a more straightforward division, with audiences and critics dividing into camps for and against; where regie is concerned critics have felt more comfortable in declaring their interest or posing as peacemakers between the two.

John H. Roberts's completion of Handel's *Giove in Argo* in 2002–2004 allowed him to stage it at the Margravial Opera House at Bayreuth in 2006 and Herrenhausen in 2007. A concert performance of the work was given in the USA at Carnegie Hall in 2008. *Giove in Argo* mostly consists of arias from Handel's earlier operas and some new ones written especially; he also selected two arias by Francesco Araja, possibly because they were already suitcase arias of his singers, Constanza and Chiara Posterla. Roberts himself supplied some of the missing recitatives.[128] A new production was included in the London Handel Festival in 2015, performed at the Britten Theatre in the Royal Academy, with established singers in the lead roles and students making up the chorus and smaller roles. Tim Ashley's review of this production for *The Guardian* was positive, as was George Hall's in *The Stage* and David Nice's in *The Arts Desk*, as Judith Malafronte's in *Opera News* had been for the CD in 2013.[129] Conversely, Mark Valencia of *What's on Stage* clearly had low expectations of pasticcio but, like the Victorian critic on discovering Handel's *Israel in Egypt* was a pasticcio, he was pleasantly surprised:

> The scholar John H. Roberts has pieced together enough bones from Handel's lost Italian opera to make a passable corpse, and now Laurence Cummings is on hand to breathe life into it. Yet *Giove in Argo* is no lurching Frankenstein creature. Patch-and-make-do it may be, since Roberts has made judicious borrowings and composed some discreet recitatives, but if I hadn't known the opera's provenance I'd never have guessed it wasn't a complete original.[130]

5.12a *Giove in Argo*, the Bayreuth production of 2006.
Source: Martin Ritter for *Online Musik Magazin*.

5.12b *Giove in Argo*, the Royal College of Music production 2015.
Source: Chris Christodoulou for *The Guardian*.

A key pasticcio skill, as we have seen, was creating unity out of disparate parts; but too much unity was felt to border on deception in the eighteenth century. Valencia praises the work but also implies that this has to be an exception to the norm, presumably because he sees pasticcio as a lesser form of opera than the neoromantic norm. Until the 1990s, comparatively few pasticcio operas had been performed in recent decades so frames of reference were lacking. Many reviewers took Valencia's line: a tone of mild surprise that it was not completely awful.

Charlotte Valori of Bachtrack was out of sympathy with the minimalist set, feeling that an archaeological curiosity should look more antique; in an otherwise glowing review which made no criticism of the opera for being a pasticcio, her final comment offered the mandatory genuflection to Romanticism: 'however, for Handel or opera newcomers, *Giove in Argo* would not be the best of introductions to the great man or his art form'.[131] Some reviewers were confident enough to move away from the neoromantic position: George Loomis, reviewing the 2007 production for the *Financial Times*, remarked '[b]ut as such it is a *pasticcio*, a form born more of expediency than of genuine inspiration, or so the theory goes. Handel apparently thought otherwise.'[132] When the CD was released in 2013, Andrew Clark of the *Financial Times* commented on the opera:

> It has become fashionable to sneer at *pasticcio* as if it's not the real thing. That argument only holds when the compilation is done in our time, as in the Metropolitan Opera's recent *Enchanted Island* ... Despite its shadowy origins (the likeliest reason for neglect), the music on both releases comes across as vintage Handel.[133]

The assumption that a consensus for sneering existed for pasticcio opera was, perhaps, truer for reviewers than for audiences, but Clark's perspective that a new pasticcio opera is not an authentic opera, but one from the past is, reveals his Romantic determinism. His underlying assumption is that the past can be forgiven its use of pasticcio as it was a more primitive place, but now that the artform has progressed to the point at which all operas are expected to be reproductions of an ur-text, the use of pasticcio today cannot be justified. Yet such reviewers regularly lament the contraction of the operatic repertoire. *The Enchanted Island* by Jeremy Sams was both an original opera and a pasticcio but Clark's denial of its legitimacy would sound less hollow if critical hostility to originally composed operas were less savage.

In 2012, Metropolitan Opera took the bold step of commissioning this richly designed pasticcio from Sams. *The Enchanted Island* used seventeenth-century pasticcio techniques to create a new baroque opera that would appeal to modern audiences who were aficionados of baroque music. The production chose to preserve the period's lyrical pace rather than tailor the pacing to current taste. It enjoyed a positive reception in 2011 and 2012, but its higher profile and greater resources exposed it to a predictable degree of hostility from critics and purist bloggers. Loved by its audiences, its very success disturbed the Romantic reflexes of critics such as Clark.

By contrast Opera Feroce, who are also based in New York, described their pasticcio opera *Amor & Psyche* in August 2010 thus:

> *Amor & Psyche* mixes elements of vaudeville, opera seria, slapstick and tableau vivant into a subtle and witty parody of baroque opera in all its gender-crossing over-the-topness. Drawn from the baroque obsession with Antiquity, the story depicts the myth of Cupid, god of love, and his marriage to the mortal princess Psyche. The piece was constructed by overlaying the music of thirteen composers spanning two hundred years onto the tale. English Lute songs, secular cantatas, as well as Italian and German baroque opera and oratorio have all been plundered in the making of this work.[134]

There is an neoromantic apology latent in this light-hearted marketing; it is a parody which plunders rather than a comedy which took a considerable amount of artistry to create. The same intention of deflecting purist ire by denying the seriousness of the project is present as it was in the Farjeon pasticci of the 1920s and 1930s. This apologetic tone is absent from Sams's more confident presentation of *The Enchanted Island* as a serious opera. Yet in 2010, *Amor & Psyche* was positively reviewed by Vivien Schweitzer in the *New York Times*, Patricia Norris in *Woman Around Town* and Howard Hurst in *Artcards*.[135] This warm critical response encouraged Opera Feroce to create a second pasticcio, *Arminio in Armenia,* in 2012. This was initially a studio work which developed into a full production in 2014 and premiered at Christ Church, Brooklyn.[136] This was less apologetic for its pasticcio form, indicating that critical reaction is a factor in companies' confidence. Julian Perkins and Stephen Pettitt's *Casanova* (2016) for Sounds Baroque drew on seventeen composers in true pasticcio style, including Vivaldi, Handel, Hasse, Gluck and Bellini. All three were new, original pastici, and although they might be placed in the antiquarian pasticcio tradition – in that their narratives are from pasticcio's golden age and their music is safely out of copyright – they might be considered avant garde today, by virtue of their deviation from the neoromantic norm.

Regie Oper

The rise of the director in the decades following the Second World War followed much the same trajectory within opera as the rise of designers such as Loutherbourg in the eighteenth and the composer in the nineteenth centuries. Many responsibilities were vested in stage directors who brought a new coherence to the conceptual, visual and dramatic components of a production. As productions grew in complexity, so they grew in management responsibilities. In the twenty years after the Second World War, stage directors tended to be steeped in the same Romantic tradition as the musical director and the critics, but from the 1960s onwards differences in approach and understanding became common. Importing techniques from spoken theatre, stage directors introduced modern dress, Brechtian ensemble practices, abstract design and tropes from theatre of the absurd and, later, physical theatre. Musical directors by contrast tended to resist changes to the score itself, which meant that stage directors tended to leave the score unchanged while altering everything else around it. Regie Oper was thus something of an historical inevitability. Press hostility was aimed more at stage directors and only at musical directors when, as in Raymond Leppard's case, they unsettled the neoromantic consensus.

Stanley Sadie disapproved of Jonathan Miller's 1974 interpretation of *Così fan tutte*, accusing Miller of superimposing a modern political message onto the opera's 'true' interpretation. Sadie believed that Mozart's eighteenth-century intentions should be uppermost, though he gave no space in his review to what he thought these might have been; Miller on the other hand sought to highlight the relevance of the opera for modern audiences by bringing to the fore themes of contemporary relevance in the opera, but which were traditionally ignored. Sadie's review outlined the director's role:

> A producer needs to respond to the music itself as well as to the ideas. One does Mozart a better service to realize the implications of the music as fully as possible, and to see the work in its context as an opera buffa of its time, with the social conventions relevant to it. The moral message may safely be let to speak for itself.[137]

As we saw earlier, Sadie also disliked a completely faithful approach to recovering the original performance methods: historically informed opera highlighted how very alien, long-vanished styles of opera could be. Instinctively, Sadie recognised that both new interpretations *and* historically accurate reconstructions undermined the core Romantic tenet that operas of genius are timeless. Reminders that things change considerably over time subverted the idea of transhistorical truths and undermined the determinist metanarratives in which he was heavily invested.

Staging *Così fan tutte* as it had been traditionally done in the previous thirty years did not make it free of political interpretation. The traditional understanding had been constructed by Marmaduke E. Brown and Edward Dent in 1890 and 1926 respectively: women, being by nature flawed, were lucky that the superior emotional maturity enjoyed by men allowed them to be forgiven for their fecklessness. Miller disturbed this tradition by reinterpreting the opera against the background of a second wave in feminism. Mozart and da Ponte's original proposition, radical for its time, was that women experience sexual desire as much as men, a point Miller restored to the interpretation. He also drew attention to the way performances of courtship and romance in eighteenth-century Vienna were designed to obscure the recognition of female sexual desire.[138] In doing this, I suggest Miller *was* allowing Mozart and da Ponte's original message to speak for itself and *was* realising the implications of the music. Sadie's objection to Miller's production concealed a political position of which he may, or may not, have been aware, that the director's role in this opera was to shore up traditional misogynies in a warm bath of Mozart's music. The critic's desire to keep the opera locked in its period is not a true desire for historical accuracy, but a means of excluding contemporary political discussion. Davison may have been at the extreme edge of fidelity advocation in the nineteenth century, but Stanley Sadie was largely representative of his profession, moderate even, when compared with critics such as Acidy Cassidy in New York.[139]

The willingness of leading companies such as the English National Opera to stage regie Oper, or director's opera, in the 1990s proved a seismic shift in Miller's direction. Instead of appeasing purism, konzept productions went on the offensive. In regie Oper, directors renegotiate the historical distance between the composer and librettist's original intentions and the needs of contemporary society. Whether or not we accept a Wagnerian origin for this, the directors associated with it such as Calixto Bieito, John la Bouchardière, Damiano Michieletto, Annaliese Miskimmon, David Alden and others have found themes within canonical operas which speak to modern concerns and debates. These themes are moved forestage through the blocking, design and the inclusion of characters or actions extraneous to the original libretto. To give some examples, in Welsh National Opera's production of

Der Rosenkavalier (Magdeburg, 2016), directed by Olivier Fuchs, another Marschallin, elderly, frail and grey-haired, looks back from 1949 at the unfolding story of her last love in the vanished world of 1911. It is as if the stage were her memory. She is unseen by the rest of the characters, busy in their world before the First World War. Bieito's production of *Die Fledermaus* for the same company (Cardiff, 2002) renegotiated time differently; depicting the hollowness and dissipation of Viennese high society, the champagne chorus was staged with the performers swigging from champagne bottles while simultaneously pissing it out into chamber pots. Philipp Himmelmann's *Don Carlo* (Berlin 2004) staged the auto da fé by having the royal family's condemned victims soaked in petrol, then hoisted high up on ropes above the family dinner table, ready to be set alight. Oblivious, the king and his family continue their meal. Purist apoplexy ensued.

5.13a Auto da fé from Philipp Himmelmann's *Don Carlos*, 2004.
Source: Berlin Staatsoper.

Yet regie Oper is, in some ways, profoundly conservative. It is an attempt to regain some of the advantages that pasticcio operas possessed: relevant contemporary themes, new interpretations through a reshaping of the story, and a new pace of storytelling to suit contemporary audiences; yet regie leaves the original score unchanged. Bieito had a new translation written for *Die Fledermaus*, to accord with the themes he was bringing out, but did not interpolate other music, change the plot, give wholly new words to arias or resequence the operetta. I suggest then that, ironically, the regie director and the purist have more in common with each other than either has with the pasticciere. Axel Englund noted of regie Oper that:

> [w]hile the musical and vocal elements of opera remained untouchably sacred and firmly rooted in the past, all sorts of images of the contemporary now began to seep into the heavily guarded bastion of tradition that is the opera house. As a result, the operatic stage became the arena for heterochronic clashes between the current and the historical.[140]

5.13b The controversial assault scene in Damiano Michieletto's *Guillaume Tell*, at the Royal Opera House, 2015.
Source: Donald Cooper for Photostage, published in the *Daily Telegraph*, 2 July 2015.

I propose that accepting the inviolability of the score has done regie Oper a disservice in that critics have been able to argue that these productions are creating the opera anew, while still purporting to be the original opera. Regie Oper directors are, understandably, shy of claiming such-and-such an opera by W.A. Mozart and C. Bieito, for example, but the main reason that only minor changes are made to the scores in regie productions is usually that the house commissioning them is still trying to appease purism. Keeping the score intact is often a condition in the director's contract, and sometimes it is a trade-off with the conductor. Given that the main purist objection to regie productions is that they are not the original opera anyway, and a new and unintended story is being superimposed on that original, a production would surely be improved if both the libretto and score were altered to better serve the adaptation the director is creating. This freedom would also mean that the more extreme dissonances between the directorial concept and the original libretto can be resolved in the director's favour. Regie Konzept is, perhaps, an attempt to broaden the canon while still retaining the canon, to tell new stories while telling the same story. This controversy is recognisable in the agonism of the seventeenth and eighteenth centuries, over how far to depart from classical rules and narratives when creating operas for the present day. They, however, resolved it by selecting and revising the music and text as they needed, to support their own interpretation of the story. This last step beckons for regie Oper.

Notes

1 'Kingsway Theatre: *An Elephant in Arcady*', *The Times*, 6 October 1938, p. 10.

2 Ryan Ross, 'Media, migration and the music aesthetic: Julius Bürger's radio potpourri (1933–1945)' (doctoral thesis, University of Southampton, 2022), pp. 7–8, 15–16, and Chapter Four.

3 Richard Traubner, *Operetta: A Theatrical History* (Oxford: Oxford University Press, 1989), p. 424–425.

4 Current legislation continues to envisage works in this way. Graham P. Cornish, *Copyright: Interpreting the Law for Libraries, Archives and Information Services* (London: Facet Publishing, 2019). For moral rights, see sections 3.4 and 3.8 on p. 14, 3.32 on p. 19, 4.22 on p. 27, 4.28, 4.29 and 4.30 on p. 28, 4.40 on p. 30 and 4.46. on p. 31.

5 Paul Rodmell, *Opera in the British Isles, 1875–1918* (London: Routledge, 2016), pp. 185–220.

6 Market research in Covent Garden's Annual Report, published in *The Times*, 9 December 1959, p. 4. Harold Blumenthal, 'The Covent Garden centenary', *The Musical Times*, May 1958.

7 Matthew Ringel, 'Opera in "the Donizettian dark age": management, composition and artistic policy in London, 1861–1870' (doctoral thesis, King's College London, 1996), pp. 142–155. Gabriella Diderikson and Matthew Ringel, 'Frederick Gye and "the dreadful business of opera management"', *19th-Century Music*, vol. 19 no. 1 (Berkeley: University of California Press, 1995), pp. 18–21. Jennifer Hall-Witt, *Fashionable Acts: Opera and Elite Culture in London 1780–1880* (Durham, NH: University of New Hampshire Press, 2007), pp. 249–250.

8 Rodmell, *Opera in the British Isles*, pp. 84, 155–162.

9 Diderikson and Ringel, 'Frederick Gye', pp. 18–19.

10 Ibid., p. 20.

11 Ibid., p. 17.

12 Rodmell, *Opera in the British Isles*, p. 155.

13 Ibid., pp. 156–158.

14 Ibid., p. 155.

15 Ibid., pp. 158–159.

16 Ibid., pp. 154, 156, 159–162.

17 *The Era*, 21 May 1892, p. 10, quoted in ibid., p. 155.

18 Note the weariness in *The Times* review of *Carmen*, 17 April 1895, p. 3.

19 Rodmell's chapter title quotes the title of William Galloway's *The Operatic Problem* (London, 1902).

20 Oscar G. Sonneck, *Miscellaneous Studies in the History of Music* (New York: Macmillan, 1921), pp. 136–144.

21 Monroe C. Beardsley, *Aesthetics: Problems in the Philosophy of Criticism* (New York: Harcourt, Brace and World, Inc., 1958), pp. 318, 571–583.

22 Leanne Langley, 'The musical press in 19th-century England', *Notes*, vol. 46 (Middleton, WI: Music Library Association, 1990), p. 591. Meirion Hughes, *The English Musical Renaissance and the Press 1850–1914: Watchmen of Music* (Aldershot: Ashgate, 2002), pp.15, 18–19, 20. Both quoted in Joseph Arthur Mann, 'Nineteenth-century music criticism and the case of James William Davison', *The Musical Times*, vol. 157 no. 1936 (London: Musical Times Publications, 2016), pp. 95–97.

23 Gillen d'Arcy Wood, 'Cockney Mozart: the Hunt circle, the King's Theatre, and *Don Giovanni*', *Studies in Romanticism*, vol. 44 (Boston, MA: University of Boston, 2005), p. 371.

24 *Music and Performance Culture in Nineteenth-Century Britain: Essays in Honour of Nicholas Temperley*, ed. Bennett Zon (London: Ashgate, 2012).

25 Peter Horton, 'The British vocal album and the struggle for national music', Zon (ed.), *Music and Performance Culture*, p. 206, but also pp. 195–208.

26 Charles Villers Stanford, 'Some aspects of musical criticism in England', *Fortnightly Review*, vol. 55 no. 330 (June 1894), pp. 826–831. Hermann Klein, *Thirty Years of Musical Life in London, 1870–1900* (New York: Century, 1903). Henry Davison, *Music during the Victorian Era. From Mendelssohn to Wagner: Memoirs of J. W. Davison* (London: William Reeves, 1912). Frederick Corder, *The Works of Sir Henry Bishop* (London, 1918).

27 Alison Booth, 'Men and women of the time: Victorian prosopographies', *Life Writing and Victorian Culture*, ed. David Amigoni (Farnham: Ashgate, 2006), p. 42.

28 Donna Loftus, 'Time, history and the making of the industrial middle class: the story of Samuel Smith', *Social History*, vol. 42 no. 1 (Oxford: Oxford University Press, 2017), p. 35.

29 Stildualismus is the view that a binary emerged in early Romantic music, between serious music that could be considered as art, and the rest that was entertainment; this was argued to be reflected in the character of German as opposed to Italian music, and totemised by Beethoven and Rossini. James Hepokoski, 'Dahlhaus's Beethoven-Rossini Stildualismus: lingering legacies of the text–event dichotomy', *The Invention of Beethoven and Rossini*, ed. Benjamin Walton

and Nicholas Matthews (Cambridge: Cambridge University Press, 2013), pp. 17–18. Hepokoski notes Dahlhaus's use of Raphael G. Kiesewetter, *Geschichte der europäisch-abendländischen oder unserer heutigen Musik*, XVII 'Die Epoche Beethoven und Rossini' (*History of European-Occidental or our contemporary music*) (Leipzig: 1834), *Die Musik des 19. Jahrhunderts* (Laaber: Laaber, 1980) (*Nineteenth- Century Music*, trans. J. Bradford Robinson, Berkeley: University of California Press, 1989). August Halm, *Von zwei Kulturen der Musik* (1913) was also used, although misapplied as Hepokoski notes, to which might be added G.W. Fink's *Musikalische Kompositionslehre* (*Theory of Musical Composition*) (Leipzig: G.F. Peters, 1847).

30 Henry Bishop and other pasticcieri sat on the same committees as their supposed detractors. Bishop was a founder member of the Philharmonic Society along with Ayrton, Smart and other reformers. He also sat on the committee of the Handel Society, along with Davison, Sterndale Bennett, Macfarren and the Smarts. Edward J. Loder, who facilitated and wrote insertion arias and other interpolations, was nevertheless a personal friend of Davison's. The pasticciere Tom Taylor attended Davison's smoking matinees in the 1840s. There is no evidence for these societies being riven with ideological disputes of the kind implied by Stildualismus, so I suggest a depiction of Britain's musical world as irrevocably divided is unsustainable.

31 George Hogarth is one example: a committed ideologue in the cause of textual fidelity, his books were intended to be authoritative and evidential: *Musical history, biography, and criticism: being a general survey of music, from the earliest period to the present time* (London: J.W. Parker, 1835), *Musical history, biography, and criticism*, 2 vols (New York: Da Capo Press, 1838) and *Memoirs of the Opera in Italy, France, Germany and England*, 2nd edn, 2 vols (London, 1851). Hogarth's disquiet over pasticcio was continued by the following who saw it as a pre-fidelity curiosity, demonstrating how much opera had advanced in the meantime: Frederick Corder's 1918 biography of Henry Bishop, O.G. Sonneck's essay of 1921 'Ciampi's *Bertoldo, Bertoldino e Cacasenno* and Favart's *Ninette à la Cour*: a contribution to the history of pasticcio', *Miscellaneous Studies in the History of Music* (New York: Macmillan, 1921) and Robert Newton's *Peter Anthony Motteux 1663–1718* (Oxford: Blackwells, 1933). These studies influenced Winton Dean and John Merrill Knapp's *Handel's Operas, 1704–1726* (Woodbridge, Suffolk: Boydell Press, 1987) and *Handel's Operas, 1726–1741* (Woodbridge, Suffolk: Boydell Press, 2006). Their perspectives even find echoes in Curtis Price's 'Unity, originality and the London pasticcio', *Harvard Library Bulletin*, new series, vol. 2 (Cambridge, MA: Harvard University Press, 1991) as well as Hall-Witt's *Fashionable Acts*, in envisioning an early termination date for pasticcio.

32 A historiography charting the recognition of the importance of performance studies in balancing textual evidence is given in Marvin Carlson, 'Theorizing the performative event', *The Oxford Handbook of Georgian Theatre, 1737–1832*, ed. Julia Swindells and David Francis Taylor (Oxford: Oxford University Press, 2014), pp. 53–70.

33 Langley, 'The musical press in 19th-century England', p. 592.
34 Davison, for example, warned Covent Garden that any attempt to adapt Mozart's *Don Giovanni* would be tantamount to blasphemy, yet two weeks later discussed how adaptation was sometimes necessary. *The Times*, 19 July 1858, p. 5 and 2 August 1858, p. 12, respectively.
35 Sonneck, *Miscellaneous Studies*, Edward J. Dent, *Opera* (London: Penguin, 1940, reprinted Greenwood Press, 1978), pp. 180–183. Hilary Poriss, *Changing the Score: Arias, Prima Donnas, and the Authority of Performance* (Oxford: Oxford University Press, 2009). Massimo Zicari, 'Expressive tempo modifications in Adelina Patti's recordings: an integrated approach', *Empirical Musicology Review*, vol. 12 (Columbus, OH: Ohio State University Libraries, 2017). Christina Fuhrmann, *Foreign Opera at the London Playhouses: From Mozart to Bellini* (Cambridge: Cambridge University Press, 2015).
36 Lydia Goehr, *The Imaginary Museum of Musical Works: An Essay in the Philosophy of Music* (Oxford: Clarendon Press, 1992). See Chapter 4, note 186, for further literature on this and Gavin Steingo's assessment of the initial critical response and the position by 2014.
37 'Minutes of evidence, taken before the Select Committee on the Copyright Acts, 1818', Paper No.280, IX, 257.1812–13, 17. Quoted in Ronan Deazley, 'Commentary on Copyright Act 1814', *Primary Sources on Copyright (1450–1900)*, ed. L. Bently and M. Kretschmer (Cambridge: Cambridge University Press, 2008).
38 Edwin Hettinger, 'Justifying intellectual property', *Philosophy and Public Affairs*, vol. 18 no. 1 (Chichester: John Wiley, 1989), pp. 47–48.
39 These were the opinions of Leslie Boosey and Ralph Hawkes throughout their careers and of the Performing Right Society, reflected in their correspondence: Boosey and Hawkes Archive, MS Mus. 1813. See also Helen Wallace, *Boosey & Hawkes: The Publishing Story* (London: Boosey & Hawkes, 2007).
40 Cornish, *Copyright*, 3.14 and 3.15 on pp. 15–16.
41 Wagner and Ludwig II is one obvious example, but Puccini and Giulio Ricordi, head of the Cas Ricordi, is another. In Britain, Frank Schuster's patronage was necessary to Elgar throughout the composer's life.
42 *Grove Online Dictionary of Music and Musicians*. Digitised by Oxford Music Online.
43 Rodmell, *Opera in the British Isles*, pp. 195–199.
44 Companies did occasionally fund new commissions: the Carl Rosa funded Charles Villers Stanford's *The Canterbury Pilgrims* (1884), although it dropped the opera from its programming after one season. Ibid., p. 313.
45 Ibid., pp. 195–207.
46 Ibid.
47 Ibid., p. 220.
48 J.A.L. Sterling, 'A short history of IFPI, 1933–2013: an interview with Professor Adrian Sterling'. Online article 2013, p. 4. http://www.ifpi.org/downloads/ifpi-a-short-history-november-2013.pdf [accessed 31 March 2023].
49 Edward Greenfield, *The Gramophone*, March 1982, p. 1239.

50 Tanya Gabrielian, 'Rachmaninoff and the flexibility of the score: issues regarding performance practice' (doctoral thesis, City University of New York, 2018), p. 27. Donald Car Meyer, 'The NBC Symphony Orchestra' (doctoral thesis, University of California, 1994), p. 37.

51 A practice which continued long into the century: in 1967 Deutsche Grammophon suppressed its recording of Wagner's *Die Meistersinger von Nurnberg*, conducted by Rafael Kubelik, in order promote its star conductor, Herbert von Karajan, conducting *The Ring*. Kubelik's recording was only released in the 1990s.

52 For this, Gilder and Haggar draw on Sterling, 'A short history of IFPI': Eric Gilder and Mervyn Hagger, 'Antinomic interpretations of self as defined by moral rights and copyrights in British tradition, spirit and feelings, and the United States Constitution', *East–West Cultural Passage, A Journal of the 'C. Peter Magrath' Research Center for Cross-Cultural Studies* (Sibiu, Romania: Lucian Blaga University, July 2011).

53 Phonographic Performance Ltd, 70th anniversary website. http://www.ppluk.com/Documents/70%20Years%20of%20PPL.pdf [accessed 11 August 2018].

54 It was against such practices that Victor Hugo championed the droit d'auteur and promoted it internationally. The Berne Convention of 1886 gave the barest protection to artists but not so as to disturb the dominance of copyright purchasers.

55 Walter Benjamin and Theodor W. Adorno made critiques of the influence of recorded music. Theodor W. Adorno, *Towards a Theory of Musical Reproduction*, ed. Henri Lonitz, trans. Wieland Hoban (Cambridge: Polity Press, 2006).

56 *The Daily Mirror*, 15 October 1929.

57 Robert J. Congleton and Sharon Q. Yang, 'A comparative study of academic digital copyright in the United States and Europe', *Research and Advanced Technology for Digital Libraries*, ed. Stefan Gradmann, Francesca Borri, Carlo Meghini and Heiko Schultz (Berlin: Springer-Verlag, 2011), p. 217.

58 Examples include the Lisburn Sufferage Society, which met at the Temperance Hall in Bridge Street, Lisburn. *The Lisburn Standard*, 30 July 1910, 3 December 1910, 6 May 1911, 8 March 1913, 4 October 1913. Mrs Metge's descriptions of their meetings can also be found in *The Irish Citizen*, 1913–1914.

59 *The Times*, 18 December 1929, p. 10.

60 James Burney, MP for Bootle. 'Copyright (Musical works) Bill.' House of Commons Debate, 12 February 1924, *Hansard,* vol. 169, pp. 814–30.

61 *The Times*, 14 August 1934.

62 In the 1920s the BBC negotiated the playing of records with copyright holders or Phonographic Performance Limited on a case-by-case basis until 1933–1935, when they negotiated a wholesale approach called needletime. Yet their hostility to fees for collective listening being paid by both the broadcaster and the listeners continued. Exemption was regularly sought based on the BBC's role as an educator, along with other learning institutions. Martin Cloonan, 'Negotiating needletime: the Musicians' Union, the BBC and the record companies, c.1920–1990', *Social History*, vol. 41, no. 4 (Abingdon: Taylor and Francis,

2016), pp. 353–374. Sterling, 'A short history of IFPI', p. 3. Michael Burden, '"Gillimaufrey" at Covent Garden: Purcell's *The Fairy-Queen* in 1946', *Early Music*, vol. 23, no. 2 (Oxford: Oxford University Press, 1995), p. 274.

63 Frank Gray, MP for Oxford. 'Copyright (Musical works) Bill.' House of Commons Debate, 12 February 1924, *Hansard*, vol. 169, pp. 814–30. Order for Second Reading.

64 *The Times*, 2 December 1929.

65 *The Times*, 10 December 1929.

66 *The Times*, 11 December 1929.

67 Phonographic Performance Ltd, 70th anniversary website.

68 Numerous operas in Welsh were created and toured in the nineteenth and twentieth centuries, while operas commissioned in Irish and Scots Gaelic occur more in the twentieth century.

69 Nicholas Matthew and Mary Ann Smart, 'Elephants in the music room: the future of quirk historicism', *Representations*, vol. 132 no. 1 (Berkeley: University of California Press, 2015), pp. 61–78.

70 *The Times*, 20 May 1935, p. 12; also Silke Wenzel, 'Dora Bright', *Musik und Gender*, Mugi im internet (Hamburg: Hochschule für Musik und Theater Hamburg, 2011), p. 8. https://mugi.hfmt-hamburg.de/artikel/Dora_Bright.pdf [accessed 26 June 2019].

71 J.P. Wearing, *The London Stage 1930–1939: A Calendar of Productions, Performers, and Personnel* (London: Rowman and Littlefield, 1976, second edn 2014), p. 782.

72 Claude Prey, *Les liaisons dangereuses* (Paris: hors série L'Avant-Scène Opéra no 5a, premières loges: *Opéra Aujourd'hui*, 1993), p. 82.

73 John Warrack, *Sunday Telegraph*, June 1967.

74 Stanley Sadie, *The Times*, 17 June 1967.

75 Wölfl, who died in 1812, had been a friend of Francesco Bianchi's widow, Jane.

76 *Birmingham Daily Post*, 1 December 1871, p. 8. By now the aging tenor's voice was causing him concern and he fought against the tendency in England to set concert pitch half a tone above that of the rest of Europe. In an excellent piece of pasticcio work he subtly rescored the tenor role in Bach's *St Matthew Passion* to accord with baroque pitch.

77 *Lloyd's Weekly Newspaper*, 22 August 1847.

78 Rachael Gray (sometimes spelled Rachel) is mentioned as a pupil of Rainforth in a concert programme for Birmingham *c*.1857 and in *The Illustrated Times*, 21 January 1860, p. 44. Otto Dene's performance is discussed in the *Evening Express*, 16 November 1895, p. 4, referring to a song of his own composition.

79 *The Musical Times*, 1 May 1860, for her Windsor concert. *Acis and Galatea* is briefly reviewed in *The Musical Times*, 1 March 1866 and the singing advertisements are in *The Musical Times and Singing Class Circular*, 1 May 1867.

80 The duet was advertised in *The Musical World*, 6 January 1877.

81 'Local intelligence', *Hull Packet and East Riding Times*, 14 January 1881.

82 The performance was recorded in *The Musical Times*, 1 May and 1 June 1891 with the Shrewsbury performance on 1 May 1892.

83 Charles Watson Mill Collection, GB 150 MILL, University of Birmingham, Cadbury Research Library, Special Collections.

84 Bluma Goldstein, 'Schoenberg's *Moses und Aron*: a vanishing Biblical nation', *Political and Religious Ideas in the Works of Arnold Schoenberg*, ed. Charlotte M. Cross and Russell A. Berman (Abingdon: Taylor and Francis, 2000) from p. 34. Kevin Bartig, *Sergei Prokofiev's Alexander Nevsky* (Oxford: Oxford University Press, 2017), p. 15. Franco Zeffirelli, *Zeffirelli: The Autobiography of Franco Zeffirelli* (London: Weidenfeld & Nicholson, 1986), pp. 203–220.

85 James Wierzbicki, *Film Music, a History* (London: Routledge, 2009), pp. 20–23, 34–37, 43, 46, esp. p. 66.

86 Ibid., pp. 18–20, 37, 48–49.

87 Dennis Sharp, *The Picture Palace and Other Buildings for Movies* (London: Hugh Evelyn, 1969), p. 70.

88 Ann Bermingham, 'Technologies of illusion: De Loutherbourg's Eidophusikon in eighteenth-century London', *Art History*, vol. 39 no. 2 (London: Association of Art Historians, 2016), pp. 376–399.

89 Ibid., p. 384.

90 Helene Furján, *Glorious Visions: John Soane's Spectacular Theater* (Abingdon: Routledge, 2011), pp. 50–51

91 'Eidophusikon, 1781', Charles Burney Playbill Collection, British Library, London, 937.f.2/8(99).

92 Ibid. and William Henry Pyne as 'Ephraim Hardcastle', *Wine and Walnuts; or, After Dinner Chit-Chat* (London, 1823), 2 vols, vol. I, pp. 292, 298, quoted by Bermingham, 'Technologies of illusion', pp. 382–383.

93 'Eidophusikon, 1782', 937.b.3, in Bermingham, 'Technologies of illusion', p. 383.

94 Wierzbicki, *Film Music, a History*, pp. 19–21. Wierzbicki weighs up the evidence for whether the earliest film exhibitions had a musical accompaniment or were listened to in silence. I suggest this neglects the evidence that audiences could be very vocal in fairgrounds, circuses, menageries, puppet shows and so on, and there is anecdotal evidence that when seeing themselves and their friends on film, workers expressed their amazement and amusement loudly.

95 Tom Gunning, 'Landscape and the fantasy of moving pictures: early cinema's phantom rides', *Cinema and Landscape: Film, Culture and Geography*, ed. Graeme Harper and Jonathan Rayner (Bristol: Intellect, 2010), pp. 31–70.

96 Ibid., p. 64.

97 Ibid., pp. 38, 43.

98 Ibid., p. 26. Wierzbicki, *Film Music, a History*, notes that, by 1908, 96 per cent of all American films told stories.

99 Gunning, 'Landscape and the fantasy of moving pictures', pp. 33–40.

100 *Sounds for the Silents: Photoplay Music from the Days of Early Cinema*, ed. Daniel Goldmark (New York: Dover Publications Inc., 2013), several examples.

An anthology of pasticcio music and short sequences from photoplay books with an introductory essay by Goldmark.

101 Wierzbicki, *Film Music, a History*, p. 37.

102 Ibid., pp. 37–38.

103 It is possible that the films previous to 1903 were also based on Berlioz's cantata rather than Gounod's. Méliès continued to produce films based on Faust operas until 1912.

104 'We have gone to considerable trouble to specify the exact music from the opera.' Ibid., p. 36.

105 *Sound Theory, Sound Practice*, vol. 2, ed. Rick Altman (Abingdon: Routledge, 1992), p. 117. *The Film Index*, 7 January 1911 (New York: Films Publishing Company), pp. 1, 25. Francesco Finocchiaro, 'Operatic works in silent cinema: toward a translational theory of film adaptations', *Music and the Moving Image*, vol. 13 no. 3 (Carbondale, IL: University of Illinois Press, 2020), pp. 50, 52–54.

106 Max Steiner scored *King Kong* in 1933, Bernard Herrmann wrote the score for *Citizen Kane* in 1941 and many of Hitchcock's film scores between 1955 and 1964. He also composed for *Journey to the Centre of the Earth* (1959), *Cape Fear* (1962) and *Fahrenheit 451* (1966). Ennio Morricone scored numerous spaghetti Westerns throughout the 1960s, but also wrote film scores for *Queimada!* (1969) and *La Cage aux folles* (1978). Laurence E. MacDonald, *The Invisible Art of Film Music: A Comprehensive History* (Lanham, MD: Scarecrow Press, 2013).

107 Alison Garnham, *Hans Keller and the BBC: the musical conscience of British broadcasting, 1959–79* (Farnham: Gower Publishing Ltd, 2003), various; also conversation with former BBC staff editor Ian Merrylees on 20 April 2016.

108 Ross, 'Media, migration and the music aesthetic', pp. 7–8, 15–16, and Chapter Four, pp. 39–67.

109 Steven Martin, 'British opera on television, 1936–1938', *Chombec News* (Centre for the History of Music in Britain, the Empire and the Commonwealth, University of Bristol, 2009), p. 12.

110 Ibid.

111 Ibid., p. 11.

112 Conversation, 20 October 2022.

113 *The Daily Mirror*, 9 February 2001.

114 Council Directive 93/98/EEC of 29 October 1993 harmonised the term of protection under copyright and certain other related rights, proposing an increase from fifty years to seventy. Directive 2001/29/EC (the InfoSoc Directive), article 2 mitigated copyright in a series of contexts but exceptions and exemptions were largely devolved to member state governments. In the USA, the Fairness in Music Licensing Act was attached as an amendment to the Sonny Bono Copyright Term Extension Act (1998) (www.copyright.gov), US Copyright Office.

115 Ian Hargreaves, 'Digital opportunity: a review of intellectual property and growth' (HM Government, Department for Business, Innovation & Skills and

the Intellectual Property Office, 2011), pp. 43–44, 68, 91. Andrew Gowers, *The Gowers Review of Intellectual Property* (London: Her Majesty's Treasury, December 2006), p. 50 section 4.29.

116 Martin Kretschmer and Philip Hardwick, *Authors' Earnings from Copyright and Non-Copyright Sources: A Survey of 25,000 British and German Writers*, a report commissioned by the Centre for Intellectual Property Policy & Management (Bournemouth: Bournemouth University, 2007), p 216. Martin Kretschmer, *Private Copying and Fair Compensation: An Empirical Study of Copyright Levies in Europe*, an independent report commissioned by the UK Intellectual Property Office (UK: IPO, 2011).

117 F.M. Scherer, 'The emergence of musical copyright in Europe from 1709 to 1850', Faculty Research Working Papers Series (Cambridge, MA: Harvard Kennedy School, 2008), p. 15.

118 Popular music names including Bob Dylan, Tom Petty, Bryan Adams and Tom Waits issued notices of intention to reclaim their rights in 2011, and industry resistance prompted many court cases including *Waite v. UMG* and *Johansen v. Sony Music Entertainment* in the USA, while UK cases included Duran Duran in 2016 and Paul McCartney in 2017. https://www.theguardian.com/music/2016/dec/02/reflex-action-duran-duran-lose-court-battle-over-song-rights [accessed 20 February 2024].

119 *Wired*, an online magazine, 13 November 2009. https://www.wired.com/2009/11/copyright-time-bomb-set-to-disrupt-music-publishing-industries/ [accessed 10 August 2018]. *New York Times*, 11 September 2013. http://www.nytimes.com/2013/09/11/arts/music/a-copyright-victory-35-years-later.html?r=0 [accessed 10 August 2018].

120 Lawrence Liang, *A Guide to Open Content Licenses* (Rotterdam: Piet Zwort Institute, Institute for Postgraduate Studies and Research, Willem de Kooning Academy Hogeschool Rotterdam, 2004). Digitised in 2015. https://monoskop.org/images/1/1e/Liang_Lawrence_Guide_to_Open_Content_Licenses_v1_2_2015.pdf See also: http://altlawforum.org/publications/copyright-cultural-production-and-open-content-licensing/ [both accessed 22 September 2019].

121 Website of The Progress and Freedom Foundation, closed since 2010 but still accessible. http://www.pff.org/ [accessed 22 September 2019].

122 *The Daily Telegraph*, 11 September 2011.

123 *The Daily Telegraph*, 3 August 2011.

124 Suzana Ograjenšek, for example, in her review of Dean's *Handel's Operas 1726–1741*, notes his hostility to directors staging Handel's works in later periods, or with abstract sets, or different acting styles (konzept Regie). '*Handel's Operas 1726–1741* – by Winton Dean', *Journal for Eighteenth-Century Studies*, vol. 32 no. 1 (London: Wiley, 2009), pp. 135–137.

125 Dean, *Handel's Operas, 1726–1741*, p. 128.

126 Ibid., pp. 129, 398 discussed in David Hunter's review 'Just the facts?', *Early Music*, vol. 35 no. 3 (Oxford: Oxford University Press, 2007), p. 462. See also Dean's 'Jupiter in Argos', *Handel Studies: A Gedenkschrift for Howard Serwer*, ed. Richard G. King (Hillsdale New York, 2009), pp. 47–57.

127 *Operatic Pasticcios in 18th-Century Europe: Contexts, Materials and Aesthetics*, ed. Berthold Over and Gesa zur Nieden (Bielefeld: transcript Verlag, 2021).

128 John H. Roberts, 'Reconstructing Handel's *Giove in Argo*', *Handel Jahr-buch*, vol. 54 (Leipzig: Deutscher Verlag fur Musik, 2008), pp. 183–204.

129 Tim Ashley, *The Guardian*, 25 March 2015. George Hall, *The Stage*, 26 March 2015. David Nice, *The Arts Desk*, 28 March 2015. Judith Malafronte, *Opera News*, September 2013, pp. 83–84.

130 Mark Valencia, '*Giove in Argo* (Britten Theatre): the first modern-day performance of a little-known Handel opera', *What's On Stage*, 24 March 2015.

131 Charlotte Valori, Bachtrack, 26 March 2015.

132 George Loomis, '*Giove in Argo*, Göttingen International Handel Festival', *Financial Times*, 1 June 2007. Hyperlink unavailable.

133 Andrew Clark, 'Handel: *Giove in Argo*, hidden Handel', *Financial Times*, 22 March 2013. Hyperlink unavailable.

134 Opera Feroce website. http://www.operaferoce.com/ [accessed 25 June 2019].

135 Vivien Schweitzer, *New York Times*, 25 October 2010, Howard Hurst, *Artcards*, 21 October 2010 and Patricia Norris, *Woman Around Town*, 7 March 2012.

136 Opera Feroce website.

137 Stanley Sadie, '*Così fan Tutte*', *The Times*, 8 November 1974, p. 13.

138 Jonathan Miller, *Subsequent Performances* (London: Faber & Faber, 1986), p. 25 and other writings.

139 Claudia Cassidy (1899–1906) was a critic at the *Chicago Tribune*, famed for her acerbic hostility to operatic innovation.

140 Axel Englund, *Deviant Opera* (Berkeley: University of California Press, 2020), p. 17.

Bibliography

Primary sources

Early thirteenth century

Aucassin et Nicolette, Bibliothèque Nationale (F-Pn fr.2168). *Aucassin et Nicolette* trans. from the Old French by Mario Roques (Paris: Librairie Honoré Champion, 1982).

Marchesini, Giovanni, *Mammotrectus super Bibliam* (*c.*1300).

Marriott, William (ed.), *A Collection of English Miracle and Mystery Plays* (Basel: Schweighauser and Co., 1838). Digitised by Internet Archive. https://archive.org/details/collectionofengl00marruoft/page/40 [accessed 27 January 2019].

Sixteenth century

Clement, Francis, *The Petie Schole* (London: printed by Thomas Vautrollier, 1587).

Fabri Wethulensis, Andreas (Andre Le Fevre de Vetheuil), *Centones, cum Diana, et iuvenilibus* (1589, reprinted Paris: D. Douceur, 1609).

Giraldi, Lilio Gregorio, *De Historia poetarum tam Graecorum quam Latinorum dialogi decern* (first edn, *Historice poetarum ...*, Basle: 104 Isingrinius, 1545).

Ricci, Benedetto, *De imitatione*, Book 3 (Venice: Aldi filii, 1545).

Vecchi, Orazio, *L'Amfiparnasso* (Venice, 1597). Trans. and transcribed by Cecil Adkins, *Early Musical Masterworks*, vol. 1 (Chapel Hill: University of North Carolina, 1977).

Seventeenth century

Anon., *The Tempest or The Enchanted Island, a Comedy, as it now Acted at His Highness the Duke of York's Theatre* (London: 1674). Digitised by the Internet Archive. https://archive.org/details/tempestorenchant00shad/page/n15 [accessed 26 January 2019].

Aubrey, John, 'Remaines of gentilisme and Judaisme in 1686–7', printed in *John Aubrey: Three Prose Works*, ed. John Buchanan-Brown (Carbondale, IL: Carbondale Press, 1972). The Folk Lore Society's 1881 edition is digitised by the Internet Archive.

Behn, Aphra, *The Lucky Chance*, ed. Fidelis Morgan (1686, London: Virago Press, 1981).

Behn, Aphra, *The Unfortunate Happy Lady, A True History* (London: printed for Samuel Briscoe, 1698). Digitised by Oxford Text Archive, Text Creation Partnership.

Burmeister, Joachim, *Musica Poetica* (1606) trans. Benito V. Rivera (New Haven, CT: Yale University Press, 1993).

Caccini, Francesca, *Il libro primo delle musiche* (Florence, 1618), critical edn by Ronald James Alexander and Richard Savino, *Francesca Caccini the secular songs from 'il libro primo delle musiche', 1618* (Bloomington, IN: Indiana University Press, 2004).

Caccini, Giulio, *Le nuove musiche* (printed in Florence, 1602, trans. Zachariah Victor for the facsimile edn, New York: Broude Brothers, 1973).

Cavalieri, Emilio de, 'Avvertimenti per la presente *Rappresentatione*, à chi volesse farla recitar cantando', *Rappresentatione di anima e di corpo* (Rome: Nicolò Mutij, 1600), trans. and digitised, Lorenzo Girodo, 1986.

Christie, William Dougal, *A Life of Anthony Ashley Cooper, first Earl of Shaftesbury, 1621–1683* (London: Macmillan 1871), Appendix One. Digitised by the Internet Archive.

Defoe, Daniel, *A Tour through the Whole Island of Great Britain* (London 1724–1727).

Divorce Exhibita, and Vicars General Books DL/C, Consistory Court of London, London Metropolitan Archives, City of London.

Dowland, John, *Varietie of Lute-Lessons* (London, 1610). Digitised by International Music Score Library Project.

Downes, John, *Roscius Anglicanus*, or, *an Historical Review of the Stage From 1660 to 1706* (London, 1708).

Dryden, John, *Albion and Albanius* (London, 1691), reprinted in The Mermaid Series, *The Best Plays of John Dryden*, ed. George Saintsbury, vol. 2 (London: Ernest Benn Ltd, 1950).

Hickeringill, Edmund, *The Black Non-Conformist* (London, printed by George Larkin, 1682).

Marana, Giovanni Paolo, *Letters Writ by Turkish Spy*, vol. 6, book II, letter X, 1662 (trans. William Bradshaw, London, 1694).

Monteverdi, Claudio, *Scherzi musicali a tre voce* (Venice, 1607) reprinted in *Tutte le opera di Claudio Monteverdi*, ed. G.F. Malipiero, 17 vols (Vienna, trans. Zachariah Victor, 1968).

Norden, John, *The Surveyor's Dialogue* (London: William Stansby and John Windet for John Busby, 1610). Digitised by Google Books.

Peacham, Henry the Younger, *The Compleat Gentleman* (London, 1622) reprinted in *Source Readings in Music History: The Renaissance*, ed. Oliver Strunk, 4 vols (London: Norton Press, 1998), vol. 3.

Pepys, Samuel, *The Diary of Samuel Pepys*, ed. Robert Latham and William Matthews, 11 vols (Berkeley, CA: University of California Press, 1971).

Sergeant, John, Letter of Thanks from the Author of *Sure-Footing* to his Mr. J.T. [John Tillotson] (Paris, 1666).

Strozzi, Giulio, *La finta Pazza* (Venice: Surian, 1641).

Walker, Clement, *The Compleat History of Independency 1640–1660* (London, 1660). Digitised by the Royal Collection Trust, RCIN 1024949.

Eighteenth century

Anon., 'Commentary on *An Enquiry into the Nature and Origin of Literary Property* (1762)', critical edn by Ronan Deazley in *Primary Sources on Copyright (1450–1900)*, ed. L. Bently and M. Kretschmer (Cambridge: Cambridge University Press, 2008).

Anon., *La villanelle rapita*, Paris version of vocal score, 1790. Digitised by International Music Score Library Project.

Anon., *La Villanella Rapita; A Comic Opera in two acts, as performed at the Theatre Royal in the Hay-Market.* (London: H. Reynell, 1790, reprinted by Ecco Print Editions, 2010).

Anon., *La Villanella Rapita, The Favourite Duett sung by Sig^{ra} Storace and Sig^{r} Buselli in the opera La Villenella Rapita* (London: Longman and Broderip, 1790). Digitised by the University of Western Ontario.

Ashley Cooper, Anthony, 3rd Earl of Shaftesbury, *A letter Concerning Enthusiasm* (London, printed for J. Morphew, 1708). Digitised by the Internet Archive.

Banks, Elizabeth to Ozias Humphry, Royal Academy of Arts, Upcott MSS 11, 67, 1 April 1778. Digitised by the Internet Archive.

Bickerstaff, Isaac, *The Tatler*, Saturday 23 July 1709, no. 45.

Birch, Thomas, *A Complete Collection of the Historical, Political and Miscellaneous works of John Milton … with an Historical and Critical Account of the Life and Writings of the Author*, 2 vols (London, 1738). Digitised by the Online Books Page.

Boswell, James, *The Journals of James Boswell, 1762–1795*, ed. John Wain (London: Mandarin Press, 1990).

Burney, Charles, *An Account of the Musical Performances in Westminster Abbey and The Pantheon in Commemoration of Handel* (London 1784). Digitised by the University of California Libraries.

Burney, Charles, *A General History of Music from the Earliest Period to the Present Age*, 5 vols (London, 1789). Digitised by International Music Score Library Project.

Charles Burney Playbill Collection, British Library, London.

Burney, Frances, *Evelina*, Letter XXXIII (London, 1778, republished by Norton Press, 1965).

Burney, Susan, *The Letter-Journal of Susan Burney*, British Library, Egerton MS 3691, reprinted in Philip Olleson, *The Journals and Letters of Susan Burney: Music and Society in Late Eighteenth-Century England* (Abingdon: Routledge, 2013).

Cibber, Colley, *An Apology for the Life of Mr. Colley Cibber, Written by Himself* (London, 1740, republished by John C. Nimmo, ed. Robert W. Lowe, 1889).

Cooper, Thomas, *A Reply to Mr Burke's Invective against Mr Cooper and Mr Watt in the House of Commons* etc. (Manchester, 1792). Digitised by the Internet Archive.

Corfe, Joseph, *A Treatise on Singing, Explaining in the most simple manner, etc.* (London, 1799).

Craftsman, The, 6 October 1733, No. 379, quoted in *The Gentleman's Magazine*, October 1733.

Crescimbeni, Giovanni Mario, *La bellezza della volgar poesia* (Rome, 1700) quoted by Robert S. Freeman, *Opera without Drama: Currents of Change in Italian Opera, 1675–1725* (Ann Arbor, MI: UMI Research Press, 1981).

Downes, John, *Roscius Anglicanus, or, an Historical Review of the Stage From 1660 to 1706* (London, 1708). Digitised by the Internet Archive. https://archive.org/details/rosciusanglicanu00downrich/page/32 [accessed 27 January 2019].

[Dryden, John], *King Arthur: or, the British worthy: A masque. By Mr. Dryden. As it is performed at the Theatre-Royal in Drury-Lane, … the music by Purcell and Dr. Arne* (London: printed for W. Strahan, L. Hawes and Co., T. Davies, T. Lownds, T. Becket and W. Griffin, 1770). Digitised by Ecco TCP, Eighteenth-Century Collections Online.

Gabrielle Enthoven Collection (sheet music), Theatre and Performance Collection, Victoria & Albert Museum, Accession No. S.57–2014. https://collections.vam.ac.uk/item/O1277982/gustavus-the-third-sheet-music-auber/ [accessed 22 May 2023].

de' Ficoroni, Francesco, *Osservazioni di Francesco de' Ficoroni sopra l'antichità di Roma descritte nel Diario Italico pubblicato in Parigi l'anno 1702 dal M. Rev. Padre Bernardo de Montfaucon, nel fine delle quali s'aggiungono molte cose antiche singolari scoperte ultimamente tra le rovine dell'antichità* (Rome: Antonio de' Rossi, 1709). Digitised by the Internet Archive.

G.O., 'To Mr Handel', *The Gentleman's Magazine*, May 1740, vol. 10.

Gentleman of Oxford, 'On our late Taste in Musick', *The Gentleman's Magazine*, May 1740, vol. 10.

Hawkins, Sir John, *A General History of the Science and Practice of Music*, 5 vols (London: 1776). Digitised by International Music Score Library Project.

Heyne, C.G., *Sammlung antiquarischer Aufsädtze* (Leipzig, 1779).

Houghton Hall, cellar accounts, M23. Record of wine at Houghton Hall 1750. Estate papers of the Cholmondley family, Houghton Hall, listed by A. Smith, February 1994. Historical Manuscripts Commission.

Hutchison, Francis, *An Historical Essay Concerning Witchcraft* (London, 1718). Ebook digitised by the Wellcome Collection.

King's Theatre, Chancery report concerning finances, Public Record Office, C38/715 Hett's third master's report, 12 November 1784. Digitised by the National Archives.

Koch, Heinrich Christoph, *Versuch einer Anleitung zur Composition* (Leipzig: Bohme, 1793).

Kollmann, A.F.C., *Essay on Practical Musical Composition* (London: self-published, 1799). Digitised by International Music Score Library Project.

Ladies Magazine, The (London: G. Robinson, 1775).

Lewis, Matthew, *The Monk, a Romance* (Waterford: J. Saunders, 1796). Digitised by Project Gutenberg.

Longman and Broderip vs Storace, Public Record Office, 24/1936: Interrogatories for the plaintiffs on 13 June 1789. Digitised by the National Archives.

Mackintosh, James, *Vindiciae Gallicae and other Writings on the French Revolution* (London, 1791). Digitised by the Internet Archive.

de Montfaucon, Bernard, *Diarium Italicum. Sive monumentorum veterum, bibliothecarum, musaeorum, &c. Notitiae singulares in itinerario Italico collectae. Additis schematibus ac figuris* (Paris: J. Anisson, 1702). Digitised by the Internet Archive.

Nugent, Thomas, *The Grand Tour*, vol. 2 (London, 1756), digitised by Pablo Günther, 'The Casanova Tour', part XVI, https://www.giacomo-casanova.de/catour16.htm#ITALY [accessed 29 November 2018].

Quantz, Johann Joachim, *Versuch einer Anweisung die Flöte traversiere zu spielen* (Berlin, 1752) trans. Edward J. Reilly, *On Playing the flute* (London: Faber and Faber, 1966).

Queen Charlotte, letter from Queen Charlotte to Prince William, later William IV, 30 March 1784. ADD4 Royal Collection Trust. Digitised by the Georgian Papers Programme.

Raguenet, Francois, *A comparison between the French and Italian Musick and Operas Translated from the French with Some Remarks. To Which is Added a Critical Discourse upon Opera's in England, and a Means Proposed for their Improvement* (London, 1709).

Riva, Giuseppe, *Avviso ai compositori, ad ai cantanti*, trans. as *Advice to the Composers and Performers of Vocal Musick* (London: printed by T. Edlin, 1727), Digitised by Thomson Gale.

Scott, John, *Critical Essays on Some of the Poems of Several English Poets* (London, 1785). Digitised by the Internet Archive.

Steele, Richard, *The Tatler*, 19 April 1709.

Steele, Richard, 'On Nicolini's Leaving the Stage', *Poetical Miscellanies* (London, 1714).

Thelwall, John, *The Rights of Nature against Usurpations of Establishments* (London, 1796). Digitised by the Internet Archive.

Walpole, Horace, *The Letters of Horace Walpole, Earl of Orford: Including Numerous Letters Now First Published From the original Manuscripts, 1735–45*, vol. 1 (London: Richard Bentley, 1846).

Walpole, Sir Robert, M23, record of wine at Houghton Hall, M23, estate papers of the Cholmondley family, Houghton Hall, listed by A. Smith, Historical Manuscripts Commission (February 1994).

The World, Tuesday, 5 January 1790, Burney Collection Newspapers.

Nineteenth century

Anon., Catalogue of old wines, part of the estate of Thos. B. Adair. December 3, 1845. David M. Rubenstein Rare Book & Manuscript Library, Digitised by Duke University Libraries (Durham, North Carolina: Duke University). http://library.duke.edu/digitalcollections/broadsides_bdsmd30948/ [accessed 11 February 2019].

Anon., *Maretti or The Brigand's Sacrifice* licensed for John Kingdom on 25 May 1853, Lord Chamberlain's Plays and Day Books, British Library, ADD. MS 52940D.

Anon., *The Mirror of Graces: Or, The English Lady's Costume* (London: Crosby, 1811).

Anon., *Salvatori or The Bandit's Daughter*, licensed for performance at the Royal Olympic Theatre 28 March 1853, *Lord Chamberlain's Plays and Day Books*, British Library, ADD MS 52938Z.

Beckford, Peter, *Familiar letters from Italy to a friend in England*, vol. 2 (Salisbury, 1805).

Bristol Theatre Collection, Playbills, TC/PB 000318.

Boosey and Hawkes Archive, MS Mus. 1813.

Lord Braybrook, ed., *Memoirs of Samuel Pepys Esq, FRS*, 2 vols (London: Henry Colburn, 1825).

Cowden Clarke, Mary, *My Long Life* (New York: Dodd, Mead & Co., 1896). Digitised by the Internet Archive.

Dickens, Charles, *The Pickwick Papers* (London: Chapman and Hall, 1836).

Disraeli, Benjamin, *Sybil* (London: Henry Colbourn, 1845. Penguin edn 1985).

Edgeworth, Maria, 'The Absentee' in *Tales of Fashionable Life*, series 2 (London: J. Johnson, 1812).

Eliot, George, *Armgart* (London and Edinburgh: William Blackwood and Sons, 1878, Cabinet edn). Digitised by the George Eliot Archive, ed. Beverley Park Rilett. http://GeorgeEliotArchive.org [accessed 23 January 2023].

Fink, G.W., *Musikalische 88 Kompositionslehre (Theory of musical composition)* (Leipzig: G.F. Peters, 1847).

Hartley, Cecil B., *The Gentleman's Book of Etiquette and Manual of Politeness* (Boston, MA: G.W. Cottrell, 1873). Digitised by the Online Books Page.

'Historical sketch of the rise and progress of scene-painting in England', *Library of the Fine Arts, or, Repertory of Painting, Sculpture, Architecture and Engraving*, 4 vols (London: Arnold, 1831), vol. 1.

Hogarth, George, *Musical history, biography, and criticism: being a general survey of music, from the earliest period to the present time* (London: J.W. Parker, 1835).

Hogarth, George, *Musical history, biography, and criticism*, 2 vols (New York: Da Capo Press, 1838).

Hogarth, George, *Memoirs of the Opera in Italy, France, Germany and England*, 2nd edn, 2 vols (London, 1851).

Hopwood, Henry V., *Living Pictures: Their History, Photoduplication, and Practical Working* (London: The Optician and Photographic Trades Review, 1899).

Hunt, Leigh, 'Thoughts on music', *The Feast of the Poets*, 2nd edn (London: Gale and Fenner, 1815). Digitised by the Online Books Page.

Illustrated London News, The, 20 July 1861, bound edn, vol. 39.

Kelly, Michael, *Solo Recital, The Reminiscences of Michael Kelly* (London, 1826, reprinted by The Folio Society, 1972).

Kiesewetter, Raphael G., *Geschichte der europäisch-abendländischen oder unserer heutigen Musik*, XVII 'Die Epoche Beethoven und Rossini' (History of European-Occidental or our contemporary music) (Leipzig: 1834), *Die Musik des 19. Jahrhunderts* (Laaber: Laaber, 1980. *Nineteenth-Century Music*, trans. J. Bradford Robinson (Berkeley: University of California Press, 1989).

Kilvert, Charles, *Kilvert's Diary 1870–1879*, ed. William Plomer (London: Jonathan Cape, 1944).

Love, James, *Scottish Church Music, its Composers and Sources* (London and Edinburgh: Blackwood and Sons, 1891).

Lumley, Benjamin, *Reminiscences of the Opera* (London: Hurst and Blackett, 1864).

Mackenzie Bacon, Richard, *Elements of Vocal Science* (London, 1824).

Minutes of Evidence, Select Committee on the Copyright Acts, 1818, Paper No. 280, vol. IX, p. 257. 1812–1813, p. 17.

Mlle Duval's *Tableaux Vivants*, programme, handbill, 1849, National Fairground Archive, University of Sheffield.

Richard, Earl of Mount Edgcumbe, *Musical Reminiscences of the Earl of Mount Edgcumbe: Containing an account of the Italian Opera in England from 1773 to 1834* (London, 1834). Digitised by the Internet Archive.

National Library of Wales:

NLW MS 6599C, letters to J.M. Traherne 1836–1856.

NLW MS 11977D and NLW MS 11973D, J.M. Traherne music book and diaries.

NLW MSS 11980–11981E, autograph albums.

Oulibicheff, Alexandre (Alexander Dmitryevich Ulybyshev), *Nouvelle biographie de Mozart* (Dresden, 1843).

Peake, Richard Brinsley, 'Memoirs of the Colman family including their correspondence with the most distinguished personages of their time', *Edinburgh Review*, vol. 72 (London, 1841). Digitised by the Internet Archive.

Penrice and Margam accounts, Penrice and Margam MS 9240 to 9280. National Library of Wales.

Pyne, William Henry as 'Ephraim Hardcastle', *Wine and Walnuts; or, After Dinner Chit-Chat*, (London, 1823).

Register of the Lord Chamberlain's Plays, vols I, II and III (Supplementary Papers, 1840–1873), ADD MSS 42865–43038 and ADD MSS 53702–53708, British Library.

[Rossini, Gioacchino], *Pietro L'Eremita or Peter the Hermit, A Serious Opera in Three Acts, Adapted to the Music of 'Mosi' Composed by Rossini* (London: Printed for John Ebers, 1822).

Sainsbury, John S., *A Dictionary of Musicians, from the Earliest Ages to the Present Time*, 2 vols (London: Sainsbury & Co., 1824). Digitised by the Internet Archive.

Sutherland Edwards, Henry, *Rossini and His School* (The Great Musicians Series, London 1881).

Stanford, Charles Villers, 'Some aspects of musical criticism in England', *Fortnightly Review*, vol. 55 no. 330 (June 1894).

Theatre, The, 1 November 1890, vol. XVI (London: Eglinton and Co, 1890).

Times-Picayune, Saturday, 24 August 1878 (New Orleans).

Trollope, Antony, *Hunting Sketches* (London: Chapman and Hall, 1865).

Turner, Sharon, 'Reasons for a modification of the Act of Anne, respecting the delivery of books and copyright' (London: Nichols and Son and Bentley, 1813).

Twentieth century

Beardsley, Monroe C., *Aesthetics: Problems in the Philosophy of Criticism* (New York: Harcourt, Brace and World, Inc., 1958).

Sonny Bono Copyright Term Extension Act (1998), www.copyright.gov, US Copyright Office.

'Copyright (Musical works) Bill'. Entry for Frank Gray, MP for Oxford. House of Commons Debate, 12 February 1924, *Hansard*, vol. 169. Order for Second Reading.

'Copyright (Musical works) Bill'. Entry for James Burney, MP for Bootle, in House of Commons Debate, 12 February 1924, *Hansard*, vol. 169.

Corder, Frederick, *The Works of Sir Henry Bishop* (London, 1918).

Council of Europe, Council Directive 93/98/EEC (29 October 1993).

Council of Europe, Council Directive 2001/29/EC (the InfoSoc Directive, 22 May 2001).

Davey, Peter, *The Theatrical History of Wales 1748–1857* (typewritten manuscript, 1945, Swansea University Library).

Davison, Henry, *Music during the Victorian Era. From Mendelssohn to Wagner: Memoirs of J.W. Davison* (London: William Reeves, 1912).

Film Index, The, 7 January 1911 (New York: Films Publishing Company).

Galloway, William, *The Operatic Problem* (London, 1902).

Klein, Hermann, *Thirty Years of Musical Life in London, 1870–1900* (New York: Century, 1903).

Lindsay, W.M. (ed.), *Isidori Hispalensis episcopi Etymologiarum sive Originum*, libri XX, 2 vols, Oxford Classical Texts (Oxford: Clarendon Press, 1911).

Lydgate, John, 'The minor poems of Lydgate, part I', ed. Henry Noble MacCracken, Early English Text Society, Extra Series 107 (Oxford University Press, 1911).

Newton, Robert, *Peter Anthony Motteux 1663–1718* (Oxford: Blackwells, 1933).

d'Osmond, Adèle, *Memoirs of the Comtesse de Boigne, 1781–1814*, ed. Charles Nicoullaud (New York: Charles Scribner's, 1907).

Powell, G. Rennee, *The Bristol Stage: Its Story* (Bristol: Bristol Printing and Publishing Co. Ltd, 1919). Digitised by the Internet Archive.

Sonneck, O.J., 'Ciampi's *Bertoldo, Bertoldino e Cacasenno* and Favart's *Ninette à la Cour*: a contribution to the history of pasticcio', *Miscellaneous Studies in the History of Music* (New York: Macmillan, 1921).

Sonneck, Oscar J., *Miscellaneous Studies in the History of Music* (New York: Macmillan, 1921).

Watson Mill: Charles Watson Mill Collection, GB 150 MILL, Special Collections, Cadbury Research Library, University of Birmingham.

Journalism

This was sourced through Gale Primary Sources who provided online facsimiles of the following national or metropolitan newspapers:

Ackerman's Repository
The Athenaeum
La Belle Assemblée
Bell's Life
The Court Journal
The Craftsman
Daily Universal Register
The Examiner
The Foreign Quarterly Review
The Gallery of Fashion

The Gentleman's Magazine
The Guardian (eighteenth-century)
John Bull
The Ladies Magazine
The Monthly Magazine
The Morning Chronicle
Morning Herald
The New York Herald
The Morning Post
Pall Mall Gazette
Quarterly Review
The Saturday Review
The Spectator
The Tatler
The Times
The Times-Picayune (New Orleans)
The World

The same service provided online access to the following regional newspapers:

Birmingham Daily Post
The Bristol Journal
The Bristol Mercury
The Caledonian Mercury
The Cambrian
The Cardiff and Merthyr Guardian
The Cardiff Times
The Irish Citizen
Lancaster Gazetteer
Reynolds's Newspaper
The South Wales Daily News.

The Burney Collection of Newspapers provided online access to the following music journals:

The Musical Examiner
The Musical World
The Harmonicon
The Quarterly Musical Magazine and Review

Gale Primary Sources, and the newspapers themselves, were used to source online copies of twentieth- and twenty-first-century opera reviews and debates about copyright from the following:

The Daily Mirror
The Daily Telegraph
The Financial Times

The Gramophone
The Guardian
The New York Times
What's On Stage
Wired
Woman Around Town

Secondary sources

Abate, Corinne S., *Privacy, Domesticity, and Women in Early Modern England* (Aldershot: Ashgate, 2003).

Abbate, Carolyn, 'Wagner, "On Modulation", and *Tristan*', *Cambridge Opera Journal*, (1989).

Abbate, Carolyn and Roger Parker, *A History of Opera: The Last Four Hundred Years*, (London: Allen Lane, 2012).

Ackroyd, Peter, *Shakespeare: the Biography* (London: Chatto & Windus, 2005).

Adkins, Cecil, *Early Musical Masterworks* (Chapel Hill: University of North Carolina, 1977).

Adorno, Theodor W., *Towards a Theory of Musical Reproduction*, ed. Henri Lonitz, trans. Wieland Hoban (Cambridge: Polity Press, 2006).

Adshead, David, 'The architectural evolution of picture and sculpture galleries in British country houses', *Art & the Country House*, ed. Martin Postle (New Haven, CT: Paul Mellon Centre digital publications, 2020).

d'Alembert, 'De la liberté de la musique', reprinted in *La querelle des bouffons*, ed. Denise Launay, 3 vols (Geneva: Minkoff, 1973), p. 120.

Altman, Rick, ed., *Sound Theory, Sound Practice*, vol. 2 (Abingdon: Routledge, 1992).

André, Naomi, *Voicing Gender: Castrati, Travesti, and the Second Woman in Early-Nineteenth-Century Italian Opera* (Bloomington, IN: Indiana University Press, 2006).

André, Naomi Adele, 'Azucena, Eboli and Amneris: Verdi's writing for women's lower voices' (unpublished doctoral thesis, Cambridge, MA: Harvard University, 1996).

Andrews, John K., 'The historical context of Handel's *Semele*' (unpublished doctoral thesis, Queen's College, Cambridge, 2007).

d'Angour, Armand, 'The sound of mousike: reflections on aural change in ancient Greece', *Debating the Athenian Cultural Revolution*, ed. R. Osborne (Cambridge: Cambridge University Press, 2007).

d'Angour, Armand, 'How did ancient Greek music sound?' BBC website, 2013. https://www.bbc.co.uk/news/business-24611454 [accessed 21 May 2018].

d'Angour, Armand, 'Sense and sensation in music', *Companion to Ancient Aesthetics*, ed. Pierre Destrée and Penelope Murray (Oxford: Wiley Blackwell, 2015).

Appia, Adolphe, *L'oeuvre d'Art Vivant* (Geneva and Paris: Edition Atar, 1921).

d'Arcy Wood, Gillen, 'Cockney Mozart: the Hunt circle, the King's Theatre, and *Don Giovanni*', *Studies in Romanticism*, vol. 44 (Boston, MA: University of Boston, 2005).

Armiger, Martin, 'The movie, the melody and you: how pop music connects film narrative to its audience', *Screen Sound: The Australasian Journal of Soundtrack Studies*, no. 3 (2012).

Aspden, Suzanne, 'An infinity of factions: opera in eighteenth-century Britain and the undoing of society', *Cambridge Opera Journal*, vol. 9 (Cambridge: Cambridge University Press, 1997).

Aspden, Suzanne, 'Opera and national identity', *The Cambridge Companion to Opera Studies*, ed. Nicholas Till (Cambridge: Cambridge University Press, 2012).

Astington, John, *Actors and Acting in Shakespeare's Time: The Art of Stage Playing* (Cambridge: Cambridge University Press, 2010).

Ayres, Michelle Elizabeth, 'Crossover genres, syncretic form: understanding Mozart's concert aria "Ch'io mi scordi di te", K. 505, as a link between piano concerto and opera' (unpublished doctoral thesis, University of North Carolina, 2018).

Banditelli, Gloria, performance of *Euridice*, composed by Jacopo Peri and Giulio Caccini, libretto by Ottavio Rinuccini, conducted by Riccado Farolfi, posted online at YouTube by 'La Pellegina 1589' in February 2015. https://youtu.be/wNIv0gQMLQA [accessed 13 September 2016].

Barker, Kathleen, *The Theatre Royal Bristol, Decline and Rebirth 1834–1943* (the Bristol branch of The Historical Association, Bristol University, 1966).

Barnett, Dene, *The Art of Gesture: The Practices and Principles of 18th Century Acting* (Heidelberg: Carl Winter Universitätsverlag, 1987).

Bartig, Kevin, *Sergei Prokofiev's Alexander Nevsky* (Oxford: Oxford University Press, 2017).

Barush, Kathryn R., 'Painting the scene', *The Oxford Handbook of Georgian Theatre 1732–1832*, ed. Julia Swindells and David Francis Taylor (Oxford: Oxford University Press, 2014).

Baugh, Christopher, 'Stage design from Loutherbourg to Poel', *The Cambridge History of British Theatre*, vol. 2 *1660–1895* (Cambridge: Cambridge University Press, 2004).

Baugh, Christopher, 'Philippe de Loutherbourg: technology-driven entertainment and spectacle in the late eighteenth century', *Huntington Library Quarterly*, vol. 70 no. 2 (Philadelphia: University of Pennsylvania Press, 2007).

Baumann, Gerd, ed., *The Written Word: Literacy in Transition* (Oxford: Clarendon Press, 1986).

Bautz, Annika, 'The "universal favourite": Daniel Terry's *Guy Mannering; or, The Gipsey's Prophecy* (1816)', *The Yearbook of English Studies*, vol. 47, *Walter Scott: New Interpretations* (University of Plymouth, 2017).

Bennett, Alana, '"Performance of excerpt from *Aucassin et Nicolette*", medievalism in Australian cultural memory' (honours dissertation, Medieval and Early Modern Studies, University of Western Australia, 2012). http://www.youtube.com/watch?v=Dcqd9j3EhZY&feature=relmfu [accessed 10 January 2019].

Bentley, L. and M. Kretschmer (eds), *Primary Sources on Copyright (1450–1900)* (Cambridge: Cambridge University Press, 2008).

Bermingham, Ann, 'Technologies of illusion: De Loutherbourg's Eidophusikon in eighteenth-century London', *Art History*, vol. 39 no. 2 (London: Association of Art Historians, 2016).

Bernstein, Jane, ed., *Women's Voices across Musical Worlds* (Boston, MA: Northeastern University Press, 2004).

Bettelheim, Bruno, *The Uses of Enchantment: The Meaning and Importance of Fairy Tales* (New York: Vintage Books, 2010).

Betzwieser, Thomas, 'The world of pasticcio: reflections on pre-existing text and music', *Operatic Pasticcios in 18th-Century Europe: Contexts, Materials and Aesthetics*, ed. Berthold Over and Gesa zur Nieden (Bielefeld: transcript Verlag, 2021).

Bini, Annalisa, '"Accidente curioso a proposito di *Un curioso accidente*", un contestato pasticcio rossiniano (Parigi, 1859)', *Ottocento e oltre. Scritti in onore di Raoul Meloncelli*, ed. Francesco Izzo and Johannes Streicher (Rome, 1993), pp. 339–353.

Bledsoe, Robert, 'Dickens and opera', *Dickens Studies Annual*, vol. 18 (Santa Cruz, CA: The Dickens Project, 1989).

Blumenthal, Harold, 'The Covent Garden centenary', *The Musical Times*, May 1958.

Booth, Alison, 'Men and women of the time: Victorian prosopographies', *Life Writing and Victorian Culture*, ed. David Amigoni (Farnham: Ashgate, 2006).

Borio, Gianmario, Giovanni Giuriati, Alessandro Cecchi and Marco Lutzu (eds), *Investigating Musical Performance: Theoretical Models and Intersections* (Abingdon: Routledge, 2020).

Brace, Geoffrey, 'Bishop, Henry Rowley', *Die Musik in Geschichte und Gegenwart* (Kassel: Bärenreiter, 1999), vol. 2.

Bradley, David, *From Text to Performance in the Elizabethan Theatre: Preparing the Play for the Stage* (Cambridge: Cambridge University Press, 1992).

Bratt, Suzanne Anita, 'Obligato/obligé: a musical etymology' (unpublished doctoral thesis, University of Pennsylvania, 2017).

Brice Heath, Shirley, 'What no bedtime story means, narrative skills at home and school', *Language in Society*, vol. 11 no. 1 (Cambridge: Cambridge University Press, 1982).

Brice Heath, Shirley, 'Protean shapes in literacy events: ever-shifting oral and literate traditions', *Perspectives on Literacy*, ed. Eugene R. Kintgen, Barry M. Kroll and Mike Rose (Carbondale, IL: Southern Illinois University Press, 1988).

Brooks, C.W., 'Apprenticeship, social mobility and the middling sort, 1550–1800' in *The Middling Sort of People: Culture, Society and Politics in England, 1550–1800*, ed. Jonathan Barry and C.W. Brooks (Basingstoke: Macmillan, 1994).

Brown, Jennifer Williams, 'On the road with the "suitcase aria": the transmission of borrowed arias in late seventeenth-century Italian opera revivals', *Journal of Musicological Research*, vol. 5 (Abingdon: Taylor and Francis, 1995)

Bryant, Julius, 'Eccentric pioneers? Patrons of modern sculpture for Britain *c.*1790', *Burning Bright: Essays in Honour of David Bindman*, ed. Diana Dethloff, Caroline Elam, Tessa Murdoch and Kim Sloan (London: University College London Press, 2015).

Budzinska-Bennett, Agnieszka, 'Musica fatta spirituale. Aquilino Coppini's contrafacta of Monteverdi's *Fifth Book of Madrigals*', *Interdisciplinary Studies in Musicology*, (Poznań: PTPN and Wydawnictwo Naukowe UAM, 2012).

Burden, Michael, '"Gillimaufrey" at Covent Garden: Purcell's *The Fairy-Queen* in 1946', *Early Music*, vol. 23, no. 2 (Oxford: Oxford University Press, 1995).

Burden, Michael, 'The lure of aria, process and spectacle: opera in 18th-century London', *The Cambridge History of Eighteenth-Century Music*, ed. Simon Keefe (Cambridge: Cambridge University Press, 2009).

Burden, Michael, 'When Giulio Cesare was not Handel's *Giulio Cesare*; the opera on the London stage in 1787', *Revue Musicorum*, vol. 14 no. 1 (St Julien de Genevois: Laurine Quetin, 2014).

Burden, Michael, 'The writing and staging of Georgian Romantic opera', *The Oxford Handbook of Georgian Theatre 1737–1832*, ed. Julia Swindells and David Francis Taylor (Oxford: Oxford University Press, 2014).

Burke, Peter, 'Oral culture and print culture in Renaissance Italy', *ARV: Nordic Yearbook of Folklore*, vol. 54 (Uppsala: Royal Gustavus Adolphus Academy, 1998).

Burkholder, J. Peter, 'The uses of existing music: musical borrowing as a field', *Notes*, Second Series, vol. 50 no. 3 (Middleton, WI: Music Library Association, March 1994).

Burroughs, Catherine, 'The stages of closet drama', *The Oxford Handbook of Georgian Theatre 1737–1832*, ed. Julia Swindells and David Francis Taylor (Oxford: Oxford University Press, 2014).

Burrows, Donald, 'Bringing Europe to Britain: Handel's first decade in London', *Handel-Jarbuch*, vol. 56 (Leipzig: Deutscher Verlag für Musik, 2010).

Burrows, Donald and Rosemary Dunhill, *Music and Theatre in Handel's World: The Family Papers of James Harris 1732–1780* (Oxford: Oxford University Press, 2002).

Bushaway, Bob, *By Rite: Custom, Ceremony and Community in England, 1700–1880* (London: Junction Books, 1982), pp. 5–8.

Butler, Judith, 'Performative acts and gender constitution: an essay in phenomenology and feminist theory', *Theatre Journal*, vol. 40 no. 4 (Baltimore, MD: Johns Hopkins University Press, 1988).

Butler, Judith, *Gender Trouble* (New York: Routledge, 1990, 2008 edn).

Butler, Judith, *Notes Toward a Performative Theory of Assembly* (Cambridge, MA: Harvard University Press, 2015).

Cage, E. Claire, 'The sartorial self: neoclassical fashion and gender identity in France, 1797–1804', *Eighteenth-Century Studies*, vol. 42 no. 2 (Baltimore, MD: Johns Hopkins University Press, 2009).

Camlot, Jason, *Style and the Nineteenth-Century British Critic: Sincere Mannerisms* (London: Ashgate, 2008).

Cannadine, David, *The Decline of the British Aristocracy* (New Haven, CT: Yale University Press, 1990).

Capp, Bernard, *England's Culture Wars: Puritan Reformation and its Enemies in the Interregnum, 1649–1660* (Oxford: Oxford University Press, 2012).

Car Meyer, Donald, 'The NBC Symphony Orchestra' (doctoral thesis, University of California, 1994).

Carlson, Marvin, 'Theorizing the performative event', *The Oxford Handbook of Georgian Theatre 1737–1832*, ed. Julia Swindells and David Francis Taylor (Oxford: Oxford University Press, 2014).

Carr, Raymond, *English Fox Hunting* (London: Weidenfeld and Nicolson, 1976).

Cavallo, Jo Ann, '*L' Orlando Innamorato*: un romanzo per la corte Ferrarese', *L'Enigma Boiardo*, ed. Silvano Vinceti (Rome: Armando Press, 2003).

Celati, Gianni, 'Le posizione narrative rispetto all'altro', *Cahiers de littérature et civilisation Romanes*, 36 vols (Caen: University of Caen Press, 1996), vol. 3.

Chamberlain, M., 'Theodore Mansel Talbot and his times', 5th Annual Lecture to the Friends of Margam Abbey. *Annual Report*, 1986. National Library of Wales, NLW C.322, Vivian Papers.

Chapman, Colin R., *Ecclesiastical Courts, their Officials and their Records* (London: The King's England Press, 1992).

Charles-Edwards, Gifford and Helen McKee, 'Lost voices from Anglo-Saxon Lichfield', *Anglo-Saxon England*, vol. 37 (Cambridge: Cambridge University Press, 2008).

Charles-Edwards, Thomas, *Wales and the Britons 350–1064* (Oxford: Oxford University Press, 2013).

Chowrimootoo, Christopher, *Middlebrow Modernism: Britten's Operas and the Great Divide* (Berkeley: University of California Press, 2018).

Chowrimootoo, Christopher and Kate Guthrie, 'Colloquy: musicology and the middlebrow', *Journal of the American Musicological Society*, vol. 73 no. 2 (Berkeley: University of California Press, 2020).

Chrissochoidis, Ilias, 'Handel at a crossroads: his 1737–1738 and 1738–1739 seasons re-examined', *Music and Letters*, vol. 90 no 4 (Oxford: Oxford University Press, 2009).

Clanchy, M.T., 'Hearing and seeing *and* trusting writing', *Perspectives on Literacy*, ed. Eugene R. Kintgen, Barry M. Kroll and Mike Rose (Carbondale, IL: Southern Illinois University Press, 1988).

Clark, Andrew, 'Handel: *Giove in Argo*, hidden Handel', *The Financial Times*, 22 March 2013.

Clark, Peter, 'The ownership of books in England, 1560–1640: the example of some Kentish townsfolk', *Schooling and Society*, ed. Laurence Stone (Baltimore, MD: Baltimore University Press, 1976).

Clark de Simone, Alison, 'The myth of the diva: female opera singers and collaborative performance in early eighteenth-century London' (unpublished doctoral dissertation, University of Michigan, 2013).

Clements, Andrew, review of CD of performances at the Berlin Staatsoper, June 2012, by the Akademie für Alte Musik (*The Guardian*, 20 February 2015).

Cloonan, Martin, 'Negotiating needletime: the Musicians' Union, the BBC and the record companies, c.1920–1990', *Social History*, vol. 41, no. 4 (Abingdon: Taylor and Francis, 2016).

Coates, Clive, *The Wines of Bordeaux* (Berkeley: University of California Press, 2004).

Colley, Linda, *Britons: Forging the Nation, 1707–1837* (New Haven, CT: Yale University Press, 1992).

Collins, Eleanor C., 'Repertory and riot: the relocation of plays from the Red Bull to the Cockpit stage', *Early Theatre*, vol. 13 (Toronto: Records of Early English Drama, 2010).

Congleton, Robert J. and Sharon Q. Yang, 'A comparative study of academic digital copyright in the United States and Europe', *Research and Advanced Technology for Digital Libraries*, ed. Stefan Gradmann, Francesca Borri, Carlo Meghini and Heiko Schultz (Berlin: Springer-Verlag, 2011).

Connon, Derek, *Anthologie de pièces du Théâtre de la foire*, ed. Derek Connon and George Evans (Egham: Runnymede Books, 1996).

Connon, Derek, *Identity and Transformation in the Plays of Alexis Piron* (London: Legenda, 2007).

Cook, Nicholas, 'The other Beethoven: heroism, the canon and the works of 1813–1814', *19th-Century Music*, vol. 27 no. 1 (Berkeley: University of California, 2003).

Cordery, Gareth, 'Drink in *David Copperfield*', *Redefining the Modern, Essays on Literature and Society in Honor of Joseph Wiesenfarth*, ed. William Baker and Ira Nadel (London: Rosemount Publishing, 2004).

Cornish, Graham P., *Copyright: Interpreting the Law for Libraries, Archives and Information Services* (London: Facet Publishing, 2019).

Corns, Thomas N., 'The early lives of John Milton', *Writing Lives: Biography and Textuality, Identity and Representation in Early Modern England*, ed. Kevin Sharpe and Steven N. Zwicker (Oxford: Oxford University Press, 2008).

Coulter, Cathy, Charles Michael and Leslie Poynor, 'Storytelling as pedagogy: an unexpected outcome of narrative inquiry', *Curriculum Inquiry*, vol. 37 no. 2 (Abingdon: Routledge, 2007).

Cowgill, Rachel, '"Wise men from the East": Mozart operas and their advocates in early nineteenth century London', *Music and British Culture, 1785–1914; Essays in Honour of Cyril Ehrlich*, ed. Christina Bashford and Leanne Langley (Oxford: Oxford University Press, 2000).

Cowgill, Rachel, 'Mozart productions and the emergence of the *Werktreue* at London's Italian Opera House, 1780–1830', *Operatic Migrations: Transforming Works and Crossing Boundaries*, ed. Roberta Montemorra Marvin and Downing A. Thomas (Aldershot: Ashgate Press, 2006).

Cowgill, Rachel, '"Attitudes with a shawl": femininity, performance, and spectatorship at the Italian Opera in early nineteenth-century London', *The Arts of the Prima Donna in the Long Nineteenth Century*, ed. Rachel Cowgill and Hilary Poriss (Oxford: Oxford University Press, 2012).

Creese, David, *The Monochord in Ancient Greek Harmonic Science* (Cambridge: Cambridge University Press, 2010).

Creese, David, Eight-string tetrachord, YouTube, uploaded by Babette Babich, 2012. https://www.youtube.com/watch?v=ZV6QDQOw4S4 [accessed 21 May 2018].

Cressy, David, 'Literacy in seventeenth-century England: more evidence', *The Journal of Interdisciplinary History*, vol. 8 no. 1 (Cambridge, MA: The MIT Press, 1977).

Cressy, David, *Literacy and the Social Order: Reading and Writing in Tudor and Stuart England* (Cambridge: Cambridge University Press, 1980).

Cressy, David, 'Literacy in context: meaning and measurement in early modern England', *Consumption and the World of Goods*, ed. John Brewer and Roy Porter (London: Routledge, 1993).

Cross, E., 'Vivaldi and the pasticcio: text and music in *Il Bajazet, ossia la morte di Tamerlano*', *Con Che Soavità: Studies in Italian Opera, Song, and Dance*, ed. I. Fenlon and T. Carter (Oxford: Oxford University Press, 1995).

Crowe, Robert, 'Giambattista Velluti in London (1825–1829): literary constructions of the last operatic castrato' (unpublished doctoral thesis, Boston University, 2017).

Crowe, Robert, '"He was unable to set aside the effeminate, and so was forgotten": masculinity, its fears, and the uses of falsetto in the early nineteenth century', *19th-Century Music*, vol 3. No 1. (Berkeley: University of California Press, 2019).

Cruz, Gabriela, *Grand Illusion: Phantasmagoria in Nineteenth Century Opera* (Oxford: Oxford University Press, 2020).

Cullen, Frank, Florence Hackman and Donald McNeilly, *Vaudeville Old and New: an Encyclopedia of Variety Performances in America* (New York: Routledge, 2007), vol. 1.

Cunningham, Robert Newton, *Peter Anthony Motteux 1663–1718* (Oxford: Blackwells, 1933).

Curtis, Alan, 'La Poppea impasticciata or who wrote the music to *L'Incoronazione*, 1643', *Journal of the American Musicological Society* (Berkeley: University of California Press, 1989), vol. 42.

Curtis Petty, Frederick, *Italian Opera in London 1760–1800* (Ann Arbor, MI: UMI Research Press, 1980).

Dahlhaus, Carl, *Analyse und Werturteil* (Musikpädagogik Band 8, 1970), trans. Siegmund Levarie, *Analysis and Value Judgement* (New York: Pendragon Press, 1983).

Dahlhaus, Carl, *Die Musik des 19. Jahrhunderts* (Laaber: Laaber, 1980), trans. J. Bradford Robinson, *Nineteenth- Century Music* (Berkeley: University of California Press, 1989).

Davies, James Q., 'Dancing the symphonic: Beethoven-Bochsa's Symphonie Pastorale', *19th-Century Music*, vol. 27 (Berkeley: University of California Press, 2003).

Davies, James Q., *Romantic Anatomies of Performance* (Berkeley: University of California Press, 2014).

Davies, James Q., 'On being moved/against objectivity', *Special Forum: Quirk Historicism*, in *Representations: Interdisciplinarity in the 21st Century*, vol. 132 (Berkeley: University of California Press, 2015).

Davies, Sioned, 'Written text as performance: the implications for Middle Welsh prose narratives', *Medieval Celtic Societies*, ed. Huw Pryce, Cambridge Studies in Medieval Literature (Cambridge: Cambridge University Press, 1998).

Davies, Sioned, 'Performing *Culhwch ac Olwen*', *Arthurian Literature XXI: Celtic Arthurian Material*, ed. Ceridwen Lloyd-Morgan (Cambridge: D.S. Brewer, 2004).

Dean, Winton, *Handel and the Opera Seria* (Berkeley: University of California Press, 1969).

Dean, Winton, *Handel's Operas 1726–1741* (Woodbridge, Suffolk: Boydell Press, 2006).

Dean, Winton, 'Jupiter in Argos', *Handel Studies: A Gedenkschrift for Howard Serwer*, ed. Richard G. King (New York: Hillsdale New York, 2009).

Dean, Winton and John Merrill Knapp, *Handel's Operas, 1704–1726* (Woodbridge, Suffolk: Boydell Press, 1987).

Deazley, Ronan, *Rethinking Copyright: History, Theory, Language* (London: Edward Elgar Publishing, 2006).

Deazley, Ronan, 'Commentary on Copyright Act 1814', *Primary Sources on Copyright (1450–1900)*, ed. L. Bently and M. Kretschmer (Cambridge: Cambridge University Press, 2008).

Delage, Roger, *Emmanuel Chabrier* (Paris: Fayard, 1999).

Dent, Edward J., *Opera* (London: Penguin, 1940; reprinted Greenwood Press, 1978).

Dent, E.J., transcript of a lecture for the Royal Musical Society, 'Italian opera in London' by Professor E.J. Dent, *Proceedings of the Royal Musical Association, 1944–1945*, 71st session (1945; Taylor & Francis on behalf of the RMS digitised by JSTOR).

Diderikson, Gabriella and Matthew Ringel, 'Frederick Gye and "the dreadful business of opera management"', *19th-Century Music*, vol. 19 no. 1 (Berkeley: University of California Press, 1995).

Diderikson, Gabriella, 'Repertory and rivalry: opera at the second Covent Garden Theatre, 1830 to 1856' (doctoral thesis, King's College, University of London, 1997).

Dingley, James, *Nationalism, Social Theory and Durkheim* (London: Palgrave Macmillan, 2008).

Dingley, James, *Durkheim and National Identity in Ireland* (London: Palgrave Macmillan, 2015).

Donnelan, Victoria, 'The English prize: the capture of the *Westmoreland*', exhibition catalogue (Oxford: Ashmolean Museum, Oxford, 2018). DOI: http://dx.doi.org/10.5334/pia.419 [accessed 30 November 2018].

Duffy, Maureen, *Henry Purcell* (London: Fourth Estate, 1994).

Duranti, Alessandro, *Linguistic Anthropology* (New York: Cambridge University Press, 1997).

Eisen, Cliff, '"In Mozart's words": perspectives on a new, online edition of the Mozart family letters from Italy, 1770–1773', *Fontes Artis Musicae*, vol. 58 (Copenhagen: International Association of Music Libraries, 2011).

Ellis, Charles S., 'Documentation for paintings by Fra Bartholomeo in the Salviati Collection in Florence', *Mitteilungen des Kunsthistorischen Institutes in Florenz*, vol. 54. (Florence: Max Planck Institute, 2008).

Emmerson, George S., 'The hornpipe', *Folk Music Journal*, vol. 2 no. 1 (London: English Folk Dance and Song Society, 1970).

Enfield, N.J., 'Language as shaped by social interaction', *Behavioural and Brain Sciences*, vol. 31 no. 5 (Cambridge: Cambridge University Press, 2008).

Englund, Axel, *Deviant Opera: Sex, Power and Perversion on Stage* (Berkeley: University of California Press, 2020).

Evans, Robert and Mary Ann Roberts (Bragod), Performance of a poem by Gruffydd ap Dafydd ap Howell from the early sixteenth century accompanied by crwth, with music from 'Kaniad y Gwynn Bibydd' in the Robert ap Huw Manuscript. http://www.bragod.com/bragodvideo.html [accessed 23 January 2018].

Everist, Mark, 'The refrain cento: myth or motet?', *Journal of the Royal Musical Association*, vol. 114 no. 2 (Cambridge: Cambridge University Press, 1989).

Ewing, Thomas, *The Correspondence of John Hughes and His Friends* (Dublin: Thomas Ewing, 1773, reprinted in paperback by Cengage Gale, Michigan, 2010).

Fabbri, Paolo, *Monteverdi* (Turin, 1985, trans. Tim Carter 1994, reprinted Cambridge University Press, 2018).

Falck, Robert and Martin Picker, 'Contrafactum', *Grove Dictionary Online*, 20 January 2001. https://doi.org/10.1093/9781561592630.article.06361 [accessed 19 August 2020].

Farahat, Martha, 'On the staging of madrigal comedies', *Early Music History*, vol. 10 (Cambridge: Cambridge University Press, 1991).

Farrell, Thomas J. and Paul Soukup, *Walter J. Ong, Faith and Contexts: Additional studies and essays, 1947–1996*, vol. 4 (Chisinau, Moldova: Scholar's Press, 1999).

Farrell, Thomas J. and Paul Soukup, *An Ong Reader: Challenges for further inquiry* (Cresskill, NJ: Hampton Press, 2002).

Fawcett, Trevor, 'Plane surfaces and solid bodies: reproducing three-dimensional art in the nineteenth century', *Visual Resources*, vol. 4 no. 1 (London: Routledge, 1987).

Feldman, Martha, *Opera and Sovereignty: Transforming Myths in Eighteenth-Century Italy* (Chicago: University of Chicago Press, 2007).

Fenner, Theodore, *Opera in London; Views of the Press* (London: SIU Press, 1994).

Finocchiaro, Francesco, 'Operatic works in silent cinema: toward a translational theory of film adaptations', *Music and the Moving Image*, vol. 13 no. 3 (Carbondale, IL: University of Illinois Press, 2020).

Firth, C.H., 'Sir William Davenant and the revival of the drama during the Protectorate', *English Historical Review*, vol. 18 no. 70 (Oxford: Oxford University Press, 1903).

Fletcher, Alan J., *Drama, Performance and Polity in Pre-Cromwellian Ireland* (Cork: Cork University Press, 2000).

Foucault, Michel, *The History of Sexuality*, trans. Robert Hurley, 2 vols (London: Penguin Books, 1998), vol. I, *The Will to Knowledge*.

Fox, Adam, *Oral and Literate Culture in England, 1500–1700* (Oxford: Clarendon Press, 2000).

Fraser, Antonia, *Cromwell, Our Chief of Men* (London: Phoenix Press, reprinted 1997).

Fuhrmann, Christina, *Foreign Opera at the London Playhouses: From Mozart to Bellini* (Cambridge: Cambridge University Press, 2015).

Furján, Helene, *Glorious Visions: John Soane's Spectacular Theater* (Abingdon: Routledge, 2011).

Gabrielian, Tanya, 'Rachmaninoff and the flexibility of the score: issues regarding performance practice' (doctoral thesis, City University of New York, 2018).

Gallo, F. Albero, *Music in the Castle: Troubadours, Books and Orators in Italian Courts of the Thirteenth, Fourteenth, and Fifteenth Centuries*, trans. Anna Herklotz (Chicago: University of Chicago Press, 1995).

Gardiner, Sir John Eliot, 'Gluck, *Orphée et Eurydice*', *The Guardian*, 12 September 2015 https://www.theguardian.com/music/2015/sep/12/john-eliot-gardiner-gluck-orphee-et-eurydice-opera [accessed 12 August 2018].

Garnham, Alison, *Hans Keller and the BBC: the musical conscience of British broadcasting, 1959–79* (Farnham: Gower Publishing Ltd, 2003).

Geraci, Mauro, 'The poetic-musical reflection of Sicilian storytellers', *Le letterature popolari. Prospettive di ricerca e nuovi orizzonti teorico-metodologici*, ed. D. Scafoglio, vol. 60 s. 4 (Naples: Edizione scientifiche Italiane, 2002).

Gibson, Elizabeth, 'Owen Swiney and the Italian opera in London', *The Musical Times*, vol. 125 no. 1692 (London: Musical Times Publications, 1984).

Gibson, Elizabeth, 'Italian opera in London, 1750–1775', *Early Music*, vol. 18 (Oxford: Oxford University Press, 1990).

Gilder, Eric and Mervyn Hagger, 'Antinomic interpretations of self as defined by moral rights and copyrights in British tradition, spirit and feelings, and the United States Constitution', *East–West Cultural Passage, A Journal of the 'C. Peter Magrath' Research Center for Cross-Cultural Studies* (Sibiu, Romania: Lucian Blaga University, July 2011).

Gilman, Todd, 'Arne, Handel, the beautiful, and the sublime', *Journal for Eighteenth-Century Studies*, vol. 42 (London: Wiley, 2009).

Gilman, Todd, *The Theatre Career of Thomas Arne* (Newark, DE: University of Delaware Press, 2013).

Gilmore, James H. and B. Joseph Pine II, 'The four faces of mass customisation', *Harvard Business Review* (New York: New York Times Syndicate, January–February, 1997).

Gissing, George, *The Unclassed* (Teddington, Middlesex: The Echo Library, 2006).

Goehr, Lydia, *The Imaginary Museum of Musical Works: An Essay in the Philosophy of Music* (Oxford: Clarendon Press, 1992).

Goehr, Lydia, 'On the problems of dating or looking backward and forward with Strohm', *The Musical Work, Reality or Invention?*, ed. Michael Talbot (Cambridge: Cambridge University Press, 2000).

Goldhammer, A., 'Histoire de la vie privée', *De la Renaissance aux lumières*, vol. III, ed. Philippe Ariès, Georges Duby and Roger Chartier (Paris: Seuil, 1985–1987).

Goldmark, Daniel, ed., *Sounds for the Silents: Photoplay Music from the Days of Early Cinema* (New York: Dover Publications Inc., 2013).

Goldstein, Bluma, 'Schoenberg's *Moses und Aron*: a vanishing Biblical nation', *Political and Religious Ideas in the Works of Arnold Schoenberg*, ed. Charlotte M. Cross and Russell A. Berman (Abingdon: Taylor and Francis, 2000).

Goody, Jack and Ian Watt, 'The consequences of literacy', *Perspectives on Literacy*, ed. Eugene R. Kintgen, Barry M. Kroll and Mike Rose (Carbondale, Il: Southern Illinois University Press, 1988, originally published 1963).

Goulden, John, 'Michael Costa, England's first conductor, 1830–1880', (doctoral thesis, Durham University, 2012). https://core.ac.uk/download/pdf/9641057.pdf [accessed 28 March 2019].

Gowers, Andrew, *The Gowers Review of Intellectual Property* (London: Her Majesty's Treasury, December 2006).

Gowing, Laura, *Common Bodies: Women, Touch and Power in Seventeenth-Century England* (New Haven, CT: Yale University Press, 2003).

Graham, William A. and Albert Graham, *Beyond the Written Word: Oral Aspects of Scripture in the History of Religion* (Cambridge: Cambridge University Press, 1993).

Grazioli, Cristina, 'Opera', *World Encyclopaedia of Puppetry Arts*, ed. Henryk Jurkowski, then Thieri Foulc (Charleville-Mézières: L'Entretemps, 2010, trans. Eleanor Margolies, 2014). Digitised by the Union Internationale de la marionettes.

Green, R.P.H., *Ausonii Opera* (Oxford: Oxford Classical Texts, 1999).

Greenfield, Edward, *The Gramophone*, March 1982, p. 1239.

Greenhill, Dr Peter, Reconstruction of a fifteenth-century Welsh stick chant by Dafydd ap Gwylim, part of the Centre for the Ancient Music of Wales's project 'Voicing the verse: Y Gerdd ar Gan' at Bangor University. https://youtu.be/ZP5IDCRjOm8 [accessed 23 January 2018].

Griggs, Tamara, 'The local antiquary in eighteenth-century Rome', *The Princeton University Library Chronicle*, vol. 69 no. 2 (Princeton, NJ: Princeton University Library, 2008).

Grout, Donald J. and Hermine Weigel Williams, *A Short History of Opera* (New York: Columbia University Press, 2003).

Grove Online Dictionary of Music and Musicians. Digitised by Oxford Music Online.

Gunning, Tom, 'Landscape and the fantasy of moving pictures: early cinema's phantom rides', *Cinema and Landscape: Film, Culture and Geography*, ed. Graeme Harper and Jonathan Rayner (Bristol: Intellect, 2010).

Gurr, Andrew, *Playgoing in Shakespeare's London* (Cambridge: Cambridge University Press, 1996).

Gurr, Andrew, 'Runs of plays in early modern London', *Notes & Queries*, vol. 68 (Oxford: Oxford University Press, 2016).

Gurr, Andrew and Mariko Ichikawa, *Staging in Shakespeare's Theatre* (Oxford: Oxford University Press, 2000).

Hadlock, Heather, 'Women playing men in Italian opera, 1810–1835', *Women's Voices across Musical Worlds*, ed. Jane Bernstein (Boston, MA: Northeastern University Press, 2004).

Hadlock, Heather, 'Different masculinities: androgyny, effeminacy and sentiment in Rossini's *La Donna del lago*', *Rethinking Difference in Music Scholarship*, ed. Olivia Bloechl, Melanie Lowe and Jeffrey Kallberg (New York: Cambridge University Press, 2015).

Hall, Peter, *Exposed by the Mask: Form and Language in Drama* (London: Oberon Books, 2000).

Hall-Witt, Jennifer, *Fashionable Acts: Opera and Elite Culture in London 1780–1880* (Durham, NH: University of New Hampshire Press, 2007).

Halsey, Katie and Jane Slinn (eds), *The Concept and Practice of Conversation in the Long Eighteenth Century 1688–1848* (Cambridge: Cambridge Scholars Publishing, 2008).

Hammond, Brean S., 'Joseph Addison's opera *Rosamond*: Britishness in the early eighteenth century', *English Literary History*, vol. 73 no. 3, (Baltimore, MD: Johns Hopkins University Press, 2006).

Hann, Rachel, *Beyond Scenography* (Oxford: Routledge, 2019).

Hargreaves, Ian, 'Digital opportunity: a review of intellectual property and growth' (HM Government, Department for Business, Innovation & Skills and the Intellectual Property Office, 2011).

Harker, Karen Elizabeth, 'Reconstructing Shakespearean soundscapes: tableaux vivants, incidental music, and expressions of national identity on the London stage, 1855–1911', (doctoral thesis, University of Birmingham, 2020).

Harling, Philip, *The Waning of Old Corruption: The Politics of Economical Reform in Britain 1779–1846* (Oxford: Clarendon Press, 1996).

Harris, Ellen T., *The Librettos of Handel's Operas: A Collection of Seventy-One Librettos Documenting Handel's Operatic Career* (New York: Garland Press, 1989).

Harris, Ellen T., *Handel as Orpheus: Voice and Desire in the Chamber Cantatas* (Cambridge, MA: Harvard University Press, 2001).

Harris, Ernest C., *Johann Mattheson, 'Der vollkommene Capellmeister': a revised translation with critical Commentary* (Ann Arbor, MI: University of Michigan Research Press, 1981).

Havelock, Eric A., *Preface to Plato* (Cambridge, MA: Harvard University Press, 1963).

Havelock, Eric A., *Prologue to Greek Literacy* (Cincinnati, OH: University of Cincinnati Press, 1971).

Havelock, Eric A., *The Literate Revolution in Greece and its Cultural Consequences* (Princeton, NJ: Princeton University Press, 1981).

Havelock, Eric A., *The Muse Learns to Write: Reflections on Orality and Literacy from Antiquity to the Present* (New Haven, CT: Yale University Press, 1986).

Heartz, Daniel, 'From Garrick to Gluck: the reform of theatre and opera in the mid-eighteenth century', *Proceedings of the Royal Musical Association*, vol. 94 no. 1 (Cambridge: Royal Musical Association, 1967).

Henderson, Donald G., 'The *Freischütz* phenomenon: opera as a cultural mirror' (Xlibris Corporation, 2011).

Hendley, Christopher, 'Fromental Halévy's La Tempesta: a study in the negotiation of cultural differences' (doctoral thesis, University of Georgia, 2005).

Henriksen, Anni Haahr, 'Roads not taken and the reflexive pronoun in the Edwardian homilies (1547)', The Danish National Research Foundation Centre for Privacy Research, University of Copenhagen, digitised on 18 May 2020. https://privacy.hypotheses.org/author/ahhenriksen [accessed 25 August 2020].

Hepokoski, James, 'Dahlhaus's Beethoven-Rossini *Stildualismus*: lingering legacies of the text–event dichotomy', *The Invention of Beethoven and Rossini*, ed. Benjamin Walton and Nicholas Matthews (Cambridge: Cambridge University Press, 2013).

Hettinger, Edwin, 'Justifying intellectual property', *Philosophy and Public Affairs*, vol. 18 no. 1 (Chichester: John Wiley, 1989).

Hibberd, Sarah, *French Grand Opera and the Historical Imagination* (Cambridge: Cambridge University Press, 2009).

Hibberd, Sarah and Miranda Stanyon (eds), *Music and the Sonorous Sublime in European Culture, 1680–1880* (Cambridge: Cambridge University Press, 2020).

Highfill, Philip H., A. Burnim Kalman and Edward A. Langhans, *A Biographical Dictionary of Actors, Actresses, Musicians, Dancers, Managers*, 12 vols (Carbondale, IL: Southern Illinois University Press, 1973), vol. 2.

Hoesterey, Ingeborg, *Pastiche: Cultural Memory in Art, Film, Literature* (Indianapolis: Indiana University Press, 2001).

Horst, Pieter W. Van der, 'Silent prayer in antiquity', *Numen*, vol. 4 no. 1, (Mexico: Brill Publishers, 1994).

Horton, Peter, 'The British vocal album and the struggle for national music', *Music and Performance Culture in Nineteenth-Century Britain: Essays in Honour of Nicholas Temperley*, ed. Bennett Zon (London: Ashgate, 2012).

Hoskins, Robert, 'Samuel Arnold', *Grove Dictionary Online* (updated 30 March 2020). https://www.oxfordmusiconline.com/grovemusic/view/10.1093/gmo/9781561592630.001.0001/omo-9781561592630-e-0000041499 [accessed 21 September 2021].

Huebert, Ronald, *Privacy in the Age of Shakespeare* (Toronto: Toronto University Press, 2016).

Hughes, Charles W., 'John Christopher Pepusch', *The Musical Quarterly*, vol. 31 no. 1 (Oxford: University Press, 1945).

Hughes, Meirion, *The English Musical Renaissance and the Press 1850–1914: Watchmen of Music* (Aldershot: Ashgate, 2002).

Hume, Robert D., 'The politics of opera in late seventeenth century London', *Cambridge Opera Journal*, vol. 10 no. 1 (Cambridge: Cambridge University Press, 1998).

Hume, Robert D., *Reconstructing Contexts: The Aims and Principles of Archaeo-Historicism* (Oxford: Clarendon Press, 1999).

Hume, Robert D., 'The value of money in eighteenth-century England: incomes, prices, buying power—and some problems in cultural economics', *Huntington Library Quarterly*, vol. 77 no. 4 (Philadelphia: University of Pennsylvania Press, 2014).

Hume, Robert D. and Judith Milhous, 'Librettist versus composer: the property rights to Arne's *Henry and Emma* and *Don Saverio*', *Journal of the Royal Musical Association*, vol. 122 (Cambridge: Cambridge University Press, 1997).

Hume, Robert D. and Judith Milhous, 'Theatre as property in eighteenth-century London', *Journal for Eighteenth-Century Studies*, vol. 31 no. 1 (London: Wiley, 2008).

Hume, Robert D., Judith Milhous and Curtis Price, 'The impresario's ten commandments: continental recruitment for the Italian opera in London, 1763–64', *Royal Musical Association Monographs*, vol. 6 (London: Routledge, 1992).

Hundert, E.J., 'The European Enlightenment and the history of the self', *Rewriting the Self: Histories from the Renaissance to the Present*, ed. Roy Porter (London: Routledge, 1997).

Hunt, Margaret, *The Middling Sort: Commerce, Gender and the Family in England 1680–1780* (Berkeley: University of California Press, 1996).

Hunter, David, 'Just the facts?', *Early Music*, vol. 35 no. 3 (Oxford: Oxford University Press, 2007).

Ingamells, John, 'John Ramsay's Italian diary, 1782–84', *The Volume of the Walpole Society*, vol. 65 (London: The Walpole Society, 2003).

Isbell, Rebecca, Joseph Sobol, Liane Lindauer and April Lowrance, 'The effects of storytelling and story reading on the oral language complexity and story comprehension of young children', *Early Childhood Education Journal*, vol. 32 no. 3 (Cham, Switzerland: Springer International, 2004).

Jacobs, René and Achim Freyer, programme note for performances of *Euridice* at the Berlin Staatsoper, June 2012, Akademie für Alte Musik.

Jagodzinski, Cecile M., *Privacy and Print: Reading and Writing in Seventeenth-Century England* (Charlottesville, VA: University of Virginia Press, 1999).

Jenkins, Dafydd, 'Bardd Teulu and Pencerdd', *The Welsh King and his Court*, ed. Thomas Charles-Edwards, Morfydd Owen and Paul Russell (Cardiff: University of Wales Press, 2002).

Jenkins, Ian and Kim Sloan, *Vases & Volcanoes: Sir William Hamilton and His Collection* (London: British Museum Press, 1996).

Johnson, James, *Listening in Paris: A Cultural History* (Cambridge: Cambridge University Press, 1996).

Johnstone, Roy and Declan Plummer, *The Musical Life of Nineteenth Century Belfast* (Farnham: Ashgate, 2015).

Joncus, Berta, 'Handel at Drury Lane: ballad opera and the production of Kitty Clive', *Journal of the Royal Musical Association*, vol. 131 no. 2 (London: Ashworth, 2009).

Joseph, B.L., *Elizabethan Acting* (London: Oxford University Press, 1951).

Joyce, Patrick, *Democratic Subjects. The Self and the Social in Nineteenth Century England* (Cambridge: Cambridge University Press, 1994).

Kaufman, Tom, 'A fresh look at Giulia Grisi', *Opera Today* (8 December 2005). https://operatoday.com/2005/12/a_fresh_look_at_giulia_grisi/ [accessed 10 January 2024].

Keller, Hans-Erich, 'Italian troubadors', *A Handbook of the Troubadours*, ed. F.R.P. Akehurst and Judith M. Davis (Berkeley: University of California Press, 1995).

Kelly, Ian, *Mr Foote's Other Leg: Comedy Tragedy and Murder in Georgian London* (London: Picador, 2012).

Kinderman, William, 'Dramatic development and narrative design in the first movement of Mozart's Concerto in C Minor', *Mozart's Piano Concertos: Text, Context, Interpretation*, ed. Neal Zaslaw (Ann Arbor, MI: University of Michigan Press, 1996).

Kitts, Margo, 'Discursive, iconic, and somatic perspectives on ritual', *Journal of Ritual Studies*, vol. 31 no. 1 (privately published, 2017).

Knight, Arthur and Pamela Robertson Wojcik, 'Overture', *Soundtrack Available: Essays on Film and Popular Music* (Durham, NC: Duke University Press, 2001).

Köster, Maik, 'Borrowed voices: legal ownership of insertion arias in 18th-century London', *Operatic Pasticcios in 18th-Century Europe: Contexts, Materials and Aesthetics*, ed. Berthold Over and Gesa zur Nieden (Bielefeld: transcript Verlag, 2021).

Kress, Gunter and Theo van Leeuwen, *Reading Images: The Grammar of Visual Design* (London: Routledge, 1996).

Kretschmer, Martin, *Private Copying and Fair Compensation: An Empirical Study of Copyright Levies in Europe*, an independent report commissioned by the UK Intellectual Property Office (London: IPO, 2011).

Kretschmer, Martin and Philip Hardwick, *Authors' Earnings from Copyright and Non-Copyright Sources: A Survey of 25,000 British and German Writers*, a report commissioned by the Centre for Intellectual Property Policy and Management (Bournemouth: Bournemouth University, 2007).

Landry, D., 'William Beckford's *Vathek* and the uses of Oriental re-enactment', *The Arabian Nights in Historical Context: between East and West*, ed. S. Makdisi and F. Nussbaum (Oxford: Oxford University Press, 2008).

Lang, Paul Henry, *Georg Frederick Handel* (New York: Dover Publications Inc., 1966).

Langley, Leanne, 'The musical press in 19th-century England', *Notes*, vol. 46 (Middleton, WI: Music Library Association, 1990).

Larson, Jessica, 'Usurping masculinity: the gender dynamics of the coiffure à la Titus in revolutionary France' (unpublished thesis, University of Michigan, 2013).

Lass, Roger, *Historical Linguistics and Language Change* (Cambridge: Cambridge University Press, 1997).

Lavenu, Lewis and James. Q. Davies, 'Dancing the symphonic: Beethoven–Bochsa's Symphonie Pastorale, 1829', *19th-Century Music*, vol. 27 (Berkeley: University of California Press, 2003).

Lazarevich, Gordana, 'Eighteenth-century pasticcio: the historian's Gordian knot', *Studien zur Italienisch-Deutschen Musikgeschichte*, ed. Friedrich Lippmann, Silke Leopold, Volker Scherliess and Wolfgang Witzenmann, vol. 11 (Böhlau: A. Volk Verlag, 1976).

Levy, Janet M., 'Contexts and experience: problems and issues', *Mozart's Piano Concertos: Text, Context, Interpretation*, ed. Neal Zaslaw (Ann Arbor, MI: University of Michigan Press, 1996).

Lewis, Judith S., *Sacred to Female Patriotism: Gender, Class and Politics in Late Georgian Britain* (New York: Routledge, 2003).

Lewis, Saunders, *Siwan a Cherddi Eraill* (Carmarthen: Dinefwr Publishers, 2018).

Liang, Lawrence, *A Guide to Open Content Licenses* (Rotterdam: Piet Zwort Institute, Institute for Postgraduate Studies and Research, Willem de Kooning Academy Hogeschool Rotterdam, 2004). Digitised in 2015. https://monoskop.org/images/1/1e/Liang_Lawrence_Guide_to_Open_Content_Licenses_v1_2_2015.pdf [accessed 22 September 2019].

Limon, Jerzy, *Dangerous Matter: English Drama and Politics in 1623/24* (Cambridge: Cambridge University Press, 1986).

Lindgren, Lowell, 'Venice, Vivaldi, Vico and opera in London, 1705–17: Venetian ingredients in English pasticci', *Nuovi Studi Vivaldiani*, ed. Antonio Fanna and Giovanni Morelli (Florence: Olschki Press, 1987).

Lindgren, Lowell, 'The accomplishments of the learned and ingenious Nicola Francesco Haym (1678–1729)', *Studi Musicali* (Rome: Accademia Nazionale di Santa Cecilia, 1987).

Lindsay, W.M., *Isidori Hispalensis episcopi Etymologiarum sive Originum libri XX*, 2 vols, Oxford Classical Texts (Oxford: Clarendon Press, 1911).

Lively, Michael, 'The narrative persona and the nineteenth-century solo concerto: an analytical study of stylistic competency and the troping of temporality', unpublished paper given at the American Musicological Society Conference 2013 (Houston: Texas Women's University, 2013).

Loewenberg, Alfred, 'Paisiello's and Rossini's *Barbiere di Siviglia*', *Music & Letters*, vol. 20 no. 2 (Oxford: Oxford University Press, 1939).

Loftus, Donna, 'Time, history and the making of the industrial middle class: the story of Samuel Smith', *Social History*, vol. 42 no. 1 (Oxford: Oxford University Press, 2017).

Loomis, George, '*Giove in Argo*, Göttingen International Handel Festival', *Financial Times*, 1 June 2007.

Lord, Albert B., *The Singer of Tales* (Cambridge, MA: Harvard University Press, 1960).

Lord, Albert B., 'Perspectives on recent work on the oral traditional formula', *Oral Tradition*, vol. I no. 3 (Bloomington, IN: Slavica Publishers, 1986), pp. 467–503.

Lord, Albert B., 'Characteristics of orality', *A Festschrift for Walter J. Ong; Oral Tradition*, vol. 2 no. 1 (Bloomington, IN: Slavica Publishers, 1987).

Lord, Peter, *The Visual Culture of Wales: Industrial Society* (Aberystwyth: Centre for Advanced Welsh & Celtic Studies, 1998).

Loughridge, Deirdre, 'Magnified vision, mediated listening and the "point of audition" of early romanticism', *Eighteenth-Century Music*, vol. 10 no. 2 (Cambridge: Cambridge University Press, 2013).

Lubrano, J. and J., Music Antiquarian Archive, University of Illinois, digitised in 2016.

Ludington, Charles, 'Walpole, Whigs and wine', *History Today*, vol. 63 no. 7 (London: Andy Patterson Press, July 2013).

Ludington, Charles, *The Politics of Wine in Britain: A New Cultural History* (London: Palgrave Macmillan, 2013).

Luff, Canon S.G.A., 'Kilvert and the ritualists: his impression of Father Arthur Stanton', *The Kilvert Society Newsletter* (Hereford: The Kilvert Society, 1989).

Luke, Carmen, *Pedagogy, Printing and Protestantism: The Discourse on Childhood* (New York: State University Press, 1989).

MacDonald, Laurence E., *The Invisible Art of Film Music: A Comprehensive History* (Lanham, MD: Scarecrow Press, 2013).

Madden, Andrew D., Jared Bryson and Joe Palini, 'Information behaviour in pre-literate societies', *Information Science and Knowledge Management*, vol. 8 (London: Macmillan, 2006).

Madry, Alina, 'The use of extracts of Mozart's operas in Polish sacred music', *Operatic Pasticcios in 18th-Century Europe: Contexts, Materials and Aesthetics*, ed. Berthold Over and Gesa zur Nieden (Bielefeld: transcript Verlag, 2021).

Mann, Joseph Arthur, 'Nineteenth-century music criticism and the case of James William Davison', *The Musical Times*, vol. 157 no. 1936 (London: Musical Times Publications, 2016).

di Marco, Salvatore, *The Italian Tragedy in the Renaissance: Cultural Realities and Theatrical Innovations* (Lewisburg, PA: Bucknell University Press, 2002).

Marsh, Joss, 'Dickensian "dissolving views": the magic lantern, visual story-telling, and the Victorian technological imagination', *Comparative Critical Studies*, vol. 6 no. 3 (Edinburgh: Edinburgh University Press, 2009).

Martin, Jessica and Alec Ryrie (eds), *Private and Domestic Devotion in Early Modern Britain* (Farnham: Ashgate, 2012).

Martin, Neill, 'The Gaelic rèiteach: symbolism and practice', *Scottish Studies*, vol. 34 (Edinburgh: Edinburgh University Press, 2006).

Martin, Steven, 'British opera on television, 1936–1938', *Chombec News* (Centre for the History of Music in Britain, the Empire and the Commonwealth, University of Bristol, 2009).

Matthew, Nicholas, 'Beethoven's political music and the idea of the heroic style' (doctoral thesis, Cornell University, 2006).

Matthew, Nicholas, 'History under erasure: "Wellingtons Sieg", the Congress of Vienna, and the ruination of Beethoven's heroic style', *The Musical Quarterly*, vol. 89 no. 1 (Oxford: University Press, 2006).

Matthew, Nicholas and Mary Ann Smart, 'Elephants in the music room: the future of quirk historicism', *Representations*, vol. 132 no. 1 (Berkeley: University of California Press, 2015).

Matusiak, Christopher, 'Elizabeth Beeston, Sir Lewis Kirke, and the Cockpit's management during the English civil wars', *Medieval and Renaissance Drama in England*, vol. 27 (Hamilton, NY: Rosemont Publishing, 2014).

McCall, Fiona, 'Children of Baal: clergy families and their memories of sequestration during the English civil war', *Huntington Library Quarterly*, vol. 76 no. 4 (Philadelphia: University of Pennsylvania Press, 2013).

McCalman, I., 'The virtual infernal: Philippe de Loutherbourg, William Beckford and the spectacle of the sublime', *Romantic Spectacle*, no. 46 (Montreal: University of Montreal, 2007), https://www.erudit.org/en/journals/ron/2007-n46-ron1782/016129ar/ [accessed 10 January 2024], digitised by Romanticism and Victorianism on the Net.

McDowell, Paula, 'Ong and the concept of orality', *Religion & Literature*, vol. 44 no. 2 (South Bend, IN: The University of Notre Dame, summer 2012).

McGeary, Thomas, 'English opera criticism and aesthetics 1685–1747' (unpublished doctoral dissertation, University of Illinois, Urbana-Champaign, 1985).

McGeary, Thomas, '"Warbling eunachs": opera, gender and sexuality on the London stage', *Restoration and 18th Century Theatre Research*, vol. 7 no. 1 (University Park, PA: Penn State University Press, 1992).

McGeary, Thomas, 'Thomas Clayton and the introduction of Italian opera to England', *Philological Quarterly*, vol. 77 no. 2 (Iowa City: University of Iowa Press, 1998).

McIsaac, Peter M., 'Rethinking tableaux vivants and triviality in the writings of Johann Wolfgang von Goethe, Johanna Schopenhauer, and Fanny Lewald', *Monatshefte*, vol. 99 No. 2 (Madison, WI: University of Wisconsin-Madison, 2007).

McKeon, Michael, *The Secret History of Domesticity: Public, Private, and the Division of Knowledge* (Baltimore, MD: Johns Hopkins University Press, 2005).

McMahon, April, *Lexical Phonology and the History of English* (Cambridge: Cambridge University Press, 2000).

McShane Jones, Angela, 'Revealing Mary', *History Today*, vol. 54 no. 3 (London: Pattersons, 2004).

Merges, Robert P., *Justifying Intellectual Property* (Cambridge, MA: Harvard University Press, 2011).

Mero, Alison, 'The climate for opera in London 1834–1865', *Musicians of Bath and Beyond: Edward Loder (1809–1865) and His Family*, ed. Nicholas Temperley (Woodbridge, Suffolk: The Boydell Press, 2016).

Michael, Lindsay, 'Audience experience during Italian opera performances in Italy in the 18th and 19th century vs. audience experience during Italian opera performances in North America today', digitised by Schulich School of Music (Montreal: McGill University, 2004).

Milhous, Judith, Gabriella Diderikson and Robert D. Hume, *Italian Opera in Late 18th-century London*, vol. II (Oxford: Clarendon Press, 2001).

Miller, Jonathan, *Subsequent Performances* (London: Faber & Faber, 1986).

Miller Marks, Martin, *Music and the Silent Film: Contexts and Case Studies, 1895–1924* (Oxford: Oxford University Press, 1997).

Minnis, Alastair, 'Medieval imagination and memory', *The Cambridge History of Literary Criticism*, vol. II, part III, 'Textual psychologies: imagination, memory, pleasure', (Cambridge: Cambridge University Press, 2008).

Moglen, Eben, *The Dot.communist Manifesto: How Culture Became Property and What We're Going to Do About It* (Chapel Hill, University of North Carolina, 2001).

Moglen, Eben, *Before and After IP: The Ownership of Ideas in the 21st Century* (New York: digital studies Group, CUNY Graduate Centre, University of Columbia, 2010).

de Molen, Richard L., 'Ages of admission to educational institutions in Tudor and Stuart England', *History of Education*, vol. 5 no. 3 (London: Routledge, 1976).

Montemorra Marvin, Roberta, 'Verdian opera burlesqued: a glimpse into mid-Victorian theatrical culture', *Cambridge Opera Journal*, vol. 15 no. 1 (Cambridge: Cambridge University Press, 2003).

Mooij, J.J., *Fictional Realities: The Uses of the Literate Imagination* (Utrecht: Utrecht Publications in General and Comparative Literature, 1993).

Moore, Helen, *Guy of Warwick, 1661*, The Malone Society Reprints (Manchester: Manchester University Press, 2007).

Morgan Barnes, Peter, 'Shakespeare in schools: understanding the oral imagination', *SEELB Educational Resources for English Literature* (Belfast: EDCO, 1998).

Murray, Barbara A., *Restoration Shakespeare: Viewing the Voice* (Madison, NJ: Fairleigh Dickinson University Press, 2001).

Murray, N.M., 'Handel and music borrowing' (unpublished doctoral thesis, Massachusetts: Wheaton College, 2009).

Nagy, Gregory, *Poetry as Performance: Homer and Beyond* (Cambridge: Cambridge University Press, 1996).

Naroditskaya, Inna, *Bewitching Russian Opera: The Tsarina from State to Stage* (Oxford: Oxford University Press, 2011).

Nash, Michael L., *The History and Politics of Exhumation: Royal Bodies and Lesser Mortals* (London: Palgrave Macmillan, 2020).

Neufeldt, Tim, 'Italian pastoral opera and pastoral politics in England, 1705–1712', *Discourses in Music*, Vol. 5 no. 2 (Toronto: University of Toronto, 2004). Digitised by the University of Toronto.

Newton, Robert, *Peter Anthony Motteux 1663–1718* (Oxford: Blackwells, 1933).

Northcott, R., *The Life of Sir Henry R. Bishop* (London: Press Printers Ltd, 1920).

November, Nancy, 'Instrumental arias or sonic tableaux: "voice" in Haydn's String Quartets Opp 9 and 17', *Music and Letters*, vol. 89 no. 3 (Oxford: Oxford University Press, 2008).

Ograjenšek, Suzana, '*Handel's Operas 1726–1741* – by Winton Dean', *Journal for Eighteenth-Century Studies*, vol. 32. no. 1 (London: Wiley, 2009).

Olsen, Kirstin, *Daily Life in 18th Century England* (London: Greenwood Press, 1999).

Ong, Walter J., 'Oral residue in Tudor prose style', *Publication of the Modern Language Association of America*, vol. 80 no. 3 (New York: PMLA, 1965).

Ong, Walter J., *The Presence of the Word: some Prolegomena for Cultural and Religious History* (New Haven, CT, London: Yale University Press, 1967).

Ong, Walter J., *Orality and Literacy: The Technologizing of the Word* (London: Methuen, 1982).

Ong, Walter J., 'Writing is a technology that restructures thought', *The Written Word: Literacy in Transition*, ed. Gerd Baumann (Oxford: Clarendon Press, 1986).

Ong, Walter J., 'Some pschodynamics of orality', reprinted in *Perspectives on Literacy*, ed. Eugene R. Kintgen, Barry M. Kroll and Mike Rose (Carbondale, IL: Southern Illinois University Press, 1988).

Opera Feroce website, www.operaferoce.com [accessed 25 June 2019].

Orrell, John, 'Scenes and machines at the Cockpit, Drury Lane', *Theatre Survey*, vol. 26 (Cambridge: Cambridge University Press, 1985).

Orwell, George, 'Charles Dickens', *Inside the Whale* (London: Victor Gollancz, 1940).

Osborne, Richard, 'Recycled Rossini receives a lively presentation at this Italian festival', *Gramophone Magazine* (2002). https://www.gramophone.co.uk/review/rossini-robert-bruce> [accessed 19 October 2021].

Osborne, Richard, *Rossini* (Oxford: Oxford University Press, 2009).

Over, Berthold and Gesa zur Nieden, *Operatic Pasticcios in 18th-Century Europe: Contexts, Materials and Aesthetics* (Bielefeld: transcript Verlag, 2021).

Oxford Dictionary of National Biography (Oxford: Oxford University Press, 2004). Digitised by Oxford DNB.

Palisca, Claude V., 'Cavalieri, Emilio de', *Grove Music Online*, ed. John Stevens, digitised January 2001.

Panksepp, J. and G. Bernatzky, 'Emotional sounds and the brain: the neuroaffective foundations of musical appreciation', *Behavioural Processes*, vol. 60 (Leiden: Elsevier, 2002).

Parker, Roger, 'Two styles in 1830s London: "the form and order of a perspicuous unity"', *The Invention of Beethoven and Rossini*, ed. Benjamin Walton and Nicholas Matthews (Cambridge: Cambridge University Press, 2013).

Parr, Sean M., 'Coloratura and technology in the mid-nineteenth century mad scene', *Technology and the Diva: Sopranos, Opera and Media, from Romanticism to the Digital Age*, ed. Karen Henson (Cambridge: Cambridge University Press, 2016).

Parr, Sean M., *Vocal Virtuosity: The Origins of the Coloratura Soprano in Nineteenth-Century Opera* (Oxford: Oxford University Press, 2021).

Parry, Adam, *The Making of Homeric Verse: The Collected Papers of Milman Parry* (Oxford: Oxford University Press, 1971).

Parry, Thomas, 'Llywelyn Fawr', *Thomas Parry: Dwy Dddrama*, ed. Dafydd Glyn Jones (Bangor: Dalen Newydd, 2015).

Pask, Kevin, *The Fairy Way of Writing: Shakespeare to Tolkien* (Baltimore, MD: Johns Hopkins University Press, 2013).

Pauly, Reinhard G., 'Benedetto Marcello's satire on early 18th-century opera', *Musical Quarterly*, vol. 34 no. 2 (Oxford: Oxford University Press, 1948).

Pearsall, Derek, 'The *Troilus* frontispiece and Chaucer's audience', *The Yearbook of English Studies*, vol. 7 (Cambridge: Modern Humanities Research Association, 1977).

Penning-Rowsell, Edmund, 'Christie's wine auctions in the 18th century', *Christie's Wine Review* (London: Christie's, 1972).

Perkin, Harold, *The Origins of Modern English Society* (London: Routledge, 1969).

Phillips, Rod, *Wine: A Social and Cultural History of the Drink that Changed our Lives* (Oxford: Infinite Ideas, 2018).

Phonographic Performance Ltd, 70th anniversary website. http://www.ppluk.com/Documents/70%20Years%20of%20PPL.pdf [accessed 11 August 2018].

Piggott, Jan, 'Milton's *Comus*: from text to stage, the fine arts, and book illustration, *c.*1750–1850', *British Art Journal*, vol. 15 no. 2 (London: BAJ Press, 2014).

Pirrotta, Nino, *Music and Theatre from Poliziano to Monteverdi* (Cambridge: Cambridge University Press, 1982).

Platoff, John, *W.A. Mozart: 'Le nozze di Figaro'* (Cambridge: Cambridge Opera Handbooks, 1987).

Platoff, John, 'The buffa aria in Mozart's Vienna', *Cambridge Opera Journal*, vol. 2 no. 2 (Cambridge: Cambridge University Press, 1990).

Pohlmann, Hanjorg, *Die Fruhgeschichte des Musikalischenurheberrechts (etwa 1400 bis 1800)* (Kassel: Barenleiter-Verlag, 1962).

Pollard, Alfred W., *Shakespeare's Fight with the Pirates and the Problems of the Transmission of His Text* (London, 1915, Sagwan Press, Classic Reprint, 2015).

Popple, Jennifer Elizabeth, *The Restoration Actress in Her Seventeenth-Century Social, Political, and Artistic Context: Nell Gwyn, Elizabeth Barry, and Anne Bracegirdle* (New York: Edwin Mellen Press, 2015).

Poriss, Hilary, *Changing the Score: Arias, Prima Donnas, and the Authority of Performance* (Oxford: Oxford University Press, 2009).

Poulsen, Frank Ebjy, 'Towards a history of privacy: conceptual and methodological considerations', The Danish National Research Foundation Centre for Privacy Research (University of Copenhagen, digitised on 25 October 2019). https://privacy.hypotheses.org/author/privacystudies [accessed 25 August 2020].

Prey, Claude, *Les liaisons dangereuses* (Paris: hors série L'Avant-Scène Opéra no 5a, premières loges: *Opéra Aujourd'hui*, 1993).

Price, Cecil, *The English Theatre in Wales* (Cardiff: University of Wales, 1948).

Price, Curtis, 'Italian opera and arson in late eighteenth-century London', *Journal of the American Musicological Society*, vol. 42 (Berkeley: University of California Press, 1989).

Price, Curtis, 'Unity, originality, and the London pasticcio', *Harvard Library Bulletin*, new series, vol. 2 (Cambridge, MA: Harvard University Press, 1991).

Price, Curtis, Judith Milhous and Robert D. Hume, *Italian Opera in Late 18th-century London, the King's Theatre, Haymarket*, 2 vols (Oxford: Clarendon Press, 1995).

Rauser, Amelia, 'Hair, authenticity, and the self-made macaroni', *Eighteenth-Century Studies*, vol. 38 no. 1 (Baltimore, MD: Johns Hopkins University Press, 2004).

Reed, Mathew, Performance of Nettuno (student production of Caccini's *La liberazione di Ruggiero* by the Cornish College of Arts, 2012). https://vimeo.com/39074777 [accessed 2 October 2016].

Reid, Charles, *The Music Monster* (New York: Quartet Books, 1984).

Reif, Rita, 'Auctions; classical sculpture', *New York Times*, 10 July 1987.

Rex, Walter E., 'Apropos of the figure of music in the frontispiece of the *Encyclopédie*: theories of musical imitation in d'Alembert, Rousseau and Diderot', *International Musicology Society: Report of the Twelfth Congress* (Berkeley: University of California Press, 1981).

Rex, Walter E., *The Attraction of the Contrary: Essays on the Literature of the French Enlightenment* (Cambridge: Cambridge University Press, 1987).

Rice, John A., *Antonio Salieri and Viennese Opera*, 2nd edn (Chicago: University of Chicago Press, 1999).

Ringel, Matthew, 'Opera in "the Donizettian dark age": management, composition and artistic policy in London, 1861–1870', (PhD thesis, King's College London, 1996).

Ringer, Mark, *Opera's First Master: The Musical Dramas of Claudio Monteverdi* (Lanham, MD: Amadeus Press, 2006).

Roberts, John H., 'Reconstructing Handel's *Giove in Argo*', *Handel Jahr-buch*, vol. 54 (Leipzig: Deutscher Verlag fur Musik, 2008).

Robinson, David, *From Peepshow to Palace: The Birth of American Film* (New York and Chichester, West Sussex: Columbia University Press, 1997).

Rodmell, Paul, *Opera in the British Isles, 1875–1918* (London: Routledge, 2016).

Rogers, Vanessa L., 'John Gay, ballad opera and the théâtres de la foire', *Eighteenth-Century Music*, vol. 11 no. 2 (Cambridge: Cambridge University Press, 2014). https://doi.org/10.1017/S1478570614000049> [accessed 3 July 2019].

Rorke, Margaret Ann, 'Sacred contrafacta of Monteverdi madrigals and Cardinal Borromeo's Milan', *Music & Letters*, vol. 65 no. 2 (Oxford: Oxford University Press, 1984).

Rosand, Ellen, *Opera in Seventeenth-Century Venice: The Creation of a Genre* (Berkeley, Los Angeles, Oxford: University of California Press, 1991; paperback edn, 2007).

Rosand, Ellen, *Monteverdi's Last Operas: a Venetian trilogy* (Los Angeles: University of California Press, 2007).

Rosand, Ellen, '*L'incoronazione di Poppea*', *Oxford Music Online*, ed. Laura Macy (Oxford: Oxford University Press, 2007).

Rosen, Charles, *The Classical Style* (London: Norton Press, 1971).

Ross, Ryan, 'Media, migration and the music aesthetic: Julius Burger's radio potpourri (1933–1945)' (doctoral thesis, University of Southampton, 2022).

Rossell, Deac, 'The magic lantern and moving images before 1800', *Barockberichte*, vols 40–41 (Salzburg: Salzburg Baroque Museum, 2005).

Rosselli, John, 'Italy: the centrality of opera', *The Early Romantic Era between Revolutions, 1789 and 1848*, ed. Alexander Ringer (Basingstoke: Palgrave Macmillan, 1990).

Rossi Pinelli, Orietta, 'From the need for completion to the cult of the fragment', *History of the Restoration of Ancient Stone Sculptures; Papers from a Symposium*, ed. Janet Burnett Grossman, Jerry Podany and Marion True (Los Angeles: Getty Publications, 2003).

Rowden, Clair (ed.), *Performing Salome, revealing stories* (Aldershot: Ashgate, 2013).

Royce, Jacalyn, 'Early modern naturalistic acting: the role of the Globe in the development of personation', *The Oxford Handbook of Early Modern Theatre*, ed. Richard Dutton (Oxford: Oxford University Press, 2009).

Saenger, Paul, *Space Between Words: The Origins of Silent Reading* (Palo Alto, CA: Stanford University Press, 1997).

Saint, Andrew, *The Victorian Church: Architecture and Society* (Manchester: Manchester University Press, 1995).

St Clair, William, *The Reading Nation in the Romantic Period* (Cambridge: Cambridge University Press, 2004).

Salgādo, Gāmini, *Eyewitnesses of Shakespeare*, trans. Matthew Steggle (London: Sussex University Press, 1975).

Sartori, Claudio, '*Dori* e *Arione*, due opere ignorate di Alessandro Scarlatti', *Note d'archivo per la storia musicale*, vol. 18 (Rome, 1941).

Schechner, Robert, 'Restoration of behaviour', *Between Theatre and Anthropology* (Philadelphia: University of Pennsylvania Press, 1984).

Scherer, F.M., 'The emergence of musical copyright in Europe, from 1709 to 1850', Faculty Research Working Papers Series (Cambridge, MA: Harvard Kennedy School, 2008).

Scholes, Percy A., *Oxford Companion to Music* (Oxford: Oxford University Press, online edition 2011).

Scott, Derek B., *German Operetta in the West End and on Broadway, 1900–1940* (Cambridge: Cambridge University Press, 2014).

Sella, Domenico, *Italy in the Seventeenth Century* (London: Longman, 1997).

Senici, Emanuele, 'Adapted to the modern stage: *La Clemenza di Tito* in London', *Cambridge Opera Journal*, vol. 7 (Cambridge: Cambridge University Press, 1995).

Sennett, Richard, *The Fall of Public Man* (New York: Norton, 1976).

Sharp, Dennis, *The Picture Palace and Other Buildings for Movies* (London: Hugh Evelyn, 1969).

Shattuck, Charles H., 'Macready's *Comus*: a prompt-book study', *The Journal of English and Germanic Philology*, vol. 60 no. 4, *Milton Studies in Honor of Harris Francis Fletcher* (Champaign: University of Illinois Press, 1961).

Shelton Reed, John, *Glorious Battle: The Cultural Politics of Victorian Anglo-Catholicism* (Nashville, TN: Vanderbilt University Press, 1996).

Siegert, Christine, 'Zum Pasticcio-Problem', *Opernkonzeptionen zwischen Berlin und Bayreuth: Das musikalische Theater der Markgräfin Wilhelmine*, ed. Thomas Betzwieser, vol. 31 (Würzburg: Thurnauer Schriften zum Musiktheater, Königshausen & Neumann, 2016).

Simms, Katherine, 'Literacy and the Irish bards', *Literacy in Medieval Celtic Societies*, ed. Huw Pryce (Cambridge: Cambridge University Press, 1998).

Simpson, A. 'Dandelions on the field of honor: duelling, the middle class, and the law in nineteenth-century England', *Criminal Justice History: An International Annual*, vol. 9 (Westport, CN: Greenwood Press, 1988).

Smith, Marian, 'Borrowings and original music: a dilemma for the ballet-pantomime composer', *Dance Research: The Journal of the Society for Dance Research*, vol. 6 no. 2 (Edinburgh: Edinburgh University Press, 1988).

Smith Atkins, Madeline, *The Beggar's 'Children': How John Gay Changed the Course of England's Musical Theatre* (Cambridge: Cambridge Scholars Press, 2006).

Sonneck, O.G., 'Ciampi's *Bertoldo, Bertoldino e Cacasenno* and Favart's *Ninette à la Cour*: a contribution to the history of pasticcio', *Miscellaneous Studies in the History of Music*, ed. O.G. Sonneck (London: Macmillan, 1921).

Southworth, John, *Fools and Jesters at the English Court* (Stroud, Glos: Sutton Publishing Ltd, 1998).

Speaight, George, *The History of the English Puppet Theatre* (New York: John de Graff, 1955).

Spufford, Margaret, 'First steps in literacy: the reading and writing experiences of the humblest seventeenth-century autobiographers', *Social History*, vol. 4 (Oxford: Oxford University Press, 1979).

Steggle, Matthew, *Laughing and Weeping in Early Modern Theatres* (Aldershot: Ashgate, 2007).

Steingo, Gavin, 'The musical work reconsidered, in hindsight', *Current Musicology*, vol. 97 (New York: Columbia University, 2014).

Stenning Edgecombe, Rodney, 'Cesare Pugni, Marius Petipa and 19th century ballet music', *The Musical Times*, vol. 147 no. 1895 (London: Musical Times Publications, 2006).

Sterling, J.A.L., 'A short history of IFPI, 1933–2013: an interview with Professor Adrian Sterling', published online 2013. http://www.ifpi.org/downloads/ifpi-a-short-history-november-2013.pdf [accessed 31 March 2023].

Stern, Tiffany, *Documents of Performance in Early Modern England* (Cambridge: Cambridge University Press, 2009).

Stevens, John, '*Aucassin et Nicolette*', *Grove Music Online*, digitised January 2001.

Stevens, Elena, 'Striking an attitude: tableaux vivants in the British long nineteenth century', (doctoral thesis, University of Southampton, 2017).

Still, Mary Helen, 'The artist and the entertainers: Emmanuel Chabrier and his imitators' (unpublished masters thesis, University of Georgia, 2013).

Strauchan-Scherer, E. Bradley, 'Lost luggage: Giovani Puzzi and the management of Giovanni Rubini's farewell tour in 1842', *Music in the British Provinces 1690–1914*, ed. Rachael Cowgill and Peter Holman (Aldershot: Ashgate, 2007).

Strohm, Reinhard, 'Händels Pasticci', *Analecta Musicologica*, vol. 14 (Cologne: Volk Verlag, 1974).

Strohm, Reinhard, *Essays on Handel and Italian Opera* (Cambridge: Cambridge University Press, 1985).

Strohm, Reinhard, *Dramma per Musica: Italian Opera Seria of the Eighteenth Century* (New Haven, CT and London: Yale University Press, 1997).

Strohm, Reinhard, 'Looking back at ourselves: the problem with the musical work-concept', *The Musical Work, Reality or Invention?*, ed. Michael Talbot (Cambridge: Cambridge University Press, 2000).

Strohm, Reinhard (ed.), *The Eighteenth-Century Diaspora of Italian Music and Musicians* (Turnhout: Brepols, 2001).

Strunk, Oliver, *Source Readings in Music History: The Renaissance*, 4 vols (London: Norton Press, 1998), vol. 3.

Surry, Nigel, 'Two early Georgian wine merchants: the correspondence of James Brydges, first Duke of Chandos with Edward Hooker and Gilbert Wavell, 1720–*c.* 1730', *Proceedings of the Hampshire Field Club & Archaeological Society*, vol. 40 (Winchester: HFC&AS, 1984).

Sutherland, Gillian (ed.), *Studies in the Growth of Nineteenth Century Government* (London: Routledge, 1972).

Tacchinardi, Nicola, *Dell'opera in musica sul teatro Italiano* (Modena: Mucchi, 1955).

Talbot, Michael, *The Musical Work. Reality or Invention?* (Liverpool: Liverpool University Press, 2000).

Tarling, Judy, *The Weapons of Rhetoric* (St Albans: Corda Publishing, 2004).

Taruskin, Richard, *Text and Act: Essays on Music and Performance* (Oxford: Oxford University Press, 1995).

Taunton, Matthew, 'Production', *Dictionary of Nineteenth-Century Journalism*, ed. Laurel Brake and Marysa Demoor (London: British Library, 2010).

Thomas, Spencer, 'Pews: their setting, symbolism and significance', *Themes in Local History*, vol. 39 (St Albans: British Association for Local History, 2009).

Thomson, David, *The People of the Sea* (Edinburgh: Canongate Press, 1954).

Thompson, E.P., *Whigs and Hunters: The Origins of the Black Act* (Oxford: Oxford University Press, 1975).

Traubner, Richard, *Operetta: A Theatrical History* (Oxford: Oxford University Press, 1989).

Treen, Kirsten, 'Stereopticon', *Writing, Medium, Machine: Modern Technographies*, ed. S. Pryor and D. Trotter (London: Open Humanities Press, 2016).

Trotter, David, 'Wanton expressions', *Spirit of Wit*, ed. Jeremy Treglowan (Oxford: Basil Blackwell, 1982).

Trowell, Brian, 'Michael Rophino Lacy and *Ginevra of Sicily*: a 19th-century adaptation of Handel's *Ariodante*', *The Handel Institute Newsletter*, vol. 6 no. 1 (London: The Handel Institute, 1995). Digitised by the Handel Institute: https://handelinstitute.org/wp-content/uploads/2021/07/61.pdf [accessed 6 June 2023].

Troy, Nancy, *Mondrian and Neo-Plasticism in America* (New Haven, CT: Yale University Art Gallery, 1979).

Trull, Mary, *Performing Privacy and Gender in Early Modern Literature* (London: Palgrave Macmillan, 2003).

Tucker, George Hugo, 'From rags to riches: the early modern cento form', *Journal of Neo-Latin Studies*, vol. 62 (Leuven: University of Leuven Press, 2013).

Underdown, D.E., 'The taming of the scold', *Order and Disorder in Early Modern England*, ed. Antony Fletcher and John Stevenson (Cambridge: Cambridge University Press, 1985).

Urquhart, Diane, *Women in Ulster Politics 1890–1940* (Dublin: Irish Academic Press, 2000).

Valencia, Mark, '*Giove in Argo* (Britten Theatre): the first modern-day performance of a little-known Handel opera', *What's On Stage*, 24 March 2015.

Veevers, Erica, *Images of Love and Religion: Queen Henrietta Maria and Court Entertainment* (Cambridge: Cambridge University Press, 1989).

Victoria and Albert Museum, 'The Eidophusikon', Theatre and Performance Collection, S.87–2016.

Vincent, David, *Literacy and Popular Culture: England 1750–1914* (Cambridge: Cambridge University Press, 1989).

Vincent, David, 'The invention of counting: the statistical measurement of literacy in nineteenth-century England', *Comparative Education*, vol 50 no. 3 (Abingdon: Taylor & Francis, 2014). Digitised by Taylor & Francis, 2014. https://www.tandfonline.com/doi/full/10.1080/03050068.2014.921372 [accessed 6 February 2023].

Visser, Colin, '*The Descent of Orpheus* at the Cockpit, Drury Lane', *Theatre Survey*, vol. 24 (Cambridge: Cambridge University Press, 1983).

Wade Evans, A.W., *Vitae Sanctorum Britanniae et Genealogiae*, Life of St Padarn (originally published 1944, new edn Scott Lloyd) (Cardiff: Welsh Academic Press, 2013).

Wahrman, Dror, *Imagining the Middle Class. The Political Representation of Class in Britain, 1780–1840* (Cambridge: Cambridge University Press, 1995).

Wahrman, Dror, *The Making of the Modern Self: Identity and Culture in Eighteenth-Century England* (New Haven, CT: Yale University Press, 2004).

Walker, F. '*Orazio:* the history of a pasticcio', *Music Quarterly*, vol. 38 (New York: Oxford University Press, 1952).

Walkling, Andrew R., *English Dramatick Opera, 1661–1706* (Oxford: Routledge, 2019).

Wallace, Helen, *Boosey & Hawkes: The Publishing Story* (London: Boosey & Hawkes, 2007).

Walsham, Alexandra, Charlotte Methuen and John Doran (eds), *Religion and the Household*, Studies in Church History vol. 50 (London: Boydell and Brewer and The Ecclesiastical History Society, 2014).

Walton, Benjamin and Nicholas Matthew (eds), *The Invention of Beethoven and Rossini* (Cambridge: Cambridge University Press, 2013).

Wangpaiboonkit, Parkorn, 'Rethinking operatic masculinity: Nicola Tacchinardi's aria substitutions and the heroic archetype in early nineteenth-century Italy', *Cambridge Opera Journal*, vol. 32 no. 1 (Cambridge: Cambridge University Press, 2020).

Waterhouse Gibson, Joice, 'A musical and cultural analysis of *Inkle and Yarico* from England to America, 1787–1844' (unpublished doctoral thesis, University of Colorado, 2011).

Watkins, Stephen, 'The Protectorate playhouse: William Davenant's Cockpit in the 1650s', *Shakespeare Bulletin*, vol. XXXVII no. 1 (Baltimore, MD: Johns Hopkins University Press, 2019).

Watt, Ian, *The Rise of the Novel* (London: Penguin, 1963).

Wearing, J.P. *The London Stage 1930–1939: A Calendar of Productions, Performers, and Personnel* (London: Rowman and Littlefield, 1976, second edn 2014).

Weber, William, 'The history of the musical canon', *Rethinking Music*, ed. Nicholas Cook and Mark Everist (Oxford: Oxford University Press, 1999).

Weber, William, *Music and The Middle Class. The Social Structure of Concert Life in London, Paris and Vienna between 1830 and 1848* (London: Ashgate, 2004).

Weintraub, Stanley, *Disraeli, a Biography* (London: Hamish Hamilton, 1993).

Weisstein, Ulrich, 'Farce oder wienerische Maskerade? Dir Französischen quellen des *Rosenkavalier*', *Hofmannstahl-Forschungen*, ed. Wolfram Mauser, vol. 9 (Freiburg im Breslau: Mauser, 1987).

Welch, Anthony, *The Renaissance Epic and the Oral Past* (New Haven, CT: Yale University Press, 2012).

Welsh, Wendy, 'Identity authority, artistic authority, markets and meaning: contemporary English-language storytellers examined' (doctoral thesis, Memorial University of Newfoundland, 2006).

Wenzel, Silke, 'Dora Bright', Musik und Gender, Mugi im internet (Hamburg: Hochschule für Musik und Theater Hamburg, 2011). https://mugi.hfmt-hamburg.de/artikel/Dora_Bright.pdf [accessed 26 June 2019].

Wermager, Sonja G., '"That hart may sing in corde:" defense of church music in the psalm paraphrases of Matthew Parker', *Yale Journal of Music & Religion*, vol. 6 no. 1 (New Haven, CT: Yale University Press, 2020).

Werr, Sebastian, 'Neapolitan elements and comedy in nineteenth-century opera buffe', *Cambridge Opera Journal*, vol. 14 no. 3 (Cambridge: Cambridge University Press, 2002).

West, Shearer, 'The Darly macaroni prints and the politics of "private man"', *Eighteenth Century Life*, vol. 25 no. 2 (Durham, NC: Duke University Press, 2001).

West, Shearer, 'Manufacturing spectacle', *The Oxford Handbook of Georgian Theatre 1732–1832*, ed. Julia Swindells and David Francis Taylor (Oxford: Oxford University Press, 2014).

Wierzbicki, James, *Film Music, a History* (London: Routledge, 2009).

Wiggins, Martin, *Drama and the Transfer of Power in Renaissance England* (Oxford: Oxford University Press, 2012).

Williams, John Graham, 'The life, work and influence of J.C. Pepusch' (unpublished doctoral thesis, University of York, 1975).

Wilson, Alexandra, 'Opera for the "country lout": Italian opera, national identity and the middlebrow in interwar Britain', *Journal of Modern Italian Studies*, vol. 26 no. 1: 'Italian musical migration to London' (Abingdon: Taylor & Francis, 2021).

Wilson, Blake, '*Cantorini* and *improvisore*: oral poetry and performance', *The Cambridge History of Fifteenth-Century Music*, ed. Anna Maria Busse Berger and Jesse Rodin (Cambridge: Cambridge University Press, 2015).

Wilson, J. (ed.), *Roger North on Music, being a selection of his essays from the years 1695–1728* (London: Novello, 1959).

Winkler, Max, *A Penney from Heaven* (New York: Appleton-Century-Crofts, 1951).

Witke, Charles, *Latin Satire; the Structure of Persuasion* (Leiden: Brill, 1970).

Woolgar, C.M. *The Senses in Medieval England* (New Haven, CT: Yale University Press, 2006).

Yates, Nigel, *Anglican Ritualism in Victorian Britain, 1830–1910* (Oxford: Oxford University Press, 1999).

Zaerrin, Linda Marie, performance of *The Weddyng of Sir Gawen and Dame Ragnell* (made by New York University, 2012). https://vimeo.com/48847736 [accessed 23 January 2018].

Zaslaw, Neal (ed.), *Mozart's Piano Concertos: Text, Context, Interpretation* (Ann Arbor, MI: University of Michigan Press, 1996).

Zeffirelli, Franco, *Zeffirelli: The Autobiography of Franco Zeffirelli* (London: Weidenfeld & Nicholson, 1986).

Zicari, Massimo, 'Expressive tempo modifications in Adelina Patti's recordings: an integrated approach', *Empirical Musicology Review*, vol. 12 (Columbus, OH: Ohio State University Libraries, 2017).

Zon, Bennett (ed.), *Music and Performance Culture in Nineteenth-Century Britain: Essays in Honour of Nicholas Temperley* (London: Ashgate, 2012).

Zubillaga-Pow, Jun, 'Plastic resistance: a psychopolitical analysis of Beethoven historiography' (unpublished doctoral thesis, King's College London, 2015).

Index

Printed in the USA
CPSIA information can be obtained
at www.ICGtesting.com
JSHW011802031224
74704JS00004B/150